MW01613465

# The Phoenix Rising

## The Case of the Blue Empress

Live Love Laugh.

### E.K. Barber

E. K. Barber

PUBLISH AMERICA

PublishAmerica
Baltimore

ISBN: 1-60836-111-X
PUBLISHED BY PUBLISHAMERICA, LLLP
www.publishamerica.com
Baltimore

Printed in the United States of America

To Ken, you have to be in love to write about love.
To Marilyn and Tony, a true love story!
To all my fans on my Facebook fan club, Fans of Books by E. K.
Barber
To Anna Rose, Hazel, Barb, and Kris, my initial readers, who help me
keep things straight.

Other books by E. K. Barber
*Flight Into Danger*
*Flight Into Terror*
*Flight Into Fate/Flight Into Destiny*
*The Phoenix and The Shield: The Case of the Hidden Truth*
Visit www.ekbarber.com for summaries, excerpts, and further
information on the author.

# Prologue

In a sumptuously furnished secret room, high above the bustling streets of New York City, she stood in front of a huge, complex board of interconnected symbols and color coded displays. Studying her strategy and her cast of players, she felt a surge of confidence and power.

It was time. Everything was set. She'd make the first move and start the round. It was going to be a glorious session. A record setting marathon!

In the game of Sovereignty there were so many variables, so many turns and decisions for each player that both the mind and the emotions were constantly engaged. Success and domination, or failure and utter destruction were twin forks in the journey. One decision, one play could send you speeding along either road. Every minute was a magnificent balancing act.

The game was free flowing and every round was richly different. Not like the hideously boring, grindingly predictable Middle World of Reality. There were parameters, of course. Rules. Still, no one could ever foresee precisely how opponents would act and react. However, with her experience, ability to set traps, bring up defenses, recruit minions, improvise and generally outthink any challenger, she'd be the victor in the end. Always had. The exhilaration was intoxicating. Like an addict on a spectacular high.

This life was called CRPG by those who still thought of it as a pastime. Computer Role Play Gaming. Today, she was going to push past all that and take the next step in its evolution. Today would mark the day the worlds merged. Reality would be revealed.

Wearing the flowing blue robes of her office, she sat down at a sophisticated computer station and logged on. Long ago she'd ascended to the role of Blue Empress and now assumed that persona exclusively. She was a legend among all the avid players in the underground Internet gaming community. BE102959.

Still, those who revered her didn't realize when they matched wits with her, discussed her in all the blogs, and put their names on her gaming queue that she didn't just play the part of the Blue Empress; she *was* the Blue Empress.

She wasn't just assuming a character in the traditional live action role playing game anymore. That was simply practice. A simulation. Preparing her for her real mission. In a moment of absolute clarity that had changed her life forever, she realized she'd transformed into the actual Empress herself. The game was nothing more than a vivid prophesy. Foretelling the world to come.

It had been an amazing journey to full consciousness. Winning had become so routine for her, so easy that there had been no challenge for years. Her cyber life was becoming nearly as boring as her real life.

Then, a little over a month ago, she found out all that had come before was mere preparation for her one true mission. Life wasn't a series of coincidental events as she had originally thought. In one explosive epiphany she knew that providence had a plan. For her! Fate had written an astounding script and now the prophesy was unfolding.

Callisto and Himalia had spilled into the Middle World of Reality. The three worlds no longer existed in parallel dimensions separated by guarded portals. The wall around the Middle World of Reality, where all the players lived and worked and went to school, had cracked and her empire and that of Avenger had blown through.

The Middle World was the new battleground! She looked around her. True. Real! The game was not just a reflection of life! It *was* life. Everything actually existed. It was the most exhilarating realization imaginable.

All her work, all the time she took over the years to hone her talents, was going to bear fruit. The years of strategizing, playing, and winning had a purpose. She'd always known she was destined for something immense, something that would make itself known to her. Suddenly, the clouded mystery of her destiny lifted and the direction of her future revealed itself in an incredible series of crystal clear signs. It was a magnificent manifestation of the one true reality.

From what she was able to determine through her observations and the logging of hundreds of extra hours of communication, she was the only one who saw; who put everything together. That meant she was the One. Born to lead. Born to conquer. Born to rule. The one true Blue Empress. And with the destruction of Avenger and the merging of Himalia and Callisto, she'd become the first Supreme Sovereign in written history. The possibility celebrated only through myth and legend. About to become reality!

Swiveling in her chair, she turned to her board. Studied it. In one strategic section were the symbols for the citizens and subjects of her empire, known throughout the gaming community as Himalia. The beautiful, lush ancient land of her mother, Adrastea. A world that belonged to her by right and one she'd been fighting for in the years since it had passed to her. Her father, Metis, had been Adrastea's first consort. A scholar, a soldier, and a seer who'd passed to his daughter the ability to read minds, and the skill to develop brilliant strategy.

Lists of code names covered the boards and were placed in teams for Tagging and Tracking. Her Minions. Taking the front line. Low risk, low points, but standing ready to earn enough to be promoted to Sentinel and receive their Boons. Several Sentinels, her tested inner circle, were in place and prepared to follow the flow of play as she moved them through her list of tasks. Text instructions for several possible scenarios were written and ready to send off.

In the upper corner was a short list of her elite militia. Hired Assassins with specific talents for specific challenges. Like critical pieces on a chess board. And finally, in the center were her potential Anointed Ones. The few true zealots who would do her bidding in order to secure their place in history as martyrs. Ones who had the potential to be reborn as Saints to rule in another dimension called Thelxinoe. The dream of every citizen of Himalia.

Everything had to be in place before the first move in the round. It was how she operated and stayed ahead of the pack. Carefully assessing her stash of valuable weapons and treasury of Boons, she thought she'd armed herself well. This round could be a lengthy one, but she was ready for nearly every contingency. On a table under a beautiful stained glass window was a detailed map pinpointing all of her hidden traps disguised as Portals to the trail of Saints, most in the City of Might, but a few scattered throughout the empire. Color coded pins indicated her Hall of Secrets, and one significant outpost in Callisto itself.

With narrow, flashing eyes, she studied the picture tacked to her board of a woman, dressed as a warrior, astride an impressive black horse. The ruler of Callisto, a hot arid world filled with beasts of all shapes and sizes. Her half sister, known as Avenger. A woman who wanted to rule all the worlds herself. Not that she had a right to any part of the empire. Ganymede, the Avenger's father, came after Metis. Avenger was second born. They shared a mother, but couldn't have been more different. Her power came from the mind and controlled action. Avenger gained ground only through physical prowess and strength.

Avenger was the main obstacle to complete domination for any Empress. The conflict between the sisters was the center of all the action. Avenger was her nemesis. Her enemy. Soon to be defeated. Forever gone. Of all the millions of players in all the years since the beginning of Sovereignty, there had never been a Final Duel. The last definitive battle between the Empress and Avenger. That end was about to become reality. She'd soon reign as the Supreme Sovereign of all the dimensions in a position of ascendancy where no one could best her. Ever. Callisto would be hers. The Middle World would be hers. Himalia, a world that was always hers, would be secure.

First things first. Her heart was thrumming with anticipation. Time to begin the round. Rolling up the sleeves of her blue robes, she turned back to her bank of state-of-the-art computers. In order to rule in this sphere of influence, she had to be cunning, calculating, courageous, and a complete computer goddess. Check, check, and check.

The huge humming LCD screens looked out of place in the elegant, elaborately decorated room. They revealed a complicated and intricate strategy that she'd been working on for weeks. Staring at the screens filled with script and symbols, she saw it all clearly. The entire series of actions and tactical moves she'd been posting and plotting. The Challenges, Tests, Quests, Trials, and possible Battles were in place and ready to activate.

All the players were strategically positioned. All the traps and decoys were set. According to her calculations and the phases of the moon, today was the day. She was going through the portal into the Middle World of Reality and take the fight there.

This was going to be brilliant. She could feel the adrenalin pour into her system. The waiting was over. The preparation was finished. The time to act was upon them. She began typing in the last minute instructions to her Minions. They were all in place and waiting for her royal authorization.

The fate of her future and the future of her empire were now in her hands. She held them up, turned them, studied them. Quick, competent, determined. The hands of a master. Her future was assured. Putting the fingers of her capable hands on the keyboard, she typed in a text message to her first Anointed One. Soon to be the first sacrifice in the last great battle for Sovereignty!

The sound of the clicking keys kept time with her accelerated heartbeat.

*This is a Test of your courage and nerve.*
*I am your Empress, it's I whom you serve.*
*In the City of Might, you face your Last Test.*
*To prove you're the One, the Anointed, the best.*
*You will go down in grandeur and glory.*
*Your name will forever be part of the story.*

# Part One:

# The Case of the Blue Empress

*I love you, not only for what you are, but for what I am when I am with you.*
~Roy Croft~

# Chapter 1

"The late George Carlin, a popular contemporary comedian, once wrote that people who dance appear to be insane to those who cannot hear the music. Think about that for a moment. It very succinctly illustrates how some people who are different and who ignore convention may appear to those who subscribe to rote conformity. We are looking for abnormal in a person's makeup, but don't get that confused with someone who just dances to the beat of a different drum."

Dr. Jette Morningstar presented her class a supposition and gave them time to formulate their opinions.

"Does that mean I can cite Carlin in my thesis along with Hippocrates, Mesmer, Charcot, Dix, Szasz and Laing?" asked an enthusiastic young woman, showing off a bit to the other students and to their professor. She'd worked hard to get into the Graduate Seminar on Abnormal Behavior. When NYU had announced this addition to the summer short course schedule, there had been a near website meltdown with everyone trying to register at once. She was one of the lucky ones who got a seat.

"I think if you cite them all, Makenzie, you may be able to slip in Carlin and still make a credible argument. Provided you draw his observations into the hypothesis you propose within the criteria used in the development of persuasive rationale," observed Jette.

Makenzie nodded enthusiastically, fully intending to do that as soon as she processed the professor's meaning.

It was an absolutely gorgeous summer day, sunny and warm, with a fabulous breeze bringing in the smell of mid July through the open windows. The landscape crew had been through early that morning, so there was an accent of freshly mown grass to add to the bouquet of summer flowers.

Jette was excited to be starting at a new university, thrilled with the facilities and the caliber of students in her seminar. She'd be spending most of her time over the next year writing her third book, but these two week interim seminars gave her a feeling of purpose and grounded her in the reality of her profession.

"When I describe the various forms of abnormal behavior and mental illness, you may recognize yourself or someone you know. But don't be alarmed. Abnormal behavior is sometimes an exaggerated form of normal behavior or what would be perceived as normal in a different context. For example, being naked in the shower is normal. Being naked in Times Square, while it would be a real attention grabber, could be perceived as abnormal."

"And in some cultures showing the face is abnormal while in others topless sunbathing is completely acceptable," added a nodding student, making the connections.

"How about giving us some longitude and latitude on the latter," grinned one of the men in the front row.

Before he could get slapped down by the culturally normal young woman sitting next to him, the whole class froze.

Suddenly and without warning, several loud cracks echoed off the corridors outside the classroom, followed by the sound of people screaming. Being raised on a ranch in Arizona, Jette knew gunshots when she heard them. She didn't hesitate. The school had protocol for this eventuality.

"Down," she shouted, running to the door to lock it. "Under your desks!"

The classroom erupted in noise and movement. Crashing desks, shouts of frightened students, scuffling of feet and the shifting of positions and people. They reacted quickly, though most hadn't yet processed the true meaning of the sounds.

Jette pushed a few of the students who were too frightened to move onto the floor. Her quick, decisive action saved lives as bullets from some kind of automatic weapon blew through the frosted glass in the top panel of her classroom door and riddled the area around them.

"Oh my God!" screamed a student as she covered her head.

"What? What is it?" asked others.

Jette moved through the room. With one eye on the door, she settled and reassured her students while making sure they stayed low and quiet. Within seconds the gunfire ceased. The silence was eerie and strangely threatening.

The room soon filled with whimpers, moans, and mumbled prayers. Looking around, Jette saw no one was injured seriously. A few cuts from flying glass, but no bullet holes. Thank God. Still, she had no idea where the shooter was and could feel the danger ripple through the air.

"Stack up the desks and get behind them. Stay away from the door." Keeping low, Jette grabbed her cell phone from her desk. "Don't call 911. We don't want to tie up their lines. I'll do it."

She dialed and clearly, concisely, and calmly she gave the dispatcher the information.

"Where is the shooter now?" asked the shocked, but well trained operator.

"I don't know."

"Any casualties?"

"Nothing serious in my classroom. No gunshot wounds, but some cuts and abrasions."

"Please stay on the line, Dr. Morningstar. Several calls are coming in. Help is on its way."

"Wow, Dr. Morningstar," whispered a student gamely, holding on to one of her fellow classmates. "You didn't need to arrange for a demonstration."

There were a few nervous giggles.

"Thanks, Stephanie, we needed that. Is everyone doing alright?" she asked, keeping her voice low and composed.

Although several responses were shaky, most of her students answered in the affirmative. Some were still in shock, they simply couldn't get around the terror. The steadier students went in quickly to give comfort.

"This is going to be on the news," whispered Stephanie. "Can I call Shawn, my fiancé, and tell him I'm alright?"

"I think that would be fine. Just keep your voice low. I don't want to attract any attention."

A petite young woman sitting alone in the far corner of the room dialed a number, her heart thumping, not from the shock or fear, but from the step she was about to take. The minute she heard the shots, she knew what she was destined to do. Opportunity had just plowed through the door without knocking and she was going to ride it to the top.

"CNN, New York Affiliate," said a voice on the other end of the line.

"Patch me into a live feed," she whispered. "My name is Evie Columbus and I'm inside NYU where a classroom has just been shot up. I have a Vidtone high-speed phone. I can feed in live video as well as audio. I already have recorded footage of the action from a moment ago."

The operator's incredulous exclamation pumped her up even more. Yes! She was the first. Calling with exclusive coverage.

All her life, Evie wanted to be an on-air reporter, and now she was about to live the dream. All the frustration, all the rejection, all the fading hopes dissolved in this one incredible break. She knew she was ready. The thrill was a tangible presence in her belly, but she buried the nerves. Hours and hours of practicing in front of the mirror behind the locked door of her bedroom was about to pay off. Big time!

"Hello. Who am I talking to?" came the voice she recognized as Connie Cottrell, the anchor of the morning show.

"This is Evie Columbus." She kept her voice low. It was more dramatic and wouldn't draw attention to what she was doing. She didn't want any of her classmates to get the same idea.

"Evie, I'm going to be putting you on live. There will be a little delay and I may interrupt to ask questions. Otherwise just keep giving us a running commentary on what's going on in there. Do the best you can. A moment ago we got corroboration from the NYPD."

"One more thing you should know," whispered Evie. "I'm inside Dr. Jette Morningstar's classroom and I have some amazing video of her in action."

There was a second's silence while that fact sunk in.

"Good Lord. To confirm what you've just said. You have video of Dr. Jette Morningstar, the author and forensic profiler?"

"Yes. And the woman your station dubbed the Phoenix this spring when she was involved in that case down in Arizona."

In Atlanta, Connie looked up at her producer. She mouthed 'wow' as he nodded. It was TV gold. There was a purposeful scramble as the research team started getting all the old background footage on Jette Morningstar and Marcus Lexington. They'd have it up and ready to fill in whenever it was needed. The Phoenix was in jeopardy in the Shield's city. Better than gold. Emmy material.

Connie Cottrell collected all of her cool and geared up to interrupt normal programming.

"Okay, Evie. I'll set you up on air," she said softly. "The next voice you'll hear is my producer counting down to your live report."

In the background, Evie heard Connie's liquid, serious voice announce a special report, then a man's low tone in her ear.

"You're on in five, four, three, two…"

"Hello, this is Evie Columbus. I'm reporting from inside NYU where moments ago…"

Evie reported everything she saw, everything she knew. At first her voice wavered a bit, but as she continued, she gained confidence. She sent pictures and short videos of the scene inside the classroom. Of Jette walking among the students, calming them, comforting them. When things quieted down, she fed in the replay of Jette flying through the room as the initial shots hit the door.

Connie and her producer just let the young woman go. It was spectacular footage. The camera was high end and there was excellent definition. Jette Morningstar crossed the small screen like someone from central casting. Her image was coming through fantastically.

The professor was a real beauty, jet black hair falling to her waist, dark, dusky skin, high cheekbones and enormous chocolate brown eyes. She'd inherited her luscious coloring from her Cherokee father and her lithe petite frame from her mother. But more than that, she carried herself with courage and confidence.

"Gorgeous," whispered the producer as they got a close up of Jette silhouetted in a background of chaos.

Evie didn't want to stop talking. It might give someone else the opportunity to deliver their own eye-witness account, so she went on with all the background material she'd been putting together since she found out she'd successfully registered for Dr. Morningstar's class.

"Jette Morningstar, you may remember, was involved in the sensational Arizona mass murder case in which she and local top New York City cop, Detective Marcus Lexington, teamed up to solve a series of tragic disappearances. Dubbed by this network as the Phoenix and the Shield, they stopped a psychopathic killer who'd been kidnapping and murdering young women in the southwest for nearly nine years. The Phoenix honors Dr. Morningstar's Cherokee roots and the Shield acknowledges Detective Lexington's commitment to his badge. In the course of the investigation, the detective was seriously wounded, but it's reported he's recovered and is back on the job this week. What a horrific time to return to duty.

"Dr. Morningstar, a renowned forensic psychologist and bestselling author, moved from Tucson and has taken a position of adjunct faculty here at NYU. Lucky for a number of students, this reporter included, that she did. Her quick reflexes and cool action under fire saved lives today."

Evie was getting low on commentary, and she knew Connie would interrupt with other reports soon. TV needed movement and the pictures she was getting of Jette comforting students and reporting to the 911 dispatcher wasn't going to keep her on the air much longer. The silence continued. Where was the shooter? She needed action. Better yet, she needed blood.

Then Evie smiled. She couldn't help it. The professor was on the move again and it would win her several more minutes on the air.

"Everyone get away from the windows. The Emergency Services Unit of the NYPD or campus security will come for you," whispered Jette as she started toward the door.

"What are you doing, Professor Morningstar?" asked an anxious student.

"Don't move," she whispered back.

"You're moving."

"I know how."

They noticed that even though the floor was strewn with debris, Jette moved through the classroom soundlessly, with incredible grace and stealth. Her Cherokee father taught her everything he knew.

"I need to see if there are any students injured in the hallway," she explained.

Keeping near the wall to avoid a direct line with the gaping hole in the door, she stopped, took a deep breath, held it to steady herself and slowly peeked through the shattered glass. There was no one in the hallway. All the instructors had performed their pre-assigned duties well. The doors were closed and no sound emanated from the long row of rooms. Perhaps the shooter was a lone gunman and had left the building. Everything may already be clear.

Then Jette shifted and looked down the opposite hall to the entrance and her heart stopped. Blood, a few bodies. And movement. They were alive. One, two, three, she counted them. Five. Pulling back against the wall, she reported to the 911 dispatcher.

"Five people down. Alive, I think. South corridor near the double doors. There's no other movement that I can see. The floor looks clear. I'm going to move out of my classroom."

"Please remain where you are," said the dispatcher.

"No. It'll be some time before you can secure this building. Those students may need help now." Her father had been a doctor and she'd learned a great deal from him in basic first aid as well.

"I'll go with you," whispered a young woman who'd been listening to Jette's call. "I'm a nurse."

"No, Hester, it's too dangerous."

"Dr. Morningstar, please. I can't stay in here hiding if there's someone out there who needs medical attention."

Jette saw the conviction on Hester's face and something else. Fear? Shock? An element of excitement? All human reactions to tragedy and intense situations. There was something more, but Jette didn't want to take the time to study the young woman. Right now, she could only accept at face value the nurse's professional need to help.

"You stay behind me. If there's any trouble, you duck back in here. Understood?" Hester nodded.

"Alright. Let's go. But be very aware of what's happening. Dalton," Jette nodded at a young man near the door. "Lock this behind us."

Jette slowly unlocked the door and she and Hester slipped cautiously out into the corridor. There was no sign of the person with the gun so Jette led the way further down the hall. Before Dalton could comply and get the door shut and locked, Evie slid out as well. There may be danger out there, but right now she'd trade her soul for video of the shot-up students and the heroic professor.

It all looked staged out of a movie set. Horrific and bloody. But this was real. Sickenly real. Several students were lying among the debris caused by ricocheting bullets. At least three were still conscious and were weeping out their fear and pain. Jette and Hester worked quickly, and as they did, other students came out from behind makeshift shelters to help.

Evie lifted her camera. Blood and carnage filled the little screen. Incredible. Fantastic. To her dismay, she saw several others training their cameras and phones at the scene. She no longer was sending exclusive images. Her stomach, completely unphased by the blood and the wounds of her fellow students, churned with annoyance at what she thought of as an invasion of her exclusive right to report. Still, she thought, her footage would be the best. No one had the sophisticated video model she had. The photos being snapped would be enough to satisfy some networks, but she was broadcasting through the best. Now if only...

Suddenly not only her dreams came true, everything she'd ever considered in her wildest desires began to unfold. Potentially tragic, of course, but there was nothing she could do about that. It was amazing. Amazing! Like an unseen hand was arranging the unfolding events with her dreams as a template. Danger. Tragedy. Impending heartbreak. Perfect!

# Chapter 2

Detective Marcus Lexington was a happy man. Over the last few weeks since his return from Arizona, he realized with some surprise that he'd never been a happy man. He loved his job, most of the time. He loved New York City, most of the time. He loved the company of women, most of the time. He loved deli food, all of the time. But he recognized now that he never put everything together to find any kind of real contentment. Gratification, certainly. Enjoyment, occasionally. Fulfillment, sure. Particularly at the resolution of each difficult case. But nothing close to happy. Now he knew it was because something was missing. More specifically some*one* was missing.

Jette. There was a feeling when he thought of her, something in his chest that was light and bright. For the first time in his life he could understand why people attributed love to the heart. All he had to do was think of her beautiful face, her fabulous lips, her gorgeous smile, her...

He glanced over at the young officer in the passenger seat of his standard plain-wrapped cruiser. Better to put the inventory on hold for the time being. Officer Kim Sommer was a newbe from the Midwest somewhere, but she was observant in the extreme. He didn't want to shock her sensibilities by boning up.

Smiling, he listened to the police chatter on the radio with half an ear. Jette had some tony New York party to go to this evening and wanted him to escort her. An uptown gathering of publishers, agents and authors with celebrities, moguls, and the established elite. And the woman who loved him, who shared his life and his bed, would move among them like royalty. She'd rule on several levels. Her beauty, her intellect, her success, her reputation, and her most distinguishing characteristic, her total lack of pretension.

He usually avoided any function that required a suit and a phony smile, and in his line of work he'd have several legitimate excuses to circumvent his duties as escort, but he loved watching her. Loved how people responded to her. Loved the feeling of possessive pride that shot through him. Just plain loved her. His smile broadened and got warmer.

Officer Kim Sommer, fresh and polished in her uniform, eyed him suspiciously. They were driving to interview a suspect in a particularly gruesome murder and the detective's usual grim, impatient expression was...was completely absent. In the two years she'd known Detective Lexington, she'd never seen him smile like that. It was creeping her out.

He was still gorgeous, of course. His thick wavy dark brown hair framed a face that could have graced the cover of People's Handsomest Man Alive edition. It looked like he was letting it grow longer. He'd get another reminder soon. It was like him to ignore the more mundane departmental regulations, like hair length and paperwork and budgets. Now that she thought of it, just about every darn rule. He kind of went his own way. Even the glint of a small diamond stud in his ear winked at his superiors.

He'd acquired a nice tan while recovering in the desert that really made those startling emerald green eyes pop. That and the frame of the longest, darkest lashes she'd ever seen on a man. They were extreme, but also deadly. When he aimed those eyes at a suspect they were like laser blasters. An amazing weapon. They'd not only pop, they'd punch.

When she'd first joined his elite squad, she had a little crush on him. That dissolved when he'd scared the crap out her with one of his celebrated meltdowns. It was a pretty classic Lexington fit, but he'd called her a naïve, corn fed, small town beauty queen with the brains of a cherry pit. Of course he'd laced the description with a whole lot of those words. She hadn't known you could pack so many 'f' words and 'a' words and 'mf' words and 'gd' words into a single sentence. She didn't mind the beauty queen part and she really was from a small town, but the other stuff stung. She didn't talk to him for a week. He hadn't noticed.

When she'd come out of the academy in the top slot, she'd requested an assignment to his Special Projects Squad, known throughout the law enforcement community as the prime place to be. Led by a fiery detective, a genius possessed by a temperament in the red zone. He lived up to his reputation. Brilliant, incredibly perceptive, unbelievably well connected, but edgy, difficult, and prone to legendary fits of temper. She knew she had a great deal to learn from him, so she stuck, as did everyone else in his unit.

"Feeling good, sir?" she asked trying to get him to reveal a reason for that unsettling little smile.

"Hmm?"

Distracted, he looked over at her. Cripes, thought Kim. Had the detective been day dreaming? The man who always remained hyper alert? Sharp as a tack? Instincts of a cat?

Since his return from Arizona he'd been different. Maybe something had happened down there. An epiphany of some kind or a personality overhaul. An exorcism, maybe. He'd been living with a psychologist, after all. Perhaps she was making some headway into his irritable and impatient character. Kim smirked inwardly at the thought. Nah. Maybe he just needed to get back to the routine of murder, mayhem, and good old antagonistic New York City culture.

"I said, um…feeling good?" she asked again.

"Yeah. Everything's nearly at 100 percent, thanks."

He was still healing from the gunshot wounds he'd suffered when he was on a case in Arizona, but that wasn't what she'd meant. That would normally only make him edgier. Right? Maybe he'd nearly died or something and had seen the face of God. That would change a person.

But, he'd said thanks. To her. Thanks? She hadn't known he had the word in his vocabulary.

He looked at her, really looked at her, then flicked a finger through her short choppy blonde hair.

"You do something different with your hair?"

That did it. She was going to the library to research alien possession. This was not the detective who left New York two months ago. She was sure of it now. Maybe she should jump out of the car. Save herself. They were only crawling along in traffic anyway.

"I cut it," she said, deciding if she was ever going to be promoted she had to show courage.

"Hmm."

"Six months ago," she mumbled to herself. "So, are…"

"Shut up!" Marc shouted so loudly and so suddenly, it made her jump. Thank goodness she was strapped in, she thought, or she might have humiliated herself by bumping her head on the roof.

"Detective?"

"I said shut the fuck up!" He turned up the radio.

"All units, all units. I repeat, shots fired. Multiple casualties. NYU campus."

This elicited a flurry of chatter and dispatched instructions, but Marc was no longer listening.

He opened his window, placed the strobing police light on the roof and pounded the button that set off his siren. Then he did a U-turn right in the middle of 7th Avenue and tore off in the opposite direction accompanied by squealing tires and blasting horns.

"Detective?" breathed Kim as her body snapped against the seat belt.

Marc's face looked lethal, his hands on the wheel were tense.

"Get Joetta Kirk on the phone. Now! Christ! Get out of the fucking intersection you fucking moron!" He shouted at a taxi stuck in the middle of a crosswalk. Marc laid on the horn and screamed out such a line of profanity that it made Kim's ears burn.

But as she dialed she felt flooded with relief. Yes! The detective was back! She wasn't sure what set him off, but the explosion was reassuring. Turning her wrist, she noted the exact time: 9:52 Eastern Standard Time. The pool was up to almost fifty dollars. Wishing she could remember what time and day she'd gotten, she knew she'd be close. Most of the people had selected the first few hours he was back on duty. She'd been late putting her money into the Lexington Meltdown Sweepstakes, so she'd been left with the remote possibility he'd hold himself in check for a few days.

She never thought she'd have a chance, but as the week went by and he seemed to be infected by some happy, happy, joy, joy bug, she figured there was hope. He'd never held his temper for so long. Even after the required anger management classes the brass made him attend. Members of his squad who drew the first few hours always won.

She punched Joetta Kirk's number while being rocked from side to side by the velocity of his sharp, erratic twists and turns. Good Lord, what bug got up his butt, she thought, and what did Captain Kirk have to do with it?

Then she remembered and could have knocked herself into traffic for her dense insensitivity.

"Jeez, sir. Is Dr. Morningstar teaching today?"

"Yes," said Marc, dread mixed with fury tightening his voice.

"Ma'am, this is Officer Kim Sommer of Special Projects." No one called her Captain Kirk to her face. "Yes, he's right here, that's why I'm calling."

"Give me the fucking phone," snarled Marc as he shot around three cars and sailed into an intersection, barely missing a tour bus and several taxis.

Kim knew a woman in uniform absolutely couldn't close her eyes, but there was nothing in the regulations that dictated she couldn't say a little prayer. Silently and in her head, of course. Trouble was she was so rocked, she couldn't remember anything but "if I should die before I wake." Didn't seem like a good fit right now. So instead she thought she'd just let her life replay before her eyes and wait for the crash.

"Joetta? Tell me what you know about the shooting at NYU." He listened impatiently. "What building? Goddamn it. Then find out. I need to know, now. I'm on my way over there. I'm going to keep this line open. I don't give a flying fuck whose precinct it's in. I'm not going there to a fucking tea party. I don't give a shit about the crime scene. Yeah. Jette's on campus today. Go! I'll hold." Marc continued to drive one handed weaving through traffic and cursing loudly whenever a car or pedestrian didn't clear the way fast enough.

"Detective, the chances that she's involved are minimal." Kim tried to reassure Marc. "It's a very large campus. Do you want me to call her cell?"

"She's teaching right now and turns it off in the classroom. But, yeah. Try. Leave her a message to call me if she can."

Kim dialed Jette's number on her own cell phone and was put immediately into voicemail.

"Hello, Dr. Morningstar. This is Officer Kim Sommer. Detective Lexington would appreciate a call." Kim glanced over at Marc. "As quickly as possible. He's concerned." She rang off. "Voicemail," she reported, although she was sure he'd gathered that already.

Marc said nothing. Probably for the best since the car was nearing light speed.

Joetta came back on the line a few minutes later.

"Marc, it's the Social Science building. We have a lot of inside reporting via cell phones. Several casualties. No firm count. From what the students are telling us, we think the shooter is armed with semi-automatic machine pistols. Tell me it isn't her building."

"I can't. Jesus Christ, Joetta. It's her building." He got a grip on his panic. He had to get his car through traffic then remain cool on the scene. Suppressing all feeling, he went into cop mode. "One shooter?"

"We don't know."

"Shots still being fired?"

"Not for the last few minutes."

"Is the shooter still operational?"

"Yes. After his initial blast he ran. ESU thinks he might be in a hole. Maybe in one of the classrooms."

"I'll be on site in less than 15. Keep me updated."

"Will do. Marc? Oh hell, I don't even know what to say. Hang in there. Jette will be alright. They have protocol and the security team on campus is first rate."

"Understood."

Kim was listening to one side of the conversation and was getting enough to give her a chill. Dr. Morningstar was in the line of fire. It wasn't fair.

Marcus Lexington was always such a loner. He had tons of friends and people really respected him, but she'd never seen nor heard of anyone who captured his attention, much less his heart. Kim was a romantic. When she found out he'd returned to New York with a woman, she sighed. When she heard the woman was Jette Morningstar, she almost wigged. She'd read both her books. Highlighted them in fact.

Then when she met Jette at the station, she could see why the detective lost himself. She was magnificent. They were very different. Opposites, really. He was all boiling passion. She was peaceful beauty. It was a stunning combination. She didn't think they even realized what a picture they made together. And when he looked at her. Whoa. Kept her in hot and heavy dreams for a week. And now, Jette was in jeopardy. Kim's heart ached for Marc and the dread that was just beneath the surface.

# Chapter 3

The scene that was unfolding on the small screen in front of her was a nightmare, but Evie knew it would play in a spectacular way on live TV.

Several of the students had positioned themselves near the outside windows, waiting for the arrival of the ESU team, ambulances, and campus security.

"Dr. Morningstar," cried one of the young women. "Look!"

Evie pointed her camera toward the street outside the window. Turning the corner and making their way down the lane toward the parking lot next to the building were three long yellow school buses. They looked like they were filled with children.

"What are they doing here? Did they take a wrong turn?" asked another student.

"I think it's some kind of band camp for the city kids. They have it every year," explained another.

"I'll inform the dispatcher. They need to contact someone inside those buses if they can. Divert them." Jette looked up as one of the students screamed and pointed. What she saw froze her one second and propelled her into action the next. The sniper was clearly visible moving quickly along the roof of the building running perpendicular to the one they were in. All three school buses currently moving up the street would soon be in his direct line of fire.

Jette tossed her phone to one of the steadier students. Where she was going, she didn't need a buzzing, ringing instrument in her pocket. "Keep the dispatcher informed. I'm going up!"

Evie's camera kept recording and sending as Jette turned and ran toward the stairway to the roof. In pursuit of the maniac with the gun. Evie used her zoom feature and followed as best she could. The stunned production crew in the news room could only watch as they continued the live feed and millions saw Dr. Jette Morningstar transform from the scholarly but sexy professor to an urban warrior.

Jette raced up the six stories at a relentless pace, her conditioning born and bred in the desert where running, climbing, jumping, and tracking were part of growing up. Jette always led the pack, a natural in everything physical. As she moved cautiously, carefully toward the door to the roof, she could feel the professor fade and the Cherokee hunter, renowned for prowess, courage, and agility, emerge. It gave her confidence. It gave her strength. Quickly, silently, she let herself out onto the roof.

Evie was several minutes behind Jette when she got to the door. Hesitating, assessing if this was all worth it, she brought out images of war correspondents. Putting their lives on the line and the accolades that came with that kind of coverage. Doing her best to steady herself and her camera, she stepped out into the sunlight.

With her camera on maximum zoom, she quickly focused in again on Jette who'd already sprinted across the roof. She prayed her Internet hook up would hold, that her camera would provide adequate color definition as it went from the dim inside light to the outside sunshine, that she'd have enough battery power. This was unbelievable footage and her equipment just couldn't let her down now.

Winded, she gasped for breath so she could narrate what was happening.

"Sorry, but that run up the stairs was strenuous. Obviously Dr. Morningstar is in much better shape," she panted, getting only a few words in with each breath.

Evie thought her dreams came true the minute she started uploading the images from Dr. Morningstar's classroom but this footage and her part in taking it were beyond career making. She was sending live feed of the most unbelievable turn of events imaginable. She'd be the darling of all the media outlets. It would always be on her resume. Bloody bodies and carnage were good, but her shots wouldn't even have been exclusive. Too many students, too many camera phones, too much competition.

But this! It was outrageous! Extreme! Heart thudding so loud, she thought the sound of it might transmit, she filmed without comment. It simply didn't need any words.

Jette ran full out, shucking her suit jacket, tying back her hair and kicking off her shoes. Viewers, now glued to their sets, stared in disbelief, as the professor transformed again, this time into an absolutely amazing athlete. Jette never hesitated. As millions held their collective breath, she sprinted, then leaped and extended gracefully, soaring over ten feet of empty air. Easily covering the space between the structures, she landed sure footed on top of a short wall running along the roofline of the neighboring building. She was no more than 25 feet from where the shooter stood. Her remarkable flight and landing had been so soundless, there was absolutely no reaction from him.

The velocity of the combined exhalations from viewers around the world could have shifted weather patterns. Cumulative relief drown the disbelief as everyone who saw it celebrated in their own unique way. People in homes held their hearts and wrung their hands, patrons in bars erupted in cheers, pedestrians and shoppers who'd gathered around sets high fived each other.

Evie felt it as electricity running through her body. However this turned out, she was experiencing the flow of unparalleled success right now. The tiny lens in her camera gave the world a stunning show.

The shooter was looking down. Down at the school buses. Evie quickly trained the camera on the buses so her audience could see what was at stake. To see the possible cost if Dr. Morningstar failed. Kids, little kids, were starting to unload. The scene seemed orchestrated for the highest drama possible. Evie had to keep reminding herself that this was really happening. Unscripted. Unplanned. With the ending to unfold with the passage of time.

Quickly, she panned back to Jette who was confidently running on the ledge. A ledge that was no more than a foot wide. Running for heaven's sake. Still no hesitation. Completely balanced. It was breathtaking.

"This is like Hollywood," Evie said dramatically. "But let me assure you, there is no safety net. No optical illusion. No computer imaging. This is real, folks. Oh my God. As you can see, the shooter has spotted the children. The children of New York City. Three bus loads of them. It's what prompted Dr. Morningstar to act. To put her own life in jeopardy." She let the pictures speak for themselves for a few seconds, then began her commentary again in the low, articulate voice of a professional observer.

"From here it looks like he has several guns. And we know he'll use them. The cries of the wounded are still ringing throughout the corridors."

This was the most amazing thing she'd ever seen on TV. The pictures she was getting were unbelievable.

"I'm going no farther. I'm standing behind a chimney, protected, but from what you can see, Dr. Morningstar is in the direct line of fire. Fully exposed. If he sees her, there is no place she can hide. Look at her agility, her balance. She's like an Olympian."

As the word spread, millions more stopped and watched their TV screens. CNN fed everything through with only a five-second delay. They would stop the film if there was a bad result. Stop it, edit it, and build a special around it.

They watched as Jette eased herself down from the ledge, now only ten feet from the shooter. Still no reaction from the sniper.

Evie held her camera in both hands, trying to keep it steady. Whatever unfolded in the next few minutes, she'd have it on disc. A permanent record. Her permanent record. Her journalistic triumph. She owned it. After today, she'd own the world.

"She must be making no sound," she continued in a stage whisper. "She must be moving as light as the air surrounding the crazed gunman. He obviously doesn't hear her coming. Pray for her folks. Pray that he doesn't, for if he sees her, there is no way her bravery and courage can save her. And if she fails, no one is left to save the children below."

She could hear the sirens now and wished she had another camera to move to the scene down at street level. But she couldn't take hers off the unfolding events on the roof. Besides, there would be others down there to record what happened from that vantage point. She kept her camera pointed at what she was sure was exclusive.

Jette could see the back of the shooter. A small young man. That was good. As sure of herself as she was on her approach, she had no real hand-to-hand training, certainly no martial arts background. Her grandfather had taught her a neat little trick when she was growing up, however. An old native warrior had taught him. And she was confident she could move quickly and without him knowing she was near until it was too late.

Cherokee warriors didn't kill other human beings except for very specific and narrowly defined reasons, so her grandfather had taught her what had been passed on to him through generations. How to completely disable someone. It didn't require a great deal of strength, but it did require swiftness and surprise. And it looked like she was going to be blessed with both.

She paused for just a second, silently chanting an ancient Cherokee prayer for strength. To center her power and activate all the adrenalin she could to channel into her hands and fingers. She visualized what she needed to do, then narrowed her vision and focused in on the shooter.

# Chapter 4

With the sirens and the helicopters screaming through the streets of New York City as a backdrop, the Blue Empress studied her board. She'd be taking a lot of time in the next few hours moving people around, assigning points, assessing her next moves. This was fabulous. Better than she'd imagined it would be. Certainly more thrilling than anything in an online challenge.

The TVs lined up near her work-station showed the ever-efficient media on the story within minutes of her putting everything into play. Live and in color. Now that was power! It was pulsing through her. The City of Might was erupting and it was on her order. She was finally battling in the Middle World of Reality. Incredible. Unprecedented. Intoxicating!

Her inside Minions were perfectly positioned. She knew one was doing her job, and would eventually find out if the others got the action she planned. They were on their own now, she wouldn't be communicating with them until they texted her later. She'd selected wisely, she thought. The game required individuality and some autonomy, but she'd chosen them, and that was how she controlled the outcomes.

Her Anointed One was coming through, that was clear enough. One could never be sure. This was, after all, a game in which the results of her choices and movements unfolded over time. The inner thoughts of this boy and the demons that drove him were clear to her. She could read minds, after all. Confidential emails were how she accomplished this in the Middle World of Reality. Minions would pour out their unhealthy wishes and dark desires and she'd feed them with her encouragement and reward them with Boons.

She'd tested this one, of course. He'd reached the status of Anointed One through several Quests of escalating violence which culminated in the murder of a homeless person in Hell's Kitchen just last week. He'd sent her several graphic pictures and shared with her that it had been a glorious Quest. She'd awarded his points and provided his Boon after she'd confirmed his supreme achievement through Internet news accounts of the kill. And all he wanted was more weapons. It was while she was arranging the drop that the idea of anointing him and giving him this Last Test became the center-piece of her first move.

Others had disappointed her. Others who thought this was only a game. It was this boy who knew the fabric of the Middle World had ripped and the Quests and Tests were real. Time would tell if he would enter Thelxinoe. It was his one and only incentive right now. But he still had to earn the privilege and she held the key.

She studied the three TV screens to see if there were nuances she needed to monitor from different angles. She'd be going to the scene herself soon. Experiencing everything electronically wasn't nearly as thrilling as hearing the sirens and feeling the thunder of the circling helicopters firsthand; of seeing the blood and counting the body bags as they were transported from the scene.

She muted the other TV's and concentrated on the student's eyewitness account on CNN. This was priceless inside information. Everything was being recorded, of course. Later she'd study the play more thoroughly in order to accurately assign points and approve promotions. An actual body count would have to be confirmed and be divided into categories. So much to do.

Morningstar was in control, that was obvious. Points for her. Lots of them. The Empress shrugged magnanimously. Had to give the enemy her due. But was this professor, this supposed forensic psychologist, the one true Avenger? The woman could be a clever decoy, but she thought not. The dramatic footage would be an excellent tool to gather the necessary clues. Points there, too.

She glanced at the ticker at the bottom of the screen and frowned. An early estimate was coming in on body count. Student reports from the inside showed five confirmed victims, no reports of deaths yet. Another two victims were found in the parking lot. Grainy pictures were being flashed on the other screens of students down. She'd look at them later.

Only seven so far. Very disappointing, but she knew her Anointed One. He'd gone in with enough fire power to bring that count up considerably. And with every casualty, every minute he held his position, she'd be assigning him points. If he got enough on his side of the board, he would transcend.

Suddenly, Morningstar flew into action. The Empress's eyes burned through the screen and her breath started coming in pants as her heartbeat thudded in her ears. Fabulous! This was extraordinary, and worthy of her level of play. Brilliant. And there could no longer be any doubt. The one true Avenger was in play!

# Chapter 5

When Marc and Kim got close to the campus, the traffic was gridlocked in all directions. Emergency vehicles, the media, police cars, Emergency Services Units, students' friends and families converging on the single location turned the streets into a parking lot. Police barriers placed around the campus kept most pedestrians contained but layers of concerned people surged toward the action.

Unable to move any further even with his lights and siren, Marc jumped out of his car and raced up the street. Kim got out and followed but couldn't keep up with his ground-eating speed.

When he pushed through the crowds and got close to the barrier, Marc pulled out his badge and flashed it to the officers in charge. He needn't have bothered. They all knew who he was. The legendary Lexington from the Special Projects Unit. They immediately waved him in assuming he was on the case.

Even though Marc wanted to go immediately to Jette's location, he knew he needed more information. Scanning the faces of the officers in the ESU, he saw someone he could count on to give him everything. She was standing with a radio along the perimeter close to Jette's building.

"Tana!" he shouted above the noise. "Hey Tana, can you tell me what's happening?" he asked running over to her and stopping as she lowered the radio.

Stunning in the regulation jumpsuit that hugged her generous curves, Tana Bentley stood tall and confident. Her bright blue eyes snapped with both recognition and pleasure. The blue grapevine had informed her that Marc was back, but she hadn't expected to see him here. She had the hots for him for years and felt the old familiar sexual tug in her belly as she responded to his hail.

"Hey, Marc!"

While she was pleased to see him, she was busy. This incident could be a career maker and she wanted to be sure she was in the middle of the action if there was any action left to be had.

"What's the latest?"

"One shooter's been subdued. He's being transported now."

"Good work. That's good." Relief released a flood of warm blood through his iced veins. Still, he couldn't settle until he saw Jette, safe and sound. "Anything more on the casualties?"

"A professor is down, looks like a head shot. No news on the condition. Nine students seriously wounded, no fatalities yet, a dozen more with minor wounds, cuts and bruises. It could have been a whole lot worse. From the preliminary on-scene report, the suspect had thousands of rounds, several semi-automatic pistols and sniper rifles."

"Do you have names of the victims?" He was breathing heavily from the sprint but his lungs couldn't seem to get enough air.

"No. You'll need to go to Dina Marcia for that."

"Where is she?"

"Over on Washington working with the media liaison."

"Was there only one shooter?"

"We're trying to ascertain that now. I'm coordinating the search, but it looks like he was solo. There have been no more shots fired since the original burst. I have to go, but how about we meet after things settle down and I can fill you in." The adrenalin surge the call poured into her system made her edgy and tense, but she had a clear idea what she'd like to do with all that energy later.

"I have to get to the scene."

"You can't, Marc. It's completely closed to anyone but the coordinated ESU teams. We're doing a room-by-room search."

"Are all the students and faculty out?"

"We're escorting them out as we clear each floor. There are still several classrooms occupied."

"Where did they transport the victims?"

Tana pointed to a Medflight helicopter. "There goes the professor now." She listened to the chatter coming through her earpiece. "They're taking her to Mount Sinai. The students are all at the NYU Medical Center."

"Her? The professor is a woman?"

"Yeah. Just a second." Tana put her finger to the earpiece. "No identification yet. We're still trying to sort out everything that happened. So how about meeting me at Gung Ho's after dark? Unfortunately, I'm not going to be needed much longer."

"Unfortunately?" asked Kim, who finally caught up and was standing by Marc's side.

Tana spared Kim a glance, her eyes flicking over the uniform. There was a pecking order in police work and she was definitely higher on the food chain.

"My unit was called to resolve this incident, but right now it seems all we're needed for is clean up and clear out. Not exactly what I was trained to do. And no matter how dangerous, I'd rather do what I was trained to do." She looked away, dismissing Kim. "It's an ESU thing."

Kim thought sincerely it was an egomaniacal thing. And she wasn't the least bit intimidated or overly impressed for that matter. She'd been working with Marc for two years so she'd been drilled by the master. Nothing this woman could do would set her back.

"Too bad it's often a bloody, terrifying thing," she said softly.

Tana shrugged, hoping to impress Marc. "It's what we live with."

"I mean for the victims," responded Kim as she turned and followed Marc, who hadn't stuck around long enough to be impressed. He was jogging across the lawn toward Jette's building.

Tana's irritation with the situation and with Kim retreated as she watched Marc work his way confidently through every barrier. God he was gorgeous. How did she ever let him go? She remembered very well his enthusiastic physical response to her own insatiable appetites. It was when she pushed the issue of commitment that he kissed her soundly and walked away. Her mistake, and one she didn't plan on making again.

Sexual frustration now mingled with the edginess. Her communicator squawked. With one last long look at Marc she got back to work. Later. She'd channel all of this excess energy into a seduction.

It was her chief, calling her unit to stand down. Return to base. Damn. Damn. Damn. Seething, she kicked at the gravel and started carrying out the order. Christ, she'd trained for years for just this kind of crisis. This situation was her dream. A sniper taking out students at random. Young people in danger, worried parents looking to you for salvation, a grateful community reminded once again of your place in protecting them from the demons. Terror. A campus in jeopardy. News helicopters circling, capturing her every move as she valiantly led her unit into the fray. Putting their lives on the line to serve and protect. And looking damn good in the uniform to boot!

Then poof. Fizzle. Pop. It was so irritating to have something of this magnitude slide through her fingers. She was an ESU commander. A position she was proud of and that few women had reached. A long, dangerous, protracted siege with a heroic ending would have gone a long way to seal another promotion. The highest ever by a woman.

Well, it was not to be this day. Everything had been resolved. The shooter was in custody, the students were being treated. No fatalities. And worse yet, not one camera was pointed in her direction.

Her reputation and career path was built on the blood of others, a fact that didn't disturb her nearly as much as having her rising star completely eclipsed by some college professor. She didn't have all the details yet, but she intended to get them. It burned her all the way to the ground that the spotlight was shifted to an amateur.

But maybe she could salvage something out of the day. Running into Marc gave her a great excuse to call him later. She could fill him in on the details. Update him. He always liked being on the inside. Maybe over breakfast tomorrow morning. Tana smiled. They'd be too busy tonight to discuss anything. Perhaps this big dark cloud had a sliver of silver after all.

# Chapter 6

Unaware he was the subject of yet another female fantasy, Marc tried calling again on Jette's cell and got the voicemail recording. When he heard a small band of students use the name Morningstar he changed direction and ran quickly over to them. Maybe they had a line on something. They were gathered around a laptop.

"I just downloaded it from CNN. Look at her."

"Oh my God! Is she nuts?"

Marc looked down at the screen and froze. Everything in his body just stopped functioning. The woman he loved, the woman who now defined his life, was running up the stairs and out onto a rooftop while the soft voice-over gave running commentary to his worst fears.

The video was shaky, but clear enough for him to see what had unfolded mere minutes before. In front of him were all the answers, he was sure of it. What he wasn't sure of was whether or not he could handle what he was about to see.

He heard Kim skidding to a stop next to him, but didn't turn. He couldn't take his eyes off the screen. And from her startled and fearful exclamation, he knew neither could she.

"Just moments before she was safe and reasonably secure inside her classroom. Now she is running toward the danger," said the voice coming from the computer.

Marc watched. It was like an out-of-body experience. He was there with her and yet he wasn't. There was a time warp and whatever happened could not be changed. By him or anyone.

"Dr. Jette Morningstar, you may remember, was involved in the sensational Arizona mass murder case in which she and local top New York City cop, Detective Marcus Lexington…"

Marc nearly jumped when he heard his own name, but he said nothing. His throat was so dry, he wasn't sure he could speak. His heart was beating painfully in his chest as he watched Jette completely expose herself, not only to the gunman, which was bad enough, but to a six-story fall, which would have been equally as fatal. The students around the laptop gasped, then cheered as she landed safely and securely on the other rooftop.

"Oh my good God in heaven," whispered Kim. "Oh my good God in heaven." She repeated when Jette ran surefooted down the narrow ledge.

The voice of the young woman narrating taunted him. Talking. Talking. Talking. He watched the camera pan over to the shooter. Crouching, the boy held a gun in each hand. Marc could clearly see at least three other automatic pistols and a couple of rifles at his feet. The ground around him was covered with hundreds of rounds of ammunition. The breath went out of him and he couldn't replace it with enough oxygen. His chest tightened, his vision narrowed. It would take only one. Only one shot. And his life would end with hers.

He watched her stop and go completely still. He knew what she was doing. The blathering reporter said Jette looked like she was psyching herself up. Exactly. In her own way, she was focusing, gathering herself and her considerable personal strength and natural instincts toward the task. Toward the danger. Toward a well armed, completely crazy boy who'd already proven he'd shoot.

Marc watched as she touched her heart. He watched as she took a deep breath and concentrated her attention on her target. He watched as she sprinted, her bare feet hardly touching the ground. He watched as the gunman realized there was someone there with him on the roof. He held his breath, his heart pounding in his ears as the gunman turned. Not even the students around the laptop had a handy word or a smart comment. No one was breathing.

Jette sprinted the last ten feet, brought her fingers around to his neck and squeezed as hard as she could. It was as if she had a tazer in her hand. Marc knew that move. She'd shown him once, demonstrated, actually. She'd squeezed the jugular shutting off the oxygen to the brain. The pressure was unbelievable and the results were nearly instantaneous. He watched as she executed the move on the gunman. Perfectly executed it. The kid went down, stunned, nearly unconsciousness.

"What was that? What was that?" asked one of the students excitedly.

"The Vulcan neck pinch or something?" asked another.

"Oh my good God in heaven," said Kim again.

Marc watched as the woman he loved removed the young man's belt and used it to tie his hands behind him, swiftly and competently. The shooter shook his head and regained his senses as she was tying his feet together with the strap from one of the rifles. She hogtied him like the cowgirl she was. He almost expected to see her raise her hands above her head and take a bow. Instead she leaned over the roof and called to the people below.

The reporter kept reporting. "I've never seen anything like that. Do you believe it? As you may remember, Dr. Morningstar is half Cherokee. It seems her genetic legacy was generous with its innate inventory of talent. She's the Phoenix and today…"

Marc didn't move. Still couldn't move. The video kept playing and the young woman kept chattering like a maniacal mechanical doll. He saw Jette settle in next to the young man, now immobilized by his bindings. It looked like she was talking with him. He was struggling, shouting, trying to sit up. Even now, she wouldn't get a safe distance away from him.

"Jesus Christ! What the fuck is she trying to do! Save his sorry fucking soul? Goddamn it!"

The students around the laptop, who'd been mesmerized by the playback, jumped as one at the fury in the voice of the stranger. Maybe the threat wasn't over. Marc's look was so dark and murderous, a few of them backed up as others nervously cleared their throats. When they saw Kim's uniform and the substantial gun on her hip, they let her handle the man.

"Let's go find her, shall we, Detective? This video is at least a half hour old. They have the shooter in custody and are transporting him. Remember?"

"I think it would be best if you don't talk to me right now, Sommer. I'm a little close to the edge," growled Marc.

"I can see that. Come on. I'm sure they'll still have Dr. Morningstar near the scene."

Hopefully they would find Dr. Morningstar soon, Kim thought. As a skilled therapist she could turn her considerable talent on the man. He was in the red zone and Kim wasn't sure she could hold him if he totally wigged out. Being armed didn't mean a thing. Drawing her gun on him just wouldn't be cool. Not that she had a chance to as Marc abruptly turned and took off toward Jette's building.

Images flashed like a slide show in Marc's mind as he ran. Jette flying over the space between the buildings. And coming up short. Falling to her death. Jette losing her balance on the ledge. And falling to her death. The shooter turning a few seconds before he did, bringing his guns around and pounding a barrage of bullets into her. Her body, splattered and shredded, lying in a pool of blood on the roof of the building. Ugly. Horrific. A real possibility given the circumstances. And any one of them sure to drive him mad.

He could feel the beast inside him rattling the cage, wanting to be released, wanting to be fed. It was a ferocious, horrible, black part of himself that felt its power growing. Anticipating its dominance, it fought to rip through the fabric of his self control.

The only way Marc felt he could live among the civilized people of the city was to focus his considerable will-power on caging the feral, untamed heart of his primal inner core. To keep it confined. But oh, he wanted to punch something. Pound something. Destroy something. Tear into the people around him. The only reason he didn't was because he knew he couldn't. If he released the beast, he'd be lost.

Kim remained silent as they slowed, then walked across the parking lot. It was such a beautiful summer day. She looked around, alert to her surroundings. A good cop. Watchful in case there was any other danger. Superimposed on the bright sunny day were the sights and sounds of the emergency crews, quickly and efficiently bringing normalcy back to the streets and buildings. Reconstructing the order, the confidence, the sense of security and protection.

Cops called to Marc as he strode by, but she knew he didn't hear them. He'd gone internal on her. It was how he coped with his temper, his seething rage. The muscles in his jaw looked like they were going to pop their sockets and his eyes shot out bullets of green fire. His friends and colleagues knew to stand back and just let it simmer until the anger channeled itself into action or focused on a target. It was both frightening and fascinating.

When he was in pursuit of the bad guys, it gave him speed and fearlessness and righteous energy. It's what made him a tireless defender of the law. On the other hand, if you were unlucky enough to be near it when it was unleashed without a specific target, you could get burned. She'd been singed a few times and she still wasn't quite sure why. She just hadn't evacuated out of the blast zone quickly enough.

It was with great relief that they spotted Jette before Marc went off. She knew Jette had some kind of super power when it came to taming Marc's dark side. When she swore she heard him growl, she slowed down.

Marc spotted Jette casually chatting with one of the ESU officers. His potent relief and love warred with his equally powerful frustration and fury. Where the hell was her cell phone? And why was she talking with this asshole who was obviously flirting with her instead of calling him?

Turning, she smiled and waved before he could shout her name. She didn't even look surprised to see him as he strode toward her.

"Marc. You know Steve Nelson. He told me that his commander spotted you here and you were on your way over. I was trying to borrow his cell phone to call you. Hi, Kim."

Kim gave a little wave and stayed back among the other members of the ESU team. There was a lot of kevlar there.

"Steve," acknowledged Marc tersely.

"Hi, Marc. I understand you know the professor. I was telling her if teaching didn't work out, maybe we could recruit her for the home team."

Jette could tell that Marc was seething and about ready to explode, so she smiled up at Steve. "Excuse us. I need to talk with the detective."

"You're taking the case, Marc?"

"No, just the professor. Out of here."

"Ah. Sure. Okay. Well, it was a pleasure meeting you Dr. Morningstar. I'm looking forward to your next book."

"Thank you."

Marc took Jette's arm and headed for the first door into the building.

"I'm not sure the area has been cleared, yet," observed Jette.

"Then we can just get your friend Steve to clear it for you."

"Excuse me?"

"Where the hell is your fucking cell phone?" Rage was screaming out of his eyes.

"One of my students has it. She was using it to communicate with the security office. I left it with her. I have a lot to tell you."

Marc stood in the foyer filled with police officers, not seeing anything but Jette, and let it rip.

"What the hell were you thinking?" he yelled. A few of the officers stopped and turned toward them, then recognizing the detective, they got very busy with their assigned duties.

"Let's see." She looked to the ceiling in a parody of a person gathering a thought. "How about…saving lives," she said softly.

"There is only one fucking life I care about. A whole lot more than you apparently do."

"Excuse me?"

"Going after that fucking asshole! What the fuck were you thinking? You're not a trained Emergency Services officer. You're not the police. You didn't even have a fucking weapon. You will never put yourself in that kind of jeopardy again, do you hear me?" shouted Marc, his green eyes flashing.

"Of course I do, darling. I think the entire campus can hear you."

Turning, he violently kicked a trash can across the foyer. The sound of it crashing against the wall was satisfying, but did nothing to dissipate his fury.

"Feel better, Detective?" Jette kept her voice low and level, knowing it would eventually bring Marc's down as well.

"No, as a matter of fact," he growled. "Wake up, professor. This city is filled with danger. If I thought you didn't have the fucking sense to run from it, I'd never have brought you here."

"You didn't bring me here. I applied for this job on my own. And may I remind you that you were shot, my horse was killed, and my mother was murdered in a quiet area south of Tucson? In Arizona. Over 2000 miles from this city?" Jette's voice was very controlled as she firmly made her point. She'd just faced down an armed sniper; she sure wasn't going to be pushed around by her lover.

Marc fisted his fingers in his long, thick hair, took a deep breath, and willed his temper back into the box. He blew out the breath. Counted to ten. Visualized the box. Hell. The length and breadth of his anger didn't fit into the goddamn box.

"Fuck it!" Marc snatched Jette around the waist with one arm, lifted her off her feet, and threw open the door to the nearest classroom.

A very disappointed group of officers looked at each other. They were really enjoying the show. Now they would just have to rely on their imaginations.

Jette's desire not to make a scene made it possible for Marc to get her through the door. As soon as he slammed it shut with enough force to jar it off one of its hinges, she started to struggle.

"Marcus Lexington, you let go of me. You put me down. Now! I'm a professor here. You will treat me with respect."

He did put her down, none too gently, spinning her around and grabbing her arms in a tight grip that made her wince. That brought some sanity back. Goddamn it. He loosened his hold, then let go, hoping he hadn't put any bruises on her. He hadn't and the beast inside him roared with frustration. It wanted out. It wanted to feed. It wanted to fight. It struggled to be released.

She'd intended to walk away and leave him to his tantrum, but saw a flash of guilt in his eyes and decided to remain still. Their relationship was still so new. He was feeling his way through the unfamiliar emotions, through his love. For him it was foreign territory and he had no map. No experience. No landmarks. No bearings.

It was far easier for her to assimilate the love between them. She was both a naturally open soul, and a highly trained psychologist. Using both her training and her strength, she was trying to help him deal with the several layers of sensations, passions, and emotions her presence in his life created.

Marc breathed and seethed. Fury was spinning through him like a tornado and he knew it was putting a strain on his rational control, always too close to the surface in the best of times. And he couldn't remember one damn thing from the anger management courses his chief had ordered him to take.

"Fuck me. Damn it. Shit." He began to pace the small room like a caged animal.

"Could you be more specific?" she asked, a tiny smile encouraging him.

"Hell, I'll try." He blew out a breath, but continued to pace. "Damn it, Jette. You had no right endangering yourself by going after that maniac."

"But he was endangering people who were in my care. Marc, really, I was out of the line of fire and had my head down until I saw the school buses. There were probably 40 kids in each of them. What would you have had me do? Stay down and just listen to their screams?"

Marc's stomach flipped. She effectively trapped him with his own fierce sense of service. Still, he carried a badge and she was a civilian. That kept his anger simmering.

"Jesus Christ, Jette. What if he'd seen you coming? He had a fucking arsenal up there." He could still see in his mind the fully loaded guns lying at the boy's feet.

"He didn't see me coming. I was careful."

"But you aren't invisible, oh karmic Princess of the Earth!" Sarcasm slashed through the words. "You aren't a magical puff of thin air or the wind or the sky, or whatever the fuck you think you are! You're fucking flesh and mortal blood."

His eyes flashed and his hands fisted as he stopped pacing and stood over her. Then he turned abruptly and side kicked a desk. It went flying across the room and hit the wall with such force the drawers flew out spilling the contents all over the floor. Jette stood her ground as he spun around and faced her. When he saw her calm face and cool manner, he tunneled his fingers through his hair.

"Oh, Christ. I'm losing it, Jette."

"I can see that. I can feel it."

"I told you. I warned you."

She looked over at the desk. "Well, I'll admit the desk will never be the same, but you did let go of me. And it seems knowing you're losing it is the first step to keeping it."

"Oh now that's a nice piece of helpful wisdom, Professor. Maybe your students will take that bullshit as truth and write a paper on it, but this is reality. This is who I am. I'm coming apart and someone could get hurt."

She took a step toward him.

"Back off, Professor."

"No, I don't think I will. Take a couple of deep breaths."

"What? Now I have to breathe in pink clouds, breathe out dark skies? Think happy thoughts? Count to ten? What a fucking crock of bullshit. I've already counted to six hundred." He looked around and eyed the file cabinets. "I'd rather hit something."

Jette almost laughed, but suppressed the urge when she saw the thunder still in his eyes. Instead she looked around.

"There's a couple dozen student desks here. They don't look all that substantial, so I'm not sure how therapeutic their destruction would be, but..."

Suddenly he gathered her up in his arms and held her so close she could feel his heart beat through his shirt. It was still racing and she could sense the stress, feel the vibrations deep inside him. "Just give me a minute here. I need to straighten out."

"Darling, I'm fine. All in one piece."

His breath came out low in his throat. "I've gone through the door with a drug-crazed killing machine on the other side, moved through a dark alley knowing the guy I was pursuing was armed and wanted to shoot me full of holes, but I've never, never felt this kind of...of delayed reaction, I guess. I know a lot of cops who get the shakes after a close encounter but this is a new one for me. I feel like I've been twisted into an impossible knot, then released without any direction or balance."

"Post-traumatic stress can manifest itself in many ways."

"Don't be a shrink right now," he whispered in her ear. "Just let me hold you. Feel you. Safe."

Slipping her hands up his broad back, Jette could feel the incredible tension in his muscles. Setting aside the therapist for the moment, she let the woman melt into his arms.

"I guess love really messes you up," he said. "Big time."

"There's a price to pay for caring." She noted he used the word love without hesitation or prompting. It warmed her heart.

"Don't leave me."

"I won't." She looked up at him. "You need me too much."

Leaning into him, she stood on her toes and kissed him. His lips were tense and unresponsive, but she was persistent. And completely irresistible.

With a moan, he deepened the kiss and all of his fear and anger flowed through his lips and dissipated in the power of her love. Her arms went around his neck and her fingers tangled in his hair. Her body fit inside his. She realized there was some latent tension in her, too and his embrace chased it away, then replaced it with a different kind of pressure. Pleasure. Heat. Lust.

His lips moved to her neck, his hands ran up her back.

"Is there a lock on the door?" she whispered. "I have an idea how we can rechannel some of that post-traumatic stress."

He chuckled. "I don't think there are even two working hinges on it anymore."

"How about we cut out of here and you take me home?"

"Have you made your statements?"

His green eyes were bright, but no longer haunted with anxiety. She looked up at him and smiled. Back to being a cop. She liked it.

"No, not officially." She moved away from him. Reluctantly. "Just a very preliminary account to the first officer on the scene."

"You'll have to be questioned for more detail and on the record."

"Can I make them to you?"

"This isn't my precinct. Unless it's assigned to Special Projects, it won't be my case. And right now there's no reason I'd get the nod. I don't think there will be much of an investigation. It appears there was only the lone gunman and my heroic Cherokee hunter bagged him."

Jette was relieved. He was finding his balance. His rhythm.

"Who will I be dealing with?"

"Probably Captain Green. This is his precinct and he likes to take the high profile cases himself."

"Do I hear some sarcasm?"

"Just that he thinks of himself as a super-cop and rides on the success of his staff. Most of the people who work for him have requested transfers to other departments."

"And have you had some dealings with the man."

"I have."

"And."

"And he hates my guts."

"Is the feeling mutual?"

"Except for you and a select few friends, acquaintances and colleagues, I hate everyone's guts."

"Of course."

"Don't use that voice."

"What voice."

"That patented and overused 'ah hum' voice that you shrinks use to suck out the psychoses. It only incites my pissed off inner beast."

"Then perhaps you'd like to tell me why he hates your guts."

"No, I don't think I'd like to."

"So it was a woman."

"Shit. Would you stop that?" She could look right into him.

She simply raised her eye brows. And waited.

"Alright, alright," he sighed loudly. "I had no fucking idea the woman was his fiancée. She was beautiful, sexy, and sent 'come bop me' signals to everything with pants. All I did was smile and her clothes were off and she was in my bed."

"Ah hum. So do you think he'd like to turn the tables?" She smoothed her hair and tucked her shirt back into her slim slacks. Her smile was teasing.

"If he even looks at you for longer than 15 seconds I'll challenge him to a duel." He flicked a finger through her hair, messing it up again and pulled her to him, pulling out her shirt in the process. "You're mine." His kiss was like a brand.

She blew her breath out. "Okay. I liked the kiss, so we'll let that bit of chauvinism pass for now. But don't make it a habit."

A habit was what he fully intended to make it. He adored everything about her. Her eyes, her hair, her scent, her mind. When he looked at her, he couldn't believe she chose him to love. To live with.

While he studied her, she studied him.

"Are you alright?" she asked.

"Getting there."

"I mean physically. It seems you've been running."

For the first time he noticed his healing wounds were protesting his sprint, jog and explosion. Little pulses of pain reminded him he was supposed to take it easy for a few more weeks.

"Seems my girlfriend thinks she's a super hero and she's making trouble in my town."

"I thought it was more like taking trouble down in your town." While she talked, she rubbed her hands together, concentrating energy in the palms, then laid them against Marc's chest where a bullet had slammed into him. Immediately there was a soothing, calming current running from her healing hands to his wound. It felt like heaven.

"Besides," she said as she saw he not only felt physical relief, he was beginning to settle emotionally. "It's now *our* town."

"I like sound of that," he said softly.

There was a discreet knock on the door. "Detective Lexington?" called Kim. "Captain Green is out here and I'm stalling."

"Thanks, Sommer," acknowledged Marc, irritated that the pleasant interlude was interrupted.

"Are you alright now?" Jette asked.

"I will be. Maybe I could use a little therapy tonight. Physical therapy."

"We have the party tonight."

"You're still planning on going?"

"Of course. This event ruined the last day of my seminar. I'm not going to let it interfere with my schedule."

"Damn."

She gave him a narrow-eyed look.

"One would think you weren't looking forward to mingling with publishers and authors and people who like to be around publishers and authors."

"One would think," he said easily. "Most everyone will be assholes."

"Maybe, but instead of concentrating on that, think about this. I'm going home after my interview with the Captain. I'm going to soak in a tub. And there will be hours of unscheduled time between the end of your work day and the party for, oh, I don't know. Use your imagination."

He grinned. "And how am I supposed to get my mind back on murder when you in a tub are the main event?"

"That's your problem, Detective."

When they walked out of the classroom, Kim was relieved to see that Marc had released the anger. Dr. Morningstar was a genius. It was a good thing too, because the detective couldn't tolerate Captain Green at the best of times.

And who could blame him. Green had already invaded Kim's personal space and asked her to fetch, yes he actually used the word fetch like she was Mollie the Collie, some coffee. In Lexington's squad they had a pecking order, of course, but if you wanted coffee, you got your own darn coffee.

On the other hand, it killed some time so Marc could chill a little. She fetched the coffee like a good little hound dog before she told Green where to find Dr. Morningstar. Hopefully it had been brewing in the pot since early that morning.

She'd knocked on the broken door of the classroom on her way back from the cafeteria. Now she thought she'd just stand back and enjoy the show. She loved her job.

Captain Green went up to Jette and extended his hand. "Dr. Morningstar. It's a pleasure to meet you. I've admired your work in criminal profiling for years. I hear you're working on a new book."

"I am."

His eyes slid over to Marc and Jette could see he was right. Captain Green hated Marc's guts. Well then, she thought. That took the captain off her list of people receiving a complimentary copy.

"What the hell are you doing here, Lexington? Trying to get a little of the reflected glory?"

"That's right, Green. I saw those TV cameras, and I couldn't resist. But maybe you should tie your shoe before they turn in your direction."

When Green instinctively looked down, Marc smirked, then didn't even try to hide it when Green caught himself and glanced angrily back up.

"Shit, you're so easy Green." The smirk transformed into an insulting grin. "Is that how Delrone got away from you? He pointed to a sign advertising women's underwear and when you looked up, he ran?"

"Get out of here, Lexington. This is a crime scene. My crime scene. And you're interfering with the investigation."

"And how would I be doing that."

"First of all, by annoying a superior officer."

"I don't see one."

Jette thought the pissing contest had gone on long enough.

"What do you need from me, Captain Green?" she asked.

"I'll need to interview you extensively and as soon as possible."

"That would be fine," she agreed.

"She's entitled to representation." Marc was not quite ready to leave. "I think I'll be sitting in on that interview."

Green laughed maliciously. "And what do you think you are, Lexington, an attorney?"

"According to the state of New York, that's exactly what I am. Would you like to see my credentials?" Marc had graduated from the NYU Law School and had passed his bar years before. He'd never practiced law, but always thought it made him a better cop. Right now it was worth all the long hours of studying and the grueling bar exam just to be able to play this card, at this time, in this place.

Green looked like he was going to implode in one huge apoplectic blast. Color mottled his cheeks and his eyes blazed. Kim nearly giggled, but she was in uniform and a police officer should never giggle.

"What did you say?" Green hissed.

"Something wrong with your hearing, too, Green?

"Gentlemen, please," sighed Jette, recognizing the battle of two Alpha dogs baring their teeth. "Captain Green, I would be happy to talk with you extensively about my observations. Would you like to do it here, or back in my office?" She effectively eliminated the alternative of going with Green to his.

Green pulled his eyes away from Marc and looked at her just as she intended. "Your office would be best. Less public."

Then Jette turned to Marc and played her own cards. "And Detective, I'm sure you're a very skilled attorney, but I don't think I'll need a lawyer at this point in the investigation." When Marc took a breath to protest, she smiled up at him. One of her best smiles, she thought. "But what I will need later is a very good massage. This was quite a day. So why don't you go on and I'll see you tonight at home."

She leaned into him, put her hand on his chest and planted a quick but substantial kiss on his grinning lips. Marc didn't miss the flash of incredulity in Green's eyes and the pucker of furious disbelief on his lips. It was more than satisfactory as a conclusion to the battle. Marc couldn't think of anything that could top Jette's action except a return peck.

"See you at home then. Call my cell if you change your mind about representation."

"I will. Now go to work. I'm sure the city of New York needs her top cop more than I need an attorney."

Marc grinned. It took considerable will-power to keep from pumping his arms like a heavy-weight boxer who'd just been declared a winner by knockout. What a shot. Jette Morningstar knew just where to slice with her unsheathed knife.

Kim had to restrain herself from applauding the really, truly excellent display of female warfare. Superior. The woman was not only a genius, she was a little ruthless, to tell the truth. That punch at Green was inspired. And greatly appreciated. The detective would be tolerable to work with for the rest of the day now. Phew. She'd have a lot to type in her journal tonight, alright.

"Coming, Sommer?" Marc asked as he moved toward the door.

"Oh. Sure." She gave Green a little wave. She just couldn't help it. "I'm right behind you."

"So, Captain Green," said Jette. "Why don't we go on up to my office where we can talk privately?"

Green looked out the open doors at the TV cameras and decided it would be best to wait to talk with the reporters. What he needed to do was formulate some short pithy sound bites that would be media friendly. That took some thought and planning. He'd practiced a few quick spontaneous comments on his way over, but none of them were relevant by the time he arrived.

When he'd gotten the call, he'd anticipated a lengthy siege with constant updates.

Huge national exposure right from the start. But Morningstar put a slice into his on-camera role. Nothing he could do about that now. After his meeting with her, he was sure he could report on something news worthy.

And he needed to find out what the hell was up with Lexington. Obviously, the man came not only to grab a few more headlines, but the woman of the hour as well. He glowered at Marc's retreating back and his eyes darkened when he noticed him brushing impatiently by the media. Damn him. It seemed the more he ignored the reporters, the more they hounded him. Well, Lexington, he thought, you may flash brightly now, but I'm going to get some real coverage on this. Straightening his tie, he followed Jette. Maybe he'd take a shot at the woman, too. A little payback.

As it turned out, when he left the building an hour later with his notes from the interview with Jette safely in his pocket, he noticed with bitterness that the cameras were far more interested in student witness accounts of Jette's heroic movements than in his take on the incident. After a few brief questions that probably wouldn't play beyond the local news, they moved as one when someone thought they'd spotted Morningstar.

Damn her, too. She was already a flourishing author and the success of her third book was assured. She didn't need all this extra publicity. On his way to the scene, he'd envisioned his own book deal. Intimate details of the tragedy from the eyes of a seasoned officer.

Some people got all the breaks. He thought maybe she'd share a little of the spotlight, but even his invitation to dinner was rebuffed. This whole incident, so promising a few hours ago, was going nowhere. The case would hardly be a headline grabber for more than a few more days. It needed a spin. Something to sustain the interest. There was still the trial. And maybe he could play a conspiracy card. If he implied there was more to the story, the news crews would hound him for days. That would be good. Maybe he could get a couple more press conferences out of this yet.

# Chapter 7

The Empress paced, her robes billowing behind her as she stared at the remaining two TV sets. The third lay on the floor, dented, shattered and clearly nonfunctioning. The set that she'd turned to CNN. She couldn't stand watching that torturous loop one more time. On an intellectual level, she knew the game spontaneously unfolded, that was its purpose after all. Each decision was unique, each outcome a manifest mystery.

But damn! Damn! Damn! This was not what she'd anticipated! Not what she'd plotted in her several probable outcomes. And most certainly not what she'd wanted.

A young woman was looking into the camera on one of the remaining TVs, her sincere, fresh face really getting under the Empress's skin.

"She saved my life. I was just standing there, you know, like I was in shock or something and she shoved me under the desk. And cripes! There were bullet holes right next to where I would have been standing. She was totally awesome."

Ridiculous, she thought. It looked like the stupid, insipid, predictable news reporters selected college co-eds for their camera appeal. Cast a few nice innocent looking potential victims and it boosts the viewer's reaction. Add a perfect tearful execution, and they get sucked right in. Ratings soar.

"I'm sure the bullet hole, singular, was nowhere near that little camera whore," muttered the Empress.

"Professor Morningstar didn't panic. I never saw anyone move so quickly," opined another student enthusiastically.

"Let's write a ballad about it, shall we?" the Empress snapped, frustration feeding her rant. "Maybe even expand the insignificant, inconsequential event into a Broadway musical. Sure. Overblown, excessively dramatic musical tributes to a puffed up, embellished potential disaster. For God's sake! The entire public is a bunch of gullible, witless, brainless, naïve zombies waiting to be fed pure crap." She paced; she fumed. "No. Broadway's too small a stage. A movie. That's it. An epic. Let's recruit a cast of thousands, shall we? Idiots!"

On another screen, a very quick and enterprising reporter was now in the middle of dozens of children from the buses, gathering accounts of what they were feeling.

"Whining brats," muttered the Empress. "Every insipid eight year old wants their 15 minutes of fame."

All she saw when she looked at them was a lost opportunity. The points generated for sheer body count would have been astronomical. Unprecedented. She hadn't known about the three buses, but that was the beauty of match play. Fate flew around and dropped incredible chances for glory like bombshells throughout the game.

"And there you have several eye witness accounts, Felicia," said the serious eyed reporter. "To recap, nine students and one professor are in area hospitals. No fatalities at this point. It appears as though this murderous rampage was in its earliest stages and was stopped before it could become a full blown tragedy."

Nine. Nine students when there were three school buses right below him? She continued to fume. Could feel herself in a slow, hot burn. There was unpredictability in the opposition, but her own people should be able to follow a simple script. Where were the hundred or more injured, dead, dying? It was supposed to go on for hours, then end in a suicide, the secrets sealed forever.

Anointed One, her ass. Idiot. Stupid, moronic, brainless, crazy freak! She swept her arm across her desk and sent files, maps, computer disks, books on gaming, and directories sailing across the room.

Grabbing the remotes like a couple of old western six shooters, she aimed them at the two TVs still standing and flipped through the channels, both local and national. The flashing images of students, faculty, police spokespeople, experts in the psychology of both heroism and mass murder, local politicians getting in their face time flipped on the screen until her stress level was teased to a tormenting but tantalizing crescendo.

She stopped her seething tirade through sheer willpower and forced herself to focus. Focus first, then act. She murmured the word like a mantra. "Focus, focus, focus. If you chase two rats, they're both going to get away! Focus!"

She flipped back to Connie Cottrell on CNN.

"In a twist of irony, the professor who subdued the gunman is Dr. Jette Morningstar, author of two best sellers on crime. *The Criminal Mind* and *Crime Scene Analysis and Profiling* both set records for nonfiction on the *New York Times* best seller list. We are told that she only joined the NYU faculty a few weeks ago. Lucky for all involved. This is definitely a case of the Phoenix Rising."

The Phoenix Rising. The words actually calmed her. Helped her achieve that much needed focus. There was a plus side to this turn of events. A huge plus. She'd accomplished one of her most important tactical objectives, after all. There was no doubt now. It was confirmed. Morningstar was Avenger. Ruler of Callisto.

Avenger had revealed herself. What a fool. Her identity was no longer a secret. Not to her, at least. After all these years, it was she who found out first. No one else had a clue. No one. In nearly a decade of gaming. It was an historic moment. Ruined a bit by the sloppy play of her own man, but splendid none-the-less.

She stared at the picture of the shooter on her board of play. Her Anointed One. He was a problem she'd need to take care of. At this early stage it wouldn't be good to have such an important character turned. Only Avenger could do it and she might be able to achieve access to him in jail.

Suddenly, something clicked in her brain. Something not so good.

Turning on the recorded video of the incident, she forced herself to look at the complete footage of Jette's actions. As she analyzed it objectively, her pulse quickened, her eyes narrowed in fury. She hadn't seen it before in the haze of anger. The movements of Avenger were too smooth. Too polished. Too perfect. They appeared to be…planned.

The Empress cursed as a new wave of rage filled her. Avenger knew about the Anointed One. She knew! It was planned! It was orchestrated by the two of them!

Somehow, Avenger had turned him. There were only two people who knew about the Last Test. She and the Anointed One. The Minions didn't know enough. They knew that something was about to unfold, but not what.

She watched the last few seconds of the tape. Yes. Avenger and the Anointed One were talking. Celebrating their victory, no doubt. He was a Blood Traitor. More points for Avenger. More points.

Alright. Fine. She'd give Avenger this Challenge. But it would be her last victory. She'd make her adjustments. Use her people. Formulate another strategy. Turning an unsuccessful match into eventual glory was her strength.

It was painful but thrilling too. Irritating because it wasn't what she wanted or expected, but exhilarating because in some ways, it was far more than she ever dreamed of. Her position would be elevated because her arch enemy's status was now clearly and forever documented at a legendary level. In this game, when you turned or defeated an enemy, your points depended a great deal on how difficult it was. Whomever was left standing got the total points. Well the difficulty on this kill was going to be astronomical! Let Avenger have her day. When the dust settled, all the points would be tallied on her side anyway!

This was going to go immediately to the next level. Her original plan was to play around in the City of Might for a few rounds, accumulate points and weapons before the Final Duel. But now she'd rearrange her priorities, revise her strategy, and develop new tactical moves. She was sure Avenger was plotting with equal intensity.

What should she do first? She saw the Blood Traitor in cuffs being helped into the back of a police car. The answer to that question was clear. She'd have to figure out a way to get to him and seal his secrets by taking him out of play.

# Chapter 8

Jette sat alone in her office, quiet now. Closing her eyes, she breathed slowly, finding her center, calming her jumping system. Everything that morning had happened so fast, she'd operated solely on instinct. Now she needed to still her soul. To purge the ugliness.

In her native Arizona, she'd have gone to her *niganayegvna nahnai,* her safe place. A small open cave where she was close to Mother Earth and Father Sky. There she could exorcize the cruelty and viciousness of the world, her world, and find her balance again.

In her new home, she'd have to find another place. She smiled. The big tub in her luxurious bathroom with spicy scented water, flutes, some fresh herbal tea. That would be a wonderful start.

But first she had to get there. Through the reporters. Through the emergency vehicles. Then through the loud and active city.

Time to make tracks, she thought as she opened her eyes and put her shoes back on. A very sweet and considerate police officer brought them back to her when she was talking to the hideous Captain Green.

He'd seemed more interested in her than in the case and what had happened, so she made short work of their interview, responding in concise answers and not elaborating in any way. She wondered about Green's skill as an investigator. Marc's opinion of him seemed colored by his dislike at the time, but now she thought he might be right about the quality of his work. He never asked her what she and the shooter had said to each other after he'd regained full consciousness. Something she'd thought would be of great interest to anyone trying to put together a solid case. Even in what appeared to be open and shut cases, details were important. She didn't volunteer any of it since it seemed hardly relevant. She'd share it with Marc. If he thought she should call Green, she would.

Putting all the students' papers she'd collected that day into her brief case, she gathered her purse and shut out the lights. Time to grab a cab. Life went on.

When she got to the front door, she was shocked to see the number the reporters still around the building. Campus security kept them out, but it seemed obvious they were waiting for someone. And she was very much afraid she knew who that was. How the devil was she going to get to the street to catch a ride home?

Then she grinned. Hallelujah. Salvation. A rather short, portly man in a uniform was talking with one of the security guards and pointing to the building. Within a few seconds, the cell phone in her purse rang. She plucked it up quickly.

"Hello?"

"Dr. Morningstar?"

"Yes."

"This is Amo Holliday, security."

"Yes, Amo."

"A Claude is here to pick you up. Do you know him?"

"Yes, I do. And a discreet ride is just what I need right now."

"Understood. If you're ready to leave, I'll send him to the side door. It should be completely clear."

"Wonderful. You can send him around now."

"Will do. And, ah, Dr. Morningstar?"

"Yes?"

"Absolutely great work today. It was amazing. Are you doing okay?"

"Thank you, Amo. I'm doing just fine. Sending Claude back and keeping the media at bay will make everything go more smoothly. I really appreciate it."

"Then you got it."

A few minutes later a hunter green Lincoln Towncar stretch limousine stopped at the side entrance. Claude jumped out of the driver's seat and came around to the back passenger's door.

"Claude. I'm so glad to see you. I wasn't sure how I was going to get through that mob out there."

"Detective Lexington called and asked me to come bring you home, Dr. Morningstar."

Jette smiled. Perfect. Her man was perfect. Or at least he was trying. And that was perfect enough for her.

"Thank you," she said as she slid into the luxurious back seat.

"We've had TV on all day in the kitchen. Excuse my presumption, ma'am but you were unbelievable. We almost had heart failure watching it, but, excuse me again, it was a proud moment. Hilda said you'd probably need a stiff drink, so she made your raspberry iced tea extra strong." He wheezed out a little laugh. Jette didn't drink spirits of any kind and Hilda knew it. What a wit. "It's in that pitcher."

"She's right. It's just what I need."

"Is there anything else I can get for you?"

"Could you program in the flutes, please? It's number five, I believe."

"It is indeed, ma'am. It will be right soothing, I imagine. Traffic is very bad right now, so it'll be awhile, but the time will be cool and quiet."

"Claude, if I weren't so crazy about Marc, I'd make a play for you."

Claude had absolutely no response to that so he just gave a delighted little cackle, closed the door softly and returned to his seat.

The back of the limo was cool and with the tinted windows up, she felt alone and private, and comforted. She poured the wonderful tea and sipped as she watched the frenzied city she'd adopted moving outside. The flutes soothed her, surrounded her with native music, creating a cocoon of serenity, harmony, and peace.

Less than three weeks ago she'd still been on her ranch in Arizona, riding her wonderful Diablo, the hot desert wind blowing through her hair. Could her world be any more different now? Marc's face came into her mind. Could her world be any more wonderful?

They'd met while he was down in Arizona working on a very personal case, driven by his heart to pursue the killer of a friend. They'd fallen in love immediately, their destinies coming together. No, that was too placid a word. Their destinies crashing together. And now they were traveling together.

When she'd decided to come to New York, to be with him, live with him, explore life with him, she knew little about his life here. She knew he was a New York City police officer. A successful one. A dedicated one. But little else about his world and day-to-day routines.

He'd asked her to move in with him and she'd accepted. She'd accepted a great deal on faith. A new job, a new home, a new lover, a whole new life. But her Cherokee blood carried with it all that she needed: trust in herself and her instincts, a knowledge that she could adjust, a love of adventure and risk, and a brave, fearless heart.

She'd left her ranch outside Tucson and resigned her position at the University of Arizona to make the journey with Marc to his city. She expected to move into his bachelor apartment for a few months before searching for something larger. A small dark place filled with mismatched furniture, dirty underwear, and old take-out debris. With a fine layer of dust to complement the unspeakable vegetation growing in the corners of his bathroom. Judging from the way he lived in his borrowed condo in Arizona, she suspected she'd have to be very tolerant of his man cave until she could shake a little order into it. But she was crazy in love and ready for the ultimate challenge. As it turned out, it was more of a shock then she ever imagined.

Jette closed her eyes and relived her first hours in New York City. It was such a fantastic memory that it deserved to be rerun frequently.

She got off the plane at LaGuardia holding hands with Marc, filled with anticipation and curiosity. She could tell he was both excited and anxious. He'd never been away from his city so long and their relationship was so new, he hadn't yet processed the idea of permanence. He was eager to get back to the familiar, and yet because her hand was in his, even the familiar felt strange. Having a resident therapist was going to be good for him. On many levels, she thought as she recalled him flipping out his cell phone and making several calls. He was back. And it seemed to feed him with pure energy.

"Okay. All set," he said to her, walking behind a cab. "I have a friend who's going to pick up your luggage, and all that completely essential cargo you packed."

Raising his eyebrows to make a point, he picked up his one small overnight bag and tossed it into the open trunk.

"Sweetheart." Jette slid into the back seat. "If we're going to successfully cohabitate, I think you need to understand a few of the indispensable rules of building a relationship."

As he climbed in beside her, he grinned. Nothing was going to spoil his mood today. Not even a few rules he was sure he could have her forgetting, or at least forgiving, by the end of the day.

"And those would be?" he asked as he gave the driver an address.

"Just one for now. Never flaunt your superiority in the selecting and packing of what is considered essential. It's a uniquely personal choice and based on each individual's definition of what is vital. In this case your one tiny suitcase is not a virtue, but a mystery."

"Ah ha. I got it. So your uniquely personal definition includes 45 goddamn shades of lipstick?"

"There were probably no more than a dozen."

"Fuck that. There were at least two dozen in the box before you panicked and went back into your stash for another essential handful."

Jette just stared at him until he shrugged. "Not that I was counting."

"No, you were cussing."

"No more than normal."

"True enough." Jette looked around. "What address did you give the driver? From what I remember, it seems a little uptown for a police officer."

He didn't think she'd been paying attention, but then he should have remembered her ability to process information on multiple levels.

"It is," was all he said and distracted her in the best way he'd found to get her incredible mind to empty. Slipping his arm around her and drawing her into a kiss, he stirred her up. Then he spent the rest of the commute simply enjoying his good fortune.

The cab pulled up to a gorgeous eight story stone building on Seventh facing Central Park. Glancing out the open car window, she saw sumptuous blossoms of colorful summer flowers spilling out of tall pots on either side of stunning twelve foot cut glass doors. Jette didn't know a lot about New York real estate, but she knew quality living when she saw it. And this was indescribably lush and luxurious. Jette looked over at Marc with amusement.

"One of your friends loan you a penthouse to impress your girlfriend?"

"Something like that."

A tall, stiff backed man in a uniform opened the back door and stood back as Marc helped Jette out onto the immaculate walkway under a rich, wide portico of gleaming brass and brick.

"Detective Lexington," said the man coolly. No eye contact, no warmth. Simple efficiency and robotic movements.

"Hey, Johnny. It's good to see you again, too. This is Dr. Morningstar. She'll be shacking up with me."

There was a slight hesitation in the doorman's demeanor that Jette could see was scandalized sensibilities warring with a rigid sense of duty.

"And Jette, this scary walking statue is Johnny something-or-other."

"It's Jonathon Waters, ma'am. I'm head doorman here at The Edgewood."

"Which is a position superior to the mayor, the Archbishop and the police commissioner, so remember to give him the proper respect. Right, Johnny? Can you escort my luggage to the apartment, your honor? Tell the scarecrow we'll be there in a minute. My girl and I are going up to the roof."

Jonathon ignored Marc as he turned and performed another of his duties by opening the huge heavy door to the lobby.

"It's nice to meet you, Mr. Waters," said Jette a little breathlessly as she walked into a foyer as elegant and spacious as the entrance to a European castle. She stepped from the busy, noisy streets of New York City into quiet luxury. Shiny hard wood floors were covered with thick beautifully patterned rugs. A huge bouquet of freshly cut flowers stood on a round marble table near discreetly positioned elevators.

"Alright, Detective. Time for an explanation." Jette looked up into Marc's glittering green eyes.

"The man hates me but can't do an overt thing about it. One of these days he'll crack under the strain and maybe hatch a human."

She just continued to silently stare at him.

"I thought it would be more fun to see it rather than have me describe it." He shrugged.

"You live here?"

"Not much, actually. But I own the co-op apartment on the top floor…"

"The penthouse?" Jette was stunned.

"Yeah. And a big chunk of the floor below it. Mostly for the, ah, staff. Up to now it hasn't been a very convenient crib. I usually spend my time working and crashing at my place in the Village or," he shrugged again. "Where ever. But I periodically come here to sleep and to annoy the people in the building."

"I have a feeling this is going to be a fascinating story."

"Another chapter in the life of Marcus Lexington."

There have been so many, Jette thought. He'd shared with her like he'd shared with no other. Even his name was an interesting and intimate secret. He had no idea what his real name was. As a quick and clever child he made one up when a social worker took him into custody after the death of his mother, an addict who'd died horribly of an overdose in a cold and grimy shelter. He'd named himself after a theater on Lexington. The Marcus Theater. And now it appeared that there was another intriguing episode. She couldn't wait to hear it.

They stood on a lush roof-top garden overlooking Central Park while Marc related his story.

"I did a lot of poaching for bucks when I first took to the streets. It was fairly easy money. No real skill involved. Anyway, I got so I'd recognize the occasional regular contributors. Mr. Clarke was one of them. Not that I knew his name at the beginning. He was just this old guy with nice threads and a big smiling face.

"Mr. Clarke always gave me a dollar outside Carnegie after performances. He had season tickets, so I knew the dates and times. I'd watch for him. It got to be kind of a game. He and his wife Betsy were, well, a little naïve when it came to the streets. Comes from being rich and privileged, I guess. As I grew and moved from begging to running numbers, doing street games, and ah…well…um…"

"Other odd jobs."

"Yeah. That's right. Anyway, I'd still watch for them. Saw them around the city. He'd pop for the buck. One night a guy grabbed some kind of necklace off her. Right there in front of Radio City, and I tore out after him. He was from a rival gang, not too bright, slow as a three-legged dog and in my territory so I took him down, gave him a little grief and repossessed the necklace. I must have been about 14 or so. The cops were all over by then, but I wasn't slow or stupid, so I got away clean. The necklace turned out to be a locket. There were pictures in it. Two little boys."

"So you returned it?"

"It was worthless. Cheap gold plate. Couldn't hock it…"

"Ah huh. So you returned it?" She repeated the question, pleased with the heart of the little boy. Still inside the man, she thought.

"Hell, why not. If the cops found it on me, I'd have been in deep shit. I bumped him when I saw him next and I imagine he found it in his pocket soon after."

Jette poked him gently over his heart.

"Softy."

"I'm going to have to disagree, professor, if you're referring to my righteously well developed pecs, they're iron."

"No, darling, I'm referring to your righteously well developed heart. So, who were the boys?"

"Found out afterward they had two sons and one of them had given her the locket. They'd both died years before I met them. One when he was a boy, from influenza, I think. The other when he was a young man. A small plane crash. Turned out the locket was from the little one. He'd bought it with his own money on the Mother's Day before he died and I guess it meant a lot to her."

"How tragic for them," said Jette softly, fascinated, touched, and all together in love with the tale. "Tell me the rest."

"One night, a few years later, a small gang of Tigers were looking for points and decided Mr. and Mrs. Clarke were good for some sport. They had the old lady pretty well buttoned up when I decided they needed to be tossed back to their territory. I broke it up. Got sliced pretty bad. The old guy got me to a hospital before I could recover and scat. Damn it was ugly. I was cussing, the admissions people were acting like bureaucratic assholes, the nurses were trying to get the bleeding under control and some old creepy hag from the public defender's office started poking at me, and the cops were all over the place. Up to that point, I'd pretty much avoided hospitals. I'd go into emergency once in awhile, get patched up, then skate with whatever I could pick up out of the locked drug cabinets, but they admitted me to this one. Mr. Clarke told them I was his grandson. Paid for top flight medical care. I guess I was pretty lucky. They'd nicked an artery and I really needed the emergency surgery.

"Anyway, the old lady, Mrs. Clarke, was cut a little and they figured I'd saved her life. Fussed over me until I couldn't stand it anymore. As soon as I could walk, I got dressed and got out. I thought I'd shaken them off, but when I was accepted into the academy, my name and picture were published in the Times. I got this card. Said they were…were proud of me. I'd see him around and the old man and I would meet for a bagel on the corner after my shift, or sit in the Park and talk about the Yankees. Mrs. Clarke would join us once in a while with sandwiches and cookies and we'd have to watch our language. The old guy died soon after I got my law degree and she followed him less than two weeks later."

Jette sighed. "You filled a hole in their hearts."

"I don't know about that, but there were times when I really looked forward to our chats. And Mrs. Clarke's oatmeal raisin cookies."

"They filled a hole in your heart, too."

"Oh I was quite sure in those days I didn't have a heart. But maybe. Anyway after Mrs. Clarke died a lawyer, some ultra conservative putz representing a real uptown firm, knocked on my apartment door. God, what a scene. I had, well, company who was…ah…"

"Not uptown."

"Yeah. Not even all that civilized, actually. We were in the middle of a pretty hardy party when the guy showed up and my mood wasn't too hospitable."

"Hard to imagine."

"He just slapped an envelope at me without saying a word about what was in it. I was cussing up a storm because I thought it was a summons or something, but it wasn't. I'd just passed the bar and recognized a will when I saw it. It was a pretty simple document. They left a fortune to each of their lifelong employees. Another fortune to the Salvation Army. And a little something for me. Said my sacrifice, can you believe that, a few pints of blood and a little pain, my sacrifice gave them something money couldn't buy. More years together. Shit. I was so shocked I never did get back to the big breasted bimbo."

Jette's eyes teared up.

"Jette, now stop that. I'm off the bimbos and I intend to stay off them as long as you live."

49

Jette gave a little laugh and sniffed. "You know your earlier, ill advised and marginally satisfying liaisons with women possessing questionable attributes are of no interest to me."

Marc just stared at her, then grinned and shook his head. "Sometimes you just give me nowhere to go. Anyway." He kissed her lightly. "You're just a sucker for a happy ending."

"And the little something?

"Eighty-four fucking million dollars, the penthouse apartment and everything in it."

Jette gasped.

"Yeah, isn't that a kicker? I knew they had class, I just figured they probably lived in a nice apartment uptown."

"You never told me. Why."

"It's not what defines me. It's not important." He looked around. "I grew up completely mobile and without things. I could put everything I owned in a plastic garbage bag."

"That kind of poverty makes some people very acquisitive. They can't stop buying, surrounding themselves with things they were deprived of earlier in life."

Marc shrugged. "I find stuff is heavy. I don't need it." He took her hand. "I really didn't think I needed anything except my job and good taco now and then." He devastated her with the look he gave her. "Then I met you." He pulled her into his arms, drew her to him, into him and covered her mouth with his, devoured her. "Better than a good taco."

"Now and then," she purred. "So how much are you worth now?"

"I have no idea. I've put it all in a blind trust so I can never be accused of conflict of interests. It's managed by some tight ass firm. A woman you'll meet soon, Hilda, acts as translator and takes care of all the expenses. I have a debit card that I use for tacos and beer."

"And your departmental salary?"

"I think the New York Police Foundation can use it more than me. It wouldn't even pay the yearly maintenance fee on this place. It, ah, comes with this roof garden."

"This is all yours?" The garden covered the entire roof and was planted with a beautiful rainbow of seasonal plants and flowers. Tall shrubs in earthen pots stood at attention along the four sides. There were several seating areas and shaded arbors. It could have been a small city park.

"I thought you might like it. A place where you can go. It's not the desert, but the sounds of the city are muted by the scrubs and the atrium is fairly quiet."

"It's wonderful, Marc."

"Ready to see the rest?"

"Absolutely. A quick tour, then I'd like to get you to bed. You're looking a little pale. I think you should take a nap."

"I can get on board that flight."

With that, Marc took her hand and walked with her into their new life.

# Chapter 9

Back in the present, her memories warming her, Jette poured some more tea as they passed Times Square. It was superbly prepared by Marc's live in housekeeper, Hilda. So thoughtful of her to send it with Claude. She remembered the first time she met the woman. She was another wonderful surprise in a day full of the unexpected. Not as shocking as the penthouse, but a surprise none-the-less. She decided she had plenty of time to play that reel over in her mind. Laying her head back and closing her eyes, she saw the moment clearly. Felt the astonishment, the pleasant revelation, the fun, all over again.

Marc took her down the front staircase, through an impressive foyer to a pair of carved oak doors, the only ones on the floor. Before Marc could put his key in the lock, they swung open and a very tall woman with steel gray hair, sharp blue eyes and a disapproving expression greeted them.

"Detective Lexington." Her posture was as rigid as a soldier at attention but her voice was soft and cultured. "I see you found your way back."

"Are you still here?"

"Aren't you the lucky one." She turned to Jette and her expression softened, became more welcoming. "You must be Dr. Morningstar."

"I am."

"Welcome to New York."

"Thank you."

"Jette, this is Hilda Adams," said Marc, pushing by her with Jette in tow. "She came with the place."

"It's nice to meet you. I sorry, Ms. Adams…"

"Hilda."

"Hilda. But I'm feeling a bit displaced." Jette looked around the unbelievably big and beautiful apartment. "I'd prepared myself for a small walk-up efficiency stacked with dirty laundry, dirtier magazines, empty beer cans, two month old milk in the refrigerator and something growing in abundance in the shower."

"You must be referring to Detective Lexington's apartment in the Village."

"I keep my apartment down there," Marc explained as he amused himself by watching Jette try to take everything in. "It's rent controlled and convenient when I'm on a case in that neighborhood."

"I had it cleaned out and fumigated while you were gone. I supervised it myself," sniffed Hilda as she closed the doors.

"You touched my things?"

"I wore gloves. Anyway, I got your message that you were going to set up permanent residence here. And with a lovely companion."

"Yeah, I decided I needed a roommate."

"Dr. Morningstar, it's a privilege to meet you." A ghost of a smile curved the woman's lips. "I hear you'll be teaching at New York University."

"I will, yes. I start on Monday. A two week summer seminar in abnormal psychology."

Hilda's eyes snapped as she opened her mouth to make a comment, but Marc beat her to it.

"Don't even say it. That was too easy an opening," warned Marc.

"You're right, of course. One need not state the obvious. I heard you were shot, Detective."

Jette smiled as the woman led them into a luxurious sitting room. Don't try to fool me with that imperious tone, she thought. The nurse's station at the hospital in Arizona told her a woman named Hilda called every day. Jette had assumed it was an old girlfriend or something. And she could see the intense scrutiny in Hilda's eyes, taking inventory of Marc's color, his weight, his energy level.

"Maybe you'd better sit down," she said. "I wouldn't want you falling and taking out the entire collection of Michela Brittany icons. It took Mrs. Clarke years to find the complete suite. Someone your size has no business around precious art anyway."

"She thinks she owns everything here because she dusts it, so don't move anything," explained Marc.

"Nonsense. Dr. Morningstar is obviously a woman of refinement and taste. It's you who shouldn't touch anything." She looked at Jette and smiled. "I caught him scraping something from the street off his boot one afternoon with the pen Ben Franklin used to sign the Declaration of Independence so he's forever banned from putting his hands on anything more than a week old."

She watched carefully as Marc sat down. He was obviously favoring his chest and side. It had been a long trip from Arizona and he was feeling the pull of his wounds.

"Would you like me to show you around, Dr. Morningstar. I'm quite sure there are rooms the detective hasn't even seen. The TV, bagels, and beer are in the kitchen so he pretty much inhabits that. And the bedroom of course."

"I'd love a tour."

"I'd love a beer." Marc gingerly leaned back against the soft cushions of the couch.

"Don't you think hot tea would be better after your long journey?" asked Hilda.

"Don't you think you're a little old to be looking for a new job?"

Not in the least intimidated, Hilda looked at Jette.

"What did his doctors recommend?"

"He's no longer under any restrictions," smiled Jette.

"I'll see to it, then. Would you like some of those incredibly nutritious and palate pleasing Doritos to go with it, Detective?"

"Oh, yeah."

Hilda thought she'd let him settle for a moment longer.

"Will you require additional staff, Dr. Morningstar, or will you be bringing in your own people?"

Jette thought of the rugged and richly seasoned ranch hands she employed in Arizona and could only imagine the impression they'd make on the proper Hilda Adams.

"I won't be bringing any of my people with me. Who is currently employed?"

"Two of us who were with the Clarkes and a few other colorful people Detective Lexington has asked me to, shall we say, keep on the straight and narrow."

"Don't know of anyone straighter or more narrow," commented Marc.

"Your wit is as sharp as a baked potato, as usual. Anyway, there's Claude. He's the chauffeur."

Jette couldn't keep the humor from tickling her voice. "You have a chauffeur?"

"No. The queen mother here has the chauffeur," corrected Marc.

"Claude is on call throughout the day and every weekday evening. He drives me when I require transportation. On weekends, the detective has put another, ah, person on staff. I'm not sure why, he never uses the car."

Marc grinned at Hilda. "Tommy is her weekend driver. She's a transvestite. Played a chauffeur in an off off off Broadway production of *Driving Miss Crazy* but that closed. No surprise. I told her she could crash in the quarters and take some coin for the weekend gig. She started life as a six foot five inch wrestler in the WWWF, then decided to grow a rack and wear high heels. Called herself He-Man the She-Man. The WWWF didn't mind the heels, but wouldn't let her go topless after she got the implants so she was looking for another calling. Besides, it has the added bonus of absolutely scandalizing this entire snooty building full of tight ass, frigid billionaires."

"People here are refined and cultured," contradicted Hilda.

"Yeah, well they couldn't vote me out of the place. Didn't know I had a law degree and could keep them in the courts forever without having to pay the legal fees."

"Some may be a bit patronizing and supercilious, but they did finally realize a resident police officer may have some merit and gave up the suit."

"Yeah right. The only reason they gave up was because they couldn't possibly raise their voices above a refined and cultured level. I got them on sheer volume."

"It was quite a revelation that someone who didn't want the place nor had any desire to live here fought so...so loudly when faced with possible eviction."

Hilda remembered their faces when Marc went into a full rant. It was a secret delight she'd never share with him. Nor anyone else with the possible exception of her priest.

Jette watched Hilda's face and it was like looking through a window. She immediately warmed to the woman.

"Back to the staff," continued Hilda brusquely. "Natalia retired when she received her inheritance, she was the cook, but since the detective rarely eats here and when he does, it's from cardboard containers, I have taken over the duties of keeping orange juice, bagels, and beer in the refrigerator. Miss Pruit assists me with household chores.

Cleaning, dusting, vacuuming. She's just barely making the grade, but I think with my watching her every move, she'll adequately meet your expectations."

"Meg Pruitt's an old hooker whose back finally gave out," Marc explained, wondering why he wasn't getting his beer considering the number of household staff he employed. "Always kept clean of the drugs, so when she wanted to get out of the game, I though dusting was a job anyone could do…"

Scandalized, Hilda just stared at him. Bringing in an old hooker wasn't the reason. Meg was quite bright and willing to do anything as long as she could stay off the streets. Dusting however, was both an art and a science. One had to use just the right stroke on just the right piece and the materials used for each surface had to be rigidly investigated for their properties.

"How about that beer," reminded Marc. "Talk about dust. There's about an inch of it collected on me since I've arrived."

"Right away. And for you, Dr. Morningstar?"

"I would love some tea."

"I got a message that you like it herbal and fruity."

Jette glanced at Marc, who just shrugged.

"Yes."

"I have some lovely raspberry chamomile. Later you can give me a list of items you'd like stocked in the pantry."

"Thank you Hilda. You're a gem. I appreciate you making me feel so welcome."

When Hilda left, Marc stared at the door she'd quietly closed, then looked up at Jette and patted the place next to him on the sofa.

"Come on over here and I'll show you welcome."

"In a second. I want to look out the windows. You have the most fantastic views."

"I like the one inside the room the best."

"And such beautiful things."

"It's just a bunch of old stuff."

"I think Hilda's right. You really should be banned from touching anything."

"Please, don't say Hilda and right in the same sentence. You'll shake me into a relapse."

Jette picked up a vase and held it to the light. "This is exquisite."

"I remember one time I broke into Polly Forns's Antiques down on 5th. I had one gang or another on my tail, so I needed a place to lay low for awhile. God, I thought, the shelter at St. Benedicts had better stuff than her old dusty crap. I hid in this huge armoire with chipping paint and creaking hinges. Imagine my shock when this crusty old dodger offered Polly $180,000 for it. And she turned him down flat. I thought what a perfect scam. I still do. Why would anyone pay a couple hundred thousand for that stuff when they could have a brand new plasma TV for a fraction of that."

"Why indeed," laughed Jette putting down the vase and flashing him a special smile.

"What?" he asked when she continued to stare at him.

"You really are adorable," she observed.

"See? You think I'm cute. Hilda thinks I'm gauche."

"Hilda isn't madly in love with you."

Marc shuddered. "Hilda doesn't have a beating heart."

"Why do you keep her here?" Jette knew the reason and thought that was adorable too.

"She'd have nowhere else to go. Nothing else to do. Just what New York needs. Another homeless unemployed person on the streets," shrugged Marc.

"Uh-huh." Jette was obviously not buying what he was selling.

"Yeah. Besides she knows just the right cleaning stuff to use on each piece. She's a maniac about her formulas. If I want to maintain the value of this crap, I need someone who was there when it was built."

"The couch you're sitting on is early 18th century."

"Well convince me the old bat isn't over 200 years old."

"You said that the staff received a bequest. Didn't Hilda?"

"Sure. Both her and Claude. Ten million each. All the others had the sense to retire to the good life, but not those two. Wanted to stay, so I thought what the hell. I, ah, suspect they're a set."

"You think they have a thing for each other?"

"In a strictly dried up eerie, unconsummated sense."

She laughed again and turned around, taking in the room, the air, the feeling about the space.

"The Clarkes' sons. Was either of them beautiful, dark, and green eyed?"

Marc stared into her chocolate brown eyes. "Think you're pretty smart, don't you?"

"Oh, I know I am."

"Okay if you promise not to get too full of yourself." Marc got up, went over to an exquisite 19th century Dutch Floral Marquetry Bureau and opened a drawer. In it were several frames, scrap books, and other family memorabilia. "I haven't been able to throw these away. Seems almost ungrateful. There is no other family that I know of. Here." He handed her a picture of a boy with thick dark brown curly hair and huge emerald green eyes. His smile held a bit of the devil.

"Oh, Marc." Jette's tender heart squeezed with sentimental delight. She'd seen only one picture of Marc as a child. Thick dark brown curly hair, huge emerald green eyes and a smile that held a bit of the angel. "Love was here. I can feel it. Love lived here and still lingers. It's a wonderful place."

"Make it your own. Make it your home. Now before the cadaver comes creeping back to show you around, how about we start with some necking on that old couch."

# Chapter 10

It took a long time to crawl through all the heavy post crisis traffic, but Jette was so entertained by her memories, she barely noticed. Claude swung up to the front of their building and before he could put the car into park, Jonathon had the door open.

"Dr. Morningstar, are you alright?"

These were the first words he'd uttered to her since the day she arrived. He nodded when she said good morning. He nodded when she said it was a beautiful day. He nodded when she asked him to call her a cab. She knew he had a voice, deep and rich and very, very pompous, but he rarely used it.

"I'm fine. Thank you."

He nodded, then gently took her hand in his huge palm and helped her out of the back seat.

Jette looked around.

"Thank the Lord, no press. I know I can count on you to protect my privacy, Mr. Waters."

"Of course, Dr. Morningstar." Jonathon's chest expanded, highlighting the ruthlessly polished buttons on his meticulous uniform. "We've had no media or other bothersome folk around. No one knows you live here but a select few. And none of us would share that knowledge with outsiders."

He said outsiders like anyone living anywhere but at this exclusive address wasn't exactly human.

"Are you going back for Marc, Claude?" asked Jette turning back to the driver.

"No Ma'am. The detective took his Harley today." His eyes slid to Jonathon, knowing there would be a blast of disapproval.

Claude secretly loved how the patented sound of the Harley revving set Jonathon's buttons vibrating. He was never sure if it was because the doorman was so revolted, or if the sound waves were just that potent. It was a powerful machine and Marc knew precisely the right amount of gas that would produce the most impressive amount of thunder. It was a kick.

"Thanks again for the rescue." She waved to Claude, then turned as Jonathon opened the door and allowed her to enter his lobby.

Feeling like a hero or something, Claude got behind the wheel again and drove it into the garage, where he would buff up the already scrupulous exterior and share stories with his colleagues in the building. There weren't many in the summer, nearly everyone was out of the city in Europe or the Hamptons, but there were enough to have a good gossip session and he knew what the topic would be. Ah, life was good.

Hilda swung open the door before Jette reached it. She tried to keep the cultivated demeanor in place but as soon as she saw Jette safe and sound, the stern mask slipped and the rigid posture softened.

"Oh, Dr. Morningstar. You've been all over the TV for the last few hours. Tommy recorded it all for you. Oh, mercy. Please forgive me."

Jette looked at her.

"For what?"

"For this." Hilda scooped Jette into her arms and hugged her.

Jette laughed with delight. "Hilda, what a wonderful welcome."

Then, completely embarrassed, but unable to help herself, she smiled and set Jette at arm's length. "Let me look at you. Are you alright?"

"Yes, I'm fine."

"Then forgive me again, but what in the Blessed Virgin Mary were you thinking? That maniac could have killed you!" She led Jette into the foyer.

Jette sighed. "Hilda. You sound like Marc. I knew what I was doing and trusted my ability to follow through."

"I see. So now you've not only jeopardized your life, you placed me in the very uncomfortable position of agreeing with the detective." Hilda's eyes narrowed, but there was the tiniest quirk of her lips.

"How inconsiderate of me," smiled Jette.

"Indeed. Would you like some hot tea now?"

"Love some, but I think I'd like a steaming salted bath first. I need to purge the rest of the shakes."

"Then you go along and I'll bring it in an hour."

"I don't think it'll take that long."

"Maybe not for you, but I won't trust myself with the good china for at least another hour. Mercy."

Jette watched Hilda's straight back disappear through the dining room into the kitchen then walked down the wide hallway to the master suite. The rich, warm colors accented by fabulous pieces of original art welcomed her home. Home. Smiling, she let the arms of her new surroundings embrace her.

She was a long way from her roots, but it was beginning to feel like her place. Some of her favorite pieces had already arrived and they were mating nicely with the most unique and fabulous collection of furniture and accessories she'd ever seen.

"Darling! I know you're off to a well deserved hot, sudsy, bath, but honestly, sweetie pie, I had to come and see for myself that you're really, really alright."

From the doorway came a huge woman, 6 5 , 240, with skin the color of rich dark chocolate, breasts the size of basketballs, and hands fluttering like pigeon's wings. She was, well, stunning. Her dramatically made up eyes were almost black, and her smile was so broad and bright, it could compete with Times Square at midnight. Her bleached blonde hair was piled high and, added to the three inch platform sandals she wore, it appeared she towered close to the twelve foot ceiling. She was in a sunny summer mood today, dressed in bright yellow short shorts the color of lemons and a white crop top with a big yellow sunflower stretched across her breasts, proudly exposing her belly with its solid and muscular six pack.

"I tell you, honey, when I saw you tearing up those stairs, I thought I was going to have a stroke. Not a little catatonic seizure, but a full brain explosion! Then I saw you go up on the roof and there was that monster as close to you as that! And those nasty, nasty guns! Such meshugass! I thought maybe you were just going to, I don't know, like scout it out or something. Like in those old westerns. Sorry about the stereotype, dear heart, but being Indian and all that. Not that any of those darn, dirty old westerns ever got the Indians right. Noble people. Did I tell you my great, great grandfather who was a slave in Georgia married a Seminole from Florida after he was freed by the sainted Abraham Lincoln? That would give me a scoshe of native blood. I'm not sure where. Maybe in my balls, 'cause honey, that's what it took for you to take off after that shooter. And if that's where the native blood is, I don't think I'll ever cut them off. I don't care how inconvenient they are."

She took Jette's hand and led her back to the bathroom. "And look at that, didn't even scratch your manicure. Oy! Did Hilda tell you I got the whole thing on disc? It's all set up for you in the den when, and if, you want to see yourself in action. Of course all you need to do is turn on the TV. It's been showing in one of those hellish continuous loops all day."

She kept up the chatter, running Jette's bath, getting out her robe, pouring lily scented bath salts into the steaming water. Jette was very much afraid she was going to stick around and scrub her back, but as she kicked off her shoes, Tommy grabbed her again, hugged her, then left her alone in the bathroom. The sudden silence was deafening, but appreciated. She adored Tommy, but wanted, needed, solitude.

Jette turned on some soulful, rhythmic native music, stripped, stepped into the bath and settled in. Then and only then did she allow herself to open up and fully feel the terror, shock, dread, horror, and fear. It was huge and her body ached with it. Her stomach jumped and her heartbeat accelerated as her mind relived the entire event. She didn't need a taped video, she could see it all, hear it all, suffer it all as if it was happening in real time. When she was in action, she never let herself consider the possible consequences of what she was doing. Now they came to her in one potent revelation. She took several deep breaths, released the burden of the distress, then began her healing meditation.

# Chapter 11

The Empress studied the board filled with lines and notes and a tumbled array of disconnected thoughts jotted hastily on notepaper. She needed to settle down and get her mind to process all the nuances. This was her strength. This was her world. She could do it. She had to study all the pieces on her storyboard and arrange them to fit the outcomes that would give her the upper hand again.

The maneuvers to get to the Blood Traitor, formerly her Anointed One, were completed. That wasn't much of a challenge. When you could read minds and hold out Boons, anything could be arranged.

The assassination needed to be public. Needed to be witnessed by her loyal Sentinels and Minions. A signal to them that she was still firmly in control. And a subtle reminder of what happened to all who considered turning their allegiance to Avenger.

Checking the clock in the corner of her computer, she reluctantly saved everything and put all of her random thoughts in a file. She needed to strip off the role of her preferred state of being and enter the Middle World of Reality. There was a life out there she needed to play. As skillfully as she performed in the world of Sovereignty, she thought. It wasn't as rewarding, but a real-world identity was part of the mystery, part of the action.

Her own Middle World identity was flawless but she hated her alter ego. Hated her. Hated her. Hated her. She wanted to stay in her true state and be the Empress all day, every day. But she knew she couldn't do that. Her Middle World role secured the resources she needed to keep her empire functioning. She still needed to eat. To pay the rent. To pay her Sentinels, Assassins and Mercenaries. To buy the drugs. She wasn't a druggie herself, but many of her Minions and Sentinels were. And it was her role to grant them Boons. Wishes. Dreams. Desires. That took real cash.

She knew it wasn't quite within the Rules of Engagement to hire Sentinels rather than to simply recruit them from the hundreds of Minions in her field of play, but she needed men and women with special skills. Not just gamers, but professionals. She added the Mercenaries when she'd decided to take the challenges and battles to the Middle World. The rules were less clear for them and their play, but that was a good thing when breaking new ground. Being the one and only true Blue Empress made her invincible, her decisions infallible.

Sighing heavily, she slowly removed her robes and mask, and went to change into acceptable attire for her role in the Middle World.

# Chapter 12

Jette checked the clock on the little wrought iron shelf over the tub. It was clustered in with several of her native ceramic pieces and together with the soothing flutes and drums, contributed to the peace she now felt in her soul.

She'd been out for over an hour. The water had lost its temperature and she felt chilled. Reaching over with her talented toes, she turned on the hot tap full blast and soon felt the relief of warm water surrounding her once again. She sighed, loving the feeling of decadence. Marc should be home soon and things could get even more decadent.

Home. It had become that to her in just a few short weeks. It was the way of the Cherokee people. In their relatively recent history they'd been uprooted from their homelands so often they'd become very adaptable. She sipped the tea Hilda had brought in. Then again, some things were fairly easy to adapt to.

Her mind wandered through time and as she bumped into memories she treasured, she re-experienced them. Everything that had happened reinforced her decision to make the move, strengthened her love for Marc, and filled her with anticipation and excitement for her new life. She recognized and welcomed the fundamental contentment she felt.

When she opened her eyes, the reason for her contentment, her exhilaration, her pleasure, her life stood in the doorway watching her. His eyes were shadowed, his expression unreadable. She could see his hesitation. And she could guess the reason for it. He could hide from most people, but not from her.

He'd brought her here to the city, and within a few short weeks its violent side had touched her. But she was a sturdy desert flower. Resilient and strong. She'd come through the trauma, thrive in spite of the risk. She smiled at him. The only way she'd convince him that she was here to stay, that she wasn't going to abandon him for any reason, ever, was to stick by him and that was going to take time.

For it was over time that he would settle into the idea that he no longer needed to run alone. That she wouldn't abandon him like his mother. She'd be by his side. Forever.

"Hi," she said softly. "Care to join me?"

He sniffed the air like a wolf. "I think if I dipped in there and came out smelling like lilies or whatever, I wouldn't be able to maintain an erection long enough to satisfy a desperate housewife. I need to shower with Eros, the manly scent of super studs."

"Excellent idea. I plan on making some significant demands on you when I get out of the tub."

"Oh yeah?"

"It's part of the live-in package. Sex on demand."

"You sound like a Direct TV brochure."

"Not like a woman in love with her roommate?"

"That, too."

She knew he was comfortable with talk of sex, but that "L" word still freaked him. A lot.

"If you aren't going to get in here with me, at least take off the hardware and come sit for awhile. I'm not done soaking yet."

Marc walked back into the bedroom, automatically unclipping his gun and tossing it on the dresser along with his cell phone, pager, radio, and badge. He stared at the little pile for a moment. Everything he used to serve and protect the public. He was proud of his service. Of his commitment to that pledge. But his lover, the one person who meant the most to him, who was now his life, moved out of his sphere of protection.

Nothing he was, nothing he did, could have stood for her today. Stood in front of her today. Would she still think he was worth the effort? Worth the risk? What had he given her, other than significant sexual pleasure? While he knew he was really good at that, what else was he contributing to this relationship?

He'd been standing in the doorway watching her. She was obviously enjoying her bath and there was something on her face. He would have said contentment, but she'd just been through a horrific experience. He knew she could purge negative feelings when she lived under the vast open sky of her native desert, but could she so seamlessly find her balance here among the often manic movement of New York City? There was nothing tranquil or peaceful about this place. About his life. About him. Could she really adapt so well? Make it her place? Make him her life?

Unbuttoning his shirt, he returned to the bathroom and sat on the edge of the tub. Maybe he should risk a loss of testosterone by joining her in the frothy, fragrant water. When he had her in his arms, when his hands skillfully played with her body, he knew his ground. He was in familiar territory. Doubts only came over him when he let his mind rule.

Jette reopened her eyes and saw what she knew she'd never get tired of seeing. His irresistible look of love. The look that fired an intense craving in her. Her belly tightened with desire.

"Are you doing alright?" he asked.

"Yes. I'm fine now. It was the reason for this soaking marathon. I needed to settle."

"I'm...I'm sorry Jette."

"I know you are Marc, and you shouldn't be. There's no reason for you to be sorry for what happened. It was horrible, brutal in fact. Frightening and traumatic. But none of it was your responsibility."

"I brought you here."

"I thought we settled that earlier."

"We didn't. I acted like a crazed maniac and all your attention was focused on my dysfunctional behavior, so we never really got back to the bottom line. You're here because I'm here."

"That's right."

"Sounds like responsibility to me."

"Sounds more like angst to me."

"Is that your diagnosis, Doctor?" Marc's eyes got harder, and his jaw set in a line that revealed to Jette her analysis was dead on.

"I took a course in angst and yes, it's my diagnosis." She continued to stare into his storming green eyes. "I can't stop loving you, Marc, so I can't be anywhere else."

Marc's stomach did a dance and words failed him. Nothing he had in his background or experience had prepared him for this kind of passion. This kind of love. Hell, this kind of argument.

"Then I could be somewhere else. We could go back to Arizona," he said more out of frustration than true conviction. He would do anything for her. Anything.

"And what makes you think I'd consider giving up this luxury apartment, my fabulous new job, and the shopping and restaurants of New York City?"

"You have a luxury ranch in Arizona, with a pool, I might add. You can reinstate yourself in the fabulous job you gave up to come here. And there's nothing in New York that compares to the Arroz de Fuegos at the Cactus Rose."

"You left out the shopping." She could see him melting, the tension easing.

"Everyone sells a perfect size 2 online now."

She raised her eyebrows. "And how exactly do you know my size?"

"I'm a detective. Besides, I've had my hands all over your perfect size 2 ass."

"I see. Well, I'm still not leaving New York City. I love it here. I love you here."

"Jette, I..." Marc gave up, overwhelmed by his feelings and still unable to release the words in his heart.

Jette sighed and stood up. Marc's heart took another hit. There was a bruise on her hip and a tiny cut on her collarbone. Put there by his city and its terror. Marc grabbed one of the fluffy white bath towels and as she stepped out of the tub, gently wrapped her in it, his arms going around her as well.

She knew he needed reassurance, but sometimes, so did she. It was part of her heart's mission to get him more comfortable with his feelings for her. Then get him more comfortable with expressing those feelings. Right now she needed the words.

"Jette...I...," he began again.

"Yes?" She looked up at him, raising her eyebrows suggestively.

This was a great relief to him because it gave him an excuse to act. He was always better with action than with words. Gathering her in his arms, he drew her to him. There was no resistance from her, no hesitation. Covering her mouth with his, he tried to pour his love into the kiss so she'd know.

Marc felt the love and he knew he could show it physically. Sometime in the future, he might even be comfortable enough to say the words as easily and as naturally as she, but somehow they still got stuck in his throat.

"I love you," she whispered as he tenderly caressed her soft, wet shoulders.

Jette knew, of course. She'd known he loved her even before he did. Now she saw it in his eyes, felt it flowing from him into her as he kissed her again deepening it until her body responded and her need for him flared up.

Should she let him off the hook? Her entire turned on, tuned up body voted an enthusiastic yes, not wanting to interrupt the moment.

But deep in her heart, Jette knew that the only way he would feel at ease with love was to find a way to express it other than physically. This method of showing his feelings worked with her because they would always have a physical side to their relationship, but she wanted for him the ability to respond to all kinds of love. Love from the friends that surrounded him. Love from family. If they had children some day, he would need to be able to say the words. So she suppressed her body's response and screaming protest and pulled away from the kiss, then pulled back from him.

She looked at him, into him. His lips curved up in an ironic smile. It was nearly irresistible. Her body made a comeback and almost pushed her heart out of the way in an attempt to react to the pull of that smile.

"Don't throw that macho, physical stuff at me," she said, making it challenging.

"We all have our strengths," he shrugged.

"And our weaknesses." She stepped back. Not far, just slightly out of his reach.

He inched forward, she inched back.

He grinned. She grinned.

"Gotta hear it, too, huh?"

"Just try. It gets easier, I promise. If you can ride a Harley through the streets of New York, you can do this."

Nodding, he took a deep breath. Like he was going to plunge into a lake. A cold, deep, frigid unfamiliar lake.

"I love you, Jette," he said in a low sexy voice.

It did it to her every time. Completely swamped her. She rewarded him by dropping the towel, jumping into his arms and delivering a kiss that could fire a ceramic pot without a kiln.

He guessed there were advantages to saying the words as she began pulling back his shirt to find flesh.

She was thinking simple stimulus-response, a basic tenant of her profession.

His body was thinking stimulus-response too, although his mind hadn't put that label on it. His hands worked their way over her body and felt her immediate and powerful response to his stimulus.

Now that he'd taken the plunge, it was easier.

"I love you," he whispered again with less difficulty as he picked her up in his arms and continued to kiss her all the way to the bed.

He wanted it to be gentle, so he laid her down softly, a fragile and precious package. She watched him as he undressed, then scooted over when he joined her on the huge old bed. He pulled the pillows out from behind the shams and as he kissed her again, positioned her on them. His hands, hands that could be hard and undisciplined, ran tenderly, smoothly up her torso, still dewy and damp from her bath. The soft touch teased her, creating delicious fingers of fire to clutch in her belly. Everything inside her gathered to meet him. To love him.

# Chapter 13

"So, tell me again why I had to get out of the sex nest and jump into a suit?" asked Marc as he came out of his huge walk-in closet and dressing room. They each had one, a fact that Jette was sure would contribute to their peaceful co-existence. Hers was well organized and tidy. His was chaotic and had a system of storing clothes that only he understood. Once a week Hilda ventured in and removed all the dirty debris from the floor, but she never put anything away. She'd leave the dry cleaning and folded laundry near the door for him to stuff where he wanted. It was a system they'd worked out after several of Marc's meltdowns.

"Darling," Jette caught a look at him in her mirror, "that's not just a suit, that's a work of art."

He crossed the room and kissed her neck, loving the domestic feel of their preparations for the party. His Zegna suit and tailored shirt were literally made for him, accentuating all of his considerable attributes.

Jette sniffed.

"And the man inside doesn't just smell like a Greek God, he is a Greek God."

"You're really good at that," he said.

"What?"

"Distracting me so I'll forget the original question. But I'm a crack detective and I can always circle back to where I started…"

"And that would be?"

"Why I had to get out of the sex nest and jump into a suit?"

"Darling, duty calls. And when I'm called to attend a function sponsored by my publisher and booked by my agent, I must be properly accessorized. Tonight, that means I need to have a gorgeous Greek God on my arm."

"So now I'm your fashion accessory?"

"We're in New York City now. You have a problem with that?"

"Works for me. So what's considered an appropriate fashion accessory in Arizona?"

"A well muscled horse with a scrupulous pedigree."

That made Marc laugh and he watched her with a smile as she finished applying her makeup.

"Shall we take the car? I'm sure Claude would be thrilled. He's been wanting to show off his new mistress at a real New York event."

"I thought I was *your* mistress."

"Not in the world of chauffeurs. You're all his. There's a definite pecking order, according to Tommy, who's new to it, but very quick on all the nuances. Claude will take us, then hang with the other drivers, subtly basking in the glory of being in the employ of the renowned Jette Morningstar."

"I'm no celebrity."

"Oh, even better. The drivers of celebrities aren't at the highest level of the chauffeur's pyramid. Too uncivilized. It's the drivers of people who are famous, who also possess class and breeding who hold the top spot. You fit that bill." He looked at her in an eye-popping tomato red silk suit with a neckline that revealed the curve and cleavage of her perfect breasts. She'd put all of her hair into some kind of intricate swirl up off her neck, her beautiful, sexy, edible neck. "Plus you're drop dead gorgeous and will be walking out of today's headlines. The poor man's going to have his first orgasm this decade if I call and ask him to take us to this function."

"Oh Marc," laughed Jette. "Stop it."

"But call him."

"Sure, why not."

"Excellent. The poor man's been suffering the life of quiet desperation since I took ownership of the car." Marc walked over to the intercom.

"But you're New York City's top cop."

"Doesn't even register a blip on the snob-o-meter. Once, I had him drive me and, ah, shall we say actress, to a Broadway premier. He almost perished from the humiliation."

"And you think I can rehabilitate his reputation?" smiled Jette.

"You'll be his redemption, darling, I assure you."

Jette studied her jewelry and decided on her mother's simple diamond studs. They'd been recently reunited and while the circumstances of having the lost one back after nine years were poignant, she was so happy to have them. Wearing them helped heal her heart. Marc noticed, admiring her ability to wash out the bad and leave only the good in all things. Even him.

As they waited for the ecstatic Claude to bring the car around, Marc made another call. He was pleased with the report. It would make his date smile.

"All of the students have been upgraded. Two are still serious, but a full recovery is expected."

His date did smile. Broadly.

"That's wonderful news. And Professor Stanley?"

"Treated and released. Apparently her injury wasn't the result of gunfire after all. She hit her head when she tripped and fell over one of the injured students. Trying to get away I'm told. Pathetic."

"Darling, everyone acts and reacts differently in stressful situations."

"This from the woman who charged an armed gunman single handed and without a weapon?"

"I was armed with my intelligence, my abilities and my native blood. I was never in any real danger, Marc."

"You terrify me, Jette. Native blood spills just as easily as blood from a mutt like me."

She remembered his precious, priceless blood running through her fingers, soaking the carpet in her library and shuddered. Finally the depth of his fear, his concern, his reaction drove itself home.

"I'm sorry, Marc. You're right."

Marc knew where her mind had gone and nodded. He didn't want her to relive the ordeal, but he did have a point to make. Since it was made and she got the picture, he moved on.

"So, do you want to give me the same statement you gave to Green? Or would you rather put it aside for tonight?"

"I'd rather just compartmentalize it for the evening. I don't have a great deal to add to what you saw anyway."

"What did he say about what the shooter said to you?" Marc got right to what he considered the most important aspect of the investigation.

"He didn't ask."

"What an asshole. So what did the kid say?"

Jette sighed, so much for putting it away for the evening.

"It was really strange, but the young man was extremely agitated as you can imagine. I think his mental state is very fragile."

"Insane?"

"Perhaps. Certainly delusional. I'd have to interview him extensively but he seemed to be in control of his actions. Calculated. He sounded like he was in the middle of a paranoid delusion, however. Playing a part in a different life rather than living in his own." When Marc didn't respond, she went on. "There was persecution. He said I ruined his place in history so there may be an element of paranoia. And there were certainly delusions of grandeur. He told me he was the anointed one. He wasn't raving or ranting, he was just expressing his frustration and his distress. When I asked who anointed him, he said the Empress, of course."

"Is this Empress a real person or in just his mind?" Marc was intrigued.

"I'm not sure at this point. I need more time with him. Right now, I can think of three possibilities. She could be a real woman who said something he interpreted in his own way, someone he believes rules his actions. She'd be a powerful woman in his life who said something he translated into attacking the school. Maybe to get her attention or earn her approval. Another possibility is that she's someone who deliberately played into his mental illness for her own purposes. Finally, she could simply exist in his imagination. That would indicate some schizophrenia. I suggested to Green to check for prescription drugs. He may have gone off his medications and a voice of a woman played in his head."

"I'll get a line on what they find out."

"Not from Green, certainly."

"No. I have a few friends in his precinct."

"The blue grapevine."

"Yeah, faster and more accurate than formal channels. Anything else?"

"Yes. I thought it was interesting that he assumed I knew what he was talking about. Like I had a part in this delusion. Almost as if he knew me and expected me to know him."

"Have you ever met him?"

"I thought about that. He's never been a student of mine, but I meet hundreds of people at lectures, symposiums, even book signings. It's possible. And one more thing. Something that reinforced the feeling that he was in a delusional state. He asked me if I would try to turn him. I thought that was an unusual term. Not punish him or hurt him, but turn him. Of course he was very angry and there was definitely some dysfunctional cognitive processing. Marc, at some point I'd like to talk with him again. Professionally. Is that something you can set up?"

"It'll depend on who's in charge. I know I'll be able to get all the lab reports, I have several contacts there. And I can get the file on his background. Actually the media does an excellent job uncovering everything from birth to current circumstances, so we can probably tune in tomorrow to get a full report on his parents, his grades in school, a personal account from his date to the prom, what his neighbors thought while he was growing up. It's really amazing how fast they can work and how much information they can get collectively. Of course it has to be filtered and rechecked, but it often gives us a place to start. Getting access to him could be trickier if Green is left in charge."

"I could ask him myself."

"Yeah, that'll work. Just don't let him make dinner a condition of his cooperation."

"I'll ask him if I can bring a date."

Marc laughed at the thought.

"One more question. Why didn't you tell Green right away?"

"I told you. He didn't ask."

"Why didn't you volunteer the information?"

"I figured I'd tell you. If you thought it was important, I could always call him."

"Jette, that's a very nice reason, now why didn't you volunteer the information?"

When Marc continued to stare, Jette nodded. He really was a remarkable detective.

"Two reasons. First of all he doesn't respect you and your work..."

"He hates my fucking guts."

"Yes, that too, and secondly I'm not about to give him an excuse to use me, my impressions, my insights, or my potential diagnosis for his own purposes. The man was annoyed that this incident didn't play out longer and was looking for an angle. He'd have loved to have some kind of exclusive information to share with the media. The young man told me things that may or may not be critical to the case. I want a competent investigator to make that call, not a glory seeking, marginally competent, arrogant hack who seemed more interested in giving me a massage than in either the victims or the serious mental illness that drove a young man to start shooting."

Marc's eyes sparkled, danced, and shot green fire. When he smiled it was a heart stopper.

"Are you real, or are you my delusion?" he asked finally.

"What do you think?"

"I think if you're a delusion, Doctor, I'll never want to seek the cure."

"Do you hear voices in your head?"

"Only when I have my ear buds in."

"You're solid, then. Now can we put this away for awhile? I think it would be good for both of us."

He looked like he wanted to continue the discussion, but restrained himself and nodded. "So do I need to be briefed on this party tonight?" he asked as he put his arm around her waist and led her out of the bedroom.

"You're such a cop."

"Why, thank you darling. But I promise to keep my gun in its holster even if provoked by homicidal boredom."

"I'd greatly appreciate that. I've had quite enough of guns today."

# Chapter 14

When they arrived at the party a half hour later, it was to a vigorous and enthusiastic reception. While Jette was originally booked to be one of several featured authors, she took center stage the moment she walked through the door.

Her agent, LeeAnn Wojnar, had obviously been waiting for her to arrive and scooped her up immediately. Tall, beautiful, sleek and polished, she was as shrewd as a top flight Washington lobbyist. An attorney as well as an agent, she was a relentless and astute negotiator. Because her final contracts were always mutually beneficial, she was a favorite of both her authors and publishers.

"Everyone, and I mean everyone, has been asking for an introduction. Even Stacy Rindy, and she never makes the first move. I'm basking in it! Hi Marc, you look absolutely fantastic," Lee beamed.

"Don't sound so surprised." He leaned over and kissed the impressive woman's cheek.

"It's just that last time I saw you, you hadn't shaved and were dressed in something that flattered your gorgeous body, but looked like you'd been rag picking. I think there was some blood on your jeans as well. Seems to me you'd just caught a killer."

"Oh, that rag picker's still in here."

"Well, you sure do clean up pretty. Think of this as an undercover assignment. Tonight I'm going to be putting Jette through her paces. You can stand at her side and be bored to a pickle with conversation designed for product placement, or you can find someone interesting to chat with and only periodically ride in to save her. Your call."

When he looked down at Jette's shining eyes, he saw he was off the hook. Nice. Life was good.

"I'll go grab a beer, find out if there's anything to eat, and surf for a familiar face."

Jette squeezed his arm, smiled, and nodded her approval, then let Lee steer her into the fray with a laugh and a wave.

Sipping a beer, Marc stood back watching proudly as the love of his life mingled and graciously accepted the accolades from the famous and not so famous; from the boorishly effusive, to the shy but avid admirers. Far from being put out by having his woman immediately taken from him and passed around to the powerful elite, Marc appreciated her and was impressed with her status. She was indescribable. And she was his. That would be enough for him for the rest of his life.

"Obviously at a publisher's party, what you need on your arm is not a man, but an agent," said Marc in her ear when he came up beside her several hours later. Lee had given him a high sign. Time to launch a rescue. Serve and protect!

"Excuse me, won't you?" Jette asked the group around her and was immediately excused by proclamation. Marc took her elbow as he led her to a relatively quiet corner.

"Thanks for the rescue." Jette took a deep breath, trying to inhale some of the remaining oxygen in the crowded room. "That was all very intense."

"That's the New York City pace and pulse."

"And I'm starving. Was there food at this event?"

Marc held up a small plate filled with stuffed mushrooms. Jette was a vegetarian, a compunction Marc couldn't understand, but was willing to feed.

"You are my God." Jette took one and popped it into her mouth.

"Your Greek God of Love and Passion. And, it appears, the supplier for your peculiar addiction."

"Are you going to have one?" She took another from the plate.

"I'd rather eat your shoe."

"Not this shoe. It took me forever to find the right color red. Do you know how many shades of red there are?"

"Falu, crimson, cerise, carmine, amaranth, alizarian, scarlet, rose, to name a few."

"A few." She laughed, loving his mind and his incredible collection of obscure information. "Sounds like the eight daughters of Erik the Red."

"He actually had three sons and only one daughter. One was the explorer Leif Eriksson."

"Really?"

"Really."

She knew that his impressive compilation of bits of data came from growing up in public libraries around the five boroughs of New York City. Libraries throughout the city were always warm in the winter, cool in the summer, open nearly every day and relatively safe for a boy on his own. But the librarians who policed the rooms and cubbies of the public facilities required visitors to be busy. To be reading. Loitering led to expulsion.

So Marc read. Everything and anything. He devoured the pages of books of all kinds with a voracious appetite and all that he read got filed away in some elaborate system in his incredibly absorbent brain. He was blessed with high intelligence and a memory that was nearly photographic so even now his mind was filled with files of facts, data, details, and obscure information.

He'd never had a formal education until he went to the police academy, but easily passed his GED's. After he'd become an officer, he got through law school in record time. As a boy he liked the thick, leather bound volumes in the Law Library and it was frequently open late. Plus everyone was always so stressed in there, they never missed the items the quick fingered boy managed to palm. He'd read many of the volumes cover to cover before he even applied to the NYU law school.

The incredibly rich field of knowledge stored in his brain prepared him to be an excellent detective. It gave him an extremely broad frame of reference for seemingly unrelated clues. In a very real sense his unique childhood experiences, while harsh and hard, led to an astounding close rate on his cases. This had come to the attention of a series of superior officers and his chain of promotions in quick succession were nearly unprecedented. His temperament was the only thing keeping him from rising even faster.

Jette swallowed the last mushroom, and sighing, put her hand to her fit, flat tummy.

"I'm as stuffed as that last mushroom. Thank you, darling. You're a wonderful provider. So where have you been?"

"The police commissioner is here so I got to talk shop. Apparently he's a fan of yours and would like to say hi. We decided to wait until the circle around you became less dense."

"I didn't know you knew Garret."

"I didn't know *you* knew him."

"I met him when I did the profile of the Watkins killer." She saw a look of astonishment pass over his face. "What?"

"I headed up the task force that caught the guy."

"I didn't know that. I mean, I followed the case, of course, but Garret was always the person who spoke for the team."

"I prefer to keep a lower profile. I hate wasting my time with the media and I tend to, well, alienate the news sluts. Besides, they get tired of bleeping me every other fucking word for their fucking 20 second sound bites. Garret's good with them."

"And yet you have a problem with Captain Green and his relationship with the press."

"Garret's a good cop. A good man. Came up the ranks. He's a team player. Like you said, Green's a headline grabbing asshole."

"I think I may have put it differently."

"But not as concisely."

"True. So, do you remember the profile on Watkins?"

"No, I was too busy following the clues."

"But as it turned out..."

He grinned. "You were dead on."

"Thank you, darling. So where's Garret? I'd like to say hello."

"He's over by the food. Grazing. Cops love a buffet. I promised to go find you and bring you over."

"Lead the way, Detective."

They spent the next half hour reminiscing and discussing the day's events with the commissioner. The shooter had been identified as Roger Flowers. Unsolicited, Garret talked about bringing her into the case on a professional basis and she agreed. The commissioner was a man she could work with.

"I've monopolized you long enough," said Garret. "I just wanted to see if Marc was bullshitting me when he said he brought you to this thing."

"He's more than my escort for this evening."

"So I gathered. I can't fault him for his taste, but I'm not sure you haven't temporarily lost your mind." Garret laughed loudly and slapped Marc on the back, taking all the sting out of his words. "But then, you can always take yourself on a patient. Thanks for turning a deadly dull obligation into a really great evening. Nothing I like better than to talk murder and mayhem and to rehash old cases. It's probably why I'm in the middle of my second divorce and came here alone."

There was a little commotion in the doorway as a woman and her entourage entered the room. Garret, Jette, and Marc immediately recognized her as Andrea Lee Jones, multiple Academy Award winning actress and star of thousands of tabloid exposés. Her brilliant smile hadn't diminished over the years and she used it to captivate and charm those around her.

"She's coming this way," said Garret. "Is it too gauche to ask for an autograph at one of these things?"

"It is unless it's on a substantial advance check or contract," laughed Marc.

"Ah. I thought so. It would probably be too humiliating anyway." He sighed, not caring if he sounded like a smitten teenager. "I've only been in love with her since I was sixteen. Oh my God, she's coming this way."

"Jette," said the actress in one of the world's most recognizable voices. "I was told you were here."

"Andi, how nice to see you again." Jette took her hand and thoroughly enjoyed the surprised and impressed look on Garret's face. Marc's face didn't change a muscle. Such control. She did hear the low hum in his throat, however.

"How's everything at the ranch?" beamed Andrea.

"Why don't you take a few days and go see for yourself. The place is mostly empty these days."

"I just might do that. So, the news accounts are true? You've moved to New York?"

"I have."

"And which of these two good looking men is the reason."

"Thanks for the compliment, but he is," said Garret, still a little star struck.

"Andrea, this is Commissioner Garret Tienstra and my escort, Detective Marc Lexington."

"Very nice to meet you, Commissioner." She took Garret's hand and accepted his greeting, then turned her full attention on Marc.

"Ah, yes. The Shield. I should have recognized you." Andrea just stared at him for moment. "Have we met?"

Marc took her offered hand, held it, and smiled broadly. "I would have remembered, Ms. Jones." He glanced over at Garret and winked, then back at Andrea. "I've been in love with you since I was…"

"Don't you dare say it young man," she laughed, still appraising him. "You'll make me feel like your grandmother."

He raised his eyebrows. "You have a mirror. You know that isn't possible."

"I also have Dr. Parfitt, an extremely talented plastic surgeon. I'm sorry, Detective. I know I'm staring, but there's something about you. Something very familiar. I wish Dr. Parfitt could turn back the time on my brain." She shook her head. "I can't get it."

"I think you're just looking for an excuse to stare at a pretty face," said Lee as she came up behind them.

"Lee, how are you?" asked Andrea as she finally pulled her eyes away from Marc.

"Fine. Ready to put together another autobiography?"

"You're writing another one?" asked Jette.

"Sweetheart, it's been 20 years since my last one. In my business that's another lifetime," laughed Andrea.

"With a whole lot of reportable living," agreed Lee, rubbing her hands together.

"And loving."

"Exactly. Pages filled with that kind of information will fly off the shelves."

"Believe me, it will be a much shorter book than the last one. Call me and we'll talk. And Jette, if that offer is genuine, I'd love to spend a few days on the ranch again."

"Oh, it's genuine. I'm not sure Jim's heart will survive another week in your presence, but with enough warning, I think he can prepare. I'll call him in the morning and tell him to expect a contact from your assistant. She still has the number, I'm sure."

Andrea smiled with genuine delight.

"Deni Marie has every number that was ever called for any reason for the last 25 years. And only she understands her filing system. She can never leave me. Thank you Jette. By the way, sweetheart, nice work at the university. I'm sure you're sick of talking about it, so I'll only say, I'm proud to know you."

"Thank you," she said with real appreciation. She really was sick of talking about it.

"Gentlemen, it was a pleasure. Lee, I'll have Deni Marie call you as well."

With one last long look at Marc, she moved on through the room.

Three pairs of eyes moved from Andrea to Jette. An explanation was keenly anticipated. Jette smiled and shrugged.

"She filmed *Riding to Destiny* on our ranch. Her production company made a very substantial donation to the Morningstar Foundation for the privilege. I found her to be as lovely to work with as she is to look at."

"So Jette, how about introducing me to the commissioner?" Lee knew nearly everyone by sight, but as yet had not met everyone in New York City.

"LeeAnn Wojnar, agent extraordinaire, this is Garret Tienstra, the police commissioner."

"Very nice to meet you. Do you have an agent, Commissioner?" asked Lee taking his hand.

Lee exuded enthusiasm and vigor, always revving up as everyone else in the room began to wilt. Perhaps she was an energy vampire, just sucking it out of the room, thought Jette as she looked at Garret and Lee. Something popped. Something good.

"What would I do with an agent?" Garret's interest was obvious, but in the woman not the idea of an agent.

"With all the real crime you deal with on a daily basis? Darling, that's a rhetorical question. You're a gold mine."

"You like murder and mayhem?"

"Absolutely. They're my bread and butter along with Prada and Rolex. There's nothing I like better than death. Talk to me about mass murder and I'm yours."

Garret smiled even more broadly. "How about we talk over dinner tomorrow?"

"Deal. I'll give you a sec to wrap it up, Jette, then I need you for round two. I'll meet you over by the bar. I want a tall glass of wine. Here's my card, Garret. Call my cell tomorrow to do time and place. My treat."

"Jette, tell me she's not married. Please." Garret pleaded as he watched her sail away in a cloud of sweet and sassy Faith Avery perfume.

"She's just divorced her second husband. Amicably, I might add."

"It's fate!" grinned Garrett.

Jette's eyes flashed in agreement. "And, she's a wonderful mother with a well-adjusted teenage son. She absolutely loves dogs and has a Maltese named Lexy she dotes on. She's a workaholic but knows how to turn it off. Bring her a small bouquet of daisies, be prompt, ask about her son, fuss over her pictures of Lexy, and you won't go home alone."

"Daisies? Are you sure? She seems more like a vivid red rose kind of lady to me."

"That's the mistake her two former husbands made. She's a very soft hearted, sweet, sentimental woman under all that motion and brass. Definitely daisies."

Garret looked at her appraisingly. "You like her."

"Very, very much."

Then he nodded. "I'll bring her daisies. Thanks."

Marc nudged her when he escorted Jette to the bar. "See a match?"

"I think sometimes fate has a point."

"Yeah, she kicked me in the ass when she put me in your path."

Lee stood by the bar, sipping her drink, talking with a woman a head taller and as pale as a bride of Dracula.

"Jette, here's the person I wanted you to meet. Klara Marshall, this is Dr. Jette Morningstar and her escort, Detective Marc Lexington."

They shook hands. Klara's long, lean fingers were strong and her handshake was firm. Marc thought she lingered with Jette's hand a little longer than was necessary, but just filed it away.

"I've read your books and enjoyed them," said Jette to the world famous mystery writer.

"Thank you and I can say the same." Klara's voice rang just short of sincere. "You certainly put on quite a show today for the cameras."

Jette didn't see the need to comment but could feel Marc shift. She took his hand and squeezed. This was a party, after all. And small talk was often, well, small.

Slightly miffed and not feeling a need to hide it, Klara went on. "I was surprised to see you here tonight. I'd have thought you'd be on the media circuit. I'm sure they'd all like a personal account. Or are you waiting for the morning shows?"

"No. I write in the mornings. I much prefer to play my life as I plan and that means avoiding all requests for interviews. Lee handles the press coverage."

Klara blinked, then looked at Lee. "She must be a constant frustration to you."

"You have no idea. Although as long as the video of her heroics keeps looping on all the news channels, I'm happy. I sometimes think the mystery keeps the buzz alive. Who is Jette Morningstar?"

"Indeed." Klara raised a brow. "So how would you answer that question, Dr. Morningstar?"

"Jette."

"So how would you answer that question, Jette? Who are you?"

Jette returned Klara's direct, almost intrusive gaze. "Anything other than a complete assessment of personality and aptitude would be a superficial description at best. A mere two dimensional snapshot of a woman and her life. So, I don't define myself. Those who know me, know me. Those who don't will formulate a picture that fits their preconceived perceptions or their individual filters. I leave it to Lee to describe me to the outside world in her glossy, four-color press kits."

Marc studied Jette in awe. A less subtle *stupid fucking question, how would you describe yourself, you superficial bitch* would have been his response. But, she got to the same place, and without alienating anyone.

Klara Marshall put his teeth on edge. He wasn't sure why. Maybe it was how she was staring at Jette. Interested? Intrigued? Envious? Resentful?

She wanted something. Was it a date or was it part of the spotlight? He wasn't sure, but he was sure Jette caught the vibe, too. She wasn't making her usual effort to charm or bring out the other person in conversation. Jette had a reserved side. It was rarely pulled out and used, but he noticed she was putting it on now.

"I can see why you're such a popular professor," commented Klara with just a touch of regal condescension. "That was well said. I can see it in print, as a matter of fact. I'd like to write a character as complex and as intelligent as you."

Jette didn't bite on the invitation. Instead she turned the focus around.

"Are you currently working on a new book?"

"Several, actually." She shifted her eyes toward Marc. Jette didn't blame her a bit. "And what about you, Detective Lexington. Have you been busy since you've been back?"

"Just some routine investigations." He wasn't about to give her material for her next book.

"You're another interesting and multifaceted character I'd like to explore. I've used New York City in many of my novels. People have such a fascination for the place. You would be an ideal archetype."

"For the hero or the villain?"

Klara laughed, a dusty, dry sound that held no real delight.

"What do you think, Jette. Villain or hero?"

"He's definitely *my* hero."

"Yes. I hear they call him your Shield. How archaic." She stared at Jette for another heartbeat, then looked at Lee. "You have my number. Please use it. I'd like to get together. I have a book signing tomorrow, but should be free until I fly to the coast for a preliminary discussion with a producer on Friday. I hate leaving the city but there is life in the outer reaches."

Her intrusive stare went back to Jette. "Have your agent set up a meeting. I'd love to dive into the complex character behind your public face."

"I think I'd like to keep that to myself," said Jette pleasantly pushing back while not agreeing to any meeting.

"We all have a duality of personality, wouldn't you agree?" Klara asked the question rhetorically, simply assuming that when she made a profound statement everyone around her would be of the same mind. Jette perversely decided not to.

"Most certainly we exhibit different behaviors based on the role we're currently playing. We have public and private personas, for example. But that's more like wearing clothes best suited for the situation. A suit for this evening's function, jeans and a sweater for riding, shorts and a t-shirt for jogging. A basic personality is well formed and consistent. One can change aspects of it through intense therapy or significant emotional events, of course. True duality is usually a sign of mental illness."

Marc felt a very satisfying flip in his chest when he saw Klara suck in air through her nose. God, he loved his woman!

"Indeed," she said finally, wanting desperately to take back the advantage but not finding any words in her normally fertile arsenal to fight this battle. "We're forced to play different parts in our very busy lives." Appearing to be bored with the discussion, she sighed heavily and waved her hand in a lazy gesture of dismissal. "It's been a pleasure meeting you all, but I'm growing weary of this role. It's exhausting to be a best-selling author in a room full of publishers and agents. Besides, I need a smoke and the insidious health Nazis wish to inconvenience the world. I will bid you good night."

Then she nodded as if she were royalty and moved through the crowd, presumably toward the door.

"Jesus," chuckled Marc. "She sounds as stilted and as scripted as her unrealistic characters. Who bids anyone a goodnight except in novels. You bid on e-bay. And I think you might have damaged any potential liaison with the freak. Maybe if you would have bowed to her not-so-superior opinion, she'd have asked you for a date."

Lee laughed. "Klara is a little much. She's written only fiction up to now, but I've heard that she'd like to introduce elements of real-life crime into her story lines. It works so well in TV dramas. Something out of contemporary headlines that people can identify with. Fictionalized, but recognizable. She wanted me to arrange a meeting with you Jette, to explore a collaboration."

"It seems to me that might be something you'd want to talk with Garret about," suggested Jette.

"True, although she's really hot to work with you. When we chatted your name kept coming up."

"Are you her agent?"

"I wish. She's mega bucks in the business. But no. Although I heard tonight she's shopping. Let's talk sometime next week."

"Alright. I'm used to collaboration in my academic research and publications. But no guarantees."

"None expected. We'll need to trust both her abilities and her integrity. I'll be asking around and getting a line on her. Then we can meet to see if there's any intersection of your interests and projects and go from there."

Jette nodded. She liked the fact that she felt no pressure to put the deal together. Her intuition was steering her away from the connection, but she'd give it fair consideration. It would probably be an excellent career move if she were interested in that kind of thing.

Lee rubbed her hands together again. "Now on to more important collaborations. Please tell me the commissioner is single."

"He will be," replied Jette.

"How many?" asked Lee.

"Two."

"Oh perfect. He has two ex's, I have two ex's. You get three strikes before you have to go sit on the bench." Lee turned, grabbed a glass from a passing tray and swung it up in a toast.

"Exactly, and it gives you some important common ground."

"Is that a professional assessment? I mean do you think that's important?"

"It can be, although at this point I think it's more important that he has fabulous eyes and a wonderful smile. And that Marc thinks he's a good man."

"Yeah?"

"And a good cop." Marc bestowed his greatest compliment.

"That's strangely reassuring, Marc. You're a very discerning man and one who's pretty hard to impress."

"That's because most people are flaming assholes. This place is full of them."

"Your sacrifice to the cause of Jette's career is duly noted and appreciated," laughed Lee.

"I've actually been enjoying myself. The commissioner and I got to take care of some business without the usual chain of command shit."

"Back to the commissioner collaboration," said Jette with a little conspiratorial wink. "I happen to know he's a real fan of Allison Gerland's work in early British criminology. She's one of yours, isn't she?"

"Yes. Do you think I should bring an autographed copy of Allison's latest book to this dinner tomorrow? I'd bring Allison herself, but she's such a knockout, I'd be afraid of the competition."

"I think just a book would be much less crowded. And it might be a faster way to his heart than food."

"Hey now, don't get carried away. That's a woman talking. Heart, stomach." He pointed to one, then the other. "Too close an internal connection to ignore. If he gives you the choice of a place to eat, he'd consider you his fantasy date if you pick Dolly Tuckers. His second wife hated the place and it's his favorite."

Marc thought he could get on board this matchmaking train. Jette's delighted look of approval was its own reward. Score.

"Marc, you're an angel. I love the place myself, but wouldn't have thought of it right off. Sorry, Jette, honey, but their buffalo burgers are to die for." She scoped the room. "Now, let's see, who else is on my must-see list. By the way, Marc, Cynthia Batton is over there. She's been discretely putting herself in your path all evening hoping you'll spontaneously catch her eye. She's getting a little more desperate and obvious with each pass. You haven't been at Jette's elbow much all evening, so maybe the pathetic creature doesn't know you're off the market."

Jette looked over to where the Broadway star was standing with a cortège of admirers. It seemed she was trying more rigorously than was natural to avoid looking in Marc's direction while obviously placing herself in his line of sight.

Raising her eyebrows, she glanced up at her escort. "You know Cynthia Batton?"

"I knew her when she was Cindy Batonowskowitz. I think she was third understudy to Rumpleteazer in *Cats*."

"Hmm. She's come a long way."

Marc gave her a devastating smile.

"So have I."

"Oh stop it you two. All that sexual static is going to interfere with everyone's cell phones, causing an end to civilization as we know it," scolded Lee.

Just then Cynthia executed a spontaneously planned shake of her head and caught Marc's eye. Her eyes widened in guileless surprise.

"A Tony-winning performance if I've ever seen one," murmured Lee.

Quickly excusing herself, Cynthia made her way toward them, a very inviting look in her eye and a pretty obvious invitation in the swivel of her hips.

"Marc. Marc Lexington. What are you doing here? Did you just arrive?" She put out her hands in a magnanimous invitation to be adored. When he took them automatically, the diva kissed his cheek and surrounded him in Seduction Serenade, her newest and, she was quite certain, most irresistible scent.

Lee practically gagged.

"Hello, Cindy. Actually, I've been here all evening." He introduced her to Jette and Lee.

"Oh my! I thought that was you," she narrowed her beautiful blue eyes speculatively at Jette, completely ignoring Lee. "Nice press. You certainly were in the right place at the right time."

Lee, nearly heaving on Cynthia's scent, now choked on the sip of wine she'd taken.

Jette felt Marc stiffen, but simply smiled and agreed. "It was pretty intense."

"Well cash in on it, darling. The publishers are all here tonight. Take it from one who knows, they can be a fickle lot. Five years ago, my autobiography was delayed when *Saturday's Game* went into rewrites after bad out-of-town reviews. When it came to New York to raves and I became the critics' darling again, they all started calling. You remember that, Marc?"

"No," he said bluntly.

Not to be deterred, Cynthia kept up the assault. "Were you two talking shop? Is this your case, Marc? How about you take a break and we can catch up on old times. You ladies don't mind, do you?"

Jette grinned. "Not in the least. Lee has people she'd like me to meet and we were just about to make the rounds."

Marc looked down at her and stared into her amused eyes. No jealousy. That was good. Wasn't it? Then she narrowed those magnificent eyes and let the deep dark pupils snap. Okay, maybe a little. Better, even.

Cynthia continued to play her cards not realizing she was beat on the board. "Marc and I go way back. Have you known him long, Jette?"

"You must not watch the news or read the *Times*," commented Lee, beginning to wonder about Marc's former taste in women. Cynthia was a beautiful, voluptuous package but there wasn't much else as far as she could see. He must have been profoundly superficial at one time. Men. Sometimes they were so easy.

"Too depressing," responded Cynthia with a little dismissive wave. "I read the trades and catch the entertainment features. I have a clipping service that sends me anything relevant. Mostly about me, of course." Cynthia exercised her well practiced laugh.

"Well, if you'd been watching news reports you'd know that Marc and Jette worked together in Arizona."

"Oh? Whatever. I had no idea." She waved her hand again, but her expression was subtly changing into something more antagonistic. "You wouldn't catch me dead in Arizona. All that sun and what it does to the skin. You'd better watch yourself, Jette. You'll pay for that tan when you're older."

Lee just stared at her. Was the woman stupid as well as dense? Jette's dusky native skin glowed and was obviously a natural tone.

Since Lee was momentarily speechless and Marc was about to pop, Jette filled in the silence that followed.

"I'll remember that. Thank you. Don't you have a performance tonight?"

"I let my understudy take the stage. It's good practice and who really cares about the summer tourists?"

"I think we all should," disagreed Lee. "They definitely contribute to our economy."

"Who are you again?" asked Cynthia, putting Lee in the same category as summer tourists.

"She's New York's top nonfiction literary agent." Marc was completely annoyed and letting it show. Obviously Cynthia was used to his bad temper, since she didn't even react to his rude tone.

"Oh. I see. Are you here securing them a book deal? Those murders in Arizona are the kind of thing people groove on."

"Neither of them are willing to write about it at this time," lamented Lee.

"Or relive it," commented Jette, wondering if Cynthia was as thick as she appeared to be. There was something underneath. Something calculated. She could be a shrewd woman playing a part. A game. Perhaps projecting what she thought appealed to men.

Then again, she might be deliberately wearing a dense cloud to get people to underestimate her.

Cynthia was a liar, that was for certain. She did watch the news and she knew about their connection. They'd said nothing about murders in Arizona.

"So, you two have stayed in touch," purred Cynthia, batting her eyes at Marc, "isn't that nice."

"Yes. We're in touch, alright." Marc slid his arm around Jette's waist to accentuate his point. "We're in touch pretty much constantly. We're living together."

Marc loved that. The sound of it. The feel of it. Living together. Something inside him jumped and it showed.

Cynthia didn't miss a beat, however. Defeat wasn't in her vocabulary.

"In that cramped little place in the Village? Marc, really. Tell me you've hired someone to come in to clean since I was there last."

"Several times. The cockroaches have actually moved out in protest."

"That I'd like to see." She winked. "Literally."

"What do you say, Jette. Want to put together a little dinner party?" asked Marc deliberately missing her meaning.

"No, sorry Cynthia," said Jette. "I like having Marc all to myself. But perhaps you can get caught up in the next hour or so. Lee will be keeping me pretty busy. Marc, I'll meet you near the front door," she said checking her watch, "at 1:30. Will that be alright, Lee?"

"Perfect."

In a territorial gesture and in front of a fuming but controlled Cynthia, she planted a playful kiss on Marc's lips. Nothing passionate. Simply sweet and teasing.

"Pretty confident," he murmured to her as he brushed his hand up her arm.

"I know my man," she whispered back. Then she looked at her gaping agent. "Let's go make some deals, shall we?"

Lee glanced over at Cynthia, then up at Marc. She wouldn't have been able to leave either of her husbands alone for five minutes with the stunning, big-breasted man eater. Then she shrugged. And that was precisely why she was currently single and twice divorced.

"It really doesn't bother you, does it," Lee said to Jette when they were out of ear shot.

"No. Marc had a life before me. She's just one of many. I'm his first and only."

"First and only?"

"The first woman he's ever loved and the only one he ever will."

"Oh Jette, you're killing me." She looked over her shoulder at the desperate, clinging actress and the completely and obviously disinterested man. "But, I have to agree with you."

"Besides, the very clear contrast in, shall we say, styles, puts me in a pretty good place," Jette added. "Advantage, Jette Morningstar."

"Whoa. Just when I thought you were without wiles, you give me a break. There's a little cat in you, Jette Morningstar."

"I predict that although she could use a good therapist to work on her incredibly obvious need for approval and attention, she'll be more likely to call her cosmetic surgeon first thing in the morning. She won't do well with the rejection. Especially when she lost to someone she considers an inferior adversary."

Lee's eyes widened. "You really nailed her. And you? Inferior?" She snorted delicately. "Using what measure, cup size?"

"She sees what she wants to see and writes a script for her life based on hopes and expectations rather than reality."

"Remind me not to ask what you think of me. I don't know if I could take the diagnosis."

"Oh, I think you could take it fine. There's nothing wrong with your self confidence or your feelings of self worth. In spite of two divorces, you have a healthy understanding of your own value. And, while they were painful episodes, they don't define you. You know the marriages weren't complete failures, but transitions. Part of growing and finding out who you are. It's why both your ex's are still on your speed dial and your son is well adjusted and happy."

"Tell me what I have to work on," asked Lee, pleased by her friend and client's insights.

"Starting tomorrow, I would say the commissioner. You need to have balance in your life. You can't let your work consume you."

"Oh boy, do I like that kind of homework, Professor." She scooped her arm through Jette's and led her toward a group of chatting guests. "Now, let's go talk with Stacy Rindy. She's been talking in the seven figures for your sixth book. Or is it six figures for the seventh book. Doesn't matter. Maybe we'll make her beg for both."

"Lee, I haven't finished my third book yet."

"I know, but you will. You're a virtual goldmine, and better yet, you're all mine. Cha Ching!"

# Chapter 15

Claude opened the door with a grin. He'd had a most agreeable evening. Probably the best of his career. He'd hit the lottery, the jackpot, the royal flush of infamy and could probably ride it to retirement. Claymore, his arch rival in the driving game, would never be able to recover from the crushing blow. He'd been surrounded by young and old, chauffeurs he knew and those he didn't. All of them wanted the inside scoop on the professor.

He was discreet, certainly, but he managed to let a few facts slip. Her Doctorate, her noble Cherokee heritage, her best sellers, her preference for meatless meals, her kindness, her extraordinary physical conditioning. Several of the others filled in the blanks from the headlines, or from earlier accounts of his employer's heroic exploits. Even the detective had taken on more polish by being connected to the fabulous Dr. Morningstar.

Truth be known, he liked driving the detective. Other than his extraordinarily bad taste in women, up to this point anyway, he was pretty exciting all in all. He made Claude laugh, on the inside of course. And they went to very unusual places.

And he knew what the man meant to the Clarkes. They'd never gotten over the deaths of their sons, but this scurrilous boy from the gutter, this scandalous man from the streets, seemed to bring them some kind of peace. And that was a fine thing.

He'd fully expected to be sent packing when the man inherited all his employer's possessions, but he was relieved that the new boss didn't seem interested in changing any of the routines. It wasn't like he needed a job or the money, he just needed a place in the world. And there was Hilda. After nearly 35 years, he felt almost ready to ask her to dinner. Maybe even dinner and the theatre.

Now that Detective Lexington had returned from Arizona with the magnificent Dr. Morningstar, the very beautiful, famous, gracious breath of class and cultivation his current good fortune was riding on, his life was perfect. It looked like she was going to stick, too. Go figure.

They couldn't have been more different. She was tranquil, peaceful, calm. He was edgy, barely controlled. She was class, he was brass. She was serene, he was extreme. They seemed perfect for each other.

"Back home, sir?" he asked over his shoulder.

"Yes. And how about we make it the long way. Through Times Square, down Broadway, around the park."

"My pleasure, sir."

See? He thought to himself. This was something the Clarkes would never have done. Not that they were up much past 10 p.m. most nights anyway. He loved New York City at night and taking the long way home filled him up with renewed life.

"So tell me," asked Jette when they settled into the back seat and Claude had discreetly raised the privacy screen. "How long did it take you to shake the lovely and talented Ms. Batton?"

"You mean the grasping and desperate bitch?" snorted Marc.

"I guess I could get behind that description if I weren't so opposed to unflattering labels."

"It took me almost the entire hour. Next time, don't leave me. Jesus I'd rather chew glass. She was very interested in you, though. Wanted to know all about your background. Searching for a flaw, I imagine."

"Did she find one?"

"Oh, several in her never humble opinion."

"Name one," challenged Jette.

"Let's see. You're too intellectual. She thinks your vocabulary is unattractive." Marc ran his fingers up her arm.

"I barely said a word."

"No, but apparently she's read your books."

"You're kidding."

"No, but I thought she was." Marc shook his head. "Actually, I was more shocked that she could read something so advanced. I quizzed her and she got some answers right."

"Maybe she's a closet intellectual."

"Yeah. Right. She just hides it better."

"She's hiding something."

"Why do you say that?" Marc asked.

"Just a feeling. Not that it's criminal or anything, Detective. I think what she's hiding is more like…like herself. What you see is definitely programmed, practiced, perfected, and performed."

"Interesting."

"Marginally so." Jette waved her hand. " I certainly don't feel compelled to study it any further."

"Me neither. I'm not even sure what the attraction was in the first place."

"Her extraordinary talent?" suggested Jette, her eyes shining. "I saw her play Madison in Monica Joy Donnelly's latest musical. She really was good."

"Oh, yeah. I'm sure that was it. So, did we make any money tonight, Professor?"

"I think so. A couple of real possibilities."

"Excellent. I'm going to need a new suit and since you're the one who starred at this gig, it's going to be your treat. That woman's horrific perfume is saturated into this one. I can't believe she actually bottles it for resale. I hope it's called *Cheap French Whore* or she'll be nailed for false advertising."

"I was going to ask you to do something about that." Jette sniffed the air. "You know, like take it off. Too bad we're in the back seat of a car."

"We've gone naked, or nearly so, in a back seat before."

"There was no Claude on that lonely stretch of highway in Arizona," winked Jette.

"I could have him put up the solid privacy screen."

"He'd know what we were doing back here," she protested

"So? My man Claude is a man of the world," shrugged Marc.

"The world of old black and white movies, maybe. Where everyone's clothes stayed on. Even during sex. If they had sex."

"You have a point. We can wait until we get to our bedroom." His hand moved up her bare leg.

"Maybe the foyer." She felt the familiar tingle between her thighs.

Laughing, Marc moved his hand higher. "How about a little foreplay?"

"What do you have in mind?" she asked, putting her hand on his knee.

"The best concrete chocolate malt in the world."

It took her a few seconds to switch gears, but she got behind it all the way. "Darling, I'm yours, but where are you going to get one at nearly 2 a.m.?"

"I have a friend who's…"

"In the ice cream business."

"Yeah."

He picked up the intercom and soon he, Jette, and Claude were trying to suck pure chocolate gold up their straws.

Claude took his seat and continued on, driving one handed. Yes, he thought, there were definite advantages of having an informal boss.

"Very clever," commented Jette when she finally got enough malt through her straw to swallow. "Freud would approve. Not only do you get the visceral pleasure of watching me vigorously suck on the straw, but it exercises the proper facial muscles."

"Are you saying the straw is phallic?" Marc thoroughly enjoyed his date's analytical mind. And her intellectual vocabulary. Cynthia was wrong. It was sexy as hell. "That's pretty insulting considering the size of the man you're sleeping with."

"Maybe I should just set this in your lap and let it melt a bit."

"Oh no. You know what happens to a guy when his manhood is exposed to the cold."

"I guess it would make the straw look pretty good, huh?"

He took a spoon from the compartment beside him and handed it to her.

"It's a little like cheating, but it'll speed things up. While I've been looking the world over for a woman who could suck a golf ball up a garden hose, I wouldn't want you to exhaust yourself."

"Thanks. I love you." Jette enthusiastically grabbed the spoon.

"You're so easy," laughed Marc.

"But not cheap," she said, her malt now disappearing at a much faster rate.

When they smoothly pulled up to the curb, they were just finishing the last of their treat. Marc tossed his cup, lid, napkin and straw on the floor of the limo while Jette neatly folded her napkin and placed it and the spoon inside her cup, reattached the lid and deposited it in the small, discreet trash box near the rear seat.

"Thanks," said Marc as Claude opened the door. "Take tomorrow, or rather the rest of today, off."

"Yes sir. Thank you sir," nodded Claude.

"Best part of this car thing is you don't have to tip him," said Marc as the night doorman let them into the lobby.

"What do you call a day off?"

"Oh, he'll be in. The man hasn't taken an unscheduled day off since I've known him. I think he sleeps in his uniform. Now, about that foreplay. Ready for something a little hotter than a malt?"

"Oh yeah. As a matter of fact, with all that chocolate and sugar in my system, I probably won't be able to sleep for hours and hours."

She laughed, then moaned when Marc began his assault in the elevator. He backed her up against the wall as one hand tilted her head for a searing kiss, and the other started up her leg again.

The thin panties she wore were no barrier to his skillful fingers. They managed to flank the perimeter, and find their objective. Once there, they launched their offensive. Expertly moving them along soft flesh, he felt her immediate response.

Vibrating now, Jette began to unbutton his shirt. Her hands finding flesh, she launched an assault of her own. Soft skin, hard muscle, all man.

"I don't think I can walk," she gasped as he moved his mouth down her jaw line and she felt shots of hot lust firing at both ends of her body.

"No need." He pushed the elevator stop button.

"Oh, this is…is…" she began, then simply lost her train of thought as his fingers, finished with their outside exploration, buried themselves deep inside her.

Returning the favor, she unbuckled his belt, unhooked his trousers, and brought down the zipper in quick, deft moves. Her hands were around him and she was on her back on the floor of the elevator before she could take another hot ragged breath.

Now he moaned as she proved that perhaps he needn't search the world any longer for the woman of his dreams. They made their own brand of elevator music as they pulled, and tugged, and touched, and joined, and came together.

Completely spent and satisfied, they rolled over on their backs to stare at the ceiling of old wood paneling. Still panting, their clothes scattered around them, each of them feeling wonderfully used.

"Elevator sex. I'm quite sure that was a first for me," sighed Jette breathlessly.

Marc chuckled, but Jette realized he didn't say it was a first for him. She smiled. He was so naughty.

"Jette?"

"Hmm?"

"Is the doctor in?"

Jette rolled over onto his chest and studied his face. He sometimes asked her that when he wanted answers to what he was feeling. To explore what were firsts for him. Not making love in an elevator, but love itself.

It wasn't a very conventional place to have a serious discussion, but then, what the heck. Her man wasn't a conventional guy. He was used to spontaneity and having anywhere and everywhere be his office. Or home. Or playground. He grew up without any of those things, so he just wasn't oriented to boundaries.

"Since you're no longer in the doctor, I think she can serve professionally. Although being naked will strain the core values of my profession."

"I'll never tell."

"That's good then. What is it, Marc?"

"Everything that happened to me today. Tonight. Just now. It's so…so…shit, hard to describe. So…"

She waited patiently for him to find his own words.

"Complex. No. Not complex exactly, although I think it is. More like unfamiliar. And enormous. There's this…this constant flood of emotions and sometimes I feel like I'm drowning in sensations I can't control." He was unconsciously running his fingers up and down her back. Touching to stay connected.

"Is it unpleasant?"

"Not like this. Not tonight. Not usually. I don't want it to stop. It's feeding me. Making me. Changing me, I think. Like that significant emotional event you were talking about with the scarecrow tonight."

"That's what can serve as a catalyst for change in personality as well as behavior."

"Well, I'd describe you coming into my life as the most significant thing that's ever happened to me. And I can feel the change sometimes. But this morning." Marc frowned, collected his scattered thoughts and went on. He knew she'd let him find a way to get it out. To say what he needed to say.

"Sommer and I were cruising to an interview. I was, well, happy, I guess. It felt like happy. I was back on the job, I knew you were working, we'd had that great morning sex and you seemed to be settling in and hadn't changed your mind about living with me. It was good…good…good." He stopped for a moment, stuck on the word good. It wasn't the exact word he wanted, but close enough so that he knew his remarkable lover, or at least the doctor inside her, would understand. "I guess you shrinks would say I was in that good place. Then I heard the call and something inside me just…just snapped. Not like my temper. That's routine. This was like everything inside me imploded. My heart, my gut, my head. My system went from smooth to complete chaos in less than a second."

Jette just let him talk. He was finding his way through a minefield of emotions in unfamiliar territory and he had no idea how revealing he was.

"I'm afraid, Doctor. Scared witless," he said after pausing again.

"Of what?"

"Of losing you and what that would do to me now. I felt myself, my soul, ripping apart this morning. I mean, at the best of times I feel like I'm being held together with only a thin web of thread. I function just on the inside edge of the world and I could fall off at any time. And be lost. But since I've met you, since you've been with me, I feel like I'm further away from that edge. I have a firmer, steadier hold on a good life. But at the same time, even though my hold on what's worthy inside me is stronger, I feel more defenseless. More…exposed."

"Love does that, Marc. It makes life riskier. But that's only the cost. The price to pay. What you get in return…"

"I know. Oh God, I know. Nights like this. Feelings like this. It's beyond what I ever expected to get back from this life. But what do I do with the fear, Doctor? With the knowledge that if you leave me, if I don't have you in my life, I won't go back to where I was before. I won't go back to anything at all."

"What do you mean, leave you? Do you mean if I die? Marc, we all die."

"Yeah, there's that. That was the very real ugly possibility I faced today. It was horrendous. Indescribable. I'm not sure what would have come out of me, where I'd be right now, in fact, if you were hurt. Or worse. I do know that I'd like to lock you in the apartment. Stand in front of it with my gun and not let the world inside to hurt you."

"I won't stop going out into the world, Marc. I can't."

"I know." He took a single heavy breath. "I know. But could you let me be a little paranoid for a while? Overprotective and a whole lot obsessed with your safety? Would you let me know where you are, keep your cell phone on, and not be annoyed when I'm calling every, oh, five minutes or so."

She laughed. "I think I can accommodate those needs. As long as we continue to talk about it." She was actually very pleased that he was able to articulate his needs so well.

"Continue my therapy, you mean?"

"Remember I told Klara that intense therapy or a significant emotional event can change a personality. Think what the combination of the two could do."

"Jesus, that woman was obsessed with you," Marc frowned. Something about that still bothered him.

"Obsessed? That's a pretty strong word," Jette observed.

"So were the vibes."

"I think that's just a natural state for her." On reflection, Jette had to agree.

"Creepy is her natural state."

"Let's get back to your therapy, shall we?" Jette stroked his cheek. "Think you can afford my rates?"

"And they would be?"

Jette bumped her naked hips against his and raised her eyebrows.

"Oh, I think I can guarantee I'm going to need a great deal of therapy." He kissed the top of her head.

"I agree. There's also the other thing, Marc. Your fear of abandonment. That I'll leave you."

"I'm not sure I have the strength to tackle that issue tonight." Marc sighed heroically.

"Darling, you have to trust me, my love for you, and the fact that I'm not going anywhere."

"That'll take some time."

"Yes, time will tell."

"Maybe in 50 years, when I wake up and you're still sleeping beside me, maybe then I'll be able to relax." Marc's voice was low, sexy and sincere.

"It's a date," smiled Jette with confidence, her heart warmed by his tone. "Now help me up and let's get to that bed. This day has just got to end."

"It's been…memorable."

"Do you think we should get dressed?"

"Who's going to see us? It's," Marc looked at his watch. "3 a.m. How about we just stay here."

"Eventually people will be wanting to use this elevator for its intended purpose."

"You mean it wasn't built to be a sex cage? But there's always that really hot, sexy, high charged music in elevators. And it goes up and down all day."

"I'm quite certain that if those doors were to open right now, we'd have to perform CPR on one of the residents."

Marc shuddered comically. "Hey. Stop. The little guy was beginning to come alive again when you bumped him a minute ago, but I just felt him scream and tuck in under my thigh."

Jette laughed again, then touched the new scars on Marc's chest and side.

"How are you doing? It's been a very long day."

"Maybe you should help me up. Now that you mention it, I think my lung collapsed again. You're an animal."

Laughing, they helped each other up. Naked and pleased with themselves, they slipped their way into the apartment and called it a day.

# Chapter 16

It was late. So late. What a day, she thought. And it couldn't end yet. Not until she put together the next day's strategy. She had to determine her moves, communicate with the necessary Minions and Sentinels, and place them where they needed to be. Then she needed to arrange the passing of the appropriate resources to her Assassin and calculate a way to take the lead. Complicated but invigorating. Her head was clear now, her pulse was steady.

This morning she only wanted to poke at Morningstar, alias Avenger, to see what would happen. Then score a few hundred points, depending on the body count. So much for her best laid plans! She'd lost an Anointed One to Avenger and the points poured into her adversary's column. For some it would have ended the game. Weaker players would have declared defeat, then played Minion for awhile until they rebuilt their points. They'd have seen the morning's events as a complete disaster. But what made her different, what made her legendary, was that she took what looked like a crushing blow and turned it into something that increased her tally at a later time.

Patience. Perseverance. Nothing was a complete failure if you learned something. And she'd learned a great deal.

"You don't drown by falling into a deep, dark pool. You drown if you give up and go under," she muttered to herself as she tacked a picture of Jette to her board.

Morningstar could have been a cleverly placed imposter. A decoy used to draw out the Empress. But the way the play unfolded, she found the true Avenger with only one push. It cost her points, but she felt the balance really tipped in her favor. Avenger revealed herself. Exposed! Glorious!

She moved a picture of Marc to the right of Jette's photo. If Morningstar was the Avenger, that plainly meant the man at her side, this Lexington, was the Dark Knight. It was unclear what his purpose was at this point, but he appeared to be staying close to his Avatar.

She also gained tremendous insight into Avenger's capabilities. Computer-generated images were nowhere near as enlightening as watching the woman in action. Over and over again, she replayed the disc. Avenger could really move, practically fly. Wait. Could she fly? That was a thought. Did she morph into a bird, or momentarily absorb some of the bird's abilities? Both were documented features of Avenger.

If she could actually fly, it would have to be entered into the log and even more points awarded. She watched the tape again. No. It wasn't really flying. Merely jumping. She wouldn't concede the points yet.

Pleasure pushed at the irritation when she walked back to her tally board. Such a fascinating and absorbing chain of events. More than she'd ever expected, really. In a flash of self analysis, she realized she'd gotten complacent. Her past triumphs had been too easy. She thought she wanted a quick victory, but realized that was just her pride getting in the way of solid gaming. How satisfying would an easy end really be? Her ego said it would be fine. Good. Great even. But her solid gaming spirit had to admit that having a formidable opponent would make the ultimate victory far more magnificent.

Even though Avenger currently soared over her in points, this game was for the long haul. A glorious, unprecedented marathon. There was no doubt who would be left alive in the end. Who would be victorious and stand alone at the top of all the worlds. Who would have Sovereignty. But in the meantime, she'd have to work on ways to even out the score.

When Avenger was just a child, the Blood Traitor High Priest had given her seven lives for the seven suns of Himalia. Coming back to life after her death assured Avenger an advantage in most every battle. Maybe she should send an Assassin to take one of Avenger's lives. Remove one of her most significant advantages while earning major points.

The Empress studied all of her reports from the field of play. Avenger had two, possibly three lives left in her arsenal. She could take another one out of play or…the Empress felt her heart pump a little faster. Another thought. Another alternative.

Wouldn't it be better strategy going into the Final Duel if she, the Empress, had one of those extra lives on her side of the board? It would require turning Avenger. Had anyone ever done that before? She was sure no one had, but would do a search just to be sure. The points she'd tally if this was unprecedented would be sky high.

Could she lift a life force from Avenger and make it her own? Was it be possible? Could she turn Avenger? Negotiate a trade for one of her lives? She'd have to take her first. How? Where? The Empress paced and planned. When Avenger was in Callisto, she probably couldn't be captured and turned. She was at full power and surrounded by her Beasts. But Jette Morningstar was bound to be more vulnerable.

The Empress worked through the night and by the time the sun came up on another day, she went to her room of rest satisfied her next moves would put her in the lead. She'd allow herself a few hours of sleep before she'd enter the real world again. Her

Middle World role needed to be played. At least for another moon. After Avenger was defeated, she could reveal herself and roam freely and openly in all the worlds, including the Middle World of Reality. She'd no longer need to keep any secrets.

# Chapter 17

"Are you working undercover at the homeless shelter this morning, Detective Lexington?" Hilda handed Marc a cup of strong black coffee.

He looked down at his faded jeans and worn NYPD t-shirt, then grinned up at her. "No. I thought I would hang around and meet and greet your book club. Maybe serve them a few pretzels and a little domestic brew."

"That won't be necessary. I called Lia Marynik's Catering and they'll be doing the serving. We'll be setting up in the west parlor, as usual." Suddenly her eyes moved over to Jette, horrified at her breach of protocol. "Oh my, I beg your pardon. How could I have forgotten? Now that you're in residence, I won't presume to use the apartment for my convenience anymore. Detective Lexington gave me carte blanche on the place, I'm afraid. He was, you see, rarely here."

"Please. Don't change your routine and your enjoyment of this space because I'm here. I'm setting up my office in the library and will spend most of my days in there. Use the west parlor."

"Nonsense, my living quarters are quite nice and more than adequate."

"But the views of Central Park from that room can add so much to the enjoyment of books and discussion."

"They do indeed. Thank you, Dr. Morningstar." Hilda smiled at the generous new mistress.

"Was that a smile I saw?" asked Marc. "I thought I heard a creaking sound."

"Yes."

"How come you never smile at me?"

Turning, she gave him an imperious look. Patented and potent. "Let me think about that. I'll get back to you."

When he got up to find his ringing cell phone, Jette caught the smile Hilda had successfully suppressed until his back was turned. The women looked at each other and for an instant, Hilda gave Jette the opportunity to glimpse the warmth behind the pale blue eyes. Jette nodded. It would be their secret.

"Dr. Morningstar. Our book club doesn't just read the classics. We love the simple pleasure of a romance once in awhile and thrillers are our favorite. While nonfiction isn't our usual genre, there was a great deal of interest in your book, *The Criminal Mind*. I'm afraid I let it slip that you were going to be living here, and the excitement intensified. Turns out nearly all of us read it."

"You read my book?"

"Certainly. Both of them. I make it a point to read all the books on *The New York Times* best seller list." For Hilda, the *Times* wasn't a newspaper. It was an institution. "You could have knocked me over with a feather when the detective told me you were moving in here with him. Anyway, I wouldn't presume to infringe on your free time, but I've been pushed to do so by the nearly mob mentality of my reading group."

Jette laughed. "Are you asking me to attend one of your meetings?"

"Oh my goodness no. Only to autograph the copies they are pushing at me daily."

"I think I can do better than that. Tell your reading group that I'd love to meet with them, in the west parlor, at a time convenient to all of us. Then I can personalize the autographs."

Stunned, Hilda nodded. "Dr. Morningstar, you have just elevated both my status and my reputation among the people I enjoy the most. If you'll provide me with a few alternative dates and times, I'm positive we can accommodate your schedule. We're mostly retired folk and can meet anytime."

She apparently was so impressed with herself as well, she turned and left without clearing the dishes.

Marc was leaning in the doorway.

"You spoil her."

Jette smiled up at him.

"It pays to keep the woman of the house happy."

"You aren't the woman of the house?"

"Oh my goodness, no. I'm not the least bit territorial when it comes to cleaning, cooking, laundry, and meal planning. And," she got up and walked over to him seductively. "I'd much rather mess up a bed than make it."

"Ah, Jette, you're a temptress."

"What time are you getting home tonight?"

"I shouldn't be too late, why?"

When she just stared at him, he just stared back.

"The dinner party. Here," she prodded.

"Oh hell, is that tonight?"

"How can you keep multiple tasks, dates and investigatory details in your mind, juggle them and never miss a step yet you have trouble with this one?"

"Didn't we just go to a fucking party?" he grumbled, ignoring her question.

"That was for business. Tonight we're having your friends over for a nice dinner."

"I never had to do that before," he grumped. "When I wanted to hang with people, we'd go get a couple of beers. When I wanted to see Tagg and Carmel, I'd go to their house."

"That was before, when you were rude and uncivilized. Now you're living with a woman and have social obligations."

"Why?"

"It's the rules."

"Whose rules? Not mine. I just grab a six pack of Corona and a pizza from Arellano's and crash a person's crib. That's a party." Marc threw up his hands, confident in his point of view.

"Not anymore." Jette successfully kept the amusement out of her tone.

"So you didn't answer my question. Whose rules?"

"Mine."

"Oh. Well, then. Let me fall in line." He scowled at her. She smiled back. "How come that never works with you." His scowl intensified.

"What, bad temper and sarcasm?" she asked sweetly.

"Intimidation and obvious authority."

She just laughed.

"That always lightens my mood," he said with an edge as he walked over to refresh his coffee. "So let's get to the important stuff. What are we going to eat?"

"I thought we'd start with wonderful stuffed mushrooms like the ones I had at last night's party, then we're going to have a nice feta and kidney bean salad followed by tofu and spinach linguini with cinnamon sweetened melba toast and slices of kiwi for dessert."

"Oh no. No. No. Just because these are your rules, it doesn't mean we all have to eat like you. Not even Lucy could live on how much you eat and I have no idea, none whatsoever, what kind of enjoyment you get out of any of that veggie shit you call food," he growled.

"It's nice to start the day with a tantrum, don't you think? It gets your blood flowing and puts a spark in your tank."

"It puts a fucking stick of fucking dynamite up my goddamn ass is what it does."

Jette laughed and kissed his stubborn, stormy lips.

"To think you eat with that mouth."

"Not the shit you're making."

"Alright. Then how about we eat up on the roof garden and you can grill half a cow. We'll have icy beer in a cooler to serve with the steaks, and a buffet of chicken wings, chili fries, nachos, onion rings, sweet corn, fresh Italian bread from Arellano's, and strawberry shortcake for dessert."

"Those are all my favorites," he said slowly.

"I know," said Jette, raising her eyebrows and smiling at the change in his expression. It was still suspicious, but had a dawning look of pleasure.

"But you'll have a tiny covered dish of tofu spinach linguini, right?" he asked.

"Absolutely, if you insist."

"We have a grill up there?" One more detail to trip her up if she was pulling his leg.

"We do now. A huge, manly, gas-powered behemoth with several lids and assorted attachments. Claude and Tommy put it together yesterday. I guess it was quite an ordeal. If I were you, I'd check all the connections before you set a match to it." She kissed a mouth that was now turned into a happy smile. "I'd hate to have that pretty face singed off your skull."

"You really are soft on me, aren't you." He bumped her with his hips.

"Oh yeah," she agreed, bumping him back.

"So, besides making my culinary dreams come true, what are you going to do today?"

"I'll be going to my office this morning. We have a meeting on yesterday's events."

"I think they'd let you off the hook if you wanted to stay home."

"I'm not going to stay home, Marc."

"Will you let Eunice Mills go with you?"

"And who would she be?"

"Private badge. The best I know. She used to be a vice cop until she decided to go out on her own."

Jette would have fought it, but his words the night before were still echoing in her heart.

"Yes, Marc."

"And Claude will drive you."

"That's certainly no hardship, although a little over the top for a professor to be driven to work in a limo. Maybe you could loan Claude your Harley and I could be his biker babe. I know he secretly covets your wheels."

"First of all you're *my* biker babe, remember? And secondly Claude couldn't handle the power, particularly with your breasts up against his back. I'm not sure I could and I'm macho man."

"So Claude drives me. Eunice escorts me. Anything else?"

"Keep your cell on and with you."

"Alright," Jette sighed. "Anything else?"

"Yes. I have a blonde wig and a long black raincoat for you to wear. With some oversized sunglasses, you should be safe."

She stared at him.

"I guess I found the end of it, didn't I?"

"Uh-huh. It ended at the cell phone."

"I told Tommy not to bring the wig over. It was her idea."

"Tommy's here?"

"Riding shotgun."

"Marc," she began, then relented. "It'll be nice to have her along."

"Thanks," he said simply then put his mouth on hers and gave her something to live for.

Eunice turned out to be a very pleasant woman. Formidable in the extreme, but with a ready laugh and because she had nothing but wonderful things to say about Marc on the elevator ride to ground level, Jette liked her immediately.

A muscular six feet tall, Eunice had a long scar running from her cheek bone to her jaw. It did little to diminish the attractiveness of her sharp-featured face and gave her a fearsome cachet. She said it frightened the little gangsters hanging in the back alleys of Brooklyn, but she looked like she could take on a whole table full of big gangsters hanging in the penthouses of Manhattan. Towering over Jette, she was filled with confident energy.

Eunice beat Jonathon to the front door, gave him a cheeky wink, opened it, and accompanied Jette to the car, scanning the buildings, the streets, and the faces of the curious bystanders. Using both experience and intuition as a guide, she nodded all clear to Tommy and Claude as she slid into the back seat with Jette. Far from being a stoic, silent body guard, she shared stories from the streets and asked tons of questions about Jette and her life before Marc. They were fast friends by the time they arrived at the university.

During the morning, Marc called several times and Jette patiently reassured him. She went to meetings, graciously and quietly accepted the accolades from her colleagues, resisted all media attention, and met with several students to comfort and encourage them. There were no classes and wouldn't be for a week, but Jette communicated with her class via email and gave them a revised deadline for their final papers.

Lee called to check on her. She and the commissioner were meeting at Dolly Tuckers that evening and she was excited about all the possibilities.

"Klara Marshall called three times already this morning to set up a time to get together. I'm going to meet with her first Jette, just to get some preliminary information. It didn't make her very happy, but I'm not liking the vibes I'm getting from her. All together too aggressive. And her sense of entitlement is a little insufferable."

"Success does that to some people."

"True. I've talked with a few honchos in the business and she's shopping for a new agent. Apparently her current one, a very good woman by the way, has informed her she needs to get more creative. Her books have gotten redundant and they don't sell well with the younger demographic. I was surprised to hear that she didn't get an advance for her latest novel. She's writing on spec, hoping to sell the manuscript after she's finished it."

"Interesting. Do you want her?" asked Jette.

"Not necessarily. The money would be great, but she's very, very high maintenance and the grapes in the vine have told me she's getting a little over fermented. I don't like high maintenance clients. Cuts into my social life."

"What social life?"

"Ouch," laughed Lee. "Hey, maybe the commish will turn out to be social and have a life."

"There you go," encouraged Jette. "Anyway, right now I'm very busy with my third book and we talked with several publishers last night who showed an interest in more. I'm not sure where Klara would fit into our plans."

"I hear you. My thoughts exactly. Jette, have you been watching any of the news shows?"

"No."

"You're sizzling. Everyone is talking about you. Do you know a Captain Markle?"

"From Tucson?"

"Yes, that's him. He's been a talking head about the case in Arizona. Gads, the man is wild about you. Did you two have a thing or something?" Lee wanted the details.

"No. We just worked a few cases together and I tutored him in the Cherokee language."

"Ah. That's another thing. It's interesting how that connection is playing. Your Cherokee blood line. It's stirred an incredible interest in their history. It's really an amazing story."

"We are an interesting and resilient nation," agreed Jette.

"I think there's a book in there somewhere. Maybe even a series," said Lee, her mind already registering several exciting possibilities. "But let's move from the speculation to reality and the main reason for my call. Do you know Maxine White?"

"Of course, who doesn't?" Maxine White was the CEO of the most prestigious publisher of nonfiction in New York. The absolute top dog. "Are you name dropping?"

"No. She'd like to meet with you personally about a project."

"This is a new development."

"Very. And impressive. She called me at 5:00. That's a.m. The woman never sleeps. Apparently she saw you last night, but wanted an exclusive meet, not just party patter. The contact could be due to your scorching press right now, but as long as the iron is hot, hot, hot, I think we should press ourselves. Will you take a meeting?"

"Hmmm. Let me check my schedule. I'll get back to you," Jette teased.

"Bitch."

Jette laughed. "Maybe we shouldn't appear too eager."

"You mean panting on my knees with my tongue hanging out appears to be too eager?"

"I'll be happy to meet with her. I wouldn't want you to hyperventilate."

"She wants a meet tomorrow," said Lee. "If you don't think it looks too eager, I could bring her around to your place. I think seeing you in that gorgeous penthouse is an excellent way to counter my overly obvious brown nosing and excessively grateful groveling."

"As it happens, I'm available all day tomorrow. I was just planning on sequestering myself there and setting up my office. To write…to produce…to manufacture what you're so hot to sell."

"Excellent. I'll call Maxine, send over all the material I have here on her, then get back to you. You can look over everything and we can…just a sec. Judy is buzzing me." Jette could hear Lee answering the interoffice page. She came back a few seconds later. "She usually doesn't interrupt, but Klara is in my outside office scaring her silly. I'll go out there and see what she wants. If I send this stuff over to you right away, will you have time to look at it this afternoon?"

"I can do that."

"Great. Maxine really is the uber achiever in this town. At least she was until one Dr. Jette Morningstar took residence."

"You flatter me."

"Flash. That's my job. Talk to you later."

As Jette hung up, she turned toward a movement in her doorway, a residual smile still playing on her lips. A woman was standing there obviously and unselfconsciously eavesdropping on her conversation.

Stunning, perfectly groomed, and expensively dressed, she waited a beat, taking the moment to set the stage for her dramatic entrance and impressive introduction. She wanted to generate the proper amount of admiration before she spoke.

Her air of poise and self assurance was translated by Jette's unerring intuition as a skewed sense of power, privilege, and entitlement. Old money and high society. More accurately New York Society. The elevated heights of which were unmatched in the class-driven hierarchy of the wealthy.

"Hello, Dr. Morningstar. I hope I'm not interrupting. Your woman out there checked all my identification and sent me back." There was the tiniest hint of irritation, like a subtle spice in a smooth and elegantly prepared marinara sauce. Otherwise her voice held the rich tones of Eastern breeding and Ivy League education. Clear and cultured. Far be it from her to spend any more time on the insult of not being immediately recognized by Dr. Morningstar's help. She'd just file it away and remember it always.

"Is there something I can do for you?" Jette's tone was respectful, but not deferential. She didn't ask the woman in, nor did she stand. Curiosity was the dominant emotion running the engine of her interest.

"Yes, of course. That's why I'm here," said the woman reaching into her exquisite Katrina Wedel bag and securing a small white card with shiny embossed gold print. She walked through the doorway and handed it to Jette. "My name is Delancy Pickford Weiss Chrysler. Mrs. Victor Chrysler," she clarified, although her husband had been dead for over five years.

Jette took the card. Well, that covered every family in the who's who of New York royalty, she thought. And Victor Chrysler. That name hit the big bell. He was a well known financier, senator, philanthropist and, if the rumors were correct, philanderer, and would have been old enough to be this woman's father.

"Have we met?" Jette glanced at the expensively embossed card.

"No. We've never been formally introduced, but I'm on the NYU board, as well as many others, and am very familiar with your work." She paused to give Jette the opportunity to return the favor and comment on her own renowned and well publicized work, but Jette simply stood and motioned toward one of the two chairs near the window.

"Please sit down. It's always a privilege to meet someone serving on the university board."

Certainly agreeing that was true, Delancy glided over and sat gracefully on the chair as Jette sat down opposite her.

"I'm here to introduce myself, but primarily to invite you to a small informal party at my home in the Hamptons this weekend. I had to fly in for the emergency meeting about that unfortunate incident yesterday. I think it can all be resolved if we're all more careful who we let on campus. Anyway, we have assigned a task force to study the options. The provost mentioned you were in your office so I thought I'd come here and get on your social calendar. My secretary is fashioning the formal invitation, but this will save us both time. Invitations to this particular event are the most sought after of the season. This is an unprecedented opportunity."

Jette could see that Delancy Pickford Weiss Chrysler sincerely thought so. When she spoke, Jette successfully kept the amusement from her demeanor and her voice.

"I'm so sorry. I'm afraid my weekend calendar is filled."

Saturday afternoon's meeting with Maxine White was tentative, but that was good enough for Jette. More importantly, on Sunday Marc was off duty and they were planning to sleep late, jog in the park, attend the opening of a friend's deli, and generally enjoy a beautiful summer day in New York City. He also had Monday free if nothing hot came up. She saw no reason to change their plans. Or at least her plans. She wasn't sure the invitation included her date.

Delancy simply blinked. Then blinked again. As if the flexing of her eyelids would replay what she just thought she heard. Would replay it with the response she'd expected.

"Excuse me?" she asked, finally.

"I already have plans, Ms. Chrysler."

"Mrs."

"Mrs. Chrysler." Jette nodded. This really was fun, she thought.

"Ah. Yes. You're still new here. From out west, I understand. Dr. Morningstar, my parties and soirées are legendary, but perhaps haven't yet made the pages of the Old West Gazette, or whatever. I think anyone, everyone really, will tell you that an invitation to one of them is the dream, the lifetime ambition of most in New York society. Your plans can be changed, I'm sure. Several people from the register who will be attending have called me since yesterday. Knew I was on the board. They expressed an interest in meeting you. Really. People you'd otherwise have to wait several years before securing even an introduction. If ever. Tiffany Mae Schmidt and her darling daughter Onnika will be there as will Melissa Leah Baade, Ramona Michelle Clark, Lisa Lucinda Chambers, Vickie Ann Murray Adams, you've heard of her great grandfather, I'm sure. Let's see there will be Michelle Lauren Cameron, the famous sculptor and Lady Lorie Ann Arrowood Williams Siler is in residence fresh from her triumph in the London revival of *My Fair Lady*. Countess Brooke Ashley Carleton and her oldest son the future Count, who, you will be flattered to know, expressly asked to have you at the table to his right, and there will be…"

Jette interrupted before the entire guest list, as impressive as it was, was revealed.

"Mrs. Chrysler, please. With all those people, I can't imagine I'll be missed." And, she thought, she sure didn't want to spend an evening sitting at the right hand of a future Count or being paraded around like a prized pet. Good Lord.

Delancy continued revealing her plans as if Jette hadn't even breathed an opinion.

"Only the top tier will be there, Dr. Morningstar. You won't have to move through the several lower levels of the New York social set to get your entre. You understand that with my introduction, you won't have to wait years, exhausting years, I might add, before you share our air. Now, logistics. Melissa lives nearest you and will arrange for transportation. Nice location, by the way. When the chair of the board personnel committee mentioned you lived in The Edgewood, I couldn't believe it. Melissa has been on the waiting list for years. She most generously volunteered to pick you up in the morning. Shall we say ten? Dinner is black tie, tennis and swimwear are a must, business casual for brunch on Sunday."

Jette knew she was blowing any chance she had to be one of the elite, but she wasn't sure their air would have enough fresh, open, breathable oxygen for her. As a matter of fact, she was sure of it.

"No, Mrs. Chrysler. Thank you, but I won't be able to make your party this weekend. Perhaps another time."

Delancy frowned and Jette felt the punch of both her disbelief and her irritation.

"May I remind you I'm on the board here?"

Mrs. Victor Chrysler considered that her trump card, but Jette wasn't playing. She deliberately ignored the subtle warning, and stood up.

"And I'm sure the university appreciates your time and efforts on their behalf. I serve on several non-profit boards myself and know how rewarding that can be."

Several coats of Delancy Chrysler's polish slid away as she also stood up. She wouldn't ask again. Ever. Anger bubbled and blossomed in her eyes.

"Good day, Dr. Morningstar," she said coolly. Looking around the office she shot her last salvo. "Don't get too comfortable here. We have standards. We might overlook a lack of solid lineage, but not a lack of appreciation."

Jette held in the laughter until she was sure the socialite was out of ear shot, then released it in waves of pure amusement.

"I'm not sure what your lineage is," she chuckled to herself, since she was far too cultured to confront the woman's delusion of superiority head on and far too busy to try to treat her. "But it was my people who greeted your ancestors when they arrived on our shores. Now that's a line. You're a newcomer, Mrs. Delancy Pickford Weiss Chrysler."

Periodically for the next hour, giggles would bubble up and escape. She wasn't a habitual giggler. Her laughter was deep and delighted; her smiles quick and dazzling, but she didn't normally respond to the irresistible tickle of ridiculous hilarity that required a little hysterical titter. But the look on the woman's face would materialize in Jette's mind, and she just had to release the pressure.

When the amusement finally abated, the predominate feeling was compassion. To be so caught up in the game of class and caste. Of keeping a tally of who you know and paying your dues to climb the social ladder, and worrying about it all. What a waste. She could tell that Mrs. Delancy Pickford Weiss Chrysler had intelligence and wit. Her card indicated she had a masters in fine art from Brown and another one in history from Princeton. Jette sighed and shrugged. She didn't get it and never would.

At noon, Eunice stuck her head in and grinned.

"I'm off to take a lunch break," she said.

"Fine. Enjoy," said Jette, filing away some of her notes. She nearly jumped when she heard Marc's voice.

"Wrong answer, Professor," he said.

She looked up into his frowning face. "Excuse me?"

"If Eunice is going off to lunch your response should be, 'who's got my back?'"

"Eunice," she called. Eunice popped her head back in.

"Yes?"

"Before you go for your well deserved and I'm sure legally required lunch break, could you please tell me who will be watching my back?"

"That would be the renowned Detective Marcus Lexington from Special Projects."

"Did you check his qualifications?"

"I believe he might be a bit overrated, but he's big and he's bad."

"Good enough, I guess."

"See you later, Marc," said Eunice. To Jette she said, "I'll be back in an hour. Don't let the kid leave until I can take the door."

"Absolutely not."

"Use your body if you have to."

"Isn't that what a body guard is for?"

"Depends on the guard."

"Depends on the body."

"I'll leave you to him, then. That for sure isn't overrated." Eunice chuckled and shut the door.

Marc glowered at the door, then back at Jette. Maybe he should have hired Ed Bailey. That man hadn't used a complete sentence in the ten years he'd known him.

"Big and bad," said Jette and smiled until he relented, relaxed, then returned it. "And better."

Not wanting to deprive himself by sustaining a bad attitude, Marc walked over to her and collected the kiss he'd been thinking about all morning.

"It seems Eunice is working out," he observed wryly.

"She's great." Jette finished her filing and closed down her computer.

"She is. Saved my ass in a knife fight with a gang of punks when I was a rookie and she was the ranking beat cop." Marc folded his arms to prevent them from grabbing her.

"Is that how she got the scar?"

"Yeah. A punk did a job on her face. A plastic surgeon could fix it, or at least reduce the impact, but she seems to like it. Go figure."

"I think it gives her cachet."

"Like that's the reason. Cachet." Marc snorted. "I think she keeps it because it enhances her rep. Talk about big and bad."

"Uh-huh. Well, I think it's interesting that she remembers that knife fight a little differently."

"Oh yeah?"

"Yes. She told me you broke it up when that gang had her cornered and bleeding already."

"Hmm, maybe. But she came on strong as soon as the odds were a little more even. Jesus, that woman can brawl."

Jette smiled imagining Marc and Eunice fighting side by side. "Where are you taking me for lunch?"

"Some place I know, then I thought maybe you'd like to walk over to my place."

"The place I originally assumed we'd be living?"

"It would give you an opportunity to see what you've been missing."

"I think it's a fine idea, but do you think we can dodge all the reporters?"

"Well, since this is my old stomping grounds, I know a way off campus that'll get us by all the media hounds, and you can wear this." His hand came up with a really old battered Yankees cap he'd found on a desk in the hallway.

Jette stared at it, then down at her lovely forest green suit. What a tease. Turning, she reached up and grabbed a broad brimmed hat from a shelf. She'd worn it one bright sunny day when she'd decided to walk to the office. Then she took out her purse and dug for her sun glasses. Tucking her hair up under the hat and putting on the glasses, she grinned up at him.

"Don't smile and maybe it'll work." He gave her gorgeous lips a little peck, then opening the door he escorted her out.

Marc didn't think she could do anything to disguise her incredibly classic face and features, but shrugged at the attempt. Most New Yorkers wouldn't recognize the mayor if he walked down the street. Nor would they care.

After they left the campus, they blended into the hundreds of people pouring out of the offices, stores and apartments for their lunch break. Marc gently held Jette's hand and acknowledged several people along the way. Mostly the strange and richly eclectic people of the street.

"Hey Folgers, what do you know?" he called to a shabby man wheeling a small piece of carry-on luggage.

"Folgers?" asked Jette softly.

"Loves coffee," explained Marc under his breath.

"Ah."

"This is Dr. Morningstar. My new girlfriend," Marc told the man when he stopped to squint up at him, then over to Jette.

"Whoa! She's a looker. Can she check out the rash on my butt?"

"No, Folgers, she isn't that kind of doctor. She's a psychologist."

"Ah. That explains why such a looker finds you fascinating." Folgers laughed, showing an impressive pair of teeth standing proud and alone in his lower jaw.

"Why does everyone always say that?" muttered Marc.

"Can't imagine," shrugged Jette good-naturedly.

"Hey, Doc. How do crazy people go through the forest?" asked Folgers.

"Tell me."

"They take the psycho-path." Folgers laughed again, delighted with himself. "Hey Snake Eyes, where do you find a legless dog?"

"Right where you left him," answered Marc and laughed when Folgers' face fell.

"You're getting old, Folgers. You told me that one last week."

"Gotta buck for coffee?"

"Where can you get a cup of coffee for a buck around here?" asked Marc.

"Yer right, kid. Gotta a fiver?"

Marc pulled out a ten. "Get some eggs with that."

"Will do!" Folgers gave them one more grin and went off in the direction of the golden arches.

"He's actually one who'll get the coffee and eggs. He's not a druggie or a drunk."

"And you're a soft touch."

"Am not. Just paying him back. Folgers took care of me once. I got pretty dented after a gang rumble and he patched me up. Took me to his palatial cardboard crib and made sure I stayed out of the game for awhile."

"What's his story?"

"He's one who never shares. I've tried to get him into permanent housing, but he always escapes. I expect I'll find his frozen bag of bones in an alley some day."

And it will hurt you, she thought.

"Why Snake Eyes?"

"It's my street name." He tapped his sleeve where Jette knew a tattoo of a cobra wrapped up his solid, muscular arm. "Partly because of the mark, I guess and I think the green eyes may have had something to do with it."

She looked into the distinctive eyes of her lover. Oh yeah. They may have. Snake Eyes was a good fit.

"I'm finding I like your family, Marc."

"I have no family. They are just throwaways. Like I was." He waved at a little woman sitting on the bench talking to her invisible companion. She waved back enthusiastically pointing him out to the person who wasn't there.

"Is there anyone in New York you don't know?"

"A few immigrants who got here in the last few weeks."

She laughed and took his arm.

"I love you."

He looked down at her. "Want to prove it?"

"Sure."

They stopped at a corner cart with an eye popping umbrella filled with celestial planets and stars and aromas to test the fortitude of any casual dieter.

"Hey, Dicey." He grinned at the smiling woman standing tall behind the steaming covered trays of her sidewalk buffet. "You got anything in there that didn't used to have a heartbeat?"

"Your new girl a veggie lover?" she asked as she carefully put out her cigarette and stood ready to serve.

"Yup."

"What the heck is she doing with you then?"

"I ask myself that every day."

"I have a wonderful rice and bean wrap that will delight her palate and not offend her peculiar preferences," laughed Dicey.

"I didn't know that."

"That's because you're a carnivore. Your usual? Or would you like to join your lady?"

"I'd rather eat that pile of day-old dog shit over there."

"I could scoop it for you. Put it in a nice bun. With what you stack on it, you'd never notice." Dicey laughed again, a hardy, gravelly blast of delight to blend with the other aggressive sounds of the New York street.

"I think not."

She opened various lids and built Jette's wrap, then handed it to her with lots of napkins and a bottle of water.

"Thank you, Dicey. It looks wonderful."

"Actually I think it looks a lot like that pile over there, but I keep it on the menu for you wacky perverts."

Jette laughed with pleasure.

"I hope you enjoy it and come often, Dr. Morningstar," winked Dicey.

"So, you're thoroughly briefed on your current events," grinned Marc.

"Oh yeah. And have you come up in the world." Her eyes held approval as she opened a bun with a practiced hand and flipped a hot dog into it dead center.

"Can't come back from a vacation in Arizona without a souvenir," said Marc as he dug into his pockets for cash.

"From what I heard, it wasn't much of a vacation. But you got the guy who murdered Fiona and that's just fine."

"You knew her?" asked Jette.

"Yes. She was quite a fixture around here. Loved to bring people to Jesus' table. With a little more time she might have been able to redeem the detective, but now it appears the task has fallen to you. Here you go, Snake Eyes. Enjoy."

Dicey handed Marc a hot dog and a Coke and made change as he proceeded to pile on as much other stuff as he could get in the bun. Sauerkraut, relish, raw onions, hot peppers, shredded cheese, chili, ketchup, and mustard. They walked away from the cart with their handheld lunch.

"Here comes the love me part." He grinned and put practically the whole thing in his mouth at once.

"Well, I guess I'll just talk to myself for the next few blocks," laughed Jette.

"Oh no," said Marc as he chewed. "I can talk with my mouth full. No problem."

She had to translate since it came out in a muffled slur, but she understood well enough.

"How about you just enjoy your lunch. I don't want to have to perform the Heimlich on you when you choke." She sampled her wrap and raised her eyebrows. "This is delicious."

"Yeah?" Marc pushed the rest of his meal into his mouth.

"Yes, absolutely." She loved her tasty wrap, the frenetic pulse of the city as they walked and chewed, and most particularly her guy. Life was good.

Marc opened his Coke and chased the last of his laden hot dog into his stomach. "Ah. That was great. Nothing like that in Arizona."

"Not quite in that combination anyway."

"I always piled on as much shit as I could when I was growing up. It helped fill the hunger hole. Now, I just like my dog coated that way. When I went to school here, Dicey would let me help myself. Not all the street vendors were as in tune to customer satisfaction."

"She's another interesting character."

"Would you believe she has a doctorate in medieval history?"

"Really? Why does she...never mind."

"You don't want to sound like an elitist academic snob and ask why she's wasting her mind and her skills selling what is loosely called food out of a cart in the street when she could be a tenured professor?"

"It did cross my mind. And yes, even though I'm curious, I don't want to sound like an elitist academic snob."

"It's simple. This makes her happy. The university rat race didn't. She taught at NYU for awhile a long time ago. Loved New York. Hated the pressure of teaching and publishing. Had a little breakdown."

"It's certainly not for everyone." She finished her wrap and opened her water. "Alright, I've now seen you rip, tear, and devour a New York hot dog with all the finesse of a rat terrier and I still love you. Any more tests of my feelings for you."

"Ah, they will be legion. Starting with giving me a kiss right here, right now."

"Hmm."

Marc grinned, unwrapped a little mint and popped it into his mouth. "Dicey slipped it to me."

"Obviously a woman of great wisdom."

Marc pulled her to him and shared his minty breath with her as he brought his mouth down over hers. She laughed when they parted and kept her arm around his waist as they continued their walk.

"Now for dessert," he said after they walked a few blocks.

"Mmm. Ice cream?"

"No, not exactly."

"Fruit?"

"No, not exactly fruit, either."

"What?"

He turned into a doorway and got out his keys.

"Me."

"Oh. My favorite."

His apartment turned out to be everything she thought it would be. Since Hilda had shoveled it out, it was scrupulously clean, but there was an odd assortment of mismatched furniture, a lounge chair with duct tape, chipped linoleum, and scarred counters. She saw a fist sized hole in one of the walls in the hallway to the bedroom.

"I recognize your work. Did you have a bad day?"

"Several, actually." He didn't elaborate; she didn't ask him to.

"Goddamn it Hilda!" he shouted when he swung into the bedroom.

Jette burst out laughing. The bed was not only made which, in Marc's opinion, was bad enough, but the floral printed comforter and bed skirt were particularly bright and, well, pretty. There were cheerful shams of the same print, and several coordinating pillows. In the center of the bed was a stuffed purple pony. On the side tables, the lampshades were the same pattern as the curtains over the windows. It was an impressive ensemble.

"This is all so together, Marc. Shows a softer side of you. Not very urban New York macho bachelor man."

"I swear to you if the sheets match, the woman is fired."

"Could you wait until tomorrow? She's putting together the party tonight."

"And why the hell do women have to have a hundred fucking pillows all over every goddamn thing?" He fired them around the room like big fluffy shrapnel. The poor purple pony sailed through the bathroom door and landed in the back of the shower.

"It's enough to make you put your fist through the wall," she said agreeably.

He turned to her in mid rant, his hands fisted in the comforter. "What did you say?"

"I was agreeing with you, darling."

"Oh, really."

"Really."

"Well, the sheets don't match."

"Thank goodness. I don't think I could run the household and catch a nooner with you at the same time."

"But they're purple."

"Do you think you can still adequately perform?"

"Are you asking if you think I can still get it up?" He grinned diabolically.

"Exactly."

"That depends."

"On what"

"On the color of your underwear."

"They're red."

"Oh yeah. That trumps purple every time."

Then he grabbed her and proceeded to completely mess up the pretty, cheery, ensemble. And his pretty, cheery woman.

# Chapter 18

They watched from across the street. It was a well coordinated operation. To all appearances they were two carefree teens out for a stroll. Chatting on their cell phones, texting their friends, ogling good looking guys, window shopping, and chowing down on diet Dew and Pizza Pringles. But they were on an important mission for the Blue Empress and their blood was up.

Their quarry was ahead of them on the other side of the street. It sure wouldn't help their point total if they got made, but the couple seemed completely unsuspecting.

With giggling nonchalance, they fell into step and crossed the street a block behind Jette and Marc.

"Oh my God. Do you believe this? There are about, like twenty teams and we tagged her first," said 2Die4.

"What are the odds?" asked IM2COOL4U.

"Oh, like twenty to one I guess," shrugged the petite red head, swinging her ponytail.

"Whatever. We're going to get the points and it's going to put us in the lead for our school," said the tall slender co-ed, impressed with herself.

"We rock!"

"Don't you think they should be more, um, diligent or something?"

"You'd think. But they don't know about the bounty the Empress set on shooting them."

"For sure. It's good to be on her side in this."

"Oh, yeah."

"The Shield sure is hot," sighed 2DIE4.

"Yeah. God. Dark Knight material for sure. If he tried to turn me I think I'd do a U-turn right in the middle of the round."

"I don't think you're supposed to talk like that. We're loyal to the Empress."

"I know, I know. It just seems like having him up close and personal would be awesome."

"I have to check the manual. Can a Minion have sex with the Dark Knight and still be loyal to the Empress?"

"Only if she doesn't have an organism," giggled IM2COOL4U.

"Yeah, like that will happen. I'm having one now just looking at him."

"Hoot! Your pants are just too tight."

"Whatever," snorted 2DIE4. "So how many points do we get for shooting Morningstar?"

"200. Plus we get to spin the multiplier because she's with the Shield and it's a two-fer."

"If we play our part just right, I think we'll rack up enough points to be tops in the house."

"Outstanding. Although we better get this right. When the Empress is in a mood, it's maul and maim."

"Don't remind me," laughed 2DIE4. "She took points from me last week when I questioned why IBHotInAZ got to advance a whole level for Recon."

"Yeah, I mean like, I heard all she had to do was to get slides of Morningstar shopping."

"Really? Why would the Empress want that?"

"Don't know. Only she sees the whole picture. The whole picture with all the pictures, get it?"

"Oh yeah. And look how famous Morningstar is now. That's so spooky."

"She reads minds, you know."

"Hey. It looks like they're stopping to secure some provisions. Is your weapon fully charged?"

"Yeah, yours?"

"Yup. God, gag me. What's she's eating?"

"Nothing I'd put on a plate, that's for sure. Shoot her now."

Both young women reached in their pockets and pulled out their weapons of choice. One pink and covered in rhinestones, the other gold with bright red lips. They flicked open their cell phones with a practiced wrist and began snapping pictures.

"Take some of other things around us," hissed 2Die4 as IM2COOL4U continued to blatantly point her phone at the cart on the corner. "We're supposed to be covert."

"What do you call being so far from Macy's?"

"Unfortunate. But you know what I mean. We can't get caught."

IM2COOL4U rolled her eyes, but began pointing her phone at other points of interest. When Marc turned toward them, they both slammed their phones against their ears and punched each other's number. They continued walking, talking to each other electronically.

"If we like, roll the dice and it's a six, we get like double points, right."

"Absolutely."

"That should get us to the, let's see, me to the third orange and you to the second, right?"

"Yeah. The field colors are like the karate colors. Black on one end, white on the other. Being turned to Avenger would be 2 levels of purple, 3 levels of red, 4 levels of brown, then 10 degrees of black. For the Empress its 2 levels of green, 3 levels of orange, 4 levels of yellow, then 10 degrees of white."

"Whew, I need my board to keep track."

"I told you to do the strings." 2DIE4 held up her wrist. On it were a white string, two green strings and one orange.

"I will when I get more. It'll be more impressive."

"I know. I feel like kind of a noob with just these strings, but it helps me keep track."

"Unfortunately the risk ratio is low on this one."

"So how do we get a Test or a Quest? We aren't going to sail to the top on Tag and Track Teams only."

"CallyinFornia did. But then she was on the Tag and Track Team for the Governator. Could you believe those pictures she got of him and his kids? They were really up close."

They watched as their quarries lunched on their individual choices. When Marc pulled Jette to him and kissed her, they both brought up their phones and took multiple pictures.

"OMG! I've got to text Candlewax. She'll just melt when she sees that! She's on the Tag team over on 5$^{th}$ and 52$^{nd}$."

"Maybe they're too hot for the Empress."

"Yeah, she's supposedly a virgin."

"Lord, that explains her famous and frequent frustrated fits."

"But it makes her power pure."

"If you say so. I would think all it does is make her more susceptible to road rage and PMS."

"Hello. She *is* unpredictable."

"Do you want to take more shots?"

"Better not. These will give us the max points. Besides, if we're spotted, we lose it all."

"Like Chutes and Ladders."

"Is that another game?"

"Na. Something I used to play with my granny."

"Your granny was a gamer?"

"If you count Candyland, Scrabble and Monopoly."

IM2COOL4U shuddered. "Not in this lifetime."

"Okay let's send the pics, roll the virtual dice and collect our points. Then I want to see if that really sweet top is still on sale at Macy's."

"I thought your card was maxorized."

"It is, but I don't intend to go back to school without it."

"You're an addict, you know."

"My bad."

"Got a good schedule this fall?"

"Oh, yeah. Nothing before noon. I'll be able to game all the a.m."

"Excellent."

Looking down at the tiny screen on her PDA, the Empress surreptitiously checked the website she'd set up for her Minions. Reports and pictures were coming in from all over the city. Tag and Track Teams she'd placed in strategic positions were giving her the information she needed. They had no idea they were snapping pictures of the real Avenger. She'd just put a bounty on Jette Morningstar and let her Minions loose. Assigning points was going to take her quite some time that night.

So Avenger wasn't going to stay safely sequestered in her Home Base until everything settled down. Interesting. She must think no one in the City of Might suspected. Even after the spectacle she made the day before. Fine. It worked in her favor. Overconfidence was the downfall of many a gamer.

Whoa. Look at that one. Taken outside the university office building. Maybe Avenger did suspect something. Not only did she keep her Dark Knight near, she was being accompanied by what must be a Guardian. The woman had to go six feet. Maybe it just showed that Avenger suspected she was on her trail. It wouldn't matter in the long run.

There were several shots of the Dark Knight walking publicly with her in his identity as the Shield. Nice code name, but not too subtle. Almost as if they were challenging the gamers in the Middle World to put it all together. Such conceit. Understandable, but it would lead to their demise.

She saw the picture of the two of them kissing. On a public street. Slut. Using her sex to reward her Knight. Sick. Apparently they were living together near the Dark Portal close to Central Park where they must pass from Callisto into the Middle World of Reality.

Wishing she could stay in the game but knowing she needed to work, she shut off her PDA and put on the persona that allowed her to walk undetected through the Middle World.

# Chapter 19

Jette arrived home early in the afternoon, a purple pony clutched in her arms. Eunice left her at the door with a smile and a hearty handshake.

"See you in the morning. You like to run in the park, right?"

"At sunrise."

"I'll bring my bike. I understand you run fast and I kind of jog like a bear."

"Make it a ten speed. Her brother calls her *Ganolvvsgv*. The wind," said Marc as he came up behind them. He saw with approval that Eunice had her gun out the minute she heard the elevator door open.

The building was what he'd call semi-secure. There was a doorman 24/7 and all other doors were locked at all times. The outside entrances were armed with a security system, but since the residents were more concerned about absolute privacy and convenience than with security, there were no cameras, and the system was pretty primitive. Simple key codes, easy to disarm. He'd been petitioning the co-op board since his arrival for something better, but hadn't given it priority since he didn't spend much time there. He'd give it another try soon.

"You're sure you wouldn't like to stay for dinner, Eunice?" asked Jette.

"No thanks. I've got a hot date." She winked at Marc. "Sorry, kid. Didn't mean to break your heart."

He laughed as she put her gun back in her holster, saluted and walked back to the elevator.

"Marc, you really do collect the most unusual people."

"What did you bring that home for?" Marc pointed at the purple pony. "I thought you took it to shove into a dumpster."

"Lucy. She's coming tonight. Wouldn't you like to give her a little something? You haven't seen her in a very long time."

"You don't think that the scorpion paper weight from Arizona would be an appropriate gift?"

"She's four."

"Yeah, but she loves me." Marc's grin was full of self satisfaction.

"This is true. But do you really want to test it with an ugly fat bug set in clear plastic."

"Hey. Luke gave it to me." Luke was her adopted brother and he and Marc had become fast friends during his stay in Arizona.

"And that's supposed to make it age appropriate for a four year old?"

"Sure."

"You're sick." Jette shook her head.

"I know that. It's why I'm living with a therapist."

"Come on. Let's change, then go up and make sure everything is ready for our guests. It's going to be an absolutely gorgeous night."

"Of course it is. You possess magic," Marc said with a wink.

"Are you saying Mother Nature wouldn't mess with the, what did you call me, the karmic Princess of the Earth."

"Don't remind me." snorted Marc. "Sometimes I have absolutely no idea why you ever unpacked."

"Because I'm crazy about you," purred Jette.

As the party began, Marc felt strange. Out of himself. The shift in his world, in his life, was so dramatic, that he had no frame of reference. He'd never entertained up on the roof. Hell, he'd never entertained at all. Except women. One at a time…mostly. Never cooked or served them more than a beer or a glass of wine.

And here he was tonight. Standing in the roof garden next to Jette. Like a couple. Greeting people whom he worked with every day, directing his best friend and former partner Tagg to get the grill going. Patting his wife Carmel's little belly when she told them number two was on his or her way. Getting a squeal and a big, wet kiss from their daughter Lucy as he presented her with the purple pony. When she hugged it like it was a precious treasure, Marc winked at his woman. Not as cool as a scorpion forever preserved in plastic, but obviously a winner.

Rachael LaFrancois and her date, a big detective from the Queens drug enforcement division named Hal Rowley, came in adding noise and laughter. Teresa Rodriguez came alone as did Raj Amed. Jette saw almost immediately that they had more than a professional interest in each other. When she asked Marc, he just shrugged.

"They've been banging each other since Raj joined the team a few years ago. It's never been a problem, so I've never made it an issue. Ah, they don't know that we all know, so we don't talk about it."

"The secret's safe with me."

Anna Martineau, the squad's fun loving dispatcher came with her husband, Arick O'Hara a firefighter with an irrepressible Irish grin and a booming boyish laugh. Dina Pacheco, a detective who'd been with Marc's squad since the beginning and her fiancé, a third grade teacher a head shorter than her, couldn't keep the shock from their faces as they took in the sumptuous surroundings. Soon the roof garden was filled with party sounds as more people arrived and mingled. Clinking glasses, shouts, laughter and loud conversation. Shop talk dominated, but was pleasantly accented with family, sports, local politics, favorite new restaurants and other social chatter. When Kim came up the stairs wearing a pink sundress, several of her colleagues whooped it up and Marc almost choked on his beer. She was, whoa, a knock out. Was she always that good looking underneath the cop?

"Yes, she was always gorgeous. All you ever see is the uniform," observed Jette. "That's why we have these parties. So you can see all of them as more than just people you work with."

"If you say so," muttered Marc, scowling a little.

"Hi, Dr. Morningstar. I brought this for the party." Kim saw Marc's frown and went for the more friendly face.

"Thanks, Kim. And if we're going to socialize, please call me Jette from now on."

"Thanks, I will."

"What's in the dish?" asked Jette.

"Tuna noodle casserole with potato chips on top." Marc handed Kim a beer. They'd gone out after shift often enough for him to know her drink preference, anyway.

"How did you know?" Kim took the beer, noting the Detective hadn't said, 'call me Marc'. Fine with her. She'd never, ever be able to get that out and make it work.

"You're from Minnesota," shrugged Marc.

"Wisconsin."

"Same thing."

"It sure isn't. The Packers eat Vikings for breakfast," insisted Kim.

"This is true," conceded Marc.

"And the Bears stalk them both," shouted Hal and led a side conversation on the Central Division of the NFL.

"How did you know about the casserole?" persisted Kim, hoping to get in on Hal's conversation soon. She knew all the stats on the Bears-Packers rivalry.

"I didn't even need to use any active detecting. You bring it to everything," smirked Marc.

"Oh. Well. Gee. It's the only thing I know how to make from scratch," shrugged Kim.

"Thanks for the addition to our picnic." Jette took it and handed it to one of the servers. "Could you take this to Hilda and have her keep it warm until we're ready to eat?"

Later, they all sat around a huge makeshift picnic table, laughing, toasting, eating everything in sight and enjoying life.

"So Kim," asked Jette, "how did you get from Wisconsin to New York?"

"By plane," said Lucy, eating some of Jette's tofu and spinach lasagna which, to Marc's revulsion, she appeared to really like.

"I studied at Julliard," laughed Kim, thinking the kid's sense of humor was keener than her sense of taste.

"Julliard!" exclaimed Carmel, impressed. "What did you study?"

"Music, specifically piano."

"Piano? Oh my!" exclaimed Jette in pure delight. "Kim. Kimberly. You're Kimberly Sommer. I didn't make the connection. I heard you play with the Phoenix Symphony."

"Play what?" asked Marc, completely clueless.

Jette looked up at him with pity. "You have no idea, do you? Some detective."

Marc hated being out of the loop on anything and could feel his blood heat up.

"We liked playing the sunbelt gigs in February when sixty inches of snow were on the ground in Wisconsin," said Kim confirming Jette's observation.

"You play the piano, Sommer?" asked Marc.

"That's like asking Michael Jordon if he plays basketball. Or Brett Favre if he plays football. Or Tiger Woods if he plays golf," observed Jette. "Do you have any idea who you've been working with these last two years?"

"Certainly not Michael, Brett or Tiger." Marc frowned, still clueless and not liking it.

"I must say I'm sorry I never made the connection," said Dina, enjoying besting Marc. It was a rare thing. "I heard you play at Carnegie when you were about, I'd say, 14 or 15. It was a long time ago."

"Not that long," said Kim. "And I was 12 when I played Carnegie."

"You had pig tails and were kind of…" Dina waved her hands looking for the right word.

"You can say it. I was kind of chubby," said the trim and toned Kim. "Came from being on the road all the time and practicing all day. I never did go outdoors much." She glanced at Jette and grinned. "I look a little different in a smaller size. Thanks for not mentioning that you didn't recognize me 'cause I barely fit on the piano stool."

"How did you go from concert pianist to cop?" asked Anna, fascinated.

Kim looked at Marc, then back at Anna. "Detective Lexington won't remember this, but when I was in my last semester, my roommate was murdered. He was assigned to the case. And when all the clues were put together, he brought the guy in. The feeling that it gave to her friends and family," she sighed. "It was so crucial to their healing. Everyone was still devastated, of course, but they got their justice. I wanted to be able to do that. I know it sounds corny, but heck, I'm from Wisconsin. Corn grows in front yards there."

"You're wrong, Sommer," said Marc.

"No. It really does. My sister grows corn in her front yard."

"I'm sure that's something the whole family gets behind, but I was referring to the fact that I recognized you on the first day you walked into the squad room. Not as any famous piano player, but as Kris Tualla's roommate. I wasn't surprised. You were a tough little witness. Chubby, but tough," he added, with a teasing grin.

"You never said anything." Kim was completely surprised.

"I figured it wasn't something you wanted to talk about. And if you did, you'd talk about it. You talk about every other goddamn thing."

"So how did your family take it? I mean you must have had it made in music," asked Carmel, trying to imagine Lucy going from a hugely successful pianist to a police officer. Since her pride and joy was currently dipping her onion rings into the dirt from one of the flower pots, she figured she needn't worry overmuch. Not yet anyway.

"They're concerned, naturally, because I'm on the streets and stuff, but after the initial shock and the record setting hysterical hand ringing, they're okay. I guess they maybe think it's a phase. But it's not," said Kim sincerely.

"That's a relief," said Tagg. "I'd hate to have to break in another one."

"Another one what?" she asked suspiciously.

"Didn't you know, Sommer? Your hire was the result of affirmative action. You're our corn fed, small town, beauty queen," laughed Tagg.

"With the brain of a cherry pit," she added, a little bit of a pout pulling out her lower lip.

"Who said that?" asked Jette horrified.

"Your boyfriend." Kim was happy to tattle and get him into some serious hot water with the professor.

"Something for which you haven't yet received an apology, I'm sure. But tonight you're taking the opportunity to do so, right Marc." Jette turned to her boyfriend.

Marc's eyes went to Lucy who was feeding the purple pony dirt-covered onion rings.

"First of all, I believe I was severely taxed and viciously provoked by one of Sommer's patented 'huh?'s' and secondly I think my exact words were..." He took a deep breath and Carmel slapped her hand over his mouth.

"Let us fill in the blanks and use our adult imaginations. Sometimes after you've been over, I have to deprogram Lucy before she goes back to daycare with a vocabulary that'll get her expelled," said Carmel.

"You can't get expelled from daycare," protested Tagg.

"You can if you call your teacher a mother f-u-c-k-i-n-g, son-of-a-b-i-t-c-h-i-n-g, s-h-i-t-face, a-s-s-h-o-l-e." Carmel spelled all the really bad words.

"Oh," snorted Tagg. "I guess she was hanging around when we were building that shed."

"I guess," laughed Marc.

"Don't spell like that Mommy." Lucy moved on to flower picking. "It'll get you expelled."

They all laughed and Kim noticed Marc got out of making an apology. Almost. Jette noticed too.

"If Marc gets back to the apology and can say it without getting Lucy expelled, will you play for us before you leave, Kim?" Jette asked.

Kim really loved Jette.

"I will if the detective takes back the cherry pit part."

Marc smiled, sipped, smiled some more.

"So you're really good, huh?" he asked.

"Considered the best by several knowledgeable critics," nodded Kim.

"Uh-huh. And have you had a tour of the apartment?"

"No. I just came up here."

"Uh-huh. Well, it just so happens that in the music room, I think that's one of the rooms off the West Parlor, there's a 1910 Steinway Louis XV Ornate piano."

Kim goggled. "No way."

"Way," said Marc. "Full Grand. I saw it on the inventory list when I inherited this place."

"If you're not pulling my leg, you can have a pass for the rest of your life on any apology, compulsory or not," breathed Kim. "Just let me touch it."

Marc winked at Jette. "Shall we move this party downstairs?"

They all got hysterical when Marc got them lost on the first pass and they wound up in the kitchen. But they took the opportunity to grab another beer or two.

"Maybe we should take a six pack," suggested Arick. "In case we get lost in a room with no refrigerator."

"Hilda's here, she can lead the way." Marc gave his horrified housekeeper a little push. "To the music room."

Hilda wasn't sure what the parade was all about, but she gamely led them through the library and into the music room.

"Holy cow! It *is* a Steinway!" Kim slapped her palms against her rosy cheeks.

"Nice piano," commented Dina.

"This isn't a nice piano," breathed Kim reverently. "This is the Grand Canyon of pianos. The Machu Picchu of pianos. The Taj Mahal of pianos. The…"

"Christ, Sommer, get a grip," interrupted Marc.

Hilda looked at Kim speculatively, whole heartedly taking her side.

"Holy cow," repeated Kim as she slowly walked around the huge ornate piano.

"I swear if she says holy cow one more time, I'm going to force feed her a fucking steak and drown her in milk," murmured Marc to Jette.

"Do you play, Marc?" asked Hal.

"Yeah. Poker down at Misciasci's. I don't even know if it works. Go ahead and see if it has keys, Sommer."

"It's in perfect condition. It's tuned every three months and the room is kept at the specified temperature and humidity," said Hilda, scandalized.

"Oh, alright. If you insist." Kim worshipfully opened it up.

When Hilda made a little squeak in her throat, Jette reassured her.

"That's Kimberly Sommer."

"It is? Oh my. What's she doing in the detective's company?"

"She's in his squad."

"They have a pianist in his squad?"

"No. She's an officer."

"Since when? I've seen her perform several times." Then she frowned. "I thought she was a lot…"

"Heavier. Yes, she was. But now she's a police officer."

"Holy cow!" Kim ran her hands over the perfectly preserved keyboard.

"Let's go back up and neck in the garden and leave her to her dairy orgasms," whispered Marc in Jette's ear.

"Just wait," said Jette, knowing what Kim was capable of.

"Detective, since this is your Steinway, do you have a request?" asked Kim. "Now that you've let me touch it, I'm going to have to play with it."

"Hell, Sommer, sometimes you leave yourself wide open," snorted Marc.

"Huh?" Kim looked over at him with wide, guileless eyes.

"See?" asked Marc looking down at Jette, considering himself vindicated. Then he looked up at Kim's expectant face. "Actually, I do. That is, if you're as good as Jette seems to think you are. If you know it, play Rachmaninoff's *Rhapsody on a Theme of Paganini.*"

Jette glanced at him completely surprised, expecting him to ask for one of his hard rock favorites or an off color drinking ditty.

Kim stared at him for a minute, then looked at Jette and sighed. Wow. How romantic was that, she thought.

"Yes, of course." Kim sat down, put her fingers lightly on the keys, accessed the music in her mind, let it flow through her…and made magic. The minute she began, she transformed. She took command of the music, then of the room. The look on her face was focused, but so lovely that it seemed the notes and chords were hers, not just their interpretation.

Jette's heart filled, then overflowed as Marc stood behind her, one hand holding his beer, the other holding her against him. It wasn't just Kim's music, which was breathtaking, it was the fact that Marc must have heard this concerto, liked it, remembered it, and had it played for her. She could tell from the beating of his heart and the absentminded stroking of her arm, the fact that he hadn't sipped from his beer since Kim had started, that it touched something in him too.

Hilda was so transfixed she forgot to run around with coasters. She needn't have worried. Everyone in the room was transported and in the cultured world Kim took them to, no one would have considered putting their bottle or glass on the exquisite old tables.

When Kim finished, Jette could have cried, not wanting it to be over. There wasn't a sound in the room.

Kim herself broke the spell. Looking directly at Marc, she dared a wink, and grinned. "Kind of puts you in a mood, doesn't it. You can thank me later."

With that everyone started talking at once. Before she could get up, other favorites were called out and Kim's fingers started flying again. From Tina Louise Itsen's intricate and energetic contemporary sonatas to the traditional Beethoven's 5ᵗʰ symphony.

Hilda reanimated and began putting coasters around after all, at the same time ordering the servers to refresh the drinks. She opened a closet that contained dozens of folding soft seated chairs that had been used for small concerts.

Jette watched as Marc laughed and chatted and listened and engaged in a shouting match over the words to *Friend of the Devil* by the Grateful Dead as Kim performed an enthusiastic arrangement of it on the antique Steinway and Tagg played the air guitar as fanatically as Jerry Garcia.

Later, Hilda topped everything off with generous servings of strawberry shortcake, huge mugs of hot, richly blended coffee, and a pot of tea for Jette and some hot chocolate for Lucy. She used the really ugly mugs Mr. Clarke bought in Las Vegas on an uncharacteristic whim, thinking this group would appreciate the incredibly intense and hideous decals of rolling dice emblazoned on the sides. She never thought she'd see the day she'd actually use them, she'd only kept them in the back of the cupboard out of pure sentiment. They were a hit.

Tommy and Claude came in, one in spandex and spangles, one in a stiff black uniform. So different, until they both went for huge helpings of strawberry shortcake and fussed over the kitschy coffee mugs.

"Hey Hilda!" shouted Kim.

"Yes, dear?"

"This one's for you. Sorry but the detective outranks me and it's the one he requested."

She played, with a great deal of improvised flourish, the theme song from the *Addam's Family*. Hilda raised an eyebrow and nodded regally as the room erupted in song and Marc howled with laughter.

"I'll remember that when I measure the starch for your underwear, Detective," she said in her cultured, imperious voice. The room erupted again, this time in good natured ribbing and speculation on how solid state underwear might cramp his style. Score one for Hilda.

A half hour later, Kim announced the last song. "This one is dedicated to our marvelous host and hostess. Hilda requested it before she left to arrange transportation for all you drunken music aficionados."

After a thrillingly elaborate introduction that created suspense for what song would be played, she began the theme song for *Beauty and the Beast*. Even Lucy knew this music and was ecstatic. Everyone else just lost it. Score another one for Hilda!

Jette looked around the odd assortment of people filling the big room. Yes, love lived here, she thought. Her eyes tracked for her beast, assuming that she was the beauty, and saw him staring at her. And still did. She smiled into his eyes as he was surrounded by people singing the words at him. Tagg and Carmel knew every line, as did their daughter, and filled in all the blanks.

So Marc didn't think he had family. True, it wasn't the usual assortment of parents, brothers, sisters, aunts, uncles, and cousins, but it was forged by trial, affection, time, and loyalty. And that made the bond stronger and more lasting. He did have family and it was adding to the legacy of love started by the Clarkes, then passed on to their surrogate son.

What they saw in him and what they felt for him were still in the walls and the feelings in this room tonight were intensifying the power of that affection, trust, and devotion. As Beauty walked over to her Beast, she basked in the bonds forged by love and nurtured by commitment. She was home. And finally, so was he.

# Chapter 20

The night was her time. No more tedious obligations in the Middle World of Reality. Her focus could be the game. She placed the picture of her former Anointed One on Avenger's side of the board. She'd relabeled him Blood Traitor. The *Times* that day had both his high school graduation picture and his mug shot. Quite a change. Troubled and compromised souls can show. In this case it did. The mask of innocence put him in one category, the transformation to treachery put him in another. Soon it wouldn't matter.

Getting a signal for incoming, she ran the pictures. A whole lot of people going into Avenger's Home Base. They looked like strong, confident Guardians. What was she doing bringing in a team that size? Strategizing? Wow. There was a huge black man with a woman and a child. So she was recruiting families into her fold. Interesting. Maybe significant, maybe not. To have a child. Why? For what purpose? Sacrifice? That had been taken out of the game years ago.

So, Avenger was calling a meeting of her Guardians. Could Avenger be anticipating a Major Conflict in the City of Might? Maybe even the Final Duel? She paused for a moment. Then came to a complete stop.

Could it be? She turned the theory around in her head and looked at it from all angles. Yes. That was it! The Avatar of Callisto had deliberately come to the city three weeks ago to launch the Final Duel here. It explained her movements. Moving from her barren world to the City of Might. Living with the Dark Knight. Calling in her Guardians. Avenger knew the one true Empress was living in the City of Might and was coming for her!

How had Avenger uncovered her location? There were hundreds of other cities and habitats in Himalia, although it was universal conventional wisdom that the Empress preferred the City of Might. Who had she turned? Was there a traitor in her field of Minions? In her Sentinels? Had the Anointed One told her? No one knew her identity, but just by tracking her latest moves, a territory could have been plotted. She shook her head and pulled back from speculation. How Avenger uncovered her location wasn't important right now. If Avenger wanted the Final Duel to be in the City of Might, she'd just have to disappoint her. It would not be fought here. Not if that's where Avenger was laying the ground work. Time to move to one of her several contingency plans. This was getting intense!

The Empress stared at her board. Where to take the fight. Where. Then she smiled. Yes! Brilliant! It would give her both the edge and the points. Since she'd speculated that Morningstar was Avenger weeks ago she'd chosen an alternate location for the Final Duel. In the deserts of Callisto. It would be riskier than in the City of Might, but in the long run the points awarded for risk and difficulty would be phenomenal.

Looking at the pictures of all the fine and fit Guardians going into the beautiful old building, the Empress expelled a quick derisive laugh. What a fool. Did Avenger think she was invisible? That her moves weren't being monitored by the greatest competitor to play the game? Avenger must still believe her identity was safe. Not a good move. Calling in her Guardians was another tactical mistake. She was about to be preempted. Since it appeared Avenger was pushing for an offensive round, she'd just have to move up her own time table. Days, then, instead of weeks. She'd go under Avenger's guard before she could structure her perimeter.

More pictures popped into the website. They were leaving. All of them. Leaving to comb the city no doubt, but leaving Avenger unguarded. Arrogant. Overconfident now that she'd surged ahead in points.

"You took my Anointed One. But now, I'm going to come after you."

She could just kill Avenger twice, then take the last of her life force in the Final Duel, but she was quite sure the only way to get through the Castle of Thunder to the location of the Final Duel was to have one of Avenger's lives. A life must be the key to open the last door, so they would both need one to get through to the other side and begin the Final Duel. Why had no other player seen this?

Turning Avenger was the next step. Turn her and negotiate for a life. Then put her back into play with only two remaining.

A daring stratagem came to mind. She studied her board. Was it possible? Ha! For anyone else, no. For her, yes. The risk points alone would be incredible. She took a mental bow. She was brilliant. A genius and an unparalleled innovator.

Daylight capture. A thousand points. A night time abduction might yield her the Dark Knight as well, but she didn't like the idea of him being between Avenger and the Extraction Team. She would consider eliminating him from the game, but that was something she could do later if necessary.

Home Base would yield her another thousand points at least. She'd have to check her table. Avenger wasn't protected by her Guardians there. One of the Tag and Track Teams she'd assigned to The Edgewood had scored a picture of the six-foot female Guardian leaving. Not a permanent Inner Guard, then. She shook her head. Avenger wasn't willing to spend points to secure the proper protection. Her loss.

There were several pieces she still needed to put together. A lot of details to see to. Was it too complex? Her quick and twisted mind flew over the huge number of tasks, the intricate planning, the critical timing. No. This was the road to the Final Duel. Nothing was too complicated for the one true Blue Empress. Nothing.

# Chapter 21

Checking his watch again, he cursed the damn bureaucrats who couldn't do anything on time. Even crouched behind the parapet, he was pretty exposed at this point. Being across from the jailhouse with a loaded and silenced sniper rifle was fairly suspicious.

He knew all about police procedure, so he was extremely careful about how he stood and interacted with the space round him. His cigarette addiction was getting to him but there was no way he was going to leave so much as an ash on the scene. He wouldn't smoke until the job was done and he was back in his car.

BE102959 herself had given him the time and the place in her communication and he'd checked to be sure the proper amount was deposited in his off-shore account. It was. She never missed. Dependable and a nice steady source of extra scratch. His retirement cush was building nicely.

This was his first real headline-grabbing kill. Most of his service up to now was in procurement. Guns, drugs, explosives. It was going to be more challenging to stay under the radar, but that just made it more lucrative. Only one person to blow down and he'd stash a nice cool fifty large to support all of his bad habits. He checked his gut. No guilt there. This little toad was ripe for road kill and a great exchange for making his life better.

His unknown benefactor with the cash and the Blue Empress fetish gave him a great deal of discretion on execution. He snorted. That was a good one. Execution on the execution. She just fed him the task, paid him the jack, and trusted him to get the job done. He liked that. No taking orders, no restraints on procedure. Being his own man was refreshing and gave him an extra boost.

He was getting itchy though. Could the transport team have been alerted and even now were they staging a sweep of the area? Everything was quiet in the alley below, but was there something happening beneath the surface?

There were no TV cameras, no pushing and shoving reporters. They'd all be staked out at the courthouse. The prisoner's time of transport was closely held, and it was hours before his formal arraignment.

His perch on the rooftop was fairly well covered, but he wasn't invisible. BE102959 was a great ongoing source of jack, but if she screwed this up, he was the one exposed. She'd found him among the less effective players of the game. He'd vented some of his frustrations, and she offered solutions. First as a hypothetical, then for real. He never bought into all the nuances of the game, but he sure bought into the supplemental income just fine. Let her believe she was the one true Empress. As long as she was a really well set up Empress, he'd serve her. If he felt she was losing control, he'd disappear. He was only a number and a bogus email address, after all.

Movement at the door of the jailhouse had him tensing. This was it. He'd either shoot and run like hell or just run like hell. Taking a deep breath to prepare his mind and body, he brought up the rifle. When he saw his target, trussed and cuffed, he relaxed. It would be a shoot and scamper, then.

He'd grown up in the Midwest where getting all dressed up in orange was how you avoided getting shot in the woods. Here in New York, it just made the target easier to spot. Like a fish in a barrel. A rat in a cage. A weasel on a stick. This would be the easiest fifty large he'd ever taken a bow for. Drill the guy and skate. Sweet.

The kid was surrounded by officers, so he'd have to take a careful shot. He'd take down the kid without remorse, but would never, ever shoot a cop. Good thing he was an ace marksman. The cops and the media would be whipped into a frenzy for awhile, then settle down. A cold case within the year.

He shifted his badge from his pocket to his belt in case he needed to blend after the kill, then with images of warm sand, an ice cold Corona, and two, no three bikini clad beauties fading in and out of his mind's eye, he lined up the shot. And took it.

# Chapter 22

Marc was multitasking, running a few background checks on a suspect, enjoying his second cup of coffee, watching Meg and Hilda cleaning up the debris from the night before, discussing a deposition with the district attorney on his cell, and staring at Jette who was on her phone with Lee getting the scoop on the dinner with Garret. From all the 'oohing' and 'aahing', he gathered it had gone well.

He didn't need to go in early today. His squad had night shift and they wouldn't start until after lunch, but that didn't mean he couldn't get a jump on the long list of things he needed to get done.

Jette was going to be working from home all day so he felt good. After her morning run, with Eunice pedaling her ass off to keep up, they all had breakfast together in the kitchen. Eunice entertained them with stories of her days as a rookie and promised to return the next day since Marc still had to curtail his physical activity. Things were going well. He was beginning to settle.

When Jette hung up, he was about to suggest they go back to the bedroom to make the bed when the phone rang. Meg answered cheerfully with "Lexington-Morningstar residence."

He raised his eyebrow at Jette who just smiled, a little kittenish, he thought. He wasn't sure when her name had been added to the greeting, but he found he really liked it. A lot. And when he heard who was on the phone, he liked it even better.

"Excuse me, Dr. Morningstar. There's a Captain Green who'd like to speak with you. First of all, would you like to take his call. And secondly, which extension would you like to use?"

Jette looked over at Marc, who shrugged, then gave a little nod. He appreciated that she looked to him for sanction, but saw no reason for her to avoid the asshole's call.

"Yes, I'll talk with him. And I'll take it right here. Would you like to get to an extension?" she asked Marc.

He thought about it, then shook his head. He'd just eavesdrop on her end for now.

"Good morning, this is Dr. Morningstar." She used her overly formal voice and made Marc grin.

"Hello, Jette. How are you this morning?"

"I'm fine. Thank you."

"Good. I'd appreciate it if you'd stop by my office today. I have something I'd like to discuss."

"I'm sorry. Today isn't a good day. Is it something you can discuss with me over the phone?"

"I'd rather talk with you in person. Will you be going to the university today?"

"No. I'll be working from home today."

"Fine. How about I come over there."

"I'd really rather not be interrupted. Is it important?"

"It could be. As you've probably heard, Roger Flowers was killed this morning."

"Excuse me?" Jette put her hand over the mouthpiece and whispered. "Marc, Roger Flowers was killed. Turn on the TV."

"Yes. It happened less than an hour ago. I just came from the press conference. I thought you might have seen it on the news."

Marc turned on the TV and muted it. There was a special report on the Flowers shooting. Green, looking appropriately solemn and official, was speaking in front of the courthouse. Jette felt a little displaced seeing the recorded press conference on the screen while talking with the man on the phone.

"No. We were enjoying a quiet morning. Why are you calling me?" She thought he'd ask her now about what Flowers said to her on the rooftop. He didn't. What he did do was stun her.

"I need to ask you if you have any idea where Lexington is this morning."

"Marc? He's here with me." She put her fingers to her lips and pushed the speaker button. If this was about Marc, he needed to hear it.

"Has he been there all morning?"

"Yes."

"Are you sure?"

"Yes."

"Can anyone else confirm that?"

"Yes, as a matter of fact."

"Who? I'll need their names."

"Are you saying you don't believe me?" The impact of his implications finally got through her initial astonishment. Not so astonished however, that she couldn't take charge of the conversation.

"I just would like some corroboration," stated Green.

"For what purpose?"

"To either confirm or eliminate him as a suspect."

"A suspect in what?"

"In the shooting of Flowers."

"Are you serious?" Jette's voice clearly communicated incredulity.

"Yes, I'm perfectly serious," said Green.

"What evidence has been gathered at the scene?"

Marc was grinning. Far from being insulted, he was thoroughly entertained by how effectively Jette went from being questioned to doing the questioning and how easily Green got turned around and maneuvered. Of course his girlfriend was the best. But still. It was fun.

"We have no solid evidence yet. There were two head shots in quick succession. He was dead on scene."

"Any witnesses?"

"No. The shots came from a rooftop across the street, we think."

"Who knew he was being transported and when?"

"Several people. We're compiling the list right now."

"Was Marc on it?"

"I told you we're still compiling it."

"Did *you* know?"

"Of course."

"Where were you at the time of the shooting?"

"I was at the stationhouse. I was in charge of the transfer."

Marc could hardly contain himself. His choking laughter was leaking out and he had to get up and away from the range of the telephone. Meg and Hilda had stopped their puttering and were watching the TV, listening to Jette, and gaping at the spectacle of Marc nearly splitting a gut.

Jette thought she'd try to get as much as she could from Green before he shut up.

"Why would anyone want to kill Flowers?" she asked.

"I'd like to explore that question with you."

Jette sidestepped and went on.

"Did he receive any death threats while he was incarcerated?"

"He received no messages or visitors except his assigned public defender."

"Was he from around here?"

"He was living in a flop in Newark."

"What did your search reveal?"

"This is something I'd like to discuss with you."

"Are you asking for a formal consultation?"

"You're an expert in the criminal mind. I thought we should discuss it. I also think you should know I just put Lexington on the suspect list. That's my personal call and I think we should talk about your safety. He was the first person who came to mind when I heard of the shooting. He's an expert marksman, he's unstable, and he had a grudge against the victim. In addition, several officers witnessed his erratic behavior at the scene."

"Don't be ridiculous. Marc doesn't fit the profile of an anonymous sniper."

This time, Marc wheezed out a laugh that could no longer be suppressed and Green fell silent.

"If you want a formal consultation, I have a standard contract," said Jette a little more loudly than was necessary. "Clear it with your chief and I'll consider it. In the meantime, I have work to do. Thank you for calling and keeping me updated, Captain."

Jette hung up and covered her face, working hard to suppress the laugh in her chest. "Marc, darling, stop it. There's something just sick about laughing when a young man has been murdered."

"This isn't about murder, this is about slaughter. Damn, Jette you make me hot. You hardly left him with enough skin on his ass to keep his pants up. And he's probably still sitting behind his highly polished solid oak desk with the phone in his hand wondering what the shit just happened."

Hilda and Meg were still watching them, speculating on why they ever found daytime dramas entertaining. Nothing was better than this.

Marc shook himself, sobering up as the cop took charge of the thoroughly amused man.

"I need to go in and find out what happened. It sounds like a professional hit and I really don't like what that might imply."

"Some kind of conspiracy? That Flowers wasn't acting alone?" speculated Jette.

"Exactly. With all the media attention Flowers was getting, it could simply be that some other wack job wanted the same spotlight. The same kind of sick fame."

"Could a parent or friend of one of the victims have been distraught enough to do this?"

"It's possible. I'd put them on the list, but none of the injuries resulted in death, paralysis or permanent injury." He'd checked the hospital a few hours earlier at Jette's request. All the students had been upgraded and three were scheduled to be released that day. "It seems like they'd be more interested in being with the victims at this point than shooting Flowers, but you never know. Retribution is a strong motivator. Not everyone trusts the legal system."

"What about the Shield? The Phoenix was threatened and I was gone for an hour on my run. Hilda, Meg, can either of you vouch for Marc's whereabouts?" teased Jette.

"Sorry, Dr. Morningstar," grinned Meg. "I only arrived after your return. I've known the boy a long time. He has quite a temper and he's a hell of a shot."

"The boy is now your boss." Marc frowned at her.

Meg raised her eyebrows, her grin intact. "Is that a threat?"

"It's a reminder." Marc couldn't sustain the frown. Meg was one of his oldest friends. When she was on the stroll and he was a kid, she'd buy him a meal once in awhile. It was the simple acts of kindness of people like her that not only kept him alive, they kept a little of the goodness inside him alive as well. "Besides, Hilda can vouch for me, and who'd question the credibility of a woman who looks like a warden?"

"Sorry, Detective. There was a debris field of clothing in your closet, evidence everywhere that you'd groomed yourself, the crumbs of a chocolate covered donut on the floor in the sitting room, a dirty coffee cup on the table in the den with the sports section ripped and crumpled and lying on the couch..."

"The Yankees lost to Boston," grumbled Marc.

"Understandable, however, these things could have been planted by a clever suspect. At no time did I actually see the Detective." Hilda never cracked a smile, never altered her severe expression.

"Are you saying I'm clever?" Marc raised an eyebrow.

"Diabolically so, I would say. So, Dr. Morningstar, I might suggest that you find a good attorney in case bail needs to be arranged." Satisfied with the exchange, she turned toward the stairs. "Meg and I will be on the roof garden replanting some of the flowers if we need to be questioned further."

A giggling Meg followed Hilda out of the room. Marc just stared at their backs and shook his head.

"In the movies, the dialogue of household staff is *yes, sir* and *no, sir*. What the hell happened around here?"

"Darling, I have no idea," smiled Jette.

Marc walked over and took her hand. "You're still planning on staying home all day, right?"

"Yes. I have a meeting with Maxine White this afternoon."

Marc raised his eyebrows. "Impressive."

"You know her?"

"By reputation only. From what I understand she could use a good psychologist."

"It's Jette, the author, who's meeting with her, not the doctor."

"Nice."

"What have you heard?" Jette was curious and knew Marc's grapevine was second to none.

"Nothing serious. Only that she feels the city was built for her convenience and nothing, including pesky city ordinances and local laws, should interfere with her plans. Calls the mayor regularly and thinks since she pays taxes every member of the police department works for her and should be available at her convenience."

"Interesting."

"Only you would think so," scoffed Marc. "If you ask most people they'll tell you she's just another pushy, powerful, rich she-bitch."

"Speaking of which, I'm going to take a conference call with Klara Marshall to get her out of Lee's hair."

"Now she's a *scary*, pushy, rich she-bitch. Transforming her into a human being could be your life's work."

"She is persistent," observed Jette.

"I think she has a crush on you."

"Then I'm going to disappoint her on several different levels." Jette shrugged off Marc's disapproving tone. "I've been reading the information Lee sent over. Some of her latest work and press reports. She doesn't seem all that stable and her attempts at fantasy fiction have not been well received. I think there's some desperation that has induced her to consider real crime."

"Well, some of us need to deal with that real crime right now."

"I'll walk you to the door, give you a kiss goodbye, then go to my office and write. I don't think Captain Green is going to follow through with the consult, do you?"

"If he calls again, let me know."

"I will," Jette agreed, "and will you call me when you get the information on Flowers? I'll watch the media reports, but if you find out anything, I'd like to know. He was a very troubled young man, but a great deal could have been done for him."

"I have a feeling this wasn't a random or impulsive act. It was an assassination."

"You think he knew something or that there was another link? That he was a part of something larger?"

"I'm not sure, but it's a possibility. So stay behind this locked door today, okay?" asked Marc.

"I intend to. You be careful out there, too."

When they got to the front door, Marc gathered her into his arms and got a send off that was both sweet and satisfying.

# Chapter 23

Marc was smiling as he came into the squad room from booking. He'd managed to find and pull in a suspect who'd been particularly slippery and had eluded his squad for the last six weeks. It had felt good to slam the door on the little creep.

His team was on late duty after taking two days off and everyone was wrapping up, shutting down and finishing tasks. It was the end of their work day, something that had never been a significant time target for him before. The end of any shift was usually blurred by ongoing events. When he was on a scent there was no beginning and end to his day. But now there was someone to go home to. It felt different. It felt good.

It had been an uneventful few days and that felt good, too. He and Jette had spent a lot of time together. The media was still in a frenzy but there hadn't been any leaks at The Edgewood, so no one bothered them at home. Eunice stuck by Jette when she ran.

Jette received several more boxes of her personal treasures from Arizona and was nesting right in. She'd become partial to sitting in the roof garden and Marc had to grin when several cacti appeared in some of the bigger pots. He was beginning to relax.

Green had frozen him out of the Flowers investigation, but he'd gotten all there was from other contacts on the force. It appeared the shooter was a troubled kid who was operating on his own. His murder was still open and unsolved. They had very little to go on. Nothing, which was a little suspicious to a cynic like him. Either the assassin was very professional or very lucky. He opted for the former.

He wished his own squad could get the case. They'd find something to move the investigation forward, he was sure of it. All Green seemed to be doing was calling press conferences. The information he provided was getting very thin and the public's interest was getting equally as thin.

Marc had been too busy to call Jette all afternoon, but had spoken to her at lunchtime. No nooner today. She'd been busy at the apartment doing research for her book and he'd been in the field early. That was fine. They had a lifetime.

He could feel the tug of happy contentment and it was a seductive sensation. Who knew he had it in him? Then he smiled more broadly. Jette. That was who.

His squad caught the happy vibe and fed on it. Always a robust group, they only put a lid on the vigorous chatter when their leader was about to blow. Tonight, there was no lid in sight.

"So Marc, how do you spell aficionado? I wanted to write in my diary the other night and I got stumped on that." Raj called out as Marc walked through the desks.

"I think you have to be one to spell it," laughed Dina, "and you can't carry a tune in a bushel basket."

"On that we have *a chord*," snorted Teresa.

"I'll take *note* of that," grinned Raj.

"The *key* is *conducting* yourself with decorum," yelled Anna.

"Or seek *harmonious* relationships," added Dina.

"And never go in without *Bach*-up," laughed Marc. "So where is the Tiger Woods of the piano set?"

"The chief called her and Tagg into her office."

"Uh, oh," said Teresa.

"Maybe you should have invited the chief to the party the other night," speculated Dina.

"Yeah, she heard there was grilling going on at your place and wanted to know who was the suspect," laughed Raj.

"Nah," said Marc, "she just wants Sommer's recipe for tuna casserole."

Teresa hummed the tune *Beauty and the Beast*, and that set them off on another round of poking and teasing with Marc in the center of the good natured, end-of-shift byplay.

They all admired him greatly. He was their prototype for cop, but they also liked him and were happy that he'd found someone special. Throughout the years, he'd gone through women so fast they were a blur of faces and breasts. Now it appeared to all the detectives and officers in the bullpen that he was hooked. His laughter and jousting blended with the others easily and the noise level heightened.

The change in mood started as a wave. A wave of silence through the sea of sound. It began at the door of the squad room and because Marc's back was to it, he felt it before he saw the reason for it. The atmosphere in the room shifted, the officers and detectives losing their playfulness one by one.

As he turned toward the epicenter of the wave, the grin on Marc's face dimmed, then fell off completely. Kim, Chief Cheskee, the unit chaplain, Garret Tienstra, and Tagg were walking through the room. Slowly, deliberately, and their eyes were on Marc. Even Kim's usual shiny face was grim.

Marc, who'd been casually leaning on Dina's desk, pushed himself off and tried to ignore the whisper of apprehension vying for his attention. This wasn't good. They were there for a reason, they were headed for him, and it wasn't to contribute to the byplay. By the time they got to him, he realized he wasn't breathing. From the unnatural silence in the room, neither was anyone else.

"Marc. We need to talk. Can we step into your office?" asked Garret.

"No," he said, his smile completely gone as his gut tightened up, "I don't think so."

"Marc," the chief signaled the rest of the squad to move away, "I think we need to talk in private."

Marc frowned, his temper being recalled to duty. Had that asshole Green actually put him on the suspect list? Were they here to question him? Had there been a complaint? Damn it to hell, had some jerk-off suspect pushed internal affairs into an inquiry. Had he fucked up somehow? Was another reprimand, or worse, in the air? And then suddenly, something cold sliced through him. This was worse. Much worse. This was…

"Jette." Her name cut through a throat so tight he was surprised it didn't bleed. His chief, his best friend, the unit chaplain, the commissioner, and Kim. The one everyone in the squad knew was the hand holder. The one who went along when there was bad news to deliver. They stood in front of him. Him. It was a sight that all cops recognized. A prospect that could be in their future, only it was usually played out in the lives of their loved ones.

"Is it Jette?" It was the only thing in his life worth shit. The only thing that would make this group necessary.

"Marc, sit down," said the chief too softly, too kindly. This was no assignment, no reprimand. This was bad. Very bad.

"No. No, I don't think so," he said, unconsciously preparing for a blow.

"Okay," she said as Kim went in close. "I'm so sorry Marc, but three unidentified intruders dressed as police officers entered your home approximately an hour and a half ago. They took Jette."

"Jette was taken in by the police?" Marc was completely confused. What had Green done now? "Why didn't she call me? Why…"

"No. No," interrupted Tagg, wanting to get it out. Needing Marc to understand. "We checked. They were imposters. Marc, they were only dressed as officers to gain access."

Marc started to bolt out the door, but Tagg grabbed his arm.

"Let me go. I need to get to the scene," snapped Marc.

"There's more," said Tagg.

"Detective Freeman and I were just there," said Kim. The tears in the corners of her eyes scared Marc more than a gang armed with semi-automatics.

"We went to get a firsthand account," said Tagg. "After she was taken from your apartment, she was apparently put in a car at the curb. We're getting conflicting witness reports, but we should get a make and model soon."

Kim took up the narrative when Tagg stopped to clear his throat. "Detective, there was gridlock on Fifth, so it looks like they were heading toward FDR Drive. Jette jumped out of the car when they got caught in the backup on First. According to witnesses, there was a struggle, she got away. Ran. They trapped her in an alley...and...and she tore up the fire escape. Fast. She was so fast. Then when she got to the roof, she...she was about to...to leap to the next roof. She'd have gotten away, too. We saw her do that at the university and this was a lot closer. You know how she can jump. How athletic she is. She jumps like a..."

"Sommer!" shouted Marc. "Report! Goddamn it. Quit wasting my fucking time!"

Kim swallowed, nodded and continued in a more controlled voice.

"Yes, sir. The intruders took a hostage, holding her at gunpoint and forced Jette to stop. She did. When they had her, they shot and killed the hostage. Jette and the man and woman holding her struggled again and they...they went over the edge and fell into the East River. Jette and two of the intruders. Eight stories. At that height, oh God, Detective, we were told that it's like falling on, on concrete." She couldn't go on, so Tagg continued.

"I talked to the witnesses. According to them, Jette and the two kidnappers went under. I'm so sorry, Marc, they didn't come back up. They're dragging the river now. I came back and the chief called the commissioner. I'm sorry. I'm so sorry."

Every word pierced Marc's skin and froze his blood. His heart exploded and the pieces collapsed into his gut. Nothing in his life prepared him for this. Absolutely nothing. This was beyond anger, grief, and shock, beyond his capacity to absorb. Everything inside him overloaded and completely burned out. He could still hear the voices, see the faces, feel the touch of someone taking his arm, but there was no connection to anything inside.

"Son," the chaplain said quietly, "let's go back into your office and wait. Preliminary reports will be coming in soon."

Marc ignored him, his mind hardly processing the words.

"Marc," said Garret, shocked and shaken himself, not knowing exactly what to do for him. "We've dispatched several units to check along the shores, but I'm told that from that height there's no way they could have survived the fall without severe injury. Because they haven't surfaced we have to assume they weren't able to. If by some miracle they survived the fall...they probably drowned."

126

No one spoke. Shock, horror and sympathy washed the room. Marc couldn't feel it. He couldn't feel anything.

"Marc, go with the chaplain." Chief Cheskee laid a hand on his arm. "I'll go to the scene and get an update personally."

"No." Marc frowned. He was a cop. An investigator. Jette was missing and he needed to find her. Shaking off the chief, he broke the paralysis he was in. "I need to go to the scene myself. Sommer, you come with me."

Everyone parted as he walked purposefully out the door. Kim looked at the chief, who nodded and she hurried out after him. The room was soundless and stunned.

"If Jette went down, it's a homicide with special circumstances. Get us the case, Chief," said Dina, tears swimming in her eyes.

Chief Cheskee looked over at Garret who nodded. "I'll get started on that. In the meantime, I think all we can do is stand by Marc." She filled them in on all she knew and they solemnly filtered out the door to go stand by their squad leader. Their friend.

"Detective, let me drive," said Kim gently as they walked out the front door of the station house.

Marc stared at Kim, but had to look away. He couldn't absorb the grief and sympathy on her face and maintain his own ability to function.

"Not a chance. I want to get there sometime today."

"But…"

Marc got behind the wheel, but had to take a few deep breaths to steady his hands enough to get the key in the ignition. He closed his eyes once, saw Jette's laughing face, then grimly opened them up to a world that might not have her in it. Impossible. The fates couldn't be that cruel. But he'd seen enough. Been around enough. Had been through enough to know that life was cruel. And unfair. And mean. And…

"Detective Freeman and the rest of the squad will meet us at the scene." Kim folded her phone. Marc hadn't even heard it ring.

"What?"

"Detective Freeman and the others will meet us at the scene."

"Fine." Marc started the engine, and peeled out of the parking lot, lights flashing and siren blaring, clearing a path to the answers. Answers that would either lead to action or to his destruction.

The flashing lights of several squad cars greeted them as they pulled up to the well maintained combination residential and commercial building. It was right on the East River. He could see several officers and rescue personnel standing on the shore looking up, then out onto the water.

"You say you've been to the scene?"

Kim nodded. It was horrible.

"Show me," he said simply.

As Kim and Marc walked up to the assembled group of police officers, it occurred to him that this was the second time in a week he approached a line of barricades with

Jette on the other side. Jette in jeopardy. Why hadn't he trusted his gut more? He should have had Eunice standing at the door. He should have taken time off, been with her himself. But as he approached the officers in charge of crowd control, he told himself he needed to stop thinking in 'what if's' and concentrate on the 'what was.'

The precinct lieutenant assigned to lead the investigation started over when she saw Marc's car pull up. She'd been the one who'd reported the incident to Chief Cheskee.

"I'm sorry about this, Lexington." Lieutenant Linda Sweeney didn't know Marc personally, but she knew all about him.

Marc just nodded. "Anything new?"

"No. Nothing."

"Will you show me where it all happened? Will you let me in on the case?"

The lieutenant considered for a moment. She was the ranking officer here, but Marc had an astounding record. She both admired and liked working with really good people. On the other hand, the detective was also intimately connected with the victim and could be considered a suspect until cleared. This was a first for her. A victim who was the lover of a New York City cop. It made the investigation much more sensitive. She used her instincts, and made her decision.

"As a courtesy to you, I'll give you sanction to see everything. I need your assurances, however, that you'll let me conduct this investigation my way. You will not interfere. You will not get in my way. And most importantly, you will not go out on your own."

Marc fully intended to get in everyone's way. Conduct his own investigation. Do anything it took to get answers. He didn't give a shit about professional courtesy. But he understood expediency, too, so he nodded.

"Let me see the scene, Lieutenant."

"They told you she jumped out of the car on 1ˢᵗ?"

Marc nodded.

"She ran into this alley and up those stairs. Apparently she outdistanced her pursuers with little trouble and was on the roof several minutes before they got there."

Marc looked up, trying to picture her feet flying on the metal treads. He had to turn off the pain to keep focused.

"Come on. I'll take you up to the roof." Lieutenant Sweeney started toward the building and the elevator.

"No. I want to go up this way."

"Suit yourself. I'll meet you up there. Officer?"

"I'll stay with the detective."

Marc climbed the stairs slowly, scanning at the same time. Looking for signs of Jette's passage. Looking for clues. This was what he did, what he could do now for her. If he wanted to find her he had to stay focused and follow the clues.

Kim watched him, knowing he was in full cop mode. She wasn't sure if this was good or bad, normal or really unhealthy. At this point, it just was. She felt numb. Jette. She'd just seen her a few nights before laughing, talking, being so darn special. And now there was a good chance she was dead. It broke her heart and when she looked up at Marc, the pieces crumbled into dust. It just wasn't fair.

When they finally got to the top, Sweeney came over.

"Find anything?"

"Nothing visible to the eye. No blood, fibers, or anything unexpected. CSI finished?" Marc was completely on automatic pilot.

"Nearly. They're where the three of them went over the edge."

Marc had never in his life suffered vertigo or a fear of heights, but he could feel himself get queasy as he walked over to the ledge. Everything felt…thick. The air around him, the blood pumping in his veins, the sounds floating through the air.

The CSI investigators glanced up. A few knew him, he could tell by the expressions on their faces. Suddenly he wanted to smash those faces. To wipe off the sympathy he saw by obliterating their features. A dark unreasonable urge to erase the compassion and thereby deny the reason for it bubbled in his gut. The beast roared inside him, wanting to be free to rip away the reality of the moment. To drown the shock in a quick, satisfying release of temper and unhinged fury.

Instead he asked for a report.

"Hey Janet, what can you tell me?"

"Hi Marc. I'm sorry about all this. I don't have much. See these scrapes here?" Janet Donlin, a young tech Marc knew was the best in the business, pointed at a pattern of marks in the dust and grime covering the ledge. "They were struggling and according to the witnesses, they fell off together."

"Any hair, fibers?"

"No, nothing yet. But witnesses put two perps and…and Dr. Morningstar here."

Marc could have choked on the terror that bubbled up his throat as he looked over and down into the river. But he didn't. And he pressed on. He had to.

"Where are the witnesses?"

"Just one up here. The rest are down in the street."

Marc saw the dark, sticky field of blood near the door to the roof and the outline of the body.

"That where they shot the hostage?"

"Yes."

He turned 360 degrees, looking at everything. Thinking. There was a little girl clinging to a pigeon standing quietly by an officer and a woman who must have been her mother. Watching him intently.

"Is that the witness?"

"Yes. The little girl." Janet motioned to the officer, who nodded and tried to take the bird from the child.

"No. Let her keep the bird." Marc walked slowly toward the young witness. He wanted her as calm and comfortable as possible.

"Hi," she said.

"Hi," said Marc. "What's your name?"

"Camryn Marie Hendrickson, but you can call me Kia."

"Nice bird."

"Thank you. His name's Nick Archambeau."

"That's a lot of name."

"I named him after this really cute guy who drives the ice cream truck." She looked up at Marc with huge, haunted eyes. "You look mad."

"I'm not mad, Kia. Just very worried. The lady that went into the water was my girlfriend."

"Oh. She died."

"Who told you that?" asked Marc a little more sharply than he intended.

"I saw it. I saw her fall," insisted Kia.

"I think she may be alive and I want to find her. Will you help me?"

"She smelled really good."

"Yes, she smelled really good. Kia, what else did you see?"

"Really bad police."

"Did someone explain to you they were fake police?" Marc's gut twisted again.

"Yes. Uh huh. My mom did. That makes them double bad."

"Yes, it does and we need to find them too."

"The lady ran over there and two fake police took her arm." Kia pointed. "She kicked one hard and turned around. Then they all went over the edge. I was hiding so I didn't see everything."

"You were hiding?"

"She told me to," nodded Kia.

"Who told you to?"

"The lady who smelled good."

"She saw you?"

"Yeah. She came up here and she told me and Mrs. Chi to hide. Mrs. Chi told her to go to h-e-double hockey sticks and said she was going to talk to the fake police. But I took Nick and hid. I hid really good."

"Then what?" prodded Marc automatically.

"I peeked out. Two boys and one girl came up on the roof and one of them took Mrs. Chi by the arm. I heard him say to the lady. 'You stop now or I'll shoot.' It was like in a movie. I was so scared. So scared."

"I would be too," soothed Marc, knowing how to get the most out of any witness and this little girl was proving to be a good one. "What happened then?"

"Well, I didn't see it 'cause I shut my eyes tight, but I heard it. A loud sound. I know one of the boys shot Mrs. Chi 'cause I saw her and there was blood in her head and on the ground."

"How do you know the lady who smells good went over the edge?"

"I opened my eyes when I heard them shouting at her. Bad words. Very, very bad words. My brother Lukas said one of them once and he was grounded for a week. The lady and one of the boys and the other girl, they went right over the edge. I heard screaming, but not long. The other boy just stood at the ledge, then got on a phone. He stood there for a long, long time. I wasn't coming out. Then when he left, I waited another long, long time. Then I went downstairs and my mom called 911."

"What did the boy who didn't fall over the edge look like?"

"He was big."

"When you stand by the ledge, where does the top of it come on you."

Kia indicated a place mid chest.

"Where did it come on the boy?"

She indicated a place just below the waist.

"He was big," agreed Marc. "Was his skin your color or lighter or darker?"

"He was tan, but he was more light."

"Hair color, eye color?"

"Um, I don't know about hair. He had a cap on. A fake policeman's cap. I didn't see his eyes that good. But they weren't like yours." She pointed at Marc's eyes. "I'd remember."

"What about tattoos or piercings?"

Kia thought for a moment, then shook her head. "I don't know."

"Anything else?"

"The man was from Brooklyn."

"How do you know?"

"You can hear it," shrugged Kia.

"That's true."

Kia stared at Marc, her sharp eyes boring through him. "What's your name?"

"My name is Detective Marc Lexington."

"Tell this to Marc, he's tall and dark," she said nodding.

"What? What did you say?" he asked, his stomach doing a little flip.

"She gave me a poem to tell to Marc. No one else. No one else. Hide. Get the real police. And wait for Marc. Then tell this to Marc. He's tall and dark."

"I'm Marc."

"Can I see your ID?"

Shoving his impatience aside, he showed her his police identification. She studied it carefully, then nodded.

"Two like in lips." She smacked her lips, then pointed at her feet. "Two like in feet, and in seven who you will greet."

"What?"

"Word association, Detective," breathed Kim, astounded and amazed. "It's a learning tool and Dr. Morningstar would know that a frightened child would be more likely to remember a number if it were associated with something."

"Word association," repeated Marc.

"It rhymes, and…" Kim stopped. Marc was obviously playing with the numbers in his head.

"227. 22. 7. 2. 27."

"Do you know what it means? Will it help find the lady?" asked Kia.

"I don't know yet, but it gives us a clue. A really good one." He handed Kia his card. "If you remember anything else, call me, okay?"

"Sure. And Marc?"

"Yes?"

Kia took a pencil and paper out of her pocket and wrote down her name and number. "When you find her, would you give me a call?"

"Sure." He nodded to the mother who came over.

"Some kid," he said.

"Yes," agreed the mother. "I've always taught her to be respectful of the police. It bothers me that those horrible people were dressed as officers. Several of my neighbors saw them but didn't help her because they thought she was being pursued by the police."

"Kia seems to understand the difference."

"She's a smart little girl. I think children understand deception quite well. I hope she was helpful."

"She was," nodded Marc absently and handed her his card.

When they left the scene, Marc looked over at Sweeney who was standing by the ledge. "Did the lieutenant clear this witness?"

"Yes. She was only waiting for you because I called ahead." When Marc said nothing, Kim went on. "Detective, she was pretty definite the clue was only to go to you. Lieutenant Sweeney wouldn't have known about it."

"It was there. She should have found it." Marc's eyes were blazing when they refocused on Kim. "Come on, let's go talk with the other witnesses on the ground and find out what else she doesn't know."

Giving Sweeney and the other officers a slight wave, he strode off the roof with Kim moving quickly to keep up. As they rode the elevator down to ground level, Marc took out his notepad and carefully wrote down the poem, glad to have something in his hands. They were feeling violent. They wanted to go out on their own and break up the tension in his body by pounding something. Best to keep them busy.

Over the next few hours, Marc talked with every witness, pushing, poking, pulling, and prodding and got everything, every little detail they remembered. Every impression. Every sound. Every facet of the scene. And several things the original canvas had not shaken loose.

The first three letters on the license plate were the initials of one of the witness's children. The kidnapper who lived and ran back down from the roof looked like a young Michael Caine but a lot bigger. His phone was a Noikia. One witness swore he heard two horrendous splashes and one swoosh. Like two bodies and one smaller object. Another had an excellent description of a driver and a fourth and fifth kidnapper who'd tried to head them off a block over.

The car was navy, not black, confirmed by three witnesses. There was a parking sticker on the right side of the windshield, either beige or white, in the shape of a triangle. Marc got descriptions of boats in the water, filled with potential witnesses. All these details could be analyzed and put together into one big picture. Maybe they were important, maybe they weren't. Maybe they'd lead somewhere, maybe they wouldn't.

Marc's investigation was impressive and even Sweeney was forced to set aside her ego and admit there were several facts she'd missed when he reported to her later. The legend was at work among them and the smart cops watched. And learned.

The one single aspect of the case that remained consistent was that three people went over the ledge. One of them was Jette.

Tagg came to the scene and reported on the squad's activities. They'd been knocking on doors in the neighborhood along with Sweeney's people. Nothing had been found in or along the river. Nothing yet.

"I need to go home and talk with Hilda." Marc was sure there was nothing more on the scene.

"I'll go with you," said Tagg.

"No. I'll take Sommer. Hilda will like having her there. I want you to stay here. They're…they're dragging the river. I need someone here." Someone he could trust to call him immediately and not mess around with channels and chain of command.

"I understand. I'll stay right here. Marc, Carmel called. She sends you her love, obviously, but she also thinks Jette has some, I don't know, some special karma that will protect her. She thinks you still might find her alive. Actually she's quite sure of it."

"Karma can't break a fall like that," snapped Marc sharply, bitterly.

"No, but it can create opportunity. We know she went into the water, so most likely she'll suffer injury. But that's not necessarily a death sentence."

"Yeah, that's what I'm hanging on to right now. It's a slippery, threadbare rope, but I got a grip on it and I can't let go. I can't."

"I'll stay right here. You go talk to Hilda."

"Hilda, Jesus Christ. What happened?" asked Marc taking a gentle tone, recognizing how fragile she looked. He and Kim found her sitting with Claude and Tommy around the kitchen table. As their ravaged faces turned to him, he raised his hand palm out to stop the flow of sympathy and horror. He needed facts right now, not support.

"Oh, Detective Lexington." Tears poured down Hilda's cheeks, as Kim sat next to her and pressed the housekeeper's shaking hands in hers. "There was nothing I could do. They, they just came in and took her."

"I know. Please, Hilda, you have to help me here." Marc's voice remained calm and low. "Tell me exactly what happened."

"Yes, yes, of course. It keeps replaying in my mind. We were sitting and chatting in the kitchen, talking about the menus for the week. Drinking tea. No. That's not important. Oh, Detective, do you want everything?"

"Yes. Everything. All the details." He knew how to handle a shaky witness. Start at the beginning and their momentum would sustain them through the horror of relating the worst of it.

"I…I'm not used to preparing vegetarian meals and she brought me her cook books and we were looking at recipes. Her favorites are marked. I'll be shopping at a specialty store for the ingredients when she returns."

This broke her. Strangely, the fact that Hilda assumed she'd be cooking for Jette soon, steadied Marc. It added traction to the slippery rope he clung to. He let Kim soothe, then moved Hilda along.

"The details, Hilda. I need to find her."

"Yes. And bring her home. I'll make one of her favorites." With that resolution, she was able to move on. "There was a knock on the delivery room door. I answered it, not even thinking that it was strange that Jonathon hadn't called before sending someone up. There were three of them. Two men and a woman. They made no effort to disguise themselves. They were in uniforms, police uniforms." She looked over at Kim. "Exactly like yours, Officer Sommer."

Marc glanced over at Tommy, whose face looked unusually solemn and set.

"You talked to Jonathon?"

"Yes. He let them into the lobby. He opened the door for them, not even thinking about security," Tommy explained. "They told him they worked with you. He checked their badges and he said they looked authentic. He asked that they use the service elevator. You know. His little dig."

"I'll interview him later." He turned back to Hilda.

"What was the story they gave you?"

"They said they were sent by Captain Green and that they needed to escort Dr. Morningstar to the precinct house."

"And Jette didn't take that at face value," stated Marc, knowing the answer.

"Oh no. I think she felt something off right away. She was very casual and polite. She said she'd be glad to accompany them. That she wanted to get her purse and would I come with her. I think if she wouldn't have wanted me out of the kitchen, she'd have pulled it off. I was confused, but got up to go with her, and that set them off. They knocked me down and pushed into the kitchen. They, they obviously wanted Dr. Morningstar. The big one said, 'take her.'"

Marc nodded at the ugly bruise and a gash over her eye. "Did you get medical attention?" he asked.

Hilda shook her head, dabbing her eyes. "It's nothing. Claude put ice on it. I wanted to wait here for you."

"Fine. No robbery? No threats?"

"No. They just went for Dr. Morningstar. It was a kidnapping."

"Then what?"

"Then everything else happened so fast. I stepped in front of the thinner man and he hit me again. Dr. Morningstar helped me up off the floor, then quicker than anyone could react, she shoved me into the powder room, ordered me to lock the door, and call 911. I did. Oh, Detective, I wasn't even thinking. I just did what she asked. I'm too used to taking orders. I heard the struggle, but I simply stood behind the door and called 911. I should come out and grabbed a knife or...or..."

"Hilda, these people shot and killed a hostage just to make a point. You'd probably be dead if you hadn't done exactly what she told you to do," said Marc.

Claude looked at him gratefully knowing Hilda would believe him. He'd been telling her that for hours and she'd get stuck on that one fact over and over.

"She could have gotten away. You've seen her run. She's so fast. She could have gotten away at any time, but she made sure I was safe."

"Not even Jette can outrun a bullet, Hilda." Marc knew Jette did try to run. Almost made it. And may have fallen to her death. "I see they put a few into the door."

"Yes, I could hear them cursing, and they shot a few bullets into the door. It's a good sturdy oak, so I was safe enough. Then I guess they realized with the noise they were making and the fact that I had my cell and could call 911 they'd better get out. I didn't hear Dr. Morningstar again, so maybe they had their guns on her. It wasn't more than a few seconds and they were gone. I called Jonathon, but by the time he responded, the kidnappers disappeared. Probably out the garage entrance."

"Why do you say that?" asked Kim.

"Jonathon didn't see them again. The parking ramp empties out onto the alley that goes right to Madison. If they had a car, it would be there. Minimum exposure on the street," responded Tommy.

"Describe them." Marc had a pretty good description, but Hilda saw them standing still in full light.

"The two men were both over six feet tall. One was a bit taller, maybe 6' 2" and was about 230, muscle, not fat, the other, a few inches shorter, was thinner, probably 180. The woman was 5' 7" and about 140." She went on to give detailed descriptions of their features, right down to the fact that the woman wore dark pink nail polish. Two had visible tattoos. The same one. The taller man had one on the top of his wrist and the woman had the same one on the side of her neck. She didn't see one on the third man, but it could have been beneath his clothes. It was a circle, like a ball. Pale blue.

"I've never seen it on the street," frowned Marc. "But we'll get started talking with tattoo artists to see if it's a gang symbol or a cult. Kim."

Kim nodded. Marc's team was standing ready and this sounded like a perfect job for them.

"I'll call. They'll start the canvas immediately."

"Good. That's good. Hilda, I'd like you to work with a sketch artist and look through mug shots. Do you feel up to it?"

"Yes. Certainly."

"Take care of that, Sommer. You can set her up on the computer in the library. Get her started on the online files. Have the artist come here. Hilda, do you want a doctor?"

"No. I want to get to those files." She reached over and took Marc's hand. "Find Dr. Morningstar, Detective. There's no way that beautiful child's light has gone out. You find her and bring her home."

Marc's throat closed. Bring her home. Home. The word echoed in his brain like a single call down a deep, dark well. For a moment the man inside him edged through his defenses. The man whose mate was lost to him. Who was paralyzed with grief so thick he couldn't breathe. He could only nod as he tried to suppress all but the cop. The cop would find her. Find her and bring her home. The man would only get in his way.

Claude, Kim, Tommy, and Hilda sat for a moment. They saw the struggle on

Marc's face. Saw the man fight with, then lose to the cop. It was both heartbreaking and hopeful.

Needing to move, Marc got up abruptly and went over the service entrance, the back stairway, and down the most logical route. There was no sign of a struggle. No blood, thank God. All the shots that Hilda heard were in the door or the paneling over Jette's head. Warning shots only.

He'd read the CSI reports later, but the scene looked clean. Near the curb, he bent down. Scuff marks. She'd dug in her heels at the last moment. He looked up and down the street, never really deserted. He'd put his own team in the neighborhood. They were the best. He trained most of them. If anyone saw anything, they'd find the witnesses.

Circling around to the front, he talked with the night doorman. Jonathon was in the back, waiting for him. He wouldn't go home until he made a statement directly to the detective. While Marc was grateful for the man's cooperation, he added little to the evidence. The kidnappers all showed badges that looked authentic. Jonathon gave the precinct number. There was no such number. He called in Rachael and had her work with him on the mug shots. They'd compare notes with Hilda later.

After getting Tommy to start canvassing the less conventional people on the street and Claude to hold Hilda's hand through the process of searching hundreds of files, Marc went back to where he wanted to be. To where his heart demanded that he be. This time Kim won the battle for the keys and she drove them back to the place where Jette was last seen.

# Chapter 24

Evie Columbus was standing outside the exclusive and bustling press area. Behind the barriers like every other civilian. And she was steaming. Apparently, there was no automatic ticket for the success train in the news business. She found out having one single moment of glory wasn't going to take her to fame and fortune, no matter how spectacular the moment was. Hoping that lightning would strike twice, she was doing her best to capture some more exclusive footage for herself and any media outlet that would meet her price.

Not that there was anything going on. Just a lot of cops standing around, waiting, watching. The footage of the boat dragging the water in ever widening circles was dramatic at first, but had quickly become monotonous. Only two bodies in over 25 hours, and one of those had been weighed down months ago. The grand prize, Morningstar's remains, were still down there.

A tall, blonde man in jeans and a loose fitting cotton sweater walked authoritatively up to the barriers. Evie stared at him. What woman wouldn't? He was gorgeous. He was…Oh my God. A shot of energy sizzled through her as she looked at him, then around at the cluster of news people she thought of as her competition. Oh, sweet! Those high flying TV and print reporters weren't reacting to him at all. No one else recognized him. Ha! So much for their research departments. It was a good thing she did her own research.

Raising her trusty camera, she recorded the exchange between the man and the cop in charge. Wow! He looked great in the camera frame. Really good looking, his thick, blonde hair casually cut. Built, too. She zoomed in on the intense face made even more intriguing by at least a day's growth of beard. It wasn't a leaping college professor, but there would be some interest on the family angle.

"Are you in charge here?" the blonde man asked Tagg.

"Who wants to know?" frowned Tagg, in no mood for another bureaucrat, reporter, or lawyer.

"My name's Luke Grainger. I'm Jette Morningstar's brother. Officer Kim Sommer told me how to get here."

"Oh, I'm sorry. Here. Duck under." Tagg held up the crime scene tape and Luke stepped into the nightmare.

"Where's Marc?"

Tagg nodded to an area near the shore where huge halogen lights carved sun bright light out of the night fog rolling over the top of the water. It was a dreary evening, made gloomier by the light drizzle falling from the dark, gray clouds.

"Anything new?"

"Since…"

"Since about an hour ago. I've been in transit and my cell battery died. Officer Sommer has been keeping me up to date."

"No. Nothing. You heard about the body then?"

"Yeah. Preliminary autopsy complete yet?"

"No, but it didn't take a pathologist to see the guy had a broken neck, at least one broken leg, and not much of a face left."

"Christ. How's Marc?"

"I've known the man for years. We went through the academy together. He's the godfather of my little girl. But, I don't know what to do for him. He's completely shut down. He just stands there like a statue. No. More like a robot because he's been going through the motions. Demanding reports, scanning updates, hounding the troops. But mostly he just stands there staring into the East River." Tagg glanced over at Luke. "I'm glad you're here. You anything like your sister?"

Luke felt his face flick a smile at the cop in the rumpled suit. "I didn't get your name."

"Sorry, I'm a little off here. It's Tagg. Detective Taggert Freeman."

"Well, Tagg, let me tell you. There's no one on this earth quite like my sister, but what I'll do is try to reach Marc in my own way."

Tagg nodded. From his quick intuitive assessment of Jette's brother, he thought that would be just fine. He watched as Luke walked toward Marc.

Evie eagerly recorded it all and started sending it out. Jette Morningstar's brother, a doctor with Physicians for Peace, had arrived on the scene.

The search team continued to drag the river. Marc's damp hair ruffled in the breeze as he watched the boat with hollow eyes. They'd been out there 24 solid hours, mobilized soon after she went into the water. He'd paced the shore, then stood for hours, like a lone sentinel, arms folded over his chest, legs spread apart staring as the boat went back and forth on its pattern. Afraid they'd find something. Afraid they wouldn't.

Eight hours into the tedious work, they'd shouted and Marc nearly went to his knees when they brought up a body, but it was a young man. Not Jette. Not Jette.

The man's appearance fit the witness descriptions and he was dressed like a cop. His neck and limbs had been broken from the fall and the preliminary report indicated that he was nearly dead on impact. Very little water in the lungs.

Dead on impact. Dead on impact. The words echoed in his exhausted mind and it would probably have driven him insane if he could feel anything at all. Normally the intensity of his mood would have been pouring out of him, but now the air around him seemed void of any emotion. Like a black hole in space. When he realized he was feeling too much, the emotion turned the corner and shot back into him until his soul overloaded and shut down completely.

A hand rested on his shoulder and he angrily shrugged it off. He didn't want to be touched. God damn it, didn't he tell everyone to leave him alone? It was his fault she was in that dark, dirty water. His fault. He brought her here, all light and beauty, to fall into hell. He wanted no sympathy, no reassurances from anybody. All they could give him were words. Empty words.

When the hand returned to his shoulder, he spun around, ready to take out his fury and grief on someone's face. Marc stared into the solemn blue eyes of Jette's brother Luke and waited for the compassion he saw in them to clear and the accusing glare to begin.

"Luke. I…,"

But before Marc could take another breath he was embraced by the man who, besides him, loved Jette best. His arms came up on their own accord and held on.

It took them a moment to settle, then Luke pulled back. Searching Marc's pale face, he frowned in concern.

"When's the last time you sat down, Marc? Damn it, you're still recovering from a very serious injury. When Jette gets back, she needs a man, not a walking corpse."

Marc knew he probably looked like shit. Mostly because he felt like shit. He was racked with fatigue and he hadn't been able to eat or drink since he heard about Jette. If he managed to get anything past the constriction in his throat, he was sure he wouldn't be able to keep it down. There were knots in every corner of his stomach, a sick sinking feeling in his gut.

"I'm fine. I'm okay, Luke." Marc made a concession to his screaming body and rested back against the hood of a car. For the first time in hours, he focused on the activity on shore. His entire squad was milling around, giving him space but standing guard. "How the hell did you get here so fast?"

"They found me pretty quickly in the town where we'd stopped for the night. I took a charter from Quito to Miami, then flew directly here. Doesn't hurt that you and Jette are considered some kind of royalty by the press. It was the Ambassador herself who brought me the message, then filled me in on what you've been up to since you got back here. Jesus Christ, Marc. I was in the hills and didn't know you made CNN again."

"That was your sister."

"Yeah. Yeah, I heard." He looked out over the cold, black water.

"God, Luke. I brought her here. Brought her to this city. I uprooted her from a place where she would have thrived in the sun to a deep, dark..." Marc's voice shook and he couldn't go on.

"So this is all your fault?"

"Feels like it. Yes."

"And how exactly did you force her to come here? Tie her up? Blackmail? Appeal to her desperate addiction for New York pastrami on rye?"

"She's a veg-head."

"That's right. She's also her own woman. Don't stand here and insult her. Now, chuck the guilt and tell me what happened."

Marc stared at him for a moment, remembering a time when Jette had said just about the same thing to him.

"You're channeling her."

"I thought I felt an urge for a sprout and avocado sandwich. Tell me what happened before she channels me to kick your ass. The way you look right now, I think I'd have a chance to take you down."

Marc felt something lift off his heart and he nearly smiled.

"They haven't found her. The witnesses said she went in. And...and she didn't come up." He told Luke in short choppy sentences what they knew, what they'd found so far. "I'll find them, Luke. I'll find out who did this to her. They're dead men."

"I'd rather you found her," said Luke with conviction, completely shook, but knowing if he collapsed Marc would too. Jette would expect him to be made of stronger stuff.

Marc looked bleakly out at the river with the droning sound of the search and recovery boat playing background to his despair.

"We're looking."

"But in the wrong place, I think. Marc." When Marc didn't respond, he sharpened his tone. "Marc, look at me." Marc slowly turned his haunted eyes back to Luke. "Do you remember that night down at the ranch when I told you the national Olympic team wanted her? That they felt she could medal in at least 10 events?"

"Yes."

"One of them was high diving."

Marc frowned, processed, then shook his head.

"But the building is probably 80 or 100 feet higher than any high dive."

"True, a high dive is about 10 meters, but I've seen her cliff dive on a dare at a height way above that. We never measured it, but the ledges above one of the lakes where we used to swim as kids were…" Luke looked up at the tall building Jette fell from and even though his stomach lurched at the sight, his voice remained steady and convincing. "Very high."

Marc felt something inside him melt. When he saw Luke, he assumed there would be shock and grief and angry accusations. This little breath of hope was completely unexpected and difficult to assimilate. He couldn't say anything, so Luke continued.

"Look, Marc, she'd know how to enter the water no matter what the height. And we both know she'd have no fear, that she'd have the clear head to do what she needed to do."

"No one saw her surface."

"And why would she do that if someone was after her? That girl can swim like a fish under water."

"But she hasn't called and there's been no one admitted to any of the area hospitals fitting her description. We've checked along the shores. It's been nearly 27 hours." Marc's voice was strained and his lungs burned. He felt compelled to fight the optimism in Luke's voice. It was just too painful to have hope.

"And you've been standing there all that time?"

"Pretty much."

"Damn it Marc, I released you to come home under the stipulation you'd take it easy!"

Marc ignored the scold and looked back at the swirling water of the East River.

"You're saying Jette may not be down there?" he asked thickly.

"Exactly. Shouldn't they have found her by now if she was down there?"

"The currents…"

"Screw the currents. She dove in, swam away from the danger and made it to shore," shouted Luke taking Marc's arms and giving him a little shake. He needed to get through to Marc. Penetrate the wall of shock and remorse that he'd been building for the last 24 hours.

Marc stared at him, trying to sort through what Jette's brother was telling him. The fact was they hadn't found her, dead or alive. Something clicked, then caught. A thought. An idea. He hadn't been thinking forward for hours. It felt good. It felt powerful.

"If she survived the fall and got to shore, they must have her. They could have been watching from the side of the river or the roof," speculated Marc.

"Do you believe they killed her?" Luke was relieved to see Marc's eyes coming back to life.

Marc looked into Luke's face. It was filled with a stubborn conviction. And it was contagious. It put Marc's brain back into gear.

"Shit. I haven't been thinking through this haze. Killed her? No. No. It doesn't fit. They could have killed her anytime between when they took her and when she got away. They were armed. They killed a hostage without provocation."

"Well then, since they didn't kill her, they probably have her," shrugged Luke.
Marc nodded slowly.

"So," Luke threw his hands in the air. "What the hell are you doing here staring at the place a few witnesses said they saw her last? You're standing still. That's not your style. She calls you *Ganohalidohi*. Hunter. This is your town. I know it's huge, but goddamn it, Marc. Go find her."

Suddenly, something released its hold on Marc's heart and unfroze his gut. It had been immobilizing him, keeping him from pursuing his natural instincts. The fog in his brain cleared. It didn't surprise Luke in the least that a feral smile formed on Marc's lips and his eyes regained their light. The hunter was back.

"Fuck me. I can't believe I've been standing here instead of working the case for this long."

"You were in shock," said Luke softly.

"That's no excuse. But I'm not in shock anymore. Jesus Christ, Luke, it's good to see you."

Luke nodded and tried to keep up as Marc pushed off the hood of the car, steadied himself and started toward the barriers. His exhaustion fell away as the energy of renewed conviction fueled him.

"If she could have, she would have contacted us. Therefore we have to assume they took her when she surfaced and have her secluded," concluded Marc.

"Do you think they took her out of Manhattan?"

Marc thought a minute. Checked his instincts. "No. There's no reason to take her anywhere else. It would be too dangerous to transport her over any of the bridges or in the tunnels if they thought we were looking for her."

"That narrows it down." Luke's casual shrug communicated complete confidence. Finding a single person in a city where there were nearly 67,000 citizens per square mile. No problem.

Marc hacked out a short laugh. "Damn, I needed you."

"What can I do?"

"First, be a doctor. I'm going to take you back to the apartment. Our housekeeper…"

"Hilda?" When Marc looked at him with surprise, he shrugged and went on. "We may not have TV, but we do have cell phones. Jette has been updating me regularly."

"Yeah, well, she took a blow and refused medical treatment."

"Sounds familiar. Is this a New York thing?"

"Very funny. Anyway, she insisted on staying in the apartment in case Jette called or came back."

When they got to where the squad was standing, watching, Marc introduced everyone. They all could see the detective was back and ready to roar. When they'd watched Luke stride confidently right toward him, they weren't sure what was going to happen. But the guy definitely snapped their man back.

Kim came running toward them and skidded to a stop in front of Marc.

"Detective. They've just brought up another body. Female."

Kim could feel the chill and went on quickly. "It's not Dr. Morningstar." When she saw the frozen tension return to Marc's face, she hardened her voice. Made sure he understood. "Detective Lexington. It's not Jette. The woman has brown hair."

"Take me there." He glanced over at Luke. "You stay here."

"Not a chance." When Marc started to argue, Luke showed his resolve. "She's mine, too."

Kim looked up at the new guy, obviously confused.

"I'm Luke Grainger, Jette's brother," he explained.

"You are?" Kim didn't bother to hide her surprise.

He ran his hands through his blonde, curly hair. "I'm sort of a blood brother. Her mom and dad took me in. They never formally adopted me."

Kim shrugged. "There's a lot of blended families all over the country. I was just expecting more resemblance. I'm Officer Kim Sommer."

"I know. I recognized your voice."

"Lead the way, Sommer," snapped Marc irritably. Even the impatience felt good after a long night and day of nothing.

# Chapter 25

The Empress could feel the rapid pulse of play heating her blood. What an exciting round it was turning out to be! All the public attention and live action was taking the game to a whole new level. The years and years she'd spent trapped by the rules of computerized engagement were nothing compared to this. Nothing but a pale stage of preparation. She had no idea it would be this exhilarating. There was anger, frustration, and a lot of wicked surprises, of course, but it made it all so much more real. So much more satisfying.

Jette Morningstar. What a competitor! All others who'd played at being Avenger couldn't compare. When they met in the Final Duel, this Avenger could only be defeated by her, the one true Blue Empress! Until that celebrated day, she wouldn't underestimate Morningstar again. Five of her most seasoned Sentinels had been selected and sent, but the numbers had barely been adequate. Sighing, she gave Avenger points for the two who'd expired. Nothing really counted until the final tally anyway and this one was already soaring beyond anything ever witnessed. For every point her arch enemy earned now, the value of taking her last life in the Final Duel went up.

She'd watched all the news accounts. Experts in the field of forensics interviewed by the major news outlets were fairly consistent in reporting that at the height of the building in question, going into water was only slightly more forgiving than landing on a concrete sidewalk. The broken bodies of her Sentinels had been found in the river proving the consensus viewpoint. Surviving the fall was an extremely low possibility. Based on what she heard, she declared a loss of life for Avenger and adjusted the weapons count accordingly.

What a blunder on Avenger's part. When capture was inevitable, she should have just surrendered.

"Not smart, Avenger, to expend one of your most treasured and valuable assets in the hopes of escaping," she mumbled as her hands flew over the keyboards. "A huge strategic blunder."

Looking back at the TVs, she saw footage of the Dark Knight.

"Immobilized without your Avatar? Witless marionette. Can't make a move without your puppet master?"

He'd been standing on the bank of the East River for hours. Searching for Avenger to bring her back and serve her. He was surrounded by Guardians. No problem. She didn't want him yet anyway. The points she'd earn for his capture or death were inconsequential at this point. Not worth the risk.

They were still looking for Avenger in the water. Fools. They may be powerful, with incredible resources at their command, but the Dark Knight and the Guardians were weak minded. They remained blind to the truth and the longer they had no clue, the longer she had to turn Avenger and win one of her lives. The Phoenix rises from the dead, after all.

Then her heart popped and her nerves jumped. She could hardly contain her excitement as she watched an Evie Columbus exclusive. More players. More action. More potential points.

The Light Knight himself had come to the City of Might. There he was. She was sure of it. Had Avenger released him from exile? She'd never seen him without his mask, but it had to be him! He was very light and nearly as tall and powerfully built as the Dark Knight.

The Empress rechecked her notes. Just as she thought. The Dark Knight could call the Light Knight into play once during a round when Avenger was either in stases or out of the field. Now they'd be working together, consolidating their power. It added to the danger, but it also increased her significant targets. More danger, more points. An easy equation. And it placed them closer together. Easier to pick off.

That was a very good thing. Fine, then. It was good. All good.

Watching as the Knights moved with most of the Guardians out of range, she considered her options. At some point taking on the two Knights and ending them would pay off. Big time. The challenge would give her the difficulty she needed to ascend in total points. After the setbacks she'd suffered the last few days, she could really use something of this caliber to acquire an advantage going into the Castle of Thunder.

Too bad her best Assassin had a thing about killing cops. It ruled out taking down the Guardians and the Dark Knight one by one. She'd have to lead them as a group into a trap. TrueBlue920 provided her with explosive munitions he thought she was going to deploy for a defensive advantage. Fool. He never thought beyond the money, really. And that made him extremely easy to manipulate. By the time he realized it was cops that would be part of the body count, it would be too late for him to lament his choices.

Still, that all could play out later. She moved those actions to the center of her game board. For the next phase of the moon, she needed to concentrate on turning Avenger. That was top priority. With one of Avenger's lives as an additional weapon, she could more boldly move through the Castle of Thunder to the portal to the Final Duel.

Taking the remote, she turned off the TVs and texted another message. *I will join you just before the moon rises. Prepare for me.*

Yes, she reminded herself as she took a last appreciative look at her board. One step at a time. Patience. This was glorious play. Just glorious. No need to rush through it.

# Chapter 26

"We're setting up in here." Marc glanced around the huge empty ballroom, mentally formulating all the things he'd need to create a command center. Dina, Tagg, Rachael, Teresa, Raj, and Kim had accompanied him from the scene. They'd taken personal time throughout the day to be with Marc while the rest of the squad concentrated on their current cases. They were now off shift and ready to work with him through the night. Eunice met them there eager to assist. Hilda, Claude, and Tommy had been alerted and stood ready.

"The chief is going to get the case assigned to us," explained Marc, "but I'm not waiting. I'll be working on it here in an unofficial capacity. I'm formally returning to medical leave on the advice of my doctor." He glanced over at Luke, who nodded.

Even though Marc looked more animated than he had when he'd first arrived, Luke knew the man was running on grit and will. There clearly was weakness in his side and he'd wince when he'd forget and let his guard down. Luke could see that wasn't going to stop him or even slow him at this point. It was a good feeling. He was worried to the bone about his sister, but he knew her best hope was Marc and he'd stand with him to make sure he didn't fall.

"Until we can move through the case officially, this looks like a good place to keep it low profile." Tagg glanced around.

"Absolutely no red tape in any corner of the room," observed Dina.

"And we all know how red tape stirs your blood," said Rachael.

"It's a pretty delicate dance right now because of all the jurisdictions and the really high profile, but I expect we'll have formal sanction soon," observed Raj.

"And taking yourself out of it will help the chief's argument to get the case transferred. Brass can't play conflict of interests," said Tagg. "With you out, I'm next in line to lead the squad. But let's be clear. There's only one pilot on this plane. Where do you want us to start?"

"What do you want us all to do?" asked Raj.

"Give us assignments," nodded Rachael.

They all realized the covert nature of the investigation made several bends in the rules, but one of their own was missing. Someone who needed the best the city had to offer. They were the best. Besides, while the process would be unofficial and maybe unorthodox, it would follow solid police procedure. When they needed official sanction or a chain of evidence, they'd feed what they had to the proper jurisdiction.

Marc looked at them all for a moment, marshalling his emotions. He felt his life was on the line, and standing on the line with him were his team. Feelings he hadn't allowed to the surface stormed through him, then settled into a special place in his chest. There'd be time later to give them what they deserved. Right now he didn't have the words or the energy. So he simply nodded.

"Let's get busy. There's a lot we can do tonight to set up. I can use all of you here whenever you can swing it until we find her."

He couldn't say her name right now. He was too close to the edge and the pain might send him over.

"We'll come right after our shifts every day," said Kim.

"None of us are on this weekend, so we'll be able to go a straight 48 then," added Teresa.

"I'm due for vacation. I'll clear it with personnel," said Tagg.

"No. I want to keep everything here under the official radar. If people from my team are out, any idiot will know, and the chief is no idiot. Tagg, when she gets the case, you'll head the team. Save the vacation for later. A lot of this I'll have to do on my own, anyway. Come in after your shifts. Claude will arrange for you to have access. Claude, get keys for everyone here."

Claude nodded, so glad to be a part of the effort.

"It's a good space." Tagg turned slowly. "We'll need tables, white boards, bulletin boards, office supplies, computers, files."

"Claude and I can get some of that from storage, honey pot," offered Tommy. "There's a room downstairs that looks like a well stocked furniture emporium." She looked solemn today. Far more like a wrestler than a diva.

"Hilda, you doing alright?" Marc asked looking over at her.

"Dr. Grainger declared me fit for duty, Detective. Tell me what I can do." Everyone could see she needed to be busy, needed to help.

"Something very specific. You're the only one who can communicate with Fartmore. Call him at home. Tell him I'm going to need a lot of money. Cash. Small bills. 200 large and before noon tomorrow."

"He'd answer your calls if you called him Mr. Farth-Moore," scolded Hilda automatically, then just stared when what he'd asked for sunk in.

"Fart-more, Farth-Moore. He's a tight ass. He'll come through for you, though."

"And to be clear, that would be $200,000?" She wasn't sure she'd heard correctly.

"Yeah, to start."

She didn't even ask what it was for, but left the room with purpose.

Marc turned to the rest of his team. "We'll need to shake people at home, but use my name. They'll wake up and reopen. Rachael get in touch with Jessica Dettinger at Compunation on 5th. Tell her I need top-of-the-line computer equipment. The absolute best she's got. Have her put it on my account. Dina, call Lindsey Hebel at Office Supply and give her a list. We'll need everything. Teresa, see if Looney Lyd is still in lock up. If she is, hell, I don't have time to do the legal work this round, call Friar Tuck. I think he got his papers back. If not, he'll know who can get her out. Arrange for the bail. Hilda will write you a check. Then get her over here. Sober her up and put her on the computers. We'll need a network. Sommer, is that super-geek who hacked into the NYPD central computer still in juvie? If so, get her sprung and over here, too. Raj, call Dalton's Donut Heaven, Shawn's Subs, Lexie's Tacos, Stephanie's Pizza Palace and get us food."

"How about the Harvest Hearth for those of us who prefer to die of old age rather than cardiac arrest?" Raj liked what he saw on Marc's face.

The request gave Marc a little stab in the heart and he nodded. Jette had just established an account there last week.

"What about phones? Shall we use our own cells?" asked Rachael seeing some other practical needs.

"No. Tagg, call Plastic. It's on the speed dial in the den. Have him bring us six dozen temps. Tell him to put three hours on five dozen and couple thousand hours on the other dozen."

"He won't take a check," said Tagg, nodding.

"Tell him to put it on my line and I'll grease him tomorrow."

"Will do." Tagg walked out to get it done.

"We'll find her well before we use up that amount of time," said Kim.

"Yeah. We will," breathed Marc. "We will."

Hilda came back in, caught Marc's eye and nodded.

"The money will be here by noon tomorrow. $200,000 in tens, twenties and hundreds."

"What did you tell Fart-more?"

"I told Mr. Farth-Moore you were remodeling. I'm sure he figures you're going to buy all your copulating statues, bean bag chairs, and neon colored lava lamps for cash under the table."

"Good enough. In the meantime how about gallons of coffee." He looked over at Raj. "And a pot of that herbal shit."

"May I recommend we bring in the old dining room table from storage and several of the more comfortable chairs from the den and library?" she suggested. "Also, if you're all going to work through the night, I'll air out the guest rooms. You can use them for rest and to freshen up."

"Good. Have Tommy take care of the furniture when she gets back."

Luke looked at Marc and asked the question that was on all of their minds.

"What the hell are you going to do with all that cash, Marc?"

"I'm going to spread the jack around this city. There will be green rivers flowing by this time tomorrow night. The walls have eyes, the streets have eyes, hell, the fucking garbage cans have eyes. I'm going to turn this city into a fucking crystal ball. I'll put out the buzz to the freaks from the condos under the stairs I'm paying for chat. And paying big time for information that leads us to the treasure. The word will spread like the plague, fueled by plenty of cash."

"Brilliant," nodded Dina, speaking for everyone in the room.

"If she's been spotted, I'll find out. It may take some time, but if the word is out there I'll get plugged in. Buzz and hum can filter through a lot of layers, some not too stable. There's always plugs and gags out there, but New York can't keep a secret from someone who's connected to the line." Marc sounded more like the young street thug from his past than the mature cop. "And green blood moves the current faster. Now let's get busy and set up this command center."

Over the next few hours, the ballroom was transformed into a bustling and efficient cop shop. As much as Marc wanted to get into the streets to start the hunt, he knew his best chance to find her, to find the people who had her, and to get her back safely was to do it with a deliberate, methodical, well coordinated operation.

Hilda was in the kitchen sobering up Looney Lyd, a computer genius who had a complete meltdown when her company went public and she'd become a multimillionaire. In an ironic twist, the stress of success caused her to have a psychotic disconnect and she spent most of her days on the streets and her nights in the bars or in lockup. She was brilliant, drunk or sober, and would be able to set up a functioning network in half the time an average techie would take to unpack the boxes. Marc wanted the best.

Tommy and Claude set up the huge dining room table to serve as a meeting space, surrounding it with portable boards. Boxes of note pads, files, pens, and other office paraphernalia were unpacked and arranged efficiently on tables serving as desks spread throughout the room.

Before midnight, a semi sober Lyd had several laptops humming and all the computers were connected and ready for action.

"Think she needs some coffee?" asked Rachael when Lyd's head flopped down on her keyboard.

Marc glanced over.

"Hey, Lyd," he shouted. "Bill Gates is on the phone!"

Lyd started, straightened, and rubbed her hand over her face.

"Tell the kid I'm not interested," she mumbled, and finished connecting all the hardware.

"Is she really a millionaire?" asked Raj carrying supplies to the dining table in preparation for the first meeting of the night.

"I think she still has several hundred left, although this week's bar bill at Bruna Young's probably set her back some."

"Several hundred dollars is all she has left?" asked Rachael.

"Several hundred million," said Marc.

"Is she going to be able to help with the research?" Dina couldn't keep the skepticism out of her voice. Lyd's shaky hands seemed to be getting the job done on the equipment, but she wasn't sure how many working brain cells were left. Certainly not several hundred million.

"When she gets clean, she can make magic, but I've got someone else on tap for the real research."

"And possible cyber snooping?" asked Raj casually.

"That too."

If he needed to get into the files of the departments working the case, he didn't want the hassle of paperwork, politics, and pissing matches. The geek he had in mind rolled in as if on cue.

Kim accompanied the tiny young woman as she propelled herself across the room in an old battered wheelchair. She'd been serving a term in juvie and was out on Marc's recognizance. She wore torn jeans, a tight t-shirt that read *Instant Gratification Takes Too Long* and had several little hoops in each ear. Her hair was short, coal black and spiky and she took everything in with pale blue eyes.

"What's your name?" asked Marc.

"Kelly Kidd," grinned the pretty girl as she surveyed the surroundings. Marc could tell that her busy mind was registering. Calculating. Speculating. He recognized the move.

"Right." If her name was Kelly Kidd, his was George Washington. Of course it could have been. He had no idea what his birth certificate said. Or even if he had a birth certificate. "What name were you given at birth."

She sighed deeply, trying to remain cool. No one at juvie or any of the foster homes ever questioned it. It was her favorite name and she'd adopted the handle several years before. Then she'd altered all the records she could find. But her fib factor was crumbling. Cripes. This tall guy had super orbs. Before she knew what she was doing, she gave him a straight shot.

"Christine Kaye Schnitger. But you can still call me Kelly. What's your handle?" She knew who he was, of course, who on both sides of the law didn't, but saw no reason to feed his ego. So she asked with a nice slice of attitude, thinking the little smirk was working.

"Lexington. Detective Lexington."

"Hey, no kidding. I like your street. Lexington. Spent some time on it before I got scooped. Any connection?"

"Not that I know of." She didn't have to know he'd named himself after the street. He gestured over at Lyd, who was now muttering to herself while testing all the connections, her left hand obsessively popping the air out of the bubble wrap that had covered the keyboards. "You'll be working with Lyd. We'll be using you for straight research."

"And to hack into secured files?" Kelly asked knowingly.

"That would be illegal," said Marc steadily. "But from what the public defender told me last week, you're incredibly…gifted."

She'd had One Police Plaza in an uproar after getting through the several layers of security their consultants had assured them were impenetrable.

"Yeah. I'm gifted. And I know no boundaries." She'd only been trying to get her juvie record erased. Marc knew that and liked the girl's audacity. It was why she was currently setting up on his unofficial team.

"That'll work. Do you need any special accommodations, Kelly?"

"Only when I pee. I need a pretty wide doorway to maneuver my wheels." She grinned at him, feeling a tingle when he called her Kelly. This guy was pretty terrifying, but he was okay.

"The bathroom off the main foyer was converted a few years ago. It should suit." Mrs. Clarke had been in a wheelchair the last few months of her life and a few adjustments had been made to some of the doorways and facilities.

"Cool," said Kelly. "So you're the Shield, huh? We've heard about you down in juvie. Lots of the 'mates point out your scratch."

Marc had carved his gang sign in several places during his own lockup. He doubted they were still there, but the legend continued.

"Tell Sommer what you need. She'll get it for you."

"How 'bout a beer and a big bag of sour cream and onion chips?"

"How about a nonalcoholic beverage of your choice to go with the chips." He was liking the kid more and more.

"I heard you weren't such a fudge on rules, Lexington."

"I'm not, but I need you clean. You a user?"

"Nah. I was just pokin' atchya. I need all my brain cells for my addiction of choice." She pointed at one of the computers. "I'm a gamer."

"Not while you're here. I don't want to see anything exploding on the screen."

Kelly shrugged. He couldn't watch her every minute. Besides, she was all caught up in her luck on this one. She didn't intend to go back into juvie, so she thought she'd bide her time, buy a ticket online to Vegas using some schmuck's credit card number and be off before the end of the week. In the meantime, she'd fondle some of the delicious keyboards in the room and make every appearance of complete and contrite cooperation.

"You going to find the professor?" she asked.

"Sommer fill you in?"

"Yeah. But only the tiniest ameba on the planet wouldn't be up to date on this story. It's scorching. So why from here? Kind of a high flavored crib for an investigation. Are we undercover or something?"

"Did Sommer tell you this is her home?"

"No. Just that we're going to find her. So, she lives here?"

"Yes. With me."

"What the heck kinda cop hides away in digs like this? You on the take or something?"

"No. Hey Lyd," he shouted over at the muttering, popping woman. "Where do you want the kid?"

Lyd looked up, blinked rapidly a few times.

"Bill here?" She looked around.

"No. This kid." He pointed at Kelly.

Her eyes lost some of their blurriness when they focused on Kelly.

"She can't touch anything until she proves worthy," she snapped.

"What is this, a martial arts movie?" muttered Kelly, looking over at an amazing set up on a table near the window. Sleek, strong, state of the art. It was not of this earth. She tried not to drool, but she did lose a bit of her cool when she let the hunger show.

"She got around your secure 5X80 system, Lyd." Marc knew precisely what would get through.

"This little geekazoid?" Lyd stared at Kelly, a tiny light of interest adding some animation to her face. "Wheel on over here, kid, let's talk."

"That was her system? Oh my God! She's Lydia Landgate? Cripes." Another step closer to heaven, Kelly thought. Lydia Landgate was extreme. A legend. Maybe she'd postpone Vegas for a week or so. She wheeled enthusiastically toward Lyd and soon they were lost in geek talk.

Less than an hour later, Marc stood in the center of the room and let the reality of it settle in. It was as good as he could do for Jette. It was all he knew how to do. Everyone was busy on phones and computers. Files were being filled with data and clues were being collected for later assessment.

"I'm going to need a picture to circulate." Marc came over to Kelly's station, already littered with empty soda bottles, bags of chips, and Tootsie Pops.

"How about the one from the university website? I can download it and make hundreds of copies," she suggested, talking around a Tootsie Pop currently dissolving in her cheek.

"No. A posed portrait is little help when trying to locate a missing person, especially with the people in the streets. She wouldn't look like that to them. I need a natural shot. Full body." He looked around, then walked over to the mantle and grabbed a framed photo of her laughing, standing next to her horse.

"Scan this one in for a body shot. Remove the horse. We wouldn't want the perverts under the bridge to fall in love with the animal. Make me a few hundred copies to start."

"Sure thing." Kelly hummed as she started her assignment. Maybe she'd postpone Vegas until this gig was over. Something inside her thrummed with the excitement of the hunt. It was like one of her computer generated games, only better. Realer.

As the printer shot out the altered photo, Kelly studied the original. Something pulled at her. The woman and horse looked familiar somehow. She'd seen the Professor, of course. They always had news on in the common room at juvie. Lots of the kids liked to watch to see if pictures of them or their relatives or their crimes popped up. Jette Morningstar was known to everyone. She didn't know the professor had a horse, though. And this one was big and black and beautiful. Something tickled her active brain, but before she could take another look at the thought, the printer needed more paper, and she set about doing her job.

Marc took the pictures and stared at them. Jette, his lover, his life, duplicated over and over. It was all so surreal. Maybe he was in a coma. Maybe this was just a nightmare.

"Marc." Luke came up beside him. "You're looking really pale. Can you sit down for a minute? Will you let me listen to your lungs?"

Marc looked over at Luke's compassionate face. Not a nightmare. Real.

"And do what? I'm not going to crawl into bed for a nap."

"No. I understand that. But I'd like to get you on antibiotics right away before your tortured immune system breaks down. You know what Dr. Schmelzer said about pneumonia."

"Go away, Doctor."

"You'll do Jette no good if you collapse in the street."

"Fine. Okay. Just don't give me anything that will make me slow and stupid." Marc snatched the pills from Luke's open hand, popped them in his mouth, grabbed a bottle of water and stalked out of the room. "Goddamn drug pusher. I'm going to take a shower and wake up."

He went into the bedroom, showered, changed, then took a moment to reconnect his circuits. He felt like he was coming unwired. Looking at the bed, the bed they shared, the bed they would be in if she was here, he felt the dread wash through him again. He wanted her in his arms so badly, his body ached. Going slowly over to her dresser, he pushed through her girl things. He could smell her. Closing his eyes, he leaned on it for a moment.

"Hang on, hang on," he said out loud and to his ears it sounded like a prayer. "I'm looking for you. I'll find you. I swear it."

Two months ago when he occasionally came into this room, he only saw furniture, only felt space. Now he saw her, felt her. How did he get to the point where he needed her to breathe? Opening his eyes, he pushed away the exhaustion, the fear. He stared at her things until his eyes burned, then turned to engage his city in the hunt.

# Chapter 27

Marc looked around him, exhausted and exhilarated at the same time. They'd accomplished a great deal in the hours since he'd left his useless vigil on the side of the river. The team moved around the room, arranging the boards, setting up files, making calls. Tommy had carried several couches and a dozen lounge chairs into the room in an over-the-top frenzy of furniture procurement. When his team needed to nap or shut down for awhile, there were plenty of soft places to land. Hilda prepared all the guest rooms for those who wanted a quiet place to rest. A table was set up with food and a huge coffee pot. From the number of mugs sitting around the room, the caffeine was flowing freely.

Marc spent a lot of his time keeping in touch with the simultaneous investigations and was pretty certain he knew everything currently collected on the case. Sweeney and her unit were searching for the kidnappers who got away using the descriptions and sketches generated by Hilda and Jonathan. With the 227 as a clue, she was pursuing several avenues, including license plates, addresses and Internet sites. They were contacting uniform vendors and would be canvassing the second hand shops and costume outlets to find out how the kidnappers outfitted themselves. Except for the fact they were looking in the wrong place for Jette, Marc was satisfied with the woman's work and very grateful that she seemed willing to share everything.

Eunice volunteered to stay with the search and recovery team while working to get as much background on the two dead kidnappers as possible. She had several sources to contact about the fake badges and would help with the uniform search.

Marc looked over at Kelly who was busy with her foray into who occupied all the apartments 227 in the buildings around Manhattan. Lyd was doing the same for private homes with addresses in all the combinations of 227. The city had a lot of streets using numbers and they were producing page after page of spread sheets. It seemed the two of them were fueled somehow by their contact with the keyboards. They looked energized even after hours of tedious work.

Because of the late hour, no other official reports were being generated and no more witnesses were being interviewed. The tip line was being monitored by Kim, who had a former classmate on the phones and email lines, but nothing of importance had materialized.

Claude located several excellent maps of the city and they posted them along one mirrored wall. Marc was planning to go out soon and begin his canvas. They'd keep track of all his movements on them.

Just after midnight, Marc called a team meeting. They'd been studying all the known aspects of the case and were now ready to address the questions and establish their direction for the short term. He began by giving them updates from Sweeney and Eunice. Nothing yet but a lot of names, and those would be fed to Kelly and Lyd soon for cross checking.

"My job will be to flush the streets. The real money won't be here until noon but I'll be going out soon to start spreading the word among the night crawlers. I'll need all of you to lead other areas of investigation. Let's begin with the questions so we can establish our direction and priorities," suggested Marc.

"Why Jette?" Tagg slapped his pen against the notepad on the table in front of him. "This was a specific kidnapping. Nothing random about it."

"There could be several reasons," mused Raj. "Three that come immediately to mind are ransom, something related to one of the cases she worked on over the years, or something that Marc has or is running."

Marc agreed with both of them, but his style was to just listen when his team was brainstorming. Not contribute until they dried up. He already knew and suspected what *he* knew and suspected. To share that with his team gained him no new insight. The only source of new viewpoints in the room was the collective mind of his team, so he remained silent. Listening. Gathering. Encouraging. Collecting thoughts and opinions from the combined intuition and experience of his team was his method of leadership. In addition, if he shared his theories and suspicions first, it could put the team on a mission that may not be the highest priority. He could inadvertently set them off in the wrong direction before they considered all the options. So it was facilitation first, then the formulation of conclusions.

He simply nodded as Kim took the role of scribe and wrote down everyone's contributions on one of the several white boards placed around the long table.

The team studied the list.

"Others?" asked Marc.

"I know this is out there, but perhaps some kind of conspiracy? Something unrelated to any of those things. She's become part of something we haven't defined up to this point," suggested Teresa.

"Explain," encouraged Marc. She was headed down the alley he took several hours before, but wanted to hear it from another perspective.

"I know we have to consider the personal angle, and some of us will continue to do that, but it might be a waste of our time and effort. This is just intuition talking, but I think there might be a relationship between what happened at the university and the kidnapping," continued Teresa. "It seems too coincidental they happened within days of each other."

"Elaborate." He looked around to get the rest of the team engaged. "Let's take that track to the end."

"It was her building at the university that was the initial target of the disturbance," said Tagg.

"And her classroom was one of the few that was blasted before Flowers took his position on the roof," added Rachael.

"Like he was baiting her?" asked Dina. "But how could he have anticipated her actions?"

"He certainly wasn't expecting her to come after him. He wasn't even looking over his shoulder," commented Rachael.

"No, but he placed himself in a position near her building," added Tagg.

"He didn't go into her classroom," considered Teresa. "Shoot her, kill her. He could have. Like with the kidnapping, he didn't want her dead."

"What about the Roger Flowers murder? That would be another link," said Kim.

"It would add to the conspiracy theory," agreed Teresa.

"Yeah, the one guy who could possibly shed some light is dead," added Raj.

"Start another line for Flowers," Marc instructed Kim. "We'll come back to him. Anything more on the conspiracy theory?"

"We don't really know enough yet, but I think it should be high on the list," speculated Tagg.

"Agreed," said Raj, and the rest of the team nodded.

"And is there consensus that the ransom angle should receive a lower priority?" asked Marc.

"On the practical side, there aren't that many people who know you're loaded. Hell, we didn't even realize the extent of it until the other night." Dina nodded at his ripped jeans and faded sweatshirt. "You hide it well."

"True enough. Everything, including this place, is operated by a blind trust and even the media has never picked up on it," agreed Marc.

"Jette has her own assets. Luke, would they be enough to bring out the hounds?" asked Tagg.

"Her mother came from a very wealthy family but the old money is nearly gone. On the other hand, that only means billions down to millions. Jette's trust is invested mostly in the Morningstar Foundation. It's got significant cash reserves, but that doesn't seem a likely target for ransom," frowned Luke. "She does very well from the sale of her books, of course. Then there's the ranch and her horses." He shrugged. "I guess there'd be plenty of hounds who'd sniff at that kind of money. But why now? Why here?"

"We'll know soon enough if there's a ransom demand," observed Raj.

"Another thing, Marc," said Tagg. "Anyone could have snatched her from the streets in the last few weeks. Discreetly and quietly. This was in-your-face. It feels more like retribution. Or challenge. Certainly something more personal than a snatch for cash."

"Let's shift our focus to the most likely scenario and put kidnapping for ransom at the bottom of our list. Agreed?" asked Marc and got unanimous assent.

"That leaves Marc's cases, her cases, or the unknown factor. The conspiracy," said Kim, moving ransom to the bottom of the board.

"You've taken down some really sick bastards," said Dina.

"And some who are very connected," added Raj.

"Okay," nodded Marc. "Rachael and Dina you've been with me the longest. Pull all my cases. You'll remember a lot of them. Find out where everyone I've had a hand in bringing down is residing at the moment. Work with Lyd. She can do a lot of your cross checking. I'll put Eunice on it when she gets back here. She has a lot of friends sitting on the archives."

It was a daunting task and one that could take weeks to do thoroughly. But it had to be started and the women nodded in agreement. They might get lucky.

"Jette's involvement in crime is a step removed from hands-on police work, but her cases were all very high profile," said Tagg.

"And her name is linked to them by the books she's published," added Teresa.

"True, but the good news is that every case she profiled ended with a conviction and as far as I know, they're all still in jail or have since died," observed Marc.

"But there are friends and family of the convicted or maybe a wacked-out fan club of one of the accused," said Tagg.

"Sommer, take that line and tug it. Her books are in the library for reference," ordered Marc.

"I'll use my own." Kim wrote on her pad. "I've read them and have written notes in the margins."

"Speaking of a fan club, what about a cracked fan of Jette herself? Maybe someone who's attracted to her because of her celebrity status. She's been incredibly visible this last week. Or maybe someone's just attracted to her. A sicko might want her as some kind of trophy," suggested Dina.

"Yeah," said Rachael taking up that line. "The coincidence of the university shooting and the kidnapping may be one of timing. Someone saw her on TV and wanted her in his collection."

Marc pressed his fingers to his burning eyes, fighting not only the fatigue but the growing sense of how dense and how huge this investigation could get. A trophy? Holy hell. He felt time pressing at him and had to push back or go mad.

"What's your gut telling you, Marc?" Tag voiced the question on all of their minds.

"I don't like coincidences," mused Marc thoughtfully, staring at the posted notes. "And I think a snatch like this is more than impulse. My gut says everything that's happened in the last week has been orchestrated. And by one hand. The university shooting, Flower's murder, the kidnapping."

"Let's go back to Flowers then," suggested Dina. "Have you ever crossed paths with him?"

"Or any of his family or associates?" asked Rachael.

"No. Never. I looked into that pretty thoroughly after the shooting. I went back three generations and questioned some of his neighbors."

They all looked at him intensely. He just shrugged.

"He took a shot at her classroom. I wanted to be sure. But I could have missed something."

"Had she ever met Flowers? Maybe he'd been stalking her or something."

"I asked her the same question," commented Marc. "She said no. And she's good with faces. He didn't have any of her books in his apartment."

"You searched his apartment, too?" asked Kim.

"Like I said, he took a shot at her."

"Open up your notes on it, Marc and we can add it to the mix," said Rachael.

"The person who shot Flowers is still out there," said Kim.

"So you believe Flowers had an accomplice, or that he's part of something organized and they shot him before he could say anything incriminating?" asked Luke, fascinated with the entire process, sick with concern, but more hopeful than he'd been in hours.

"I think it was someone who wanted what Flowers knew to die with him." Marc looked at his team. "He did talk a little on the roof."

"Yeah, I saw that in the video. Could be a motive for the kidnapping. What did Green make of it?" asked Tagg.

"Green didn't ask about it."

"Ah ha." Tagg knew Marc would have slapped any one of them seven ways to Tuesday if they hadn't asked. "So what did Jette tell you he said when *you* asked her about it?"

"Some very strange shit. Maybe we can find a context for it now, something that will shake some sense into it. He said she ruined his place in history. That he was the anointed one. He said the Empress had given him a final test."

"What was Jette's preliminary impression?" asked Luke, sure she had one.

"She believed he was both paranoid and delusional. She wasn't sure if this Empress was a real person, perhaps someone in his life that he elevated to royalty, or was part of his delusional world. After he was murdered, she speculated that someone might have pushed him over the edge. Perhaps this Empress discovered his fragile mental state and played him, then wanted him to be silenced. He wasn't under a doctor's care and there were no prescribed drugs in his system or his apartment."

"So Jette thought he might be part of a bigger picture, too," said Luke.

"Yes. She wanted to have another meeting with him."

"Interesting. Would she have gotten access?" asked Dina.

"The commissioner already mentioned it at a party we attended last week."

"But someone prevented that from happening," frowned Raj.

"Anyone watching the video would have seen them talking. Maybe someone wanted to find out what he said to her," said Teresa.

"Yeah. Anyone, other than Green it seems, would have been curious," agreed Tagg.

"They could have thought he said something important. That Jette knew something," thought Kim.

They all nodded. It felt right.

"At least five people took her. Maybe more. That's a lot of players," observed Tagg.

"What would be their motive for shooting up the school, then kidnapping a woman they thought knew something long after she had an opportunity to share the information? And in such a flamboyant fashion?" asked Dina.

"That's something we need to find out," said Marc, convinced that's what happened.

"Did Flowers say anything else?" asked Tagg.

"Yes. One more thing that seemed significant. To him anyway. He wanted to know if she was going to try to turn him."

"Turn him? Like turn him in?" asked Kim.

"Maybe."

Kim wrote *anointed one, last test, Empress* and *turn him* on the board.

"Alright, another question." Rachael was ready to move into another area. "How did the perps know where Jette lived? It's easy enough to get in the building, really. But they came right to The Edgewood. Didn't you say this place is owned by a trust?"

"Yes and we use a post office box for all our correspondence." Marc moved on with his team.

"It wouldn't be impossible to uncover this address electronically, but it certainly wouldn't be on anything with easy access," speculated Rachael.

"So maybe they know her personally. Or professionally?" asked Raj.

"Or they know you personally and the fact that she's living here with you. She hasn't been here long, but it's not a secret," Kim pointed out.

"It's still a relatively small and select group of friends and associates. And until a few weeks ago I didn't consider this home. It was just a place I'd come to if it was closer than my apartment in the Village when I needed a bed or a beer. I've always used the Village address on all my legal documents and employment records," responded Marc.

"Jette probably emailed this address to close friends and associates. People she trusted. Hacking email isn't that difficult," shrugged Tagg.

"Someone could have heard her give a cab driver the address," offered Kim, sure she saw that on an episode of *Law and Order*.

"They could have followed her," thought Teresa.

"How'd they know which apartment?" asked Raj.

"They wouldn't have needed to know which apartment. Jonathon thought they were police officers and gave them the penthouse floor," responded Kim.

"True."

"Sommer, you coordinate the lists," assigned Marc. "All these things are possible. Make a note to get Hilda to start her own list. I know her book club meets here and Jette was to speak to them in a few weeks."

"Not too likely that eleven elderly book buffs are going to mastermind a kidnapping," said Tagg.

"No. But we need to follow that line. Maybe one of them gave birth to an international terrorist. And who knows how many people each one of them told."

Kim wrote the assignment on her pad. "I imagine we can assume everyone in the building knew. I'll call the dean at the university to find out how many people there have access to her address."

"Good. Luke, give us a list of any family members or Arizona contacts who may have known. I'll contact her agent. Anything else?" asked Marc.

"Yes. Something pretty significant, I think," said Luke, caught up in the process. "Why was it so important to have her alive? I'm sorry Marc, but there has to be a reason she was taken and not killed right there in the kitchen."

There was silence. No one had an answer.

"I don't know. I only know I'm glad they want her alive. Hopefully alive and well," said Marc through the constriction in his chest. Rubbing it distractedly, he hoped it was emotion, not fluid building up in his lungs. It was getting difficult for him to take a deep breath. "Maybe I'll get a ransom call, although at this point it's unlikely, then we'll know she's alive because she's a bargaining chip. Otherwise, we can only assume she has something or knows something they need or want."

"Then she'll know just how to play it until you find her." Luke held Marc's green eyed glare with his own intense stare. "She knows the criminal mind. She understands abnormal behavior. Trust her to keep whomever has her off balance."

Marc nodded, noting the pain deep in his chest did back off a bit. Anxiety then, he thought. When Luke looked at the hand still rubbing his chest, he quickly dropped it to his side and pushed on before the doctor got out his instruments, shots, and pills.

Eunice came in just as an undeterred Luke got to his feet and his intent to examine Marc got shoved into the back seat. All eyes shot to her as she quickly put up her hand.

"Nothing," she said quickly. "The boats are still out so nothing to report is really good news right now. I hope you know that."

When they all nodded, she held up the folders in her other hand, then gave them to Marc. "Sweeney asked me to bring these to you. She sent her team home to catch a few hours down time, but will remain with the rescue boats and call if there's anything to report. It's information on the corpses. Very superficial background checks at this point. A student and a bouncer. The bouncer has a short rap sheet, mostly assault. The student is criminally clean so far, but was expelled twice from an exclusive private school up north. She was very much into the martial arts and was booted for using fellow classmates as practice dummies. It may indicate some criminal inclinations frosted with really good lawyers. We'll need to cross check them against any of your cases and contacts."

Marc scanned the case files of the kidnappers, handing the preliminary autopsy sheets to Luke, who'd worked his way to his side, determined to do a quick check on Marc's lungs at the first opportunity.

"Short form," Marc requested.

Luke read the reports. "Both died of massive injuries. No obvious drugs in their systems, although a more complete toxicology report will follow. Number one broke her neck, but also sustained internal damage. Ruptured colon, shattered sinus cavities, crushed facial bones, dead on impact. The other had a torn cerebellum and extensive brain stem damage. The brain shifted in the skull due to the abrupt deceleration. He survived the fall. For a few minutes. Wouldn't have been able to move. Sorry bastard. There was some water in his lungs. There's more, Marc, but nothing that should alarm you."

"You are joking. Every fucking thing in that report alarms me," snapped Marc.

"Marc, remember what I told you. These two were panicked and flailing when they went in the water. Jette would have positioned herself to go in smoothly. A diver displaces the water. In other words, the water gets out of the way. If that doesn't happen, the liquid becomes solid. These two ran into the solid surface, Jette would have cut into the water differently."

"Cliff divers go from 20 to 30 meters," added Kim. "Several people have even survived a fall or jump from the Golden Gate Bridge and that's 220 feet high or about 66 meters. This was only around 28 meters." She shrugged like it was all just a piece of cake.

Marc glanced at her. "Been at the Internet, Sommer?"

"Yeah, and from what Dr. Grainger…"

"Luke," Luke said automatically.

"From what Luke has been telling us, I'm sure she came out of the East River alive. Eunice is right. Finding nothing is good news. They haven't found her because she isn't there." Kim shrugged again, absolutely convinced and wanting to say what was on her mind. "Now we just have to find out who snatched her when she surfaced. I mean that must have been a real bummer for her. She fights, runs, gets away, has to stop because she doesn't want them to hurt the hostage. Leaves a clue. Then they shoot the hostage anyway. So she pulls away from her kidnappers and executes an incredible dive into the water, and who's to say she didn't do that deliberately by the way, did you think of that?" She stopped for a shallow breath and went on. "And then when she survives all that and gets to shore...these...these miserable creeps snatch her again. She must have just about popped a gasket. I mean, really."

"Miserable creeps?" asked Marc after staring her into silence. "They're fucking cowards."

"Yes sir." She nodded soundly. If she swore, that's what she'd say alright.

"So you think she might have gone into the water deliberately?" Marc gave her version some thought.

"Yes, I do. It was either that or go with a couple of armed kidnappers who'd just shot a hostage in cold blood. I think she knew exactly what she was doing. I think she calculated the risk and took the dive. Smooth, clean, professional. And I think she came out of it in good shape," nodded Kim emphatically.

Marc looked over at Luke who nodded.

"And since we can assume that she's not caught in traffic somewhere in Queens, or that she decided to just keep swimming to Canada, she had to have come out somewhere," concluded Marc.

"Yes."

"Then I'll take on the task of finding that location. Someone saw it. I just have to find the eyes," said Marc.

"It's a long shot, Marc." Dina glanced over at the maps pinned to the board.

"Not so much when you know nearly all the mouths attached to the faces of all the eyes in the areas around the river." Tagg smiled grimly. It felt good. "And we all know that our man Marc here does."

"True. Detective Lexington is the only cop on the entire force who could pull this off," agreed Kim with confidence.

"My misspent youth just keeps paying off. Now on to the most tangible piece of information." Marc deliberately moved away from Luke. "227."

"She obviously overheard something and it has to do with those numbers and wanted to leave us a clue," sighed Dina.

"Man, she thinks fast," admired Eunice.

"Yes, she'd have a clear head through all of this," agreed Kim.

"227, 272, 722." Tagg looked at Marc. "There's too many combinations. Hundreds, probably thousands, if we also consider two digit possibilities."

"Let's take them in order then. I'm thinking there was a reason she gave them to us like that," said Marc. "They could be a partial so we can add to them but I don't think she'd confuse things with three digits if there were only two."

"They could be in other combinations, though. An apartment number combined with a street or avenue," speculated Eunice.

"Lyd and the kid are collecting names at addresses and street numbers. I'll have them start on phone numbers. Cross match them with names we get from the files. Tagg, you stay with the license plates since you'll need clearance to do that," Marc suggested.

Tagg slapped a file he held. "Sweeney got the names and the makes and models of all cars with 227 in its various combinations on its plates. There are 60 possibles coinciding with the type of van the eyewitnesses described."

"I'll help you run them down," offered Dina. "You know Marc, we could use some of the troops down at the station."

"No. Too public. People coming in and out. Eyes and spies. People connected to the media. And we still don't know how the Flowers information got leaked. I don't want any of our leads in tomorrow's headline."

"Plus staying away means no one will see your movements. Our movements," speculated Tagg.

"Exactly," nodded Marc. "I think it's important that whomever has her thinks they've won this round. Luke is here. I've left the scene. They might believe we've given up, started the grieving."

Marc didn't even want to think about the possibility of that actually happening. He felt his weapon on his hip. It wasn't just her life they were trying to save. He really thought at this point it was his life too. One fast bullet to the head would end the agony for him if she was found dead after all.

"Anything else?" he asked, shaking the awful ache by taking the next step.

No one had anything to add, so notebooks flipped shut and the team prepared to scatter.

Just then, Hilda, limping slightly, came in with a platter of huge meatloaf sandwiches and Tommy followed balancing plates, napkins, flatware and bowls of potato salad, chips, fruit, and deli pickles. The entire team turned to them like sunflowers to sunshine.

"Detective, you need to eat something." Hilda set the platter down on the long table.

Marc frowned at her. "Why aren't you in your room?"

"I was slaving over these sandwiches. Now don't be ungrateful. If you don't eat, you won't have the energy to find Dr. Morningstar."

"Consider it doctor's orders." Luke looked directly into Marc's drawn face. "I have this feeling that if you fall, so will she."

Marc stared at him for a few seconds, then deliberately walked over and picked up a sandwich. It smelled like heaven and his mouth immediately began to water of its own accord. Hilda knew meatloaf and deli pickles were among his favorites. Comfort food, Jette called it. Saying nothing, he snatched the mustard, squeezed on enough to make Hilda cringe, then stuffed as much as he could into his mouth. Hilda pulled a cold can of Coke out of her apron and handed it to him.

"You'll need this to get that unearthly mouthful down your throat," she scolded.

Again, Marc just stared for a few moments, then he grabbed the can, opened it and gulped it down. The rest of his team fell on the food and soon the room was filled with the sounds of grateful eaters. Hilda replenished the platter and Claude brought in gallons of coffee, iced tea, and soda as well as plates of homemade cookies.

Fueled up and feeling better, Marc studied the map.

"I'm going out on my own for awhile. I have to start spreading the word, throwing around the green." He looked over at Hilda. "Where's the cabbage?"

"There was nearly five thousand in the household account and another three thousand in the contingency fund. Will that be enough to start?" Hilda handed him a thick brick of bills.

"Yeah, it won't take much to prime the pipeline. I'll follow through with the major flow tomorrow afternoon." He looked at his watch. "I mean later today."

He took the cash from Hilda, quite certain it contained everything she had in her own personal emergency stash. He'd settle things with her later.

"Detective, should you be going out alone with that kind of money?" asked Kim.

"No one will talk to me unless I'm alone."

"Be careful out there," cautioned Tagg simply, then turned them all back to their assigned tasks as Marc strode out of the apartment.

Standing solitary on the elevator, Marc looked down at the floor where he'd made love to Jette only a few nights before. It seemed like a lifetime ago.

"Jette," he whispered. He wanted to hear her name. Hear it from his lips. "Jette."

It nearly broke him. Leaning heavily against the wall of the elevator, he could feel desperation welling up in his chest and throat, but on the ride down to street level, he fought and won. When the doors to the lobby slid open, he rolled his shoulders and stepped out the determined, confident, focused cop. He left the despair in the elevator with the memories of the sweetness and strength of his lover.

# Chapter 28

Returning to the penthouse at sunrise, Marc was exhausted, but had lost that floating feeling of disconnection. His city recharged his confidence. Hundreds of familiar faces welcomed the cash and began the wave. By noon the word would have legs and the whispers would ripple throughout the streets. When he took some serious jack out that afternoon and evening, he'd get something back. Something he could use. Sifting through all the shaft would take time, but he had a nose for bullshit and would only pay for good intelligence.

The sun was just coming up, casting shadows over the converted ballroom. His team was there. All of them. Teresa and Eunice were in the soft leather arm chairs, their feet up on ottomans, catching a nap. Kim was at a computer with her hair wrapped in a towel so she must have showered. The kid was gone, either to knock off for awhile in one of the guest rooms or taken back to the shelter Marc had arranged for her.

Lyd was mumbling to a computer in the corner, trading one addiction for another. There were about a dozen half filled coffee mugs littering her table and huge empty bags of chocolate stars.

Raj and Dina were quietly posting information on the boards for the morning briefing. Luke had finally fallen asleep on a couch and Rachael's head rested on her folded arms as she slept at her table.

Tagg looked up and nodded. He was on a phone, and from what Marc could hear, he was talking with a warden in a Texas prison.

Marc stared at an empty chair near the fireplace. Did he dare sit down? When he was walking the streets, he felt okay. Certainly better off doing something, having a plan. Now he was afraid if he sat down, nothing in his system would operate effectively enough for him to get back up.

The coffee and pastries looked fresh and he thought of refueling, but for the first time in his life, he rejected the thought of coffee and the caffeine he was sure he was now immune to. His stomach felt raw and ached terribly. No more coffee, then. Fine, if he couldn't take the caffeine, he'd take a hit of oxygen. Stretching, he took a deep breath and frowned. The deep inhalation didn't contribute the usual shot of extra oxygen to his system and with it more energy. He tried again. Nothing. He could feel his chest expand, but no air seemed to come in. Like he was climbing in high altitude.

Then he felt his chest tighten up. Recognizing trouble, he frowned. During some of the rumbles in his past, he'd taken a direct hit in the solar plexus. Getting the wind knocked out of a diaphragm and not being able to gasp wasn't terribly painful, but horribly unpleasant. This was worse. It was both unpleasant and painful. Could his lungs be filling? Was pneumonia going to be a problem? Damn it. He didn't have time to get sick.

He'd swallowed the antibiotics Luke nagged him to take, hadn't he? Maybe that was what was eating away at his stomach lining. Damn drugs. He glared over at Luke. Unreasonable resentment licked at him, and he pushed it back. Knowing it was unreasonable meant he still had a few working brain cells.

He took several shallow breaths. Something was happening in there. Something that was squeezing the air out of his lungs, making the urge to cough overpowering. He glanced at Luke again. Should he consult with him? Acknowledge his difficulty? It wasn't like anyone could restrict him even if his weak lung was putting in for retirement. He was in his own place. Who was going to stop him from what he wanted to do. Needed to do?

Then, like a declaration of who was boss, a cough forced its way through his will. Fine. Why fight it. Maybe he'd have another one. He coughed again. A little quiet exhalation to clear the horrible constriction in his chest. Damn. The next cough was louder. Longer.

Luke's eyes shot open, alert and focused. Frowning, he stared at Marc, who turned immediately and grabbed a report off Rachael's table, startling her and waking her up. He hoped her moan and expletive would divert Luke's attention.

It didn't.

As Marc paged through a report he couldn't read, his eyes, already burning from fatigue, began to water with the effort to suppress the next cough.

"Marc." Luke spoke softly. "You may as well let it out. There's a good reason your body wants you to cough."

Marc did let it out, and because it had been building and had been denied too long, it was long and fierce. And it led to another. Then another until Marc could no longer catch his breath. Luke was out of his chair and beside him in an instant.

Kim, Raj, Teresa, and Tagg hurried over as well. Tagg clapped a gasping Marc on the back.

"That won't help at all, Dr. Freeman," said Luke. "Go into the den and bring me a tall glass of brandy. We need to relax his diaphragm. Kim, go get my bag out of the guest room. Rachael, ask Hilda to brew up some of Jette's healing herbal tea. The special black stuff. I'm sure she'll have it among her stash. Have her put a tablespoon of honey in it."

Everyone scattered as Marc glared at Luke.

"My...my...team...not...yours," he managed to rasp before another fit of coughing made it impossible to talk.

"It's a bitch not being able to bark at me, isn't it? Damn it Marc. Don't try to fight it. Sit down."

Luke led him to a chair and gave him a little shove. Marc fell into the soft cushions. It felt like the warm embrace of a benevolent, bosomy grandmother.

Marc resisted the wonderful feeling of being off his feet and tried to continue his protest, but could only growl and snap. And cough. Now everyone was awake, and that made Marc's mood even blacker.

Tagg came in with the brandy and at Luke's nod handed it to Marc.

"Drink that. All of it. You need to loosen up."

Desperate for air and some kind of relief, Marc snatched the glass and between coughs, tossed it back in three huge swallows. It burned all the way down his aching throat and sizzled in his tortured stomach. But it did its work on the rest of his system. Instantly, he could feel his body relax, and the tight vise on his chest eased back a little.

Luke grabbed the bag from Kim and removed his stethoscope, thermometer, and a small inhaler. Marc might not have been able to catch a breath, but when Luke came at him with the thermometer, he batted it out of his hand. It went sailing across the room and landed at the feet of Hilda who was just entering the room with a tray. She bent over, picked it up and without saying a word handed it back to Luke.

"This goes in your ear, you idiot. Do that one more time and it's going up your ass. In your shape, Tagg can hold you down. Hell, in your shape, Lyd can hold you down. Now stop fighting me on this. We need you. Jette needs you."

That worked. Still frowning and coughing, Marc stopped pushing at Luke, then nodded. Luke put the inhaler to Marc's mouth and had him take the medicine directly into his lungs with a few short blasts. Then he read Marc's temperature, and opened his shirt to listen to the lungs. After a brief exam, Luke let out a breath.

"Amazing. You have the constitution of an ox."

"And the disposition of one, too," muttered Tagg.

"Agreed. Marc, you have a slight temperature and your lung has some fluid in it. It will lead to pneumonia. When that happens, you'll be in some serious trouble. Frankly, I think anyone else would be down already. I want you to keep coughing. Don't suppress it. Keep this inhaler with you. I'm going increase your antibiotics and you'll drink the tea that Jette swears by."

"I'd rather have the thermometer up the ass," wheezed Marc.

"Can't blame you on that one. But she's a shaman and she grows it for healing. You'll feel better and it'll be by Jette's hand."

They stared at each other for a moment. The two men in the world closest to Jette. As the rest of the team stood by, they watched Marc's face lose its irritation and saw something like grief take its place. It faded quickly and was replaced with determination. Marc reached out and Hilda handed him a mug with the steaming brew. Without a word and without a grimace, he sipped at the tea between shallow coughs. It soothed him. On several levels.

"Marc. This was a warning shot."

"I got that." His coughs were reduced to annoying little hacks. Now that his lung was letting go, he could feel the healing wounds on his chest and side throb. He felt like one big, bad bruise.

"And speaking of shots." Luke reached back into his bag for a hypodermic and a small bottle of liquid.

"What's that?" growled Marc.

"I'm going to send Claude out for the oral version, but in the meantime, I'm giving you two mega doses of antibiotics and a mild sedative."

"Oh no. No." Marc coughed, holding his chest this time. "I'll take the fucking medicine, but the brandy was enough to relax me. No sedative."

Luke stared at him for a heartbeat, then gave Marc the victory. He hadn't really expected to get the sedative into him anyway. "Okay, but I want you to take this."

"What is it?" The petulance in his voice would have been amusing had the situation not been so dire.

"Vicodin. For the pain."

"I'm fine. Go away."

"Don't even try to hide the pain, Detective," shouted Luke glaring at Marc. "I can see it. Now you'll take everything I prescribe. Everything! I promise I'll step back on the sedatives, even though they'd help you, you stubborn son-of-a-bitch. Nothing I give you will slow you down. Only help you stay on your feet. I'm the doctor here. I won't tell you how to run the investigation, but you, by God, will not tell me how to treat a man on the verge of some very serious medical trouble."

Everyone in the room stopped and gaped at Luke. He was such an even-tempered man, the blow up was unexpected. And pretty impressive. Then all eyes flew back to Marc, waiting for the answering explosion. He coughed, stared up at Luke, then calmly took the small pills and swallowed them with the rest of the tea.

"Not a bad fit, all in all." Marc stared into Luke's snapping blue eyes. "But around here, that wouldn't get you out of amateur status."

"It wasn't my best effort," said Luke, regaining his equilibrium.

Marc's eyes swept the room and suddenly everyone else got very busy. Except Hilda. Standing by with a pot containing more of the honey laden tea, she moved right through Marc's intense glare and poured more of the dark liquid into his mug.

"When you find Dr. Morningstar, she'll be glad to hear you two are playing so well together. I'll get breakfast started for the rest of your team."

With that, she set the pot down and walked out of the room.

Luke hovered for a few more minutes, then went over to a table to write a prescription. Hoping he wouldn't need it, he also ordered some oxygen. Marc was walking a fine line and so far he'd been able to keep his balance, but eventually pure strength of will wouldn't be enough against pneumonia.

Marc put his head back for a minute and concentrated on taking air into his lungs. The boulder that had been resting solidly on his chest was beginning to dissolve. The pain was easing as well. When he felt he could speak with reasonable volume, he forced himself to unfold out of the chair, stand, steady himself, and assemble his team.

No one had anything of importance to share. Lists were being formulated and Kelly would be in shortly to begin to cross reference them to see if there were any links. Soon after breakfast, the room emptied as the team reluctantly put the Morningstar investigation on hold to attend to their other cases.

"Hopefully, the chief will get us officially assigned soon." Tagg was the last to leave. "Are you sure you don't want me to request vacation time?"

"No, you've already given me a great deal to work with. At noon the real money will be here and I'll start pouring it through the streets."

They both turned as Kelly wheeled into the room.

"Geez. Somebody just found out where you live. Be sure to use the back door. There must be a hundred reporters out there. Hey Lyd, whatchya got for me today?"

Lyd looked up.

"Let me check my brain barf," she muttered snatching one of the thousand yellow sticky notes decorating the wall near her computer station. Everything in her life got written down or it dissolved in the fog within seconds. "Lucky you. Finish the run on 22nd and 27th Avenues. Then we got a long list of rascals to cross check."

"Can I bring you a cup?"

"Sure. I'll have a little of what the boy had."

"What boy?"

Lyd nodded at Marc and pointed to a glass on the table next to him.

Kelly sniffed the glass and could smell the brandy. "Oh, no. You're not going down that road. Not Lyd the goddess of software. You have way, way too much to teach me before you burn out."

Lyd just shrugged, thought of something, grabbed her pad of sticky notes and began scribbling.

It was the first time Marc registered that Lyd hadn't had any alcohol since she'd arrived. It would become problematic when the DT's hit. The tremors could get bad. He'd have to talk with Luke about that. He didn't even get turned around when Luke came up beside him, seeing where Marc was staring and noticing the dawning look on his face.

"She isn't a true alcoholic, Marc. More of a binge drinker. I'm going to keep an eye on her, but I've started her on some benzodiazepines. In the long run, maybe she just needs someone to hang on her every word and consider her a guru," observed Luke as they watched Lyd and Kelly discuss a point, with Kelly waving her hands and Lyd nodding her head.

"Detective." Hilda came into the room. "LeeAnn Wojnar and the commissioner are here. I put them into the front parlor."

"Good." Marc looked around the room. The commissioner didn't need to see what they were working on in here. Obviously Hilda knew that.

Lee was standing near the windows when he walked in, the commissioner right beside her. She crossed the room quickly and grasped Marc's hand, staring sadly into his bloodshot eyes.

"God, Marc. I had to come. I don't want to intrude, but can you tell me what's happening?"

"Not much." Marc pulled away from her grip. Her terror wasn't something he wanted to deal with right now.

"How are you doing?" asked Garret, gently leading Lee away and into the room.

"Fine. I'm fine." Marc tried not to let his impatience show.

Garret waited a beat, then asked, "So then the next question is *what* are you doing. You haven't been seen since yesterday. Obviously you haven't spent the time resting. What do you know?"

Marc hesitated.

Garret looked into Marc's eyes and signaled his support. He knew there was an unsanctioned investigation going on behind the scenes, but to ask about it, to acknowledge it could put both their careers in jeopardy.

"Speculate, Marc," pushed Garret, his lips twitching. "I don't need to see it."

Garret had been a detective once. A good one and that was the only reason Marc gave them a few of the bare bones.

Lee closed her eyes against the sudden rush of tears. "You think she's alive? When Garret told me you'd left the scene, I thought you'd given up. I should have known better."

"You saved me a trip to your office. I want to ask you some questions." Marc indicated the chairs and they all sat down.

"Sure."

"The people who kidnapped Jette, who we believe have her now, knew where she lived. It's not a state secret, but it isn't widely known. I need to have the names of anyone you might have told."

"Yes. Yes. Let me think. Judy Naylor, my executive assistant, of course. Our research aides, Sara Thacker and Amber Blaeser. They've delivered things here. Brilliant young women. Lots of friends. They might have said something to any one of them. I'll find out. Jason Torreano, my driver and Sheryl Jones the florist I use. But she's the best in the city and very discreet. There's probably more. I'll make a list, along with contact information."

"Appreciated. You brought Maxine White over a few days after the party."

"Yes."

"Jette told me she made an offer."

Lee actually smiled.

"An understatement, I'd say. It was something I'm sure Maxine never intended to do after just one meeting. She usually plays a closer game than that. The dominant position has always been her preferred play. She exercises her control in the extreme. Sometimes she waits weeks before returning a phone call or sending an acknowledgement. And she never, ever RSVP's. She just shows up when she wants to, or not. No one gets the upper hand with her."

"She'd never met Jette," stated Marc.

"No and it was something to watch. Jette controlled everything, right from the beginning. Maxine walked in, I guess you could say she swept in like an imperial queen, and asked Jette if she'd mind if she smoked. She already had the cigarette out of her purse. Jette said yes, but Maxine was welcome to go up to the roof terrace at any time. She was so gracious, it was like she hadn't denied Maxine anything. I just stood there trying to keep the cartilage in my knees from dissolving, thinking that I could perhaps find work on the West Coast under an assumed name when Maxine banished me from New York. Then she put the tobacco away and demanded coffee, thinking that made her the winner."

"What was the offer? Jette didn't say."

"She didn't?"

"We got...distracted."

"Aha. Well, Maxine cut me right out, which was probably my punishment for not offering the palm of my hand as an ash tray, and offered Jette a staggering three book deal, a personal senior editor to work with, and a marketing campaign that was unprecedented as far as I could see. As a matter of fact, from my years in this crazy business, the whole package was over the top."

"What do you mean, she cut you out."

"I should say, she tried to cut me out. She wanted Jette to sign directly with her. It was like I wasn't even in the room."

"What was Jette's response?"

"Also unprecedented as far as I know. She looked at me and said something like it was a very flattering offer. She brought me right back into the game so smoothly, that Maxine never flinched. She said we'd be happy to look over all of the paperwork once the offer was formalized. She laughed and asked questions, then listened in that way of

167

hers. The most powerful woman in the industry was playing it close, and Jette, just opened it up. Opened her up. And we were discussing details that are never, ever put on the table during a preliminary meeting. Marc, we're talking about millions."

"So anyone in her office would have access to her address?" Marc dismissed the millions and got to the relevant point.

"Yes. Her legal department, their messenger service, probably even their publicity department since Maxine would just assume it was full speed ahead."

"I know her. Do you want me to talk with her, Marc?" asked Garret.

"No. I'll do it." He noticed Lee's shifting body and heard her little gasp.

"I'll try not to fuck up the deal," he said sarcastically

"Oh God, Marc. Just ignore me." Lee waved her hand in self recrimination. "It doesn't matter for heaven's sake. That little gesture of alarm was knee jerk. Go at her if it will help. I really don't care."

"It'll just be a formality. And it's low on my list right now."

"With all of Jette's coverage this week, there was probably a profit in selling her whereabouts," observed Garret. "From the paparazzi outside, I'm assuming your location is now out."

"Yeah, I heard. But the list of who knew before the kidnapping is still relatively short."

"Could someone have followed her here?"

"Yes. We've thought of that."

"Give me something more to do, please," begged Lee.

Marc's instincts were dulled by fatigue, but he felt he could trust her. Jette certainly did. And she could be very helpful in pursuing a potential line of investigation.

"It's possible, although we've all placed it low on the list, that the kidnapping has something to do with the cases Jette's written about or is currently working on."

"I have all her notes and early drafts. I'll make out a complete list of everyone she interviewed. Not all the names are in the books. She visited prisons and morgues and mental hospitals. She talked with a lot of really sick people. Marc, it's going to be a very long list."

"You're an intelligent woman, Lee. Cull it the best you can. Make a priority list. Try to include contact information so we can make inquiries."

"I can help you with that," said Garret to Lee. "I'll stop by your office later today and look at your lists."

Marc nodded. He didn't like going outside his team, but the possibility the kidnapping had anything to do with Jette's books was low anyway. It would free up time and effort that could be better spent on the more relevant lines of investigation.

"Chief Cheskee is really pushing to get this whole investigation moved to Special Projects. I realize you're on medical leave, but as a consultant, how broadly do you think you'll need to define your jurisdiction?" asked Garret.

"All the way, Garret. And we need to keep the FBI out. If they take the case because of the kidnapping angle, it'll bog us down."

"Sweeney is pursuing this as a homicide just to keep that from happening." Garret was firmly in his corner.

"Yeah, I got that and it's appreciated."

"So you want to consider her dead to uncomplicate things?" asked Lee, a little taken aback.

"Pretty much," said Garret. "Well, Lee, I think we should leave and let Marc get some, ah, rest. You start collecting information and I'll work on getting everything moved to Special Projects. That will take some time and some delicate politics."

They both left, knowing rest was not something Marc intended to do. They weren't even at lobby level before Marc was back in the ballroom with his notes.

Soon after, Tommy came in dressed for the streets in unrelieved black leather.

"I'm going up to Harlem, honey," she said. "It's not too likely our sweet Jette is stashed in any crib up there, but I'm going to tap my flow and cast my net."

"Want to wait until the green is delivered so you have some lubricant?"

"Nope. Gonna spread the charm and push the muscle. Take jack in where I'm going, lover, and you get bashed. Plenty of my boys are still back there in the neighborhood who remember the big bad ass kicker with the red high heels."

"Careful. Not everyone up there appreciates the fashion statement."

"Honey, people remember when it's a three inch heel planted up their ass. It redefines pain. And I know when and where to tip toe, never fear. Besides," Tommy stuck out her prodigious chest, testing the stretching capacity of the high grade leather. "There's enough tit here for a truck load of tat."

Marc turned to Kelly when she giggled.

"Don't encourage her."

Marc nearly burst with frustration when Hilda entered the room and interrupted again.

"I'm sorry, Detective Lexington. There's a Mrs. Greta Sorenson downstairs insisting she be given entry. She says she's Dr. Morningstar's grandmother." The look on Hilda's face was concerned and sympathetic. "The poor woman must be frantic with worry."

"Oh, fuck me." Marc's last encounter with Jette's maternal grandmother had been unpleasant and frigid. Greta Sorenson was a wealthy, spoiled, self centered woman who wanted nothing but the best for her granddaughter. Her own narrow high brow definition of best. She had a glacial reaction when she found out Jette took up with him. Her idea of a suitable mate was absolutely everything Marc was not.

He looked at Hilda, poised and perfectly groomed after only a few hours rest. "You'll probably bond like Velcro. I can't talk with her now."

"I think she deserves to be informed of what is happening to her granddaughter," said Hilda tightly.

"Goddamn it! We don't know what's happening. Tell her to…"

Before Marc could blow, Luke stepped in. "I'll go unpack my backbone and talk with her, Marc. What do you want me to tell her?"

"No. No." Marc held his pounding head for a second. "I'll see her. I'll tell her something."

"I'll come with you then. Tell Jonathon to send her up," instructed Luke. "I'm going to go put on some light armor. How about bringing her into the den."

"Perhaps she'd be more comfortable in the front parlor?" suggested Hilda tactfully. She'd heard snoring coming from the den earlier.

"Oh, yeah. That's right. Lyd's taking five on the couch in the den." Luke had given her a light sedative when her hands began to shake more than normal.

"I'll get Mrs. Sorenson settled in then." With one last disapproving look at Marc, Hilda left the room.

"Hilda's a perceptive woman." Luke shook out some pills and handed them to Marc with a bottle of water. "I give her five minutes before Cruella blows any possibility of being on Hilda's Christmas card list."

It was a sign of how distracted he felt that Marc didn't even ask what it was Luke was giving him. He just grabbed the pills and swallowed.

"All of five minutes?"

"She's traveled through two time zones so she'll be a little off her game."

Hilda opened the door to a tall, beautiful, sophisticated woman dressed impeccably in a dusty rose colored suit. Jette's mother's mother. Her thick blonde hair was pulled back and perfectly shaped into a balanced and elegant twist. A skilled plastic surgeon and expensive spa treatments had her looking more like Jette's mother than grandmother. Since Jette had inherited all her coloring from her father, there was little resemblance.

"Hello, I'm Greta Sorenson," said the woman in a soft, cultured voice.

"How do you do? Please come in. The detective and Dr. Grainger will be with you in just a few minutes."

"What a magnificent penthouse. Oh my. Are those Tiffany lamps authentic?" asked Greta, taking in her surroundings, curious about the relationship between the woman who'd opened the door and her granddaughter.

"Yes. Certainly."

"And is that an original Carol Young Feller water color?"

"Everything in here is original." Hilda thought Greta's interest in the accessories was a bit inappropriate under the circumstances but maybe she was still in shock over Jette's disappearance.

"I'm a little confused. Is Jette living here with you?"

Hilda was far too disciplined to allow surprise to register on her face. Obviously Jette and her grandmother weren't very close if she didn't know about Marc. Or rather *all* about Marc.

"I'm the housekeeper, Mrs. Sorenson," she explained, then had to suppress a little wave of resentment when Greta's attitude toward her completely changed. Gone was the sheen of interested civility. It was replaced by an imperious attitude and a dismissive tone.

"Housekeeper? Well finally. I've told Jette a hundred times she needed to get help. It's too bad really good help is so difficult to procure now days. I'm sure she can find a younger woman given more time."

Hilda nearly stumbled at the insult, but busied herself opening the door to the parlor.

"May I offer you some refreshment?" Hilda asked automatically.

"Some tea would be wonderful. I have a dreadful headache."

"I'm sorry." So she was upset about Jette, Hilda thought, compassion coming in for another try.

"Yes. The inferior scotch they serve on the airlines does that to me. I'd bring my own, but those idiots holding things up in the name of security won't allow it through. I usually don't touch blended scotch but I simply needed something for my nerves."

"Of course. Your granddaughter."

"Bridgette?" Jette's given name was Bridgette, but it was shortened to Jette when she was a toddler and the shortened name was a better fit with her raven hair, dusky skin and dark brown eyes. "Oh, I'm sure she's just off on one of her native spirit journeys or some such thing. Her heathen father contaminated her at a very early age and I haven't been able to breed it out of her. I came to convince her to accompany me to Europe. Get out of the spotlight after that horrible incident at the university. She needs to get away from this cesspool of a city."

The compassion Hilda had for Jette's grandmother evaporated. Hilda, born and bred in the cesspool, nearly forgot herself and said something scathing. Better to go and fetch the tea, she thought.

When she returned, she could tell from the slight variation of each sculpture in the room that the woman had picked up every piece to assess its authenticity.

"I can see it didn't take long for that man to move in on Jette's wealth," sniffed Greta more to herself than to an invisible housekeeper. "I had no idea there was so much money in writing books."

"Pardon me?"

Greta certainly wasn't going to repeat herself to a servant. Instead, she took the tea and pulled out a cigarette. "Get me an ashtray."

"I'm sorry, ma'am. Both the doctor and the detective prefer there be no smoking in the apartment."

"That's their choice, now get me an ashtray."

When Hilda didn't move, Greta snatched a small bowl off a side table.

"Never mind. I'll just use this."

"That's a 15th century Ottoman bowl."

"What's your point?"

"I'll get you something."

Marc and Luke entered the room and caught the exchange.

"Five minutes flat," muttered Luke.

"You just have to know how to handle help, or they'll start handling you." Greta snapped her lighter and touched it to the end of her cigarette. "So, where is Bridgette? What have you done with her?"

Luke glanced over at Marc and realized he wasn't going to be able to tackle the task of handling Greta. There was too much fury. So he walked over before there was an explosion. Putting away the annoyance and resentment and pulling out the little bit of consideration he could still feel for Jette's closest relative, he kept his voice calm and sympathetic.

"Greta, I'm sorry. Jette's been kidnapped."

Greta just stared at Luke. There was no shock or horror or any visible reaction.

"Excuse me?" she asked finally.

"The day before yesterday, Jette was taken from here. We've been working around the clock to locate her."

Hilda walked in with a plain glass saucer and placed it near Greta.

"I'm so sorry, Mrs. Sorenson," said Hilda, still trying to relocate the compassion for the woman.

Marc knew he should tell her something. This was Jette's grandmother. Her blood. A woman who, for some reason, she loved.

"We believe it has something to do with the incident at the university. I think she called you when she knew it had been broadcast?"

"She did. Not that I ever watch any of those hideous news stations. I told her how indecorous it was. How unfortunate for her, her reputation, her career. That's why I'm here. To talk her into coming with me to Florence until this all dies away. Bridgette led a discreet life. Albeit one that I would not have chosen for her, but without a lot of this, this sordid media exposure. Since she decided to take up with you, she's been shot at, been involved in murder of the most explosive sort, has created an unseemly exhibition of herself at that college, and now you're telling me she's been kidnapped?"

"Yes."

"Hmm. I think not. Who'd kidnap her? That's just nonsense." She waved her smoldering cigarette. "More likely, she's come to her senses and returned to her ranch, or she's gone off somewhere to do that ridiculous native thing she does. Will you have time to give me a quick exam, Lucas? I want to be sure that cross country trip didn't weaken me too much."

"We're a little busy here at the moment."

"Oh, fine. For heaven's sake! I'm sure she'll be alright. She's been involved in one disgusting spectacle after another since her mother died. This fascination she has with the criminal element is most distressing. Perhaps she's finally snapped out of it and is simply hiding from this Lexington person. I knew she'd regret it the moment she hit this filthy city. I wouldn't be surprised if he's done something to her." She didn't seem to care that Marc was standing in the room. "Inferior choice. I told her so and I can't wait to say it to her again in person. She gets mixed up with an alley cat and she'll come to no good. God! It's that heathen blood in her. It just never stops. I would wash my hands completely of her, but she's my blood, too, and there's always hope."

"You said you were on your way to Italy, Greta?" interjected Luke, when he saw Marc's fury flame up. He'd given up long ago arguing with the woman, or trying to change her perceptions. Taking Jette's lead, he mostly ignored everything she said and kept up the conversation by just moving on.

"Yes. I need to get away. With the burdens I have to bear, it's no wonder I have a heart problem."

"Yeah," Luke mumbled to himself, "it doesn't beat."

"I haven't got time for this," snapped Marc.

"Nor have I. I have a plane to catch in less than four hours," stated Greta.

"You're leaving?" Hilda couldn't help herself. She was appalled that Jette's grandmother would leave the city before Jette was found.

Greta simply glared at Hilda imperiously, revolted that a servant would even enter the conversation much less use that tone of voice. Not responding to her, she slapped the untouched tea on the table then maliciously and deliberately stubbed out her cigarette in the delicate Ottoman bowl instead of the glass saucer.

"Tell Jette to call me when she returns from her little voodoo party with that blasphemous god of her father. And be sure to let me know if you find her body in his freezer." She glared back at Hilda, looking her up and down. "You may see me to the door."

Leading the way, Hilda opened the foyer door. Marc and Luke followed to be sure she left. Without another word or backward glance, Greta swept from the apartment.

For the first time since Marc laid eyes on the woman, Hilda blew her cool and slammed the door. Nearly off its hinges.

"How did that darling girl come from such a creature?" snapped Hilda. "That perfume may be $450 dollars an ounce, you Grace Kelly wanna be, but one need not bathe in it to make a statement."

Turning on her heel, she stalked back to the parlor to air it out.

Marc looked at Luke. Luke looked at Marc. And the two of them exploded with unexpected laughter, a little edge of hysteria making the reaction nearly uncontrollable, until Marc dissolved into a fit of coughing so fierce it had Luke staggering to the closet to pull out the tank of oxygen. After giving Marc enough to calm his lungs, he took a hit himself.

"Jesus Christ, that woman is entertaining," gasped Luke.

Marc sat on the bench in the foyer and put his aching head in his hands. Even though the coughing fit left him weak and he was no closer to finding Jette, he felt better than he had all morning. There was balance somehow in having this moment. Luke was here. Cruella was still an evil bitch. Hilda did have a temper. Hope somehow sprung from that.

# Chapter 29

Sipping a wonderful glass of Ciel du Cheval Merlot, the Empress studied the new pictures coming in. The Knights summoned several Guardians but without Avenger they seemed to lack direction.

Minions were placed all around The Edgewood and with her well timed tip to the press, they were nicely hidden among the chaos. The points for a sighting of the Shield were high enough to keep them planted among the usual shoppers, tourists and now the curious and the media. Of course the Minions thought it was Detective Marcus Lexington, the New York City hot shot cop they wanted. Only she and a few of her trusted Sentinels were privy to the full truth.

What were the Guardians doing in there? If the Dark Knight made a move in her direction, she needed to know about it. The pictures only gave her a superficial look at the movements of Avenger's people. She needed to get into the inner circle and thought about ways to work on that. Opening a file of the true names of her Mercenaries, she thought through a few options. What people revealed about themselves over the years gave her clues and she was able to pinpoint their Middle World identities. It was a pretty interesting list. For the next hour she studied the names, then made her moves.

"Insurance," she muttered to herself. "Just a little insurance. There's no way they'll be able to find their Avatar until I'm ready to reveal the location. And by that time she'll be long gone and the trap will be set. Boom! Points for me."

She reached for the beautiful hand crafted face mask she'd purchased at one of the Sovereignty conventions she attended. She laughed, remembering all the delusional men and women who swarmed around the conference, talking strategy and theories, and building coalitions. Let them attend their lectures and speculate on what the Final Duel would be like. They were lemmings. Pitiful peons trying to gain a bit of glory by pretending to be something they could never achieve. She'd surreptitiously gathered a lot of code names and email addresses from those who had that maniacal look in their eye. The look that indicated they really, really wanted to believe that their sorry lives were as fulfilling, exciting, and richly rewarding as the world of Sovereignty.

Trying on the mask, looking through it at the image reflected in her mirror she felt totally, fully, completely free. Alive. Invincible. It was exhilarating.

For the first time, she was planning on taking a daring journey into the Middle World of Reality as the one true Blue Empress herself. While she drove through the streets, she'd need to remain in her current role, but when she reached her destination she'd emerge as the Empress, her Middle World identity safely hidden behind the traditional mask.

Time to meet with her people in person. Time to come out and take the next step.

# Chapter 30

At noon the money arrived by bonded couriers. There was curiosity in their eyes as Marc opened the cases, but they said nothing. They were used to the eccentricities of the very rich.

"You want us to wait until you count the money, sir?" asked the young uniformed woman.

"No."

Taking the order and scribbling his name on the place the guard indicated, he let Hilda show them to the door as he stared at the cash. He was anxious to get started. Eager to set his plan into motion. Hell, ready for any kind of movement. He'd worked through the maps for the best way to proceed and had a detailed grid already seared into his mind.

Stuffing each of his pockets with folded handfuls of cash and small cell phones for some of his better informants, he considered transportation. Should he take out his Harley, call a cab, or hop the subway? He had an unmarked police cruiser, but even the savvy first graders in this city could spot one a mile off. He knew he was sluggish when the decision seemed to be a fairly big one. Disgusted, he strode out of the room. He'd work out the weighty problem of how he was going to get around the city on his trip down the elevator. Because of the media trucks parked out front, he pulled down his cap, threw on his shades and pushed the button for the parking garage.

The decision was taken out of his hands when he stepped into the deserted concrete structure below the building and Claude was there with the limo.

"Hilda told me you were leaving the apartment," he explained, standing next to the opened back door.

Marc stared at the limo as if it were an alien space craft. How could he have forgotten he had a car and driver? The fact that it wasn't the usual transportation choice for a cop was no excuse.

Marc turned as Hilda came out of the other elevator door. In her hand was one of the cases containing the cash.

"I thought you might want this. You won't have to return every time you need more, ah…jack."

Marc scowled at her, his overtaxed brain processing what she'd said.

"We figured this could be, well, sort of your rolling headquarters, sir," suggested Claude.

"Shit. My batteries must really be drained if the two of you are a step ahead of me," mumbled Marc as he irritably snatched the case and climbed into the back of the cool, comfortable car. His weary body nearly betrayed him with a moan as he settled in.

"This should help your batteries, Detective." Hilda handed him another bag. "You forgot to eat again."

Marc could smell leftover meatloaf and this time his body beat his willpower to the finish line and he did moan.

For Hilda, that was enough gratitude. Slamming the door, she stepped back and moved away as Claude got in and pulled out.

"Where to, Detective?"

Marc gave him the first corner of his grid. Back down to the river area where she was last seen. By a little girl and her bird. His gut did a little rattle when he thought of it. Assuming it was hunger, he opened the bag and devoured its contents.

In the front seat, Claude glanced at the rear view mirror and nodded, satisfied they were doing their best by the detective and his lady. Smoothly, competently, he drove to the water's edge.

Marc spent the afternoon in the streets and when the sun set, he went back over the same ground to pick up the night time population.

Nothing credible came to light. Several informants, street people, pushers, peekers, seekers, and pawns said they saw her in order to increase the grease, but Marc knew a con from a credible scoop. The kind of money he was spreading invited both, and it was up to him to do the sifting.

When he found himself flagging, he'd meet Claude at an assigned location, sit in the back of the car, plow through whatever food he'd grabbed at a local deli. A few times, there was a bottle of water and a couple of pills on the polished shelf under the side window. Because his chest constantly reminded him of the need for a blast of antibiotics to bolster his exhausted immune system, he'd take them.

Periodically, he'd just sit and consider what he'd picked up. It was basically nothing. Yet. But it was early and at least with each passing hour he knew places where she hadn't been seen.

Vaguely, on the edge of his consciousness, his buried sense of the absurd appreciated the incongruous nature of a decorated New York City police detective riding around in a limousine, pouring thousands of dollars into the streets, and pinning his hopes for finding his lover on the dregs of the population he probably should be arresting rather than financing. It certainly wouldn't make it past the scriptwriters for a movie of the week. Too bizarre.

God, he was tired. When he felt himself floating, or starting to drop off to sleep, he'd heave himself out the limo and start moving through the shadows once again. Echoes of his childhood blended with the noises of the here and now. There were times when the sights and sounds and smells would take him right back to when he was living on the streets himself. Some of the same faces, more decayed and weary than he remembered, listened and tried to comprehend his questions. Finally, checking the time, he decided to let the word spread and thread on its own. He needed to get updates from his team.

"Home, Claude," he said as he climbed into the back seat. Yawning and rubbing his throbbing chest, he called ahead to be sure everyone was assembled. They were.

"Why don't you close your eyes, sir," suggested Claude. "There's a little traffic on Fifth and it'll be awhile before we get there."

Marc didn't even hear him finish the sentence. His fatigue had asserted its own formidable power, and he drifted off in less than a heartbeat.

When Claude pulled into The Edgewood garage and parked, he was startled when he glanced at the rear view mirror and saw Marc shifting to let himself out. It hadn't even been an hour and he thought that Marc was completely out. He'd intended to go upstairs and inform the team that the detective was getting some much needed sleep.

Without a word, Marc shoved out of the back seat and slammed the door. Claude looked over his shoulder and shook his head fondly. The back was filled with debris. It would take at least an hour to shovel it all out and get the limousine back to pristine order. He nearly jumped out of his skin when there was a rap on his window. He was even more startled when he saw the detective.

Marc didn't wait for him to roll it down. He just saluted him, then turned, strode over to the elevator and pushed the button.

Claude's heart filled with…with, well something. Something great. Just great. Now if they could only find Dr. Morningstar. It would go from great to perfect. As he watched Marc walk through the open elevator door, his heart filled a little more. He'd find her. Of that Claude was certain.

The briefing was long and lively. Everyone had accumulated a great deal of information to share. The investigation was going well, but to this point still going nowhere. Kim had Lee's list and was working with Lyd and Kelly to get them into a data base. No cross matches yet. Teresa and Eunice were tracking down names from Marc's cases. Nothing new to report, but several had been eliminated due to death or continued incarceration. Rachael had Sweeney's files and was trying to get in to see Green. There was excellent follow-up from Sweeney, but nothing very promising. Green wasn't cooperating at all. Tagg and Dina were fielding a steady flow of calls on dozens of phones that Marc had left in the streets.

"Marc," shouted Dina. "A call from someone named Sergeant Pepper. Do you want it? He says he'll only talk with the Commander, code name Jude."

"I'll take it." Marc was standing by the maps making notations. He automatically reached out and Dina slapped the phone in his hand.

"Yeah, Sergeant." He listened for a second then said, "Eight days a week. Okay. Fine. I'll meet you there in ten."

He glanced over at his team who'd looked up from their laptops, lists, and leads.

"Sergeant insists on code names and passwords. Beatles fan. Doesn't trust anyone. It makes it a little complicated to get a conversation started, but a report from him is good news."

"I could use some air." Tagg got up and grabbed his jacket. "I'll drive."

"I could use some air too." Luke stood and stretched.

"Think I need a body guard and a personal physician?" asked Marc.

"Just covering your backside," said Tagg.

"And your internal organs," added Luke

"I've been out there alone all day," muttered Marc as the trio headed for the door.

"True, but I still need some air," said Tagg, undeterred.

"And so do I," added Luke.

Marc shook his head. "Just don't slow me down."

The uniformed man standing at attention when they arrived was a former Marine with a serious head injury who now lived in a low rent room and spent all of his nights hunting for enemy combatants on the streets of New York. He was unarmed and harmless, but he didn't miss much.

"Sir." He saluted Marc. "I'm the eggman."

"I'm the walrus," responded Marc solemnly.

Tagg looked at Luke. They felt like they'd stepped into a spy movie. A really bad spy movie.

"Good to see you Commander. Who are they?" Sergeant nodded suspiciously at Tagg and Luke.

"They're here on orders from the President. I don't know their names and neither can you."

Sergeant nodded solemnly. "Understood, sir. I have a report from down under."

"From Australia?" asked Luke.

Marc glanced over at him. "Hardly. From under the bridges. Go ahead, Sergeant. Report."

"Mostly what hasn't been seen, sir. Nothing from 71$^{st}$ through 82$^{nd}$ in the last seven hours. We have people stationed at all the checkpoints you recommended. Here are some shoes and items our team dragged up from the river or found abandoned in the alleys. Nothing that looks like what your special agent had on. Hanky Panky saw a floater a few days ago in the river, but she was sure it wasn't a dark haired woman and her description matched a body recovered this morning a few miles down. It was a stabbing. Lemonade said he saw a lone woman with long black hair walking down 7$^{th}$, but upon further investigation, it was Steal Toe's sister up from Alabama. That is confirmed. I repeat. Confirmed. Snort was telling some of the pop heads that he saw alter gratis or something. Pretty excited about it. Came right out of the water, I guess. He isn't too easy to understand…"

Marc's brain ticked off something and gave him a nudge. When that happened, he always stopped. "Repeat that last bit, Sergeant."

"He isn't too easy to understand?"

"No. What did Snort say?"

"Something about an alter gratis."

"Atargatis. Did he say Atargatis?" Something in Marc's belly rolled.

"Yes sir, that could be it. Like I said, Snort isn't easy to understand. Why?"

"Snort's a Syrian scholar," said Marc.

"Snort's a burned out coke head, sir," clarified Sergeant.

"Yeah, well that too. But before he burned his circuits, he was a scholar. Myth and history. Whenever something reconnects in his head he shows real brilliance." He was already moving out of the alley. "Thanks, Sergeant. Now, go get some rest. You've done well tonight."

Sergeant saluted solemnly, then proud and satisfied he executed a perfect 90 degree turn and started back to the meticulous little room Marc had been paying for since they'd met in a dark alley years before.

"What's Syrian myth and history got to do with Alter, Altra gratis?" Tagg followed confidently even though he was completely in the dark.

"Atargatis," Marc corrected. "I think Atargatis was a Syrian mermaid. I want to go confirm that with Snort."

"And…"

"If he thinks he saw a Syrian mermaid, that may mean he saw a woman with long dark hair in the water." Luke and Tagg looked at each other when they climbed into the car with Marc. He really was the best man to find a single grain of sand on a crowded, busy beach.

"Stay in the car," insisted Marc when they arrived at a bridge a few minutes later. "I need to go under and find Snort."

Tagg looked over at the men and women milling around, the few who'd already gotten their evening fix and were sprawled on the ground, the several who were sitting and hitting on the same lit cigarette.

"I think I'll go in and take your back," said Tagg.

"No. I have to go in alone or they won't talk. They aren't the same as Sergeant. I'll get off a shot if I need assistance."

"Do you think any of them need medical attention?" asked Luke.

Marc looked over at the genuine concern on the face of Jette's brother. The man had guts. And compassion.

"I'll let you know." Marc knew most of them were beyond medical redemption.

Tagg and Luke watched as Marc confidently walked up to a group standing around a barrel with fire licking up the sides. Then they lost sight of him as he went into the shadows beneath the bridge.

"Don't worry," said Tagg softly into the silence of the car. "This city loves him."

"It's not the city I'm worried about. It's the psychotic, burned out drug dealer that sees Marc as the enemy that concerns me."

Tagg nodded. It concerned him too. A lot. "We have to trust him on that as well."

Marc walked in unmolested, however. And Snort was in his usual spot, flat on his back, his knees pulled up, stoned on whatever was in the burning butt between his fingers.

Marc got down, his face not revealing the thundering of his heart. He didn't want this to be another dead-end and he'd soon find out if it was. Most investigations were a whole series of dead-ends. But this time the stakes were so much higher.

"Hey, Snort."

Snort opened his eyes and tried to focus in on Marc's face.

"Hey, Snake Eyes," he said finally. "You got some green to share?"

"A lot of it for the right trade."

That made Snort shift and sit up.

"You wanna hit?" He remembered his manners and offered the butt. "It's laced."

"No. I want you to tell me about Atargatis. I heard you saw her." Marc hoped Snort had a few working brain cells and that he wasn't too stoned to access them. He'd hate to have to take him in. It would be a real problem getting him through the mass of people who saw Snort as one of their own. The fact that Marc was a cop was rarely an issue since he didn't bust anyone for possession or panhandling, but it would quickly become an issue if he pulled Snort out.

Snort took a hit and appeared to be thinking. "Ah, yes. Atargatis." Marc noticed that Snort's voice became more cultured, less vague. It was a good sign. He could still pull out the scholar. "She crawled out of the water. A beautiful siren. Beautiful. I would have liked to have seen her lovely breasts, but she had on clothes…"

"Snort," Marc interrupted. "What did she look like?"

"Atargatis is not of this world. She lives in the sea. Her long black hair should be flowing in the water. That's how I see her. But curiosity pulled her out of the river and on to the land."

"Atargatis has long black hair?"

"Indeed. But she was wearing clothes. A grave disappointment."

Marc very discreetly pulled out a fifty dollar bill. Over the usual payment, but this was no bullshit or delusion or hallucination. He was sure of it. She was alive. Alive! Something inside him was smoothing out. He could feel it lose its jagged edge. The urgency was there, but the terror had backed off.

"Snort. Show me exactly where and this is yours."

Snort snatched the money and hid it before anyone else saw. Then with Marc's help, he slowly got up and led him to a low abutment about 50 feet from the bridge and pointed.

"She came out right here."

"Did you see where she went? What happened to her?"

"No. I was quite disappointed I didn't see breasts, so I went on with my business."

Marc looked around. There were abandoned warehouses and run down tenements, both filled with people who would want to do more than look at a pair of breasts. Could she have been attacked? Was she dazed or injured and could she be lying in one of the rooms? Could someone inside be holding her?

He'd call in a team to do a forensic analysis of the spot Snort indicated and begin a search. But he'd do that later. Right now, in the darkest hours of night, he needed to do his own canvas. Alone. His own way.

"Snort. Do you know citizens in there?"

"Lots of two legged rats and slime with teeth. People who want more privacy than under the bridge."

"I figured. I'm offering a lot of money for information. Useful information. I'll know the difference. Start the wave now and let it ripple through the cribs. I'll be here for the night and will talk with anyone, anywhere. I need to know where she is."

"You leave your badge on the street?"

"Guaranteed."

Snort thought about it for a moment. There was a great deal in the building that frightened him, but he knew he wouldn't get stuck and torched for getting someone hauled in. When Snake Eyes said he left the badge on the street, he never went back and pushed it. He licked his lips. "My cut?"

"Double anything I give for useful information."

Snort nodded like an agent getting a once in a lifetime deal for a popular client.

Business was business everywhere, anywhere. He turned and disappeared into the deep, dark mouth of the building.

Marc went over to the car and reported his news. Tagg and Luke were both relieved and excited. It seemed like a solid break.

"This is good stuff, Marc. Do we bring in a forensic team?" asked Tagg. "Search and rescue?"

"No, not until morning. I don't want police down here spooking the citizens. If she's in there or if someone has her, we need to go in soft," replied Marc.

Both Tagg and Luke ignored the fact that Marc was the police. "Luke, why don't you go back to the apartment and get some rest? Tagg go home." He reached in and grabbed a flashlight. "I'm going down to take a preliminary look."

When he got to the concrete abutment on the side of the river, Marc turned and saw both Tagg and Luke behind him.

"I'm not all that tired," shrugged Luke.

"Carmel told me I couldn't come home until we found out what happened," said Tagg.

Marc stared at them both and nodded. At least they didn't look like a couple of beat cops or even detectives, for that matter. They both needed a shave, hadn't attended to their clothing in awhile, and wore grim expressions.

At just after midnight they found a hair. A blessed single long black hair on one of the nail heads attached to an old wooden dock. Marc carefully placed it into an evidence bag, then stared at it under the flashlight.

"Jette," he said simply and the other two nodded. "We'll get a positive match. Tagg, can you take it in...and...and then ask Hilda to..." Marc simply couldn't finish the sentence. He knew it was necessary to find Jette's DNA in the apartment for comparison. A hair from her brush would be best. But he couldn't get the reality of it past his throat.

"Let me." Luke reached for the evidence bag. "Tagg, I think you're the man to stay here. I'll call Kim and have her meet me at the apartment. I'll take care of it," said Luke when Marc didn't let go right away. "Marc. I'll take good care of it."

Marc shook himself. It was just a fucking hair. But it was Jette's hair, he was sure of it. Jette who came out of the water alive. Right here. Right where he was standing. Where was she now? Who had her?

"Yeah. Sorry. Good." Luke gently pulled and he released his grip on it. "Tagg, you hold here at the scene, then call in Sweeney to get CSI at dawn. I'm going into the building."

Tagg started to protest, but he knew that Marc was probably safer alone.

"Call me if you need back up," he said. "Punch my number every half hour. No chat necessary, just a short signal so I know you're on the job."

It was a good plan. Annoying, but solid. Marc nodded and walked into the dark, dank cave of the nearest building. Alone and determined.

Soon after he entered, the inhabitants Snort flushed started hissing at him to come into hallways and dark rooms. The stench and the filth hit him and he was often transported by memory back to his days on the streets, some of his nights spent moving through buildings and rooms just like this. The only ambition was survival. Live another day. Live another hour.

By the end of the night he felt like a priest in a confessional. He heard all manner of declarations, data, and dribble. The sun was turning the morning from a dark bleak gray to a dull bleak gray when he heard his first really important bit of information. He was leaning against the brick wall of a dusty, odorous interior office, standing up in order to keep himself awake and found that wasn't working any more. He kept drifting and would have to catch himself before he fell over. It wasn't a good thing to be so vulnerable with the dregs of the city floating around but he figured they'd have no way of knowing he was nearly dead on his feet.

He'd caught a glimpse of his face in a broken pane of glass when he took a leak against the wall. He looked hideous. Pale, unshaven, wild unfocused eyes. He looked like a resident.

A shaggy young man came and leaned on the wall next to him. When he heard the words, the words he'd been waiting for all night, they didn't register at first. They seemed to spin around in his head. Meaningless phrases, sounds that were familiar but far too disconnected. A pop of adrenalin hit his starving system when he heard the strung out addict mumble that he saw a woman, wet and struggling put into a van.

"Woman. Wet. Struggling," Marc repeated, then startled the young man with his reaction. Probably scared him as well as he reanimated with a vengeance.

"Did you see where she came from?" he demanded loudly, grabbing him and giving him a fierce little shake.

"No, man. Maybe Mars. I don't give a shit. My bitch said you'd pay for information on a woman. I gave you information on a woman. I want to sheen the green or my face shuts down."

"Describe her and green will roll."

"Black hair. Real long. A looker. Mad as a wet cat. Had a cat once we tried to drown in the tub. Looked just like that. Three big guys, two chicks. The wet cat took out a couple, but they were too big. Too many. Had one limping and one gonna maybe lose an eye."

"What did they look like?"

"It was dark. Just guys and chicks."

"We'll come back to that. What about the car."

"It was a 2005 Chevy van. An Express. Yellow. Fully paneled sides and rear."

"Anything written on it?"

"No. No rust, no marks. Hadn't been in any kind of accident."

"Nice description on the car. Why so clear?" Marc couldn't keep the suspicion out of his voice.

"I used to sell cars, man."

"After you stole them?"

"Hey, Snort said the badge was burned."

"I could care less. License?"

"Didn't see. Didn't notice. Didn't care."

"Let's go back to the perps. Can you describe them?"

"No."

"You can tell me the make, color and year of the car, but can't describe the people?"

"Never sold people."

"Okay. Were they black, brown, or light?"

"Guys were one black, two cream. Chicks were one brown, one light."

"Tall or short?"

"Neither."

"Means they were average."

"Yeah."

"Color hair?"

"Didn't see hair. Musta wore caps or somethin'"

"But you're sure there were five of them."

"Yeah."

"Here's a phone. It's programmed with my number. Call me with anything else you remember or can find out."

"Green exchange?"

Marc pulled his hand out of his pocket with the cell phone and $500. It was a fortune but he knew he'd get more if there was more. The addict slid the money into his filthy jeans and faded back into the building.

Alone again, Marc took a second to process the information. She wasn't in here. There was some relief in that. He'd need his team now, but wanted a few moments to take it in. Jette. Out of the river and physically well enough to fight her captors. Not great news, but news that would keep him on his feet for another month if that was what it took to find her.

# Chapter 31

Dressed in her long blue robes and solid silver face mask, the hood from her cape brought up over her hair, the Empress stood among her Sentinels staring through the one way mirror. Their curiosity was evident in their sidelong glances and quiet stares, but it was immaterial. Her identity was sacred and no one would ever uncover it. Perhaps when everything was over, when she'd risen to the top, after the complete destruction of Avenger and her ascension to Supreme Sovereign, she could finally come out. Reveal herself to the millions of followers in the Middle World of Reality. Her admirers. In the end, her subjects. This would be her choice. Later.

She studied the beautiful woman asleep on a mountain of pillows in the impressively ornate four poster bed. Like a heroine in a fairy tale waiting for the kiss of her one true love. Her long black hair was shiny and loose, her exotic features were flawless. Precisely the picture of the legendary Avenger she was sure all Sovereignty gamers everywhere held in their minds.

The room was a suitable setting for someone of Avenger's status. She'd be given every courtesy, every luxury. When Avatars were captured and kept, this was the sacred rule. She'd be treated with the respect she'd earned over the years of play.

Because the room had been a shelter at one time for the unfortunate in the City of Might, there was graffiti all over the walls, but everything was immaculate. The small bathroom and shower had been scrubbed and sterilized. She'd supervised the cleanup herself. The furniture was expensive and comfortable. It was a cage, but a gilded one.

"Has she given you any more trouble?"

"Not since the shots." The Sentinel stared at the bed where Avenger lay drugged and docile. For now. He had scratches and bruises to prove she fought like the wolf many thought she could morph into. He had no doubt the Empress was right. She was the one true Avenger. "They tame her."

"Tame her, then they will turn her,"

"Yes. Exactly so."

"Jette Morningstar, she calls herself. A fabulous Middle World identity, all in all," she observed.

"And the Phoenix," said her most trusted Sentinel.

"Yes."

"A confirmation of your sight."

"It was a mistake to allow the media to call her that. At this level of play a little mistake is the difference between victory and defeat."

The title had been another of the clear signs that Avenger was walking in the Middle World. Maybe her ego delighted in having that modest inside nod to her secret. Ego was a huge advantage in the game.

Then a thought sizzled through the Empress. Maybe Avenger fed the name to the media herself to give her people a signal. A wink. A wave. Perhaps a heads up. A signal could mean that Avenger had been planning a major move of her own.

Interesting. Had she, the Empress, averted a preemptive strike by bringing down Avenger at this time?

She laughed. A sharp, nearly maniacal sound that filled the room. Perfect. Just perfect. She'd add the points for an Aversion to a Battle to her side of the board. Yes, she would. And document it for review later. If anyone challenged it, she'd have all her proof of providence ready.

The Empress continued to stare at her nemesis. She wanted to feel every moment of triumph. Every wave of pleasure. Every second of incredible power. Avenger was here. Avenger was hers. Captured and caged. It was beginning to really sink in. The glory of it. Underneath the placid, expressionless mask, she wore a wild and vicious grin.

She'd known that Avenger would rise out of the river and had moved all of her Sentinels and Mercenaries along the shore. The Phoenix would regenerate. And she had. Right back into the grip of her people.

No one knew precisely how many of her seven lives Avenger had used in her fight for Sovereignty, but the current wisdom had it at four. Losing one in the fall meant she had only two more.

Two lives left. One for the Empress to acquire in her own weapons column to get through the Castle of Thunder. Then the last one for her to take in the Final Duel.

Since Sovereignty's introduction into the CRPG market nearly a decade before, the Final Duel had only been a distant possibility. Something even avid gamers were never sure would happen. Ever. But she'd do it. It would be a single explosive, celebrated victory. A complete and total triumph that would end the conflict forever. The game would be finished, but the story would be told and retold in legend. In print. In documentaries. The glory would be overwhelming. She'd become the mythical Supreme Sovereign and it would give her complete dominion over all the worlds.

It would be a magnificent finish. To have Avenger dead and stay dead was the goal of every Blue Empress ever to play the game. And it was within her grasp. The plan had no flaws and everything was being executed perfectly.

An Empress's strength came in awarding points, then Boons from her galley of treasures. It was how she recruited and retained her legions of Minions and closely held Sentinels. And in the Middle World of Reality, it was how she contracted Mercenaries to follow her command and rewarded Assassins who took care of anyone who deviated from the path. Compliance was assured by her control over both the rewards and the punishments.

She had a Boon that she was sure even the human manifestation of Avenger would find irresistible. It was an unblemished plan. Simple. Straight forward. Brilliant.

Avenger was going to turn, she was sure of it. A few more weeks and she'd be begging to negotiate a trade.

"I think everything is under control here." Her voice was low. A bit raspy. And the mask muffled it further. Still it was strong and authoritative. "You know how to contact me if anything manifests. Carry on."

With that she swirled out of the room.

# Chapter 32

Marc's team stood around waiting to give reports and receive additional assignments. They'd been napping in the apartment when Luke came from the river with the news. By the time Marc returned with Tagg, they were ready to follow up on all the leads. Kelly and Lyd started early and revised their runs to include the information on the van. There was a great deal of excitement and renewed energy as they drank coffee and shared information. That night they would be into their weekend off and could stay with the investigation for a solid 48.

Marc revised the maps, drawing in the location of Jette's exit from the river. It was almost a mile from where she went in. Tommy reported no legitimate Jette sightings from 110th to 125th so he took out a red highlighter and blocked off the area.

"Red will indicate blank areas that have been covered and won't be high priority," said Marc.

"We aren't going to wait for forensics to confirm that the hair is Jette's?" asked Dina.

"It's hers," replied Marc with conviction, then moved on. He held up a picture of the van. "We're now looking for this. So Tommy, time to change the channel. Go back into the alleys. Start with the population running in all directions from this location." He pointed to the place where he'd found the hair.

"Gotchya, sugar pie. Lots and lots of eyes down there. Too bad they can't all focus."

"All we need is one. And take brew." Marc looked at his watch. "They'd have trouble making a score right now and that's what they'd be trading for the green anyway."

"And smokes. Addiction is a powerful pull and can open even tight lips. Too bad we can't offer smack," she lamented.

At Marc's long stare, she shrugged.

"Nicotine is more powerful anyway. We'll stay on up and up street. I'll just go empty the bladder, refill the tanks, touch up my fading face, and be off."

"Okay, now how about some reports." Marc turned to the rest of the team. He was eager to be out in the streets himself, but knew there was more to the investigation than random pursuit.

"Nothing on cross checking the van and the number 227 in that order but we have several matches with those numbers in them," reported Teresa. "I'm going to start there."

"I have the list of street addresses and apartment numbers with 227. Raj and I are going to narrow it down." Dina scanned the hundreds of names on the spreadsheet. "There's quite a few with all three numbers. Phone interviews first to see what pops."

"Good. Anything more on the perps who took the dive?"

"No. Nothing that we've been able to connect with Jette. There's been no intersection of their lives at all that we can find. Sweeney's been real cooperative which is a plus."

"Anything on the tattoos?"

Rachael was consolidating the information gathered by the team.

"It's quite a popular tattoo. It's a moon."

"A blue moon?"

"Yes."

"Any significance to that?"

"We're looking into it. Nothing so far."

"Did both bodies have the tattoo?" Marc looked over at Luke.

Luke consulted the autopsy file and nodded.

Absentmindedly rubbing the spot where his own gang brand snaked up his arm, Marc frowned. "Could be a new crew mark. I'll ask the citizens I talk to. What about my cases. Anything pop there?"

"We have the list of people out and about," said Rachael. "Dina and I are working it, but nothing that looks too promising. Only one interesting lead. Stoneface Brace is out again and the first three numbers of his cell phone are 227. We're trying to track him now."

"This isn't his style. He's too stupid, he has no friends who'd help him pull this off, and he'd come after me personally if he was that pissed. Last time I saw him, he thought I was his brother-in-law. Thought I owed him money. It's worth a check, though." He glanced at his watch. "He'll be at Jody Hogan's Deli on Nova Scotia. Orders rye toast and cops all the pickles people leave on the tables."

Dina wrote it in her notes. "If only we could just clone him," she muttered to Rachael, who'd spent several hours coordinating uniformed officers to check his known addresses.

Tommy came swirling back in with food from the kitchen. "That darling Hilda has been doing kitchen duty again, boys and girls! She heard the bossman stomping through the apartment and figured he needed a nutritional transfusion."

"Get away from me with that shit," snapped Marc irritably. He was hot on a lead and didn't want to be interrupted.

"Speaking of shit, it's what you look like right now," said Tagg.

"Go to hell, this isn't a beauty contest."

"True, but you need to eat."

"Tagg's right, Detective." Chief Cheskee said from the doorway. "You need to eat."

The room fell silent. Even Marc didn't respond. It appeared he was about to be interrupted, like it or not. The chief, his superior, was striding into the room taking everything in.

"How'd you get in here?" he asked finally.

"Your driver let me in. After checking my badge and calling it in, I might add. I'm sure he figured I was a part of all this. Now tell me why I'm not."

Marc ignored her question. Everyone else stood mute. Finally Marc broke the silence.

"Why are you here?"

"I followed the dots, Detective. My top man requests a medical leave and the rest of his inner circle goes home precisely at the end of shift. They come back the next morning right on time, not looking at all rested. This morning a hair comes into evidence and the lab is checking it against one belonging to Jette Morningstar. I was a detective before I was a chief, Lexington. Now fill me in on what you have. I expect that this will all be officially yours by Monday morning anyway."

"Tagg will be heading the formal investigation," said Marc. "I'm remaining on medical leave."

"That's a little hard to support given that you're up to your neck in evidence."

"I'd prefer to keep some of what we've learned here. There was a leak in the transfer of the university shooter. It hasn't been plugged and I don't want this investigation compromised."

"What has that incident got to do with Dr. Morningstar's kidnapping?"

When Marc didn't answer, her temper pushed through.

"Detective, if you have information pertinent to that investigation, you'll be in serious trouble if you don't report. Now!"

Marc stared at her for a moment. Long enough to electrify the air between them. She stood silent, not about to repeat the question that lay there like a stone.

"Jette's life is on one side of the scale, Chief. You've always backed me…" Marc began.

"But…" the chief prompted.

"You're brass. You follow procedure."

"Someone in this department has to." She swept her arms at what they all knew was an active investigation. An unsanctioned one.

"Chief," said Kim softly, ever the peacemaker. "Detective Lexington has done more in the last 72 hours to locate Jette than any department could have on its own. His methods have been unorthodox and while they are all legal, they wouldn't have been possible within this timeline given the policies and procedures you must adhere to. Not to mention the budgetary implications. The detective has financed the whole operation and it's been quite an expensive proposition."

"Nicely shoveled, Sommer," nodded the chief when Kim stopped to take a breath.

"Thank you, Chief. But true."

"You said locate Dr. Morningstar. You mean her killers, don't you?"

No one responded. The chief stared at the faces in the room. In her opinion, the best group of officers and detectives in New York. She wasn't going anywhere.

"Okay, Marc. You win. I guess I'll stow my badge in the same place you all have put them. Call me Lauren, pour me a cup of that coffee, and let's keep this here. For now. Give me something to do. As luck would have it, my calendar's light today. I'd planned on giving a push to getting the case transferred, but as it happens, I don't feel the same sense of urgency."

The rest of the team looked at Marc. It was his move and they'd go where he'd lead them. He respected his chief and could use her connections and expertise. Should he let her in? His instincts were completely short circuited on this case, but she'd always been straight in the past. He nodded.

"Appreciated." He poured her a cup of coffee. It was the signal the team was looking for that the chief was now in. "Because of what we've discovered in the last few hours, this case is definitely a kidnapping, not a homicide."

"Dr. Morningstar is alive? You know this for sure?"

"Yes." And that simple word. The conviction that it was true kept Marc on his feet. It fueled him.

"And she's been kidnapped?"

"Yes."

Lauren nodded. She knew what that meant. The FBI. She felt the familiar tug of territorial control. If the FBI got the case, her people would be in the loop, but not at the same level. It would complicate things dramatically. No one wanted that.

"The hair could have floated in from the river. From a body. We can still pursue the homicide angle. Let's see how far we can push this before we have to share."

"Understood," agreed Marc, appreciating the support.

"Same perps have her?"

"We don't know. The van used by those who currently have her wasn't the same one driven by the people who took her from here."

"What's your best guess at this point?"

"I'd say we have more than one team of kidnappers. She was taken nearly a mile from where she went into the water."

"This is much bigger than a simple abduction."

"Yes, it appears to be."

"And since you're on medical leave, Marc. I think you should take some down time. Now. Go take a nap. Freeman can fill me in. You look like death warmed over."

"Well, since you've stowed your badge, Lauren, I guess I'll just ignore that order."

There was a moment of silence in the room. No one called the chief Lauren. Ever. Not even behind her back. True, she'd invited him to do so, but several of the squad hadn't even remembered that was her first name.

The chief sipped, stared. Then she decided to take a step back and just keep an eye on him.

"By the way, Marc," she said. "We're narrowing down the source of the leak on Flowers. It was a very closely held bit of information."

"I'm interested in the name. I'd like to add it to our list of accomplices."

"Explain."

Marc took her through the investigation and their theories to date. Then assigned her to what they called the 227 team.

Kelly watched the detective stride around the room. He was so intense. So dangerous looking most of the time. And he had a rep. He'd been a chief with the Cobras when he was younger than her. He seemed straight now, but once a Cobra, always a Cobra. And that could be hazardous to your health. She'd been listening. To everything. The scut work she was assigned took little active gray matter. Absorbing information flying around her was one of her specialties. Most people underestimated her, thinking her brain was as defective as her legs or something. Or they ignored her because she was a kid, and pretty much a throw-away at that. Well she heard everything that was going on and she filed it all away inside her active mind.

Excusing herself, she rolled into the bathroom. Looking into the shiny, gold framed mirror, she pulled back the collar of her t-shirt. The blue moon stood out near her collar bone. She'd erased that little detail in her records. Good thing. She eased the material back over the mark and thought about her next move.

# Chapter 33

Inside the suite, Jette came out of her meditative state to full consciousness. Shifting and stretching, she felt the bonds of her captivity. The fleece lined restraints were the same used in hospitals to control patients who might hurt themselves or others. They were gentle, but very strong and confining. She didn't like them, but mostly just tried to ignore them.

How far was Marc in the investigation? When her captors had been caught in traffic and were bickering over the fastest route to this place, she'd jumped out of the car. Then she'd left the little girl with the bird the clue to find it. Had Marc questioned her? Had the girl remembered? Jette had no way of knowing if the name and the street she'd overheard them shouting about was where she was currently being held, but it felt right.

After that beautifully orchestrated and somewhat painful dive into the East River and the long deep swim under the surface, she'd figured she was safe. Thought she'd shaken her captors. She remembered her odd combination of exasperation and exhaustion when she got out of the river and was greeted by five more pursuers. If she hadn't already swum full out for a mile, she may have been able to out run them yet again. But they took her. Right on the dock. Sentinels, they called themselves.

She knew she was being drugged. Periodically these Sentinels would hold her down and the effect of the fluid running through her veins after the needle punctured her arm was unmistakable. Something she suspected was a strong narcotic based on her body's reaction. First a thrilling euphoria, then a light headed contentment, then a pulsing emptiness, then an edgy craving. It was interesting, but from first to last it wasn't pleasant. Not even the initial ecstasy because she knew it was false. It was a trap.

The fuzzy condition of her brain was both foreign to her and aggravatingly difficult to deal with. Mental discipline helped. After a period of meditation, her brain could still focus with some precision. She could still shake off the haze floating between her sharp, analytical mind and the world around her.

Right now she felt a little groggy and lethargic. They'd be giving her another shot soon. That was good. As much as she hated them, she gained the most knowledge when they came to administer the drug. There was danger, of course, so she tried to remain hyper-aware when people were in the room. She played along, absorbing as much information as she could, assessing what was happening. Identifying people and patterns. Action would only come after she knew enough to dictate the direction.

When she'd first been brought there, something had told her not to give in too soon.

Not to be an easy mark. So she'd resisted them physically and fought their attempts to subdue her. Then with the administration of the drugs, she calmed and became watchful. She was still and silent. Never speaking, no longer resisting. Some of it was due to confusion and the need to remain unresponsive until she could get her mind in gear. And some of it was the way she interacted with her environment.

Her native father taught her the way of the wilderness beast. Lay low. Lay quiet. Use all your senses to identify the danger. Act only when you have the advantage. This she had no problem with. They couldn't chain her active mind. Her intuition. Her scrutiny.

In addition, as a therapist, she was trained to listen and gather data before delivering a diagnosis. So even though she wasn't in physical control, this was her professional milieu. So far, she knew there was an obvious delusional reality for a few of the people she came in contact with. These men and women didn't worry her over much after the first few hours. For them this whole scenario was a symptom of mental illness. Some kind of psychotic disorder. They didn't seem to be hallucinating, so she wouldn't diagnose schizophrenia. For them it was all a game of sorts and she felt sure she could manipulate their more fragile truth.

Those people who called themselves Minions and Sentinels were pathologically delusional, but since they seemed more benign in their delusional state, she'd encourage their fractured reality. In her professional opinion, she'd be safe as long as she played into their fantasy and resisted the temptation to try to shine a light on their distorted views. Her role and their expectations of her were most important to understand at this point and that was beginning to come into focus.

She'd learned a great deal in a very short period of time. The game, its characters, its rules were beginning to become familiar. She had no idea what the motivations were at this point. There would be time later to sort it all out. They called her Avenger. Was that a TV program? A movie? Some kind of cult heroine or video game character? She'd never heard of her, but she was woefully ill informed on some of the pop culture phenomenon.

On the other hand, if these mentally fragile people wanted her to be this Avenger, that was precisely who she'd be. For now she felt relatively secure. Woozy and out of her body, but certainly not physically injured. The drugs were worrisome of course, but other than the injections, her treatment was more than humane. In actuality, she was being indulged like royalty. Apparently she ruled Callisto, and was to be treated with respect. She liked that part of the delusion. Very much. Her food was prepared perfectly, obviously by a chef familiar with vegetarian cuisine. Her private bathroom was devoid of anything that could be used as a weapon, but was filled with all of her favorite cosmetics and body lotions. It was uncanny and oddly threatening.

The ones she needed to study more carefully seemed to be garden variety thugs. They were less committed to the game being played out. They carried guns and did what they were told, but their conversations were only vaguely related to this world of Sovereignty and they used the codes and names assigned to them without much conviction. Certainly with no interest or passion. She suspected they were being paid.

Mercenaries could be dangerous, but these knew how to take orders and didn't deviate from them. She'd tried to bribe them early on with promises of monetary rewards and they'd all refused, so whomever was in charge had their loyalty. Perhaps on some level they bought into elements of the delusion.

It put a chip in her heart that she'd be able to give Marc a definite ID on the person giving her the shots. Her shape, her touch, her voice all betrayed Hester. She'd shown remarkable courage under fire and had become the darling of the morning shows. Rumor had it that Oprah herself was putting together a show of heroes with Hester as the centerpiece. Another charade in a world filled with deception.

The most amazing and personally painful revelation was that she'd been the target of the school shooting. The connection with Flowers was shocking, but immediately apparent when she discovered the context for his comment on the Empress. And the turning. Around here being turned was quite a theme. She suspected that the reason for the drugs was to make her dependent. To turn her.

Well, she'd turn and spin like a top when she felt she needed to. Right now she was going to remain diligent and in control of her own decisions. Her part would be played with one single purpose. To get her out of here with as much information as she could gather in the best shape she could manage. Marc was out there and he'd find her. Or at some point, Avenger would find a way to break free.

# Chapter 34

When things were humming in the command center, Marc went out again. It was where he felt the closest to the possible break the case needed. He spent a very frustrating afternoon trying to rouse informants, fanning out from the point Jette left the water. No luck. He knew it was a matter of time and persistence. He had plenty of the latter, he only hoped he had enough of the former.

Marc's cell phone rang as he came up through the parking garage. It was nearly time for the daily briefing and he wanted to check all the cell phones for calls before going back out to sweep the night crawlers.

"A woman to see you, Detective." He heard Jonathon's voice and frowned. Answering the phone had been so automatic, he'd forgotten he'd put it to his ear.

"Not a reporter."

"Please."

"Fine, I'll be right there."

When he got off the elevator and strode into the lobby a woman stood up. Tall and slim, she had shoulder length hair, expertly highlighted and cut. She was wearing a sleek tailored suit the color of ripe olives. She walked over to him on slim Prada pumps. At first he didn't recognize her, then he nearly gaped when she smiled.

"Dicey?"

He'd never seen her without her stained apron and her hair under a cap.

"Hi Marc, I know you're busy, but can I talk with you for a moment?"

"This isn't a good time."

"I know. But what I have may be related."

"To Jette's disappearance?"

"Yes."

"Sure, then. Come on up."

As they rode the elevator, Marc took two calls from informants and set up times for meets.

"Sorry," he said automatically as he closed his phone and let Dicey into the apartment.

"No problem. You're pressed for time and I'm just here to help."

If she was impressed with the penthouse, she didn't show it. Marc thought maybe she'd grown up in luxury and was used to sumptuous surroundings. As he indicated the living room, he took a good look at her and recognized her suit as a designer brand. Her hair and makeup were impeccable enough to get her admitted to the private showrooms on Fifth Avenue. The simple jewelry she wore looked real. Maybe she came from money. Or maybe she'd become a millionaire one hot dog at a time. It occurred to him how little he really knew about her.

"I'd offer you something, but the clock's ticking."

"I understand."

As they both sat down, she started without preamble.

"I noticed something the other day you may be interested in."

Marc frowned. "The day Jette and I stopped at your cart?"

"Yes. I didn't think anything of it at the time, but looking back on it with a new context, I believe I'm right."

"Right about what?" Marc never discounted information. Sometimes it was useful and sometimes it meant nothing, but he never made that determination until he heard it. Processed it. Filed it away.

"I believe you were being followed. At least that's what it looked like to me."

Marc's instincts buzzed. He got out his notebook. "Just tell me what you remember, and I'll ask follow up questions when you're done."

Dicey told him about the two young women she'd observed and gave descriptions, including what they were wearing and an accurate accounting of their actions.

"They looked like they were playing, I don't know, Super Spy or something. At first I thought they were just attracted to you or to Jette or to both of you as a couple. You for obvious reasons. You're eye candy. Jette because of her beauty or her style. Of course they could have recognized her as the Phoenix, but you had her pretty well covered and no one else was stopping and pointing."

"You recognized her."

"Mostly because I know you, Marc. And I knew you were together. Maybe they were watching you as a couple because you were acting so darn romantic and it attracts attention. Especially with two young girls out for the day. They took several pictures with their cell phones and it looked like they were sending them or at least they were doing a lot of texting. Nothing that would attract a great deal of attention, just a couple of teens acting like teens. But you and Jette were definitely the focus of their attention."

"How long did they follow us?"

"As far as I could see you. When you turned the block at Washington, they did too. On the other side of the street."

"And you said they were young?"

"Yes. Teenagers I would say, but college age. 17, 18 or 19. I had enough college freshmen to know that would be about right."

"I'd like you to stick around and work with a sketch artist."

"You think it might be something?"

"I don't know, but we do have one question on the board that needs an answer at some point. How did the kidnappers know where she lived?"

"Isn't that part of the public record?"

"No. We use my address in the Village for all our public records and a box number for mail." He frowned. "How did you know I lived here?"

"Folgers told me."

"How did he know?"

"Menace told him, and I think he found out from Earl the Pearl, who got the scoop from Miss Lissy, who…"

Marc held up his hand and nodded. "A New York secret…"

"Which isn't a secret at all really. But Marc, you'd have to be connected to the network. Not everyone would be able to find her that way. I mean there's the World Wide Web, then there's the street wide grapevine, but you have to be one of the grapes."

"Or tap into one."

"She's only been here a short time. And whomever took her would have to know about your connection."

"It was all over the news."

"True. Anyway, I'll stick around and do what I can. Little Dicey has the cart and she can hold until I get back."

Marc indicated her new look. "I hope you go home and change first."

"Oh yes. I know how to play my part. This is my going to The Edgewood outfit. I didn't want your snooty doorman to call 911. And it worked. He let me right in."

"I hear you."

"You must be quite the topic of conversation around here."

"To say the least."

Marc took her into the ballroom and introduced her. She looked around.

"Unusual décor for a cop command center. I believe that's a Canakkale Ceramic. I've never seen one outside a museum."

Marc shrugged. He'd take Dicey's word for it. "This is Officer Kim Sommer. She'll arrange for you to work with an identification program to reconstruct the faces and body shapes of the girls."

Soon Kim and Dicey were working in the corner with a state-of-the-art computer generated face program. Within a few hours, 2DIE4 and IB2COOL4U smiled off the pages.

"Sommer, take these to the university and see if anyone knows them. It could be that two of her students recognized her and wanted to send out pictures of her and her boyfriend."

"Will do."

"And can you take Dicey home while you're at it?"

"No, Marc. I'm going to take a cab. You just find her. And when you do come on down to my cart for a rice and bean wrap on the house." Dicey stood, took one last long look around, then patted Marc's hand reassuringly.

"If this helps me find her, I'll buy you a house."

"No need for that."

"Nice suit, by the way. Is it a Liz Este?"

"Yes. It is. I knew her back when she was Elizabeth Estervig and she never forgets a friend. Had the color blended just for me. She calls it Dicey Black."

"I think Jette would look great in that color."

"She would. Have her call Beth after you find her. I think she's back from opening her Paris studio. Your beautiful young woman will probably be needing a therapeutic shopping spree after her ordeal."

Marc just nodded.

# Chapter 35

The Empress watched from behind the glass. It really was unbelievable. Avenger was hers. A beautiful pampered prisoner in an impressive luxurious cell. The points for this unprecedented capture would have to be calculated outside the usual grid.

"She can mesmerize and control with her gaze so don't stay in there with her for long," she warned her Sentinels.

"No, Empress."

Avenger was watched constantly, but no one would enter unless they needed to make a delivery or to accompany the Minion with the shots.

"I have more to place in the room. Take these things." She handed the Senior Sentinel several bags. "We'll vacate under the full moon and move her to another location. The animals in the walls will do her bidding, so we need to keep changing locations. This Temple will be the first step in the trail I want to lay for her Guardians.

A trail to their destruction. After we have her relocated and locked in, I'll have a Minion reveal this location to her Knights. They'll follow the crumbs I leave for them right to the sites we have prepared. It'll only take one. The Dark Knight will want to take the lead, take the glory. Too bad he won't find his Avatar, but an open portal to his end."

"Brilliant, Empress. Her Dark Knight and her Guardians are officers of the law in the Middle World, used to following clues. Your plants will lead them like lemmings to the slaughter. The points for their annihilation will be valuable."

"Yes. And be sure that TrueBlue920 doesn't participate in this round."

"Understood. We have him ready for other actions."

"He procured the explosives, but has an aversion to destroying Middle World officers of the law. It's a deep flaw since so many of Avenger's Guardians are police, but we'll keep him on the reserve team. Now go. I'll watch from here."

The three Sentinels moved through the room unaware that Jette was awake and knew the minute they'd come in. Her passivity was feigned and purposeful. She wasn't completely functional, but she was conscious and aware.

She could hear three people. Two men, one woman. Tinman, Darth Vader, and Barbie. She wanted to be sure she'd recognize features, voices, and even scents when called upon to do so after they were taken into custody and charged. She'd labeled them all and had assigned everything she could see, feel, and assume to their names.

Tinman was tall, solid, pale, and without a heart. He was the one who'd killed the hostage on the roof. It was shockingly violent, considering he'd shown her nothing but polite deference since he'd placed her in this room several days before. Obviously he was caught up in the darker edges of the delusion.

Darth Vadar was as big as Tinman with dark skin, dark eyes, a shaved head, and a deep melodious voice and was probably a Mercenary. He called her Morningstar once and was rougher than the other two. On the other hand he seemed completely under the control of the woman they referred to as the Empress.

Barbie was tall, curvaceous, blonde, and vapid. Jette was fairly sure she was in the game because she was easily manipulated, liked the costumes, and really liked the drugs.

All three had tattoos. They looked like moons. Blue moons.

They were whispering as they placed items around the room. Good thing her sense of hearing was acutely honed by years of practice in the desert. Every word came through. She'd have to think later about what it all meant, but nothing got past her.

"The Empress wants the trail to be obvious. The Guardians will eagerly follow the bread crumbs," murmured Tinman.

"They'll walk right into the traps. She has three of them set up among several decoys. Rooms of Destruction. Hopefully they'll be together."

"Certainly the Empress will be able to take the Dark Knight out of play with one of them."

"And several Guardians."

"And they'll think they're going to find Avenger at the end of the trail."

"They'll only find the doors to their end."

"What's the point of that?" asked Barbie, trying to keep up.

"Kaboom. Bombs. No more Guardians. No More Knights. Big points," simplified Tinman in a sarcastic tone.

"Oh, yeah. Cool," giggled Barbie.

Jette felt a wave of urgency. The Dark Knight? She'd already figured that was Marc. Destruction? Bombs? No. Not if she had anything to do with it. Time to get in the game. Time to meet the woman behind the mirror. God, she felt like Snow White. *Mirror, Mirror on the Wall, Who's the strongest of them all?* Taking a deep breath, she willed her mind to get in line. *Time to meet me, Time to fall!*

When the Sentinels fell silent and started walking toward the door, she made her move. She felt it was a good sign that her system was at its lowest level of drug induced miasma. Her wits scattered quickly when she felt the prick of the needle in her arm.

"Tell the Empress I'd like to see her," demanded Jette, keeping her voice and tone authoritative. "But release me. I need to be standing when we meet."

Tinman and the others jumped. They hadn't known Avenger was awake. Tinman turned. He was the Sentinel in charge. He whispered to Barbie and Darth Vader and they stood by the door as he cautiously walked to her bedside.

Avenger was fearsome, even in captivity. He'd seen her on TV, of course. Without armor or sword, she all but flew to take out the Anointed One. No hesitation. And more importantly, with one touch, she'd turned him to her will.

The fear intensified when he looked into her open eyes. With the pupils dilated from the drug, they looked black with just a hint of the dark brown iris surrounding what seemed like the doorway to her soul. Deep and shadowy and dangerous.

Jette deliberately remained silent, just staring into his eyes.

Nervously, Tinman pried his gaze away from Avenger and looked over at the mirror. He couldn't make this decision himself. Walking to the door, he hesitated, then opened it and left the room.

# Chapter 36

Marc swayed and sat down hard on the chair next to the table where the files were beginning to tip over from their weight. He rubbed his eyes, afraid if he did so they would pop out of his head, but finding the urge irresistible.

"It's been days since you've done anything more than close your eyes," frowned Luke, coming over and squatting next to the chair. "Marc, you can't sustain the pace. You won't rest, you eat only when your body warns you that you need fuel. The stress has been astronomical and you're still recovering from serious wounds…"

"Go away, Luke. You aren't helping."

"Damn it Marc, you don't even have the energy to lose your temper. That should tell you something."

"She's out there. What have these days been like for her?" snapped Marc, feeling ill. Tired and discouraged and sick to the bone.

"I'm a physician, Marc. I'm telling you that you can't push yourself physically like this anymore." He took Marc's arm and waited until his exhausted friend shifted his bloodshot eyes to his. Luke knew he had to get through to Marc or he'd have a seriously ill man on his hands. Keeping his voice even and reasonable, he gave it his best shot. The only one he knew would work. The only one he had left.

"Marc, you're our best hope of finding Jette. Of finding my sister. If you don't shut down now, you'll start missing clues. Damn it Marc, you probably already have."

That got Marc's attention. Something cold started to swirl though his gut. Probably already have. Already have. What had he missed?

"Luke, I close my eyes and I see her falling. I see her struggling. I see her waiting for me to find her. God, I can't sleep."

"I want you to take something."

"Absolutely not," sighed Marc automatically. To him drugs of any kind were the enemy.

"Fine. Then at least do what Jette does. Try a little relaxation. You haven't been around her long, but you know the drill."

"Yeah. Surround yourself with comfort and stillness, shut down the senses one at a time and close in. Hell, like that would ever work with me. Luke, she's naturally tranquil, at peace with herself when she shuts down. I'm, well, more complicated. I don't think I can ever get to the place she seems to find so naturally."

"Try or you'll burn out and be of no use to her. Try." Luke put his hand on Marc's shoulder. "Do it for her."

Marc just stared. Another symptom of his extreme exhaustion. He couldn't even sustain an argument.

For her, he thought. For Jette. He nodded and Luke let him go.

He dragged himself up to the roof garden. A place where he could still hear, see, smell, taste, touch his city, the city that gave birth to him. Raised him. Held him in Her arms as he grew into a man.

Collapsing onto a thick comfortable lounge chair, he pulled up his feet and toed off his shoes. His entire body screamed with fatigue, his chest throbbed relentlessly, and his eyes burned when he closed them.

Shut down, he thought. He'd seen her do it. Rest. Relax, then float gently into a meditative state. For her, it was second nature. Or maybe pure nature. Could he do it? Shut down for Jette? Yes. For her, he'd try anything. Do anything.

Remembering her patient instruction he started with his five senses, turning them off one by one. There was no sight now, nothing but the darkness behind his closed lids. As the sounds faded and the scents retreated, he felt himself loosen up. Lighten up. Float. Help me, Jette, he thought. Come with me. Be with me. He imagined her in his arms. Not hot and passionate, but soft, sweet and lovely. Her familiar form filled his mind and the world retreated farther. His body began drifting. He could no longer feel his limbs, there was no pain. His heartbeat was the only sound in his head. The steady rhythm sent him further into a state of rest. Deeper into relaxation. Deeper. Deeper.

When his eyes slowly came open, everything was dim. He frowned. What the hell? Had his eyes finally blown? Had he stared so intently at the maps, the computer screens, the files, that they finally got used up? Shifting, he nearly moaned. Damn, he was stiff. All over. Stretching out the cramps in his lower back, he rubbed his chest and side. He may be going blind but at least the old wounds no longer pounded.

Painfully bringing up his arm, he flexed his hand and wrist and looked at his watch. It took a moment to focus. Blinking, he waited until the face of it shimmered into detail he could read. It looked like 8:30. He sighed, scrubbing his rough face, then sat up with a jerk. 8:30! He'd come up to the roof at noon. He'd been under for over eight hours. His eyes hadn't blown, it was approaching dusk.

Standing up, he shook out his arms and legs and rolled his shoulders. No wonder he felt like his bones were made of concrete, he probably hadn't moved a muscle the whole time. Shaking his head, and running his hands through his hair, he stretched out the contracted muscles throughout his body and realized his brain had lost that fuzzy other-worldly feeling that was beginning to make him punchy. He felt hungry and, if not refreshed, then at least more human.

Knowing someone would have come looking for him if there were any new developments, he decided to take another few minutes. Slipping his shoes back on, he walked over to the edge of the garden and looked down over his city. Lights were blinking on. Another day had passed and she was still out there waiting. Waiting for him. Expecting him. The fact that she had to endure another night thinking he'd let her down tore a piece out of his heart.

Move, he told himself. And finish this. Turning, he walked quickly and with renewed determination down the stairs to the apartment. As he strode though the deserted kitchen, he snagged an apple, two chocolate donuts, a chicken leg and a mug of coffee. He could hear people in the ballroom on the phones and computers. Not wanting to talk with anyone, he ate, showered, and finished waking up. When he went back to the command center, he felt so refreshed, he was almost sure he could fly if called upon to do so.

"I'm going out for awhile," he called to his team as they turned and watched him stride out of the apartment. He needed to be in his city. The heart of it. At street level he debated walking through the park, then seeing the people and press milling outside the door, he decided to hop on the Harley. Seconds later, he roared out of the garage and onto the crowded busy streets of New York City.

Blaring horns, hawking vendors, loud voices from open windows, and muted music behind club doors surrounded him as he weaved through traffic and gave him what he needed. Life. Energy. Even optimism. She was here and he'd find her if he had to take the town apart brick by brick.

Something was poking at him and he wanted to wander until his internal compass found its destination. Before he even realized where he was going, he was back on the rooftop where Jette had taken her dive. There was a solitary recovery boat still out there. Sweeney met with the press every morning and announced that they hadn't yet found Jette's body. That was fine with Marc. It actually played well. If the people he was looking for thought the police assumed Jette was dead, he'd have a freer rein.

He spun around, hand on his weapon when he heard a whisper of sound behind him. The little girl with the pigeon stood staring at him.

"Hi Kia. Shouldn't you be in bed?" he asked, relaxing a bit.

"It's hot in the apartment and I need to feed Nick. You don't look so mad anymore."

"No. I got some rest."

"Have you found her?"

"No. No, not yet."

"And you're sad."

"Very. But I have to keep looking." Start at the beginning, his refreshed mind whispered. Go back to the beginning. "Kia, tell me again what the lady told you to tell only me."

"Sure. Two like in lips, two like in feet. And in seven who you will greet."

227. They'd been chasing those numbers with very little success but it was only a matter of time before they uncovered the meaning behind them. He hoped he had enough time.

What were you trying to give me, Jette, he thought. Maybe the clue was in fingers, feet and greet. No. It wasn't a riddle. She'd want to make it obvious.

His eyes traveled around, looking at buildings, rooftops, church steeples. Thinking. Processing.

"And in seven who you will greet." His eyes snapped back to a church. "Kia. Say it one more time. Very slowly."

"Okay. Two like in lips." Kia said the words slowly, deliberately, without the rush of emotion she'd felt that first day.

"Two like in lips," he repeated.

"Uh hum. Then two like in feet."

"Two like in feet." Marc's heart was thumping. It felt too big for his chest.

"And in seven who you will greet," she finished, seriously, quietly.

The thumping became a buzz in his blood.

"Kia," he said just as quietly, just as deliberately. "Could the lady have said heaven, not seven? And in *heaven* who you will greet."

Kia frowned, thinking, considering. Then she nodded enthusiastically.

Marc closed his eyes. Luke was right. His mind had been so misted, so filled with anxiety, he hadn't pushed on Kia's recollection. She was a child. In shock, for God's sake. Terrified. He should have considered other possibilities the first time he questioned her. Seven never really did make sense. It wasn't seven. It was heaven.

Now that all the static from fatigue and shock and worry had lifted, he played the information differently. His blood rushed with a geyser of hot, potent hope. Not just a clue. An obvious, simple, directive.

"Thanks, Kia. I have to go." He turned with renewed energy.

"Do you know where she is now?" asked Kia, really, really liking what she saw on the man's face.

"Not exactly, but I think I'm one step closer."

As he ran down the stairs, he flipped open his phone. He wanted to have a complete report by the time he got back to the apartment.

Tagg answered on the first ring. "Hi Marc. What's up?"

"Who will you meet in heaven?"

"Excuse me?"

Marc told him the new version of the poem. "I for one am not counting on getting there, but legend has it you'll meet St. Peter, isn't that right?"

"Right. St. Peter," agreed Tagg.

"Is there a St. Peter's church on 2nd? 22nd?"

"Just a minute. I'll get Kelly right on it."

A few seconds later, he was relaying the information "There's a ton of St. Peter's right around here. It's a popular name, but not on 2nd or 22nd. Here's one on Lexington at 54th."

"No. There's something about 2 or 22. Most likely 22."

"Come on in, Marc. We'll have a list by the time you get here."

"I'm there in five."

# Chapter 37

Remaining calm and quiet, Jette resisted the temptation to look over at the mirror herself. It was obviously a window on the other side. She'd been behind enough of them in her career to recognize the texture and depth of the device. They were watching. Always watching, it seemed.

The exception was during her time in the bathroom, thank the Great Spirit for small favors. Her exhaustive search was made in a drugged state, but she was quite sure there was nothing in there projecting her image to some perverted observer. A Sentinel stood outside the door, but otherwise she was given complete privacy. She'd made good use of that privacy over the last few days, taking short showers, then keeping the water running until the impatient guard would pound on the door. They must think she had the world's tiniest bladder because she'd ask for frequent bathroom breaks, then use the time to stretch out her muscles, do yoga, run in place. She wanted to be physically ready to take off if given the opportunity. Her cosmetics were being used up at a record rate and a pair of pale blue panties would never be the same.

Who was this Empress? Did she have a real world part to play? What were her motives? Was she using this game to trap people to do her bidding, or was she also caught in its delusion?

All her questions needed to be put on hold. Later. When she was alone she could reflect. Right now she needed whatever wits she could harvest for her meeting with the Empress.

Tinman reentered the room carrying a long black scarf.

"You will not look upon the Blue Empress." He secured the scarf tightly around her eyes.

Fine, she thought. I'll use my other four senses. She heard the door open and footsteps. Confident, no scrape or shuffle. The woman had no congenital defect in her legs. Seven steps in about 14 feet. A woman with a long stride. Tall. Take that Tinman. I learned something.

"Hello, Avenger," whispered the Empress, her voice distorted by something. Something over her mouth? Low and raspy. A deliberate attempt to disguise her tone? No identifiable accent. Something familiar? She wasn't sure. "Are you comfortable?"

"I am." Jette had no idea what the expected responses were from Avenger so she said nothing more.

"Your captivity is shaking the Middle World. The legend begins."

"How long do you think you can keep me here?" If she was going to be part of this legend, she wanted to be in on all the details.

"I'll keep you as long as I need to. You're well hidden."

"You're a clever woman."

Silence. Was she not to be called a woman, thought Jette. Or did she have a problem with the word clever. Or was it the praise. Should she be more defiant? Less complimentary? She took a deep breath and went on instinct.

"It will make my victory more satisfying, Empress. Prepare for your defeat."

The angry reply was immediate. "I thought for a moment you were weakening."

"You can't keep me long enough for that to happen."

"You will turn, Avenger. You will grant me one of your last lives. It's just a matter of time. Your Dark Knight won't save you. He hides while your Guardians run around the City of Might without direction."

Inside Jette, a low-grade fury signaled for a significant shot of adrenalin and helped cleanse her system of some of the drug. It took her a long time to anger, but she had the blood of the Cherokee warrior and when the simmer turned to a boil, her temper could be formidable. She could feel her blood thrumming though her veins and it brought strength to her voice, punch to her posture. Her fists balled up and tightened, her jaw clenched, and to those observing, she became every inch the Avenger.

It was an unintentional transformation and everyone familiar with Jette knew it was in her repertoire. Those in the room and those watching through the mirror, however, had seen her go quiet and passive in captivity. Now before their eyes she was morphing into a powerful and dangerous adversary.

"Untie me now," she demanded. "Now. Let's end this." The volume of her voice was low, but the tone was menacing, confident, with a whiff of condescension.

The Empress was thrilled. Here was the woman who ruled Callisto. Avenger. Born under a full moon like she herself had been. Who'd been banished from Himalia to be raised by wolves.

And she was her captive.

"You lose track of time, Avenger. It's not yet the full moon. First you must turn, pledging your other remaining life to me. Then I'll take your last life in a Final Duel."

"If you're so powerful, so filled with destiny, then get there sooner. Fight me!"

"No, I think not. I think…"

"Coward," interrupted Jette. She could hear the quick intakes of breath from the Sentinels in the room and an air of disbelief pushed in on her heightened senses. "Fight me now, Empress."

A heavy blanket of silence fell in on the space around her.

"Are you still there?" demanded Jette as the seconds ticked off toward a full minute. "At least remove this ridiculous blindfold. What are you hiding? I know you're a Blue Empress."

"I'm not *a* Blue Empress, Avenger. I'm *the* Blue Empress."

Jette let out a short derisive laugh meant to insult. To incite.

"Empress to your weak minded Sentinels, maybe. But to me you're a coward."

There was more silence. Had she overplayed?

"I can see you aren't ready to be turned. Perhaps another week."

Suddenly, she felt strong hands grab her arms followed by the presence of a familiar Minion and the prick of a needle.

"Another week?" breathed Jette heavily as the drug began to alter her mood. Fighting its seductive pull, she held on to her anger. "In another week my Dark Knight will have you caged. Your Sentinels, Mercenaries and Minions will be defeated. I'll be free and watching as your power dissolves into nothing. Nothing. Surrender to me now, Empress. Surrender to me now and I'll find a place for you when I rule. Fight me and you'll be crushed."

The drug in her system wouldn't be denied and Jette fell back on the pillows, flush with her diminishing anger and caught in the ecstasy of her heated blood. What they were giving her was extremely potent and she knew she'd have a time of withdrawal when she got out of there. Right at the moment, that seemed far, far, away. Everything seemed far away. She floated.

Her mind stayed tethered to the reality of the room, however. She forced a part of her brain to stay alert. Over the last few days she learned that her captors would talk more openly right after a shot when they thought she was out of it. So she went still. Like a stalking mountain lion. And listened.

"Shall we punish her for the insult, Empress." The Tinman sounded like he'd relish the duty.

The Empress was still keeping her voice low and rough. Disguising it. The thought was a bit fuzzy, but it occurred to Jette that the Empress was keeping her identity from her Sentinels and Minions as well. Interesting.

"No. What good will it be to turn her if she isn't at full power when I do. Use your limited mental acuity. Are all the explosives rigged in the traps in the Halls of all the Saints?"

"Yes, Empress. Your points for annihilation and kills will be assured."

"Excellent. Award yourself another 500 points and a hundred each to your team. Distribute the Boons as well."

"The same as you give Avenger?"

"Of course. But only to the Minions. We need our Sentinels to remain alert."

"Their Boons will be of greater value. Sentinel TrueBlue920 has finally decided, Empress. He wants a Porsche. A red one."

"Simple enough. I'll see to it."

"You're a generous Empress."

"Are you content with your lot?"

"Yes. My account is growing nicely."

"Excellent. We have two other temples prepared. I prefer not to move her through the streets of the City of Might until we have to. Her Guardians are about. Their pursuit is feeble and without direction, but they could accidentally stumble onto a clue. I'll communicate time and place. Remember the codes."

"Yes, Empress. This has been an exceptional run. Do you think she'll turn?"

"I have no doubt."

Jette smiled, satisfied for now. She's learned one thing for sure. The Blue Empress was caught in her own full blown delusion. While the drug sent part of her brain on a clouded journey into a psychedelic netherland, another part planned and plotted.

# Chapter 38

"St. Peter was a popular guy," said Kelly. "Was he a pope or something?"

"I don't know. A saint for sure," muttered Tagg.

"There's a Church of St. Peter on Barclay."

"What's the address?" demanded Marc. He was leaning over Kelly, impatient, but knowing she was the fastest they had.

"16."

"No."

"St. Peter's Episcopal on 20th."

"Closer."

"St. Peter's religious medals at 22 East 115th. If we go with just Peter, yikes, there's hundreds of hits. Let's see. Peter's Bar and Grill on 2nd, here's Peter's Beauty Emporium on 22nd," muttered Kelly, reading off her screen. "If we go with Pete's, the list is off the page."

"No." Marc's energy was beginning to dissolve in the frustration. They would check them all out, but none of them felt right. "Let's stay with the Saint."

"Okay. Here's a St. Peter's school on 22nd but it's over in Jersey. I arched the search to a 50 mile radius, just in case."

"It would probably be empty in the summer," said Rachael.

"Oh my God!" whooped Kelly. "Look here! There used to be a St. Peter's Mission on 22nd. The address is on an old website, down about 30 hits, but it could be something."

"A mission? Get me everything you have." Marc's intuition sizzled.

"It was established by Dominican sisters right after World War II." Kelly quickly skimmed the articles and website. "It moved. The mission site on 22nd was abandoned for a bigger building on 53rd about two years ago. It wouldn't have been on our list."

"What's in there now?"

"Um. Just a sec. Nothing. No business or citizen has that address. I can't find anything that's in there now."

"Lyd, check city records. Any permits for reconstruction?"

"Hey, hey, hey, kid," shouted Lyd after a few seconds. Her voice never went much above a whisper or snarl, but she was caught up in the thrill of a new clue. "Nothing on reconstruction but here's a two year lease on the entire property. To a corporation called Dominion."

"Dominican?"

"No. Dominion. Like in…" Lyd waved her hand. "Like in taking over the world or something." She clicked the thesaurus. "Power, authority, control, command, rule, sovereignty."

Everyone had stopped listening, everyone but Kelly, who stared at her for a few seconds before getting back to the search.

"Raj, find out everything you can in the public records on this corporation. Everyone else, get ready. We're going in." Marc's heart pumped with certainty

"No. Wait. Marc. Listen." Tagg grabbed Marc's arm before he could tear out of the room. "You can't just go in with guns blazing. If she's at that location, she's been there for over four days. An hour to think, plan and bring in ESU isn't going to matter. We need their equipment for recon. We need to know what we're up against."

Marc fought against Tagg's restraining hand.

"Let go Tagg. You don't want to stand between me and Jette."

"Marc. I'm not, but listen to me. You go off without backup and a plan and she could die in the crossfire. You could die trying to free her. Remember. We figure this is connected to the university shooting. The boy had amazing firepower."

"If she's in there…"

"Marc. Tagg's right. If she's in there, let's give her the best chance of coming out alive," urged Eunice. "I hate bringing this up, but remember the Peroni case. I was there."

We were too late to keep the lieutenant from going in and his whole family was killed. Including the lieutenant."

"Okay. Okay, you're right."

Tagg slowly released his grip on Marc's arm, expecting him to push away and run out the door. But Eunice had reached the cop inside of Marc and it was the cop in charge now.

"Sommer, keep working with Kelly to get what you can about this mission and the building. Tagg, call the chief and get the warrants in place. Then let's get Tana Bentley involved. She's the best. We'll make this official. Raj, call her. The number is on my speed dial." He threw his phone to Raj. "Everything we need is on record. Kia made a formal statement and our current interpretation is drawn from it. Dina, call Sweeney. This is still her case and she should be in on the take down. She's given us everything we need to return the favor. Eunice, grab the maps from 15th to 30th. Teresa, call procurement and get gear here. Riot guns, vests, everything we'll need for a major push. Rachael, arrange for transport. We go in," he checked his watch, "at 10 p.m."

By 9:30, all the necessary warrants had been procured by the chief and Tana's team stood ready. Sweeney and her team were taking the perimeters and keeping civilians out of the area. Marc's squad was to serve as backup only, something that burned right through his gut, but good sense and a solid plan prevailed.

The structure on 22nd was a fabulous old building with wonderful gothic architectural details. One of thousands of buildings in transition, standing ready to be restored. There were large windows in the front that were now covered with plain brown paper. The sidewalks and alleys around the building were neat and well maintained. It didn't have an abandoned look, but it did appear empty.

Time crawled for Marc. Was she in there? Was she alive? Was he ever going to wake up from this horrible nightmare? There had been eyes and ears in and around the building for over 15 minutes. Electronic signals were being sent to the mobile command center in a van a block away from the target. There was no sound, no motion detected.

At 9:45, two black and whites silently blocked off both auto and pedestrian traffic on 22nd. At 9:50 Tana sent a quarter of her unit to the rear of the building. At 9:55, she positioned another quarter on strategic rooftops above and across the street from the former mission. At 9:59, everyone simultaneously removed the safeties from their assigned weapons and made sure their body armor was secure. At 10:00, the well coordinated team orchestrated a perfect incursion. Locks were expertly released and darkly clad men and women swarmed quickly and silently into the building.

By 10:10, the first floor was declared clear. Clear and empty. Tana gave the signal for Marc's team to enter and start checking the rooms in the rear for forensic evidence while she and her unit continued up the four floors of warehouse space and offices.

Marc walked through the large reception area, now illuminated brightly by the overhead fluorescent lighting. He could hear the ESU team moving in and out of the stairwell, shouting all clear into their radios. The place had a deserted feel and Marc was quite sure they'd find no human inhabitants.

"Commander Bentley told us to go look in the rooms down this hall." Kim glanced over at Marc to be sure he didn't slip into some kind of breakdown. But he was cool. All cop now. Focused and ready to work any clues the building held.

Marc led them down a hallway and into what looked like a small apartment. The lights had been turned on by the ESU team and they stopped just over the threshold, astonished. While the rest of the floor was completely empty this area was a luxuriously furnished suite. Bedroom, bathroom, a tiny kitchenette. It was neat and tidy, although the beautiful bed was unmade.

Marc sniffed and scented his mate. Jette. She'd been here. And not that long ago. He wanted to rave. To stomp and swear and throw his fist through the wall. But he pulled on the mantle of discipline and ordered his team to begin gathering evidence.

Go through the motions. Take the next step. It was the only way he was going to make it through the hour. Through the night. Make it through until he found her.

Marc noticed the two way mirror in the wall. Walking to the hallway on the other side, he saw the cots, TVs and garbage cans overflowing with fast food wrappers. This was where the kidnappers watched her.

Tagg came up beside him. "Marc, I'm sorry. Maybe I should have let you follow your instincts. Maybe…"

Marc held up his hand and cut him off. "I can't deal with maybe's right now, Tagg. I can hardly deal with this. Inside my head I know you were right and that has to keep me on track right now." He nodded at the automatic weapons in the corner. "If they abandoned that arsenal, I can only imagine what they carried with them. I have a feeling she wouldn't have come out alive."

He walked away and Tagg let him go, then turned and joined the rest of the team. No one said anything as they quietly and efficiently went about their work. Disappointed but determined.

Marc walked into the bathroom. It was fresh and clean. His stomach clutched when he recognized the scent of her shampoo. She'd been a prisoner, but if they'd gone to the trouble of getting her favorite shampoo, she'd probably been kept safe. That fact had his terror taking a step back from the brink.

Tana came in to report, looking around at the heavy, dark furnishings. "Nothing upstairs. This room is creepy. Looks like a gothic headquarters. What are you dealing with here, Marc? Some kind of cult?"

"I don't know. I do know Jette was here."

"Fingerprint matches already?"

"No." He nodded at the cosmetics lined up neatly on the dresser. "These are all her brands."

The hot stab of jealous fury penetrated Tana's kevlar, but she kept her voice cool and detached. "I see. If you want my opinion, it looks like she may have been a part of this whole thing. Are you sure she was snatched? This is a pretty luxurious way to be held against your will and no kidnapper I've ever encountered supplies the victim's brand of shampoo, for Christ's sake."

As Tana took a jar of exotic cream with her gloved hand and sniffed it, she had no idea how close she came to being taken down and slammed to the floor. Tagg saw it, however, and stepped in quickly.

"There's evidence that the door was secured on the outside and over there is a two way mirror. There are soft restraints on the bed. She was being held and being watched. For some reason we'll eventually discover, they wanted her to be comfortable."

"Hmm." Tana's skepticism was obvious. "I hear she's working on a third book. Maybe she wanted a little more publicity. Maybe that stunt she pulled at the university didn't give her enough media attention. Or maybe it gave her a real taste for it. Could be she's a media junkie, a news whore. This would be a way of sustaining the interest. It wouldn't be the first time a pseudo celebrity staged a crisis to capture the spotlight."

This time Tagg had to restrain Marc. Grabbing his arm as he started for Tana, he turned him toward the doorway. "Marc, just chill out here. We have to work this room. Glove up and start going through the drawers. Maybe she left us something. Remember, she gave us the location," he said in a low voice.

Dina came in on the end of Tana's comments and took Marc's other arm, pushing plastic gloves into his hand.

"Detective, the CSI team is here, but I thought you'd probably want to search the drawers yourself." Then, when he didn't move toward the door, she whispered, "Marc. Come on. It's not worth the paperwork."

Marc seethed, but nodded. Nothing could be gained by knocking the head of the elite ESU team unconscious. He almost turned around despite the paperwork, when Tana thought she'd score another hit.

"She gave you this address? Interesting. Laying a trail for you to follow? What a waste of city resources."

Tana's dental work was saved only by luck and chance when she was called to the third floor to check out what looked like the crib of a homeless person.

"I sure hope we aren't needed for any real emergency tonight." Tana took a parting shot as she strode out of the room, satisfied that she'd created a cloud around the sainted Jette Morningstar.

Marc's vision blurred with rage, but as soon as Tana was out of his range, he turned it toward the task at hand. Angrily pulling out of Dina's and Tagg's firm grasp, he walked into the room where Jette had been held. The fact that there was no sign of any violence was the only thing keeping him from falling off the ledge of sanity.

He did a quick visual scan. Nothing obvious jumped out at him. He'd study the forensic photos later. Lots of stylish antique pieces and accessories. This took a bankroll, he thought. And planning. He walked over to the stacks of books on the night stand. Library books.

"Rachael, make a list of these and see who checked them out. Chances are they were purchased at a used book sale, but we need to follow this up." They all knew that it probably wouldn't be that easy, but sometimes they got lucky and the perps got stupid.

There were several receipts, all for cash purchases, but they carried names and addresses of retail establishments. High end label clothes were hanging in the closet, all Jette's size.

"This is just getting stranger. It's like she was a guest, not a prisoner," observed Tagg.

"I think this is really, really good news, though," added Kim loud enough for Marc to hear. "It means that they want Jette to be comfortable. That's a little bizarre, but if they take the time and effort to get all of her favorite stuff, that means they aren't going to hurt her. Right? Don't you think that's what it means, Detective?"

Glancing over at Kim, Marc gave her a ghost of a smile. He'd come to that same conclusion and it was keeping him relatively calm.

"Yes, Sommer. I think that's exactly what it means."

Tagg discretely left the rooms when he heard Tana coming back down the corridor. He'd decided to handle the liaison role.

"All done here, Tana?"

"Yeah. All done. There's nothing here for Emergency Services."

"Let me remind you that the kidnappers shot and killed a hostage."

Tana narrowed her eyes, assessing how much damage she could do to her rival. Not much, maybe, but there was opportunity here. Tagg had a great deal of influence over Marc.

"Look, Tagg. Between us, this is how I see it. Morningstar wasn't kidnapped. She staged the whole thing. No one could have survived that fall into the river. For some reason, things got out of hand on that rooftop. A hostage was shot. She or her minions were upset and sent the two who'd done the shooting over the edge to their own death. Then they walked away and came here. And hey, as it worked out, everything got even more dramatic. Her specialty, from what I know. I suspect she'll leave a clear trail and will set things up so she can be found before the end of the week. Then it's the talk shows and another best seller. Just don't call me for backup the next time she leads you to her location."

Tagg was nearly speechless, but not quite. "There were witnesses," he said angrily.

"Yeah. I read the reports. First this elderly maid, who was locked in a john and saw nothing, really. Then Morningstar gets away. How convenient. She's chased by thugs., but maybe she's leading the pack. Then a little girl gives an account of what she thought she saw after Morningstar gives her a clue. A clue that sounds like it was written beforehand and rehearsed. Damn, you have to be a rookie to swallow any of that whole. Well, I'm no rookie. I personally think her role in the university shootings should be investigated further. I'm going to give Green a call."

Tagg just stared at her as she spun around and strode out of the building, yelling commands to her unit.

Dina came up behind him. "Is she nuts?"

"No," frowned Tagg. "Her and Marc have a history. She'll give Jette the boot any chance she gets. I think she still hopes for a chance to take her place."

"Hmm. Then she's not nuts, she's delusional."

"Yeah. Well, let's not be distracted by it. We've got a lot of work to do to keep this trail hot."

Back in the room, Marc walked over to Janet Donlin, glad to see she caught the call. She was running a blue light over the bed linen. The throbbing question got caught in his throat, but she anticipated it and gave him the information he wanted to hear.

"No ejaculate, no sign of sexual activity. No blood or anything to indicate rape or violence of any kind," she reported softly, kindly.

Marc only nodded. The rest of the team let out their collective breath and kept working.

"I'll be outside," he said abruptly. "I want to see if there were any eyes or ears out there earlier."

He needed air. He needed to get out of the room that held her scents. When he got to the street, he took in huge lungsful of oxygen and paced like a caged animal. He felt like a caged animal. Unhinged by his intense frustration. She'd been there and he might have had her if he hadn't waited. If he'd put the clues together sooner. He knew he followed logical, intelligent procedure, but his gut was neither logical nor intelligent right now. It was filled with raw emotions released by his fury.

"Pssst. Pssst." Marc looked around and saw a ragged little woman standing behind an alley dumpster. Most of her face was concealed under a large brimmed black hat and a pair of oversized sunglasses. She looked like a movie star who went overboard on the punk, shabby chic look.

"SueTee?"

"Hey, traitor." SueTee had never forgiven him for getting a law degree. Her deep seeded issues with lawyers remained a mystery. "Hear you've been spreading the green really thick. True or false."

"True."

"You're here and the people inside the old mission are not. You interested in an eyeball account? Yes or no."

"Yes."

"Hear you're willing to pay for word. True or false."

"True." The pace was aggravating, but he knew he'd get more information by playing SueTee's game than by interrogating her. And he was too much a cop to torture or beat it out of her.

"Will you go as high as 50? Yes or no."

"Yes." Hah! Her game just bit her in the ass, he thought with a sliver of satisfaction. He would have gone as high as $500 if she'd ask him an open ended question.

"People were here until 23 minutes, 6 seconds before you arrived. Are you interested in more? Yes or no."

"Yes."

"Three men, two women, one I couldn't tell. It was dark. No street lights. Would you like to have descriptions? Yes or no."

"Yes."

"Let's see the green. Do you have 5 ten's? Yes or no."

"Yes." Marc took money from his front pocket and discreetly pulled off five bills.

SueTee had an aversion to coming in contact with anything still warm from someone else's touch, so she opened her huge purse and watched as Marc dropped in the cash.

"Too bad, you dirty collaborator. Ha! That'll teach you. It was too dark. I can't tell you what they looked like. Too dark, I said. But they were dressed strange. Hoods and capes to the ground. Saw the outline of titties or I wouldn't know two were women. Smaller though. The size, not the titties. You want to know if they knew you were coming. This is worth more green. True or false.'

"True. More green if…" Marc forgot the game in his eagerness to get more.

"Ah ah ah! You're sorry for interrupting. True or false!"

"True."

"They knew. They were in a hurry. They were here for the last four days. La de da. In and out. Only at night but not a problem. Then a big ass delivery truck comes around and in a tizzy they move out of here. Three men. Two women and a body. Three men. Two women and a body. You want the body. True or false."

"True." Body. Hell. He nearly exploded with the pressure of playing SueTee's game.

"It's not a corpse. Not a corpse. Was yelling and punching. Plenty of life. You want to know about the truck. True or false."

"True." Marc felt his own life return. Jette was alive. Alive. He had to hang on to that. And he had to pay attention to the details. He lost her, but he was still on her trail.

"You want to know the color. Yes or no."

"Yes." He continued with the odd questioning until he was sure he got everything he could from SueTee. Her purse was full of cash, but she'd turned out to be an exceptional witness and Marc had an excellent description of the truck. Not the same one that had brought her here. They were switching their vehicles. Smart.

Walking around to the back alley, he snapped on his flashlight. SueTee told him precisely which door they'd come out. Getting down on one knee, he ran the beam back and forth. Something blue caught his eye. Reaching down, he picked it up. It was a piece of blue cloth. A tiny piece that was incongruous with the other clutter in the alley. He found two more pieces between the door and the place SueTee had told him the truck was parked. Then four pieces in a cluster, then nothing. It wasn't much, but it was something. She was leaving him a little trail. And he'd go over every square inch of the city to find the rest of it if he had to.

The fact that Jette was alive and alert enough to do this also gave him confidence. They had time. He had no way of knowing how much, but they had some time. She wasn't dead, nor, it appeared, incapacitated.

Opening his cell phone, he called Tagg and asked him to meet him outside.

"SueTee says they were here until 23 minutes before we went in and all indications are they left in a hurry."

"They knew we were coming! How?"

"I don't know but from now on, this investigation is conducted with only our first team."

"But…," began Tagg.

"No one else is to be brought in. No one. I want a complete list of people who knew we'd located the mission. Complete. Leave no one out no matter who they are."

"That include the chief and ESU?"

"Everyone."

"How do you want to divide the tasks?"

"I have to leave those questions to you, Tagg. I need to go on a hunt while the trail is hot." He filled Tagg in on the truck sighting. "It was on the streets and the streets are mine, goddamn it. I'll tack in the streets like Jette tracks in the desert. Keep this information close. Very close."

"Fine, but Marc listen." Tagg could see Marc's condition was a contradiction. Exhausted and frustrated to the point of collapse, yet shaking with urgency. "Can you come back with me and shut down for awhile? Settle yourself before you go out there? You need to be sharp."

"No, damn it. We were 23 minutes too late! I need to get moving before the trail fades. The attention span of the city is short."

Tagg watched Marc jog across the street and into a deep, dark alley. Turning, he went back into the mission to do his part.

Toward dawn, the team staggered back into the ballroom. The highly charged exit made the return seem even more silent and somber by contrast. Hilda, Tommy and Claude were in the kitchen putting together food and coffee for the morning briefing. Kelly and Lyd, discouraged by the news, retired to the guest rooms for some much needed rest.

They'd spent hours bagging and tagging all the evidence. There were hundreds of pieces of it: fingerprints, hairs, receipts, plastic flatware filled with DNA, wrappers, clothing, books, newspapers, magazines, a watch, cigarette butts, and several hypodermic needles. While it gave them a wealth of leads, the volume was daunting.

Still, they all knew they needed to continue putting one foot in front of the other. Fueled by the fragrant and filling buffet Hilda set out, they started sifting through the clues with dogged determination.

Marc came in a few hours after sunrise, showered, then worked the maps. He placed bright green dots on the locations where the truck had been spotted. Traced by his own private army. The people of the streets. Vendors, vagrants, maintenance workers, hawkers, peddlers, even a few drug pushers. Separating the legitimate sightings from the vague or bogus accounts was the most frustrating part of the process. There was no end to the people who admitted seeing it in exchange for a payoff. He'd held back the fact that the truck had front end damage and an *I Love New York* bumper sticker. Whenever one of these details was added to the sighting, he knew he was on the right track.

They'd taken her down 22$^{nd}$ and had turned south on Broadway. Smart. A lot of traffic. The angle of Broadway indicated a move to the east side. Three separate people had seen it on 17$^{th}$. He was closing in. Unless the truck had left Manhattan, he'd find it soon. And if it had left, he'd chase it to California if he had to.

Marc called for a team meeting and they all gathered around the boards. For days they didn't have enough forensic evidence to go on. Now they almost had too much. The evidence bags containing the items found at the scene were on their way to police headquarters, but they had everything catalogued. Raj was printing hundreds of photos taken from every angle.

"What can I help you with?" Eunice walked into the room. She'd just come in from talking with several owners of the make and model van used in the original snatch. Marc wasn't inclined to tell her the vehicle had now changed.

"How about your report," Marc asked causally.

"Nothing. Absolutely nothing but nice families, small business owners and a few nervous teenagers."

"I'd like to have you take another crack at it."

"Talk to the same people?"

"Yes, you might have missed something."

Eunice looked him in the eye. "I'm not your informant, Marc. I know you're sending me out of here, putting me on shit detail so you can work with your team. Let me in or cut me loose."

Marc stared at her and did a gut check. It cleared her, but he was so tired and burned out. "This is too important," he said finally. "I'm sorry. I'm cutting you loose."

Eunice surprised him by laughing. "God, you're one hard-headed sorry son-of-a-bitch. I'd kick your ass if you weren't so pathetic. I think I'll just wait until we find Jette and let her figure out the best way to make you pay. And don't think I won't rat you out. First thing I'm going to do after we get her back is tell her you froze me. She'll make you burn, boy. Now I'm not going back over the same territory so give me some different shit work and let me get out of here so you can talk to your team."

He almost relented, but she was right. He was a hard headed son-of-a-bitch. Hard hearted as well, it seemed.

He handed her an inventory of the high-end cosmetics found at the scene.

"Find out where these are sold. We want a complete list of places and purchases. Start in the city."

Eunice nodded, pausing to give him an opportunity to change his mind. He didn't. He let Eunice walk out of the apartment without an apology.

After they heard the front door slam, he looked around at his team. Dina, Rachael, Raj, Teresa, Tagg, Luke, and Kim. Solid. He was sure. He had to be sure.

"I want no one else in on this phase. No one. Write your notes from this board, then we erase it."

They all nodded. "What about the chief?" asked Rachael.

"No."

"Lyd and Kelly?" asked Kim.

"They're both computer geniuses and they both have flaws. We need to see if one of them is snitching for the other side. We did talk about conspiracy as a theory." He looked into their shocked eyes. "Which of you is the most computer savvy?"

"That would be me," said Kim. She shrugged. "I'm the youngest. Did any of you go through Computer Tots when you were 3 years old?"

They all shook their heads.

"Lucy just showed me how to turn on my new cell phone," griped Tagg.

"I need you to trace where Kelly and Lyd have been electronically. Can you do a history or something? Find out who they've been communicating with while working on our investigation?"

"Yeah, sure" Kim displayed little enthusiasm. They'd all come to like the strange duo.

"Tagg, you take a look at the chief, Sweeney, Eunice, and Tana. Be very, very discreet," ordered Marc.

"Goes without saying," muttered Tagg.

"There were several dozen people on the Emergency Services Unit," said Dina.

"But they didn't know the location until they drove there," countered Marc.

"You already know, don't you?" asked Rachael.

"Yeah. But I'd like the proof. My senses are a little dull. I could be wrong."

The team looked around.

"Shall we look at each other?" asked Dina with just a trace of bitterness. She agreed that there was a leak, she just didn't like looking at other cops. Eunice was an old friend, the chief was her boss, and even though Tana was off on this case, she was one of the few women holding a place of incredible authority in the elite ESU. She was proud of her. Sweeney was cooperating with everything. Lyd and Kelly were new, but had become an incredibly important part of the team.

"Would you have a problem with that?" asked Marc.

There was a penetrating silence.

"What color is my underwear," Dina asked.

"Blue," said Marc without hesitation.

"Ah hum. You've been in my locker?"

"I was looking for a Band-Aid." He held up his index finger. "Paper cut."

"Nasty. Maybe Luke should take a look at it or maybe I should just kick your ass and give him a leg and an arm to set."

Marc glanced over at Luke, who was standing with a cell phone in his hand, staring at the two of them like the rest of the team, then looked back into Dina's stormy face.

"I think I'd rather you kiss it and make it better." Marc put his finger closer to her. He waited. The team waited.

Dina snorted. The team relaxed.

Dina grabbed his finger and made a show of giving it a big smacking kiss while at the same time twisting it. Marc's eyes teared a little with the shock of pain shooting through his finger and up his wrist, but he took it like a man and maintained a grim little smile. The tension in the room cracked and they all started talking at once.

Marc brought them back to order with quick, authoritative assignments. "From what we saw, this operation requires a lot of grease. We need to find the money. Raj, start with the Dominion Corporation. Dina, Rachael go back to the make and model of the original van. We used the 227 to narrow the field. We need to take that out of the equation."

"At least now we can divert all the time we spent on the 227 connection to other tasks," nodded Rachael.

"Yeah, that's something. Luke, there were hypodermic needles at the scene. Here's the number of the tech in charge. We put a priority on it. Teresa, you and I can start on the catalogue of evidence and begin prioritizing."

They knew they had to just keep moving forward. And they did. For hours. Then brought everything back to the midday meet.

"I can find nothing on the computers that would indicate either Kelly or Lyd leaked through email messages," reported Kim. "Of course they're both miles beyond my talent and there's still phones, faxes, and face-to-face."

"The Dominion Corporation was established a month ago and it finalized the lease of the building less than two days after they filed their articles of incorporation. Cash transaction. The names and addresses on the paper are all bogus. Dead people," said Raj. "Dead people, dead end."

"The books we found at the scene were all purchased at various branches at used book sales. They haven't been checked out in years," sighed Dina.

"Here are the photos we took of the scene." Teresa pinned them up on the board. "We'll divide the area into quadrants for further investigation."

Marc shuffled the reports and the inventory of evidence. Looking up at the boards, he sighed. They were rapidly losing focus.

"Is it me, or is there something wrong with this picture. There seems to be almost too much incriminating evidence. I could understand it if they thought their location was to remain a secret forever, but don't these people watch crime TV? They have to know almost everything they left is traceable."

"I think someone is very familiar with police work and wanted us overwhelmed with leads," speculated Dina.

Teresa nodded. "I agree. It's just a feeling, but it's like they want us to be insanely busy. Anyone understanding police procedure would know we have to track everything we find on the premises."

"I'm thinking of the number of hours it will take to pursue everything. Far more than what a squad can put together in any kind of timely manner," commented Raj.

"And I think these clues will take us everywhere but where they're keeping her," speculated Marc.

"Why do you say that?" asked Kim.

"It's all been planted."

"Oh." Kim looked around and saw there were other surprised faces.

"Not that I don't want you all to stay on the clues. It's still evidence."

"But you'll stay with the truck. Something they didn't plant," said Tagg.

"Exactly."

"And we'll keep sifting through everything hoping for a hit." Tagg's feeling of frustration was obvious in his voice.

215

Luke stared at the pictures while the hum of the investigation swirled around him. He wanted to see the place where Jette had been held. He'd been left back at the apartment with Tommy, Claude, and Hilda. It burned him, but he accepted it, not wanting to be in the way. The pictures took him there and made it all real. She'd been in that room. Slept in that bed, walked in that space. His heart ached. When he got to the shots of the bathroom, he shook his head, then bent over to take a closer look.

"Damn it, Jette. You wily creature," he said out loud. "Marc, Jette left us a message. You need relevant evidence, I think you got it!"

Everyone shifted their attention as he looked up from the colorful shots of the graffiti ridden walls.

"What?" Marc asked sharply. "I didn't see any message from her."

And he'd looked. They all had. There'd been no lipstick on the mirror. No words ripped out of a magazine. Nothing.

Luke pointed at several colorful swirls. "Very clever. Hidden. Not obvious. No one would know."

"Know what?" demanded Marc impatiently.

"These are Cherokee symbols."

"What?"

Everyone gathered around Luke and stared at what looked like graffiti. Luke began pointing at various shots of the bathroom walls.

"The Cherokee people were one of the very few native populations who had a written language. It's not an alphabet exactly. They call it syllabary," Luke explained with excitement. "It's survived. Jette can read it and write it. She obviously wanted you to have information, but didn't want them to know she was leaving you something."

"It looks just like the graffiti," breathed Kim with admiration. "All blended in. No one would have perceived it and if they did, they would have thought it was just a series of geometric designs."

"So what does it say?" Marc considered this the only important thing.

"I don't know. Sorry. I picked up some of it when we were kids, but I've forgotten. You can call anyone at the Cherokee Nation in Tahlequah. They'll give you a translation."

"What about Captain Markle? He's Cherokee. And he's a cop," asked Marc.

"Yeah. Perfect. He'd know. Jette's been working with him for years, and he's absolutely obsessed with it," agreed Luke.

Marc quickly dialed the number for Markle and a very sleepy voice answered the phone.

"This better be important, Lexington. I just got back from tracking in the desert and was looking forward to a full eight in the sack."

"Chuck, I have you on speaker. You heard about the incident at NYU?"

"Hey. We sure did." Captain Markle perked up at the mention of Jette. Marc always thought he had a little crush on her. "She really did a job on that maniac. We're all very proud of her."

"You haven't heard she's been kidnapped then?"

"Kidnapped? What the hell? No. We've been in the desert on a training exercise. First a sniper nearly takes her out, now she's been snatched? Can't you keep her safe? You're a cop, goddamn it!" Maybe more than a crush, thought Marc with a horrible pain near his heart.

"Look, let's not get into that right now," he said wearily. He was a cop. And he hadn't kept her safe. He'd deal with that later. "We think the incidents are related. Right now I could use your help."

"Sure. I can be there later today."

"I don't think you'll need to travel. We need your expertise in the Cherokee written language. Jette left a message on the wall where they were holding her. If I email you pictures, can you translate?"

"Yes, I can. Let me put some pants on and get to my computer. Want to hold on or shall I call you back."

"I'll hold."

Chuck gave Marc his email address. Kim scanned the pictures and sent them on. A few minutes later, Chuck was back.

"Okay. I've got your email. I'm downloading the pictures now. Marc. Do you think she's okay?"

"Yes, we think so. They're killers, but they want her alive."

"Good. Good. Is Luke there with you?"

"I'm right here, Chuck."

"Forgot all your basic Cherokee, huh?"

"I only learned it in the first place so she couldn't keep secrets from us."

"I'm looking at the wall now. Very clever. She drew them so they looked like part of the landscape. What were they drawn with?" Some of the symbols were in blood red.

"Cosmetics."

"That's good. Alright the first symbol is like a warning sign. An indication that the message is of critical importance. Are you getting this or do you want me to write it down."

"No. We have a scribe." Marc nodded at Kim who took up a marker and began writing on the white board next to the pictures.

"The first word is flowers. Wasn't that the name of the shooter?"

"Yes."

"Was there a connection?"

"We think so, yes."

"Well, this confirms it. Hunts. Earth princess. Earth princess? Does that mean anything to you?"

Marc didn't think his heart could take much more, but then he turned another corner and it got hit again. But this time there was something soothing about the words. Like a little wink and poke.

"Yeah, I think she's telling me she's alright."

"Good. That's good. Okay. Um. Let's see. This is ten. Here's areas, places, locations. Okay, ten locations. The symbol for empty. Seven are empty. This isn't making any sense."

"Don't worry about that, Chuck. Just give us the words or concepts."

"Right. Okay. Track, or follow the trail. This one is, ah, traps. Traps. Damn. This is harder than I thought. Not everything has a modern equivalent."

"Give us the basics and we can work on the interpretation later."

"Sure. Sure. Trails are, um, false. Untrue. Deception. Whoa. Hold the phone. Deadly. Traps. Marc, there are traps and they are deadly. Danger. The word is repeated. Thunder? I'm sure this is thunder. Dangerous thunder?"

"Explosives? Could she mean bombs?" asked Marc.

"Yes, good. We have no word for explosives, so dangerous thunder would be right. And the symbol for destroy or destruction is next to it. Christ, Marc. Who are you after?"

"We haven't identified them yet. Mostly we're working on finding Jette. This is a completely unexpected development, although we suspected a deeper conspiracy."

"Well, if Jette has accurately read the situation, and I think we would all agree she wouldn't be leaving you a message like this based on speculation, you have more than a kidnapping to worry about. Let's see. There's more here. Three. Three locations have the thunder. In the next line there are several symbols relating to play. Game. Battle. War. I have no idea what that means, but she repeats game."

"Not a real war, then."

"That's my guess. Let's see. Here's one for house or home. This one is for deity. House of gods? This one is warriors. Two of them. Then there are the words for night and day. "

"Night and Day?"

"Yes, or dark and light. The color of sky, so that would be blue. Ruler or leader. So blue leader. That's all I see, Marc. I'll keep studying it. If it's alright with you, I'll show it to some people I know to confirm my translation, but I think I got everything right."

"Thanks, Chuck. Yes. Show it to whomever can help. But don't share the source."

"Got that. Are you sure you don't want me to fly out there?"

"No. But thanks. You've been a big help."

"I'd appreciate it if you'd keep me informed."

"I'll do that."

Marc left Luke to make nice and walked over to the board where Kim had written down all the words. Now to interpret the translation.

"Deadly traps," said Tagg. "Marc, I know you want to find Jette but we have another urgent situation here."

"Bombs. Explosives. We're going to have to bring in the Bomb Squad," agreed Dina.

"Yeah. So much for keeping it close," frowned Marc. "Take care of that, Dina. Talk with Tony Nippard. He's someone we can trust."

"I know him. You're right. He's a really good man. I call him now and ask that he stand by."

"Ten locations, seven of them decoys. Deities? Gods? Saints?" asked Kim. "She was kept in St. Peters. Maybe her captors are keeping with that theme."

"That really doesn't narrow it down very much," frowned Teresa.

"What's all this business about games and dark and light?" asked Rachael. "Should we be looking at paramilitary groups?"

"Or terrorists, maybe?" asked Kim.

"One step at a time," ordered Tagg. "We need to find these locations before they have the itch to detonate the bombs."

"I think at some point they were going to give us this location," Marc mused. "And with all the evidence…"

"We'd have followed the well marked trails right into death traps," breathed Teresa.

"Thank you, Jette," said Rachael with feeling. The rest of the team murmured their appreciation.

"They had no way of knowing we were so close," said Dina. "Maybe they haven't had time to lay the explosives."

"I don't think we can count on that." Marc drilled his fingers into his pulsating temples. "I know this is priority, but I have to stay with the hunt for the truck. I have to. I trust all of you to work the clues, find the locations. Let's plan our next moves."

Kelly wheeled into the room, then took a deep breath. The thought of initiating contact with the detective made her stomach roll around. He'd become even more scary and intense after his strike on the shelter. This may be bad timing, but tough. She'd spent all the time the team had been out of the ballroom looking over every scrap of evidence tacked to the boards. After what she'd eyedropped from them, she knew she was right.

Taking off to Vegas had been her mission, but that had switched off. There was something even more compelling about being a part of this hunt. This team. It had pulled a layer out of her she didn't recognize, but she knew she liked it.

The detective trusted her, utilized her, made her feel, sort of powerful or something. He yelled at her, but he did that with everyone. Even that made her feel connected somehow. The wheelchair made some people soft, some people freaky, some people way, way over-the-top considerate. Totally awkward and never real. Not the detective, though. And none of his team either. He treated her just like everyone else. Sometimes it was pretty low, but that was all part of the package. Now she was going to see if he'd listen to her.

She'd put it all together. Like she'd seen him do. He'd take everything he knew, study what he'd learned and formulate a conclusion. Well, she'd done the same thing. She was a champion gamer because of her ability to strategize and outthink the challengers. It was what separated leets like her from the noobs who just used speedy fingers and quick reflexes to blast and burn. Leets worked the gray matter, not just finger dexterity.

She looked over at Lyd, who gave her an encouraging nod. Lyd listened to her conclusions and thought she was completely on the right track. Okay, so not the best sounding board, but not all of Lyd's ability to connect with logic had washed away. She quoted some bloke named Will Rogers. He said even if you're on the right track you'll get run over if you just sit there. So she intended to forge ahead. Giving Lyd a little wink she imagined the wheels of her chair moving over the rails to the detective.

Marc was standing in the middle of his team. Good. She wanted them all to hear. To see. To know. How was she going to get their attention, she thought. How was she going to present this? She shrugged. Just use her usual sharp-edged push. If there was room in the NYPD for a former Cobra, maybe they could find a place for a big brain with no legs.

"I know why Dr. Morningstar was snatched," she said loudly. "And if you buy me a deluxe set of new wheels, and pour me a sixteen ouncer with ice, I'll tell ya."

# Chapter 39

Jette sat on her bed, propped up against a sea of soft, velvety pillows. Another location. Another sumptuous room. She was blindfolded and knew that meant a visit from the vaulted Empress. The rhythms and relationships were becoming familiar. Too familiar. She needed to get out.

The flight to this place the night before had been fast and unexpected. It was obvious they were being pushed. Marc. He was in pursuit. She was sure of it.

They hadn't traveled a long distance, so they were still in New York City. His city. It warmed her blood and gave her a surge of confidence and energy.

A thick dark hood had been placed over her head as they prepared her for the journey, but she'd used her senses to assess as much of her environment as she could. Even though distinctive sounds penetrated the thick material, she wasn't able to pinpoint their location from them. New York City wasn't her home ground. No real help there.

On the other hand, there was no doubt what she smelled in the air. It was faint and from the building's past, but it would give Marc a clue if she could get a message out to him. That would be her next move in this round.

Now to keep the Empress occupied. Feeling the woman's presence, Jette concentrated on the task at hand.

"I've put you in the Hall of Secrets. Your Knights and Guardians will not be able to penetrate the extra layer of concealment," whispered the Empress.

"That's not fair." Jette wasn't sure if it was or not. It just seemed like a good thing to say to keep this woman comfortable with the upper hand. She wanted the mastermind of her kidnapping to feel superior, confident and, if possible, safe. It would allow Marc to get closer.

"Oh, but it is. All within the rules of play. So tell me Avenger. Are you ready to turn?"

Jette hesitated. She was perfectly happy to turn, but didn't want to give in too soon.

If she was this mystical character, Avenger, she'd be a pretty tough woman. Some kind of ruler. And a warrior. On the other hand, the drugs she was getting, while not life threatening, were doing things to her system she deplored.

There was a delicate balance here, but she went with instinct again. Time to play a hand.

"Tell me what you want and I'll calculate its impact." Her tone was reluctant, suspicious. When the Empress hummed her approval, she knew she was getting the rhythm right. It was frustrating, but relatively simple to play on the woman's psychosis. It wasn't a particularly fair fight considering the deep mental illness driving this Empress, but the thought of the blood of the innocent victim on the roof took away all need to play fair. It was easier to encourage the delusion than try to help the woman see reality. As a matter of fact she was sure it would also be less dangerous. So she pushed. And she played. "I'll calculate the impact, think about the consequences."

"I want one of your lives. Give it to me and we can end this round."

"Interesting. How will you go about transferring the life?" If it was a matter of a verbal declaration or signing a paper, she'd cave right now.

"I did some research. It's never been done before."

"Then let's break new ground."

"I think you need to do it."

"Do what?"

"Die by your own hand, then pass the life to me when you rise again."

So it involves dying, Jette thought. That couldn't be good. Maybe she could get the ball rolling in a different direction.

"I need to think about how to make the transfer. In the meantime, let's discuss other trades." She knew that was part of this game.

"What do you have that I want?"

"How about my Dark Knight. He must be worth an incredible amount of points right now."

"He has had several successes," revealed the Empress to Jette's delight, "and that would make him a valuable asset."

"I'll deliver him to you as a Boon, if you wish," offered Jette with apparent nonchalance. "I can bring him here. One call. He does my bidding."

Could it be this simple, Jette thought as she waited for her answer. The seconds ticked by.

"An interesting offer. I've been working on a plan to just remove him from play."

That wasn't what Jette wanted to hear.

"Don't be short sighted, Empress. You'll disappoint me if you take the easy way."

Push the right buttons, thought Jette. This may not have been the easy way in the nuances of the game they were playing, but sometimes simply saying it was so planted that fact in a mentally fragile mind. She decided to fertilize the seed she'd just planted.

"Take the easy way and your followers will start looking to me for courage and leadership. Go ahead and eliminate the Dark Knight, but everyone knows that the more complicated and daring move would be to place him at your side. I'll consider releasing him from my control and putting him there. Perhaps for a single round."

This was wild improvisation now, but with solid elements of ego manipulation and reverse psychology. When there was no immediate response, she knew it was working and stopped before she overplayed.

"And the Light Knight?"

Light Knight? Who the heck was the Light Knight?

"He's of no consequence. You want him, you can have him too. He's become more of a drain on my power than what he contributes to the play."

She sincerely hoped the Light Knight, whoever he was, would forgive her for that.

"Interesting. So that's why he was banished. But he's a known healer in the World of Reality. That should put him into a higher category."

Oh good Lord, the Light Knight was Luke.

"Perhaps for you and your hordes of Minions, but a healer is useless to me."

The Empress considered this. It was true. When you could rise from the ashes, what good would a healer be in the arsenal. She felt a rush when she realized that Avenger may be a formidable warrior, but she was a lousy negotiator. The Dark Knight had accumulated a huge amount of value with his pursuit and her Light Knight was relatively insignificant to her, but would be a real asset in Himalia. She should have considered that.

Both Knights in a trade. It really was something to think about. The Empress smiled behind her mask. Another long step toward Sovereignty. Ha! For all her might and power, for all her show of physical prowess, Avenger was a pathetic strategist.

"And what do you want in return," she asked.

"Release me."

Yes, it was her weakness, thought the Empress with a surge of confidence.

"No, Avenger. Only transferring one of your remaining lives carries enough value for you to get that in return."

"Then free me here inside the Hall of Secrets."

Jette waited for the answer. She was desperate to get free of the restraints. To be free to run.

"Let me calculate the points, then we can discuss the trade."

"Don't take too long to decide, Empress," said Jette with impatience. "I feel the pulse of the full moon in my blood." She'd learned that the moons determined arbitrary deadlines and were timelines of some sort. Timing was important in this game.

The Empress laughed. It was low and ended in a little cough.

"In a few weeks, Avenger, you will be so deep in my control, I will get anything I want. Everything I want. There are several full moons remaining in the year."

"That's still just speculation. I can bring the Dark Knight to me today. One call and he's yours."

"Ah, more than just speculation, I think. You're trying to pull down my wall of patience."

That was exactly what Jette was doing. Get her to act without thought.

"The offer only stands for another moonrise."

"You're in no position to make any demands or deadlines. I'll go work with the tables and consider your trade."

Jette could feel the room empty. That must have been the Empress's last word.

The medicinal smell of alcohol forecasted the next shot. Jette was ready to make her move there, too. Because she hadn't resisted the last few shots and played at panting for them, the Sentinels no longer held her down. She needed to be alone with the nurse.

A woman in robes and a mask removed the blindfold and placed it on the bed. Jette fisted the dark fabric and worked it under the duvet. Maybe she could use it later for something.

Looking around, she saw her plan worked. There was no one else in the room.

"Hester," whispered Jette. "You need to help me get out of here."

She could feel the young woman jump at the sound of her name.

"How? How did you know it was me, Avenger?"

"I can see."

"But I'm wearing a mask."

"You always have, Hester. I can see through that, too."

"Even...even in the classroom?"

"Of course," said Jette with casual confidence. She realized Hester was going to be easy to play, and she didn't feel the least bit guilty twisting her up.

"Oh, God. Oh my God." Hester glanced at the mirror. The mask revealed nothing, but Jette could feel the tension mount. "Okay then. You know. But you can't turn me like you did the Anointed One," she said. "You have nothing I want."

"I think I do, Hester." Jette kept using her name, personalizing the communication. "What Boon did the Empress give you?"

"Fame and the respect of people around me. She arranged for me to be in the spotlight. My parents are so proud. It's been a wonderful week. I wanted to be a hero. Like on all those TV shows. Brave. Running and helping victims of disaster. She made it happen."

Jette thought so and was glad this was the only Boon. It would have been more difficult to turn her had it been some unique offering.

"Hester, I can give you more of it." Jette stated it clearly and with commitment. She was sure the impressionable Hester would believe it to be true. Now to cement the concept firmly so the young woman would follow through after she left. Hester had a very suggestive personality so Jette interjected 'you know' into her communication to transform fiction into fact "In your heart you know that. You know that every media outlet will grant me air time. Help me out of here. Be by my side and be a hero again. This time be the kind of hero who's legitimate. You know you were only featured because you were in the right place at the right time. With my influence, your status will be genuine. You'll save even more lives. You're a healer. And a fine one. Let's get out of here and walk into the spotlight together. Your future will be assured. You know this is the best play right now."

"She said you'd try and tempt us. But I made my choice. You turned the Anointed One and we all saw what happened to him."

"I did turn him and he would have thrived under my protection." Jette was certainly not above some creative fabrication. "But he rejected it. He wanted to play on his own and he wasn't strong enough. You will join me and stay by my side. I'll be able to place you in my protection. The Empress won't be able to touch you."

"Let me think about it."

"Hester. Your fame will grow faster and last longer if you align with me. Look at what you know. I've consistently beaten the Empress. Her light is fading. Don't go down with her. She can't protect you." Jette knew she was pushing all Hester's exposed buttons.

"You're here. You're the captive of the Empress," declared Hester loudly, not wanting anyone who was watching to see, to hear that she was tempted.

"I'm exactly where I want to be," declared Jette with what she hoped was an appropriately Avenger-like attitude. "The pitiful Empress only thinks she's in control. Do I look beaten? Think about it. I've won every challenge. All I want you to do is get a message to my Dark Knight. Make your decision soon or I'll withdraw my offer of protection and you'll lose along with all the other Minions after the Final Duel. You'll lose everything. Your family will see you go down. They'll be humiliated. How will they explain your fall to their friends?"

Hester stared at her, pulled and pushed by the war of reality vs. fantasy. But in the end, she was too grounded in the Middle World of Reality. She knew this wasn't a game anymore. And she knew who would win in the end.

"Okay," she whispered, "but I expect you to keep my secret. You'll get me interviews and talk with your agent about a book deal?"

"I'll talk with my agent." She could even keep the promise. Lee wouldn't be getting her any kind of deal, but the young woman didn't need to know that.

"What do you want the Dark Knight to know?" Hester kept her back to the mirror and covered the low murmur by reaching over and plumping up Jette's pillows.

"My location," whispered Jette simply.

"I don't even know that. I'm picked up at my apartment and brought here in the back of a van." Hester kept busy, smoothing Jette's sheets and checking the water decanter.

"You have a clue."

"Maybe."

"And you can pay closer attention when you're taken back. Time the trip, count the number of left and right turns, listen for distinctive sounds. Go to the Dark Knight. He'll be able to use what you know. And the next time they pick you up, he can follow."

"I'll think about it."

"You'll need something that will show him you're on my side."

Surreptitiously, Jette removed the delicate silver and turquoise ring from her finger and gave it to Hester.

"A sign so he knows you are now a Guardian. Give it to him. Now go," she whispered.

Hester took another long look at Jette, then slipped the ring on her little finger. This was going to be good, she thought. Maybe Avenger could get her a cover story in some magazine. Her mother had been clipping the newspaper articles, but a cover would be something she could put in a frame.

Turning away from the bed, she put her hand in her pocket as she walked toward the door. It wouldn't do to have anyone on the other side of the mirror see it. She knocked on the door signaling the Sentinel that she was finished. He'd assign a driver and if she played it right, maybe she could sit up front with him and get the exact location.

# Chapter 40

Marc turned his glare on Kelly as the others stiffened a little. Interrupting his operation was never a good idea, but pushing into this one was almost suicidal. Kelly didn't back down however and met his glare, amp for amp. If a sprite in a wheelchair could swagger, she did so as she rolled into the circle of the squad.

She thought she'd let her statement stand through the silence that followed. There was no way she was going to let her trembling nerves clog her throat and shake her voice. Conviction dominated her attitude as she rolled right up to him without looking away, without even blinking. Marc reined in his annoyance and gave her an impatient little nod.

"If you know why Jette was snatched, I'll buy you any mode of transportation you want, and pour the juice myself. If you're just shoveling shit for your own perverted pimp, you're trashed. You're out. And you won't get out of juvie until you're old enough to vote," snarled Marc, freezing her with his laser green eyes.

"Detective," interrupted Kim, ready to step in before either one of them crossed a line.

Both Kelly and Marc diverted their eye battle toward her and said in nearly identical tones, "Back off!"

Kim raised her hands, palms out and did just that.

"Deal." Kelly rolled with plenty of attitude to one of the boards. Everyone noticed she had a lap full of pictures, papers and printouts.

Marc watched as she pinned the top picture to the board. A picture of Jette on her horse Diablo at her ranch in Arizona. It had been ripped from the cover of one of the many supermarket tabloids that had featured Jette and Marc during the flurry of press interest following the case down there. It had been snapped with a long range lens by some enterprising paparazzi before they could set up a secure perimeter around her property.

Jette was mounted on the powerfully built black stallion while he soared over a fence. The horse was magnificent, but it was the rider who captured the imagination and owned the frame. She was as comfortable and confident in the saddle as she was sitting behind her desk. Her long black hair flowed behind her. There was a slight smile on her face, brilliantly accentuated by bright red lipstick. She was dressed all in black, jeans, boots and tank top. The muscle definition in her arms and shoulders was impressive. It was a breathtaking shot and it shook Marc to the soul as he stared at it.

"I copped this from Tommy's stash of mags. Thought I'd use a visual to grab your orbs and open my case. Obviously this is Dr. Morningstar. It coated several of the supermarket rags over a month ago, but was also in a lot of legit media too. And this," she held up a disk. "Is from my own personal prime hit collection."

Pulling the cover off a CD case, she pinned it next to the picture. It grabbed the orbs, alright. On it was a nearly identical picture. A beautiful dusky skinned woman in a mask, with long black hair flying, bright red lips smiling, sat comfortably on a muscular black horse jumping a stone fence. The black tank was replaced with a form fitting vest of shiny ornately detailed black metal, but the similarity was electrifying.

"What is that?" asked Tagg, the awe obvious in his voice. No one else said a word. Marc couldn't. He was too stunned. "Some kind of video game?"

"No. Something far, far more extreme," explained Kelly. "As a matter of fact, Sovereignty is the most extreme. A true MMORPG, a massively multiplayer online role-playing game. More than just a CRPG, a computer role playing game. It's rated intense and only the highest sphere of players can survive the pace and strain."

Kelly tapped the tabloid picture of Jette. "I think this picture might have sparked some kind of freak gene in a master gamer out there. You see, a lot of live action players can get pretty into their characters, quests and challenges. Some hard-core leets get wacked out on the adrenalin and the thrill and can start thinking and acting more in the character than in their true self. Then it's shrink time if you're a kid, and maybe babbling street time if you're a little more age advanced. Some nerds are pretty much riding the edge of reality anyway. A few players go…"

"You got our attention, don't lose it. Make a point," interrupted Marc, finding his voice. Something about the picture and the cover sizzled. His skin felt hot and his pulse jittered. This felt like a lead. A good one. He could tell everyone in the room had already started making the connections to Jette's clues, particularly the word 'game.' He wanted to hear more.

"Yeah. Well. See, there's a lot more. Give me just a little space here. I need to get everything out and then I don't think I'll need to make any kind of point. I think the point will pop."

When Marc didn't interrupt again, she nodded.

"In this game there are two Avatars. Ah, let's see. What's civilian speak. Hmm. Okay. That would be two major entities, characters within the game who lead the creatures of two worlds, Himalia and Callisto. One rules the empire of Himalia and the other has been banished to Callisto. They are half sisters and are the source of the conflict." She took another breath, knowing she sucked them in with the pictures, but this was going to shoot them up. "In this game, the sisters, Orthosie and Lysithea are known as Avenger and the Blue Empress."

She got just the reaction she'd anticipated. Marc jolted. The rest of the team glanced over at the notes Marc had pinned to the board on what Roger Flowers had said to Jette after she'd restrained him. To the clues Jette left behind. Empress. Blue leader. Blue Empress.

Kelly nodded. "Yeah. Pop, huh? When I read that bit about what Flowers said on your board, I knew. Everything clicked into place. Okay, so. Um, there's more. Remember that time I saw Dr. Morningstar with the horse on that first day? When you asked me to make the pictures? My brain did a little dance. Like I recognized her. But I'd been watching the tube like everyone last week when she did her super hero act, so I didn't go back at it. Then on one of my breaks, I flipped through some of this stuff you collected and it kept calling her the Phoenix and you the Shield. Things really started clicking. Like a Geiger Counter near hot rocks. I just about freaked."

When Marc shifted impatiently, she picked up the pace and got back on track.

"You see, each character has her own powers, her own set of skills, and weapons and stuff. One of Avenger's is that she has a number of lives. She gets knocked off and poof, she comes back to life. It costs her a lot of points, but hey. Rebirth. Her symbol is...a Phoenix." Kelly was on a roll now, fed by the gasps of several of the team, and the interest she saw in Marc's eyes. Turning over the cover of the disk, she showed them the back. A picture of a Phoenix. Slam dunk. But she had more. A lot more. "She has two trusted High Guardians. Elite fighters by her side. The Dark Knight and the Light Knight. This may be a little bit of a stretch, but you're pretty dark, and you aren't a knight or anything like that, but they call you the Shield."

"And a knight would carry a shield, just like a police officer," breathed Dina. She just couldn't help it. It was all so incredible. "We call our badges shields."

"Yeah," nodded Kelly enthusiastically. "And well, the doc is pretty light. He's really the next closest male to her, so I figure he could be the Light Knight. When Avenger went missing, it could look to this loony leet like you called in the Light Knight to the City of Might, New York City to you civilians, for this round. It would reinforce the mad, mad trip her mind is on. "

"It's a perfect fit with Jette's clues," nodded Kim.

"Yeah. Like Cinderella's slipper," agreed Raj.

Marc raised his hand cutting off further discussion. "Let's hear from the kid first."

"Jette's clues?" asked Kelly, momentarily stopped.

"Later. Go on," ordered Marc. Everything in his brain, his heart, his gut was buzzing and popping. Only his training was tethering him to the floor. His entire body was on fire.

"Anyway, I really think an extreme player put this together and slid off her rocker. She saw these things, she'd think they were signs I guess, in the Middle World of Reality and pow! A brain cell popped and she thinks the game has become reality. You see, each of the characters, all of us, have identities in the Middle World of Reality, our world, the one where we all are flesh and blood.

"I think some wacked out psycho Empress thinks Dr. Morningstar is Avenger's identity here in the Middle World. And when Dr. Morningstar moved to the City of Might, it must have seemed like Avenger was going for the Final Duel to Supreme Sovereign. I think the Empress staged an ultimate Last Test to an equally wacked out Sentinel promising him the position of Anointed One to shoot up the school and see what Dr. Morningstar would do. To get her to reveal herself. And wow, she did in a big way. I mean, really! She didn't even hesitate. She just…"

When Kelly saw the fierce expression on Marc's face, she shrugged.

"Well, excuse me, but you're used to her, you know. Pardon me if the rest of us have to catch up here."

"The game…" Marc prompted.

"Okay, sure. Sovereignty is very complicated game and I could take you through all the play rules and roles, but I don't want to get into all that now."

"Good decision. Just those things you think are relevant," suggested Marc.

"Yeah. Anyway, here's a fact I think will work for you. I, ah, I hacked into Roger Flowers's accounts and emails and all his facebook stuff. Plus I hacked into his text messages. He was a gamer, alright. And a Soviac for years. That's what we call geeks who get spaced out on Sovereignty. Real fanatics. And I think he took it to a whole new level. I found a message. It wouldn't have a whole lot of meaning outside the game, but it's a final Quest, called the Last Test. Only the most elite players would get a chance to complete one. The ultimate in earning points. To be an Anointed One and get your name on the Hall of Saints would have you retiring on top. No more than, I'd say, a hundred or so of the millions of players get the opportunity and even fewer pass the test. I'm the best I know and I'm not even close. I think Flowers was as cracked as this Empress and brought the Final Test into the Middle World."

On the board, she pinned the message that had sent Flowers on his rampage. She looked up at Tagg.

"I printed it in 18 point type, so you wouldn't have to take out your glasses."

*This is a Test of your courage and nerve.*
*I am your Empress, it's I whom you serve.*
*In the City of Might, you face your Last Test.*
*To prove you're the One, the Anointed, the best.*
*You will go down in grandeur and glory.*
*Your name will forever be part of the story.*

They all read it, absorbed it. Marc's burn turned into a full blown fire in his gut. Still he said nothing, letting Kelly take the lead.

"Yeah. Powerful stuff, huh? She sent him out to poke at Avenger. Not to kill her, or even wound her. Just do a thrust. Then he was to take as many collateral creatures down as he could before he dissolved."

"It was like a suicide mission?" asked Teresa. She was a CRP player too. Not at this level, but it was all making a kind of sick sense when put into the gaming context.

"Oh, yeah. He'd become a Saint and go straight to Thelxinoe, the most beautiful and wonderful of worlds. Off limits to those who still have a heartbeat. Now you gotta understand that for players, well, this is all a game. No blood, or real offing. So when you transcend, you take a bow as a Saint and go hang at the corner and brag it up or sit down with the solid parental units and eat pork chops. You don't really get dusted."

"Flowers was killed," said Raj.

"Oh yeah. That's what would happen in a failed Last Test. Not so real on the death charts, for sure, but if you don't dissolve in glory, there's a huge point bounty on your head. He was totally dead the minute he didn't complete his Quest and was captured. She'd have one of her Sentinels take care of him. Usually it's with explosives or with a sword, but this is the Middle World and she'd probably use whatever. The Empress is ferocious."

"Is this in any of Green's files?" Marc looked away from Kelly at Raj.

"No," said Kelly and Raj simultaneously. Kelly shrugged without a shade of repentance when Marc turned his glare back to her. The spotlight was on full power and while she was under it, she was going to push its limits.

"I took a peek at the Green scene myself. Either he has no geek of my caliber on his home team, or he doesn't put everything in his computer files. Not even the message on the Final Test was in what he has on Flowers."

"Or they could have been sanitized," speculated Teresa. "The chief is working to get us the Flowers case too but he might be keeping his own book."

"We'll put that on a list for later. So if this Avenger looks like Jette, what does the Empress look like?" asked Marc.

"No one knows. She wears a full face mask. It has to do with one of the big reasons for the rivalry. It's assumed that Avenger got all the looks, and that the Empress is on the side of hideous and revolting."

"No hair color, eye color, anything?"

"No, she always wears a silver face mask and hooded robes." She showed them all a picture of a tall woman in long flowing blue robes and an elegantly designed silver mask.

"Anything else?" Marc gave no clue as to what he was thinking.

"Yeah. Sure. Plenty. Okay, so, anyway, the Avatars give players Challenges meant to test and train Minions in Himalia or Beasts in Callisto. Stuff like planting flags of our sovereign nations in audacious locations, performing physical feats of endurance or daring, finding hidden treasures through maps and clues. To pass into the role of Sentinel for the Empress or Guardian for Avenger, Challenges are more rigorous and difficult like, um, calculating solutions to brain stretching problems or solving mind burning riddles. I'm champ at those and a little light on the physical stuff. There are battles, plenty of them. Leading the battles between the worlds is reserved for the Sentinels and Guardians. Empresses or Avengers lay all the strategy."

Marc frowned at her. "Got a point in there?"

"Sure do. One of the common Challenges is following and photographing famous people. It's a training exercise called Tagging and Tracking. You get points. Lots of them if the face is a cover creature. A famous person you'd see if your eyes scanned the mag section. Dr. Morningstar would be one of those. Remember when that uptown skirt came in and said you were being followed by two Betty's? Sounds like Minions to me. I know you put them way down low on your assignments, not knowing how it all fits, but I think there's probably a ton of teens all over the city sending pictures to this screwy Empress for points. I could take those you got there and put them through the face recognition program on facebook if you want. I'm sure they have accounts. All of us millennials have a home page."

"Teresa, get those pictures for Kelly." Marc nodded at the two sketches that were above Kelly's head.

"You certainly absorbed a lot of information," said Teresa, going over to the board to get them.

"Yeah. I'm a sponge. Most people don't pay much attention to me, or think my brain is as defective as my legs, but I hear things. When Lyd did her thesaurus thing with the Dominion corporation and sovereignty was one of the meanings she spewed, well, it pushed everything I'd tucked away into the light. Pow. It all came together when I took a sec to revisit the epiphany. Anyway, I'm on a roll, so to speak." She used her gloved hands to rock her wheelchair. "Although by this time tomorrow I expect to be optimized and motorized! One more thing then I can get to the questions and answer part."

She took the sketches from Teresa and went on.

"Sovereignty rides on conflicts, some are booked around adventures, but mostly they're built on quests, tests and challenges. Each round is like an episode. Each carries a certain amount of points. Like, I know why Avenger was snatched from here. It's her Home Base. Wow. The Empress and the Sentinel gang that made it out alive must have taken a thousand points or more for that alone. There's a lot of improv, but the Empress can have what we call multifarious scripted encounters. I think she has an overall strategy for this. I can't read it all, but forcing Avenger to reveal herself, then doing a snatch. Wild. It's seriously sick, but totally sweet."

Kelly's eyes fired up with admiration. She just couldn't help it and it appeared that no one in the room was going to hold it against her.

"Okay, let's use all of this to..." began Marc, shifting to move on.

"Ah, one more thing," Kelly interrupted. "It's kind of a big thing, I guess. Maybe. I don't know." She hesitated, then looked over at Lyd, who nodded encouragingly. "Full disclosure is best."

She pulled back the collar of her shirt and showed Marc the tattoo.

"When you get enough points to move up to Sentinel or Guardian, you can wear the mark of the blue moon."

The team's attitude chilled. They'd been associating the tattoo with the enemy since the investigation began. It was hard to see the symbol in their own camp.

"Does that mean you fight on the side of the Blue Empress?" Marc's voice was calm, but hard.

"Does the fact you got a cobra running up your arm make you a cheating, lying, drug dealing, murdering gang banger?" she countered sarcastically.

Marc said nothing. He simply stared. As confident as Kelly was, she was no match for Marc, and was the first to crack.

"No," she said with a snap of temper. "The tattoo just means I'm a really good player. Great even. I earned the right to wear the mark of the blue moon when I passed the test for Guardian. That's a Guardian, like in the army of Avenger. I prefer her side. Avenger is like a rebel. Anti-establishment." Kelly's tone was sincere, but had a nervous undertone. "So, um, are we cool, Dark Knight?"

He stared at her for a minute longer. It didn't seem to unnerve her in the least. She'd let everything speak for itself now. His team held their opinions. Held their breath. He shifted and studied the picture of Jette and the horse, the cover of the game, the print out with the final test, then he walked over to the large table holding food, water, and soda. Grabbing a sixteen ounce bottle of Mountain Dew, he deftly used his other hand to finger off the cover of an ice bucket, dip a glass into it, and fill it to the rim. He brought it over, placed it on the table near Kelly. Slowly he unscrewed the top of the bottle and poured the yellow liquid over the ice. No one spoke. Kelly allowed herself a cocky grin, then reached for her reward.

"You'll get the wheels by tonight."

"Here's the website." Kelly handed him a piece of paper. "I'd get it myself, but I'd have to hack into your bank account, and that might get me into trouble with the law."

Looking around, Marc saw the subtle nods. For the first time since Jette disappeared, Marc's eyes lit up with something more than just determination, frustration, and fear. He liked this kid and not just for her excellent information. It was time to bring her in. All the way in.

"There's more I'd like you to see."

He moved to the pictures of the room where Jette was held and filled in his young partner.

"Give me your impressions."

"Wow. This is extreme," said Kelly, sipping and thinking. "Providing you with intelligence like this? And from the inside. Wicked. It's unprecedented for sure. I'm processing as I speak, but I think you can swallow this bit whole. It's really good news. Avenger is going to be kept alive for now. That's a definite. This is a temple. Plush. Not a crypt to lay her out, but a soft and easy detention room. I'm thinking maybe since this play is so extreme, she may be trying to turn Avenger, or she may push a trade."

"Trade?"

"The Empress gives Boons to her Minions. She trades something from her treasury for action. Most times she gives points or weapons or extra time for a Quest, but I'm thinking if she's gone into the Middle World for real, she'd be giving out Boons that real Soviacs would crave. So it would be tech equipment, drugs, fine threads, cars, other stuff. I'm not sure what she'd have that Dr. Morningstar doesn't already have in spades. We could put our heads together on that. There's more, do you want me to keep moving?"

Marc just waved a hand and she did.

"The messages that Avenger left for you on the wall. The decoys. Classic play.

They're like multiple doors and only one holds the prize. Having explosives behind some of the doors is routine. She'd want you to be in one of the exploding locations for sure." She nodded at Marc. "Taking out the Dark Knight would give her a ton of points."

"You keep saying 'she'. The perp behind this is a woman?" asked Tagg.

"Oh, yeah. I'm sure of it. If this psycho believes the fight for Sovereignty has come to the Middle World of Reality, being a Blue Emperor wouldn't fit. It wouldn't compute. Her brain may be on the blink, but I think it would all have to fit or none of it would fit. Men are only pawns in this game. The developer didn't much like the male gene."

"And everything Jette has done since the first shot has only strengthened her delusion," thought Rachael.

"Yeah. All the really physical stuff she can do. Heck, if I had just one less card in my own deck, I'd probably believe it," agreed Kelly.

"Why is there a wolf on the back of this cover?" Marc turned over a CD, his pulse pumping. It felt good after the horrendous misery of not finding her at the 22nd Street mission.

"It's pretty well tuned by us historians that she was raised by them after being banished to Callisto. It's CW, conventional wisdom, that Avenger can morph into one."

"Jette is a member of the wolf clan." Marc couldn't take his eyes off the face of the magnificent black wolf on the back cover. It had to be a good thing. It had to be.

Now Kelly's eyes nearly popped.

"What?"

Marc looked over at Luke.

"There are seven clans in the Cherokee tradition, Bird, Blue, Paint, Deer, Wild Potato, Twister, and Wolf," explained Luke, overwhelmed by the sign and feeling a thick flow of confidence. "The Cherokee are matriarchal and trace their affiliation through the women in the family. *Ulisi*, her grandmother was of the wolf so Jette is of the *A-ni-wa-ya*, the wolf clan. The clan that's produced the most war chiefs and warriors."

The room was silent, the air bulging with one huge collective unspoken *wow*.

"Look out Blue Freak," murmured Tagg.

Not deterred by the wonder she felt, Kelly threw in one final bit of information she thought was important.

"Avenger, and sorry, but now I'm just going to have to worship her as the one true Avenger given the wolf thing, and the Empress were both born under a full moon. That's why the Final Duels can only be fought at that time of month."

"Kind of the ultimate PMS," offered Dina.

"Yeah," agreed Kelly quickly. "And um, Dr. Morningstar was born under a full moon. I checked and so would the Empress. So there you have it."

"Does it feel right?" Marc asked his team after he felt his heart beating again. The room erupted. The frustration and disappointment they felt after the raid faded with the surge of renewed energy from new, solid intelligence.

"It feels like a bull's eye to me," said Tagg with enthusiasm.

"I'm looking for any lack of logic in this, but it all fits," agreed Kim.

Everyone else shared their animated assessment, then stopped and waited for Marc's thoughts and assignments.

"This information connects everything. Confirms our suspicion that the attack on the school was related to this. To her." He stood firmly with Kelly's assumptions. His intuition was screaming, and the adrenalin pouring into his system punctuated his certainly. "Anyone who would start living this instead of just playing at it would have to be seriously cracked. In addition, they'd have to have some solid money. Not just a salary or regular paycheck, but be thickly set. I think it's time to shift the investigation on who did this, who has Jette, to wealthy, unhinged, females who are long term gamers."

"Someone in the City of Might," added Kelly. "Soviacs all agree that the City of Might is really New York City, probably Manhattan. It's an island with a Times Square and a Central Park."

"Fine. Someone right here in the city, either a resident or a frequent visitor. We need to know everything we can about the game." Marc looked at Kelly. "We're going to need you to light the way in that tunnel."

"Sure."

"Who wrote the game? Who was its author?" asked Marc.

"Crap. Your first question and I have to flush out. I don't know, but you could use your push to find out."

"Zena Brightson developed the game." Lyd's voice was clear and direct, her pride in Kelly obvious on her face. "Wacked out worse than me. I'm a lush, but she's a psycho."

Marc looked at her. "You know her?"

"No, not really. She wanted me to develop the software for her game, then started spouting all these rules and characters. I couldn't get her to think in a straight line and I need that in order to communicate with anyone."

"Raj, get me a name and address."

Raj pulled out his cell phone.

"Is there any reason these characters and places carry the names of Jupiter's moons?" asked Marc.

The team looked at each other. Jupiter's moons? Why would they ever need Google? Just ask Marc.

"Hmm. Not that I know of," said Kelly. "I think they were just cool names. Moons are a theme but it's the earth moon that carries the weight."

"Okay, then. Back to where Jette might be right now. Will knowing about the game help us there?" asked Tagg.

"It could," nodded Kelly, eager to get back to being the resident expert. "I scrounged all the photos of the fortresses and hideaways online. People's renderings of what is described in the game. Books that have been published on it. If the Empress wanted to dig into a place that would follow her play pattern, she might choose one of these."

She handed Marc a short pile of printed pictures, mostly of buildings and landscape, and pointed to the one on top.

"The shelter," he said and she nodded in agreement. He took the pictures and posted them side by side on another board.

"Are any familiar?" asked Kim. They all looked pretty gothic to her.

Marc nodded. "Yeah. This one." He pointed at a very ornate stone building. "That's St. Bartholomew's."

"The one on Park Avenue?" asked Dina, not seeing it.

"No. No," said Marc thoughtfully. "An abandoned old hospital in Harlem. It's a branch of the library now. Damn it! I need the evidence from the site. Dina call the station. There was a copy of *Trail of Tears* in the table drawer near the bed. It was a library book. Check to see what branch it belongs to. I'll bet it's the one in St. Barts. And this one." He tapped a picture of a stone building with gargoyles. "Looks a little like the All Saints Museum. Tagg, find the picture of the receipt that was on the dresser. I think it was for the Molly Kelly cafe. That would be on the same block. Saints. Saints. Bitch! She gave us a trail. Making it easy enough for a rookie to follow. She wants us to find these locations."

"Eventually," agreed Tagg. "But it would have taken time and she doesn't know you're right behind her. We're in the game."

"That's our big advantage right now," nodded Rachael.

"Yeah!" Kelly felt the familiar gaming surge. "The play uses decoys and Avenger's messages confirm it. The Empress has created a path to ten sacred sites and three are traps. This isn't important for you, but she's racking up points for every minute you're seeking. She'd expect you to take days, maybe even weeks to find them."

"Are these all the pictures?" asked Marc.

"Yes. At least all I could find," nodded Kelly.

"There is a solid two dozen possible," mused Tagg.

"True, but I think I can place a lot of them." Marc's eyes darted from one to another. "The Saint's angle is a real push. We can use any evidence we found to confirm. This one's St. Frances rectory. Do we go into these buildings openly or should we keep a low profile?" Marc glanced away from the board to look at Kelly.

She hesitated. It was one thing to be asked questions about the game, it was another to be asked for opinions on how best to play it. What if she was wrong.

Marc felt her reluctance.

"Kelly, it would take too long for any of us to get up to speed. Your best guess at this point."

"She'll have Minions out everywhere. Like the teen team she had on you. There will be a feed into her main play board. She probably knows where you are right now." Kelly bit her lip. "I'd say you play her. Make like you're all over the place, but don't show your face at the locations until you have them all nailed. Then go in all at once. One big sweep. Quiet, late at night when the amateurs are tucked away at home for the night. You miss one and she'll know it. If it isn't a decoy, she'll detonate for two reasons: one to get points and the other because she's seriously bent and your actions will make her head implode. She'll do it because she's seriously pissed and wants to take a punch at the city."

"Let's work on getting the locations. Then the team…"

"We're called Guardians." Kelly wanted them all to think inside the box. "You're the Knight, we're called Guardians."

234

"Right. Then you Guardians can all go anywhere and everywhere but to the places we identify."

"I think this is St. Phillips' over on 9th." Dina tapped a picture.

"Lyd, get the website up on that."

The rest of the hour was spent putting everyone's memory to work. Marc got several more and pretty soon, they were down to only a half dozen that needed identification.

"This one." Marc tapped a picture of what looked like a small thatched cottage. "Something about it's giving me that buzz."

Everyone stared at it.

"Nothing that small in Manhattan," squinted Tagg.

"It must have something to do with a saint," reminded Kim.

"Something inside of a museum? A display?" asked Dina.

"It looks a little like a peasant's hut," thought Rachael.

"Yeah, lot's of those around here," said Tagg.

"Maybe not here, but Russia, I bet…" thought Kim.

"Too bad we aren't in Russia."

"Got it," said Marc. "Thanks for the shove."

They all stared at Marc.

"Huh?" asked Kim.

"The Prince of Kiev restaurant. A mural."

"I love Chicken Kiev," said Kim before she could stop herself.

Tagg snorted at her while she blushed. "I thought we needed a saint, not a prince."

"He's also known as St. Vladimir. He was this medieval Ukrainian prince who converted to Christianity." Marc waved his hand distractedly.

"How do you know that?" Kim asked and when Marc ignored her, she turned to Tagg. "How does he know stuff like that?"

Tagg shrugged. "I asked him once. Said he read a lot when he was a kid."

Marc walked over to the intercom and shouted at Hilda to come into the ballroom with Claude and Tommy. They were there within seconds.

"Tommy, I want you to drive Hilda and Claude down to The Prince of Kiev restaurant. Take your own car." He pointed at the astounded couple. "You two are going out to lunch."

"We will not," insisted Hilda. "We aren't going anywhere until we find Dr. Morningstar."

Marc ignored her and gave Claude a phone. "Take this and send back a picture of the mural on the back wall. Have lunch, look around, then come back here."

Hilda opened her mouth to refuse again, when Tommy tumbled to the mission.

"Oh my God. Claude, Hildie, we're going undercover. Claude, dear heart, wear that darling dark blue sweater. It looks awesome with your lovely gray hair. And Hildie, we are going in style, so wear the rose colored silk. And the pearls. Oh, and don't forget to change your shoes. No one will believe you're out on a date in those."

Hilda just stared while Claude blushed scarlet over the word date.

"Let's see." Tommy looked up, tapping her cheek. "Now, should I be a uniformed chauffeur or a doting friend or maybe just a hired driver for the day? Maybe I can be a visiting niece or something."

"I didn't write a fucking script for this, Tommy," snapped Marc. "Be their long lost love child, I don't give a shit. I just want them covered."

"Sure thing, sweetie pie." Tommy was completely undeterred by Marc's snarl. "Covered like a handmade quilt. Oh my, I just had the perfect brainstorm. I have this awesome quilted jacket that will look like a uniform. If you two don't mind, I'll take on the role of hired driver. Let's see, I can be Kayleen. And you two can be the Jensens. I always wanted to be a Kayleen and I think Jensen is the absolute perfect name for you…" Tommy kept up the chatter as she took Hilda in one arm and Claude in the other and led them out of the room.

Tagg stared after them. "She's like a cartoon character come to life. Maybe she is. Maybe she's from the Outer Dimension of Stardust and Sunshine here to live out some computerized fantasy."

"Yeah, but she's solid as stone underneath. She knows what I want," muttered Marc, catching the sigh that threatened to escape his chest.

"Got it," called Raj from the other side of the room. "The developer of the game is a New Yorker! Here's her address."

"I want to go talk with her myself. Tagg, Kim, come with me. Dina, call Tony Nippard. Fill him in. Meet somewhere away from here and give him all the locations we have. They can discretely take their dogs into the buildings. Have them in plain clothes."

"The dogs can go under cover as seeing-eye dogs," suggested Kim with enthusiasm. "And the Bomb Squad can be visually impaired tourists. Cameras, brand new Reeboks, and maps. Lots of maps."

Marc stared at her. "I think Tommy has been a bad influence. I'm going to have to spend some extra time with you when this is all over."

Kim shrugged. Fine by her.

"Want any of the action?" asked Dina intending to pass on Kim's idea.

"No. Right now I'm only interested in finding Jette. Hand it all over to the experts, but stay with them. Remember. We don't want anyone to know we're on the inside track. That includes everyone not in this room. Eunice is already on scut work. Rachael, Raj, Teresa, I want you to race around this city like headless chickens. Do your real detective work via cell phone and lap top. Don't worry if these Minions are taking pictures. Just stay away from the locations we've identified. You'll be our own brand of decoy."

"Right," they said as one, ready to play the game.

"Kelly and Lyd, you're looking for narcissistic, wealthy female New Yorkers. Intelligent and computer savvy."

"Well that narrows it down to about 2 million suspects," bitched Lyd.

"She's a gamer," said Kelly, rubbing her hands. "And completely off her rocker."

"Something not as easy to assess," grumbled Lyd.

"Feed names to me in the field. If I feel a pop, we'll track them down. Tagg, Kim, and I will interview. We'll start with Sovereignty's developer."

Everyone nodded and scattered. Guardians in pursuit of their Avatar.

# Chapter 41

"Detective Marcus Lexington."

Zena Brightson read the name off his card in a soft, breathy voice so icy and controlled that Kim felt a shiver up her spine. Then she just stood like a statue and waited for him to continue. She was obviously used to having people quake in her presence.

Marc was completely unaffected. His fatigue was a barrier to all emotion at this point. Nothing prevented him from studying her, however. Analyzing her. Watching her.

People reacted differently to police officers, guilty or innocent. When suspects were idiots, they exhibited false bravado, threatening to call their lawyers or denying everything before he had a chance to outline his reasons for the interview. When he had a suspect who felt remorse, guilt, shame, or concern, their actions and expressions were transparent to him. Those who had something to hide could rarely do it well enough to get by his radar. He was good at reading faces, great at feeling the vibrations of conscience, and unequaled in intimidating suspects until they confessed sins and infractions dating back to childhood.

But Zena was difficult to read. There was nothing coming off her, coming from her. So he waited. Stared. Waited. Stared. He was good at this game. Better than her. She blinked.

"What can I do for you?" she asked with just the right accent of indifference. It was a logical question, but her apathetic tone and stiff demeanor tipped the scale in Marc's mind. There was far more apprehension behind her facade than she wanted to reveal. Just a bit too unconcerned. It could be because all inquiries by people she just met had her putting on a mask or it could be because she had something to hide.

"I'd like to ask you a few questions concerning your game called Sovereignty."

"Do I need a lawyer?"

"Have you broken the law?"

"No."

"Then we can keep this a friendly inquiry for now."

"Are you a player?"

"No, but I'm familiar with various aspects of the game."

"One cannot just be familiar with various aspects of the game," she said with a hint of sarcasm, each sound pronounced with exquisite care, as if she were unused to the spoken word. Given all the incredible equipment in the room, perhaps she really did spend little time communicating face-to-face with people. When Marc didn't respond, she continued with the same exacting, precise tone. "Sovereignty is more than a pastime or a diversion. It's a lifestyle. For many of us, it's more demanding, more rewarding, and more satisfying than anything that can be found in the so-called real world."

"You've made millions in our so-called real world on the game," stated Marc.

"True. My rewards have accumulated and my coffers have filled. I choose to think of it as a consequence of my play rather than as commerce. A Boon for my efforts and my skills. I have a staff of very acute commercial Minions who handle the details of the empire."

"You don't get involved in the day-to-day decisions?" Marc noticed she peppered her conversation with game lingo. It was an interesting blend of fantasy and reality.

"Never. I've delegated everything. I spend my days playing. What my marketing Minions call research and development. My strategic plans involve Challenges, Quests and Tests, not market share or any other such thing. I'm not interested."

Marc looked around the sumptuous office.

"And yet you enjoy the fruits of your little hobby," poked Marc.

"Hobby? Hobby?" Zena voice was a breathy snarl, sounding disturbed and almost sinister but with the volume so low it was like she was talking to herself. Again Marc held his questions, waiting for her to go on. She was in a mood now.

"This is no hobby. I told you it's a lifestyle. I developed the world of Sovereignty when I was in college. I needed the fantasy, the stimulation. I needed the people in it. The fact that it spawned an empire was a side effect, never the main focus."

"You say you needed the fantasy, why was that?"

"That's none of your business," she snapped.

"It must have been pretty dramatic to push you into such a violent and brutal pastime."

"This is not a pastime any more than it's a hobby. You bait me with your words, with your observations. You are playing me."

Marc continued to stare. Her eyes bore into him as her hands clenched and unclenched. Many people could control their faces, few people could control their hands. Marc noticed but maintained eye contact.

"People are too unimaginative to understand," she said finally, for indeed Marc was playing her and he was a master. "They live insipid and ordinary lives with one dimension and few rewards."

"Do people in the game ever come to life?" Marc asked, watching her intently, talking, he was sure, to the Empress. Maybe not the woman who had Jette, but certainly to a character who lived in the world she'd given birth to.

"Come to life? They don't come to life. They're already alive. They live in the world of Sovereignty. They breathe, they fight, they plan. They risk all. It's a glorious life and it's only after they leave Sovereignty that they perish from the sheer boredom of their ordinary existence. We all come to life, but only in the world we create."

"But it's not real."

"Oh yes it is. We live, we laugh, we fear, we do battle, we have glorious victories, and stunning defeats."

"You're talking about a virtual world of make believe." Marc pushed. "I think it might be time you grew up."

Whoa, that got her, he thought, as she looked like she could go berserk at any moment. Her hands fisted tightly and stayed that way, she actually got a little color in her cheeks, and her eyes were murderous.

"State your purpose. I must get back to my boards, back to my world."

Marc noticed she never called him by name or by rank. She still held his card, glanced at it a few times, but didn't call him detective, or Marcus, or officer. That was very unusual. And the phrase 'state your purpose' was certainly not something he heard every day.

"I just need some background."

"For what?"

"For a case I'm working on."

"What kind of a case?"

"How many gamers do you estimate participate regularly?" he asked instead of responding to her question.

"I have no idea. I believe it must be millions. The game sales alone exceed that."

"Where is Avenger?" Marc asked abruptly.

Zena frowned, but didn't respond. "Avenger is allusive and very, very clever. I believe right now she's taken another shape."

"A Phoenix?"

"No. I believe she has taken the form of a wolf and hides among us."

"Like a werewolf?"

"That's fiction."

"You haven't answered my question. Where is she?"

"I know who you are," she whispered abruptly, staring intently into his eyes.

"Who am I?" Marc didn't blink, challenging her with his equally intense glare.

Abruptly, Zena shook herself, pulled her eyes from Marc and looked out the window to the beautiful East River, now looking peaceful and calm. Flicking his card, she shrugged.

"You are the Shield. You are one of the many who inhabit the City of Might."

"I inhabit New York City and I'm a detective with the NYPD. That's reality. Do you sometimes have trouble distinguishing reality from your game, Ms. Brightson?"

"No," she said slowly, not turning from her study of the river. "I just prefer the world of Sovereignty to the pain and disorder of your world. And I think I'm finished with you and that world. Please leave now."

Marc nodded at her bookshelf, ignoring her request for the moment. "I see you have Jette Morningstar's books."

*The Criminal Mind* and *Crime Scene Analysis and Profiling* were buried among the hundreds of volumes on gaming, medieval art, computer graphic design, and other relevant topics. Kim looked over at Tagg. She'd completely missed that. She could see from Tagg's expression so had he.

"Yes. They're very interesting, considering they're born of your reality." Zena didn't even turn in the direction Marc indicated. Interesting, Marc thought. Had she recently put them there? Was she presenting an air of nonchalance for his benefit? Was she composing herself behind that mask?

She didn't stop him as he walked over and took *The Criminal Mind* off the shelf. His heart and gut took another hit as he opened the cover and saw her beautiful script, personalizing the book.

*The world can be healed. One person at a time. Thank you for your interest in my work. Jette Morningstar.*

"You've met the author?" asked Marc when he felt steady enough to speak. His eyes were all but glued to the page.

"Dr. Morningstar is a famous author. And I know about your relationship with her. Who doesn't? So don't try to impress me with your formal inquiry."

"You didn't answer my question. You've met Jette." Marc's voice remained detached, his eyes and hands steady.

"I wouldn't say I met her. I attended one of her lectures and book signings. I don't have her delusional optimism, nor any of her hopefulness. I believe the Middle World of Reality is doomed."

Marc ignored her prediction.

"How many times have you talked with her?"

Zena turned then and slid into the doomed real world for an instant. Pulling herself through the tunnel from her fantasy, she assumed the appearance of a CEO of a multi-million-dollar corporation.

"This interview is over, Detective. I want to get back to my world. If you have reason to contact me again, you'll have to do so through my attorney, Lori Horton. Call Madelyn, my assistant, and she'll give you her number."

"We'll be talking again," said Marc. "Nice tattoo, by the way."

Zena automatically glanced down at the top of her right wrist. The edge of a full blue moon was barely visible under the long sleeve of her blouse.

Nodding at Tagg and Kim, Marc left the office without another word. He'd gotten all he needed for the moment.

"Whew. Is she a head case or what?" asked Kim when they got on the elevator.

"I know that gaming can be addicting, but that woman's left the building of sanity and is on her way to commitment." Tagg glanced over at the silent Marc. "Or confinement. Want me to pick her up and take her in?"

"No. We don't have enough. Besides, I'd rather have her out and about. I'm getting in a tag team of my own. 24/7. It's someone like her. Someone like her who has Jette."

"Yeah?" asked Tagg.

"It feels right and frankly, it seems less ominous somehow. If they really believe she's this mythical character, this Avenger, they'll act in a predictable way. I don't like the fact that they think she has a few lives to spare, but it seems they're more interested in turning her."

"Will they hurt her? Threaten her?"

"If they do, she's not holding state secrets. She's smart enough to, well, turn. According to Kelly that means the Avenger does the Empress's bidding. I'm not sure what the Empress will want her to do, but she'll play it just right."

"Yeah, she will." Kim brightened. She'd been so worried. Certainly not at the level of Marc, but heartsick. Now something lifted inside her. "Jette would know just what she'd have to do. She has no reason not to play along. To do what they ask. At least to a point. She'll know you're looking for her and that you'll find her soon. She knows, well, she knows you're out here. Buying time is all she'll have to do until…" Her voice trailed off as Marc's intense green eyed gaze moved to her. Sometimes he just unnerved her. "Ah. I mean, you know, she can get into their heads. The criminal mind. Read it like a book. Some diabolical gaming superstar hasn't got a chance against Jette's experience. And maybe she'll get an opportunity to run. Crack open the door and she'll blow right through it. And then…and then…" When he just continued to stare, she gave up.

Tagg took pity on her, as usual.

"You're right, Kim. She'll protect herself until we get there. So Marc, tell me we're closer."

"There's probably hundreds of suspects, but yeah. I think we're closer. It's a Blue Empress. We just have to find the right one." He pulled his eyes off Kim and checked his phone. "I've got a bunch of calls to return. Maybe someone's spotted the truck."

He walked briskly back to the car, leaving Kim to mutter.

"Why can't he just cut me off? Tell me I'm right and put me out of my misery."

"Kim, I've told you. He does that deliberately," Tagg responded under his breath. Hope had lifted him, too. "If you had a big brother, you'd have heavier armor. It's what they do. Stare you down until your basic insecurities reduce your IQ to that of a rock."

"But he's the only one who does that."

"It's part of his charm."

"Sure. Okay. I guess so."

When they got back in the car, Marc formulated their next moves.

"Something happened to Brightson during her early years. Tagg, call Dina and have her do a little research on that. Get Lyd to dig into her company. I bet there are significant lawsuits. Family of players or former players who have taken this game too far. Have her feed it to Dina."

"Where to now?" he asked.

"Nothing new on the truck, so let's go see Maxine White. She fits major elements of the profile and she was very interested in Jette last week."

# Chapter 42

"What can I do for you, Detective?" Maxine White was a polished professional and clearly the queen of her sleek and uncluttered domain. Everything around her was set up to put her in the spotlight. The monochromatic color scheme was all soft cream and white with the only splash of color being her designer suit of bright canary yellow. The bulbs in the recessed lighting were pointed in the direction of her shining ivory desk and there was no artwork on the walls, just mirrors. Jette had said her ego was both her greatest asset and her biggest barrier.

"You visited Dr. Morningstar at her residence, is that correct?"

"If confirming what you already know is the purpose of this interview, Detective Lexington, we can end it now. I haven't the time to waste."

Completely unphased by her laser blast of condescension, Marc went on with his questions.

"Your company published several books on gaming and most particularly on the history of successful strategies in Sovereignty."

There was a slight hesitation. Either from his abrupt change of topic or because he didn't cower and beg forgiveness before proceeding.

"That's right. But I'm confused. When I consented to see you, I thought this would be about Dr. Morningstar."

"It is. Indirectly. These books on gaming don't exactly fit into your usual selection of publications."

"We have a very eclectic catalog. Exactly what's your point, Detective?" The temperature and timber of Maxine's voice chilled and lowered. She was clearly becoming more annoyed with each question.

"I really don't have a point yet, just more questions."

Maxine was nervy, Marc thought. Getting tenser. Edgier. Was it because of something she wanted to hide, or just her usual impatient need for control?

"You sued Zena Brightson a few years ago for breach of contract."

"I don't sue anyone. Someone from my legal department on the second floor may have initiated action for some reason, but that isn't what I concern myself with on a day-to-day basis."

"What do you know about Sovereignty?"

"It's a computer role-playing game."

"Do you play?"

"Who has time for such nonsense?"

Marc thought the answer might be Ms. Maxine White, that's who.

"Some insane, self absorbed lunatic has been entering the fantasy world of this game and has been recruiting people with shaky mental health. Would you know anything about that?" Marc thought he'd give it a shot. If the Empress was in there, maybe she'd pop out and call him to a duel or something.

"No." There wasn't a flicker of either interest or challenge.

"Why did you set up a meeting with Dr. Morningstar?"

"I think that would be obvious. I wanted her next book. Headlines translate into millions."

"Fifteen minutes of fame doesn't extend to the months or even years it will take to bring her next book to market."

Maxine stared into Marc's eyes for a moment.

"You're smarter than that, Detective. You know as well as I do that Dr. Morningstar is not a fifteen minute wonder. That wouldn't even get a phone call from me. She had classic appeal. Lasting charisma. Her aversion to media exposure actually worked in her favor. She wouldn't have burned out by burning too hotly. I regret that her death will end the negotiations. I was determined to have her."

"Dr. Morningstar isn't dead, Ms. White."

"Then where is she?"

"That's what I'm trying to determine."

"Then I fail to see why you're looking here in my office. As you can see, I'm not entertaining any authors at the moment." Deliberately exaggerating the glance at her watch, she stood up into the lights. "But I do need to get back to business. I'm a very busy woman and I'm sure there's nothing more I can tell you that is germane to this whole business."

Marc didn't move. Taking their cues from Marc, Tagg and Kim didn't either.

"Was there something else?" Maxine prodded, a little taken aback that her obvious dismissal didn't result in the vacating of her office.

"Tell me, Ms. White, do you know of anyone who plays the role of the Blue Empress?"

"No."

"What CRPG do you play?"

"I told you I don't have time for such things. Now I must ask you to leave because I'm getting the feeling you're playing with me."

"This isn't a game. This is real. Have you ever heard of Avenger?"

Again, a slight hesitation. "I'm done answering questions, Detective."

"I could make this official and take it downtown."

"How clichéd. We both know that would afford you no new information since I'd bring a bevy of those lawyers on the second floor with me. It'll only waste time for both of us."

That stopped him. She was good. Time was something he didn't have and she did. Without another word, he stood up, nodded his acknowledgement of her advantage and led Tagg and Kim from the room.

"She knows who Avenger is, either because of those books, or because she has Jette. I'm going to have her tagged," he said when they swung out of the building.

"I'll call the chief and get a team out here," offered Tagg.

"No, I'll take care of it." Reaching in his pocket, Marc pulled out a phone and a couple of fifties. Trotting across the street, he chatted briefly with an elderly man reading magazines at a news stand. The man nodded, then went back to a copy of *Teen People*.

"Who's that?"

"Name's Library."

"Library?"

"He borrows the reading material, then puts it back. Never buys. The guys at the newsstands have no problem with him because while he's reading, he drops plenty of green on snacks, smokes, and coffee. Never creases or greases the pages. He'll drop nearly twenty while reading a three dollar magazine."

"He'll be able to follow her?"

"Sure, plus he blends in better."

"Where to next?"

"Back to the apartment. The team needs to debrief. Impressions?" Marc asked as they got back into the car.

"She's rich, single, computer savvy, narcissistic and if she reads the books she publishes, she understands at least the fundamentals of gaming," reported Tagg.

"I agree. I think she's a gamer with at least one preferred CRPG. I'm just not sure she's a kidnapper and a murderer."

"I think it's interesting that when you told her Jette was alive, she didn't ask any questions. I mean, I'd be so curious, I'd have a million of them," observed Kim.

"I think she was completely distracted by Marc's questions about gaming. Jette became less important than evasion," speculated Tagg.

As they got out of the car, Marc startled Tagg and Kim when he spun around, walked out of the garage and grabbed a young man's wrist. The boy had been there when they'd left a few hours before and he was still there. It appeared he was taking several surreptitious pictures with his cell phone while pretending to talk on it.

"Are you one of the Empress's Minions?" asked Marc angrily. The young man's eyes nearly popped out of his head.

"Ye…ye…yeah," he stammered, then groaned when Marc twisted his wrist. "Hey! You're hurting me."

"I'll do more than that if you don't cooperate," growled Marc, feeling his control slip.

"What are you offering. I'll consider turning for the right Boon," moaned the kid, not knowing how close to real hurt he was.

Marc pulled him into the garage. "How about I don't break your goddamn arm and rearrange your fucking face. Is that enough of a Boon, you little piss ant?"

"What? Hey, man. This is just a game, ya know?"

"Oh really? Where's Jette?"

"Who?" He decided quickly that getting out of the garage without needing a cast would be Boon enough.

"Avenger," snarled Marc, giving the wrist another painful twist.

"Oh. Rumor has it she's being held by the Empress." He couldn't spill out the information fast enough.

"Where?" Marc released his grip a bit, giving the boy some relief.

"I don't know. I'm just a Minion, orange class."

"Is she in the city?"

"The City of Might?"

"New York City, you stupid putz!" Marc shouted. He'd just about had enough of this gaming shit.

"I...I think so," gulped the Minion. "Yeah. I think so. The Empress said she'd be turning Avenger in the City of Might. There's a bounty on you. Major points for shots of the Shield."

"Where did you email the pictures?"

"We download into a special room on the Empress's website. You have to have a code and a password."

"What room? And what's the password?"

"The code is sacred. I tell and I'm banned," sniffed the Minion, horrified at the prospect.

"Tell me or you'll have to pick your nose with your toes."

One reason Marc consistently got information from suspects was because he always looked like he meant his threats. On the other hand, most of the time he did.

"Okay. Okay," cried the Minion babbling out a website. "The room is Phoenix and the password is Diablo."

Marc shook himself. Diablo. Jette's horse. Pulling the boy toward the car, he shoved him at Kim.

"Get his name and address then call in a black and white to take him home."

He wanted to get to Kelly. He needed to see what was in this room. She was into the site in less than a minute and Lyd projected the contents up on a screen. Marc and the team studied the pictures downloaded from hundreds of cell phones around the city. There were hundreds of shots of Jette. Alone, with Marc, talking with students, speaking to people she met, laughing at a street performer. Walking, running, shopping. In New York City. In Tucson. From their different textures and perspectives and various levels of quality and clarity, it was obvious there were dozens of photographers.

"That's how they knew her brands," murmured Dina, fascinated. And a bit taken aback when she saw herself in several shots.

"Jesus Christ, Marc. They have pictures of Lucy." Tagg's voice snapped with anger.

"I think these kids, these Minions, are harmless, Tagg. They think it's a game. They're doing this for points," observed Rachael.

"Still, I want these so-called Minions traced if we can." He looked over at Kelly, who'd been listening to the exchange. "Can you find out who put these into the room?"

"No. Not specifically. But I can get all the game names of every geek who had access to the room. From them, I can get their email addresses and it should be a breeze to trace them back to at least a name they use on their accounts. People who are committing fraud will have phony street addresses and stolen credit numbers, but not these kids. They're just gamers who were chocking a thrill chill. They may try a few layers, but that only means it'll take me another couple minutes to peel them."

"Get us names and addresses and we'll start the interviews." Marc sighed and rubbed his tired eyes. "I don't like the odds of getting anything from them, but we have to take the steps."

"We can assign this to internal teams. I'll have the case by this time tomorrow and can keep the reason close," suggested Tagg, still shook over seeing his little girl up on the screen.

"Look at all the pictures around The Edgewood. Somehow the puppet master found out where Jette lived. I think we need to go back to that question," said Dina.

"She could have been followed. There are pictures of her everywhere," added Teresa.

"You'd never spot these kids. Cell phone cameras are so ubiquitous, and they only took a dozen or so pictures apiece," said Rachael.

"No. There are none between 30th and Central Park South," observed Marc.

"How can you tell?" asked Raj.

"I know my city. There's a big gap between the University and The Edgewood," frowned Marc. "I agree with Dina, we should…"

His cell chirped and he quickly checked the number. "I need to take this. Yeah? Call me when she lands. Thanks." He signed off. "That was Library. The very busy Ms. White is on the move. She came out of the building a few minutes after we left her office."

"Is Library following her?"

"No, he was in the middle of a movie review."

"Jeez, Louise," said Kim with disgust.

"But, he's on the phone with the cabbie who picked her up."

"You knew that. You knew he'd use his own network," she replied admiringly.

"Oh yeah. Library hasn't lost a mark in all the years I've known him."

"So where is she?"

"Cruising down 42nd."

"You know where she's going, don't you?"

"I have a pretty good idea, but I'll wait for confirmation. Lyd, can you and Kelly trace the person who set up the account these kids are dumping the pictures into? We need a name, a location, anything."

Lyd just waved at him like she was batting away flies.

Marc looked over at Luke. "She doing okay? I mean with withdrawal?"

"She'll hold," nodded Luke.

Marc's phone chirped again. He listened, nodded, then just sat and stared at the phone.

"Who?" asked Tagg.

Marc recited the address. When it didn't register with anyone, he said it out loud. "The chief."

"You knew," breathed Kim into the stunned silence. "That's why you didn't want me calling in a team to follow Ms. White."

"Could she be the Empress?" asked Tagg trying to shake the shock.

"I don't know. She doesn't have deep pockets, but she has very useful contacts. She knew Jette was alive. I saw that when I briefed her the other day. And she was too willing to keep everything unofficial."

"But you explained that to her."

"It was out of character."

"Do you think they could be working in tandem? A duo?"

"My sources tell me they're definitely a couple. White pushed herself into this apartment for a meeting with Jette. It could be that the chief was pulling the strings. Or the other way around. White has the cash for this kind of operation. But right now, I don't care if together they think they're a pair of fucking high priestesses. If they have Jette or know where she is, they're going to drown in their delusions."

Marc was glad his circuits were completely burned out. There was nothing left in him to be angry or disillusioned or even surprised.

"Do we pick them up?" asked Tagg. He wasn't as burned out and was feeling angry, disillusioned *and* surprised, as was the entire team around him.

"Based on what proof? I have a powerful, wealthy, self absorbed woman visiting a chief of police. Besides, I want to watch them. See where they go. Jette isn't there. I want them out of custody, feeling on top of things and moving around."

"Um, back up, Marc. How do you know Jette isn't there?" asked Tagg.

"I know the chief's cable guy. He arranged a little outage, then came and did his magic yesterday. He was in every room. Absolutely no sign of Jette or anything else incriminating, but she's does have a copy of Sovereignty in her collection."

They all just stared at Marc.

"What color is my underwear?" asked Raj.

Marc looked at him, up and down. "Raj, you're a man who enjoys silk next to the skin. I don't know the color today, but you're a boxer guy and like to make a statement with the ladies." Then he shocked them all by winking at Teresa. "For now, I'll keep the two of them covered with my street teams. Then at the right time, we'll do a sweep."

"At least we can bring Eunice back in," said Rachael.

"I thought it was Tana who sold us out. I mean. The way she was acting," observed Kim.

"It still could be, but I think the probability is low," said Marc.

"So she's just a garden variety jealous, egotistical, self serving witch," nodded Kim.

"Christ, Kim, let yourself go," smiled Raj.

"So for now we just watch them?" asked Tagg.

"Yeah. And get Kelly and Lyd to dive into the chief's cyber life."

"With no boundaries," said Tagg grimly.

"None," agreed Marc.

"What's next?"

"Let's put together files on the other women we've identified." Marc made the assignments.

"What about Eunice?" asked Tagg. "We could use her."

"Bring her back in."

# Chapter 43

Marc could feel himself getting bleary again. If he wasn't so afraid of drugs, he'd take a few amphetamines. Speed, ice, crystal, glass, crank. Maybe a whole handful. He knew he needed to stop. His movements felt fragmented. Someone had told him once that sometimes people were so busy mopping the floor, they'd forget to turn off the faucet. During the course of a normal investigation, he'd routinely stop to process all the data. To think about how things fit into the big picture. To let inspiration catch up to him.

Sitting down on the soft leather chair in front of the fireplace, he put his head back and brought his feet up onto the ottoman. Closing his eyes, he let the faces of the suspects float into his consciousness, hoping something from this subconscious would push through the clutter of details to give him a clue.

His mother's face and form invaded his mind. Unbidden. Unwanted. A gaunt, burned out skeleton of a woman sitting hunched over and rocking on a filthy cot. His memories of those last days were faded and flawed, but he remembered clearly that she'd sold him to an old man for the price of a fix. Maybe the very same envelope of smack that killed her. Greed for the drug drove her to inject the entire amount into her emaciated system and it overloaded. It would have been the kind of hard street justice he'd come to appreciate, especially after he'd run from the old guy. She'd beaten on him pretty bad when he finally came out from where he'd been hiding. Then she'd shot up and checked out. He'd still had the bruises when the people at the shelter called the cops and social services took him away.

He hadn't realized he'd given into his body's need for sleep until he felt a light touch on his shoulder and forced himself back from the swirling dream of shelters, his mother, the streets, the pain.

"Marc?" It was Luke. "Your team's assembled."

"How long?" He had to clear his throat, but noticed the tightness in his chest had eased back. "How long was I out?"

"Just a couple of hours. But enough, I think. You look less like a corpse."

Shaking his head to clear it, he got up and gratefully accepted the coffee mug Luke pressed into his hand along with the inevitable pills that came with it.

Marc walked over and stared at the board devoted to strong, wealthy women. They'd collected several who'd intersected with Jette within the last few weeks. Klara Marshall was up there as was Mrs. Victor Chrysler. Marc had found her card when searching through Jette's office. It had been difficult going into her files and correspondence, but he'd wanted to do it himself. It seemed less invasive somehow.

Marc started the briefing by placing Maxine White's picture next to the chief's.

"This command center is now off limits to anyone not currently in this room," ordered Marc solemnly. "The chief is not likely to come back since she'll have the case by tomorrow and expects to stay on top of things there. Tagg you'll be in command. The formal investigation will take a traditional path using all the evidence from the mission."

"But not the syllabary or how much we have on Sovereignty," said Tagg.

"Exactly," nodded Marc grimly. "White will give her everything we discussed in the interview, but if either of them have Jette, it might get them to move. We have them covered."

"So you deliberately baited White," stated Tagg with approval.

"And she went right to the chief."

"Could be she just wanted to know what the hell one of the chief's detectives was doing in her office."

"Could one or the other of them be this Empress?" asked Raj.

"Their names go to the top of the list, but either of them or both could just be feeding the woman behind all of it," said Marc.

"Do you think the chief deliberately passed on information, or could it just be pillow talk?" asked Rachael.

"Based on what we know, the information on the 22nd Street mission was passed immediately to the people holding Jette." Marc took another sip of coffee.

"They could have been together when Tagg called the chief for the warrants," speculated Eunice, glad to be a part of the team again.

"She secured the warrants from her home, so it's possible White was in the right place at the right time. We have them covered and they're still together, so let's move on. Concentrating on them too much may prevent us from other lines we need to pursue. Raj, did you get the lab report on the contents of the syringe?"

"Heroin. Pure. Top of the line."

"A remnant from the previous tenants?"

"No. Fresh. So either one of these Minions or Sentinels is a user, or…"

"Or they're popping it into Jette." Marc's flat, hard tone sent a shiver through the room.

There was silence as everyone absorbed the fact. Finally, Kim voiced the only positive conclusion.

"If this Blue Witch is trying to turn her, it's really good news she's doing it with something like drugs. There was no blood. No signs of sexual abuse. It could be a whole lot worse."

Marc tried to shake the picture of his mother's face, still so close to the surface, and the residual despair and disgust that went with it. It wasn't the same. It wasn't the same.

"Detective?" Kim wasn't sure Marc had heard her. The haunted look in his eyes framed by the deep shadows of fatigue was painful to look at.

"You have no idea," murmured Marc, as if no one else was in the room. "No idea."

His detachment was alarming his team. Could he have reached his limit? They'd all been expecting it. Speculating on when he'd hit the wall. Fearing it, actually.

As one they looked over at Luke. He'd been able to go in and bring him back before.

Luke nodded and went up to Marc, who was still staring at something no one else could see. Luke knew about Marc's background. Sympathy nearly swamped him, but they needed Marc too much to let him float away from them.

"Marc," said Luke with authority, then waited until Marc's eyes refocused and turned to him. "While it's physically invasive and an affront to everything Jette is, the core of her will shake it off when we get her back. You know that. She's smart enough to realize what they're doing to her and strong willed enough not to let that keep her from protecting herself. Remember the syllabary she left for us. They were drawn with a firm hand and a keen mind. The drugs will affect her, we can't protect her from that, but underneath, she'll remain alert."

"She's already addicted, Luke. At some point her body's need…" How could he say it? He swallowed hard. "Her need for the drug will push the animal inside her to do things her civilized nature can't stop her from doing."

"Then we better get busy, Marc. Because the animal that lives inside her is the wolf. God help those who have her if that's unleashed. Let's go find her. Let's bring her home before there's nothing left of those Minions but bits of bone and flesh."

The team watched as Marc's face cleared and his lips turned up. Luke was a magician. He'd found the hidden button and pushed it. Hard.

"Right." Marc turned his eyes, now fierce and determined, to his team. "Dina, explosives report."

"The bomb sniffers, going undercover as seeing-eye dogs," she winked at Kim, "found buried treasure in a storeroom at St. Barts, in a platform near the stage at the All Saints Museum and in a dumpster in an alley outside the Prince of Kiev restaurant. The photo Claude sent back from the restaurant was nearly a perfect match. Good eye, Marc. Very, very discreetly three squads went in as tourists, plumbers, and garbage collectors and carried out the explosives leaving in the triggering mechanisms. Remotes. Not very sophisticated. They attached electrical detection devices on each one. We'll know if the Empress tries to detonate."

"Good job," approved Tagg.

"Yeah. Score a big one for the Guardians," nodded Dina. "Jette did a job on the inside that saved both lives and property."

Marc moved on before the emotional burst in his chest clogged his throat. "And you think the eyes and cameras in the vicinity are clueless."

"Yeah. Tony swept the area and saw several teens lounging around without any apparent purpose. They didn't suspect a thing so he left them alone."

"Good work."

"Yes. Tony was an excellent choice. He personally swept the other sites we identified. Nothing." Dina knew Marc had been hoping Jette might be found in one of them and was sorry she couldn't bring him good news.

They all took a moment to observe the victory and process the disappointment, then pushed forward.

"With the bombs out of play, we're completely clear to snatch Avenger out from under the Empress's nose. She won't be able to take out her temper on innocent bystanders." Tagg wanted to add more weight to the positive side of the scales.

"Rachael, you have the chief's biography. Didn't she spend some time in the Bomb Squad?" asked Marc.

"Six years. It's how she made a name for herself. Damn, she was a good cop, Marc. I find it hard to believe she'd have a part in blowing up parts of our city."

Marc nodded. "So do I. But something else occurs to me. There's still the person who took out Flowers. Check the chief's marksman status."

Rachael paged through her notes.

"Lousy. Barely passed the mandatory tests."

"What about vice? Did she ever work in the drug and alcohol division?"

"No. But any beat cop worth her salt could name names if she wanted to score some smack."

"Hell." Marc rubbed his face. "Could we be looking for another cop? One who's a high level marksman, an explosives expert, and knows how to score drugs?"

The team sat silent. This was a real possibility and it both stunned them and made then angry beyond measure. There was nothing worse than a cop with a dirty core.

"Let me take that one, Marc," suggested Eunice. "I have a lot of connections and can be real discreet."

Marc stared at her. "A marksman, an explosives expert and a former vice cop with connections. Sound familiar?"

"Yeah. Fits me like a wetsuit. You want to make an arrest?"

"No. You were testifying in Judge Lynda Jones's courtroom at the time of the Flowers shooting and besides, you don't even own a personal computer."

Eunice stared at him.

"A part of me is real proud of you, Detective. And that part is keeping me from planting a fist in your pretty face." She hesitated for only a second. "So what's my bra size?"

"38 D," said Marc without hesitation.

Raj just whistled, then realized he was the only one who made a sound. As a matter of fact the room seemed devoid of all movement making his loud and appreciative whistle nearly echo. A flush changed Raj's cheeks from a fine coffee color to a shade near mahogany. He sincerely hoped his face was pretty enough to be spared Eunice's fist.

"And real proud of that, too." Eunice nodded at Raj, then looked Marc in the eye. "So are me and my 38D's in this or not?"

"You're in. All the way to the end." Marc's eyes flashed once, then moved to Teresa. "What about your decoy duty?"

"We've been putting on a pretty good show of tearing around the city in an undirected pattern. Periodically we pose for the cameras with perplexed, confused looks on our faces. The pictures going in to the Empress will keep her happy."

"We don't want them to move Jette again. If she thinks we have no real direction, she'll be complacent."

"I'm in constant touch with Sweeney. Her team is still running the mountain of evidence from the mission. It's slow going. Nothing new."

Marc's cell phone chirped. He looked at it and took the call immediately.

"Hola, Franco."

He listened for a few seconds, then jumped up and started toward the door.

"Sí, sé la ubicación. Si es el derecho uno, usted ha ganado cinco grande. Permanezca donde usted es. No toque una cosa." He snapped the phone shut as he crossed the threshold. "I think we have the truck!"

"Want a team?" asked Tagg, but got no response, then heard Marc slam out the front door. "I guess not," he murmured.

"I think he already has an entire posse," observed Kim.

"Translation?" asked Raj.

"Marc knew the location," Tagg interpreted. "If it's the right one, you've earned five large. Remain where you are."

"Don't touch a thing," Dina finished.

"Sounds promising," said Raj.

"Our man in action." Tagg turned to his weary band of Guardians. "Let's do background checks for some more of these women."

Marc turned in a circle, looking over the neat row houses surrounding the tiny park. The truck sat in a tidy little alley behind a church. St. Marks. The Empress was getting cute.

Franco was a cab driver who'd dropped off a fare near the church and saw the truck. The cabbie grapevine had him on the alert and he appreciated the night's bonus Marc slapped into his waiting palm.

Forensics would prove the truck was the same one SueTee saw, but all he had to do was step in and sniff. Jette. Her scent lingered. A tiny piece of blue fabric stuck behind the wheel cover confirmed it.

She'd either been transferred to another vehicle, dropped before the truck was abandoned, or she was in one of the surrounding buildings. His guess was a drop. A careful inspection revealed no subtle blue trail around the truck. She may have been unable to leave anything for him, a thought that pushed his alarm button, but he thought it meant she hadn't been taken this far.

Still, he needed to set up a door-to-door sweep. Since no one outside his team was going to get the word on this location it was going to tap all his resources. His instincts told him they wouldn't find her in this neighborhood. Her kidnappers wouldn't have left the truck near their lair.

Would the driver have taken public transportation back to the nest? Called a cab? Walked? Been picked up? His head pounded with too many possibilities. All the alternatives would have to be checked out. But what did his gut tell him?

Shutting down his spinning mind, he opened himself up. The driver would want to stay with the prize. He'd go back to Jette. They were nearby. Not in this neighborhood but within walking distance. How far would a Sentinel walk before a ride or the subway became a preferred option. This was New York. People walked. It was often faster than calling a cab and certainly more circumspect. So how far? If the person was a New Yorker, he'd walk several miles. Fine. Then that would be the perimeter. He'd find her somewhere within a four mile radius. Unfortunately that left hundreds, even thousands, of possibilities.

Marc returned to the apartment to set up teams for canvassing. It would be their highest priority right now. A four mile circle was drawn around the perimeter of St. Mark's. They were pinpointing any building or business associated with saints and found twenty churches alone. Pictures from websites were being printed and posted.

Lyd waved a phone at Marc from her corner. "Hey Snake Eyes. It's Chuck Markle."

"Put him on speaker," he called.

"I'll get right to the point," came Chuck's disembodied voice. "Then you can have one of your team update me on your progress."

"I really appreciate that."

"I've been studying the pictures you sent and have one more word for you. One that was separated from the others. I think it's important. Healer."

"Healer? Luke? Do you think she wanted us to contact Luke?"

"I don't know, but it's female, so I don't think so. Do you think one of her captors is a doctor? Or a nurse?"

"It's possible. Although the idea of a medical person being one of the players is chilling."

"Yeah. It can't be good."

"But thanks for the information, Chuck. Every little bit helps. I'm going to connect you to Tagg. He'll fill you in." Marc turned from the phone and began pacing. His nerves felt on fire.

Tagg nodded, took up the receiver, and went to the corner of the room to give it all to the Tucson Captain.

"The Empress must have brought in a nurse to administer the drugs." Kim looked at Marc and hoped the mention of drugs wouldn't make him space out again.

Something pushed at Marc. The subliminal nudge was strong and he was grateful that the few hours rest reduced the barriers to his subconscious. His instincts rocked when Chuck had said nurse. Nurse. The Empress's specialty was to grant Boons. What would a nurse want? To be able to save lives? To be...

"Get me the name of the nurse who was in Jette's class. The one who went out and helped those students who were down." He slammed up against what he thought was the right conclusion.

"You don't think...," began Kim.

"Jette said she was incredibly cool. Unnaturally so. The fact that Jette mentioned it means on some level she thought it was a bit off. This nurse has become quite a celebrity. A hero."

A few minutes later, Kim had the name and she and Marc were on the way to her apartment.

# Chapter 44

Jette's dreams were vivid and filled with splashes of intense color. Clinically, she knew they were enhanced by the drugs flowing through her system. Objectively she knew this experience was going to make her a better therapist, but on the most fundamental level of her heart and soul, she hated what the narcotics were doing to her. She didn't like having her wits scattered, faded by the intensity of the euphoria the alluring liquid granted her. When she wanted to lay a plan for escape, or battle intellectually with the Empress, she felt dull and sluggish. At times, the drug gave her a false sense of invincibility that she considered very dangerous.

From a very early age, guided by her native father and loving mother, she found her center. From that solid base, she never lost her balance. Choosing a life free of anger, artificial stimulants and even meat, she remained firmly grounded. Her mind, body, and spirit were synthesized into one complete and happy whole. Now she felt fragmented. While this experience was interesting to the therapist inside her, it was upsetting to her soul.

Tonight was different. After another shot, her dreams circled out of her sleep and swirled into the room. Her heart sang when she saw her father sitting in the soft leather chair near her bed.

Thrilled, she sat up and patted the bed next to her.

"Come sit with me, *Adadoda*. It's so good to see you."

"No, *Uwetsi*." He stood and held out his hand. "Not here. I want you to come with me."

Without hesitation, excited and happy, she took his warm hand and they journeyed to her special place in the hillside near their ranch. With father sky over them, they sat cross-legged on the warm, dry earth and grinned at each other. Identical smiles, identical hearts.

Wood was laid carefully for the fire. South to embody happiness and peace, east to symbolize blood and success. Fire sizzled out of her father's fingertips as he ignited the dry logs and golden flames soared toward the Great Spirit.

"Now that's impressive," she laughed.

"No, *Uwetsi*. That dive into the East River was impressive. Flaming fingertips are just drug induced magic. As soon as you detoxify, I'll go back to being a common spirit, but you'll still be able to leap across buildings."

"*Adadoda*. It's so good to see you. So much has happened since you left me."

"Left you?"

"Since you went into the arms of the Great Spirit."

"It true, I've transcended to another form, but I've never left you. I'm always with you."

"Always?" she asked a little sheepishly.

Laughing, he chucked her under the chin like he did when she was a girl.

"Well, no, *Uwetsi*. Not always. I know when to close the door."

"It's just that I don't want to wake up from this lovely dream and think of you watching everything I do."

Her father laughed again with the abandon of a free spirit.

"We just check in on your big days. We saw you receive your doctorate. It was a proud day for us. Brains as well as beauty and a brave heart. Your mother and I were only able to give it one shot, but we certainly gave it a good one."

"Is she with you?"

"She is, yes."

"Will she come with you next time?"

"And what makes you think I'd let him journey alone?" A soft gentle voice floated on the air.

"*Unitsi*!" Jette's joy soared around them when a stunning fair haired woman stepped into the fire light. She jumped up and ran into the open arms of her mother.

The embrace felt real. It was *Unitsi*. Her scent, her touch, her beautiful voice. Jette's senses filled her heart and soul with indescribable delight. When they parted, her mother's sparking blue eyes warmed her with their familiar shine.

"You and your father can talk about your predicament later. Tell me about your man."

"I'm so in love."

"I can see that. He seems so unlike you. A little intense, isn't he?"

Jette laughed. "To say the least. But the moment I met him, I knew he was my destiny."

"It isn't an easy companion you've chosen for the journey."

She could feel herself laugh again. It was so good to talk to her mother about the man who'd changed her life forever.

"And since when did the Cherokee ever choose the easy way? We've survived because we can adapt and because of our bravery in the face of adversity. I'm determined to bring Marc to the light, *Unitsi*. To help him find peace."

Her mother sighed, but with fond approval more than with exasperation. "You always liked jumping the highest fences, facing down the wild mountain lion, running the most difficult mile. And you tamed the bitter little beast inside of Luke. He's a fine man, isn't he?"

"I only jumped the fence because I could feel the horse's confidence in my own heart. I faced down the mountain lion because I knew she meant me no harm, and I run anywhere, anytime because it gives me the freedom of the wind. And Luke is the man he was always meant to be. The seed of hostility and malice wasn't able to flourish." She grinned at her parents and winked. "But if the general population thinks it's due to my mystical connection to all of earth's rhythms…"

"They would be right, *Uwetsi*," laughed *Unitsi*.

"Now sit here and tell me about this Empress and how you will defeat her," instructed her father.

Jette and her mother sat down near the fire.

"By knowing her, *Adadoda*. She wears a mask and disguises her voice, but her mind and motives are open to me. She hates the world she was born into and has created another that fits her needs. Her personality is seriously flawed and I'll drive my will into that flaw and push. Marc and I together will meet her in a Final Duel."

"She hasn't a chance," stated her father. "By the way, your man is right behind you. He's a great tracker."

"He is."

"It won't be long," he assured.

"We're going to go now," sighed *Unitsi*. "You have to get moving."

"No. Stay. Don't leave."

"Darling, every time your heart beats, our combined blood flows through you. We are always with you."

"*Adadoda* told me not always," said Jette, her voice thick with tears.

"No," her mother laughed. The same musical sound that echoed through Jette's mind and heart whenever she thought of her. "When that blood runs hot, your father and I go on a picnic. But we are never far. We love you."

With that, her mother and father rose, clasped hands, looked to the sky and faded.

Sighing, Jette woke up in the bedroom. Still in captivity. There were no windows in the room, but from the hush all around her, she judged it was night. Rubbing the tears from her cheeks, she glanced at the door leading to outside. To freedom. It was just a door. Her life was on the other side.

Sitting up, she followed her routine and pressed the button to summon her keepers.

The warm, mellow, loving feeling that came from her conversation with her parents lingered throughout the morning. It was ironic. The Empress, her adversary and apparently her blood enemy, had given her a gift. In a detached, clinical way, she knew it was a drug induced hallucinatory dream, but on a very basic level she didn't care. In her heart and in her mind it was a wonderful respite.

When the Tinman came in and released her, she steadied herself, then walked to the bathroom, showered, and made herself presentable. Maybe this was the day Marc would find her, or maybe she'd find a way to check out of the luxury suite of this creepy castle and get back to her own world. Either way, she'd reunite with Marc looking her best.

As she studied her face in the mirror she saw the dilated pupils and felt the pull of her body's desire for another shot of the liquid rapture. A false need for a fickle prize.

Her lips quirked up at the thought of being in the arms of her lover. Now that was real rapture. Real and true. And it was amazing how much she missed it. Missed him.

Opening her fist she looked at the diminished handful of what she thought of as little blue bread crumbs. Securing them in her pocket, she stretched and went through her entire yoga routine. It took nearly an hour, but she felt physically better when she opened the door and let Tinman escort her back to her bed.

Hester didn't give her the shot today, and Tinman wasn't nearly as skilled. There was pain before the rush. She hoped Hester's absence meant the young woman was now working with Marc. She'd give it one more day. Then she'd move to Plan B. What that was, she hadn't determined, but she was confident she could outwit her captors.

The narcotic began to erode her resolve, seduce her determination, but because she started with so much of both, her mind began to formulate a Plan B.

# Chapter 45

Marc and Kim returned from a frustrating search for Hester. Her neighbors hadn't seen her, and her family hadn't heard from her.

"Marc it's the hospital," called Raj. "Your hunch paid off. They have a Jane Doe fitting your description. She was brought in last night. Overdose. She would have bought it but a resident of the cardboard condos had a brand new cell phone to call 911. Looks like one of your plants bore unexpected fruit."

"Tagg, Sommer, let's go," ordered Marc. "Luke, I could use you on this run."

Luke nodded and followed them out the door. Less than twenty minutes later, they stood over Hester, lying in a drug induced coma.

"Is she going to make it?" asked Kim.

"Yes, I think so, but not any time soon." Luke studied her chart, then checked her vital signs himself. "It was an overdose that put her in the coma. No other trauma. Could be an attempted suicide. She had a huge amount of heroine in her system. With her height and weight, it would have been lethal."

Marc turned her arm. "No other needle marks on her, so she wasn't an addict. If this was her first shot, she could have just miscalculated."

"Agreed. But look here. There's slight bruising around her elbow. As if someone held her arm tightly," observed Luke.

"Attempted murder, then," Tagg concluded.

"She had no identification, no jewelry, no money?" Marc asked the attending physician.

"No. Nothing but the clothes on her back."

"Who called it in?"

"The person didn't give a name, but they'd have a number at the 911 dispatch center." Marc nodded at Kim who stepped out to get it.

Tagg stared at the Hester. "Why do you think they wanted to dispose of her now?"

"Jette got to her and the Empress knew it," guessed Marc.

"Poor kid," frowned Luke.

"Before you waste a lot of your sympathy, remember that she was probably a part of what went down at the university," snapped Marc.

Kim came in with the number. "Kelly checked your log. You gave that phone to someone called Lizard Breath."

"Let's move. I want a look at what LB took off the body." Marc turned toward the door. "Kim call in and get an officer down here. I want to know the minute she wakes up."

"You think she was robbed?" asked Luke as they all walked quickly down the corridor.

"More likely picked over. There was a slight tan line on her wrist. She was a habitual watch wearer."

"He stripped her valuables, but still called in 911?"

"Most people who take to the streets aren't killers or thugs, but they can be opportunists and wouldn't pass up a chance to mine for gold."

Within a few minutes, Luke, Kim, and Tagg watched as Marc rousted several of the alley citizens until he found the one he sought. A short, thin, Asian man in a brand new Yankees cap stood squinting up at Marc. Somewhere in the city a capless tourist was walking around wondering where he left his souvenir.

"Give me the loot from the Betty you found doped, LB," demanded Marc gently.

"Is there a reward?" asked the little man without any guile or guilt.

"Depends on the cut and caliber."

"It's prime."

"So is the number on the green. Let's see it."

LB dug deeply in his pocket and produced a wallet, a watch, a chain with several charms Marc recognized from the Sovereignty website…and Jette's ring.

"That's…" Luke began.

"Yeah, it is." Marc reached for it and nearly broke LB's arm when the withered old man closed his fist and shot his hand behind his back.

"Show me the presidents."

Marc's mind stuttered for an instant and Luke reached in his own pocket for cash. LB surrendered the items instantly when he saw the president was George himself. Marc took the three items, handed the wallet and chain to Kim and held the ring up to the light.

"Why would Hester have the ring?" asked Kim.

"I think Jette turned her and this ring was somehow supposed to get to us," replied Marc.

"And that's why they shot her with the heroin. Why they tried to kill her," concluded Tagg, electrified by the sight of something from Jette. Knowing she was working it from the inside punched light through the dingy alley. Through all of them.

"Think she drew a symbol on the stone?" asked Luke.

"I'm betting she tried," nodded Marc.

When he held her ring, he swore he could feel her hand on his arm. Turning the ring, he forced his brutalized eyes to focus on an inside inscription. Not her hand on his arm, but a clear message.

"Luke, is there a reason she'd have the word beer etched in here?"

"Maybe she was starting a shopping list for the homecoming party?" Luke took the ring and looked for himself. "Beer. Why beer? A bar? Do you think there's a bar near where they're holding her?"

"No. She'd etch bar. Fewer letters."

"She'd be gathering as much about her environment as she could."

"Maybe she smelled beer? What's in beer?"

"Hops, malt, yeast, and water." Kim shrugged when everyone turned and stared at her. "Hey, I'm from Wisconsin. Beer, cheese, the Green Bay Packers."

"Well there's no field of hops in New York City," said Tagg.

"Plenty of weed, though. Isn't marijuana in the same family as hops?" asked Kim.

"Yeast could mean she wants us to look for a bakery," speculated Tagg.

"And malts are served in diners, fast food places," added Luke.

"Stop. I think we're flying too far afield. I think it's beer she wants us to look for. Let's start there," said Marc.

"Liquor stores?" asked Kim.

"No. A brewery." Luke was excited by the thought. "If you've ever toured one or driven by one, they have a very distinctive smell. She'd be using her senses to give us a trail to follow. Her sense of smell is amazing and not always an asset, let me tell you. But if she smelled a brewery…"

Marc flipped open his phone.

"Eunice, have Lyd and Kelly look for breweries inside the perimeter. We're on our way to St. Marks now. Call in the team and meet us there."

Within twenty minutes, Marc stood behind the church. His confidence ebbed and flowed like a tide. They hadn't found a working brewery within the perimeter, so Lyd and Kelly were looking in historical records of the city. If there'd never been one, his assumption on the perimeter was off.

"Talk to me, Lyd," he said on the phone. "I need an address."

Tagg, Kim, and Luke were at his side, the rest of the team were on their way.

"Here. Here it is! About three blocks from where you're standing," laughed Lyd a little hysterically. This high was better than booze, she thought. She rattled off the address.

"Get me a warrant, Tagg. Judge Lyndsey Elmer is standing by," shouted Marc, already running toward the car. He got on the phone with the rest of the team and fed them the address. They wouldn't be sharing this information with anyone this time. Just one judge he trusted and the team. "We go in silent. No lights, no sirens."

If they had any doubt the building was their target, it evaporated when they saw the façade. Marc took a picture and sent it to Kelly. She texted right back. *Empress's Armory. Perfect match.*

"Eunice, you take Rachael and Teresa and cover the back. Raj, Sommer, Tagg, take the loading dock. Dina, you and I go in the front. Luke stay back. As soon as we secure the building, come on in. I don't want to tip my hand until we're well into the building, so as soon as we get the warrant, I'll work the outside lock. We'll announce our presence before going through any internal doors."

Less than ten minutes later, Marc moved through a huge empty warehouse. Completely deserted. No furniture, no equipment, no debris, no life. There were three doors in the rear, but even as he, Tagg, Kim, Raj, and Dina moved cautiously toward them, Marc knew they'd find nothing.

Taking the steps and methodically going through the doors, they confirmed they were alone. One room held a huge heating and air conditioning unit. They checked behind it, around it. Nothing. The office was empty except for some built-in shelves along one wall. Behind the last door was a bathroom with a separate stall and a single sink.

Standing in the middle of the huge warehouse, turning slowly in a circle, Marc holstered his weapon. What the hell was he doing? Taking advice from a fifteen year old delinquent and being led around by the delusions of some gamer? Getting sucked into her fantasy? Who was more cracked here? Him or this Empress?

"Jette," he shouted. "Jette!"

No response. Just an echo in the vacant space. It didn't appear that Jette had ever been there. The entire team felt the bitter sting of defeat. Another dead end.

"There's nothing here. It's absolutely clean." Luke walked up beside him.

Clean. Marc's head pounded with fatigue, but there was an itch about the place. It was, in fact, unnaturally clean. All the surfaces had been dusted, scrubbed, and sanitized. Even the metal furnace had gleamed in the dim light. Just like the mission on 22nd.

No. Not a dead end. Not yet. In fury and frustration, he yanked out his phone and called Kelly.

"Let me see the space," said Kelly.

Marc pointed his phone at the huge room. Three stories. Old wooden rafters, floors of slick gray tile. The entire left side was a bricked common wall with the building next door.

"Okay. Clever. I think it's supposed to be the Hall of Secrets."

"Hall of Secrets?" Marc was getting damn sick of playing this game.

"Yeah. This is really, really sweet. The Empress can only invoke this once during play. See, the two Avatars have access to a building that's filled with concealed spaces. The bricks would hold a code. It's great strategy. Another layer between you and her. No one serving Avenger can read the code so you'd have to turn a Sentinel but that's not important right now 'cause we're not playing by game rules. Look for hidden rooms. She'll have Avenger stashed."

"There's a hidden room," shouted Marc to his team, already scanning the walls.

After a half hour of careful inspection, Marc was beginning to doubt the entire theme. They'd been over every inch of the walls, from floor to ceiling. There was no evidence of any recent modifications.

"Here's the blueprints," puffed Kim, running in from the street.

"Let's go outside. The light's better." Marc felt the walls closing in on him and his body ached for fresh air.

Tagg unrolled the building's plans and laid them out on the hood of his cruiser.

"I measured the interior space. Let's see if the dimensions are accurate," sighed Rachael, taking out the paper she'd written on.

"Maybe it's another decoy." Dina slammed out of the front door. "Hell," she said softly. "Pardon me while I take out my frustration on that little grunt across the street. Looks like a Minion to me."

Turning suddenly, she took off after a very startled young man who'd been pointing his phone in their direction. He didn't have a chance against the streaking fury of Avenger's Guardian and within a minute, Dina dragged a sweating, swearing privileged puppy to the car.

"Want him in the Palace of Pain or do you want me to take him to the Tower of Torture."

"Screw you! Take your points and let me loose. I got karate practice in a half hour," shouted the kid.

"Practice, huh? Well, this isn't practice, you creepy little cockroach." In an accomplished move, she spun him around, forced him up against the wall and cuffed his wrists.

"Hey! Who do you think you are! Cops?" squealed the now frightened boy.

Taking out her badge, Dina flashed it in front of his face.

"That's exactly who we are."

The boy paled.

"Hey, so what. I took a few pictures to send to the Empress. There's no law against that."

"Actually there is. It's called aiding and abetting."

"Catch another one?" asked Raj from the doorway.

"Yeah. Come and take him, will you? Get what you can from him." She glanced over at Marc, who was still studying the maps, apparently unimpressed with her collar. Tagg looked up and answered her original question.

"Call a black and white and take him in. I've had about enough of these preppies dogging us." He looked over at Marc. "It's a good sign, though. That wasn't a random meeting. This location must be something."

"Yeah, I get that."

Marc went back to the blueprints. They showed the big room. An office. A bathroom. Right locations. Another wave of exhaustion had the lines blurring. Suddenly he jerked and the rest of the team came to full alert.

Wrong dimensions! He didn't need Rachael's measurements. The abandoned office was smaller than in the blueprint. And...

"The bathroom," he muttered.

"What?" asked Tagg. "You need a bathroom? There was one in there."

"One. Not big enough. There were hundreds of employees. I should have seen that before. Come on."

They poured back into the building, guns drawn, cautious, but optimistic. In the small bathroom, pipes disappeared into what appeared to be an old wall. On closer inspection, the materials were indeed old, but several of the screws and nails holding up the stained drywall were shinier than they should have been.

Dina flipped the handle on the toilet. It didn't flush.

"It's not connected to anything," she whispered.

Marc motioned for Tagg, Teresa, Kim, and Raj to take the office while he studied every inch of the floor and wall. They found no entrance, no hidden doorway.

"Marc." Rachael pointed at the mirror. "Hinges. Do I open it?"

Marc hesitated. Anyone behind the mirror must know they were in the building. Would they hurt Jette if they thought rescue was imminent? It wouldn't be a way in. At best it was an observation window.

He shook his head. Better to find the doorway so they could get in fast if they needed to.

Just then, Tagg appeared in the doorway grinning.

"The built in bookshelves are hinged. Thought you'd want to lead the way," he said softly.

Marc nodded, realizing his throat was dry with tension. This was it. They'd found the location Jette led them to. She was on the other side of this wall. Jette. After all these days of searching, she was just yards away. Still, they needed to exercise caution. He had no idea what or who was between them.

The entire team positioned themselves around the bookshelves. From the placement of the hinges, they could see the door swung into the room beyond. It would give them cover as they entered. Marc would go in first, the rest of them at his back.

Marc felt he would burst with the need to move, but waited until everyone was in place. Drawing a deep breath, he gripped the corner of the bookshelf and shoved.

It moved easily and they poured into the room, fast and ready for anything. Within seconds they were standing in the middle of another beautifully furnished suite. Another beautifully furnished *empty* suite. The bed was made, the lamps were off, the room was deserted.

Marc nearly cracked under the strain of disappointment. Too drained for any emotion, he didn't join in the cursing, the speculation, the sounds of frustration.

"They were warned again," growled Tagg looking around at all the irritated faces.

"You think one of us tipped her off?" Dina snapped, at the end of her endurance and speaking for everyone.

"No." Tagg, holstered his weapon. "But there's another leak."

Marc looked at the exhausted faces. Did the Empress know they were coming? Did he have to hunt alone now? Could he trust anyone? Discouragement dogged his fatigue.

He scanned the space, sniffed the air. The odor of the old brewery was strong, but there was nothing of Jette.

"No," he said. "There wasn't a leak. Jette was never here. It was a decoy. Call in CSI, I'll be outside."

No one followed him. No one offered any words of encouragement or comfort. No one had it in them.

Marc pushed out the front doors. He needed to move. But there was nowhere else for him to go. He'd been so sure this was where he'd finally find Jette that he hadn't seen beyond it. Fear clutched at him. There wasn't much left in him and he knew it. Rubbing his throbbing chest, he wondered where he'd find the energy to keep going, to keep thinking, to keep hoping. Jette was still out there and it was killing him.

Shaking his head and stretching out his back, he looked up and got a different perspective of the building. His dull brain flickered, then focused. The old brewery was part of a block-long series of buildings. Together, they looked like a connected village of sorts. Could there be another secret room? An entrance from the outside? Kelly had said look for secret rooms. Plural.

There was a common wall shared by the apartment building to the left. On a hunch, he walked into the dark, narrow alley space to the right. Turning the corner, he started slowly down the back alley that ran the full length of the block. As in the interior, the space around the old brewery was unnaturally clean and ordered. Carefully scanning the exterior façade, he saw nothing unusual.

He glanced over at the less tidy back entrance to the building next door and froze. Literally froze. Then a slow, feral smile took the place of exhausted frustration. There *was* more inside him. The tiny reserve of strength, of energy, of hope put purpose in his stride. Walking over, never taking his eyes off the tiny blue shred of material, he felt the electricity of success. Jette. She'd left him a message. She'd left him a trail.

He picked up the piece of fabric, rubbed it between his thumb and fingers. Identical to the pieces he'd found leading from the shelter, the one in the truck. Jette.

Getting on his radio, he ordered the team to the alley. They were there in seconds. Scanning the ground now, he saw another piece a few yards ahead of him and another a few yards ahead of that. Not so many to be conspicuous, but enough so he followed steadily and confidently.

Hearing the excited comments of his team as they matched his pace, he almost didn't trust the ease of this last step to her. Could this be another deliberate trap? No. It was Jette. It was a trail she left for him. Two pieces were scattered among the debris near the rear door to the building that shared the west wall of the brewery.

Marc signaled for silence, then drawing his gun, tried the door knob. It was locked. Irritated, but not surprised, he took a minute to contemplate his options. The legal ground here was shaky. Any evidence gathered from this scene would be vulnerable if he didn't wait for an expansion of the search warrant. On the other hand, he was engaged in a chase. There was clearly imminent danger to the hostage. Hell, he'd worry about all that later. Jette was in this building. Reaching in his pocket for a jackknife, he studied the lock on the door. A piece of cake. In seconds, the door was unlocked and he was swinging it inward.

There was no one in the dim hallway. It was a typical modest New York City apartment house with narrow corridors and several doors on either side. Marc could see the light from the small foyer at the opposite end of the building. Crouching down, he looked carefully along the floor and baseboards. Here was another short hallway to the left with more apartments. He spotted no blue specks of fabric. Maybe she ran out. Maybe they'd been swept away by a conscientious landlord. Then his eyes moved up and he saw it.

"There." He pointed at a piece tucked into the door jam of the rear apartment. This time he didn't even stop to think about the consequences, he stood up, walked to the door, and decided to just go through it.

The door blew off its hinges as Marc put all his pent up fury into one ferocious kick.

"Police," he shouted as he went in low, sweeping the apartment with his gun. Tagg and Kim were right behind him providing back up, and the rest of the team followed. There was nothing in the spacious living area. Nothing in the open kitchen. It was a vacant, empty apartment.

Marc turned his head, scanning the room, then like an animal scenting his mate, he ran straight at the closed door in the back, put his shoulder into it and burst through.

It was like falling into a different world. The room beyond the door was opulent. Dark, heavy furniture, tapestries, thickly woven carpets, all reminiscent of a medieval castle. Perfectly staged. In the center of the room was a huge four-poster bed covered with a spread of luxuriant gold-trimmed maroon velvet.

And lying in the center, on a mountain of soft fringed pillows was Jette.

Jette! If an army of enemy Minions had been in the room, Marc wouldn't have seen them. Wouldn't have been able to react. After endless days and nights of suppressed terror, there she was. Only five feet away. He only had to take a few more steps.

Like a sleeping princess in a fairy tale, Jette lay still and beautiful. Her eyes were closed and for a single horrible moment, Marc thought he might have been too late.

Paralyzed for that second by the sight of what might have been a tragic ending, Marc's body seized. Then his eyes locked on her chest. It moved. She was alive. Alive. It echoed in his head as he ran to her side. His team poured into the room and automatically checked the closets and adjoining bathroom. She was alone.

"Jette." He slapped her cheek lightly, trying to bring her around. At the same time, Luke pulled at the restraints and had her free in seconds. The rest of the team stood back, letting Marc and Luke take point. And privilege.

"Jette, baby, can you hear me? Wake up." Marc remembered Hester. The coma. He nearly stepped aside for Luke to examine her when a sound came from deep inside her. It was a combination of a moan and a sigh. She was completely stoned. He gently turned over her arm and saw the tracks of needle marks. He felt nausea punch through him. She ate nuts and berries, for Christ's sake, never taking into her body anything she considered toxic. This was more than a crime, it was an invasion, it was profane. A murderous rage settled into his gut. Only his concern for her went deeper and kept him from immediately taking up the hunt for the Empress with blood in his eye.

"Jette." He gave her a little shake and could see she was trying to throw off the lethargy and come around.

Memories of trying to get his mother to wake up when he was a very small boy flooded his veins with ice. Suddenly he was back there. He was hungry and wanted her to get up, get him something to eat. A picture of the woman's tortured, emaciated body and her haunted, lifeless eyes resurfaced from the imprint on his brain. No. No. This was Jette, not his mother. Jette. He gently took her in his arms and whispered in her ear.

"Jette. It's Marc. You're safe. I'm sorry. Sweetheart, I'm sorry it took so long."

Jette heard his voice echoing down a long dark tunnel. She was floating, lighter than air. A smile formed on her lips. Marc. Marc was here. There was a reason she was distressed, but she couldn't remember it. She couldn't seem to hang on to any thought very long. But everything was alright now. It was Marc's voice. She should get up, go with him. She wanted to go home with him. Home. Now.

"Marc?" Her voice came out as a soft, breathy whisper. Her eyes slowly came open, but they weren't tracking. His face looked like an impressionist's painting. She tried to blink him into focus, but she couldn't. She couldn't. What was the matter with her? Was she ill? Had she been sick? "Marc?"

"Yes, baby. It's me." He checked out the rest of her body, barely able to breathe. If they'd touched her they wouldn't live, in custody or out. But she had no bruising or other marks. Her clothes were intact.

"*Ganohalidohi*. You found me." She smiled dreamily. "Nice work."

"Jette, listen to me. Try to focus. Did they hurt you?"

The tone in Marc's voice sobered her up and brought her mind in for a landing. Her voice was still breathy, but the volume was more determined.

"Hurt me? No. I…I don't feel a thing. I can't even feel my feet. Are they still there, Marc?" Somehow the need to know if her feet were still attached to her ankles was overwhelmingly important. Odd.

"Yes, sweetheart, your feet are still there."

"Ah, that's fine then." Jette's eyes fluttered. Now that she knew for sure, time for a nap.

"No." Marc gently shook her. "Don't go back under. Stay with me."

"Of course. Forever." Her head settled into one of its favorite spots between his chin and chest.

Caressing her hair, he noticed it was clean and shiny. It even had the familiar smell of spicy apples. Now that the relief was washing out of his system, he started taking in the details of her appearance. She looked polished and ready for a press conference. Her makeup was expertly applied. Her way, not by some other hand. Even her manicure looked fresh.

"She looks…wonderful," breathed Kim over his shoulder.

"Over here," called Tagg. He pointed at a hole in the brick wall covered with what looked like a metal plate. "I bet this leads back into the brewery. Probably in the furnace room. Maybe behind the circuit breaker."

"We'll check it out later."

Jette's eyes focused on her grinning brother.

"Luke? Why are you here? Is something wrong?"

"Jette. You were kidnapped. Remember?" Luke's heart was beating with excitement and swelling with gratitude, but he was a little concerned over her disorientation.

"Yes. I dove into the river. It was a 10. Perfect dive. It was a high dive or death, I thought." Then her eyes teared up. "Marc, they killed a woman. Just shot her. Have you found them?"

"Not yet. I was busy looking for you."

"I knew you'd find me. This is your city. You'd find me."

Marc's gut took a hit at the certainty in her voice, in her eyes.

"Are they out there? There were three." She blinked several times, but Marc's face was still a blur.

"No, honey. No. They're gone."

The colors were wrong. "Why are the colors so...so bright? What happened? Did I hit my head?"

"You're under the influence of a narcotic, Jette. I think heroin."

"No. I never," she began, trying to muster up indignant, but only managing mellow. Then she remembered. "Oh yes. They injected something. The last shot was a doozy. Tinman gave it to me. Way too much, I think."

"Luke?" Marc looked up at the doctor, alarmed. "An overdose?"

"No. No," assured Luke quickly. "She'd be in a coma. It's the reason for her confusion, but she's in no danger."

"Hester. Hester gave me the other shots." Jette's eyes shifted conspiratorially. "I turned her. Did she find you?"

"I got the message in your ring." He would tell her about the nurse later.

"Was it a brewery?"

"Yes."

"Can we go home now?"

"I have to take you to a hospital, Jette. You need to be examined."

"Luke's here. He can examine me."

"No, honey. We have to have a chain of evidence. Did they...did they touch you?"

"No. No. Treated me like royalty. Darling, they only wanted to turn me. So I gave her the impression I'd be willing to dance for them. Eventually." Jette smiled up at him. Both of him. Twins. As intriguing as it was to double her pleasure, she blinked until there was only one of him. "Played her. She's in desperate need of therapy, Marc. A real case study, let me tell you. But I'm not going to treat her. If she asks, my schedule is too full. Remember that, okay?"

Unable to believe that he held her in his arms, Marc just stared at her and didn't realize she'd asked for a response.

"Okay?" she asked again.

"Okay," he said, ready to agree to anything.

"Are you the Dark Knight?"

"Yes," he said automatically.

She smiled, admiration clearly etched along the dreamy expression. "You figured that out too. Brilliant. I have more. I have more for you, Marc. Let's go round up our Guardians and make a move. I'm ready to knock this Empress off her throne."

"We'll do that, but I need to make sure you're alright."

"No. That's not the next move." A sense of urgency pushed at her. Suddenly the danger penetrated the syrupy coating of confusion clouding her consciousness.

"Traps. Marc. There are explosives."

When she tried to get up, Marc gently held her tighter. "We got your message. The Bomb Squad located the devices. Her traps have been dismantled."

"Oh boy." Jette breathed out and a small, delighted chuckle came with it. The drugs exaggerated the euphoria of her rescue. Suddenly there had never been a better day. "That's definitely going to fry her circuits. Not that they're too well connected at the moment."

"Is that a clinical diagnosis?" Marc asked, smiling at the sound of her laugh.

"No. I said I'm not treating her and I meant it. I'm going to help you defeat her. Let's go push her into a complete mental break down." Sighing, thinking that was about as evil as she cared to ever be, she fell asleep in the arms of her Dark Knight. Secure. Safe. United.

Marc stood up with her cradled in his arms, closed his eyes for a moment to harness the rush of emotions flooding his circuits, then walked with her through his team. They parted, nodding, smiling. Proud, silent, touched beyond relief. The tears pooling in their eyes, some slipping over, punctuated the feelings pouring from all of them. A collective feeling of release and wonder soared from the space around Marc and Jette. Marc caught each of their eyes as he carried his treasured woman out of the room. He could have walked through stone.

# Part Two:

# The Phoenix Rising

*I love you, not only for what you have made of yourself, but for what you are making of me.*
~Roy Croft~

# Chapter One

Marc took Jette to a special emergency room for forensic testing and her blood was taken into evidence. He sat with her through all of it, not willing to let her out of his sight. He scandalized the doctors and nurses when he got into a shouting match over the impropriety of him being in the room during the examination for sexual abuse. Jette coolly and calmly informed the attending physicians that she wanted him near. More awake than her rescuer, she answered all the doctor's questions, waited for the lab results, and chatted with the little girl with the bird after Marc placed the call personally. She and Kia had quite a conversation as Marc sat, then fell asleep in the chair next to her bed.

Marc came to full alert with the click of the door opening nearly an hour later. Completely awake and ready to take on murderous hordes, he relaxed when Luke came in leading a bevy of specialists. They assured her and Marc that other than the injections, she was in perfect health. No signs of any abuse or mistreatment.

When she begged the doctors to let her go home, they agreed with the stipulation that Luke be in attendance. Another shouting match ensued when Luke enlisted a few of the more courageous physicians to suggest that Marc be examined. When it ended in a coughing fit and a small bedside table being knocked on its side, everyone backed off and Luke was left standing alone.

Knowing her man, Jette moaned slightly and shifted in the bed. Marc immediately stopped his rant and moved swiftly to her side. His coughing concerned her greatly, but seeing her brother shaking his head, she realized this was an old and ongoing battle. Luke was an excellent physician. He'd just have to deal with two patients and he'd have to make it a house call.

"Do I need to be interviewed?" she asked as Marc opened the door and checked the hallways. Clear. They'd kept the rescue close, but the hospital personnel was another matter. A leak would fill their path with reporters.

"Yes, but not now." As much as Marc wanted to arrest the people who took Jette, it had to wait. She needed to get straight first. It was his single priority at the moment.

"And will I be making my statements to you?"

"Yes."

"Good. I can fill you in and we can get started…"

Marc interrupted her. "Sweetheart. I've never wanted anyone more than the bitch who took you, but we have a more pressing issue."

"More pressing than finding the woman who thinks she's this Empress?"

"Yes." Reaching over, he gently rubbed the bend in her elbow that had been the injection site.

"Oh. Right. That's going to be a bit of a problem, isn't it?"

More than a bit, he thought, but he wanted to get her home before facing it fully. "Yes."

"Alright then." She raised her arms, knowing he'd be carrying her. "Get the door, Luke. I want my own bed."

Luke had arranged for Claude to transport them back to the apartment in the limo. He was waiting for them at the back door.

"Claude, how lovely. Thank you," smiled Jette, as if nothing had happened and they were going to take a ride through the park. She touched his cheek, now wet with a few tears, when he opened the door for them.

"Let's get you home, Dr. Morningstar," he beamed then watched as Luke helped Marc tuck her into the back seat.

Hilda had set up a nest with a downy soft duvet and several pillows. Luke smiled as both his patients took full advantage of the make shift bed. With a small sigh, Jette was asleep in seconds and Marc, knowing she was safe and in his arms, followed her moments later.

They both came awake as Claude pulled into the garage and up to the elevator. Jonathon abandoned his post for the first time in his career to come down to the lower level. It was he and he alone who wanted to open the limo's back door and hold the elevator.

"Welcome home, Dr. Morningstar." He broke into a smile so rusty and little used that his face fairly creaked.

"Thank you, Jonathon. It wouldn't be home without you at the door," replied Jette, making Jonathon's smile grow along with the breadth of his chest.

Marc scooped up Jette, shifted her weight and stepped out of the limo. Luke thought Marc needed to be carried himself, but after a very brief debate, he stood aside and let Marc claim the privilege of taking his sister up.

As Jonathon gently closed the limo door he said under his breath, "Nicely done, Detective. Nicely done."

Turning precisely on his well-polished heel, he went back to stand at his post before Marc could comment. Jette planted a peck on Marc's cheek.

"I do believe he's melting."

"The screaming reporters have finally wacked him out," disagreed Marc. "You could shoot that titanium poker he has up his ass into the center of the sun and it wouldn't bend a molecule."

The three of them walked into the apartment with a great deal of fanfare and fussing.

The entire squad surrounded her. They'd left the rescue sight to the CSI folks, eager to be a part of the homecoming.

Seeing Marc's penetrating glare over Jette's shoulder, they refrained from pelting her with the hundreds of questions they'd accumulated and just raised their coffee cups in a salute to her rescue. Jette smiled and graciously thanked each of them for their part in finding her. She made them feel like heroes.

Eunice laughingly shoved a huge mug of coffee into Marc's hand as she took Jette from him and effortlessly carried her into the front parlor. Kelly and Lyd had left for the day, but Jette heard all about them and the part they played as they started to fill her in despite Marc's growls and glares. They just couldn't help it.

Tommy squealed and patted her heart and promised they'd go out for pedicures as soon as she was able, then had a complete meltdown, weeping until her false eyelashes melted off her face.

Jette spent a private moment with Hilda, comforting her and quietly reassuring her that she had sustained no serious or permanent injury. Then, knowing Hilda's needs, she asked if she'd get her a cup of tea and a whole plateful of her wonderful molasses cookies. Jette's favorite. Hilda reinflated immediately and soon Jette was sipping perfectly brewed tea out of delicate antique Meissen cups and everyone, including Claude, who'd come up to join them, was helping themselves to cookies.

Even though Luke joined Marc in trying to get Jette settled in the bedroom, she happily ignored them both and insisted on greeting everyone who wanted to see her. To give her a kiss, a touch, a few flowers, a hug.

Lee brought her daisies and thought she exercised magnificent restraint when she didn't even mention a potential book deal about the event. The commissioner made a brief appearance with an armload of desert flowers, then insisted on taking Lee home.

Lucy visited with Carmel, proudly presenting a handmade card. It had horses all over it. Jette sincerely thanked Carmel for putting up with Tagg's long hours and the pregnant woman burst into tears, declared a hormone emergency, and ate a dozen cookies.

Marc sat next to her, touching her, holding her, snapping at everyone but not being able to override Jette's gentle need to reassure and show her appreciation. People orbited her like she had a gravitational pull. Her energy and inner strength seemed to transfer to all those around her until, utterly exhausted she fell asleep telling Lucy an old Cherokee legend about the first fire.

Luke, who'd been standing as sentinel, gauging both his patients' vital signs and not inclined to interrupt as long as they were sitting down, pushed and prodded and finally got everyone to go home. Marc put his entire squad off duty on compensatory time until he called them back, so they all headed out, intending to carry the celebration to the nearest cop approved bar. They still had a lot of police work to do on the case, but not this day. Luke agreed to keep them updated.

Marc carried Jette into their bedroom, laid her gently on the bed, then went back out to check on the security measures he'd put into place. Eunice had planted herself in the kitchen where she, Tommy and Claude engaged in a lively game of three-handed euchre while watching the back door. They were going nowhere. The human wall of protection, combined with all the additional electronic equipment Tommy had installed satisfied him that while she was in the apartment, Jette would be safe.

When he walked by the command center, Marc saw Hilda sweeping some of the debris into a pile in the center of the room. He paused, then strode into the room, grabbed the broom from her hands, and threw it in the corner.

"Enough. Until you need this tomorrow to ride off to the market, I want it to stay right there. Now go to your rooms and get some rest."

"I'm not six years old, Detective."

"No, but you're not twenty-six either. Now that Jette's back, she's going to insist I can't work you 24/7 anymore." Marc just stared at her for a moment. He could feel his heart in his throat. "Now that we have her back," he began, hoping his deep seeded gratitude showed so he wouldn't have to force the words out. "Hilda, I…"

"Very well, Detective Lexington. Not that referring to my age is at all a polite thing to do," Hilda interrupted, removing him from the hook he was dangling on. She heard the 'we' in the sentence and felt the pleasure pulse through her. "I think I might just fix myself some tea and retire."

Marc grinned. "Did you say retire?"

"For the evening. Just for the evening."

Snorting, Marc turned to go back to Jette.

"Detective?"

"What?"

"I never doubted you'd bring her back home. Not for a single second."

When Marc stopped and glanced over his shoulder, she'd already turned and walked out the door. He took a minute, staring at all the trappings of detective work. Cop stuff. His life. Or what had been his life before Jette. Files, boards, computers, phones, lists, photos, empty coffee cups, crumbs of all sorts, and just let it sink in.

Jette was home. Jette was home. Then scrubbing his face, he strode out of the room.

Luke was in the master bedroom waiting for him. He couldn't stop staring at his sister. It was just so good to see her lying among the pillows. So good.

"It was like a goddamn parade around here." Marc removed his gun and laid it on the dresser.

"They all wanted to see her first hand. Wanted to see for themselves she's really okay. It's amazing how she worked on getting everyone else's head straight. Damn it, Marc she was held against her will for a week and the trauma just slid away from her."

"Yeah. It's going to take us longer to shed the shakes than her. The insult never got through her defenses."

They stood silent for a moment watching Jette breathe.

"You know she'll take you through her ceremonies to return you to balance," said Luke. "I hope you like to sweat. When something this big happens, they can be grueling." After another moment, he added. "You may want to make a run for it while she's still sleeping."

"No good. She'd find me."

"You're right. She leaps tall buildings."

"Avenger."

"What about the investigation? Are you going to interview her when she wakes up?"

"No. As much as I'd like to get her statement and continue the investigation, we have a much bigger problem to deal with right now."

"Yeah. She looks so good to me, I can't even imagine what she's facing." He looked at his watch. "And soon. I'm sorry, Marc. I know from what you've told me that you've had far more experience in this than I have. What can we expect? Can someone's body really get addicted so quickly?"

"Yeah," Marc rubbed his stomach where it was cramping up. "You inject straight heroin into the bloodstream and the addiction is full blown within a few days. After that, it just takes more and more to get the same high."

"That's what I was afraid of," sighed Luke with concern.

"First she'll experience mild discomfort. She'll feel pretty good until her body needs another fix. We saw that the last few hours. Then the craving will start. Followed by the pain. Excruciating. Indescribable. We have to get her…"

"Don't talk about me like I'm not in the room, boys." Jette's eyes came open and they saw that she was awake and alert. "Sorry I clocked out for awhile. But I'm back. You can ask me directly, Luke, how I'm feeling."

"So tell me, Jette. How are you feeling?" He grinned.

Jette's eyes slid to Marc's. "I feel relatively good, but the craving is beginning to make its presence known. It's…it's a little like hunger. What was it they gave me, Marc?"

"The lab says pure smack, heroine, uncut. It would turn you within days. Create a powerful addition. From the number of injection sites on your arm, it looks like they popped you every four hours or so."

"That seems right. I never felt any significant withdrawal and an addict can begin to suffer within a few hours after deprivation." Turning her arm, she stared at the marks on her arm. "It's rather interesting. A direct experience. I wouldn't recommend the process, but since it's happened, I might as well learn from it."

She was, in fact, beginning to feel the grip of intense need and the faint whisper of the pain to come.

Marc stared at her. He wasn't fooled. He'd seen the signs far too often. But he'd let her play this in any way she wanted, so he said nothing. He and Luke went over to her and he sat down on the side of the bed as Luke took her wrist to check her pulse. When Luke was satisfied, he passed the hand to Marc, who held it softly in his grip. He could feel the slight tremor and knew Luke had felt it too.

"What do you recommend, Marc?" she asked directly. "I'm so sorry, but Luke is right. You have experience in this area that far exceeds ours."

"You should be in a hospital or treatment center," he began and put up his hand when she took a breath to protest. "But I stand behind your preference to be home. There needs to be added security. Luke is here and I know from firsthand experience, he can handle himself."

"Why thank you, Marc." Luke reached into his bag for a hypodermic and a bottle of potent antibiotic. The Vicodin would be next. "At least with gunshot wounds, paper cuts, and pneumonia."

Luke wasn't above making a little trouble. Now that Jette was safely home, he wanted Marc off his feet.

"Pneumonia?" Jette's attention snapped immediately to Marc's pale face. "You have pneumonia?"

"No." Marc glared up at Luke. "This isn't about me."

Ignoring Marc, Luke looked at his sister. "He hasn't let me listen to his lungs in days, but judging from that coughing fit in the hospital, lucky they didn't arrange for a transplant by the way since your lung came up and out of your throat, and his flawless but chalky complexion, to be featured on the cover of the next edition of *Vampire Monthly*, I'd say he's in trouble."

Marc's flawless but chalky complexion flared.

"Better color, Marc, but I'd rather it be from good health than from temper."

"I've been taking your fucking pills," growled Marc. "Now…"

"No you haven't," Luke interrupted. "At least not as I've prescribed them."

Marc couldn't believe that Luke wasn't dropping it. If he could only get a complete lungful of air, he'd shout him down or shove him out. The truth was he'd been feeling horrible and the pain pounding from his wounds almost took his mind off the pressure in his chest.

Luke calmly filled the hypodermic.

"And now I have Jette I can enlist. We both know if you don't take the shot, she's going to insist I put more of that sludge she calls tea into you."

"I think we've had enough of fucking needles around here," growled Marc.

"For Jette maybe, but it's your turn. Can't have her get ahead of you on injection sites. Now present arms." Luke smirked.

Jette remained silent letting the boys flare, glare, and stare. Finally Marc rolled up his sleeve and sat still while Luke injected him.

"They better just be antibiotics," he snapped. "If you've given me something to put me down, I swear I'll find you and pound you into barbecued beef."

Luke shrugged, unconcerned.

"I'll just have my sister stand in front of me."

Knowing he'd have to get the job done quickly, Luke filled another hypodermic with the powerful pain killer and got that into Marc too.

"You drank my tea?" asked Jette softly, wanting to distract Marc and liking the feeling of warmth the fact brought to her heart.

Marc stared at her, knowing that Luke had been right about how it would touch her, but refusing to acknowledge it.

"We rubbed it on his chest and it cured him overnight. Now let's get back to your treatment." Luke put away his bag for the moment, satisfied Marc's lungs would get no worse. "Tell us what to do, Marc."

Scowling, fighting a nauseating wave of pity, Marc presented his best advice.

"Your general physical health and conditioning are far better than the average addict, but they pumped some powerful stuff into you and it will push your system into intense withdrawal. You need to be taken off slowly, through a gradual process. I think we should do a standard withdrawal treatment. The doctors at the hospital sent some methadone along. Luke, you'll administer it periodically then get more as Jette needs it through prescription. It's intensely regulated, but we won't have any trouble getting what we need. Morphine should take care of most of the pain."

Jette raised her free hand, palm out. "Stop right there. That's not acceptable. I will not allow another toxic substance in my body. No methadone. As a matter of fact, no additional drugs of any kind."

"But you can't do this cold," argued Marc.

"That's precisely how I'm going to do this."

"I won't let you. You have no idea." Marc released her hand, desperate to save her from the intense agony of withdrawal. He got up and began to pace. He could hear his mother's screams echoing in his head, her weeping, begging. Then her whimpering until he went out and begged for enough coin to score something for her. Enough to get her back on her feet so she could go out and score for herself. "You have no idea," he repeated. Anger bubbled up and drowned out the worry. "You'll go through standard treatment. In a few weeks, no more than a month, you'll be able to function normally."

"No."

"No?" Marc shouted. Temper took control and Luke stood back. He was staying out of this one. He knew who would be the victor, but didn't want to be caught in the crossfire.

Marc went over to the edge of the bed and glared down at Jette. She calmly looked back, struggling mightily against the licks of fire already beginning to burn her from the inside.

"I can see you're already feeling it, Jette. Don't try to hide it, don't try to deny it." Only his concern kept his temper from snapping completely. "I've seen it. I know what it can do."

"Your mother?"

"Yes, damn it. Among others. Don't be a goddamn idiot. I'm not going to stand by while you go into hell. Because you will, Jette. You take the treatment, and take it soon, or you'll go into the burning flames of hell!"

"Marc, darling. I know this is tough for you, to relive it, to see it again. If you want to leave, I'll completely understand." Her voice was losing some of its power, but none of its steel.

"I don't give a flying fuck about what this does to me." And it was doing plenty. His stomach was in knots; his nerves were frayed to breaking. How could he protect her from an enemy that was inside her? He was helpless and it made him crazy. "It's you I care about."

"Marc. Darling. Sit down and let's talk about this. We have some time yet…"

Instead of sitting, he started pacing again, too agitated to settle down. His temper was pushing him, keeping the fear from taking possession.

"Okay," he snarled, deciding to blow discretion and subtlety out of the argument. "Okay. Let me tell you exactly what to expect, Jette. First you'll sweat and have indistinct pain. Cramping. Like you ran a marathon without any prior conditioning. Then the pain will intensify, like the grip of a vice. Tightening. Pressing. A horrible irresistible hunger overlaying everything."

He knew he was being vicious, but he had to get her to understand. Let her be disgusted with him, but she was going to get some relief. Striding to the bedside, he towered over her in a cloud of unfocused fury. "Then intense, hideous waves of pain will go through you like a spreading wild fire. No respite, no relief. Pure torture, pure unrelenting pain. There will be no break in the agony. You'll no longer be civilized. All of your instincts will fight your humanity. You'll shake and your body will scream for the drug. Then *you* will scream for it. You'll lose your cultivated, educated outer layer. You'll become an animal. A snarling, savage monster. You'll do anything, say anything just to get more drug into you. You won't feel love, you won't feel anything close to human. You'll hate me Jette, because I won't be able to take the pain away. You'll hate me when I say you can't have what you think you need to live. You'll hate all of us."

There were tears of utter exhaustion in his eyes, and his hands were balled into tight fists. She could feel the horror pour out of him. For a moment she considered going in to treatment just to spare him the torment.

"That's enough," snapped Luke, stepping in, stunned and sympathetic, but angry. "I think she has the picture." It was making him ill. Marc's memory was so vivid, it filled the room, throbbing in the space around them, sucking out the light. Luke bravely put a hand on Marc's vibrating shoulder. "Take it outside if you can't put a lid on it. Now."

Jette stared into Marc's blazing eyes and tried to smile. Her lips couldn't pull it off, so she gently patted the bed. "Darling come sit here. Come sit by me." When he didn't move, she used what she knew would work. "Please, Marc. I need you. I need you to hold me."

Marc shook off the dread, the anger, the guilt. He unballed his fists, took a deep shuddering breath and sat down. He opened his arms and she went into them. He wasn't sure if it was him who was trembling, or her. Probably both of them, for different reasons.

"I want to do this on my own. No more drugs. Marc, please," she begged when she felt him tensing up for another rant. "I know I can. I'm not your mother. I'm not an addict and I have skills I can employ to keep the pain from completely taking over. I know it'll be terrible, but I'll prepare for it. Marc, please. I want this stuff out of me. Completely. Now. I'm so sorry this is affecting you this way."

Pulling back, she looked into his tortured eyes. "Darling, I want you to go do your cop thing. I'm sure there are a lot of things you have to do to move the investigation forward. Go find the Empress. Luke will stay with me and perhaps get some additional assistance."

She looked up at Luke and he nodded, not at all sure he'd be able to stand it. The picture Marc presented was horrific and he'd been consulting with colleagues. But he loved her and would stay with her.

"No," said Marc, clenching and unclenching his jaw. "No. If I can't get you to listen to reason, I'll stay. It would be worse not being here. I'm not going to let you do this without me."

"Thank you," she said simply, not wanting to dwell too long on her victory. "Well at least you've given me a pretty clear picture of what to expect. Before I do battle, I want to shower and change into something fresh."

"How about a hot bath. It can soothe the first stages," suggested Luke.

"Sounds lovely. Marc?" she looked up at him. "Can you start the water?"

"Hot as she can stand it," said Luke.

"Sure. I...I'll get it ready for you." Marc gave her a light kiss, then eased her back on the pillows.

As Marc went into the bathroom, brother and sister stared after him. "That is one stand up guy you have there, *Ganohvsgv*."

"This is going to be hell for him, too. Promise me Luke, that if he cracks, you'll take him out of here."

"Yeah, me and what army. I try to take him away from you and I'll need a hospital bed."

She looked him up and down. "You have a point. But please. I can't have this breaking him."

"I understand. I'll let him bend, but if I see him breaking, I'll call in reinforcements. Tommy or Tagg do you think."

"They're about the same size, but Tagg won't be slowed down by three inch heels."

"True. And Tagg has balls."

"Oh, Tommy does too."

"She does?"

"Yes. She's never been able to really commit. She's still quite conflicted."

"How do you know these things?"

"I'm a therapist, remember? And Tommy's pretty open."

"Not open like running around naked."

"No. Open like sharing her thoughts."

"Thank the Lord." Luke ran his fingers through his hair and gave an ironic snort. "Hell, I don't believe we're talking about Tommy's anatomical choices."

"I think it's healthy. We can't let this...mmm..." Jette took a deep breath against a shock of pain, then went on. "This drug business be our only point of conversation. Good heavens. Life goes on around us."

"Yeah, but I think I'd rather talk about world peace than Tommy's balls."

Luke's face changed to an uncharacteristic solemnity. "Jette, are you sure you want to do this. It's scaring me to shakes to think about what's in store for you on this one. I know you have an incredible will, but this is an enemy you've never personally faced."

279

"I understand the nearly irresistible power of this enemy, *Alisdelisgi*, but I intend to win the battle."

"Don't call me protector, *Ganolvvsgv*," he said referring to her use of his Cherokee name. "There is nothing I can do to fight this with you."

"I know. But you can stand with me while I do. You know I've studied addiction. I'm not going in without some very basic respect for its control, but this is my choice. I just don't want Marc to suffer, too."

"I don't know. I think he needs to suffer."

"What?"

"He's feeling incredibly guilty about all this, Jette. He feels he brought you here. Uprooted you with the hope that you'd find a home, happiness, fulfillment, and success here. Instead, he feels that he and his city let you down."

"So, if I can think clinically for a moment, by being at my side on this journey through hell, he'll be doing penance?"

"In a manner of speaking, yes." Luke glanced back at the bathroom door. "I also think there may be an element of fear there, too."

"But I'm safely back home."

"You say home and I know you mean it, Jette. But I think there's a part of Marc, maybe a significant part, that expects you to abandon him. And with all this ugliness entering the picture, he may be feeling you won't think he's worth the pain."

"I can only prove myself with time and that's something that takes, well, time."

"I've been with him a lot this week, Jette. He really is remarkable, but he has deep seeded insecurities and you're the biggest gamble he's ever taken."

"You'd make a good therapist."

"Helped you through adolescence, didn't I?"

"You put Vaseline in my hairbrush, scrambled all my CD's into different cases, and hung my Annie Oakley doll from my bedpost. I'm surprised I survived the trauma."

"Hey. It toughened you up."

Jette smiled affectionately at her brother. "Honed my coping skills."

"And here comes the big test."

Marc came over to the bed and held out his hand. "Ready?"

She got up and swayed. "I guess I'm more unsteady than I thought."

Marc scooped her up and took her into the bathroom. When he returned, Luke was pacing.

"Let's get all the curtains closed in here and dim all the lamps. Light will hurt her eyes." A picture of his mother screaming at him to turn out the lights flashed in his mind. He was only six years old and could barely see in the gloomy dingy little room, but she swore at him vilely until he found the switch to the lamp in the corner.

Luke saw his expression and suspected where his mind was parked.

"She means to do this, Marc. She's not going to take our advice."

"Yeah. Yeah, I know." He took a deep breath, purging the image of his mother's contorted face. He had Jette to think of now. "So let's get ready. This is going to be pretty straight forward. The drug will leave her system, but not willingly nor happily. Once the pain starts, it will be relentless. I would say we have 24 to 48 hours of intense battle, then a few weeks of skirmishes. There'll be nausea with the initial stage, so let's get her something to combat that. Also, lots of water. She'll be dehydrating fast and that can be uncomfortable, as well. Have the morphine and methadone ready just in case. There might be a point where she changes her mind. You have no idea what she's about to face."

"Fine. I must admit this is beyond my medical expertise. I…ah…appreciate what you're doing here."

"It's going to be hell."

"I get that."

"We could wait a few hours, then knock her out with something and take her down the easier path. It would be against her will, but there may be a way of making it up to her later."

Luke considered it. "No. I think we play it her way. We still have to live with her after this and I don't think either of us have the necessary internal fortitude to face the full blast of the Cherokee Freeze."

Marc nodded, running his fingers through his hair. Luke noticed Marc's hands weren't completely steady. That was a first.

"Are you going to be alright? You know she'd completely understand if you passed on this. She wasn't just saying that. I'll be right here."

"No. I can't. This is making me sick." He caught Luke's expression. "Okay. Sicker. I'm not sure if I have what she needs, what it takes to get her through to the other side, but I'm sticking."

Luke knew what this was costing Marc, but followed his lead and nodded. He'd have a shot ready for him, too. Just in case.

The bath was soothing, but Jette could already feel the shards of intense pain begin to cut her from the inside. The sharp edges were slicing away at her and she wasn't sure she'd be able to make it back to the bed. Just as she was about to call for Marc, he came in with a nightgown, a glass of thick liquid, and a very worried expression.

She smiled up at him, her dark eyes made even darker by the expanded pupils. Marc swore he could see into her soul. He saw courage and resolve and something else. Love. It didn't mask the pain, but it gave him what he needed to stay in control.

Her eyes went to the liquid and she frowned. "What's that?"

He almost smiled at her suspicious expression. A little role reversal.

"It's something Luke had for nausea. It'll help."

Nodding, she drank the liquid. Everything hurt, like there was nothing covering her nerve endings. Even the soft nightgown Marc helped her into punished her skin. He knew and he suffered, too. Gently, tenderly he kissed her and gathered her up in his arms  At her sharp intake of breath, he stopped, let her settle, then carefully carried her to the bed.

Jette shifted, tried to get comfortable, then gave up. She looked up at the two men, her Knights, and smiled. Even that hurt as her face and lips tingled with a whisper of pain.

"Here is what I'm going to do. I'll go into a deep meditative state, like a trance. You've seen me do this before."

"Yeah. Going native," nodded Marc.

Luke had seen it often as they were growing up. She used the method to battle both physical and psychological pain. And she always came back stronger.

"Exactly. Anyway, I'll put myself into deep relaxation and fight the pain through visualization and projection. On one level I'll be far away from you, so don't expect me to respond. On another level, I assure you, I'll feel you here. It'll help. I'll try to surround the pain, but if it's as intense as you say, I may only be able to chip away at it and absorb the pieces." Her body stiffened with the sharp punch of pain. "Okay. That hurt."

"You okay there, Jette?" asked Luke, frowning.

"No, but I will be."

"Are you sure?" asked Marc. "You just got your first clue and that's only a phantom of what's coming. Are you still sure?"

"Positive." She gritted her teeth. "Marc, if you'll hold me, I think it'll help. I'll be drifting between levels of consciousness, so I suggest you get as much rest and sleep as you can while I'm down. Luke, I probably won't surface for at least eight hours, so don't freak out and start resuscitation or something."

"What about monitoring your vital signs?"

"That would probably be good." It would give him something to do, she thought. "You're familiar with my numbers."

"Alright." Luke leaned over and kissed her cheek. "Happy trails. I love you."

"I love you too. Thanks."

"Marc, call me if you need me. And take this opportunity to get off your feet. I can hear the breath whistling through your lungs."

Luke stepped back, stared at them both for just another minute, then turned and left the room.

Marc got into bed, settled in, then opened his arms to his courageous Cherokee warrior. She shifted and curled up in his arms.

"Now kiss me goodbye, darling and give me something to hold on to."

His mouth came down on hers and he poured all of his love into it. She returned it the best she could, but when he opened his eyes and moved away from her lovely face, he knew she'd left him to begin her journey. Her painful passage to hell. Her breathing became shallow, her features softened and her body relaxed.

"Good luck, darling," Marc whispered, his own emotional pain so intense his heart shattered. He watched until exhaustion had him surrendering and he closed his burning eyes.

When Luke came in several hours later, Marc's eyes immediately opened. He blinked away the fatigue, unable to believe that he'd fallen asleep. He immediately looked down at Jette, who remained motionless in his arms.

"What time is it?"

"1:00. Time for your meds." Luke handed him his pills and was pleasantly surprised when Marc took them without a battle. "Can I get you something to eat?

"No, thanks. I'm not hungry."

"I can watch her for awhile if you want to get up and stretch."

"No. I'm fine."

"Okay. But I'm right outside. Just shout."

"Yeah. Thanks. It helps."

# Chapter Two

Morning came. Marc hadn't been able to sleep for long periods, but felt more rested. Whenever he closed his eyes, nightmares from his past haunted him. They chased him until he gave up and just let his mind wander over the case. He knew there were several pieces of the puzzle he needed to look at, place on the board to review and find the connections. He just couldn't focus.

Luke came in with coffee and maintained the watch as Marc slid his arms from around Jette, placed her gently against the pillows, went into the bathroom and took care of business. He showered and shaved but went through the motions without much awareness. He was numb.

When he came back out, Luke pushed food at him and he pushed it back until they started shouting at each other about the benefits of nutrition, the idiocy of not eating, the irrelevance of a lack of appetite, the very uncomfortable placement of each of the pieces of flatware up and in Luke's body, and the immaturity of New York's top cop, until the door slammed open and Hilda rushed in. Her sharp tongue, withering admonishments, and aggrieved manner had them both stuffing eggs into their sullen faces. As Hilda put it, for the benefit of Jette and her wellbeing. She went over to the bed, smoothed the duvet around Jette, and satisfied herself that all was well. Coming back to the sitting area, she stood, hands on her bony hips until Marc and Luke finished everything on their plates, then grabbed the tray and stomped out of the room.

"I still don't understand how our eating an omelet helps get Jette through this," muttered Marc.

"I wonder where she got her military training." Luke forgot for a moment that he'd been trying to get Marc to eat when the shouting match began.

"Fort Hard Knox. That is one scary old bat," grumped Marc.

"Yeah," agreed Luke and the men folk bonded in the aftermath of their mutual grievance, all earlier harsh words forgotten in their shared complaint.

Just then a horrible, intense wave of pain wracked Jette and her eyes flew open.

"Marc?"

Marc was sitting on the bed next to her in a heartbeat. "I'm right here. Right here, sweetheart."

"It's so, so huge." She moaned. She just couldn't help it.

"I know. I know. What can I do?"

"Hold me. Hold me."

As Marc positioned himself on the bed and gathered her in, he looked up at Luke with haunted eyes.

Feeling his arms around her, she went back under, but there was too much there for her to suppress. It wasn't localized but was hitting her from everywhere. Another moan escaped her lips and her eyes came open again, then lost focus.

Marc felt it and could hardly breathe from the intensity of his empathy for her. Her hands were clenched into tight fists and she couldn't control the tears running freely down her pale cheeks.

Luke came over and checked her pulse, ran his hand over her forehead.

"Pulse high, but steady. A slight fever, but nothing out of the ordinary."

Marc wasn't sure if he should hold her tighter to minimize the impact of the shudders wracking her body or loosen his grip to allow her more freedom to find some position that would give her comfort. He felt powerless and it nearly killed him not to be able to fight the enemy inside her. He remembered his mother and the frightful nights she spent when she was getting close to the withdrawal stage. She'd always come out of it looking years older and horribly diminished.

"Should we knock her out anyway?" Marc looked up at Luke. He was desperate to give her some relief.

"Marc. I…I've prepared a shot of morphine and one of methadone. You'll have to tell me. God, you'll have to tell me if you think she needs it."

"I don't know. I don't know. At this point, I think we'd only be giving it to her for our own comfort. To save us from having to watch her go through this. She said no more drugs. You know she meant for us to stand by that. How can we give in if she won't?"

"Yeah. Yeah, you're right." Luke swallowed hard to push the lump in his throat aside. "Jette. Jette sweetheart. Here. You need some liquid. Can you drink something?"

Luke held the glass while Jette drank deeply.

"Cold." She started to shake violently. "Cold."

They piled on blankets, then when she started to sweat, they removed them.

Marc continued to hold her as she moved in and out of consciousness. Luke brought out cold compresses when she was feverish, and had her drink hot water when she started to shiver again.

Hilda hovered and would change the sheets every time Marc carried her to the bathroom or held her in the chaise by the window. She made sure there was always ice water in the thermos and hot coffee for the men. Just before lunch, she knocked and came in to deliver a message. Jette had settled for the moment, deep in a meditative state.

"I'm sorry, Detective Lexington. But there's a Captain Green in the foyer. He's insisting that he talk with Dr. Morningstar. He's very...rude, but I thought I'd better let you know." Hilda sniffed disapprovingly.

"Tell the asshole to go fuck himself," snapped Marc.

Hilda paused for a heartbeat, then nodded. "I think having him masturbate in the foyer would be very distasteful, so I think I'll just go get Tommy to help me sweep him back into the street."

With that, she turned and closed the door softly behind her.

Luke looked at Marc. Marc looked at Luke. And the two of them laughed like a couple of truant teenagers tripping on some contraband brew. They didn't stop, couldn't stop, until Hilda brought lunch. Then they sobered up the best they could and ate the sandwiches without a fight.

The day passed slowly, but it passed. Just when they thought they couldn't take her pain any more, she'd calm and put herself into a shallow trance. When she felt the pain retreat, she'd wake up and want to move. Luke would offer his arm and they'd stroll slowly around the room, usually depleting her energy in a few minutes.

Then Jette would sit up or take a bath. Luke brought her soup that Hilda kept hot on the stove and she ate it to please them but every time she finished a small bowl, she'd be violently ill within minutes. They gave up on the food, realizing she was in no danger of starving to death.

Marc never left her. Tagg took over the investigation completely and made brief reports. Nothing new really. The Empress knew she'd lost her prize, but there'd been no overt reaction. All the suspects they had identified were being followed and their lives turned inside out.

Marc couldn't concentrate on the case. When he watched Jette fight the pain, nothing mattered but her. His impotence when the pain intensified ate away at him, but he stood.

Luke stood with him, both as his backup and his doctor. Since he was taking his medicine without comment, and caught naps with Jette when she calmed, Luke just kept a close eye on his color, his motions and his posture. Marc was running on fumes, but still running.

The day faded and night brought only slight relief for Jette. It was hell and they all felt the flames. Several times, she was so exhausted, she'd pass out and fall into a restless sleep. Toward midnight, it looked like she was going to stay under for awhile.

"Get some rest, Luke," insisted Marc. "She seems calmer. I'm going to get in bed with her and hold her."

"Can I give you something Marc? Something to help you sleep?"

"No," snapped Marc. "I don't want to sleep."

"Not all drugs are evil, you know. You're beyond exhaustion and could use a little help."

"You're a goddamn pusher," Marc hissed.

"And you're a goddamn martyr," Luke hissed back.

"Asshole."

"Idiot."

"I'll call you if I need you," insisted Marc, feeling very shaky and wanting the doctor out of the room.

"Get some sleep. Your disposition is deteriorating."

"No it's not. It's always been this nasty."

"Oh yeah, I forgot. It's what attracted my sister. The psychologist. You've become her lifelong project."

"Let's hope it's a long life."

"It's going to have to be long just to be able to take you out in polite company."

"Night Luke,"

"Night Marc. Call me." Luke took one last long look at his sister, then left the room.

Marc stripped down to sweat pants, got into bed and took Jette in his arms. He wouldn't admit it to Luke, but his healing wounds were pounding like a bitch and it felt good to get horizontal. Taking a deep breath, smelling the scent of his mate, he fell instantly asleep.

His eyes snapped open a few hours later when he felt her shuddering violently.

"What is it? Jette?"

"I can't go down." Another vicious shudder went through her as pain wracked her body. Tears gathered in her eyes and trailed down her cheeks. "I haven't the strength to stay under. I thought I'd be able to fight it by shutting down and going through the usual healing rituals, but it isn't working."

She was breathing shallowly, trying to fight the agony by forcing it away from her. "I need to go up. Marc, darling I can't fight this alone. Help me. I need to go up. Only you can do this for me."

"What can I do? I'll do anything." And he really meant anything. A surge of energy pumped into him with the thought that he may be able to help her. "Do you want me to get you something? Give you something?"

He was willing to go out on the streets and score some smack if it would give her some small relief. God help him, he'd put the needle in her skin himself.

"Love me, make love to me. We can only fight this with something stronger," she whispered.

"What? I don't understand."

"Put your hands on me. Transport me. Take me away from this pain."

"Are you sure?"

She smiled weakly, tears flowing down her cheeks in spite of her attempts to keep them in check. "I'm the doctor."

He wasn't sure if she was right, if this was what she needed, but he would follow her lead. Do whatever she wanted. He peeled off her soaked nightgown. Her skin was on fire, every nerve ending open and ready. He touched her all over, his lips following his hands. Her senses were heightened already by the pain, and now the pleasure came in the same way.

"Can you feel this? Can you feel me?" he breathed feeling his own powerful response. He moved his hands up her torso and cupped her breasts, then brought his head down and flicked his tongue over her body. Tenderly, he continued to taste her, tease her, turn her on.

"Yes. Yes," she whispered and it enflamed him. He touched her everywhere as she opened herself up to him.

"Yes. Oh, Marc. You're doing it. I can feel the desire. It's building, it's wonderful. Don't stop."

Her breath came in hot, heavy gasps and he was relieved to hear the subtle difference. There was pain in the deep throaty moans, but there was also a heavy dose of pleasure. Stroking, caressing her all over, the feel of his hands, his mouth, his tongue traveled along the open and supercharged nerve endings on her body. Waves of pure primitive sexual need helped put out the flames of pain.

His hands moved up her thighs feeling her shudder with anticipation as his mouth covered hers and their tongues met in a burning sensual dance. His fingers found her hot and wet and throbbing with desire and he played a prelude to the pleasure yet to come. She writhed as the craving for him inside her gathered in her belly and there was no room for anything else. Her pulse was racing, carrying the promise of more. Of satisfaction only he could give her.

"Now. More. I need to feel more," she moaned and he realized gentleness was fighting the pain, but not winning the battle. So he pushed aside his need for control, his need to protect, his tenderness, and channeled some of his frustration and anger into a frenzy of movement. He'd fight. He'd fight with everything he had. With love. With need. With life.

He drove himself into her. Over and over, his mouth covering hers to swallow her moans, his hands moving roughly from her belly to her breasts as he shattered the tortuous ache in her body. Each orgasmic thrust took her farther from the edge of the pounding pain and drowned her in a red hot sea of pure lustful primordial heat.

"Yes, yes, yes," she groaned as they rode each other to another climax. Then another. He was relentless. She asked him to fight with her and he could do no less. Her hunger, her need, her moans gave him stamina and strength. He aroused her, fed her, drenched her in sensation, then brought her to climax, and over the edge.

His body responded without thought. Never had anyone demanded so much. Never had he found so much inside him to give. Their movements were primal, their instincts ancient. They came together as mates. A man and a woman who knew each other, loved each other, trusted each other.

He made love to her over and over throughout the rest of the night. He touched her, savored her, penetrated the wall of pain, then exploded it from the inside. She moaned with both ecstasy and agony, shuddered with both sexual release and stubborn shooting pain.

They were covered with sweat, riding the waves of desire, completely lost in each other. Her need for him would gather in her belly, reach a plateau, then they'd keep moving until they found a new, higher peak. Finally, toward dawn, fully spent and panting with the final thrust of one last orgasm, Jette sighed deeply with triumph.

"It's surrendered," she whispered. "It's over. We won."

Marc collapsed against the pillows and rolled her body over his. They were still connected, he was still inside her. But he wasn't at all sure he was still alive. As they got themselves under control and the world around them began to rematerialize, he could feel his heartbeat. Or was it hers. Their pulses seemed to sing a duet. Alive then.

"I think we might just be welded together. All that heat must have melted something," gasped Marc when he could talk again.

Jette laughed deep in her super-satisfied throat.

His heartbeat still roared in his ears, pounded wildly in his chest. Her small, delicate hand settled lightly over his heart. He looked down at it and remembered all that little hand did through the night. His bright sweet angel had more than a few surprises. He couldn't help smiling.

As the sun came up, Marc carried her into the shower and they washed away the night in hot steamy water. She was nearly unconscious as he placed her gently on the chaise. He stripped the bed of the tangle of sweaty, damp sheets, and put on fresh, clean linen. His knees were weak and he had to lean against the headboard a few times before the task was complete.

By the time he carried her back to the bed she was sleeping. It seemed to him natural and deep. Marc laid her gently on the clean sheets and brushed her damp hair from her face. It was still horribly pale and the dark circles under her eyes were far too prominent, but the pain was now at a level she could contain. Sliding in beside her, he gathered her in.

She felt him, felt his closeness and his love. A little sigh came from deep inside her as she nestled into his chest. Marc looked down and with his last bit of energy, whispered his love and kissed the top of her head.

Marc was satisfied, both body and soul. He'd never had a night like this one. He was able to do battle for his woman. Only him. Like an ancient warrior, exhausted and completely used up from combat, he too slipped over into the sleep of the dead.

When Luke came in quietly a few hours later to check on Jette, he found her sleeping naturally in the arms of her lover. Luke's breath caught in his throat. The picture they made entwined in each other was stunning.

They looked like the first man and woman, the prototype for what came later, a modern day Adam and Eve. Each was beautiful, but together they were nearly indescribable. Sunlight coming from a slit in the drapes bathed their bodies in a golden hue. Her acres of black hair tumbled over his bare chest. His arms, even in sleep, were wrapped tightly around her, one securing her waist, the other over her smooth, bare back.

His tough muscled body, scarred by injury and with a gang tattoo of a snake running up his arm, spoke of a hard life. Lying safely against him, her dusky skin perfect and glowing, her hand open and trusting over his heart, she embodied his salvation. At one time Luke wasn't sure they belonged together. Now he was sure they belonged nowhere else.

For the first time in his life, other than when he was unconscious, Marc didn't wake instantly with the presence of someone in the room. On some basic level he knew it was a friend and couldn't find the energy to open his eyes. They were both completely, thoroughly, utterly spent.

Hilda came up beside Luke. "I've never seen him asleep before," she whispered.

"He's like a cat. Never really goes all the way under. Comes from growing up in the streets, I guess."

Hilda nodded. "Beautiful, aren't they?"

"Magnificent. Like Kanati and Selu."

"Who?"

"First man and first woman. Cherokee. Jette knows more about the folklore than I do. She can fill you in someday. I always thought she should write a book on it."

"Well, there's the picture that should be on the cover. Gorgeous. Makes me wish I could paint."

Luke's eyebrows went up. "That's a little whimsical."

Hilda shook herself, appalled at her lack of discretion. "So, I'm a little mushy, Doctor. I'm entitled. All these people disrupting my normal routine, tramping around the apartment."

She tiptoed in and snatched the sheets off the floor where Marc had dropped them. As they let themselves out, she was muttering under her breath.

"The floor isn't a hamper, for crying out loud. Thought maybe she'd be able to breathe some civilized behavior into him. I guess a beast doesn't change his habits just because he's loved by an angel."

Luke smiled. All was right with the world.

He knew there was nothing to be done for them but let them sleep. It looked like his sister was over the worst of it. She'd found her way, her own way, and that was good. He went to the kitchen to secure a cup of coffee and make some phone calls. People all over town were waiting for his report.

# Chapter Three

It was midday when Jette stirred, then woke.

"Marc?"

"Yes?" He'd been awake for a few minutes, feeling their heartbeats and letting the pleasure of it feed him.

"What day is it?"

"Wednesday, I think. Give me a second and I can check the *Times*."

"It doesn't matter. Are you alright?"

"As soon as the feeling returns to my extremities, I'm sure I'll be fine."

"What a night."

"I must say it was beyond my experience. Extreme sex." He shifted and felt the ache everywhere. It felt wonderful. "How are you doing?"

"As long as I don't have to move quickly, I think I'll be fine. You were magnificent last night, *Unaligohi*."

Marc didn't say anything. She'd called him her mate. Something was happening inside him. A wound was closing and it felt…good. Better than good. Liberating.

"I was going to say, glad to oblige, but…" He sighed and stretched and took inventory of his feelings. "But there's more."

"Do you want to talk about it?"

"No. Not now. I haven't got enough firing brain cells to find the right words. So, are you still jonesing?"

She stretched and moaned. "I can still feel the cells of my body seeking their fix, but it's distant. They aren't happy with me and will continue to make me pay. Their craving is singing in my brain."

"Damn, Jette. How you put things. You make withdrawal sound like a fucking teaching moment."

"Well it certainly has given me a new perspective on addiction."

"It seems the worst is over."

"Just some minor discomfort."

"It was pretty brutal, wasn't it?" He turned her into him, her breasts pressing against his bare chest. He knew he'd come to some kind of sexual burnout when it felt more sweet than sensual. Warm and comfortable. He liked it.

Jette sighed, feeling the comfort too and enjoying the flavor. "I won't try to minimize it, Marc. It was horrific. On the upside, I think the intensity of it prepared me for childbirth."

Marc went completely, absolutely still, the hand that had been stroking her back stopped. Finally, she took pity on him and laughed.

"Don't worry darling, we won't test that for years."

Marc's heart thumped beneath her palm. Childbirth. Shit. Where did that come from. Kids? Was she serious? He concentrated on Lucy, Kia, and Kelly. Not all kids were scary little assholes, after all. But there was nothing in him that could connect in any way with the concept of fatherhood. He'd never had a father and was completely sure he must lack the capacity for it. What the hell. One problem at a time. Jette would come to realize his deficiency. It made his gut shift a bit to think that it might disappoint her to such a degree that she'd give up on him. When he felt her stretching out some kinks, he came back to his current concern.

"What can I get you? Could you eat something?"

"I'm not really hungry, but I think I could keep something in my stomach."

"Good. It'll give Hilda something to do. I can feel her lurking out there."

"She's a dear."

"She's a menace."

"I want to freshen up, then come back to bed and sleep for awhile. I still have to fight some, go back under and try to purge the residual impact of the drug. I also think after last night's marathon, my muscles may appreciate a little respite."

"Aw. And I was going to suggest we take a jog through Central Park."

"Aha. And what if I call your bluff?"

"I'd have to do something manly like accidentally shoot myself in the foot."

Jette laughed, kissed him lightly on the chest and pushed herself into a sitting position. Her hand went immediately to her stomach. "Whoa. Hold the breakfast for awhile. I think I'll take a long hot bath, then reassess my ability to retain food."

Marc frowned. "Are you sure you're doing okay?"

"Yes. Although it's all relative, I guess." When the room stopped spinning, she swallowed hard. "Better. But I don't think I need to prove anything, so if you want to carry me to the bathroom, I won't fight you."

Marc grinned. "Does that mean I can join you in the bath?"

"Sure. I could use someone to wash my back."

"Can I do the front too?" Marc swung his legs over the bed and in one graceful move stood up with her in his arms.

"Of course. And Marc?"

"Yeah?"

"I love you."

"Yeah."

While taking their bath, they discussed how to proceed with the case. Marc was torn between his need to be with Jette and wanting to get back into the investigation and bring the bastards behind her abduction to justice. With Jette smiling at him and appearing relatively solid, he felt himself caring about the pursuit again.

"I'm sorry," he apologized. "But I need to talk to you about everything that happened. I need to get a statement."

"Are you heading the investigation?"

"Not officially. The commissioner got it assigned to our squad but Tagg is heading it. I've been put back on medical leave."

"Hmm. That might be difficult to support that after last night."

"I don't know," smirked Marc. "Last night nearly killed me."

"I want to know everything that went on here as well. I got a little of it the other day, but I'd like a context for everything that happened to me. And frankly, I was stoned and in seclusion most of the time, so I'm afraid there won't be a great deal I can offer."

"Not so stoned that you didn't participate in your own rescue. You led us to where you were. Safely, I might add. And we got all the traps. Those boomers were powerful. They would have done serious damage, to my team as well as to property. You saved lives, Jette."

She nodded, feeling his admiration as well as his anxiety. It was good.

"Tell me everything," she said as she settled in his arms to listen.

Marc went through the investigation from his end. He tried to keep it concise and detailed, like a report or a testimony, but there was a great deal of residual fear and pain and anger. Some of it was less intense now that she was with him, drown in the relief of having her home, but he hadn't been able to purge much of the dreadful week of searching since he'd moved right from her rescue to dealing with her addiction.

Jette could tell from the haunted expression in his eyes, that it would be some time before he'd be able to cleanse all the extreme shock and anxiety. The doctor would have to be on call for a long, long time. And that was fine with her.

First, however, he needed to rejoin the formal investigation. She knew work was his way back. To search and find the Empress would bring his world to balance. Justice. The scales. On one side what was done to them, on the other, what they would now do back to her.

"Are you going to keep the task force here?" she asked.

"No. It's formally in the hands of the Special Projects Unit now. Our official board and debriefings will be in the office. We will, however, keep a duplicate board here and when we're in the field, we'll meet here. Not everything needs to be in the official record."

"You think you have a leak?"

Sadly, Marc told her about the chief.

"We didn't want to show our hand while you were still out there, but now I'll call the commissioner and get the search warrants to take her down."

"I'm sorry, Marc."

"Not as sorry as she's going to be. Now tell me about the Empress and the people around her. I want all your impressions. And I'll need the times she was in your presence. We've been watching a lot of the suspects for days now, and we might be able to eliminate some of them based on that."

So Jette filled him in from her perspective. By the time they'd finished their bath, they both had a pretty good picture of each other's movements.

When they'd tucked back into bed, Marc held her and told her about Hester. There'd been no change in her condition. They thought she'd live, but there could be brain damage. Jette was appalled and distressed and found there were tears for the woman who'd betrayed her.

"I'm going to have to deal with some guilt on that, but not right now," she said when the tears dried up.

Marc nodded, thinking there should be no guilt at all, but knew he couldn't remove it with words. She'd do that for herself.

Jette placed her hand on Marc's chest, concerned by the difficulty he had catching a full breath at times.

"So you're on medical leave?"

"Yes, and right now I feel the need for a little more bed rest before I return to active duty."

He wasn't ready yet to let go of her. It wasn't more than a minute later, after a few sweet kisses that they both were deeply asleep.

They spent the rest of the day in bed, sleeping, sharing thoughts, touching, healing. They shared meals in the room feeling safe and cocooned. A few visitors kept them in the game, and Luke monitored their vital signs, but for the most part, they spent the time resting and reconnecting.

The next morning, they awoke not completely back to normal, but refreshed and revitalized.

"Feeling better?" Marc stretched, thinking he'd never had a better night's sleep.

"I still feel the tug of the heroin, but it's more like its echo. I want to spend the morning containing the rest of the discomfort and cleansing my system. And I want you to get back on the streets, Marc. Go be a cop."

"I'm not leaving you," he began, but she put up her hand and stopped his protest.

"Darling, I'm going to be in deep meditation for awhile. You've made sure the apartment is secure and Eunice and Tommy will be able to stop any army she may send."

When he just scowled, she pushed.

"You have to arrest her for me to be completely safe. Now give me a kiss, wait until I'm all the way under, then go make me proud."

Just the right words. Marc nodded. He would do as she asked. His kiss was soft and sweet and soon she was as still and quiet as an undisturbed summer meadow.

Marc was strapping on his weapon when there was a light knock on the door. He went over to the bed and pulled the sheet over Jette's bare shoulders.

"Come in," he called, not able to take his eyes off his sleeping warrior.

Luke entered balancing a large tray. It was filled with fabulous smelling food and drink, fresh bagels, bowls of fruit, granola and hot tea and coffee.

"Great. You're up." He walked over to the sitting area and set the feast down on a table. When Marc came to help himself, Luke noticed his weapon. "You planning on going out?"

"Yes. I need to get back into the investigation."

"Kicked you out of bed and told you to start the hunt again, did she?"

Marc laughed. It felt like heaven.

"That's exactly what happened."

"It amazing how insidious her methods are. You're making a perfectly good point, clipping along on your own righteous path, then zap, the world spins on Jette's axis and you're right by her side headed in the same direction she's going."

"I thought maybe since you've known her longer you could give me a few tips."

"Sorry, my friend but I truly think you're doomed." Luke helped himself to a piece of toast. "You don't have to agree with her…"

"But it's quicker."

"God, we're pathetic. So, how's she doing?"

"She's unbelievable. There's some residual pain. She calls it an echo. I'm glad you're here. Can you stay in the room and make sure she's okay?"

"I was asked to pitch the first game at Yankee stadium, but I'll call and cancel."

"I'd appreciate it." Marc stared at her, sleeping, her head pillowed on her hands. "Damn, I hate to leave her."

"Serve her in another way, Detective. Find the bastards who did this to her."

Luke's face hardened. Marc nodded.

"I intend to."

"Time to go fire your boss?"

"Yeah. Now that I have Jette, I can open the case up."

"You ready for it?"

"As long as I have her to come home to, I'm ready for anything."

"Taking your antibiotics?"

"Jesus, Luke."

Luke laughed softly. "Just asking. Your color is nearly human today."

Marc hesitated for a moment, then spoke softly. "Look, Luke. I…ah…I haven't had time to tell you. If you hadn't been here this week. If you hadn't…hadn't…well. Been with me on this. She wouldn't be here. You know that."

"You would have found her, Marc."

"Yeah, okay. Maybe." Marc lifted a hand, then just blew out a breath. "Ah, fuck it."

He walked over, pulled a startled Luke into a sincere man hug, then strode from the room. A cop on a mission.

"Well, hell," mumbled Luke, a little flustered. "I guess I love you too."

Jette shifted as Luke walked over to the bed. Her eyes remained closed and there was a shallow frown line between them. She wasn't ready to surface yet. There were still a few fingers of deeply rooted pain she wanted to pull out. She knew Luke would understand. He did.

Luke grabbed the *Times* and a big mug of coffee. Feeling pretty good, he stretched out on the chaise, and fell sound asleep before he'd read a single paragraph of the sports section.

# Chapter Four

Chief Cheskee looked up as Marc knocked on the door jam and walked in. Immediately setting aside a folder she'd been reading, she stood and indicated one of the chairs on the other side of her desk.

"Detective. This is a surprise. I thought you'd be cloistered with Jette. How is she today?"

Marc stared for a moment at his chief. Why hadn't he ever seen the slight shiftiness in her eye contact, the weakness around the mouth? Because he hadn't been looking, he told himself.

"She'll be fine, but she took a walk through hell." He decided to sit and keep the conversation civilized. For now.

"Tagg's been reporting. Minimally. I hope you're here to give me more than the bare bones he's been willing to share." There was a sharp edge to her voice that nearly brought Marc's temper up and out. Knowing she'd end the morning in lock-up kept the lid on.

"Actually, I'm here to do more than report. I'd like to ask you some questions."

"Sure. Anything."

"As you know, there were several leaks during the investigation."

"Leaks are a common problem. I recall several times you've cultivated them yourself, encouraging fellow officers to provide you with inside information. I have here somewhere a complaint from Green. He thinks you know more about his case than you should."

Marc just shrugged. He knew she'd back him. Absorbing complaints in favor of his superior police work was something she consistently did. There was a tiny ping of regret for what he was about to do. Ignoring it, he went on.

"I think this time we have the source."

"You have other information?"

"I will have. A warrant is being executed as we speak."

"How come I don't know about it?"

"It went through the commissioner."

"That's unusual."

Marc passed her a file. "Not when the suspect is a high-ranking member of the NYPD."

The chief's face still didn't register any apprehension. Nothing to indicate she had anything to worry about.

"Who? Green? That man can't keep his bloody mouth shut."

"An opportunistic asshole for sure, but that's not against the law. And he didn't know about the raid on the 22nd street mission."

"That premises could have been vacated long before you got there."

"True, but it wasn't. According to my sources they left just before we arrived and in a hurry."

"Marc, your sources are drunks, degenerates, and the disenfranchised. And why wasn't that fact in your report?"

"I wanted to be sure I could back it up. It's in the one you're holding."

She opened the file, read, then slowly brought her head up. No confusion or shock. But there was a thin layer of cool concern on her face. Almost indefinable, but Marc could read it. The confirmation churned in his stomach.

He'd expected her to look differently, sound differently, act differently, but she didn't. Projecting competence and confidence, she slowly closed the folder. With an unchanged air of authority, she used the same detached voice she always used when questioning his reports.

"This appears to be a search warrant for my apartment, my office, my phone, and my computers. You said you had some questions. I'm assuming there's an explanation for this as well."

"I'm thinking I don't need to provide you with an explanation. You already have one. And I only have one question. Why?"

"Marc, I've been a cop, a good one, by the way, for nearly all my adult life. I'm not going to answer that question. I'm going to remain silent."

"I'm not wired, Lauren." Marc deliberately used her first name and was delivering no bullshit. "This is between you and me. I haven't read you your rights, so anything you say can't be used. I just need to know."

"I can ask you the same question, Marc. Why? Why do you need to know?"

"First, because it's just in my nature. The need to know why people do the things they do. Secondly, because I want to know what was more important than the job. Than your integrity. Than…"

"Than the department? The city? You? You and the woman you love?"

Marc hesitated. Was it personal? Hell, yes. He nodded.

"Then between you and me Marc, it's simple. And unfortunately for me it will soon be patently obvious. Money. I did it for gobs and gobs of money. I would have retired by the end of the year. Retired and disappeared into the sunset. You'll find hundreds of thousands of dollars in a numbered Bahamian account I didn't think to hide. Didn't think I needed to. My mistake."

"Money?" Marc was astonished. A part of him thought of, perhaps hoped for, more dramatic reasons. Blackmail. Love. A hidden past. Secrets. Something that would have absolved her from responsibility. But money?

The chief smiled sadly.

"Marc, for as savvy and seasoned as you are, you're still a bit naive. You are so single minded about the job, about your unwavering sense of duty to this city, you don't see the bigger picture."

"I see corruption."

"Yes, but you don't see how a person can be both dedicated to the job and motivated by other needs. I want a lifestyle that my salary can't give me, yet I love my job. Therefore, I make compromises."

"Compromises? Is that what you call betraying your trust?"

She sighed. "Nothing quite so evil. I haven't sold my soul to the devil. I only sold a little of my time and a tiny slice of my integrity. It was a very, very lucrative trade. Unfortunately, it appears I'll need to spend the entire amount on my defense. You really are a fantastic cop. And I want you to remember, that 99% of the time, I was too."

"Well, that one percent is going to tarnish the entire package. I'm going to Mirandize you. A team from Internal Affairs is outside the door and will be conducting the search. The commissioner himself will escort you to booking."

"What's the charge?"

"Conspiracy to murder."

"You're overcharging. That will work in my favor."

"Working with me to bring down the Empress will bring more favor into the negotiation."

"I have no idea what you're talking about."

"What is your relationship with Maxine White?"

Marc could see that one startled her.

"Maxine and I are friends," she said after a brief hesitation.

"Oh, I think there's more to it than that."

"Maxine and I are more than friends, but that's hardly controversial in today's society."

"How long have you been friends?"

The chief paused again, but she was willing to provide information they could easily acquire elsewhere. She was well aware that some level of cooperation could keep her connected to Marc. And she'd recognized long ago that was a good thing.

"A few months."

"How did you meet?"

"At a NYPD benefit breakfast."

"Did she approach you?"

"I don't recall."

Marc had a feeling that she remembered every detail. "Is she the Empress?"

"I still have no idea what you're talking about."

"You play Sovereignty."

"I do."

"So you know who the Empress is?"

"She's a fictional character, Marc."

"Are you the Empress?"

"I think I'll exercise my right to remain completely and utterly silent."

Marc knew she meant it, so he recited the Miranda warning, then rose and went to the door. His chief never moved as the team poured in, followed by the commissioner. Marc was surprised that when he left her familiar office and walked through the buzzing bullpen, he was more sad than angry.

# Chapter Five

Yawning and stretching some life back into his limbs, Luke looked down and smiled. There was a blanket over him. Glancing over at the empty bed and hearing running water, he put the clues together and figured his sister was up and about.

"Are you hungry?" he asked when she came out of the bathroom, all fresh from her shower.

"Starving."

"Ready for some bird food?" He handed her granola and raisins.

"Yum." Jette took the bowl and settled into a chair next to him. "Now that we're alone, I want you to fill me in from your perspective."

"Well, I came to New York to see the world premiere of *Flight Into Danger* and thought I'd drop in. Marc told me he'd lost you, so I decided to stick around."

"Luke."

"Jette."

Then with a laugh and a shrug, he told her of Marc's incredible connection to the city and what went on behind the scenes.

It warmed Jette to see the high regard in her brother's eyes when speaking of her lover. Family approval wasn't essential to a good relationship, but it did help. She laughed when he told her of Greta's visit. On the other hand…

"Feel up to seeing people?" he asked when the saga came to an end. "Marc hasn't called the team in yet, but Tommy and Claude are hovering around the kitchen, hoping to get their chance to pamper the princess. It goes without saying that Hilda's baking. I swear so much came out of that oven we could have built a cathedral of bread, meatloaf, cookies, and fried chicken."

"His favorites."

"Yeah. She was incredible through all this."

"Still is."

"So, you ready to join the Guardians in their quest for retribution?"

"Yes, but give me a little time. I want to do some stretching, then I'll need to put on a ton of makeup to look alive," she lamented, catching a glimpse of herself in the mirror.

"Better get started then. You really are hideous. You don't want to scare the troops."

When she went into the bathroom, Luke called Marc.

"Where are you?"

"Working through dumpster alley, interviewing roaches," said Marc.

"That sounds appetizing. The Phoenix has risen from the ashes once again and is ready to fly. I thought you might want to know."

"I'll be right there. Thanks."

A half hour later, Marc let himself into the apartment. He'd called the team on his way back and they were all in transit. When he didn't find Jette in the bedroom, he felt a little punch of anxiety. Would that ever go away, he thought? Passing the ballroom on the way back to the kitchen, he saw her standing among the boards, files, and fragments of evidence. It gave him another little jolt. Not anxiety this time, but a bit of wonder.

He stood in the doorway and stared. She'd been such a presence in the room during their long search. It was as if she'd materialized from the specter that had haunted him through the days and nights into flesh and blood.

Jette turned when she felt him and caught the look on his face.

"Now that I'm back, it hardly seems real, does it?" she asked softly.

"We'll get this cleaned out soon. Get this out of your life."

"Taking away the tangible evidence of your work won't exorcize the ghosts, Marc. Only time can do that."

They met in the center of the room and he folded her into his arms.

"Stay with me," he whispered into her hair, breathing her in.

"I'm not going anywhere, Marc."

"I thought I'd lost you. I thought I'd brought you here to your death." As he stroked her back, his eyes fell on the board crowded with names, locations, pictures of perpetrators, and random theories. The dread and misery he'd felt while compiling all of it, the hours of rage and frustration, of grief and pain seemed to pulse through the room.

"I have many methods of purging all of the negative energy in this place, Marc."

"More intense therapy?"

"There's that. But I was thinking of a ceremony. A cleansing ritual."

He pulled her back, still holding on to her.

"Seriously?"

"Seriously. Leave a few of the papers and files you don't need. I'll want something to burn."

"In here?"

"Yes. Don't worry, darling. I'm not going to build a bonfire in the middle of this lovely floor."

"I don't give a shit if you do."

"I understand that, but the fire marshal of this city would probably frown on it. And poor Hilda might not survive what it would do to the exquisite bamboo flooring. I'll adapt my usual methods and use the fireplace. The heartache and anger the files symbolize will be destroyed by the flames and heat. We'll take the ashes to the roof and disburse them."

"Will there be chanting?"

"There will."

"I like what chanting does to my heartbeat."

Jette looked at him. He meant it. It was a simple statement and it touched her. She felt exactly the same way.

"When this is all over, when the worlds are in balance, we'll come into the quiet room and cleanse it together."

Marc loved what the sound of the word 'together' did to him. "What about what's inside of me? What this room does to my gut?"

"We have cleansing ceremonies for the body and soul, as well."

"Does it have anything to do with that black sludge you drink?"

"Perhaps."

"Maybe we can just move."

Jette laughed. "On second thought, I think we can resolve the imbalance inside you with love."

"I love you, Jette," he said with profound gratitude shining in his eyes.

"Then everything else will settle. I promise." Seeing something else in his eyes, feeling it in his heart, she asked. "Tell me about this morning. Was it horrible? Confronting your chief."

"Not as bad as I thought."

"But she breached your trust."

"More like the trust of the city."

"And the badge."

"Yeah."

Jette stared into his eyes, into his soul, and went on. "A significant older woman in your life disappointed you, Marc. Let you down. It would be psychologically reasonable for you to project your mother into the situation, reinforcing your resentment and fear surrounding abandonment and rejection."

"If you say so."

"I am the therapist."

He shrugged.

"Talk to me, Marc. It hurt you."

"Some."

Standing silent and still, Jette waited. Marc thought he'd just tough it out, then found himself talking.

"We really don't have time for this. Plus it isn't necessary. I'm fine."

"Are you?"

"Yes. Move on."

"Can you, Marc? Can you move on?"

"Jette. Turn off the fucking head channel, will you?"

"Your deep-seeded anger comes from unresolved emotion."

"Well we aren't going to resolve it here."

"Why?"

"I don't need a fucking shrink."

"Yes, you do."

Clearly aggrieved, Marc crossed his arms and decided they could stand there until she fainted from hunger. He'd catch her, of course. Remaining stoic, he stared down at her.

Undeterred, she returned his scowl with a kind, patient, steady stare of her own.

He glared. She waited.

"Okay. Okay. Fuck it! First of all, I like my deep-seeded anger. It gives me an edge."

"Agreed, but if it's too sharp, it will cut deep and the wound won't heal."

"Oh, now that was a clever turn of a phrase."

"I thought so. Marc, that anger poisons your peace of mind."

"That anger blows the peace in this entire neighborhood."

"So purging it will help with the noise abatement initiatives of New York. Darling, one day that anger may cost you something more than you're willing to pay."

"You. Will it cost me you?" There was a touch of bitterness in his voice.

"No. I'm here to stay. You need me too much. Now quit stalling and tell me what's inside you."

"You already know."

She didn't reply.

"Okay. Fine. Damn, you're perverted." He threw up his arms and started pacing, anger pouring from him and into the room. "Hurt. There was hurt mixed in with the anger. Disillusionment with the disgust. God, the woman was my boss. She wasn't a friend, but I trusted her. She always backed me, found ways to make things work for me. I thought she admired the job I did for New York."

The air throbbed with his anger, but the poison was losing its potency.

"Damn her. Damn her to hell. Her actions could have seriously sabotaged this case. This case. Fuck her. This wasn't just a case. This was about you. She knows how I feel about you and instead of setting aside her greed and own personal issues, she worked against me. I'm so angry with her I could take her into an alley and punch her. Stomp her. And yet caught up in all that fury are memories of her giving me a hand, advocating for me, standing in front of me at the review board. I can't hate her. I'm trying to hate her. I do hate what she did."

While he talked, he gradually stopped his manic pacing and settled. Then stopped.

"I can hate what she did," he repeated, finally able to separate the woman from the actions. His emotions from his feelings. "But I don't have to hate her. I can bring her to justice. And I can regret having to do it."

"Exactly." Jette patiently listened until he reached his own conclusions, found his own path to a better frame of mind. "She was two women. Not schizophrenic, but certainly she played two completely different roles. You can still remember and appreciate all that she did *for* you all those years while abhorring what she recently did *to* you."

"Yeah." He raked his fingers through his hair and nodded. Something inside him settled. "Yeah, I can."

"Feel better?" asked Jette after a moment.

Mac shook himself. "Yes, Doctor. I do, actually. Now, can we move on?"

"Not quite. What else is in there?"

"Nothing."

"Don't make me come in there after you."

"Jesus, sometimes I think you're the nut case." He sighed, both exasperated and somehow liberated. "I look around sometimes and I wonder. Who's next? Who's next to let me down? The chief's deception hurt, but what if it had been one of my team? I handpicked them. Every one. Or Tommy or Eunice or Lyd. Or, heaven help me, that pushy little teen geek. If they would have turned on me, turned on you, we'd have to blow out the walls in here to fit all the dark and dangerous crap I'd spew. I liked the chief, but I didn't, didn't..."

"Say it Marc," prompted Jette gently.

"I didn't really, *really* like her," he finished in a rush.

"You didn't love her," translated Jette.

"Yeah. Yeah, I guess you could say that."

"No, you could say that. But we'll save that for later."

"Thank God. Are we done now?" More relieved than aggrieved, more settled and clear headed than he'd been in days, he decided she'd have to read his mind because he wasn't about to admit it out loud.

"Yes." She read his mind just fine. "The clouds of dark emotion you released can now be purged from the room."

"We're going to need one big fucking exorcism."

"It's not an exorcism, it's a cleansing. And since this is a ballroom I have a great idea. We'll do more than cleanse the room. We'll replace the ache and fury with a time of dancing and celebration and forgiveness. We'll celebrate the Green Corn festival in here."

"You told me about that once. A celebration where you can get absolution for all of your sins. The Cherokee believe you start fresh every year."

"Yes."

"It better be one big mother of a party. I have a lot of sins."

"It doesn't matter."

"Like one big flush, huh?"

"Exactly," laughed Jette. She really did love her man. On so many levels.

"When is this festival?" asked Marc, circling her waist with his arms, liking the change of subject to something more domestic.

"During the full moon when the corn is ready for harvest. Sometime in the fall."

"We don't have a lot of corn growing in Central Park."

"We'll improvise. I'll call my father's cousin in Oklahoma as the time gets near and he'll give me the date. Then we'll fill this room with laugher and music. It's all about a new beginning, Marc. It's meant to chase away this ugliness."

"Full moon, huh," he brooded. "Back to the phases of the moon."

"It's a very compelling pull. But for us, it will bring light to a wonderful celebration, not a final duel."

She smiled, kissed him to seal the promise, then stepped back as she heard voices in the hallway. Looking around, she felt the air in the room lighten as the bright life forces of Tagg, Dina, Rachael, Raj, and Teresa burst in. Their combined energy filled the space and chased the gloom to the hidden corners.

"Hey, Jette! I never thought I'd say this in a sentence, but you're looking a little less stoned today," laughed Tagg, giving her a gentle hug and a huge kiss. "If you really wanted to lose five pounds, there's better ways of doing it."

"She lost them, I found them. They kind of snacked up on me." Teresa, smiled broadly, looking like she didn't hold it against Jette in the least. She scooped Jette against her in an expansive hug. "I swear the only way these guys can fuel any kind of investigation is with high fat and refined sugars."

"There's nothing refined at all about how we fuel our brain cells," chuckled Dina, kissing Jette. "I think there's something to that donut, cop relationship. Sugar sharpens our senses."

"And redefines our booties. I'm going to have to go to the gym an extra hour every day for a month," laughed Teresa.

"Hey. You're in shape. Round's a shape!" teased Raj, who clearly had enjoyed exploring those extra five pounds that morning.

"Yup." Teresa shook her redefined booty.

"I see a few of you used your better judgment." Jette flicked one of the Harvest Hearth wrappers on the table.

"That would be me," saluted Raj, grinning as he grabbed the wrapper and kissed Jette's cheek. "I don't consider the four food groups to be Fast, Junk, Frozen, and Chocolate."

"Seriously, you're looking great, Jette. I can't believe you're standing right here. Frankly, I can't believe you're standing at all. Luke kept us informed all the way," said Rachael, giving Jette a hug.

"Someone talking about me? If the praise would embarrass me with its stunningly flattering content, I could retreat and come back in a few minutes." Luke's cheerful voice came from the open doorway.

"No," they all shouted when they saw he was carrying mugs of coffee and the ultimate cliché, a huge platter of assorted donuts.

"When you want to be greeted like the second coming, always come bearing the addiction of choice." Luke set down the tray. When both Raj and Jette just stood and looked at the plate of fat and caffeine, he laughed. "Tommy will be right in with your perverted choices for a morning pick me up."

On cue, Tommy bounced in with a small tray of tea and oatmeal raisin bars.

"Here you go sugar pie, or should I say granola girl. Time to get that five pounds back. And there's enough for you too, handsome." She winked broadly at Raj, standing half her size. "Tell me true, Raj honey, is this green tea, oatmeal combo how you maintain that complexion? My spa has been slapping that stuff on me from cheek to cheek, but on the outside, darling. If I could keep my hide as creamy as your really fine shine, I'd eat rat tails and a penguin's frozen balls. Is it like that all over? Hmm?"

She raised her well-plucked eyebrows high and waved a hand at him when his cheeks got a little pink.

"And that shade. Sweetie, it's a perfect complement to your mocha cream. For that, I'd dip those tails in motor oil and roll those balls in kitty litter." Laughing hysterically at her own wacky chat, she turned her attention on Jette. "Now don't you look all perked up today. I know that's not oatmeal, hon." She sniffed like a puppy. "That's Crème de la Mer, $125 an ounce at Saks and worth every penny, dear heart. Now move over, boys and girls, 'cause Tommy has her appetite back and wants donuts by the dozen."

Jette looked over as Marc was swept to the table by his own revitalized appetite and the pull of cop chatter. Everyone started eating and talking at once, with Marc shouting the loudest and eating the fastest. She smiled. The cleansing ceremony had already begun.

Rachael snapped her phone shut. "Kim will be here in twenty with Kelly. Lyd's still sober and is on her way too."

"I'm looking forward to meeting them and getting started on developing a profile for the Empress," said Jette, already feeling like part of the team.

"You're the only one who communicated directly with her. We'd like your impressions. Your professional impressions," said Tagg.

"To begin with you understand she's very, very sick."

"Oh yeah, we got that part." Teresa mumbled around a donut, determined to do the gym thing at the first convenient moment.

"In spades," agreed Raj, thinking nothing really beat donut-fueled sex.

Jette's report on the delusional state of the woman and various reasons for it was clear, concise, and well thought out. Everyone felt they knew her, now they had to identify her and put her out of the game.

"What about a physical description?" asked Tagg.

"I was blindfolded, but judging from her stride, she's fairly tall, not heavy. She had no trouble disguising her voice. Low, raspy. No identifiable accent. It could be she's a woman used to performing. Her vocabulary would indicate a more mature woman. She laughed once and it ended in a little cough. I think she might be a smoker or have a health issue related to the lungs."

Jette walked over to the board filled with women's pictures. Each had a number that referred to files, some thick, some with just names, addresses, and brief biographies.

"What's Lee doing up here?" Jette tapped the picture of her agent and friend.

"She fit several of our criteria," responded Marc unapologetically.

"I want her off," insisted Jette.

"She stays on until we unmask the Empress," disagreed Marc.

"Lee is an open woman who has no layer of artifice," persisted Jette, steel giving substance to her calm manner. "An important part of profiling is taking people off the suspect list. People who don't fit."

"I'm the cop. She stays," argued Marc.

"I'm the profiler and the only one who's met the Empress."

"You were drugged and blindfolded."

"The drugs actually enhanced my senses and the blindfold only took one of them out of play. The other four were still collecting."

"Give me something tangible then."

"Tommy isn't the only one who can identify a specific scent. Lee always wears Faith Avery. Bathes in it. I would have smelled it. The Empress doesn't routinely wear perfume. Even if she showered and scrubbed to remove it before coming in, some residual would have remained."

"We'll put that into the mix, but we remove no one until this is over."

"I think I may have met the Empress at some point in my life. She felt familiar, but I didn't know her. Lee isn't the Empress."

"That doesn't make any sense." Marc's voice got sharper.

"It does to me." She reached over to remove Lee's picture. "Tagg, with your permission?"

She looked over at Tagg, whose eyes widened with surprise and some alarm. He'd stepped away, not wanting any part of the little feud brewing. He noticed the rest of the team had deserted the field completely, falling back behind the various tables and boards, their heads going back and forth like spectators at a tennis match.

"Marc told me you were in charge." Jette's hand still rested on the picture.

"Ah…," Tagg began, glancing over at Marc for leadership.

"Ah, fuck it," shouted Marc. "Take the fucking picture down if you want a symbolic grand gesture of fucking loyalty. It's still up here." He tapped his forehead.

"Thank you, Marc. That's quite a symbolic grand gesture of partnership and team spirit." Jette aimed an easy smile at her furious lover. "I just won't mention it to Lee and the commissioner when we invite them over for dinner next week."

"Any others you think we need to remove?" asked Marc sarcastically, glaring around at Tagg and the rest of the team as if they'd been part of some kind of insurrection. "Or better yet, feed?"

"Why not introduce me to all of the women here, and I'll give you my best professional opinion," replied Jette, resisting the urge to kiss Marc's angry petulant mouth.

"No," said Marc, glad to get back on track and assert himself again as a working cop. "I'd rather you look over the board and tell me if any of the women are familiar first. Then we'll go over them and brief you."

"That makes sense," conceded Jette, grateful to be able to say that. She tapped Zena Brightson's publicity photo.

"I know her," she said thoughtfully trying to put the face together with a memory.

"How? Where?" asked Marc on full alert. He wanted to prompt her with more information but restrained himself. She'd come to it and he didn't want to contaminate her recollection.

Jette stared at the picture. The woman wasn't a friend, wasn't a colleague. Not a neighbor or someone she ran into frequently. Then it popped. A fully formed experience and an impression.

"At a book signing. The last time I was in New York. She was very resistant to some of my ideas on both psychological and spiritual healing."

"Did she seem threatening?"

"No, not at all, just sad and a little disconnected. Who is she?"

Marc filled her in. "And my impression is that she's seriously unplugged. Dina, you put together the bulk of this file. Anything new?"

"Yes. There were several lawsuits against her company, both judicated and pending. Some for millions. Mostly from parents whose kids went off the deep end and took the play for real, or from victims of those kids."

"This has been a real eye opener," observed Tagg. "I think from now on when we have a bizarre murder, seemingly random, we should open gaming gone wrong as a line of investigation."

"We have a few cold cases we could revisit after we close this one," nodded Rachael.

"The simulated conflict and potential violence seems to touch something in all the gamers, but really plays havoc on those who are on the edge. It feeds something inside them," mused Jette, thoughtfully. "I'd like to do some research into the whole phenomenon. Although you have to realize the vast majority of live-action players are in it for the fun, recreation, and stimulation. It's not an obsession, it's a hobby."

"There are hundreds, even thousands, who reenact the Civil War, but they don't take the battles back home to the streets of Savannah," agreed Rachael.

"And there are renaissance fairs with period costumes and jousts and huge turkey legs and sword fights. As far as I know, the people who go limit their journey to the Middle Ages to the weekends," added Teresa. "No jousting with the neighbor's Toyota."

"Did you find what induced the creep factor on Brightson?" asked Tagg.

"Not yet, but there's a sealed juvenile record and we've petitioned a warrant. It must be fairly significant since it was sealed by Judge Sue Kane herself before she became a member of the Supreme Court," responded Dina. "Zena was thirteen when the records were sealed."

"I know Sue. I'll give her a call and see if I can give it a shove. It would help to know if Brightson was the victim or the perpetrator," said Marc.

"It would, but either way, adolescent trauma could easily make her fragile enough to prefer a fantasy world," observed Jette. "I see Maxine White is up there. She fits the profile. Does she have alibis?"

"No."

"My times were accurate, but I don't know about the a.m. or p.m."

"We checked both against the log. We've already been able to eliminate a few of the suspects based on timing. It helps."

Jette actually smiled when she tapped Delancy Pickford Weiss Chrysler's picture.

"What did she have to say when you talked with her?"

"We haven't interviewed her yet. Her staff here tells us she's in Newport, and her housekeeper up there tells us she's in the city," said Marc.

"Interesting. But she could just be avoiding the inconvenience of speaking to the authorities."

"Or she could be bopping her best friend's frustrated husband. Or maybe her best friend. But I have a feeling she's deliberately eluding us," thought Marc.

"Besides her recent contact with me, why else is she up there?"

Marc went to her file and pulled out a copy of a newspaper clipping. On it was Delancy with a teenage girl.

"That's her daughter. Look at her wrist."

There were several strings visible as the girl waved to the photographer.

"We had the paper send over the original."

He handed Jette the blowup showing the strings circling the girl's wrist.

"Are these symbols of some sort?" asked Jette.

"Yes. According to Kelly, they're used by a less intelligent species of player to keep track of their points. What do you think? Would she fit the profile?"

Jette thought about it, then nodded.

"I really didn't get much of an impression, but on reflection, I think you can leave her on. The fact that she has a daughter may exclude her. Maybe it's a natural bias, but I just can't picture a mother in this role. On the other hand, she was extremely persistent that day in my office and very angry when I refused her invitation. She turned quite nasty and aggressive. The invitation could have been a ruse to get me into a car. An easier snatch than taking me from here."

Marc handed the file to Theresa. "Any of the others on the board feel right?"

Jette tapped Abigail's picture.

"I'd put her close to the top. She not only fits the profile, she fits the role."

She moved from picture to picture, getting reports and giving her best advice on priorities. "How many players are there in the city?"

"An estimate is a little over 100,000," said Tagg.

"That's a lot of potential suspects."

"And a whole network of possible accomplices."

"True, although I suspect most are unwitting and are only playing. They have no idea this has moved from fantasy to some kind of fanatical reality."

Jette laughed when she saw her grandmother's photo on the board.

"And whose idea was that?"

"Luke made me do it," Marc said quickly, his lips quirking.

Luke looked over and frowned at him.

"Jette, did I mention that Marc makes faces behind your back whenever you ask about the vegetarian choices on a menu?"

Jette slanted a glance at Marc, who was making a face at Luke.

"Really. Hmm. Does Grandmother have an alibi, Detective?"

"I never checked, actually."

"Well, she *is* a smoker," speculated Hilda. She'd come in to serve coffee and stayed for Jette's analysis. She clearly bonded with the men on this issue. "However, with your acute sense of smell, Dr. Morningstar, you'd have picked up the tidal wave of Chanel."

When she turned and left the room with the empty plates and mugs, Marc and Luke pitched into a fit of laughter so powerful they had to hold each other up. The sight of Marc gasping for air and Luke's eyes watering with hilarity soon had everyone hysterical even though none of them really understood the joke. Jette just let them go. It was better therapy than a month of formal treatment.

# Chapter Six

Kelly was eager to work with the magnificent Dr. Jette Morningstar, alias Avenger. For that's how she thought of her now. She brought all of her notes and the several versions of the game itself when Kim picked her up from the group home.

Her new shelter didn't suck. Detective Snake Eyes must have a lot of clout if he scored a bed in this facility. It was top of the line as far as she was concerned. They had a separate room with accommodations for kids with special needs. There was stuff like bed checks and backpack searches, of course, but the food was great and the evening snack of popcorn, extra extreme butter flavored, thank you very much, and root beer was sweet. The man and woman who ran it seemed on the up and up. The real deal.

"Hey, slim Kim," she called as she rolled up the retractable ramp into the van Kim was driving.

"Hey, kid." Kim smiled as she buckled in all the wheels. The new chair was fire engine red with more bells and whistles than a luxury automobile. A heated leather seat, a hydraulic lift so she could raise and lower the chair, a small entertainment unit with a built in DVD and MP3 and smooth electric controls that could have her turning on a dime. Even a deluxe cup holder. "Got everything you need?"

"On my person. You want to stop at Starbucks?"

"Sure."

"It's my treat today."

"You don't have to…"

"No, really. I'm flush, and no one at the home lifted it while I caught the z's. Detective Snake Eyes pays me and lays it on thick."

"Think you should save any of that for college?"

"Nah. I say live large and live now. So I think I'll get double chocolate sprinkles."

Kim smiled. Living large was double chocolate sprinkles. Life was good.

"Hilda always has the kitchen stocked," Kelly went on. "So we don't have to spring for the sweet grub. She'll have cookies, donuts, brownies, even Rice Krispies squares. She's tight."

When they pulled up to the apartment, Kim unhooked Kelly, who never hesitated as she shot out over the ramp and up to the front door.

"Hey, J-bird," she called to the rigid and serious doorman. "I gotchya a straight jo. No foam, no frills, no flavor. Strong and black as your back!"

Kelly handed Jonathon a tall cup of coffee.

"Why, ah, thank you little lady. Shall I call up and let them know you've arrived?"

"No, thanks. They're expecting us."

"You are such a suck up," said Kim as they got into the elevator.

"And proud of it!" giggled Kelly as she loudly sucked the foam from the top of her latte.

"I didn't even know he could smile."

"He's just shy. But I think I'm wearing him down."

"Hard to believe that could happen."

Eunice met them at the door and escorted them into the ballroom. When Kelly saw Jette in the flesh, she nearly lost her voice. It came back to her strong and filled with bubbling awe.

"Oh my God. Oh my God. It's her. Ah, I mean you're her. Avenger. I'm going to ask you to excuse me for a minute while I have a seriously special moment for myself and gamers everywhere. I need to just sit here and stare, so pardon my eye popping."

And she did. She completely stopped in the middle of the room and stared at Jette.

"You must be Kelly." Jette smiled as she walked up to the chair and extended her hand.

"Oh, wow. Your voice. Her voice. It's exactly, I mean exactly, what Avenger would sound like."

Jette laughed as Kelly grabbed her hand and pumped it.

"And I bet that's Avenger's laugh, too." Kim rolled her eyes, but secretly agreed. "Get a grip, Kelly. This is Dr. Jette Morningstar."

"By day, maybe. But by night, she's Avenger. Ready to fight the Blue Empress for Sovereignty."

"Actually this is very enlightening," smiled Jette. "If this is how a bright, intelligent young woman reacts to the game, I think someone in a deep delusional psychosis could easily transform fantasy into reality."

"Has Snake Eyes shown you the stuff from the game? The pictures and stuff?" asked Kelly still holding Jette's hand.

"Yes. The fence jumping picture was most certainly the catalyst for the initial delusional breakdown. And the rest of the coincidental similarities really solidified it in her mind. Enough so she completely ignored the inconsistencies."

"Yeah, like you didn't really share a mother, your father was a doctor and didn't die at the hands of a crazed cleric, and you're too short. Avenger is supposed to top six feet. Plus Avenger tears into meat and sucks wine like a French monk."

"You not only know a great deal about this game, it appears you know a lot about me."

"It's pretty much public knowledge. Stuff the Empress should know or could know with very little research. Before I presented my theory, I played a little 'oh no, she isn't' with myself."

"We call that playing the devil's advocate. A very smart move before drawing a conclusion."

"I'm a player. A good one."

"Could you come join us? I'd like to ask you some questions."

Kelly looked down, noticing for the first time she was still holding Avenger's hand. Cripes. What a rush. Or maybe it was the triple caffeine from the latte. Either way, it had her nearly floating out of her chair as she zipped over to the group by the boards.

"Shoot the questions. I'm here to serve."

Jette crossed her arms and leaned back against a table.

"Could you review my powers?"

"Yeah, sure. You have several, actually. You're a brilliant warrior. You really kick righteous ass, ah, butt. You communicate with animals. Some suspect you can change into one. The mountain lion, the wolf, the eagle. Did they tell you Avenger was supposedly raised by wolves?"

Jette nodded. "And I suppose they told you I am of the wolf clan?"

"Yeah. It gave me the maximum skin bumps, up and down. Anyway, highest power on the scale is that you're a Phoenix. You rise from the dead. It's why the Sentinels were waiting on the shore when everyone in the real world was dragging the river. They knew you'd pop up even if you broke your neck. It's written in the legend that you were given seven lives by the High Priest. Some Soviacs think you were knocking sneakers at one time, you know, kind of, well super duper close, shall we say. " Her eyes slid to Marc. "Sorry, Dark Knight, but you're not usually in the running when Avenger makes the booty call."

Shrugging, Marc winked.

"And need I remind you again, it's only a game?"

"Sure, if you say so. Anyway, conventional wisdom is that you've died four times. I think the fall into the water and your survival would count as a forfeit of one to this particular Empress. She wanted to turn you to get another one. If she succeeded, you'd have had only one left. Your next death after that would be a permanent defeat."

"I was blindfolded when she came into the room. I had the feeling she was talking through a mask, disguised from her followers, so why do that?"

"First of all, she'd definitely be in a mask. A full silver one. Some say it's because she's hideous. You'd have your eyes covered because you have incredible power in them. Not like x-ray vision or anything, but it's how you communicate with animals and how you can bend Minions to your will," explained Kelly. "And excuse me for saying this, but you really do have a potent punch on the peeper scale. Not scary like his," she nodded at Marc. "But nothing I'd want to mess with. I think it's a good thing they didn't blind you."

"I certainly agree with that. Tell me about the Empress's powers."

"The most mondo is she can read minds."

"And she reads minds in this world by reading what pours out of players in their email communications."

"Yeah. People share really deep stuff online. Also, she trades for things. She has a practically a bottomless stash of Boons because she controls the empire's treasure chest."

Kelly continued filling in the blanks of the game and expanding Jette's understanding. When they were finished exchanging information and insights, Jette stared at the boards, then looked around the room.

"In my professional opinion, here's how I think we should proceed. I'm going to go public and challenge the Empress directly. Avatar to Avatar."

"How would you do that?" asked Tagg.

"I'll call a press conference..."

"A what?" Marc was incredulous. And furious.

"A press conference. I want to get in her face, figuratively speaking." Jette's eye's flashed.

"You never talk with the press," snapped Marc.

"I'll give one of our reporters in the city an exclusive interview. You tell me which one, Marc. I'm sure Lee will have no trouble setting it up. It's the best way to go public and in a big way. I'll play into her delusion. At this point I don't want her to slide out of it for long."

Jette could see Marc was seething, but would deal with that after she laid out her plan.

"She's into staging and symbols so I want Marc and Luke to stand with me during the interviews. My Knights. She needs to see them solid and in their places. That will push her a little further into the illusion and really boil her blood. I'd offered them in a trade at one time but she took too long to make her decision. Now they're still mine and that fact will slap at her."

"Nice move," whistled Kelly.

"You were going to trade us?" Luke put his hand over his heart in mock horror.

"And what would a Phoenix want with a healer?" She grinned at him. He was such a goof sometimes.

"Hey, the Dark Knight's my bud. Watch it or I'll get him to kick your ash."

Kelly giggled. Ash. That was a good one.

Since the Dark Knight was getting darker by the second, Jette decided to move on quickly.

"Kelly, you said I have a High Priest."

"Yeah. Sure do." Kelly saw where Jette was going and really got behind it.

"Describe him."

"Well he's really big and dark. No one has ever seen his face. He wears a hood."

"Tagg, you're really big and dark."

"Tommy's bigger and darker," said Tagg quickly. He'd never gotten over stage fright.

"Yes, but she'd see the camera and want to sing and dance," observed Jette.

"Well, I'm not going to wear a hood," grumbled Tagg.

"No, I wouldn't expect you to, but I'd like to have you stand with me. Who else is in my inner circle?"

"The BeastMaster." Kelly looked around. "No one here fits the bill. She's short and kind of troll like."

"The Empress will have to assume she's off mastering the beasts," said Jette.

Kelly giggled again.

"We'll set the stage in the front parlor. Kelly, I want you to take Tommy and scout out the apartment. Pick out pieces you think would be found in Callisto."

Kelly nodded, completely on board.

"I'll weave a message to her into the interview. A direct challenge," said Jette.

"Wicked." Kelly nodded with enthusiasm. "Now, you're looking really hot and ready to do battle, and all that, but be sure to let her know you're at full power. Say the words if you can. That will totally sink her ship. All she did to try and turn you didn't even phase you. Ho! She might just want to go straight to the Final Duel."

Marc was getting more and more annoyed and soon his anger began to send negative vibes throughout the room. Jette looked up and over at him. The first duel of the day came as deep, rich brown eyes clashed with green ice.

"I want a face-to-face confrontation," Jette said softly, talking to the room, but pushing her resolve through the connection with Marc. "From everything you've told me and everything I felt when she was in the room, if I push her, she'll come right for me. When she does, I'll rely on all of you to stop her, take her, and finish this game."

"There's nothing you can say that will convince me that you should put yourself in jeopardy." Marc's tone was sharp enough to cut facets in a diamond.

"I am already in jeopardy, Marc."

"All the more reason you're going to stay here behind a blue wall," he demanded. Everyone else in the room held their tongues and held their breath. Everyone but Jette.

"If I hide, she'll just pull in, lay low, and wait," countered Jette.

"You aren't hiding. You're staying inside protective custody."

"Custody? You want me in custody?" Jette's brown eyes flared.

"Not officially." Marc was determined to ignore the hot blast.

"You just released me from a gilded cage. I will not agree to be placed in another one, Detective."

"Stay here. Trust me to find her."

"This isn't a matter of trust. I trust you. I trust all of you. This is a matter of working together. Of using all the expertise we have. I know this woman. I've been in her head. Kelly knows the game. If I don't show myself and challenge her directly as this mythical Avenger, if I don't get into the game with her and use it to get her to come after me, she'll push the psychotic button of another Anointed One. "

"You're talking about a fucking game. A fantasy. We're in the real world now," shouted Marc.

"No, we're not because she's not and to get her we have to play in her world. Marc, if I push her openly, she won't be able to resist the challenge. She'll have to make a major move," insisted Jette.

"I agree," said Kelly enthusiastically, getting in the middle despite Marc's furious scowl. "She's probably calculating several singular scenarios as we speak. Get out there soon or she could blow in a hundred different directions. And man-oh-man I sure wouldn't want to be in her path, because she'll come out blasting."

Kim put her hand on Kelly's shoulder and squeezed hard before the little gamer could take a breath and make another observation. Recognizing the rumble of a volcano about to erupt, she didn't want her young friend to be in the path of friendly fire.

Jette didn't either, so she stood up and put an end to Kelly's enthusiastic observations.

"I think we need to channel all our energy into developing a workable plan, not into obstructing it."

"So now you're taking tactical advice from a goddamn fifteen year old?" growled Marc angrily, glaring at Kelly, glad to have another target for his rage.

"You're the goddamn cop who brought me into this, remember?" Kelly glared right back, not at all intimidated. At least not with Avenger herself in the room.

"Watch your fucking mouth," shouted Marc.

"You watch it," fumed Kelly, not backing down. "Watch it move and pay attention. I'm the goddamn expert here."

Jette took a step between them.

"Kelly, they wouldn't have been able to put this together without your expertise. I'm sure everyone not only appreciates your input, they are in awe of it. I know I am. How about you take a break. Hilda is baking. I bet she could use an expert on chocolate chip cookies right about now."

Kelly snapped a final eye bullet at Marc, then felt herself calm in the wash of Jette's presence.

"Fine. I can take a direct and not very subtle hint." She smiled at Jette, completely ignoring Marc.

Jette smiled back as Kelly expertly spun her chair and shot out of the room.

Marc walked over and slammed the door. "Goddamn smart ass kid. One more fucking show of 'tude from her and she's back in juvie."

Jette gave him a steady look. "Does she remind you of anyone you used to know, Detective?"

Marc completely ignored her and stalked over to the window to begin his count to 100, but Tagg and Eunice thought it was hilarious. Not even Marc's furious muttering could stop them from laughing out loud. As a matter of fact, it seemed to fuel them.

The rest of the team, amused but exercising better judgment, held in their reaction. They were neither as large as Tagg and Eunice, nor as terrifying.

"Okay," said Tagg when he got himself under control, "since I'm inclined to believe our 15-year-old expert, this message that you'll deliver publicly through the interview will be counted as a major Challenge and she'll have to come at you, Jette. We just don't know how or when."

"True, but this is going to get very personal very quickly, I think," assured Jette.

Marc was pacing now, obviously working on another round of counting. The sound of his boots pounding the hardwood floor punctuated their discussion. Jette ignored the sound. The others took her lead and did the same.

"She lost the big prize, one of my lives, but she still wants it. And, according to Kelly, she's probably been declaring a Time Victory, accumulating credit for days I'm not sighted. If I were out of the game for a week or two real time, that's a lot of points. So, when I show up on television this afternoon, she won't even earn those. It will be a real hit. Win, win for Avenger. Lose, lose for the Empress."

"Will you quit talking about this like it's a goddamn game?" Marc exploded. His head was pounding, his chest hurt and he felt his guts clutch up. He prowled around the room one more time, then stood over Jette. "You don't have seven fucking lives, you have one. And if she takes it, you're all out of lives. You're not a Phoenix rising from the dead, professor, you're flesh and blood!" He glared fire at everyone else in the room. "And the rest of you aren't helping."

The rest of the team couldn't think of one thing among them to help, so they remained silent and let Jette continue.

"Marc." Jette waited until he refocused his glare at her. "The point is this game *is* reality to the Empress. That's been the reason for all of her actions up to now. I, for one, am grateful that she seems to play by a set of rules that governs her decisions. Marc, we're very lucky that she wanted to turn me rather than just remove a life from my arsenal. Her players could have killed me right in our kitchen."

Marc froze on the thought, then thawed in the heat of his anger. "Okay, Jette. It's a game. This whole thing is a fucking game. I, the Dark Knight of all that's holy in hell, declare war on the freaky Blue Empress. There's been a fucking overthrow and I've taken over the fucking world. I'm now the Dark King and you're out. I've put you into the tower."

"No. That's the one thing you can't do. First of all, you can't declare anything. Only I can. It's her rules we need to abide by, not yours. Secondly, and probably most importantly, if she can't find me, if she loses track of me, I think she'll do something horrible to draw me out. We were lucky at the university, but how many other Roger Flowers' does she have lined up? I want her to know where I am. That I'm back in the game. I want her focused on me."

"But how do you know any of this for sure, Avenger?" He leaned over Jette, his hands resting on the table behind her. "Are you a fucking mind reader, too?"

"No, I believe that's the Empress's strength." Jette replied in a voice of velvet-coated steel the team was beginning to recognize and admire. "In reality, we know she doesn't literally read minds, but she has access to them. People's dreams, desires, inner thoughts through the emails she receives from everyone in her network. She uses those inner thoughts to get what she wants. When she gets it, she awards Boons. It's a very powerful form of behavioral control."

"Well, lucky her," Marc snapped sarcastically. "So if I email this insane bitch, she'll give me what I want? That would be a hell of an improvement over what's going on in this room!"

"It's a thought," shrugged Jette calmly. "But since there are probably 5,000 Empresses in play, I think my way will be more direct."

Marc straightened and continued pacing. He felt she was right, knew she was right, but it didn't stop the rush of dread. He looked around for something he could break. Something he could throw. The frustration and rage inside him were building and waves of his foul mood were flooding the room. He stared at the chairs, then looked at the fragile plates lining the wall. Everyone could read his mind and they didn't need the Empress' power.

"No, Marc. Don't even think about it," warned Jette.

He drew his gaze away from a large bowl sitting on a beautiful credenza. "Is every fucking thing in here over a fucking century old?"

"I'm not." Tagg stood up. "And I agree with Jette. How about throwing me?"

Tagg didn't anticipate the hit. It had been a tongue-in-cheek challenge, but it was his cheek that took the punishment. When Marc's fist slammed into him, he staggered back and would have fallen had Eunice not grabbed him and given him balance.

Really pissed at what she saw as a sucker punch, she spun around at Marc and went in low, throwing her strong muscular arms around him and keeping him from pounding another shot into Tagg.

It barely slowed Marc down, however, as he swung her roughly around his body and gave her a mighty shove, sending her sailing through the air and ramming into a card table filled with files. Papers sailed in all directions. The beast inside Marc liked the sight and sound of the chaos, fed on the rage. He kicked the board over too, then turned to face Tagg, who'd shaken off the powerful punch and was ready to rumble.

Jette calmly, confidently stepped in front of Marc as he went for his former partner. Heat was shooting through his veins, his devil clearly in control now. Just as it looked like he was going to push her, she placed her hand on his chest. And braced herself. She needn't have bothered to prepare for a physical response, however. Her hand on him turned him into a statue. A tense, angry, shaking, resentful statue poised to leap back into the fight, but he did stop.

"Everyone! Get the fuck out of here. Now!" shouted Marc, his chest heaving, his fists clenched at his sides, staring into the serene face of his lover. Right now his adversary.

"Jette?" asked Eunice. After all it was her job to protect the woman. Even from the man who hired her. Truth be told her own blood was up. Her hip was going to have an impressive bruise on it and she wouldn't have minded taking a shot at Marc to even things up. She respected a ripe and boiling temper, and Marc's was first-rate, but so was hers and it was getting an outing right now. "Give me the word, Jette, and I'll remove this maniac from the room."

Marc turned his searing green eyes on her.

"Try it," he growled. "Go ahead. All of you. Try it. I'm in the mood for a brawl."

Jette's voice cut smoothly through the heavy tension. It was low and soft and sure.

"Thank you, Eunice. I appreciate your dedication to my safety. I have no doubt you could take down an entire gang of Sentinels and the Empress herself. But if you all would excuse us for a moment, I think Marc and I have some fighting to do."

Eunice nodded. "We'll be right outside the door. And boy," she returned Marc's glare with a potent one of her own, "she asks for our help and you're down. You aren't above the rules of law. Or civilized behavior, for that matter. You touch her and so help me I'll have you arrested."

That did it. Something else snapped inside him. The thought that anyone, particularly the people he trusted and admired the most, would think even for a moment that he'd lay a hand on Jette so appalled him, his temper immediately turned back from full boil to simmer.

Eunice saw his reaction and nodded. Satisfied, she led the rest of them out, leaving the Phoenix and her Shield to come to an agreement.

When he heard the door click, Marc stepped back from Jette, turned and angrily strode to the window. It was another beautiful summer day. The blue sky taunted him, the sights of New York in full bloom mocked him. The world was moving in a reality that had nothing to do with the darkness inside him or the danger surrounding the only thing in his life that really mattered.

"Can a man love a woman too much?" he asked finally, knowing she was patiently waiting for him to say something. She wouldn't shout or rant or criticize. He was seething with dark clouds of pain and anger and she'd absorb it into her soul.

"No." Her answer was simple but her visceral reaction to his question was far from it. It hadn't been what she'd expected, and her love for him, always potent, surged.

"I think you're wrong, Doctor. I'm almost sure that what I feel for you is," Marc took a deep breath, "unprecedented."

That made Jette smile. It was just so…so Marc. Strong positive emotions were pretty foreign to him and difficult for him to assimilate. Particularly his love for her. He was far more comfortable with rage and frustration and disappointment and hatred.

Walking around in front of him, she put her arms around his waist. Laying her head on his shoulder, she breathed him in. Gradually reducing her heartbeat, she used her connection to him to draw out his anger and bring his own heartbeat down.

Slowly he brought up his arms and gently, tenderly hugged her. Kissing the top of her head, he opened up his soul and felt her quietude flood in.

"I'm still so fucking furious with you. With them. With fate. What the hell have you ever done but been, I don't know, amazing. And hell opens up and shakes your world." He held her away from him, looked down at her, seething, but controlled. "And a part of me includes myself in that hell. And that's what makes me even crazier than I was before I met you."

She waited a moment, giving thought to what she wanted to say. She could have just kissed him into a softer stance on the world but she couldn't separate the doctor from the woman and he needed help.

"Darling, your love for me, while adding risk to your life and depth to your potential for frustration and anger, opens up another level of passion. You may be crazier, I'd have to test you in order to treat you, but I know for a fact you'll be a better man because of it. I love you Marc…"

"But you're a loving person, Jette," he interrupted. "I'm not. I'm a hating person."

"As a therapist, I'd have to disagree with your label. You're a man who hates, that's true, but darling, I've seen you interact with friends, colleagues, people you know all over this city. Your affection for them isn't the same as what you feel for me, it's not supposed to be. I'm your mate, the woman in your life who draws out your unbelievable capacity for a deeper, more intimate love. And that love, your passion, and mine for you can't be hell. It's the closest thing to heaven we can experience on this earth."

Marc stared. Frowned. Thought about what she said. Frowned some more. He really did need therapy but had avoided it his whole life. He'd always been afraid of what he'd find under all the shit in his questionable character. Now he was living with a therapist. One of the best. Fate had a perverse sense of humor, that was for sure.

Jette remained silent. She'd never be able talk him into a state of ease with his love for her. That took self discovery and with her as his guide, he'd get there on his own someday. Hopefully, in her lifetime.

Her calming bond was taking care of his exploding temper and tension was leaving his body. Finally, he thought he'd be able to go back to work.

"I suppose I have to apologize to Tagg." Marc sighed. "Even though he asked for the punch," he added sullenly, not ready to completely concede responsibility.

"Yes."

"And Eunice?"

"Yes."

"That's going to hurt. Can't I just ask them to punch me back? You know, like a free kick in a soccer game?"

"No."

"Hmm. Maybe if we stay here like this for awhile, they'll go away."

"Darling, I can hear them pacing around in the hallway."

"What about the delinquent? Do I have to make nice?"

"No, not necessarily. You don't even phase her. Actually, your temper seems to feed her."

"Well then, she'll never starve."

"Plus she adores you."

He snorted at that one.

"Something I can identify with completely." Jette gave Marc's gorgeous mouth a peck. "There, I hear her chair out with the others."

"I'll get them back in here. But before I do, I need to ask you one more time. Will you leave the city? You can go anywhere in the world. I can rent a jet and it can take you to a secluded safe-house in the Canadian Rockies. Will you do this for me?"

"First of all, that last condition was an unfair use of my love for you. Putting it into the request is emotional blackmail."

"Dr. Morningstar, you really are a fucking pain in the ass. Fire the damn doctor, will you, and just let me work with the woman."

"If you fire the cop and just let me work with the man."

"I can't."

"That makes two of us. I'm not leaving and I'm counting on the cop to stand with me to keep me safe."

"Will you follow my direction on all the details?"

"Of course."

"Will you let me stand in front of you?"

"You've done that before." She gently touched the scar on his side.

"I know. It hurt like hell, but it made you so indebted, you moved in with me. I scored big and all it cost was about two pints of blood."

Finally he smiled, then thawed a little more and kissed her inviting mouth.

"I love you, Marc. Let's get back to work on this case. Are you ready?"

"I think so."

Jette let everyone back in the room. Kim went immediately to the mess on the floor and began reorganizing.

Marc's 'you doing okay?' to Tagg and Eunice served as an apology when they both nodded and began rearranging the board assignments. Kelly beamed at him when he tossed her a can of her favorite soda. Jette put her own healing touch to Tagg's swollen cheek and they began to plan, laying out schedules as if nothing had happened.

Marc lost it a few more times, but it never came to blows again and finally they had a plan of action meant to take down the Empress. The Phoenix was rising and with an army.

# Chapter Seven

Evie Columbus was so freaking excited. To be called by the woman herself. It was the most sought-after interview of the day. Of the year! Maybe ever! Bigger than any Hollywood celebrity or political figure, that was for sure. Bigger than the President or the Pope or the latest pop star.

She decided to spring for a cab rather than take the subway. What the hey. She'd be able to sell this interview for thousands. Maybe hundreds of thousands. Score one for higher limits on her credit cards! And then there was the professor's connections. Maybe she'd share her agent. What a life!

When she pulled up to The Edgewood, she could only stare. She had no idea that Dr. Morningstar was so well set up. She'd have to get that into the bio-documentary she wanted to do on her. Glancing over at the press being held at bay on the other side of the street, she grinned. She'd have waved, but that wasn't the kind of image she wanted to project. Getting out of the car, she walked purposefully toward the door Jonathan held open, much like she'd seen Heather Fox do it.

Jonathon passed her on to Rachael, who checked her credentials, searched her purse, then escorted her up to the penthouse.

Hilda greeted her formally and announced her to Jette. Evie just couldn't help it. She stared at everything like a slack-jawed tourist. When she was led into the formal parlor, her brain nearly drained from the sensory overload. The place was like a freaking palace. She sure hoped Dr. Morningstar would let her film in this room. It would be a perfect backdrop.

"Hello, Evie," Jette said pleasantly, leading the young woman to a grouping of chairs near the magnificent marble fireplace.

"Dr. Morningstar." Evie was breathless with the effort of trying to keep her composure. This place was exactly what she wanted for herself someday. Her daydreams now had a clearer focus. Shaking herself back to the job at hand, she sat on the edge of a chair as Jette took hers and tried to look like a concerned and competent reporter.

"You look wonderful, Dr. Morningstar."

"Thank you."

"Do you mind if we tape this?" She reached for the small recording device in her pocket.

"Not at all. But before we go formal, I want to talk with you."

"Sure." Evie inwardly gave herself a high five. The doctor didn't say those insidious words 'off the record'. Everything that was said could be paraphrased later.

"Tell me, Evie. What's your heart's desire? What do you want from this life?"

A little surprised by the question, but game, she gave an honest and immediate answer.

"I want to be famous and I want that fame to be based on my work as an on-air reporter. I want to be rich, although one will follow the other, I suppose."

"It appears as though you're well on your way to that dream. Tell me, how does it feel?"

Evie leaned forward.

"Great. Really great."

When Jette continued to look at her without comment, she found herself elaborating. Honestly and without prevarication. It was how Dr. Morningstar was looking at her. Encouraging her.

"Well, maybe not so great. I guess I expected a little more. It seems you have to sustain the pace of spectacular stories to get any attention. To get any respect. Frankly this interview will help."

"Do you feel you're qualified to sustain that pace?"

"Yes. I do. I'm as good as the women I see in front of the cameras every day, better than most. I only needed a break to prove myself."

"You certainly were in the right place at the right time that day in my classroom. Is that the break you were waiting for?"

"Are you kidding? It was a dream come true!"

"What about the students who were shot? The children who could have been killed?"

"Hey, there was nothing I could do about any of that. Reporters don't make the news, we only observe and provide the lens for the world."

Evie's eyes were shining with the fervor of a fanatic. It was a well-structured, well-rehearsed answer, Jette thought.

"Do you share your dream with others, Evie?"

"All the time. Ever since I was a kid. A lot, and I mean a lot, of my friends and family were skeptical, but this last week they've been eating their hearts out, that's for sure."

"It must feel wonderful," Jette prompted.

"Oh yeah. Over the top. I want more, though. I want it all."

Evie was loving this conversation. She realized it was all about her and eventually she needed to get Jette's story, but it felt so unreal. Sitting in the kind of apartment she'd have one day, chatting with the woman of the hour, describing comfortably all that had been happening. She wondered where Jette got that really fabulous suit. The cut and color were beyond gorgeous and she'd need to be upgrading her own wardrobe soon. She was about to ask when Jette posed another question.

"As a journalism student, why were you so eager to get into my class?" Jette's tone and manner were still conversational.

"Don't be modest, Dr. Morningstar. Headlines follow you like pelicans on a shrimp boat." Evie hoped she'd remember that one. It would be a clever color comment that she could interject spontaneously. After she practiced it about a thousand times.

"And you wanted to write some of those headlines, I suppose?"

"Wanted to and did! A lot of stations are still using my report and the Internet is full of sites that have the whole video. It's number one on NewsNation."

"You're a star."

"I am, yes." It was about time someone recognized that. This was really going well. Maybe she could talk Dr. Morningstar into a series or something.

"The Empress chose well. You're clearly someone who's easily manipulated by her desires."

"What? What did you say?" Evie was utterly shocked, dead in the water, completely without any wind in her sails. She could hear her heartbeat in her ears, and the world around Jette's face faded.

"And what if the students had died, Evie? What if Roger Flowers hadn't been stopped? There were busloads of children in his sights."

Jette's gaze was direct, but Evie now noticed the steel behind the softer demeanor.

Evie felt her dream dissolve as a pulse of pure, electric shock hit her system. What now? This was completely unexpected. Could she bluff through this or should she move to her contingency plan? Sweat began to trickle down her spine.

"I...I don't know what you're talking about," she stammered, her polished prose completely deserting her.

"Yes you do. Your face and demeanor are well practiced and nicely controlled, but your heartbeat has accelerated and you're beginning to sweat. Bodies betray thoughts and are more transparent than we would like them to be." Jette's tone was still calm but compelling with a hint of command. "Tell me about it, Evie. Tell me how you compromised your soul."

Her soul? Now that was over the top. She'd just made a little deal. Okay then, time to try and make another one. Hoping to keep her well-trained voice from losing its strength, she cleared her throat, tilted her head, and pushed.

"What the hell." She thought a nonchalant shrug would be both sophisticated and project a lack of real concern. "Busted. Big deal. Instead of fighting to stay in the news game, I'll switch tactics. It's what us gamers are really good at."

"Your ability to improvise would be admirable if your ultimate goal wasn't so despicable," replied Jette.

"Oh, please. Take the train to the real world, professor."

"Is gaming the real world for you, Evie? Is it what you substituted for living your life?"

"I do just fine in both."

"No. I think you need to define the differences. Your willingness to put real lives in jeopardy to fulfill the fantasy could be a symptom of a deep problem. Or maybe it's just a result of a truly damaged sense of ethical judgment."

"Oh I know the difference, Doctor. I use one to help me fulfill what I need in the other."

"Then you need a better moral compass."

"No thanks. I like my direction just fine. And I really don't care what you think of me. I hope you release a statement condemning me. Make it big and splashy and public. That will put me right in the middle of all the hype. In the center of the action. Me. Evie Columbus. With a firsthand account, no less." Evie got up, her breathing accelerated, her fists clenched in desperate determination. "If I can't report the news, I'll be the news. I'll sign a huge book deal. Huge! The public will eat it up. All about me being on the inside. Right from the beginning. I've got all my notes, the emails. There's a publisher out there who'll give me millions for the rights to my account of the case of the Blue Empress."

Marc walked in with Kim and Tagg. It startled Evie, but didn't stop her.

"Want to share the name of your agent, Dr. Morningstar? You're not the only one with a story to tell, you know."

"Don't forget the 'Son of Sam' laws originated in this state," observed Kim.

"The Supreme Court reversed that law in 1991," snapped Evie. "I'm protected."

"And it was rewritten in 2001. Go ahead and sell your story. Write a fucking best seller. Make a million. The victims of this crime will be needing some extra funds to deal with the trauma," snapped Marc.

"What victims?" asked Evie, still trying to calculate the angles. The odds. The best way to play it.

"The nine students to start with."

"I'm not liable. I didn't shoot them."

"You didn't stop it either," reminded Jette. "So you do share some of the responsibility."

"All I was supposed to do was record what I saw. To get your actions and reactions."

"And Hester?"

"Who?"

"The nurse in class."

"I don't know who you're talking about."

"She's another Minion. And she's in a coma."

"What?"

"The Empress ordered her execution. She's lucky to be alive."

Evie's color drained, but she wrapped herself in a protective cocoon of denial.

"Fine," said Evie, pacing mentally. "I'll have to put the book deal on hold. It doesn't diminish the value of my firsthand account. I'll still get millions. And interviews. And screen time. I'll weep and talk of my possession by the Empress. Better yet, my addiction. I'm a gamer, after all. There are always ways to win. And I know how to win."

Evie stared into the fireplace. A new angle occurred to her and she liked it. Turning, she looked at Jette and calmed. "Let's see how this works, shall we? You fully participated in Sovereignty and it got out of hand. I was as much your Guardian as I was her Minion. You loved being Avenger. You knew all about the attack on the school and staged the whole thing with Flowers. It's not true, but so what? The tabloid junkies don't care about that. There are legions of people who'll believe you're a sleazy attention-grabbing, publicity-seeking bitch. They want to believe you're not as perfect as you seem. Stupid, ignorant people will eat it up and love it."

Jette did nothing. Said nothing.

Evie was clearly warming up to the idea. "And a druggie, too. You insisted on heroin as your Boon. You weren't kidnapped, it was a drug deal gone bad. And you disappeared for a week. Was it for rehab? I took a journalism class on how to prevent smearing and slanting and spinning, but if you look at it differently, it was like a how-to manual on getting it done."

"And what will happen to you, Evie? What will happen to your own sense of right? Your integrity? Your heart? How can you survive the lying and its result?" Jette gave Evie one last chance to grab the line she offered. "If you sit down, I'll get you help. Do it now because I won't offer my compassion again."

"Oh, screw you. You think you're all that! Well you're not. You're just this week's favorite flavor. I'll take the facts and add layers of my own interpretation. You can't stop me. I'll say that everything the cops are doing is one big cover-up to protect one of their own. I can spin this and make a fortune. I mean you even live with a former gang leader, for God's sake! Someone rumored to be out of control most of the time." Her eyes narrowed, then focused on Marc. She needed one more thing to make her plan really work. To give it weight and the headlines she needed.

"It's time to arrest me, Detective, then watch me fly. I really believe that crime does pay, you see. It's not a bad back-up plan all in all."

Marc stared at the young woman, glanced over at Jette and with her slight nod, gave Evie a knowing, vicious smile. "No, I don't think I will."

"What?" screeched Evie, absolutely shocked. Then appalled. Then panicked. Holding out her wrists, she set her demand. Her next move. The necessary step in her contingency plan. She had to be formally tied into this whole affair or no one would take a meeting. "You have to arrest me. I broke the law!"

Marc calmly reached down and turned off the recorder Jette had placed on the table behind a huge bouquet of fresh flowers.

"I think I'll cut you loose and send you out there to try to find anyone who'll believe you. You've had your fifteen minutes of fame and without anything else to back it up, that's all you'll have. And since it's already been fourteen minutes and fifty-seven seconds, you're done. Enjoy your obscurity. You're pathetic."

"No. No. I confess. I knew everything." Evie was really panicking now. In order for her back-up plan to work, she needed credibility. And the only thing that would support her claims would be an arrest and a wonderful public trial. And a wardrobe of simple dark dresses. She'd cut her hair. In her revised dream, her contingency plan, there was a public defender and a long stint on the witness stand. Then she'd go to jail for a little while and come out fit and famous. Like Martha Stewart, only younger. She was prepared for that, but not for obscurity.

"And email your Empress that soon she'll be as finished as you," added Kim.

"I can't. I can't. She's changed email addresses again. I've been trying to communicate with her since the day of the shooting. Everything comes back undeliverable. Okay, wait. Wait. I'll help you. I'll help with the investigation. I'll tell you everything I know and give you copies of all the emails."

"Kim, take this freak home and get what she has. I want everything," said Marc.

"Okay. Good. That's good." Evie's mind was spinning, trying to calculate the possibilities.

"Evie. You're too easily seduced by your whims. You need help in developing better judgment," suggested Jette.

Evie grabbed on to the thought. Another angle. A good one. Being close to Dr. Morningstar in any capacity would afford her some celebrity. And if the doctor treated her wouldn't she be under some kind of obligation not to reveal any of the stuff she'd just spewed.

"You're right. Okay. I see that now. I need your help. Will you take me as a patient?"

"No. That I can't do. I'd have trouble remaining completely objective." Jette walked over to a small table near the door and took out a pen and paper from its drawer. "This is the name of the person who works with students at the university's mental health center."

Evie reluctantly took the paper, but saw the closed look on Jette's face. Seeing the name of a person written in the doctor's own hand gave her another idea. She could sell this on e-bay. Write up a little story about the trauma and how Jette Morningstar herself recommended this therapist. She carefully put it in her backpack.

"I'll call her." Evie fully intended to do just that. Maybe she could get a book deal on how to move through a traumatic event.

When Tagg and Kim left with her, Marc rounded on Jette.

"Do you have to try and save everyone?" snapped Marc, obviously trying to keep a lid on his frustration.

"Yes, I do." Jette smiled up at him. "And aren't you the lucky one."

"Don't you think there are some people who aren't worth it?"

"No."

"Not even this Blue Empress?"

"No."

"Well, I want to fry her, what does that make me?"

"A work in progress."

"I'll be in the exercise room. I need to pound on something."

"I think that's best. Did you get your heavy bag hung back up?"

"Tagg did it."

"Good man."

# Chapter Eight

The cameras were ready and Heather Fox, the most well known of all the investigative television reporters in the city, was in her chair in the corner of the West Parlor being fluffed and buffed. Even though she'd been around a long time, she wasn't inclined to look it.

She'd been briefed and appreciated not only the exclusive interview, which would be a real ratings grabber, but being a part of something bigger. Everything she'd been told off the record she'd honor. It was her reputation for integrity that got her the interview in the first place.

Jette sat across from her, gorgeous and composed. Damn her, Heather thought with amusement. The Native American beauty was sitting confidently in the bright unforgiving lights with very little makeup, her complexion flawless, her dark eyes bright. Why the woman shied away from all media was beyond Heather's comprehension. She was a natural in front of the camera.

In a taped version to be run as a special later in the evening, her producer was planning to combine this interview with shots of Jette running and jumping and taking down a gunman. It was such a contrast to the composed, elegant woman sitting in front of her that it was going to be the very best visual display of contemporary news television had to offer. It made everything she did, worked for, and believed in important. She wondered if Jette needed a new best friend.

"Now everyone just relax. We go on live in five," she said.

"We'd like the woman who was behind the conspiracy to know as soon as possible that I'm alive, well, and ready to be seen," said Jette.

"We've been doing promos since you called us. I can guarantee you'd have to be in a coma not to know about this interview. All the networks have been given a heads up and permission to use excerpts has already been issued." She turned to Marc. "Marc, it wouldn't hurt if you smiled."

When Marc's frown deepened, she gave it up. Either way, he was exquisite, so it didn't really matter. He was wallpaper anyway. It was clear that the focus was Jette.

"And just so you know, Dr. Morningstar, we'll be on a five-second delay."

Jette glanced at Marc, knowing that meant the producer could bleep out any of his more colorful descriptors.

"Understandable," she smiled, obviously comfortable in front of a camera crew.

Jette staged every detail for maximum effect. They were there to flush out an Empress. In this context, she was Avenger. Kelly chose for her a heavy antique chair, with dark maroon leather seats, ornately carved details on the back and arms and brushed brass nail heads. On a high roughly hewn table behind her was a wrought iron candelabra with heavy hand-dipped candles. She'd even lit them and let the wax flow over the sides to give it just the right look. The aura was medieval.

Jette was dressed in a long sleeved, high necked sheath of black knit that Kelly picked out of her closet. On the shoulder was a gold phoenix pin. There was no mistaking the bird for anything else. Her thick black hair was long and loose. Kelly had critiqued her efforts with an enthusiastic thumbs up, then spun around a picture from a Sovereignty play book. Avenger was masked, but otherwise the similarity was uncanny. The book had been published by Maxine White.

Marc, his face set and grim, was dark and dangerous sitting on a matching, less elaborate chair on her right. Her Dark Knight. Luke was on her left, bright and smiling and relaxed. Her Light Knight. Behind her Tagg was standing as her High Priest, dressed in black leather, his arms folded over his chest giving him an air of both mystery and command. It was a perfect tableau. They were ready.

Heather smiled comfortably when her producer gave her the high sign. Rolling. "Good afternoon, Dr. Morningstar, it's so good to see you safe and home again, along with your wonderful team." She looked around, leading the watcher's eye through the introductions. "Surrounding Dr. Morningstar are a few of New York City's finest, Detectives Marcus Lexington and Taggert Freeman, and her brother, who flew in from Ecuador, Dr. Lucas Grainger. I imagine you won't let her out of your sight again anytime soon, Detective Lexington."

"That's right." He didn't elaborate. Heather had known him for years and hadn't expected him to. Her next question was already programmed and for Jette.

"Before we begin with the details of what happened to you, let me ask you how you're feeling after your ordeal."

"Fine, thank you. I'm at full power and more than ready for the next major challenge." Jette looked right into the camera, her brown eyes piercing the lens, her gaze clear and unguarded. Take that, Empress, she thought.

"Would you agree with that Dr. Grainger?"

Luke smiled broadly and Heather felt her market share take a little bump along with her heart. This man was a camera's dream.

"Oh, yeah. There's no way to keep her down for long. Her abductor's attempts to hold her and to harm her were heinous, but totally ineffective." His dismissive tone would burn the Empress and he knew it. "She's like the Phoenix the media is so fond of calling her. Indestructible."

"Was she like that growing up?" asked Heather, hoping she could arrange a follow up with this man.

"Now, that's the kind of question I'd better evade, Ms. Fox. 'Sister growing up' stories are filled with potential pitfalls and minefields and unlike her, I'm destructible." He nodded at Jette, his smiling eyes clearly communicating his affection. "And you've seen her in action. Terrifying."

Heather laughed, delighted. Maybe he'd be good for a whole series. "Since I'm not her big brother, I'd say formidable rather than terrifying."

"Whatever word you use," Luke himself looked into the camera. "Don't mess with her. All you'll do is lose points."

"I'll remember that," Heather said, although no one in the audience would mistake his challenge for anything else but a direct message to the woman behind the abduction. She turned her attention back to Jette. "I have so many questions for you Dr. Morningstar, but let me start with the one most people will want to know. Can you tell us if the attack on the university, the shooting of Roger Flowers, and your abduction were related?"

"Oh, quite clearly. Because there's an ongoing investigation, I can't tell you much, but Roger Flowers was part of a larger conspiracy."

"And you got right in the middle of it?"

"Yes."

"And do you know who's behind it?"

"We do."

"Willing to share?"

"Not at this time."

"Do you have a suspect in custody?"

"Not yet, but because her behavior is so predictable and her moves so unimaginative, it won't be long. Her ego has her believing she's in charge, that she is, shall we say, the avatar in control. That kind of ego is blinded by power and self aggrandizement. She made incredibly bad decisions without seeing the consequences of her actions, her moves, or her so-called strategy."

Jette emphasized the words she knew would bait the Empress. In the woman's delusional state, she'd clearly hear what others in the audience would assume was casual conversation or a clinical diagnosis.

"Can you tell us who this woman is?"

"Not at this time. Her identity is being closely held. Not that she can hide for long. The team assembled here is on her trail."

Heather thought she'd give Marc another shot.

"What can you tell us about the investigation, Detective?"

Although he felt more like ripping the microphone off his lapel and wrapping the cord around the reporter's exposed neck, he looked into the camera.

"Nothing."

"Have there been any arrests?"

"Several."

"What are the charges?"

"Conspiracy."

"Conspiracy to what?"

"Murder."

Alright, Heather thought, sighing inwardly. Jette Morningstar was the focal point anyway.

"Dr. Morningstar, did you meet the mastermind behind this conspiracy during your captivity?"

"I did, yes. I was blindfolded during our brief conversations, but I saw her clearly."

"You mean you profiled her?"

"Exactly."

"Can you tell us what you think?"

"I can tell you what I know. The woman behind my abduction and the university shooting fanaticizes she maintains an exalted position while hiding behind a mask. Her sense of entitlement and her false impression of grandeur won't hold up in the world of reality. The vision she holds is not based on anything solid, but on her own lofty ideas and opinions and her skewed perceptions of her place. The control she seeks through rewards is an illusion. The people she thinks she maneuvers and manipulates relate to her in a very superficial way. Very soon now she'll find herself abandoned."

"Is she crazy?"

"Oh no.

"Is that your clinical opinion?"

"Yes, although I'd need to interact with her further to make a more accurate diagnosis. I intend to do that shortly."

"Confident," observed Heather.

"She hasn't a chance of winning. She hasn't had a single victory." Jette hoped her smile looked more like a dismissive smirk.

"I certainly can see that taking you on was her downfall." Heather suspected that comment would help whatever they were planning to do. When she saw Jette's tiny nod of appreciation, she knew it was right on target. "What a welcome New York City has given you. First your classroom is shot up, then you're abducted. Ever think about going back to Arizona?"

"No. I love this city. It's mine now." Kelly had instructed her to claim the City of Might as hers if given the opportunity.

"On to another topic. Although, as you have stated, a related one. I'd like to ask about your heroism at the university. Why did you go after Flowers, why not just do your job and keep your head down?"

"Instinct. Those in my care and those children on the buses were being threatened. There was no real cognitive calculation. I saw the danger, I felt the need to defend and to protect, and I acted on it. My risk was quite minimal, actually."

"Jumping a ten-foot span, running along the ledge of a six-story building, then sprinting toward an armed and dangerous killer? I think most people in the viewing audience would have been inclined to remain safely behind that door."

"Don't underestimate the human need to shield those in their care. To defend those who look to them for protection." Jette continued to take Heather through her movements.

"Fascinating. A Captain Green gave daily press reports and updates on both the university shooting and your, how do I put this delicately…"

"My suspicious abduction? My unfortunate and tragic death? The lack of any connection between the abduction and the university shooting. No concrete action by the exalted Special Projects Unit headed by the overrated Detective Lexington? The Detective's own suspicious seclusion?" Jette used Green's exact words.

"Was he ill informed or was he being deliberately obtuse to throw off your kidnappers?"

"He was never involved in my case. The Special Projects Unit and Detective Lexington were solely responsible for my rescue, have been my guardians all along, and were one step ahead of my abductor all the way. I'm not quite sure why Captain Green was meeting with the press on this topic or why anyone listened or recorded his reports. He certainly wasn't privy to any part of the investigation."

Heather smiled fiercely. Green had jumped at the chance for a personal interview with her and she could feel a satisfying ambush in his future.

"Well, it sure appears that the reports he was issuing about your death were very premature."

"One could speculate that I rose from the ashes, I suppose." Jette gently touched her pin.

"And since you're sitting here suffering no ill effects, I think the Special Projects Unit can score another astounding success."

Heather looked up at Tagg and smiled, hoping he'd be more inclined to smile back. He wasn't.

"We'll take our bow when the game is over and the dust has cleared," said Tagg in his deep, rich 'media voice.' The camera petrified him, but he imagined Carmel and Lucy watching on their TV at home and controlled the urge to bolt.

"Detective Freeman, you headed the formal investigation?"

"I did, yes," nodded Tagg.

"How did you find Dr. Morningstar so quickly?"

"We followed her trail. She was able to communicate with us."

"You were able to communicate with the team looking for you?" Heather's looked back at Jette with a wide, appreciative look.

"I was," responded Jette.

"Tell us more about that, if you can."

"I'd rather not elaborate at this point. Let's just say I left them messages that they were able to effectively translate."

"According to a few of my sources, there were teams spreading out through the city disarming improvised explosive devices planted by your abductor. Is this…"

"Bombs," interrupted Marc. This time he acted on his fury. "Jesus Christ! Improvised explosive devices, my ass! What's wrong with the word bomb? Fucking bombs planted by a goddamn maniac who's lost what's left of her fucking mind if she thinks she's in the same league as Jette. She couldn't outthink a fucking New York cockroach!"

Whoa, thought Heather. What a show. Give me a few more bleeps, Detective. Talk about an IED. This was a classic Lexington rant. She'd been a little concerned that he'd restrain himself around Jette. Marcus Lexington always made terrific television, even with all the bleeps. Maybe because of them. Apparently his lover thought containment wasn't necessary because Jette made no move to stop him. Halleluiah.

"Are you saying that she was out of her depth when up against Dr. Morningstar?"

"Out of her depth?" Marc's green eyes flashed. "That fucking freak would be out of her depth in a fucking fifth avenue pothole puddle!"

"I think we get the picture," said Heather with a broad smile.

"Then, excuse me. I'm just going to go find and arrest the fucking lunatic before she accidentally pulls off one of her idiotic moves in this fucking game she's playing. The goddamn royal bitch of fuck ups doesn't have enough juice to rule a fucking toad parade and it's my job to scrape the scum from the city's boots."

Marc stood, pulled the microphone off his lapel and slammed out of the room. Jette sat firm and smiled serenely into the camera. Far from apologizing, she turned up the steel in her own voice.

"In other words, and I'm sure you'll need them to air this, our adversary has taken no points on anything she's tried up to now. With every round, she's come closer to her own destruction. No one like her will ever acquire sovereignty. There are people in this world, my world, people like Detectives Lexington and Freeman, who will fight. Who will do what's right." Jette looked directly at the camera and Heather could honestly say she'd never seen a more effective use of the eye of the lens. It was like Jette was staring into the soul of the viewer. She not only commanded attention, she demanded that the person on the other side of the screen take notice. The challenge in her voice, the dare in the set of her posture, the complete confidence came through. "In this world, she can't win. She hasn't got the intellect. She hasn't got the power. And, because I met her and talked with her, I know she hasn't got the vision."

Heather did have a sharp intellect. Sharp enough to let the words stand for a moment before she went on.

"I hope you'll be able to elaborate when this is all over."

Jette smiled. "Perhaps."

"I'm sure your agent will want you to hold the story for your next book."

"I write to put together a body of knowledge in order to educate. I'll let you report the details of this case."

"Deal. You have my number. I understand your previous work is used in courses in both psychology and criminology. Tell us about the topic of your third book. Have you had any time at all to work on it?"

The rest of the interview was a publicist's dream come true. Chat about Jette's projects, both current and projected. About her heritage and the Cherokee people.

"Dr. Morningstar, it's been a real pleasure and I'm sure I speak for our viewers, who include many of the students whose lives you saved and their families, when I thank you for your broader service to the community. You didn't stand by and simply watch events unfold. Thank you. Sincerely."

"You're welcome," said Jette simply. "Our world thrives on the thoughtful and proactive connections we make with each other. When you feel the life of another, when you feel the bond, their pain is yours. All things in nature are connected, intertwined. If we follow our instincts, we'll move to protect. That's the only reality."

When the cameras had been folded up and the crew escorted downstairs, the apartment seemed unnaturally quiet. Like it was holding its breath. Then Kelly shot into the room, followed by Lyd and the rest of the team.

"Oh my God! Oh my God. Sweet. Sweet. Sweet! That's exactly, I mean 100%, right on target, exactly what Avenger would say! The Empress is going to stroke out. Full power? Ready for the next challenge? Predictable and unimaginative. The Empress is going to have a brain implosion. The City of Might is yours? Lost every battle? Pow. Take that. And that. And that!"

"I passed the Avenger test?" laughed Jette.

Lyd added her congratulations. "I'm not the gamer the kid is, but I've been reading up on it. I mean, look at you."

Jette noticed that Lyd's eyes were clear and there was actually a little life in the deep dark pupils. It warmed her heart when Lyd high fived Kelly.

Dina's cell phone rang.

"That was Tony Nippard," grinned Dina as she pocketed her cell phone. "The Empress didn't seem to like your interview. His bomb-a-dears report the remotes were activated right in the middle of it. But no thunder today. Take that you Blue Horndevil. And that and that and that." Dina mimicked Kelly.

Everyone started talking at once.

"We thought she'd detonate when we snatched Avenger from the Hall of Secrets," said Raj.

"That'll teach her to bring her sorry blue and broken ass into the Middle World of our reality!" snorted Eunice.

"No points for taking out the Dark Knight and a few of the Guardians. The trap had no ka-boom!" laughed Tagg.

"Now she'll know even that move was foiled. No points for you today, Blue Loser!" hooted Rachael with a little dance.

It was fascinating to Jette how the team got into the lexicon of the game. It was both a tactical advantage and a brilliant investigative strategy. Getting into the minds of the perpetrators helped them find the trail

"Where's Marc?" she asked, knowing it was time to put away Avenger and put the doctor back on call.

"He's in the gym working two phones and kicking the hell out of the heavy bag," said Tagg.

"Kicking it?" giggled Kelly.

"He knocked it clear off the chain again. It's rolling around on the floor and he seems to get some kind of charge out of seeing the stuffing fly out of it. Tommy's calling the boxing supply store now to order a replacement," laughed Tagg.

"Better get a heavier chain while you're at it," sighed Kim.

"I think I'll go make that suggestion," smiled Jette.

They all watched as Jette went to tame her beast.

As it turned out, it didn't take much. Most of Marc's temper was absorbed by the stuffing from the heavy bag scattered all over the hardwood floor of the exercise room. When he turned, he saw her standing in the doorway watching him. She looked drained. He'd wanted a nice row with her to top off his kicking and stomping frenzy, but her exhaustion popped the cork on his temper and released it into the air. He walked over and gently drew her into his arms.

"You look beat."

"Not as beat as your poor bag."

"I'm not sure why they call them Everlast."

"Darling, your voracity goes well beyond their quality control parameters. It's made for boxing, not rage reduction." She looked at his bruised hands. "Did you forget gloves again?"

"I wasn't thinking about accessories."

Jette rubbed her palms together, then took his hands and sent the healing heat through Marc's abraded knuckles. He sighed heavily, but took the relief she offered him.

Jette looked around at the piles of stuffing. "At least it wasn't an animate object."

"How about you take a nap?"

"How about you join me?"

"You need to sleep."

"No, I need my Dark Knight."

"Everyone is confident she'll come after you now."

"Then I'll step aside and you can punch the stuffing out of her."

"Deal," he sighed with resignation. "Still love me?"

"More today than yesterday."

"I think my lips need a little of that heat," he said and went in for some relief for his heart.

# Chapter Nine

The Empress watched. And burned. When her Minion sent pictures of the Dark Knight and his Guardians swarming around the Hall of Secrets, she'd called back her Sentinels as a precaution, certain they wouldn't penetrate the protection of the hidden room. But they did.

She had to keep reminding herself she was battling the true Avenger, not the inferior gamers who'd challenged her in the past. Had the birds in the air and the beasts that inhabited the alleys of the City of Might carried messages from their Avatar? The rats and bats and even the skittery bugs under the damn floorboards probably did her bidding. It was the only explanation.

Then, when the exclusive interview had been announced, she felt another, more powerful punch of disbelief. How had Avenger recovered so fast? The idiot nurse had assured her the addiction would be absolute within a few days and Avenger would be out of play for weeks after she'd forfeited the life.

Based on this, she'd declared a conquest for Time Out of Play when she knew the Dark Knight had taken Avenger back to their Home Base near Central Park. It wasn't much, but at least it was something. Now the hundreds of points would have to be removed with penalty.

Then another thought hit with the force of a stiff slap. The little conniving bitch. The nurse had been in Avenger's camp from the beginning. Perhaps being turned while still sitting in the professor's class at the university. She hadn't administered the heroin at all!

There she was looking out from the television, the true Avenger, sitting in Callisto, surrounded by her Knights and the High Priest. Unscathed.

Focusing on the device in front of her, she pressed three buttons for simultaneous detonation of her carefully laid explosives. She'd wanted to do this ever since she lost Avenger, but had successfully pulled back on her seething temper. She was proud of her ability to remain coldly calculating. She'd wait. Wait until she could lead Avenger's Guardians and Knights into the traps.

But now all bets were off! She didn't care about the death count anymore, she just wanted to blow. To cause pain.

"Death, destruction, devastation," she chanted. "Detonate, detonate, detonate. That will move you out of the spotlight when they break into your special report with my special report. Never a single victory? Ha! Take that Avenger!"

Random destruction wouldn't give her huge points, but right now she'd take what she could get. Picking up her remotes, she turned on the other TV's to the local channels. Muted them. And waited. And waited. The minutes passed. Where were the reports on the three blast sites? They should be breaking in by now. The time ticked by. Still nothing. She'd send Minions over for a firsthand look. For some reason, the media was lagging behind events.

Then the truth was revealed in the interview.

"...teams spreading out through the city disarming improvised explosive devices planted by your abductor. Is this..." asked Heather.

Even through the buzz in her brain, she heard the Dark Knight say she couldn't outthink a New York City cockroach. In a cold, nearly trancelike state, she punished herself by watching. When it was over, she replayed it from the beginning. Listening again to every word. Every painful, galling word.

Even with all the treachery, she could have accepted the events as a part of a complicated and high flying round, if it weren't for the comments by the Dark Knight and the mocking tone of the Light Knight. Their comments echoed in her mind and fanned her fury. Their confident, condescending attitudes pushed her over the edge. The slow burn became a full-fledged conflagration. She tore through the room destroying, smashing, vowing vengeance to the empty room.

According to the rules of play, when she destroyed Avenger, any Knights and Guardians her stepsister used in the battle were hers to command. Her victory would give her sovereignty over them. She'd originally planned on making the survivors of the Final Duel minor Minions, adding humiliation to their defeat, but not now. She'd sacrifice them, annihilate every being and beast who'd aligned themselves with Avenger. There would be no amnesty. No acceptance ritual for turned Guardians. No pardons for Callisto's beasts who wanted to join the Empress. And most particularly, no place in the empire for the Knights. No matter what. Just complete and utter destruction. It would break new ground, but that was her destiny anyway.

Finally calming to a point where she could think, she sat in the rubble and got back in the game. She was the best. There was only one outcome. She'd be the victor in the end. Now, how to get there. How to get there.

She sat staring at her devastated game board. It was her move and she needed it to be bold. Something unpredictable. Something to strike at the heart of Avenger. Hate throbbed and boiled in her. She needed to make the move soon or she'd burn up from the inside.

As she breathed in and out, finally able to calm herself, a spark of inspiration penetrated the fog of her anger. A smile replaced the pained look. She had it! Something Avenger would certainly fight for. And that would mean another run at one of her precious lives.

Pouring over her notes and folders, she checked to be sure. Yes, this would draw out Avenger. Place her firmly into a hot trap. The play that had been there all along. Buried. This was good. No, grand! Brilliant! Cockroach indeed. Nothing was more difficult to kill, to eradicate, and to catch as a New York cockroach. Texting her messages furiously, she put into motion a contingency plan. But with a twist.

# Chapter Ten

Marc came awake when Jette slid out of bed. She'd been restless in the night. The craving for the drug was still buzzing through her, he knew, agitating her system. He debated leaving her alone. She had ways of dealing with everything, mental, physical, emotional. Ceremonies, rituals, customs. He watched her as she put on a robe and walked out of the room.

Should he intrude? He looked over at the clock. 4:37. It was early, but she was an early riser. Maybe she was going for a cup of tea. Did she need him? Hell, she could tell him to bug off if she wanted solitude. She'd done it before.

He got up, pulled on the sweatpants he'd discarded the night before and found her standing in the library, looking out the window onto Central Park. The lush summer green of the trees faded to black and blue in the harsh lights of the city. It was the closest thing to her beloved natural surroundings she had here.

In Arizona, she'd walk only a few yards to lose to herself in what she called the Mother Earth and the Father Sky. She had a special place there where she went when she needed to retreat, reflect, and refuel. Did she feel uprooted? Did she miss the open spaces and stunning sunrises that seemed to energize her?

"I love this view," she said softly, knowing he was there.

"Do you want to be alone?"

"No. I was just feeling…edgy."

Marc walked over to where she was standing. "I don't ever remember looking out this window before."

She looked up at him. "You need me to be your guide in all things. Stop. Look. Appreciate."

"Alright."

He slid his arm around her narrow waist and brought her up against him. She felt thinner to him and he didn't like it.

"I'll gain it back, darling. Perhaps by this afternoon. Hilda's been preparing all my favorites and I have enough chocolate to open my own candy store."

"Tommy was a little distraught while you were gone. And she heard that chocolate could soothe the cravings."

"Exchanging one addiction for another?"

"Something like that."

"I didn't like it Marc."

"Didn't like what?"

"I didn't like being under the influence of the drugs. I know some people think the rush, the high is exhilarating. It gives them a sense of freedom. I found it to be a trap. The lightness and lack of focus seemed so deceptive. Intoxicating, but truly ugly underneath." She turned and Marc could see the reflection of tears in her eyes. "And yet, there are parts of my body that even now are craving the drug. Marc, can I talk to you about your mother for a moment?"

"Whoa. Where did that come from?"

"I've been thinking about her…"

"Well stop it."

"Please, you have such hatred for her."

"That's my privilege. Back off, Doctor."

"It's such a fearful weight, Marc."

"Then it's mine to carry."

"It feeds the anger that burns through your soul." When he didn't respond, she went on. "I know she was lacking."

"Lacking? She was a fucking abomination." Some of the anger she knew was always there beneath the surface bubbled up. Making her point, she thought.

"Darling, please. You have to forgive her. Carrying resentment like that is unhealthy."

"Look Dr. Morningstar, I said I want you to back off. My resentment is justifiable. She starved me, neglected me, sold me for a goddamn fix. She never called me by a name, only boy. Hey boy, see if you can score some coin. Hey boy, give me your blanket, I'm cold. She never told me she loved me, never showed me she cared." It seemed to Jette that this was what bothered him the most. "I think some people are born without parental instincts."

"Is that why you always go so still when I talk about children?"

Marc sighed. "Please, Jette. Don't make me jittery. You'll turn me off of sex."

"We wouldn't want that to happen." Jette gave him a little nudge and a smile. "Anyway, we were talking about your mother."

"The woman who gave birth to me."

"Okay, if you prefer to think of her that way."

"I prefer not to think of her at all."

"But until you look at it, deal with it, talk about it…"

"Cut it out."

"Cut what out?"

"That therapist thing. Putting your hands into my brain, my gut."

"Marc. Do you think I'm a strong woman?"

"The strongest I've ever known."

"Darling, I'm telling you it's taking all of my strength to fight the force within me that wants more of the drug."

"There's still some inside you. You aren't completely straight, yet. It'll take awhile to get totally clean."

"I understand that, but do you realize your mother, once hooked, was in a constant state of this…this overwhelming need?"

"I don't want to hear it. I don't want you to put yourself in the same species as my mother."

"I understand that, too. I just want you to think about it."

"No."

She hugged herself as he rubbed her arms. "This whole incident has made me see things, feel things I had no way of experiencing before. Your mother's maternal instincts must have been overwhelmed by her addiction. What she did to her son, her baby, you, was ghastly. I just don't want you to assume she never had those feelings. At some point, darling I think you should try to mitigate the bitterness, the hate you feel, with some compassion. Try to understand."

"No."

Jette shook her head. "I actually think your single-minded stubbornness may have been the sole reason you survived the neglect. But I'm warning you, my love. I'm relentless."

"And you smell good, too." Marc sniffed her neck.

"Are you trying to distract me?"

"Oh, yeah. I want the doctor to take a break and I figure if I pull out the woman, she'll fade out of here and leave my neuroses alone."

Just as he was going in for a kiss to lay another trap for his woman, she shuddered in his arms. He stopped, pulled her back, and looked into her eyes. "Was that desire, or are you hurting?" Concern etched a frown on his face.

"Make love to me, Marc," Jette whispered pulling him to her. "I need you. I need you to help me fight this. Love me. Take me away from this awful ache inside me."

"Jette." He laid his lips on hers, putting himself between her and the hideous painful pull of the drug.

Their lovemaking was not a gentle skirmish but a fierce battle. Marc's mouth worked its magic, his skillful hands transporting her to a safe place. Fueled by both love and lust, they rolled over the carpet sharing their time on the top, staying connected, each thrilling thrust taking them to the final intense explosion of complete release.

Later, sated and satisfied, Jette lay on top of him as he studied the ceiling.

"I've never seen this view, either." He stroked Jette's cooling back. "I think I like having you as my guide in all things."

"Mmm. My pleasure."

"So, how do I explain the rug burns?"

"Who's going to see them?" she asked, raising her smiling eyes to his.

"Good point."

"Let's go back to bed."

"I'm not sure I can walk."

"Hilda will be up soon. Do you really want her to find us naked on the Persian rug?"

"Whoa, that forced some fiber back into my bones." Marc moaned as he slowly sat up. "I'm all for the bed, but how do we get there?"

"You aren't going to carry me, caveman?"

"Damn. I was going to ask you to carry me."

# Chapter Eleven

Marc smiled a little looking in at the Persian rug and feeling the slight burn of a few places on his body that had been rubbed raw the night before. He was enjoying his second cup of coffee waiting for Jette to shower and get ready for the day. Hilda was doing her thing on the Revere coffee table with a white cloth and some secret cleaning solution. It was so domestic, so normal, that Marc took a moment to let the ordinary in to chase the disquiet from his day. When she looked over at him, he knew he had to deal with all the reasons things weren't normal after all.

"Hilda, I want you out. Go visit your sister in Crystal River for a few weeks. Put all of your expenses on the household charge account."

"I'm not leaving." Hilda moved on to the tables lining the wall.

"As long as you work for me, you'll do as I say." Was there anyone in the entire world who would do what he asked without a fight?

"I will not leave here," Hilda replied firmly.

"Alright then, you're fired!"

Hilda stared into his furious eyes and proceeded calmly. "Under the explicit stipulations of the Clarke's will, if you release me from service, I have three months to find other accommodations. I will stay in my quarters on the premises until the end of that three months."

"Jesus Christ, Hilda," Marc shouted as he paced. He was ready to tear out his hair. "What the fuck are you going to do if these armed Sentinels or whatever the fuck these people think they are, come here? Go after them with your goddamn vacuum cleaner?"

"I could try that approach, but I think this will be a bit more effective." She pulled a Beretta 92 out of the deep pocket of her apron.

"Where the hell did you get that?" he exploded when a quick glance determined it wasn't one of his.

"It was Mr. Clarke's gun. And don't think I can't use it, young man. Anyone coming in to harm Dr. Morningstar will have to get through nine shots. I won't be locked in a bathroom again!"

Marc looked down at the gun, his anger trumped by his amazement. She appeared to know how to hold it at least. She was confidently and competently gripping it in her right hand.

"Do you have a permit to carry a concealed weapon?" he asked.

"No, but if I'm arrested, I have a few contacts in the New York Police Department."

"I'm not going to bail you out."

"Goes without saying, but Detective Freeman will probably serve and protect my right to bear arms for the promise of a few chocolate chip cookies and a pecan pie."

"Tagg's too fucking easy."

They stared each other down. When Marc suddenly went for her, she dodged, moved quickly behind chair and raised the gun to eye level.

He was impressed. She was angry and determined.

"Did I pass, Detective?"

"You'll hold. And don't be afraid to use all nine shots."

"They won't get her again," declared Hilda, then surprised them both when her eyes teared up. She managed to get herself under control before she shed even one tear, but it touched something inside Marc and he smiled. For just a moment, a fleeting look of fondness touched his face, then it was gone as quickly as the unshed tears.

"No, Hilda. I don't think anyone will ever take anything out of this apartment again." Stretching, he shook out his tired muscles. "See that you take it off safety if you ever get serious and don't shoot one of my original Jewels Katrenicz figurines or I'm taking it out of your paycheck."

"The pitiful pittance you call a paycheck wouldn't even pay for the insurance on any one of the lovely pieces," she sniffed. "And since it seems I've been rehired, I'll go see to Dr. Morningstar's breakfast."

"Don't get too comfortable. As soon as I find someone who can operate that freaky, temperamental stove, you're out."

"Fair enough," she retorted, not looking worried in the least.

# Chapter Twelve

"Hi Hilda." Luke walked into the kitchen feeling great. Rested, relieved, and reinforced by the fact that Marc and his team were on top of things.

"Hello, Doctor Grainger. Would you like some breakfast?"

"No, thanks. I'm going out for awhile. No one here needs a physician and those who do won't listen to me. There's a free clinic over in Queens that needs a hand to cover for one of the doctors who just had a baby. It's time I make myself useful."

"How did they know you were in New York?" asked Hilda suspiciously, thinking the good doctor had been plenty useful the last week.

Luke laughed. "You sound like Marc. Physicians for Peace have an office here. I checked in with them this morning."

Just then Jonathon buzzed the kitchen intercom.

"Yes?"

"There's a Detective Hal Rowley here. His identification checks out. He's here to pick up a jacket he left at a party Friday last."

"Oh yes, send him up, I'll let Detective LaFrancois know he's here."

"Detective LaFrancois?" asked Luke.

"I believe they have a personal relationship. Detective Rowley was her date at a function here."

"Ah." Luke thought Rachael was quite a fox and had fleetingly considered hitting on her. But when a very large man was allowed to come into the kitchen after passing two layers of security and Hilda's intense scrutiny, Luke changed his mind. The man was supersized. Introductions were made and Hal's firm, muscular handshake put a prominent 'out of bounds' field all around Rachael.

"Hi Hal." Rachael smiled when she came into the room with a coat. "I could have brought this on Saturday."

"I was in the neighborhood finishing up an interview," he grinned. "And truth be told, I wanted a firsthand look at all the excitement here. Marc really has everything covered."

"Like a blanket," Rachael nodded proudly. She made the introductions then frowned when Luke shrugged into his jacket.

"Going somewhere?"

"Yes. I'm going out to Queens."

"Making a house call, Doctor?" asked Hal pleasantly.

"More like a clinic call."

"Which one?" asked Hal and Rachael together. They looked at each other and laughed.

"The one run by Physicians for Peace," responded Luke, glancing over at Rachael. "Why?"

"How did they know you were in New York?" she asked.

Luke glanced over at Hilda and grinned. Things were tighter here than at CIA Headquarters. "I called them."

"Okay, hold here and I'll secure you a ride. The team's in the park, but I can get a squad car here in a flash," said Rachael.

"Hey, don't bother Rachael. I have to report back to the precinct," said Hal. "The clinic is only a few blocks out of my way. How about I drive him over and make sure he's tucked in. FYI, they have the best security in the neighborhood. A top-notch private group."

Rachael looked up at her huge fellow officer, and a man she really liked. It made sense. "Let me clear it with Tagg. Hold for a minute, alright?"

Both men nodded. Luke looked over at Hal with amusement. "Do you think the mayor has this much trouble getting around?"

"Not even the President of the United States, my man. Marc runs a very, very tight squad. It's why they're the best." Hal had put in for a transfer into Marc's unit and had been turned down. He started dating Rachael soon after.

"He called them," said Rachael into the phone, obviously answering the same question she and Hilda had put to Luke. "He wants to go in and give them a hand."

She went on to explain Hal's presence, his observations about the security at the clinic, and his offer.

"Excellent. I'll have him do that." Rachael folded her phone and nodded at the two men. "It's a go. Thanks, Hal. Bring your car around to the parking lot elevator. The officers outside the door will take Luke down and load him in. Then if you'll escort him into the clinic and call in when you've made your delivery, that would be great. Tagg is going to call and check out their security, but he thinks it should be fine. He knows some of the people there."

Luke just stared at her. "First of all, I appreciate the ride, it beats going down and calling a cab, mostly because Jonathon scares me. But I've been opening my own car doors for the last, oh, almost three decades or so. And I'm quite sure I can make it from the car to the front door of the clinic."

"Do you want to face Marc and Jette if something happens to you? If you think Jonathon is scary, put that picture in your head," insisted Rachael.

"You have a point."

"A good one I think. Call us when you're ready to leave the clinic. We'll send Tommy over to get you."

"You have my complete cooperation, Detective," winked Luke, then turned to Hal. "Ready to make a delivery?"

"Give me five to bring the car around." He saluted Rachael, knowing a kiss wouldn't be appropriate on the job. "See you Saturday."

She saluted him back. "We may have to change our plans to doctor sitting detail."

"That's the life of a cop," he grinned.

A few minutes later, Luke stood with his hand over his heart to give homage to the sleek sports car. "Nice car! Cops must do pretty well in this town."

Hal laughed. "Not hardly. But this is New York, home of Wall Street investments. My brother's a stock broker and has turned my meager paycheck into, well, this."

"That's better than a fairy Godmother."

"I was thinking. I'd like to come back here to see Rachael after shift. I'll give you my cell number and you can call me when you're ready to leave the clinic. I'll clear it with Marc."

"Sounds like a plan. Thanks, Hal. So. Do you think I could drive this baby back here?"

"You're Jette's brother, a good person to volunteer at the clinic, and probably a fantastic doctor, but man, there's not a chance in hell you're going to get the left seat."

Luke laughed and slid into the passenger seat of the new red Porsche, settling in for a fine ride.

# Chapter Thirteen

"You're the cheese," Eunice said to Jette, studying the computer-generated map. It was a 3D program that had all the buildings in Manhattan illustrated in both scale and image. "You'll go where we say."

When Jette opened her mouth to protest, it was Eunice, not Marc who raised her voice.

"No arguments, Jette, or the commissioner himself will authorize protective custody and you'll be compelled by court order to stay where we stash you."

Marc flashed Eunice a quick grin. Jette wanted to remind them that they were supposed to be feuding, but she suppressed the little push of resentment and petty pique in favor of team unity. And to keep the promise she made to Marc. She'd trade her autonomy for his support.

"There will be a series of traps set," said Marc. "Here, here, and here." He indicated the three positions Jette was to place herself that day. The park, Lee's office, a small salon on 7th. All civilians in the office and salon would be replaced by officers. "Ready? We go in 30 minutes."

Precisely a half hour later, Jette left The Edgewood with Eunice and crossed to the park. Running was the first outing. It was routine, as was Eunice's presence. The twenty other officers dressed as vendors, joggers, tourists, and homeless persons were a new addition.

Marc was sitting on a bench as one of his favorite undercover characters, Christmas Nick. An elderly, brown-eyed, beat-up old man in a scruffy, dirty, red and white Santa suit. He smiled a little when he thought of Jette's reaction. He wondered how long he could hang around before she knew it was him. Getting up from the bench, he shuffled toward her, enjoying the sight of his lover stretching out for her run. He was three feet from her when she glanced over at him and smiled.

"Come no closer. My lover is a cop and extremely volatile. Even though I've had a thing for you since I was five, I can't risk your jolly old self." She talked softly, her voice barely carrying the three feet.

Marc stared. The brown contacts really changed his appearance. And the dental apparatus reshaped his mouth and produced an impressive set of rotten teeth when he leered at the pretty women.

"Tagg told you," he griped softly in a high, clipped, voice reminiscent of Bart Simpson.

"No, darling you did," she said softly as she handed him a dollar. "And be sure you bathe before you come home."

Eunice stepped between them. "Move on, you ugly degenerate. You're a disgrace to your uniform."

"Tagg told *you*, then."

"Yeah, a long time ago, Nick. I wouldn't have known otherwise."

"She did." Marc nodded at Jette.

"She's the Avenger."

Eunice boarded her bike. "Ready, cheese?"

"Ready," said Jette.

"Everyone is in place. All we have to do is run and ride," grinned Eunice.

Jette took off down the path, with Eunice peddling after her. The twenty cops, hand chosen by Marc, including Kim as a street performer dressed in full clown regalia, and Tagg, as a vendor with an exceptional beard, watched them blow past each checkpoint. There were several people holding up their cell phones taking pictures of Jette and Eunice and each one was tagged for further investigation by the team.

They might have been Minions, or they might have been tourists. Or they might have just been impressed with the two extraordinary bodies streaking by. All would be checked out, however.

When nothing happened out of the ordinary, Marc was both relieved and disappointed. They regrouped and met in the ballroom soon after Jette had cleaned up and changed. Eunice showered in one of the guest rooms where she'd be living until the Empress made her move and they sent her into the land of padded cells.

"So how did you know it was me?" demanded Marc when he walked into the room. Jette was a little unsettled by the brown-eyed gaze. It changed his appearance more than any other aspect of his disguise. He still wore the brown contact lenses, but had removed the offensive outer layer of dirt and grime. A lot of undercover cops were spotted because the folds in their skin simply weren't dirty enough or their hair was too clean, or they didn't carry enough body odor. He had his own formulas and was quite proud that he'd never been detected, not even by the savvy street people he knew. Nearly a half hour in the shower was necessary to make it possible for him to be in a closed room, however.

"Darling, there were several things. First of all, I figured you'd place yourself as close to the entrance of the park as possible. Secondly, your walk was far more confident than it should have been."

"I shuffled over to you," protested Marc.

"Yes, but you did so confidently." Jette waited until everyone finished laughing. "Thirdly, you changed everything, brilliantly, I thought. But your nose has a little bump in it. You wore the same nose."

"It's been broken a couple of times," scowled Marc.

"Yes, I know, and even though it's been beautifully put back to its fine, patrician shape, there is that flaw."

Marc rubbed the bridge of his nose thoughtfully. "Anything else?"

"Nothing tangible."

"So let's compare notes on what we saw and who we saw, then we can move to the next trap. I'm convinced you were being observed this morning, Jette. There were several Minions in the Park."

"She's watching just to see if it's the true Avenger and not a decoy," said Kelly. Marc looked over at her. She was a little creeped out by the brown eyes, too. They actually fit his coloring better, made him look exotic and, combined with his tan, almost Latino, but she was mad about his green eyes and thought of them as his signature. She could understand why the contact lenses were critical to any disguise. "Um, now she'll know. No one runs like Dr. Morningstar. Having her streaking through the park was a great idea."

"She'll be making her move soon," predicted Jette.

"I agree," said Kelly with confidence. "She needs a mass of points to overcome your evasions. Soon. Before the next full moon."

"When's that?" asked Marc.

"Three nights from now," said Kelly. She'd already looked it up. She wanted to join the force someday and thought showing off her research skills was a great way to get an internship with the NYPD.

"So that's her deadline of sorts."

"Yeah."

"My guess is she will try to lure her into a deserted warehouse or theater…" began Tagg.

"Or a building under construction or renovation," added Kim.

"Agreed. Let's check out the route for possible locations," suggested Marc.

Hilda entered the room.

"Detective Lexington, Cynthia Batton is here to see you. I'm afraid even with the added security, Jonathon was so dazzled by her, he called the elevator himself."

"Jesus Christ, what does she want?"

"Since I'm not clairvoyant, I have no idea, but I thought you might want to see for yourself. She's female, very wealthy, narcissistic, a woman used to playing roles…"

Marc gazed at Hilda and nodded slowly. "She fits the profile. You're thinking like a cop, Hilda."

Hilda's eyebrows shot up. "I merely like to know everything that happens in this household."

"Security?"

"Jonathon called up as instructed. I looked through the eyehole and made sure it was her. I didn't frisk her, take her fingerprints, or ask for identification, but I'm certain the woman is Cynthia Batton, and that she is not accompanied by anyone."

"I still think I'll have a talk with Jonathon," said Marc, standing.

"He'll enjoy that, I'm sure." Hilda turned to leave, then stopped and looked over her shoulder. "And one more thing. You may have to smooth over the fact that I'd replaced my dust cloth with the Beretta when I opened the door."

Marc grinned at her.

"Yup. Thinking like a cop."

"Hardly. I'm just a little more cautious since my lock up in the bathroom, that's all."

She left the room and quietly shut the door.

"Hilda has a gun?" Jette was little appalled.

"Clearly a case of badge envy," grinned Eunice, liking the fact that Hilda was carrying.

"Maybe you can help her, Doctor," chuckled Tagg glancing at Jette. "Better pop the eye coats, Marc, unless you want to explain the look to a civilian."

Marc nodded and expertly removed the brown lenses, restoring the vivid green.

"I think I might come with you," said Jette.

Marc looked over at her and held out his hand, a move that mystified him, delighted Kelly and Kim, and made Tagg shake his head and smile. Marc was such a goner. He never thought he'd see the day, but fate was sure a generous old broad.

"A little jealous yourself?" he asked as Jette took his hand and they started toward the door.

"No, not at all. But Hilda's right. She fits the profile. She obviously knows about this address. I understand that you're nearly irresistible, darling, but she was really pushing last week at the party. And she lied when she said she didn't know about me or my background. I definitely had a feeling she was hiding something. There was a tension that couldn't be explained with simple sexual attraction or desire."

"Greed? Connections? Need for police intervention on some issue?"

"Something. And it was definitely specific to you."

"Or you through me?"

"Agreed."

"Darling," cooed Cynthia when they entered the room. Jette caught the subtle jump away from a tall curio cabinet. Apparently, so had Marc.

"I don't mind providing a little hospitality, Cynthia, but that doesn't extend to sharing my stuff. Even though I think some of the things I inherited in this place are hideous and hardly my taste, they are nonetheless mine. And now Jette's. Put it back."

Cynthia's talent for facial and body control were obvious. And impressive. She registered neither surprise nor alarm. Her demeanor revealed nothing. Until she decided how she was going to play the scene, her expression was an ambiguous palate. When she realized Marc was not going to let it go, she opted for amused playfulness. The perfect mask of it formed on her face and was accompanied by the precise body language to accent the picture. She looked youthful and full of mischief.

"You're right. It is hideous. I was going to leave it in the foyer on my way out for all the world to see. It isn't valuable, is it?"

She removed the small statue from her enormous Louis Vuitton purse with a little delighted laugh. Jette was quite sure she knew it could sell at auction for over $25,000.

"And what was with that biddy and the gun?" She changed the subject quickly.

"Added security. What can we do for you, Cynthia? We're busy." Marc made no effort to keep the annoyance out of his voice.

"Not too busy for old friends, I hope." Turning her magnanimous pose to Jette, she was clearly ready to accept Jette's appreciation. "Darling, I saw your interview on television yesterday and wanted to see for myself that you were doing alright. I told Sebastian he'd just have to reschedule the rehearsals."

With that statement of unbelievable generosity standing for an eight count, she walked over and confidently sat on a floral settee. Stage left, thought Jette as Cynthia rearranged her skirt and smiled up at them. "I wouldn't say no to a martini. Double olives. I skipped lunch." Again she laughed, looking at Jette, obviously assuming she was going to turn right around and procure her drink order. When Jette didn't leave Marc's side, she decided to flick her out of the competition. She was used to taking most of the lines for herself anyway. "Marc never had anything but beer and maybe a bottle of water at his apartment in the Village, not that we did much drinking there. But I imagine there's a fully stocked bar in this palace somewhere. Remember the brand of gin I insist on, Marc?"

It was Beefeaters, thought Marc, but he certainly wasn't going to say it out loud.

"Cynthia, now that you've seen Jette and the fact that she's in perfect health, I'm going to have to ask you to excuse us. We're working."

"Working? On what, darling?" Cynthia had no intention of budging off the settee.

"That would be our business," began Marc, but Jette put her hand on his arm.

"Why don't you get Cynthia that martini."

Jette wanted some time to observe Cynthia. To listen to her voice and determine if there was an underlying tone and rhythm that had been hidden in the disguised voice of the Empress.

Marc looked down at her. There was no way in hell he was going to leave her alone with anyone, much less someone who fit the profile.

"Don't you have a performance tonight?" Marc turned back to Cynthia. "You wouldn't want to throw off your timing."

"You're right, of course, darling, but one martini will do no more than relax me nicely." She smoothed her hair and Jette noticed her hand trembled a bit. Looking over at Marc, she saw he noticed, too.

"Fine. Want anything, Jette?"

"I'd love something cold."

Jette watched Cynthia watch Marc as he moved to the phone and pushed the button for the kitchen. She couldn't blame her when her eyes locked on Marc's butt.

Marc directed Hilda to bring in a martini and a raspberry iced tea.

"You aren't having your usual domestic brew, Marc?" asked Cynthia coyly when he hung up.

"No."

"Don't tell me she's tamed you."

"Pretty much."

Cynthia sighed. "Are you in a mood, Marc? You're looking a little dark today."

"Thanks."

Giving up, Cynthia turned to Jette.

"My oh my, Jette, sweetie. He doesn't appear very happy. It didn't take long for him to fall from bliss into boredom." She sighed and winked conspiratorially. "Good heavens, I was able to entertain him for more than a few weeks. Maybe you have to play many parts to keep him fresh."

Far from being insulted, Jette was totally absorbed studying Cynthia. All human behavior fascinated her, but Cynthia was as compelling as an intense episode of reality TV. She was creative and cunning. Confident and contained. But also, desperate and very much on the edge of a breakdown. As was her manner, Jette said nothing. She serenely watched as Cynthia deconstructed.

Marc sincerely wished they weren't in the middle of a complicated investigation. What a show. His woman was a wonder to him. It was the ticking clock, not compassion, that had him getting back to cop business. The comment on playing parts could have just been a spontaneous dig. Or maybe not.

"I heard your understudy delivered again for the Sunday matinee. You better beware. The *Times* gave her high marks the next morning."

Cynthia snorted. "She couldn't touch my hem in talent. Besides, like I said when we were together at the party the other night, it's just the summer tourists in the audience and they're barely literate. Always laughing over my lines, applauding in the middle of a song, singing along when they recognize something from the sound track they bought at their local Target store. They are ghastly."

Marc would have reminded her that they weren't together at the party, but Hilda walked in and the moment passed.

Cynthia took her frosted martini off the tray a bit too eagerly. Her face clouded when she saw the servant give Jette a little smile with her iced tea. Lord. The deference and what appeared to be affection by the staff twisted fingers of jealousy around the strong ball of envy in her gut. The pressure behind her eyes was building and becoming unbearable. Only her fury born of desperation was stronger at this point.

After taking over half the drink in one ravenous gulp, she thought she'd work on digging into Jette. Seeing her among all these expensive things like some pampered princess was just too much.

"So Marc, could you explain to me so I can take it back to the boards and satisfy everyone's curiosity, how you came to connect to such a straight arrow as Jette?" She put her fingers to her lips and laughed with perfect self deprecation. "Oops. Can I say arrow about an Indian without getting sued?"

Marc's temper was about to erupt, but Jette's gentle hand cooled the flow of lava. Her voice was slightly amused, completely professional.

"I have no problem with that." Jette's eyes remained steady, her demeanor self-possessed. "But as you may know, Cynthia, I'm also a therapist. I think if you let me, I can help you more than Marc can at this point."

"Excuse me?" asked Cynthia, set back by her failure to get Jette into the cat fight she knew she could win. "Marc, are you going to let her talk to me like that?"

"Sure."

"Well, I think it's clear if you and I are going to continue to be friends, we need to meet somewhere other than here."

When Marc said nothing, she drained her glass. Stalling. Calculating. She couldn't get any more obvious. She couldn't get any more desirable. Her spa bill that morning had been through the roof. Her eyes narrowed on Jette but before she could launch a counter offensive, Marc had another question.

"I'm curious. How did you know where I lived? I never brought you here and I certainly never told you about it."

"Yes, it was very, very bad for our relationship that you kept so much from me." Cynthia turned her entire body toward Marc. If Jette wasn't going to be pulled in, she was just going to ignore her. "That darling new morning anchor, Donna Neubauer, called me because she knew we were an item and wanted a lead. She'd heard a rumor you had a place on the Upper East side. I laughed and told her I knew firsthand that wasn't so, but my driver overheard the conversation and set me straight after I hung up. Apparently he knows your chauffer, Claude. You've fallen into high-grade silk here, Marc."

"It appears that makes a difference," he observed.

"Why of course it does, darling. Don't be naïve. If you'd have been more open, we'd still be an item."

Marc just frowned, not sure how he felt about being measured by his bank account.

"Everything about a person has the potential to make a difference to someone, but would you have us believe you'd be that shallow, Cynthia?" asked Jette.

"You appear to be very comfortable here," snapped Cynthia, reaching the end of her rope and letting go. "Are you saying you'd rather live in that hovel he brought me to? Frequently, I might add. The bed was lumpy, the décor disgusting. It was a dump."

"I could be happy anywhere with him, but now that you mention it, I think we'll invest in a new bed for the hovel." Jette's smile remained calm and serene.

"Cynthia, we really have better things to do than stand here and entertain you. You've had your drink, now relax on out of here," suggested Marc.

Cynthia decided it was time to retreat and cut her losses. She got up, considering her last line. Something dramatic. No, something mean.

"You know my number, Marc. I haven't changed it. Call me when the little squaw goes back to the reservation."

"You really do need help, Cynthia. On so many levels," observed Jette. "I can understand that it would be too painful for you to introduce me to your private demons, but please get some help. Your talent is a gift. Honor it."

"Go to hell. You'll be heading there soon enough when Marc forgets you're here and moves on to the next of his bimbos. As a matter of fact rumor has it that he already has."

With that, she made her dramatic exit.

"For someone who has delivered the lines of the masters, you'd think she'd have come up with something more original," said Jette when they heard the front door slam.

"You know what she said..." began Marc.

"You mean you really did spend all of your time searching for me rather than taking advantage of my absence?" Jette smiled up at him.

Marc just snorted. "Where else am I going to find the same combination of wolf, warrior, and shrink?"

"Exactly." Jette stretched and sighed. "By the way, you can take her off the suspect board, Marc."

"Based on..." he prompted.

"Two reasons. First, the Empress is not a thief."

"The blue bitch is a murderer, a kidnapper, a certifiable psycho, but you don't think she's a thief?"

"That's right. And since I'm the person doing the certifying, the Empress isn't a psycho. She's a fractured woman who's now almost completely folded into her delusion. She isn't playing Sovereignty, she's living it and in Himalia she isn't a thief. So in this world she isn't a thief."

"Maybe she's a klepto."

"Cynthia isn't a kleptomaniac, she's a thief. And yes, that's a clinical diagnosis. She needed the piece she nearly had in her purse for the money, which brings me to the second reason she isn't the Empress and why I think she wants to get back into your life so desperately."

"It's not for my body?"

"Well there's that, too."

"My charm?"

She just stared at him.

"Okay, fuck that, but we can still count my body," he conceded.

"As desirable as you are, darling, I think at this point your bank account is a bigger attraction. Her addiction is serious and is becoming obvious. Was she a user when you knew her?"

"I have no idea. It never came up. Our, ah, connection was very brief and very superficial." Marc shrugged. "I'll make a few phone calls. In the meantime, on your recommendation, I'll bust her back to the minors, but I'm not going to cut her yet. She was unaccounted for during all of the Empress's visits. An understudy was used several times this last week. She's a role player, and not as stupid as she looks."

"Fine, but you're going to find she has a cocaine addiction that is causing her to lose function. Her absences from the stage are primarily due to her inability to perform at those times, not from making a visit to me." She sighed. "And my empathy for her at this point is very strong. Stronger even than my annoyance for her obvious and desperate play for my man. See if you can get her some help."

Marc just stood looking at her.

"She really needs it, Marc. And if she doesn't respect her talent, I think we should." When he continued to stare, she gave him a sidelong glance.

"What?"

"It's not your kind and giving heart or your professional integrity that stands out for me at the moment."

Her eyebrows came together.

"It's the casual reference to 'my man'. So nice and primitive." He made a little growl in his throat.

"Before you walk around beating your chest, remember underneath the wolf, the warrior, and the shrink is a very possessive woman in love."

"I can live with that," he grinned.

"You certainly are," she said, then purged Cynthia's negative energy with some hot, spontaneous necking.

# Chapter Fourteen

Sitting alone in her car near the rented jet, the Empress studied her portable board again and recalculated the point distribution. She still needed one of Avenger's lives and she was certain she was moving in the direction that assured her that necessary key. The Castle of Thunder was prepared and the Physical Test was set up and ready.

This was an incredible logistical challenge, but that added to the points she needed to even the score. Several of her Sentinels were traveling separately on commercial flights; many of them were already in transit. Her forged and phony identification was tucked safely in her carry-on luggage. She'd be going commercial herself within the hour. Disguised, of course. Other recruits who'd been dormant were activated at the site. Local players at various levels of performance were lined up and ready.

The operation was draining her resources and straining the budget, but it couldn't be helped. Everything had to be kept close and that meant private transportation for the cargo and plenty of professional firepower.

Avenger had blocked and evaded every one of her moves. Frustrating, but exciting, too. It was time to pull out all she had. In the scheme of conquest she'd just calculated, she could still achieve Sovereignty and without equivocation when she took out Avenger herself. The Final Duel was going to take place during this phase. The end was near.

There was motion on the tarmac. Her team. She felt a rush of power and anticipation. This was going to work. Soon they'd be jetting cross country to her Western Fortress. And Avenger would face her toughest test yet.

# Chapter Fifteen

Jette looked at the familiar number on her cell phone. Luke. She was on the roof garden, purging some negative energy from her soul though shallow meditation. The intrusion of the tinkling phone was a necessary byproduct of her connection to reality, so she pushed out of the pleasant state she'd created and answered.

"*Alisdelisgi.*"

"I have your Light Knight, Avenger. Do not in any way indicate to your watchers that I'm on the phone." Jette's blood froze as she recognized the whispering, raspy voice. "If you try to calibrate my location, I'll begin his torture."

"I'm alone. It's just you and me, Empress." Jette responded calmly, even though her throat nearly closed in fear. Luke. The Empress had Luke. Or maybe just his phone. Her mind raced. How should she play this? Straight. Play it straight. The woman was most likely in the grip of a full-blown delusional psychoses. Dangerous in the extreme, but somewhat more predictable.

"Tell me, Empress, how did you capture my Light Knight?"

"He was taken from the City of Might. You left him unattended."

"Very clever. Extra points for you."

"Yes, too clever for you, it seems." The Empress paused for drama. "He's Themisto, your brother, is he not?"

Jette frowned. The Empress seemed quite excited by that fact. Kelly hadn't mentioned this Themisto, but he was her brother, so she played along. "He's my brother, yes."

"Not just the Light Knight then. Very smart to hide him in plain view."

"Points for me."

"But I have him now. You should have protected him better. Very arrogant of you to allow him out of your Home Base this close to the Final Duel."

"My mistake, Blue Empress. You are formidable and fearless. I underestimated you."

"You did, yes."

Jette knew she'd said just the right thing when the Empress couldn't keep the smug attitude from coating her voice.

"Your move, Empress."

"Do as I say or I'll drain his blood. The blood of Adrastea and Ganymede. Rumors of his existence have been in play for years, but few believed that our mother had a son with your beast of a father. It's told in some obscure original documents that she abandoned and banished him as a child because no man can ever rule Himalia. His blood would be a great source of added power for you."

"And useless to you. What must I do to get him back?"

"You know."

Jette wracked her brain. Kelly had been tutoring her. What would Avenger do? Trade? No. A Duel? No. That was just between the Avatars. A Quest? Yes. She had to engage in a Quest to find him. Once she'd completed the Quest, she'd be faced with a Physical Test to open the door behind which would be the item she sought. She hoped she got this right. She needed the Empress to stay in her delusion.

"Tell me my Quest, Empress. Your ability to hide him versus my ability to locate him. If I find him, and pass the Physical Test, he's mine. If I don't, you get the points and the prize."

"Tell no one. This must be your Quest and your Test. No help from your Guardians or the Dark Knight."

"I understand. I do this alone."

"I have Minions who'll be watching. They are legion. They are everywhere. If any one of them records a Guardian by your side, I'll start taking apart your Light Knight. First his hands will be mine. I'll take their power to heal for my own. Then his eyes. His sight will be tallied to my side. Then I'll open his jugular and drain his blood."

"I understand. Tell me my Quest and I'll begin immediately. I'll do this alone."

"I need your Blood Oath on that."

"You have it."

"I need to hear it. I need you to say the words."

Jette pushed through the terror she felt for her brother, his hands, his eyes, his blood, and recalled the chant for the Blood Oath.

"By our mother Adrastea's blood, this sacred oath I swear. What I promise binds my will, by the common blood we share."

"Listen carefully. I'll only say this once." Jette heard a paper rustle.

*"This is your challenge, this is your Quest,*
*Follow the sun, go swiftly, go west.*
*In my fortress of glass and white stone,*
*Come find your Light Knight, come all alone,*
*You know the place, you know the land,*
*It's familiar to you, it rises from sand.*
*To find his location, you have 24 hours,*
*Then I'll open his throat, drain all his powers.*

*Once you've completed this part of the Quest,*
*A feat you will face as a Physical Test.*
*Ten Sentinels you'll fight with a sword and a knife.*
*Get through them all and you take back his life.*
*A thousand points for finding your Knight.*
*A thousand more if you live through the fight.*
*Two thousand for me, and the Knight for my own,*
*If you fail either Challenge, or don't come alone.*
*So don't try deception, don't try a trick,*
*At midnight tonight the clock starts to tick."*

When she finished, Jette's heart and mind throbbed. Could she be any more cryptic? Then she thought of Luke. Open his throat? Could she be any more clear?

"Starting at midnight, I have 24 hours to find my Light Knight and battle your Sentinels?" She wanted to be sure she understood the timeline.

"Yes. At midnight tomorrow night, if you haven't completed the Physical Test, I'll begin his assimilation. You may choose to sacrifice your Light Knight, but because he is also your brother, I'll automatically take the lead."

"When I've destroyed your ten Sentinels and recaptured my Light Knight, will I meet you in battle?"

There was silence. Had she made an error? It was a very complicated game.

"Only under the full moon, Avenger."

That's right, she thought. They could only face each other in battle under a full moon.

"I'll meet you in the Final Duel when the moon rises in three nights time, Empress."

"Only if you fulfill your Quest and pass your Test. Formidable barriers to our next meeting, Avenger."

"Prepare, Empress. I plan to do both."

"Come alone with sword and knife."

"I've got that part. Now I need to consult with my Light Knight. I need to determine if he has enough power to make the journey worth it. I'll be fighting alone and I won't do that if my prize isn't intact."

"Certainly. Say hello to your brother."

"Light Knight?" Jette asked, holding her breath. Maybe the Empress was only using a decoy. A false knight meant to be bait.

"Avenger," said Luke in a calm, steady voice. It was him. The anguish she felt was reduced slightly by relief when she realized he was playing the game. That was good.

She wanted to tell him she was sorry. That she'd intended for the Empress to come directly for her. That she loved him and would do anything, anything to get him back. But that wouldn't be something Avenger would say or how she'd act. So she suppressed the sister and pulled out the role of Avenger.

It was interesting to her that she was actually feeling more like the ruler of Callisto than the civilized professor and therapist right now. Anger was squeezing her heart and avenging sounded pretty good to her at the moment.

"Are you at full power, Light Knight?"

"I am yes, but I think you need to pitch her the points. Count this one as…"

"That's enough," hissed the Empress. "No more interaction. I've given you your Quest. If you can figure it out and if you choose to meet the challenge, your Light Knight will remain in play. Otherwise, I'll meet you back in the City of Might and you'll never find his grave."

"I'll see you soon. I accept your challenge." Jette wanted to make it clear that she was in the game and that she'd play by the rules.

"Fine, but you still have to find him." With that, the Empress hung up.

Jette checked her watch. It was 6:00. Marc would be home soon. He'd gone out with Tagg to check the perimeter of the park for her evening run. That was a relief and a bit of good luck. She needed to clear her mind and think. Uncover the answer to the clues. The Empress wanted her to find the location, she was sure of it. Luke was just the bait. Whether it was a conscious desire or an unconscious compulsion, the Empress wanted Avenger to step into the trap.

She replayed the poem several times in her head. Were they still in New York? A fortress of glass and white stone. There were several buildings, probably hundreds, in the city meeting that description. It was west. On the west side? Or had she moved Luke out of the city now that Avenger had claimed the City of Might.

West. Follow the sun. The sun. A picture of Arizona's state flag punched through her churning mind. The 13 rays of the western setting sun!

Rising from the sand. That sounded like Arizona. Would the Empress take Luke home to Arizona? Right where Avenger grew up? Oh yes. It would give her a real boost, both in points and in creating a legend. Bold, just like the kidnapping in Avenger's Home Base. It fit her ego perfectly. She needed to feed her bruised and battered self esteem with a daring and splashy victory over Avenger.

But where in Arizona? It was a large state. How would she find the location in 24 hours?

Closing her eyes again, she replayed the entire conversation. There was something in the background that her initial alarm had blocked out. A kind of whistling, whooshing sound. Familiar somehow. Forcing herself to relax, she cleared her mind of clutter and her soul of fear.

"I know the place. I know the land," she repeated. Then suddenly she did know. The whistling, whooshing sound of screaming spirits. It was astonishing, but it fit. Everything in the Quest. It fit!

She pushed the button on her phone that would give her confirmation. Please, please. If this wasn't right, she didn't have a next step.

"Morningstar Ranch," said a familiar voice.

"Jim?"

"Hi Jette. How are you feeling?"

"I'm fine, thank you. How's Moonshine?"

"She's missing you, but Becca takes her out every day and she goes like the wind. I think Diablo's getting a little anxious that his handsome self is going to be bested by his little sister before the year is over."

Jette's breathing calmed with the familiar voice and the chatter of a dear friend. "Jim, has the Haunted Hall of Shrieking Leaks been sold?"

"Why? You looking to buy that old monstrosity? Tear it down and put it out of its misery?"

"No, I just need to know if it's occupied."

"As a matter of fact, it's funny you should ask. Jaci said she saw some extra lights up there the other night. I heard it had been rented to someone from South America, but didn't really believe it. Won't take long before the leaks and shrieks will empty it out again."

Not only was the place a sieve every time it rained, but when the wind of the desert kicked up, the sounds echoing through the house were like fifty drunken ghosts singing opera. Badly. It was a stone and glass atrocity of architecture that had been designed by the devil and built by a psychotic mason with a grudge against nature. An eyesore on the beautiful desert horizon.

It rose from the sand on a high mesa and the whooshing sounds blowing through the place where, according to local lore, the sound of screaming spirits offended by the place. And it had been built by a man named Pitcher. Luke told her to *pitch her* the points. Strange words to use until it was put into context. And wasn't the original owner a Count of some sort? Luke put a little more emphasis on the word count. Nicely done Light Knight.

Jette's heart soared. Another severe miscalculation by her fictional half sister. Lord, the woman was on a losing streak. If her brother wasn't in so much danger, Jette would have celebrated. The location was as close to home field advantage as she could get. Score one for Avenger.

The building was practically in her own backyard. Several times after it had been abandoned, on a dare and a prayer, she'd climbed up the steep rock cliff it was built on and planted a flag on the balcony. Luke was often the one instigating the adventure. In later years, they'd made themselves at home, walking through the huge house, creeping each other out with tales from the crypt. It had been many years since she'd been a chronic trespasser, but her hands and feet had their own memory and were eager to make the ascent.

Better yet, her Light Knight would remember this and be expecting her. It gave her heart a soft sweet squeeze knowing that some of the fear he'd be feeling would be mitigated by his certainty that she was on her way.

She chatted with Jim awhile longer, hoping her anxiety would be chalked up to some residual edginess from the withdrawal, then called the airline immediately. She needed to be out of the apartment and on her way to Arizona before Marc got home. And she had to ditch her guards. Eunice was riding the door to the roof and the rest of team including Hilda, Claude, and Tommy were between her and the street. On the street were several undercover personnel.

Looking around the roof garden, she shrugged. Her rooftop escapades were getting redundant, but it seemed the theme was going to be continued. She'd need her identification, but didn't want to grab her purse. That would be a clue to her crowded entourage that she was planning on leaving.

She'd causally go down to her bedroom, grab her ID, some cash, and a credit card, then come back up with a nice cup of tea to meditate. Then jump the fence. Literally.

# Chapter Sixteen

Arriving at LaGuardia after hailing a cab on 7<sup>th</sup>, Jette checked the departing flights. Less than an hour before the flight left. Looking around, she spotted four, possibly five young people very interested in snapping her picture. Minions. Marc could get their identities off the security tapes later. Right now she was comforted. Luke's life was in the balance. They'd send pictures to the Empress and she'd know Jette was following her clues and her instructions. She was traveling solo.

Looking again at her watch, she thought of the note she'd left. Marc would be finding it right about now so if there was any seismic activity shaking out of Manhattan, she'd know the source. His fury was something the team would have to deal with. She told him she'd call later to explain.

The flight to Tucson was direct, on time, and far, far too long. There was too much time to think about the consequences if she'd guessed incorrectly and some South American millionaire would greet her in the screaming house of horrors. Her gut told her she was tracking the right trail, but her mind kept flashing on other possibilities, other alternatives. There were a lot of sites that could fit the description.

Rather than call anyone from the ranch, she rented a car and was soon streaming down the familiar highway and back roads. Taking in the pulse of the land, her land, she felt better in the arms of her home territory. The smells, the bright night sky, and the heartbeat of Mother Earth comforted her, calmed her, and reassured her.

Parking just inside the gate of Morningstar Ranch, she jogged up the long driveway and after decoding the alarm, let herself into the beautiful ranch house. The evening song of the night birds greeted her warmly and the creak of the back door welcomed her home. Not stopping to enjoy her homecoming, she immediately headed to her bedroom.

It was after midnight, so she was the only one moving. The Minions watching the ranch would be able to forward a favorable report. They'd seen her go in, she'd made sure of it, but they wouldn't see her leave. From childhood she knew every way possible to sneak undetected into and out of her house. The Empress would assume Avenger was inside and preparing for the next night's Physical Test.

"Sorry to disappoint," muttered Jette.

Stripping her street clothes off on her way to the bedroom, she shook out her travel-weary muscles and chanted an ancient prayer to the Great Spirit. A prayer to keep her brother surrounded with protection until she could get to him. From her closet, she pulled out black jeans, a long-sleeved, black turtleneck and soft knee-length, leather moccasins. She needed to be sure-footed tonight.

After dressing quickly and quietly, she strapped a beaded sheath to her thigh and slipped her knife into it. She only hesitated for an instant before she went into an old trunk in the back of the closet and pulled out another, older knife. Her father's. She'd go in prepared. That one slid nicely into the top of her moccasin.

From a shelf, she grabbed a leather shoulder scabbard. She'd get a rifle and ammunition from the gun rack in the library.

Eyes snapping, mouth turned up in a tight, determined smile, she reached over and snatched her grandfather's ceremonial eagle feathers off the wall and weaved them into her long hair as she braided it and tied the plaits with soft leather strips.

When she turned around, she caught her reflection in the dressing room mirror. Gone were the professor and doctor of forensic psychology. The Cherokee warrior in the glass was both formidable and focused. The Empress was now her quarry and she was ready for the hunt.

With swift efficiency, went into the library and unlocked the gun cabinet. Choosing a light-weight rifle, she opened the ammunition drawer and took what she needed. She sincerely hoped she wouldn't have to shoot the weapon, but she was going in loaded. With quick, capable moves, she punched cartridges into the rifle then put spare shells in a pocket on the scabbard. Never in her life had she aimed a gun at another human being, but tonight she knew she could. Flipping the rifle into the scabbard as she walked, she felt her blood sizzle.

She'd go up the side of the mesa and gain access to the glass house from there. No one would be watching the cliff side. They'd assume nothing but high flying birds could gain access from that direction. 265 feet of sheer cliff with a substantial wall once she got to the top. No problem.

There was the matter of getting there. She wanted to leave her rental car in the driveway near the gate for the Minions to see, snap, and send, so she'd go in on horseback. Thirty miles by the relatively safe soft road or 10 by the back country trails. Even though there was nearly a full moon, galloping in the desert was a dicey prospect. She looked at her watch. There was plenty of time. The safer road, then.

Which horse? Diablo was her fastest, but Moonshine was more sure footed at night. Diablo was used to a saddle, Moonshine had just started her training so she'd have to ride her bareback. She was wearing the war feathers of her ancestor. She'd ride her horse like he might have when leading his people west. Bareback on Moonshine.

A window in the rear of her brother's room opened right into a small copse of squat desert trees. Great cover. Sliding it open, she listened. Feeling nothing move in the dark, hearing nothing but the sound of night birds and tiny creatures, she jumped silently out the window and ran over the soft sand to a small shed near the new barn. Inside, she opened the cabinet containing the ropes and other equipment she and Luke used when they climbed. Pulling on gloves, she wrapped ropes around her shoulder and attached spikes to her belt. Hoping she had everything she'd need, she went to the barn to find Moonshine. The fine, fit filly softly pawed her stall when she recognized the scent of her mistress.

"Shhh. We must be silent as the night," she whispered to her horse, stroking the strong neck and feeling the steady heartbeat of her beloved horse. Diablo, waking up in the stall next door, gave her a baleful look.

"Not now, boy. You'll have your turn later."

Opening the doors in the back, she led her horse out of the barn, re-secured the doors, and moved a safe distance from the bunkhouse. Then she grabbed Moonshine's mane in a tight fist, leaped on her back in one smooth, strong motion, found her seat, and galloped out into the desert. Her desert. Her home.

Moonshine sailed over the fence at the far edge of their property and they rode hard into the night, the light of the moon shining off the sand, illuminating their way. Every inch the Avenger.

The jutting rock off the back side of the mesa was black against the blue gray sky. The house that sat atop it was visible from miles away.

As she approached, she saw lights. Lots of lights. Inside and out. While it was something she'd have to avoid in her approach, she was relieved to see them. It confirmed the presence of people. People who were awake and alert after midnight.

"Okay, Shine. Let's approach from the rear."

She rode over to the foot of the steep summit, then dismounted quickly. Knowing the easiest route to take up the cliff face, she decided there was no pride in trying to make this difficult. Shaking out her muscles, she stretched a few times to move more blood and oxygen to her arms and legs. Chanting another prayer, she slung the scabbard with the rifle over one shoulder, the rope over the other, inserted her foot into a familiar hole, and started the climb.

It was a physical test, alright, just not the one the Empress had anticipated. Jette moved swiftly, but surely from handhold to foothold. Using spikes and her rope when necessary. Her muscles chanted back at her as they were pushed in both endurance and strength. Jette never slowed, never stopped. Hand over hand, grabbing onto rock ledges, then finding another, pulling herself up, her body reacting to the memory of the many climbs she'd made in the past.

When she got to the top without incident, she gave herself a moment to rest. To recapture her breath and settle her racing heart. She still needed to get over the wall, find Luke, and get him out.

When she'd recovered and refocused, she stood and with sure feet and strong arms, jumped, hooked her hands on the ledge of the seven-foot wall, and shimmied up. Laying down flat on top of the ledge, she looked along the wide terrace. No sign of a sentry. No sign of life. Score a few more points for Avenger!

Dropping soundlessly down onto the terrace, she shucked her ropes and stakes and ran from the edge of the wall to the house, then moved along the exterior, peeking in the windows. It was like a muted TV inside. Lots of movement and action and absolutely no sound. The huge insulated double paned windows gave her a clear picture, but she couldn't hear anything. Her reconnaissance netted her a lot of information, but not her main objective. There were several people crowded around a bar in one room, a few others in a bedroom next door. A kitchen with evidence of habitation and a lone cook making sandwiches.

Dread began to tug at her and she started to wonder if perhaps she'd guessed incorrectly. Then she found him. She had to take a second to blink away tears of relief. She hadn't realized how close to the edge of total terror she'd been.

Luke was alone in the room, a huge partially furnished bedroom, his arms and legs taped to the chair he was sitting in. Beautiful, breathing, and unharmed. Sleeping or drugged. Thank the spirits.

She cautiously tried the handle of the French doors leading into the room. Unlocked. It was almost like a trap. Too easy. Hesitating, she looked around.

Closing her eyes she pushed out with her intuition. What did it feel like? People scattered around the house. No real tension. No one alert or nervous.

Not a trap, then. Arrogance. Classic egotism. The Empress had an image of how this was to play out and she saw little else.

If her Minions were on duty in the airports and near the ranch, she'd know that Jette was in Arizona, but she'd be looking for her the way Avenger would arrive. Coming through the front gates, on horseback, when the moon rose the next night. Armed with sword and knife. Sneaking in during the middle of the night was not something Avenger would do. Chalk one up for the professor. Smarter in the long run.

Suddenly, Luke stirred, looked up at a clock on the wall, then directed his gaze out the window. He couldn't see her in the shadows of the night, but unlike the Empress, he was expecting her. Jette smiled. He'd know if there was a trap. There was no warning on his face, just anticipation. Faith.

Taking a step forward, she entered the faint wash of light from the room. Luke saw her, smiled, and winked. It was all clear.

Without hesitation now, she opened the door.

"Did you call for room service?" she whispered.

"That was the suite next door, I called for rescue."

"Ah. I guess that's why the concierge told me to bring a rope and come armed."

She strode over to where he sat, kissed him lightly on the cheek, then drew her knife. It glinted huge and menacing in the light from the lamp.

"Whoa," said Luke. "I'll talk. I'll tell you everything."

Jette chuckled and quickly and competently sliced through the duct tape.

"You're right on time." He rubbed his chaffed wrists. "A little early in fact. I figured the 9:05 flight out of LaGuardia, the drive from the airport to the ranch, a ride through the desert, a record-setting climb up the side of the cliff."

"Are you alright? Have you been drugged?"

"Not since the first shot outside the clinic in Queens. Got it in the neck and went out like a light. I'm just bait, Jette. Other than that phone call, I've been completely ignored."

"Nice clues."

"Why thank you, Avenger."

He stood up and swayed.

"Are you sure you're alright?"

"I'm as hungry as a hibernating bear and thirsty as a camel, but otherwise, I'm just stiff and my limbs were napping. Did you bring any food?"

"As a matter of fact…" She brought out one of her nutritional protein bars from the pocket of her jeans.

"I'll wait thanks. These may be my final hours and I don't want to die with the taste of wood bark in my mouth."

"How about chocolate?" She handed him a candy bar from her other pocket.

"Live each day like it's your last, 'cause one of these days you're going to be right." He ripped open the wrapper and devoured the candy in quick, ravenous bites.

"Can you rappel down?"

"I could, but I'm not."

"Please. I need you to be safe."

"No. I can tell from the look in your eye that you're not planning on moving to safer ground. You're actually looking a little terrifying. But first things first. Excuse me. Watch the door a sec, will you?"

Luke quickly let himself into the adjoining bathroom. He came out a few minutes later, drying his hands on a towel and sighing hugely.

"That's even a bigger relief than seeing your smiling face in the window. I think I can now comport myself like a man. So tell me. What's the plan?"

"Now that you feel a little better, will you go down the side of the mountain?"

"Not unless you lead the way."

"Fine. Stay."

Luke snuffed like a dog. Jette rolled her eyes, shrugged, and decided not to waste any more time trying to convince him to leave. She reached into her back pocket and pulled out her cell phone. Pushing a number, she waited until she heard the familiar voice at the other end.

"I've recaptured the Light Knight. Yes, he's fine, but he won't leave. No, I won't either." She held the phone out and Luke could hear Marc shouting. When he wound down, Jette interrupted. "Are you in position? Give me twenty to recon. I'll call you with a report. Yes, Dark Knight. I will."

Luke stared at her.

"Recon? You didn't come alone?"

Jette's grin snapped wickedly, the adrenalin pushing up its intensity. Talk about formidable. "Do I have a degree in idiocy? That kind of thing only happens in the movies."

"But she said come alone or she'd cut off my hands."

"That would have been inconvenient."

"To say the least."

"I'd have to take back those leather gloves I got you for your birthday."

"I wouldn't want to be such a bother." He wiggled his fingers. "I must say I'm glad we never had to test the Empress's resolve on that issue."

"Oh, I have no doubt she'd have followed through. But I figured you'd still have your mind. And your mouth."

"Well thanks."

"Don't mention it."

"I won't."

"You okay to move? We may have to go fast."

"Yeah. Lead the way, Avenger. I'm right behind you."

She grinned at him.

"Hey, I'm not the super hero here." Luke shrugged. "My ego has no problem following the person who can shoot straighter, run faster, climb mountains, and chuck knives. You're a tough lady, Avenger."

"I can't transplant a kidney." She grinned at her brother and handed him her rifle.

"Not successfully, anyway." He was more comfortable with a scalpel than a gun, but stood ready to fight and defend.

"I want to go back outside to get a read on the location of the people through the windows. I saw six in the living room, two in the bedroom, and one in the kitchen so far. Stay in the shadows."

"So we're not going to go through the doors, guns blazing?"

"God, I wish the *Die Hard* series would just…die."

# Chapter Seventeen

The Dark Knight folded his cell phone and put his night vision binoculars back to his eyes. He and his Guardians had been watching Jette from a safe distance since she began her ascent. His heart seized up so many times, he was surprised it hadn't just stopped. Jim kept reassuring him, but Tommy wasn't helping with her gasps and her *oh my gods*.

"She coming back down?" asked Captain Markle.

"Not the way she went in." Marc was half relieved she wouldn't be hanging on the side of a sheer cliff, half anxious that she was in the middle of a band of armed and dangerous criminals.

"Told 'ya not to worry. That girl's got goat in her blood," chuckled Jim.

"I swear, she should just bottle it and be done with it," huffed Tommy while she fanned herself with her flattened hand. "Just this minute, I wouldn't be surprised if she jumped off the balcony and flew through the night sky with Luke hanging from her beak. Like Hawkwoman or some such thing?"

"You read too many comic books," muttered Tagg.

"Well, I thought she was amazing going flat out on straight land, but her vertical technique is pretty impressive too. I actually think she'd make a brilliant comic book hero," speculated Eunice in her low scratchy voice.

"We could use more women in that genre," agreed Kim.

Marc just turned and stared at them.

"Well, we could," retorted Kim defensively. "There aren't that many, you know." When Marc didn't say anything, she didn't stop, couldn't stop. "Well, there aren't. Name more than five. I bet you can't. I bet no one could. And the way they dress them. They show more of their double D cups than their muscles. I'll bet no more than a handful are drawn by women. I mean, really…"

"Don't respond to the great green glare, Kim," advised Eunice, throwing a lifeline to her younger, less seasoned sister in blue. "Pretty soon you start babbling and he never says a word. It's a hideous thing to watch the disintegration of a suspect under that stare, but its humiliating to see a competent officer crumble and collapse under its weight."

Kim's eyes moved to Eunice with gratitude. She knew she was babbling, could feel it bubble out of her. Nerves mixed with the snake eyes just did it to her. If Eunice hadn't interrupted, there would have been no place to go but a meltdown into a jabbering, prattling puddle.

Marc finally blinked when he realized neither woman was going to take up the comic book argument again and looked around at his team. Tommy, Tagg, Kim, Raj, Dina, Rachael, Teresa, and Eunice from New York, Jim and the hands from the ranch and Captain Markle and his team, the local law. It was an odd assortment to be sure, but he'd go through any door with them.

While she'd waited to board her flight in LaGuardia, Jette had called Marc and relayed all the information to him in a private bathroom stall in the VIP section of the airport, where no Minion would be able to follow. They'd argued about the best way to proceed. Actually he shouted and ranted like a maniac while she calmly leaned against the sink and told him her plan. By the time she'd boarded, she'd won, and he still couldn't remember clearly how that happened.

She'd fly to Tucson and give every appearance of following the game plan. He'd assemble a back up team who'd surreptitiously report to the general aviation terminal at Kennedy one by one and board a private jet. It was nice to have deep pockets when transporting a covert team cross country. Claude and Hilda stayed back to simulate activity in the apartment.

They'd arrived soon after Jette and immediately loaded vans with the body armor, guns, night vision equipment, and restraints Captain Markle procured, then drove to the site Jette suggested. When the locals arrived, they approved the location and all stood ready, armed with a search warrant and enough artillery to wage a small war. Jette's first priority was to secure the Light Knight. No movement toward the house would be made until they heard from her.

The Minions reporting from the ranch, teams of excitable college students, had been rounded up quickly and quietly and were now sitting in lock up. It had been easy to spot them all in the wide open spaces of Arizona.

Jim and the hands prepared the horses and rendezvoused with Marc, Chuck, and their teams in the dried up arroyo near the mesa. Jette figured they could get a lot closer undetected if the backup team came in from the desert. Marc and Kim had ridden before as had all the locals, but the rest of his New York posse got a quick lesson on how to stay in the saddle. It wasn't pretty, but Jim had them ready to ride by the time Jette called.

Marc swung up on Diablo, who picked up on his bad temper and danced around in agitation. Marc's strength got him calmed as he watched everyone mount. All the backup vans were parked and ready to be driven by the deputized ranch hands as soon as they were given the signal to move in from the road. They had to be convinced to stay back, but it didn't prevent them all from bringing their own rifles, two or three to a man. They were a fearsome force.

"Let's go take down this blue bitch." Marc turned the giant black horse and led the way through the desert.

# Chapter Eighteen

Jette stalked silently from window to window. Dim nightlights revealed what she assumed were sleeping Sentinels under blankets. In other rooms, several more were playing cards or watching television. When they reached the end of the long terrace, Jette punched in Marc's number again.

"Do you have the map of the house?"

"Captain Markle has one right here." They'd stopped and gathered in a low dry river bed. It was all uphill now and they were discussing whether or not to go a little farther on horseback, or proceed on foot. The house was surrounded by loose rock and shale and the welfare of the horses was becoming a concern.

"Here's the number and location of all that I can see from the outside."

She gave him the information.

"Fine. Now stay there. We're less than a half mile from your position."

"I recommend coming in on foot. They probably have outside sentries. I haven't seen the Empress, but I'm betting she's in the master suite on the third floor. It would be a great space for her own command center. I need to neutralize her so the rest have no clear leadership. Without her dictating the moves, your job should be easier. I'm going in. Be careful, Dark Knight. See you inside."

"You come on down and meet us at the west entrance. Jette! You will not go in that house! Jette. Jette!" Marc cursed and tried to redial, but Jette wasn't picking up.

"Marc. This is my jurisdiction, but you're going to want to coordinate this I assume?" Captain Markle admired Marc's rant, but wanted to get back on point.

"Is that a problem?"

"No, but it's becoming a habit. You actually make my job easier. How do you want to play this?"

"Thanks, Captain. We'll exercise this search warrant. Go in fast. Arrest everyone in the house as either material witnesses or suspects." He made assignments to squads, then brought everyone around the map illuminated by the flashlights of the squad leaders. "Alpha group, block off all exits. Beta, place yourselves along the eastern perimeter. Delta, the west. I'll take the south with the New York contingent. We'll create a net, move in, and make the sweep. The north is straight down. Let anyone who wishes to take that route out go to hell with our blessing."

"Roger that," agreed Captain Markle.

"We have to assume they're all armed and dangerous. We have the locations of most of them, and can work through the house room by room. Some of these suspects are professionals, others appear to be pawns. We have two friendlies within the perimeter. Jette and her brother Luke. Can everyone here identify them on sight?"

Everyone nodded.

"All groups take out any lookouts stationed around the house in their area. Arrest, restrain, Mirandize and call in someone from Alpha to take them down to the road to await transport. Jim and his posse are bringing in the vans. Clear?"

Everyone nodded again. It was a solid plan. They'd all been issued full body armor, riot guns, and extra magazines. They felt confident and well prepared.

# Chapter Nineteen

Jette turned to Luke. "You stay here. I…"

"Oh no. I'm not staying out here alone. It's dark out here." Luke was going to stick to Jette. "Besides, you think I want to face Marc without you by my side? That man's a maniac. I'd rather face the Sentinels, if it's all the same to you."

Jette nodded, then slowly opened the door into the first floor hallway. She vaguely remembered the layout from all the forays she'd had on the premises when she was a teen, and her memory didn't fail her. She found the back stairway to the second and third floor with no problem.

The second floor appeared to be deserted and empty. No lights, no furniture, no signs of life. Jette took a moment to call the outside team with the inside intelligence.

"Keep your head down, professor," warned Marc, not wanting to distract her or his team with another cursing marathon. It was time for action and all attention needed to be focused on the operation.

"I'll say the same."

She and Luke continued up the stairway. They could hear computer keys clicking and a voice. A woman. Upbeat and excited. The Empress? Who was she? Jette felt sure that she'd be a familiar face. Well, she'd soon find out. The voice was different. Undisguised now.

"The Minions texted in their reports. Avenger is still in the ranch house, her rental car is parked just inside the gate. No movement from the house. She's probably sleeping and preparing for tomorrow night."

"You mean tonight, Empress," said a tinny voice over a speaker phone.

"Yes, you're right. Tonight."

"What do you hear from New York?"

"There's been activity around the apartment. No one has followed her or accompanied her. She's alone. If she shows up here, she'll collect the 1,000 points for her Quest, but that will be her last tally. Her very last."

Jette unsheathed her knife. Avenger's weapon of choice. She nodded at Luke, who had his own weapon up and out. For all his talk, he was competent and confident with a gun.

Stepping silently into the room, she saw a woman sitting straight and tall at a computer. She was masked and wore long blue robes. No weapon that Jette could see. There were notes tacked everywhere in the room. And hundreds of pictures of her and her life in New York over the last few weeks.

"You've done well, Empress. By this time tomorrow you'll have everything you ever wanted," said the voice on the phone.

"Yes. I'll talk with you tomorrow," replied the Empress and pushed the button to disconnect. Getting up gracefully, she walked over to the picture board.

"Tomorrow, Avenger," she muttered.

"Why wait?" asked Jette.

The Empress whipped around and Jette thought she heard a low growl. The eyes were hooded through the mask but were wild when they registered Jette's presence. They jittered back and forth from Jette to Luke and back again.

"Did you fly? Did you fly? Did you fly?" she asked, obsessively stuck on the one thought, the one possibility.

"Yes, I did." Jette felt the woman's mental state slipping away, but wasn't inclined to catch her and rescue her from madness. Remembering the face of the hostage shot without provocation, Flowers killed on the jailhouse steps, the agony of withdrawal, Hester in a coma, the threat to her brother, she pushed. Hard and direct. Right into the woman's most vulnerable psychological spot.

She flicked the eagle feathers in her hair. "I can transform now. I flew in as an eagle and released my Light Knight. My brother. Born of Ganymede. I will rule Himalia. You lose, Empress. You lose everything." Jette thought she'd give the Empress one more push into a psychotic break. "And I'll bring my brother with me. He'll sit at my side and rule with me."

"Whoa," murmured Luke. "That'll put her in the tank."

"No," screeched the Empress. "No man can rule. You are not worthy. Not worthy. Not worthy. I declare a draw. A draw." She held up her hand. In it was a remote. "You're standing in the Castle of Thunder! I push this button and we both expire in the explosion. We end the session in a draw."

"Oh crap." Luke instinctively took a step back. "Truth or dare?"

"Truth." Jette watched the shaking hand and the stiff fingers holding the remote. "Tread softly."

Jette sheathed her knife and held up her hands.

"No draw, Empress. You win. I prefer to play another session in this round."

"Fly out now. Fly out now then," the Empress shrieked. "Take your prize, but you must return to the Castle of Thunder for your Physical Test when the moon rises."

"I will. I'm leaving with my prize. Award the points. I'll be back with the moon. Light Knight, shall we fly out of here?"

"Do your thing, Avenger. I'm in your claws."

Luke lowered his weapon and they backed out slowly as the Empress continued to wave the hand with the remote. It looked like she was about to hyperventilate. Her chest was heaving, her eyes were still jittering. But there was victory there, too. She'd survived to play another day. Avenger and her Light Knight were retreating while she stood in the high tower.

"Gently," said Jette softly. "We don't want her to accidentally detonate. She's very, very fragile."

"Hey, so am I. An explosion would definitely break through the force field," whispered Luke, following Jette's lead, walking backward in smooth, unhurried steps.

When they got into the hall, Jette immediately raced down to the end of the corridor and got on the phone. They could hear the Empress muttering, talking about the Physical Test, the Final Duel, Sovereignty. Papers were fluttering, but no explosions.

"Where are you?" asked Jette when Marc answered.

"Right outside the gate. We're waiting for one squad to get into place then we'll all come in together."

"Abort the direct assault, Detective. She has the place wired for explosives."

"Are you sure?"

"Yes."

"Then what the hell are you still doing in there?"

"I'd like to stay in here. Monitor her. She doesn't want to blow this place up, Marc. I will rise from the dead, but she'll have to begin again as a Minion. There is no way she'll want to do that while I exist at full power. I suggest we stay in touch. Bring in your teams quietly and take people out of here slowly. When it becomes obvious, we'll want to know where she is."

"Let me talk with Luke."

She passed the phone to her brother.

"Luke, do you think you can pull your sister out of there?"

"No. Besides I think she has a good read on the situation."

"Watch her back."

"I'm on that."

"We're all in place. We'll start with the extractions in the lower south side of the house. Try and get her down there."

Luke closed the phone and handed it back to Jette.

"He actually thinks I might have some influence over your movement in here."

Jette grinned in spite of the dire situation.

"Our relationship is still so new."

"Yeah. He'd like us to join up with him. They're starting in the living room on the south side."

"I'm going to keep this position for awhile. I want to see what she does."

Luke sighed.

"There really is no end to how much bother you are, Avenger. I have your back."

# Chapter Twenty

Marc got on the radio and checked in with the squad leaders.

"Alpha, any movement out there?"

"None."

"Beta, are you finding lookouts?"

"We've bagged a couple." Captain Markle tried to keep the excitement out of his voice. He was used to spending his nights making sure the citizens of his county were all tucked up. His world didn't include a raid on a house full of potentially homicidal cultish game players. "We're moving in closer."

"Delta, are you ready to come in from the west?"

"Roger that. We'll start with the den and move through the kitchen. All quiet so far."

"Check your mark. We're going in 60 seconds."

In exactly one minute all units moved as one. Marc and his team tried the front door, found it unlocked and just walked right in. Stealthily, they made their way through the foyer and fanned out. Tagg and Marc went to the right, Teresa, Tommy, and Raj took the left, and Kim, Dina, and Rachael went straight through. Eunice stood at the door to protect their rear position. They needed to make their arrests and get everyone out quickly and quietly.

In the first room on the right, three men were lounging in front of the television, two were asleep and one was completely stoned. Marc and Tagg had them cuffed and Mirandized in a few minutes.

After sweeping the closets and bathrooms, Marc met his team and their collective haul in the foyer. "Where's Tommy?"

"She went up to be sure the second floor is empty," replied Raj, helping Teresa with the four they'd found and cuffed.

Marc nodded.

"Take these out to the wagons. I'm going to find Jette."

Suddenly they heard muffled gunfire from somewhere inside the house. The Delta leader's voice, cool but urgent, came over Marc's radio. "Engagement with armed suspects. Could use backup."

"Go find Jette," suggested Tagg when he saw Marc hesitate. "We'll split. Kim, Teresa, Dina take out our catch. Raj, Rachael, Eunice, with me."

They scattered as Marc raced up the front stairway. The sound of gunfire was an echo in his mind and he was desperate to find her.

The top of the stairs spilled into a huge triangle-shaped living room. Just as he was about to declare the area empty and clear, he caught movement from behind a long bar to his left and was immediately confronted with more than just a game-playing geek. The man was huge, bold, well trained and completely unafraid of taking on an armed police officer.

Rushing Marc with amazing speed and agility, the giant executed a blazing series of kicks and punches managing to disarm Marc and send him sailing across the room, upending a tower of boxes and crashing into a huge, old glass coffee table.

"That hurt," Marc muttered feeling the bruises already forming on his shoulder, side, and back. He was momentarily stunned, but managed to shake it off and come to his feet as the big man circled him. His gun was somewhere still in orbit, he thought, glancing around. Certainly not within his reach.

"Martial arts training, Dark Knight." The Sentinel came in gracefully for the kill. "You're worth a great deal to me."

Marc shook his ringing head, spit out the blood pooling in his mouth and in one graceful dance, spun away from the leaping man, reached down, grabbed his backup piece from inside his boot, raised the weapon and shot the Sentinel in the thigh and shoulder. The man went down screaming. Marc could swear he felt the floor heave.

"Gang training, you fucking moron."

Walking over, gingerly favoring his side, he flipped the man and restrained him. He texted Jette, giving his location and asking if Luke could come down and look at a suspect.

She texted back immediately that they were on their way. Within a few seconds, Luke walked in.

"Where's Jette?" asked Marc, his eyes snapping.

"Hi Marc, nice to see you too. No, really. Don't make a fuss, I'm fine."

"Where's Jette," asked Marc again.

"She's on the hunt. Staying with the Empress. When she heard the gunshots, the batty broad flew out of the room with a handful of papers and, we assume, the detonator. Jette followed."

"Fucking stubborn…" Marc took out his frustration by stomping on the already abused coffee table. "See what you can do about this asshole."

Luke quickly bound the wounds with strips of the man's shirt while Marc called in Teresa and Dina to get him out to the waiting EMS unit.

"He'll live," said Luke. "What about you? It looks like you took a hit."

"I'm fine," snapped Marc, finding his gun in the center of the fireplace. "Let's go find your sister."

# Chapter Twenty-One

Jette followed the billowing Blue Empress down the long dark hallway. She was shrieking on her cell phone.

"Where's the gunfire coming from? I swear if Sentinels are shooting at Avenger, I'll have them destroyed."

Punching another number on her phone, she paced in front of a door.

"What's happening? Are you sure? How many? How many? This can't be. This can't be happening."

Muttering, she called another number.

"Prepare to leave. I'll be there in a few minutes." The door opened and Jette saw with frustration that it was an elevator. She'd forgotten about that. The Empress stepped in and saw Avenger as she turned and punched the button for the ground floor.

"Back. Back," she screamed as Jette started running down the hallway. She held up her hand with the remote. "You forfeit. You forfeit the points. You didn't come alone!"

Jette stopped and put up her hands in surrender, playing the game.

"You win this entire round, Blue Empress."

"You lose. You lose," screamed the completely mad woman as the elevator doors shut.

Jette texted Marc that the Empress was now on the ground floor, armed with the detonator and extremely, extremely dangerous. Turning, she saw three Sentinels sneak into one of the empty rooms down the hall. She was about to call in reinforcements when a vision came running up the stairway to her right. A grinning, almost indescribable apparition.

Tommy, obviously in pursuit of the Sentinels, was dressed in a blue skintight mylar jumpsuit, red patent leather low-heeled boots, a snappy red scarf tied expertly around her neck, and two hammered gold brackets cuffing her wrists. Her exotic honey colored hair was tied up in a matching blue scrunchie and a line of ruby studs decorated each ear. She was dazzling to the eye.

"Sugar pie!" Tommy called in a loud whisper. "Oh, my! Aren't you the picture of a daring Cherokee warrior!"

"Tommy! You look…heroic."

"You think the outfit's too much? You do. Don't you. I was kind of thinking Wonder Woman, you know?"

"It's perfect. Now, is your kickin' outfit just for show and style, or do you want to go show those Sentinels what a couple of righteous ladies on a mission can do!"

"I'm with you, honey bun!" Tommy drew a pair of matching pearl handled derringers from inside her prodigious pushup bodice.

Jette removed the rifle Luke left with her from the scabbard on her back and together they tore down the hallway. With one swift kick of her red leather boot, Tommy took out the door standing between them and their target. Three Sentinels stood at the windows, their rifles out and ready to fire down on any officers in the large courtyard. Their expressions were almost comical as they turned and tried to bring their weapons around to hold off the huge mylar clad woman and the native warrior.

"I don't think I'd move a muscle if I were you, sugar," ordered Tommy bringing her derringers up, covering two of them while Jette trained her rifle on the third.

One of the men made the mistake of smirking at the tiny weapon and testing the resolve of the big blonde holding it. It was Tinman. His eyes went wide with shock when he saw Jette.

"Don't move a muscle and I won't turn you into a snake," she hissed.

Clearly off balance, he jerked up his rifle, but before Jette could react, Tommy put a tiny, but effective hole in the man's eye.

"Now I have one more little bullet in this baby and two in this one. Either of you want to be called One Eyed Bob at the prison hospital where they're going to plant your vegetated ass?"

The man and woman wisely dropped their guns as Marc and Luke blew into the room.

"Hey Tommy," grinned Luke. "Looking good."

"Yeah?" asked Tommy, primping her curls. "I'm feeling a tad ungepatched right now. Had to shoot the beast over there. He just wouldn't take me seriously."

"Can't imagine why," muttered Marc. "See what you can do for him, will you Luke?"

Marc got on the radio. "Send up a," he looked over at Luke, "paramedics or medical examiner?"

"Paramedics. The bullet didn't have much punch."

"I wouldn't want to actually kill anything, honey pot." She waved her two darling Derringers. "Just sort of stop them."

"Well there's nothing wrong with your aim," admired Luke. "Looks like you two didn't see eye to eye."

Members of the Alpha squad came in to take the prisoners out. Tinman regained consciousness. He'd lose the eye, but otherwise his brain was intact.

"You'll never beat her," growled the injured Sentinel, then grinned through the blood running down his cheek as they heard a helicopter firing up.

"Oh no. Oh no. She's going to get away," squealed Tommy, slapping her hand against her heart, obviously frustrated beyond measure.

Before Marc could stop her, Jette bolted out the terrace doors and saw the helicopter. The Empress was running toward it, deserting the field with a half dozen other players. Without hesitation she grabbed the long metal pole holding the flag of Himalia. Narrowing her eyes, she chanted in Cherokee to get focus. In her mind she could see the rotor spinning, then she slowed down time, held her breath, and with perfect precision launched the metal pole like a javelin. Right into the heart of the rotating propeller.

"Duck," she shouted running back in as the shattered propeller disintegrated into a shower of lethal shrapnel. The Empress and her escaping Sentinels scattered like lemmings faced with a fiery torch. Two of them fell, bloodied by pieces of flying debris but the rest got to shelter under the low roof of the terrace.

"Whoa!" squealed Tommy, clapping her hands like a child at a circus.

"Holy shit," shouted Luke.

"That's my girl!" grinned Marc.

Jette just turned and threw a fierce narrow-eyed glance at the prisoners being led out, two of them passively accepting their fate and Tinman shouting obscenities.

"Now let's go make the final move!" she said in the voice of Avenger.

Marc called into his radio. "The Empress and what's left of her team are scattered around the outer courtyard. Extreme caution. They're cornered and they're loaded."

"Roger that," came multiple voices.

"Is Luke up there?"

"Yes."

"We have an officer down. Not serious, but could use a medic."

"Where?"

"Front yard. Should be out of the line of fire."

Marc looked over at Luke, who nodded and started toward the door.

"I remember the direction."

"Would it do any good to ask you and Tommy go with Luke?" asked Marc looking into the blazing eyes of his lover, who'd retrieved her rifle from where she'd tossed it before her sprint and throw. She really did look like an Avenger at this moment, but he preferred to have the woman underneath, his woman, safe and secure.

"Don't even waste your breath." Jette neatly sidestepped a pile of debris and led the way out the door.

"I go where she goes, sugar," said Tommy, not as deft, but game as hell. "We're the female posse."

"Let me give you a man's gun then, for God's sake," muttered Marc as the three of them raced down the hallway toward the center courtyard.

"Sweetie, I tucked my man's gun away long ago." Tommy giggled like the girl he always wanted to be.

Marc just shook his head. This was the strangest tactical detail he'd ever had. He suppressed his concern for Jette and her safety as he caught up with her at the doors to the outside. "We need to coordinate this. Did you see any radios or other communication devices on the blue bitch?"

"She communicated with cell phones only."

"Fine. Then she won't be able to eavesdrop." In less than a minute, he secured the locations of everyone on the teams and had given them new orders.

"Roger that," came the calls of the group leaders.

"I could use some backup over here," requested Marc.

"Sending three over to you now, Detective," came Captain Markle's voice. "Is Jette secure?"

"She's right here."

"Send her out. Alpha is clear and can stand cover."

Jette just looked at him and frowned.

"Captain, she's wearing war feathers in her hair. You tell her."

"Understood. She'll be standing with your squad," said the Captain, proudly feeling the buzz of his own Cherokee blood. "We'll move in on your command."

"Hold all fire. We move in one wave."

"Roger that," confirmed all the leaders.

# Chapter Twenty-Two

Everyone moved on Marc's command and the well-coordinated operation was nearly bloodless. The superior fire power and training of the police units quickly subdued the resistance. A few of the more committed Sentinels and Minions tried to fight, and several had sophisticated martial arts training, but when faced with assault rifles and a few well placed warning shots, they got on the ground.

The paid professional Mercenaries were almost easier to subdue. They had no real commitment or loyalty. They realized they were busted, surrendered. and remained silent, knowing their rights under the law. The prisoners were muscled into waiting police vans and the air was filled with shouts, flashing red and blue lights, and that strange nervous chatter fueled by post combat relief.

Marc was on both the radio and phone, trying to locate the one person he was most interested in. None of the squads reported a visual, nor would any prisoner confirm a position for the Empress.

"She may have a hole in the house or the grounds. Let's set up a grid for a search. As soon as the dogs locate the boomers and they've been disarmed, we can do a room by room," he suggested.

"I have the entire property layout here, I'll assign the teams. ATF are ten minutes out," reported Captain Markle. He'd ordered a team from the Bureau of Alcohol, Tobacco, Firearms, and Explosives as soon as they'd been informed of the presence of bombs.

"Get everyone out as quickly as possible."

"Roger. We're sweeping as we go. Found a few more squirrels."

"I'll join you in five." Marc walked over to where Jette stood looking up at the windows, trying to spot a swish of blue fabric. "Do you think she stripped the costume and is going out with the other prisoners?"

"No, she's not going to get out of character. She was wearing her full mask and robes even when she was alone in a room. She's fully devolved. You'll find her somewhere. The fact we haven't located her has more to do with our caution than her cleverness."

Marc stared at her for a second, then grinned and ran his hand down one of her braids and their feathers.

"Talk about fully devolved. Will you wear those to bed tonight? I'm caught in this old western fantasy. The cowboy and the Indian princess."

"Cowboy?" asked Jette, raising an eyebrow.

"Hey. I rode a horse to this gig."

"Uh-huh. And tell me, city boy. How long have you had this fantasy?"

Marc looked at his watch.

"It's been about an hour, I guess."

"And do you think it might have anything to do with riding cross country with a really fine animal between your legs?"

"Better turn off that program, Avenger. I'm sure Diablo's a really great lay, but my tastes run more to the human form. And the female human form in particular."

"And…"

"To your form, exclusively." Marc saw Jette's eyes flicker and assumed it was an invitation. He lowered his head to steal a kiss.

"Marc?" she whispered seductively.

"Yes?"

"Move very, very slowly."

"Not exactly what I had in mind, but…"

"She's right behind you and to your left. I have her in my peripheral vision. She thinks she's hidden. Behind the Laurel."

"Armed?"

"She hasn't been to this point and if she does have a weapon, it'll be knife or sword."

"My gun is holstered."

"I'm more concerned about the detonator. Put your arms around me. My knife is in the sheath. Grab it as you go. I have another in my boot. I'm going to get to it and go for the detonator."

Jette loved her man. He didn't even hesitate or question her plan. As he put his arms around her and drew the knife, Jette could see the Empress take tentative steps toward them. She had a sword in her right hand now and was holding something in her left. Aim for the left hand then. Jette closed her eyes as if in passion as Marc's lips came down on hers. She pictured her moves, the knife flying, hitting the left hand, the detonator falling to the ground, her diving and scooping it up.

"Cover me," she whispered. "She has a sword."

Then like lightning, the two of them moved as if they'd planned, practiced, and performed the duet a hundred times. Marc spun around, armed with Jette's knife and drawing his gun. Jette bent and in one swift action drew her father's knife and sent it straight and true right through the left wrist of the Empress. The detonator didn't fall to the ground, but sailed into the air as the Empress screamed and dropped her sword. She pulled out the knife, tossed it at Jette, and ran onto the terrace.

Marc caught the detonator on its downward arch as Jette dodged the knife and tore out after her. When Jette reached the terrace the woman was on top of the ledge. Blood was pumping out of the wound on her wrist, but she didn't seem to notice.

Marc ran up beside Jette. "Goddamn it, Jette. The detonator is a fake."

"Are you sure?"

"Yes. It's a decoy."

"Then she still has one. The real one."

"Maybe it was all a bluff?"

"No. There are explosives in this house. I called Kelly. The Castle of Thunder is the last obstacle before the portal to the Final Duel."

The Empress shouted at them. "You may think you beat me Avenger, but you haven't. You'll rise up alone, your Knights and Guardians will be nothing but a memory under a pile of rubble. Without them the Blue Empress will have full advantage."

The woman on the ledge laughed maniacally and reached into a pocket in her robe. Another electronic device. Larger with a switch instead of a button.

"Behold, the real thing," muttered Marc.

The Empress paced on the ledge, ranting, waving her injured hand throwing fine lines of deep red blood into the air and across the stones. As mentally distraught as she was, she had presence enough to keep her body between Jette and the detonator, firmly gripped in her uninjured hand.

"She's going to blow this place up, Marc," murmured Jette under her breath. "I'll try to stall. Evacuate."

Nodding, Marc grabbed his radio, turned his back, and put out the all call. He kept his voice low and calm, but the truth and urgency came through. "Everyone out. Now! Seek cover. Explosion imminent. Get back behind the outer walls. Move! Move!"

"Blue Empress," Jette took a step forward, projecting deference and defeat. "I want to negotiate a trade. I'll reveal the secret of the phoenix if you leave me the Dark Knight and a dozen Guardians."

The demented woman stopped pacing and ranting. It appeared she was thinking. Calculating.

"No. No. No. The Dark Knight has to die. I want him in the inferno."

"Let me think. Let me think about it, Empress," stalled Jette.

"No. You have no time left in your reserves," shrieked the Empress, taking up her pacing keeping the switch behind her back and out of the line of fire. "The advantage is mine. I win this round. In the end the one true Blue Empress will triumph. The Castle of Thunder will be the doorway!"

"Alright, you can have my Dark Knight."

The Empress laughed with triumph.

"Order him back into the Castle of Thunder!"

"Clear," whispered the Dark Knight, not at all offended that his lover just offered to make him cannon fodder. "All are out of the house. Rush her, shoot her, or run?"

"Run." Jette backed up. "A bullet might not stop her hand's reflexive action. I think setting a new record for the fifty yard dash would be a really good plan. Go!"

Marc snatched Jette's hand and they ran, vaulting down the terrace steps and picking up speed as they covered the lawn in record time.

The Empress loved the sight of it. A perfect way to end this round. "That's it! Run! Run! Cowards! The Blue Empress will find you! Find you and beat you! Prepare for your downfall!"

With that, she turned, opened her arms wide, her long robes billowing like wings. With no hesitation, she stepped off the terrace wall and tried to fly.

Marc and Jette streaked across the lawn. Ahead of them was his New York squad. They'd been the deepest in the house and the farthest from the eight-foot outer walls, but they were used to flat out running a New York block and managed to get behind the wall before the house erupted into a huge fireball.

The initial detonation set off a chain reaction and the night air was ripped with the sounds of explosions, shrieking stone missiles, shattering glass, and thundering rock slides. The ground shook with the impact of the multiple blasts. Marc and Jette were caught in the sonic thrust and flew through the air.

"Jette," shouted Marc, picking himself up, coughing and gagging on the smoke and dust. "Jette!"

"Here," she called, then spit out the grainy debris that filled her mouth when she'd opened it.

"Well, now. That's quite ladylike." Marc limped toward her out of the cloud of smoke.

Jette spit again, then glared up at him in a very unladylike manner. "I'm no lady, Dark Knight. I'm the Avenger."

Marc took her in his arms, and together they stood among the falling ash and acrid smoke. Feeling wonderful. Feeling alive. He thought he'd finish the kiss the Empress interrupted and that felt pretty wonderful too.

"Who was she, Marc? You recognized the voice, didn't you? Who was she?"

"I'm pretty sure when they pick up what's left of her, they'll find Zena Brightson."

"The woman who developed the game?"

"It sounded like her. Seriously off her rocker, but I think so."

Jette stared up at what was left of the terrace and its wall. "I need to go back up there."

"Why?"

"To see if I can locate the knife I threw into her. It was my father's."

Marc pulled two knives from his belt. "Would one of these be what you're looking for?"

"Oh Marc," she smiled up at him. "Thank you."

"I grabbed it just in case my little knife chucker needed more ammo." When she reached for it, he held it up and just out of her reach. "Now about that fantasy."

"I think we should seriously shower first."

"Is that what they did after the fade out in the old west?"

"Most definitely. First thing."

"Fine." Marc gave her a quick peck. Looking around, he sighed deeply. "Although I have a feeling it's going to be hours before we can get to first base."

Jette looked at the rubble.

"Every bomb cloud has a silver lining," she concluded. "The hideous blight on the beautiful Arizona skyline has been removed. Our side wins again." Then she sighed as exhaustion knocked on the door. "What a night."

"What a week."

"What a month."

"What a life."

Arm in arm, they walked toward the line of squad cars, police vans and arriving ATF trucks. The Phoenix and her Shield.

# Chapter Twenty-Three

They gathered at the ranch house living and reliving every detail and toasting each other repeatedly. Telling and retelling the story soon to become a local legend on the successful rescue of the good Dr. Luke Grainger by the incredible Cherokee warrior, aided by her amazing Dark Knight. And of the destruction of the glass fortress and the Empress.

"I tell you, honey," hooted Tommy to Jim, who was completely smashed and knew he was because Tommy was looking pretty good to him. "I decided out there tonight to have the operation. You know, go all the way. No more schmeckle. Lord, a few times that saddle horn just did it to my equipment."

"I don't know," responded Jim seriously. "There are advantages to taking a leak standing up. Especially in these parts where there are snakes and other nasty little critters slithering around in the sand."

Luke, who was truly glad to be tipping his beer with his attached hand instead of taking it through a straw, joined in the debate.

"Have a few more beers, Tommy, and I think one of the guys here can take care of that pesky detail for you. They do that to steers and geldings all the time. Snip snip and the he-cow and the he-horse are done with the swinging and the poking."

All the male ranch hands had unconsciously, yet simultaneously, crossed their legs.

"Let's order some pizzas," suggested Kim enthusiastically, quite sure a change of subject was what the party needed.

"You still have that jet revved up, Dark Knight?" called Luke. "We can fly to Chicago for some really fine take-out deep dish."

"I'd rather fly this Jette tonight," smiled Marc, only a little tipsy and feeling mighty fine having his lovely Avenger safe in his arms.

The team howled at what they thought was the ultimate wit. Marc took his manly bow, then Jette led him out onto the terrace. She breathed in the cool pre-dawn air of the desert while Marc held her and breathed in the scent of his mate. He decided just a breath wasn't enough, so he turned her and took possession of her mouth.

"I need to go off, Marc. I need to get back into balance," she said softly when he pulled back.

Marc looked at her, into her. "Alone?"

Jette nodded slowly, knowing what the response would do to him, hoping he had accumulated enough trust to let her go. Not just trusting that she'd be safe, but trust in her love for him, their love for each other. To know she'd come back and she'd come back to him.

"Is this a test?"

Again she nodded. "Darling, my core is chipped and a little fractured. I need to be whole again."

"Can't you do that while I keep watch? I need to be with you."

"Darling, a healthy, happy, long-lasting relationship needs to be built on the attraction of two complete souls. It should always be a choice based on our feelings of love and what we make together, not a dependency based on a need."

Marc knew her words made sense, but his heart still ached a little that she needed and wanted to do this alone. "Can't I be a little dependent?"

"Until you have completed the journey to harmony, I think that's fine."

"But you don't need me?" he asked reluctantly, not sure he wanted to hear her response.

"Darling, what I have for you is something far more powerful, and far, far more enduring than simple need. I'll always need you and the things that you are uniquely qualified to contribute to this partnership, but it's the joy of my love for you, that heart bursting feeling of bliss that will keep me by your side. Forever."

Marc let her words sink in, then opened his arms, not even sure if there was a word for what he was feeling.

"Go," he said simply. "I'll wait here."

Giving him one last long look, she turned and ran into the night. Marc didn't move from the spot. What was he feeling? It was strong and it was positive. It was…certainty. It was complete trust. He was sure she'd come back. Back to him. Back to their life together. And he realized she was right. That was stronger than anything.

Luke came up beside him, noticing the look on his friend's face. He thought of the haunted man who stood vigil on the shores of the East River. Quite a transformation. Marc stared at the lightening horizon. On his face was not only the love, but a hint of contentment. Interesting. And just fine.

"She's gone off, then?" Luke asked.

"Yeah."

"Tough to let her fly."

"Yeah."

"When she comes back, she'll be ready to move forward without looking back."

"My biggest fear is that she'll find something out there that will remind her of what she's given up by following me." Marc gave voice to what he'd been thinking since he arrived in Arizona. He couldn't believe he'd said it out loud. Luke was working on him nearly the same way as Jette.

"Trust her, Marc," Luke said simply.

Marc looked around. The ranch, her horses, her birthplace. The serene and warm horizon coming into relief as the rays of the sun touched the land. Then he thought of the pain, the pressure, and the problems he'd brought into her life. How could that be a good trade? But did he trust her? Yes. With his whole, jaded heart and his entire damaged but awakening soul, he trusted her.

"Alright," he said softly.

"So. Ever thought of making it legal?" asked Luke.

"Like a contract or something?"

Luke gaped at him, then sat down hard on the ledge, put his face in his hands, and roared. He laughed so hard, he nearly dislodged a rib.

"You really are a pathetic putz. Quit thinking like a lawyer."

Marc frowned down at him. "Huh?"

"Now you sound like Kim. I'm talking about taking the next step."

Marc looked around.

"Asking her to marry you, you idiot!" Luke threw up his hands.

Marc stared at Luke. Mute. There was absolutely no air in his lungs.

"Don't tell me you haven't given it a thought." Luke's eyebrows shot up.

Marc stood frozen, still unable to accumulate enough air to push any words through his throat.

Luke just stared. "Good Lord, you look like a guppy. You mean you never thought about marriage, wedding, wife, china patterns, frenzied women picking out table favors and the perfect shade of vanilla beige, hysterical caterers, bridezilla?"

Marc slowly shook his head.

"Well, let it sink in. It could hit a brain cell and stimulate the growth of an idea." Luke laughed, stood, and thumped his friend on the back. "And hey! Let this sink in with it. I come with the deal. You marry my sister and that makes us brothers!"

"Her parents never formally adopted you," Marc mumbled through numb lips, that single irrelevant fact the only thing that seemed to come to the surface.

Luke howled and nearly collapsed. "Let's go make some coffee. You need to wake up."

"Do you think," began Marc, ignoring his need for coffee. "Do you think…"

"Frequently," chuckled Luke thinking how this whole conversation would play and replay in the annals of family folklore. It was destined to become a classic.

Marc cleared his throat, then turned and stared into Arizona's beautiful rising sun.

"She's like that sun, Luke. Bright, warm, chasing away the darkness inside me. In every corner it touches, there's no room for night."

"Jesus, Marc," sighed Luke, touched but still tickled to death. "Talk like that and the wedding is in the bag. Forget the coffee, let's go rent a couple of tuxes."

Marc looked at Luke, some of his air returning in the rush of promise. With one last look over his shoulder, he turned and went inside with the man destiny decreed would become his brother.

# Chapter Twenty-Four

Jette was looking out her favorite window. They'd flown home after a few wonderful recuperative days in Arizona. The charge of energy the desert air, sun, and sky gave her showed in her glowing skin.

As soon as they got back to New York, Rachael insisted she lead the team that took down Hal Rowley. Something that the therapist in Jette got behind. He'd served in Vice, the Bomb Squad, and was an expert marksman. He fit the suspect profile right down the line. The gun that was used in the Flowers' assassination was found in a storage locker after Kelly scraped through several layers of clever false identities to secure the location, then worked her way around a few more blocks and screens and found all the money. He didn't have a brother who worked on Wall Street. Hal's future was cast in gray stone.

Luke was staying on in New York for awhile filling in at the Queen's clinic. Jette suspected he wanted to be sure she was completely clear of the drugs and Marc's lungs were going to remain operative before returning to Ecuador. It was great having her brother near, so that was fine with her.

Lyd and Kelly were meeting with a very sympathetic judge to arrange for Lyd to assume guardianship of Kelly. She'd remained completely sober. Finding her maternal instincts and pride in her prodigy were stronger than her need for a drink. Kelly was in heaven.

Marc's team had all gone home after a day of sorting through files and data. Tommy was driving Claude and Hilda out to dinner on a real date of sorts. Progress, it seemed. Now it was just the two of them in the apartment and Marc appreciated the privacy. He had intended to make good use of the time.

"Am I interrupting?" He hesitated when he saw the serious, thoughtful expression on Jette's face.

She shook her head, but didn't turn around. "I've been thinking. I need to talk with you."

"We aren't going to talk about my mother again, are we?"

"No. Not today." She turned around and in the rays of the late afternoon sun, her exquisite beauty nearly robbed Marc of his kneecaps. Finding he needed them to cross the room, he located the necessary cartilage and moved toward her.

"Although, as I recall, after you stopped pounding me about the woman, we had a pretty vigorous exorcism. All over the carpet."

"Is that how you remember it? I pounded you?" asked Jette.

"No. As I recall I think I pounded you. Even though the rug burns were mostly on my ass."

"You're evading, Detective."

"It doesn't appear to be working."

"Marc. Stop. I don't want my inquiries and, in my professional opinion, your need to resolve the issues with your mother, to be perceived as pounding."

"I thought we weren't going to talk about her today," scowled Marc.

"Can I talk about her tomorrow?"

"Talk about her all you want, I don't have to listen. As a matter of fact…" He started to turn away from her, but she gently took his arm.

"Not tomorrow then either."

He looked at her speculatively. "Maybe I should negotiate a moratorium for, say, the rest of my life?"

"That would be unreasonable."

"So," he shrugged. "Just add that to bad-tempered, difficult, and perverse."

"I'll do that. Anyway, you've sidetracked me."

"In that case, want to have hot, sweaty sex on the carpet again?" He took her in his arms.

"Maybe later. Right now I want to talk to you about the case. The Blue Empress case."

He could see she was serious. "Alright."

Keeping her eyes fastened on his, she shared her thoughts with both the man she loved and the detective she trusted the most.

"Marc, I've been going over all the events in my mind. Everything happened so fast that I needed time to put it all into a framework. A few things don't fit. You taught me that if something doesn't fit, take another look at it. Don't try to explain it. Don't try to make it fit."

"What doesn't fit?"

"First, and most important, the Empress wouldn't have committed suicide."

"Why not? She had no way out. She was looking at significant jail time and, I think, most importantly, the Avenger beat her."

"Trust me, darling. It doesn't fit her profile. She'd have retreated, regrouped, then come back after me some time later."

Marc did trust her, but to him profiling was still a soft science, far from the facts that developed theories in a case. Far from the tangible evidence that he used to find and convict the criminals he tracked.

"She said she was the Empress. It looked like she was running the show," argued Marc.

"Only because we *assumed* she was running the show. From what we learned about Zena, she was a woman who fought severe depression and horrible manic periods ever since she killed her family. She wasn't stable enough to be the woman who challenged me."

Zena Brightson's records had been opened. At the age of 13 she killed her mother, father, and brother after years of sexual abuse and neglect. Taking a ceremonial sword from a collection of her father's, she methodically sliced them in a ritualistic way that assured her an insanity plea. Until her 21st birthday, she'd been institutionalized. Released from the system, highly medicated, she went to college and excelled at everything. Except social interaction. Her full and fertile mind conjured up the game of Sovereignty when she found a way to combine her love of history, her passion for computer engineering, and her need for bloody violence. The product quickly became a commercial success when she introduced it on the newly emerging World Wide Web.

"She had the pathology of a woman barely able to function in the real world. Her medications were the only thing keeping her from being institutionalized again. The Empress I met was far more controlled and would be able to move through the Middle World of Reality very well. She's completely invested in her delusion so she'd play all her parts perfectly. Her identity in the real world would be flawlessly executed."

"Then why was Brightson in Arizona?"

"I think she was being used as a decoy," Jette concluded. "She was being manipulated by the real Empress. I don't think it's over. I think the real Empress was on the phone with her when we arrived at the house in Arizona."

Marc was silent. Thoughtful. Did he miss something? His focus wasn't on the clues or on the suspect. His focus was on Jette. It was more than possible that a significant piece of evidence got by him. His usual single-minded attention to solving a case was hijacked by his pursuit of Jette.

"Anything else?"

"A few more things. We were so centered on why the Empress thought I was Avenger, I think we let the question of why she thought she was the Empress slip by. I think we need to find a woman who was born under a full moon. I had Kelly check. Zena Brightson was not. Metis, the Empress's father, was a scholar or a soldier. Perhaps a prophet of some sort, although that's less likely. Zena Brightson's father was a successful auto dealer. I think we should look for a suspect whose father was either in education, the military or both."

He stared at her a minute. She used silence to allow him to think and formulate his own conclusions. Then he nodded. It was possible. And when something was possible, it had to be pursued.

"Come on," he said. "Let's go back into the command center. We're boxing things up to be transported to headquarters. It's a good opportunity to go over everything again."

Jette smiled up at him and took the hand he offered. They made a good team, she decided.

His hand tensed when they walked into the chaotic ballroom. In addition to the files, computers, boards, boxes and other cop debris, the space was filled with the residual strain and stress of the investigation.

"We'll do the cleansing as soon as everything is out," assured Jette softly, feeling the pulse of the room and the man.

"It was horrible," said Marc. She turned into him and held on for a moment. He took a deep breath and felt hope and humor return to his heart. Return to the room. "I'll need therapy for years and years. Maybe we should keep the couches in here. Something for me to fall on when I feel myself going psycho. I'll just take to a couch and you can sit with a very, very thick notepad and write another book."

Jette let go. He'd be alright.

"Let's do this." She walked over to the first box.

"Okay, but this wasn't how I was planning to spend our home alone time."

They went methodically through the room. It amazed Jette how much his team had accomplished in so little time. She found a stack of one hundred dollar bills under a pile of folders and another one just sitting near a silent computer.

"This is getting to be like a treasure hunt. Maybe you need to put these in the safe." She waved the blocks of money at him.

Marc stared at it. Cash. They hadn't yet found a money trail back to Zena Brightson. All the transactions they'd traced originated in cash. The jet had been paid for and secured by a thirty thousand dollar cash transfer to the owner's account. Money transferred from three separate accounts that had been opened the week before under the name and social security number of an obscure and unsuccessful actor who had died years earlier. The red Porsche had been paid for in cash. Drugs, weapons, rents and other purchases were all cash transactions. The Sentinels and paid Mercenaries the team had rounded up, including the chief and Hal Rowley, made cash deposits in their accounts. How much total would it have taken to finance this operation? Hundreds of thousands of dollars. In cash. Cash.

Feeling the buzz accelerate into a full hot hum in the blood, Marc dove into the box containing the clothes Jette had been wearing the day they found her.

Jette sensed the change in Marc. "Got something, *Ganohalidohi?*"

"Yeah. I'm on the scent." He found the scarf she'd stuffed in her pocket. "Is this the scarf that was used as a blindfold?"

"Yes."

"So it could have belonged to the Empress."

"Quite possibly. She would have liked that connection."

Marc ran it though his fingers and held it up to the light. And thought. And processed. A fresher mind did perceive the evidence differently. No cloud of concern faded the clarity of what was right in front of him.

He went back over everything. Every conversation, every clue. Then he looked up at Jette and talked it out. Yes. It fit. He made a few phone calls, then hit pay dirt with an old neighbor. Events clicked into place. The picture was nearly complete.

"Her father died when she was eight or nine. Her Mom remarried less than a year later and a baby sister came along shortly after," he told Jette who'd come over to hold his hand. "The sister died as a toddler."

"How?"

"A horrible accident. She fell from the terrace of a hotel in Miami while on a family vacation. Does this sound like the kind of early traumas that could set her off?"

"Yes, especially if she didn't get any help."

"Especially if she helped her sister take the dive."

"Marc, she was just a child herself."

"Children can kill, Doctor." He looked steadily into her dark, compassionate eyes. She knew what he was thinking. He'd killed when he was a child.

"It's not the same," she said softly, then added. "Do you want to talk about it?"

He surprised her when he just laughed. "Christ, you are such a shrink. But to answer your question, no. Not now. I have to call the team in, and the commissioner will want to know the case has been reopened. We'll get Kim on finding out about the moon and getting more on her father. What he did. We probably won't need it in the end to close it, but it will give us more fuel."

"Kim, not Kelly?"

"This is official now. We do this by the book."

Jette nodded, deeply saddened, but resolute. One more step needed to be taken before the scales of justice would balance.

# Chapter Twenty-Five

As Marc and Jette walked down the familiar streets of the Village, Jette had the distinct feeling of déjà vu.

"Ready for a little lunch, Avenger?" asked Marc.

"Even an Avatar has to eat, Dark Knight."

"Hi Dicey." Marc casually walked up to the familiar cart, Jette by his side.

"Hey, Marc. Hello, Dr. Morningstar. How great to see you." Dicey beamed at them. "Thanks for the personal call. I appreciate it. Don't forget, these are on the house. Or rather on the cart."

Laughing deeply, she began to automatically put up what she thought of as their regulars. Her dexterity and timing were impressive as she orchestrated the wrap for Jette and the hot dog for Marc.

"I appreciated you coming in with a report," said Marc.

"Did you ever find those two who were following you that day?"

"Yes, I think so. A couple of college girls who got caught up in the game. From what we've been able to get out of them, they had no idea they were being used in a real abduction. Never put two and two together, even after Jette's kidnapping."

"Not very bright. They won't go far in that game they were playing."

"You'd know all about that, wouldn't you Dicey?"

Marc put the scarf on the cart.

"Nice scarf." Dicey placed their food and drink on the narrow cart ledge. "Be careful with it. You don't want to get your assorted condiments all over it."

"Dicey Black," observed Marc.

"I'm glad to see that it's caught on. Told you the color would look nice on her."

Dicey looked into his eyes, then glanced over at Jette.

"It was used as a blindfold. Careless of you to leave it behind." Marc nodded at the cash drawer in her cart. "A millionaire, three dollars at a time. And all in cash."

Dicey dragged her eyes from Jette's.

"I beg your pardon?"

"Remember what brought down Al Capone? You're too dangerous to leave on the streets while we gather the evidence. Agent Elliot Cooper from the FBI is standing over there. He's representing the interests of the IRS and wants to talk with you."

"Turning me in for not declaring a few bucks, Marc? That isn't like you."

"It's the most expedient way to chain you until we execute the search warrants and take you down on conspiracy."

Dicey just raised her eyebrows as she glanced back over at Jette.

"And what do you have to say about this?" she wondered.

"Hello, Empress." Jette selected her words carefully. "Consider this the Final Duel. I declare a victory. I am the Supreme Sovereign of all the Worlds. Himalia is mine, Callisto is mine, and this world is mine. You're done."

Dicey remained silent, but looked directly into Jette's eyes. Deeply. The seismic sizzle could be felt by everyone within a 20-foot radius. Jette knew. And Dicey knew that Jette knew. It was enough. For both of them.

"Prove it," she challenged, snapping back.

"I intend to," Marc declared solemnly. "Elara Dicen, you're under arrest. You have the right to remain silent." He continued the Miranda warning. "Do you understand?"

"Oh, yes, I understand," said Dicey as Marc put restraints on her wrists. "And I think I'll remain silent. Completely silent."

"That's your privilege." Marc handed her over to Dina who came up to the cart with the rest of the team.

Dicey stared at all of them for a moment. Then her eyes flashed and she let them see the Empress. What the hell, it was only the first step in a follow-up round. It wasn't over until she declared it over. She'd remain silent and be out on bail in less than three hours. She walked cool and collected with Dina and got regally into the back of Agent Cooper's car.

"Does Dicey fit your profile a bit better, Dr. Morningstar?" asked Marc.

"Yes. She does. I know it hurts you, Marc. You liked her. Plus she was a positive female role model who turned out to be a deceiver."

"It will probably contribute to my abandonment issues."

"Not if I can get you into therapy right away."

"It's a date. At least she won't get out on bail right away with all these federal tax fraud charges. We'll need some time to build the conspiracy and kidnapping case."

"No you won't. After Agent Cooper is finished with his interviews, get her alone. You and her. You'll get a confession," assured Jette.

"Is that your professional opinion, Doctor?" asked Marc.

"It is. She's dying to tell you. To give you all the details. Every one. She considers this world and its rules immaterial. On some level she's convinced they can't hurt her. They simply don't apply. In addition, and most importantly, the Empress is the dominant personality right now and she'll tell you because she wants desperately to come out from behind the mask. To take her bow with gamers everywhere applauding her genius. In addition, you'll find everything documented in great detail somewhere. Having it written down for posterity is both part of the game and part of her pathology. You'll find her logs and have everything you need for a solid conviction."

"It's extremely circumstantial, but it doesn't hurt that she was born under a full moon, that her father was a professor of astrology, and that Elara is a moon of Jupiter. She was always Dicey to me and everyone on the street. I never knew her given name. I guess there was a lot I didn't know."

Dicey threw him a confident smile as the nondescript federal vehicle pulled away from the curb. He got a glimpse of a newly formed portrait covering the familiar features. Like a transparent mask. In the look she gave him, he could see that Jette was right on target. She'd tell him everything.

"Pssst." The sound came from behind them. Marc turned and smiled at Folger.

"Hey, what's up, man?"

"Just thought you should know, Snake Eyes. Razor said that Bunny told her that Minty told him that Junior Stokes saw the perp coming out of the diamond shop on 6th. The street won't talk to anyone but you. If you got any of that green left after all the planting you did this last week, you could pop him. He'd roll for a twenty. Don't let him talk you up."

Marc smiled. "And when did I ever overpay?"

"Ah, kid. You're a soft touch and everybody knows it."

"Right. Hungry?"

"Always. You think Dicey will mind if the roaches feast on her turf?"

"I think Dicey has bigger problems. Did you know she wasn't playing straight?"

"Knew she was a rich bitch, but she always played straight as far as I saw. Go figure. Some people just don't show."

"Yeah. Here. Get yourself a steak." Marc gave him a folded fifty.

"And who would sell me one of those on a bun?" he chuckled. "Think I might use it to tuck into a room on dive street. Like to shower and brush my tooth once in awhile."

"Makes you more attractive to the ladies."

Folgers winked at Jette. "Sure could give you a run for your money. See ya, Snake Eyes."

Marc stretched his back and let his eyes travel over the light and shadows of the street as he watched Folgers shuffle down the sidewalk.

"I didn't even know she was a rich bitch." There was sadness in the tone.

"Your city didn't abandon you, Marc. Your City Mother and your family stood beside you. Supported you," Jette spoke gently, understanding the fog in his heart.

Marc turned and looked at her for a few heartbeats.

"I get the message, Doctor," he said, then glanced in the direction of the diamond shop on 6th. It had been all over the news that morning, and sounded like a job for super-cop.

"Go do your job, Shield," Jette insisted. "I'll meet you at home later and we can start that therapy."

"There are potentially hordes of freaky defectives out there still playing Sovereignty and you're still their prey." Marc was clearly torn. He wasn't sure he wanted life to go on quite yet.

"I'll put an end to it."

"How, morph into thick-skinned, ill-tempered rhino and hide in the fucking zoo?" snapped Marc, irritably.

Jette laughed at her Knight. He really was a case.

"No. I am going to take a more clinical approach. I'm calling Heather and we're going to have a follow-up interview. For immediate release. To the small population of players who are actually caught in the delusion, I'm Avenger and I'm ascending to Supreme Sovereign. I've traveled through the Castle of Thunder, and have defeated the Blue Empress in the Final Duel. The conflict between the worlds is finally over. The last chapter has been written and there will be a thousand years of peace and harmony."

"Is that part of the game?" Marc frowned. He thought he'd read everything.

"No, it's a Supreme Sovereign diktat. It's my platform, so to speak. It'll work, darling. People mired in the deep delusion will serve my command."

"You better beware," warned Luke, who'd come up to join them. "Sounds like she's beginning to get off on all this. *Serve my command.* I never thought I'd hear that out of your egalitarian mouth, *Ganolvvsgv*. You know what they say about absolute power. Corrupted. First it's a diagnosis, then it's a diktat."

Jette's smile was that of an absolute sovereign as she nodded regally.

"I have a very public track record, so to speak. I'll make them believe."

"Do we have to call you, your majesty?" asked Luke.

"Only in public."

Luke laughed uproariously as Marc's skeptical scowl deepened.

Jette continued outlining her plan. "For most players of Sovereignty, the people who simply enjoy the gaming, the Final Duel set up by Dicey will become a classic they can analyze and discuss for decades. According to Kelly, without yearly updates gamers will move on to the next hot product. With the death of Zena Brightson, there will be no more updates. It's over, Detective. Now go assume your true identity, the part you were born to play and catch a jewel thief."

Marc stared at her, clearly torn.

"I command it," she added.

Seeing the sparkle in her beautiful dark eyes, Marc whistled at Eunice and flicked her a wave. She nodded and crossed the street.

"Would you make sure Jette gets home safely?" he asked.

"Hey, what about me?" asked Luke.

"And see that the doctor gets home as well," added Marc grinning.

"I think you should ask if she could make sure I get home safely," snorted Eunice. "Really, Marc…"

"I wouldn't mind the company," interrupted Jette, knowing her man.

Eunice glanced over at her and nodded. "Alright then. As long as you promise to take a cab and not run. I didn't bring my bike."

Jette smiled up at her. "I couldn't sustain the pace in these shoes."

"Honey, you could sustain the pace in three-inch heels, carrying a briefcase, a laptop and an open umbrella. Now kiss your Shield, Phoenix. I can tell he's revved to go after another headline."

The Shield flashed his grin, glanced over at the media that had collected on the corner, then thought what the hell. Let them record an eyeful. He grabbed his Phoenix around the waist, lifted her off her feet and gave her a kiss to sustain the pace of her heart until he could get her alone.

"You're perfect," he whispered, then turned and went in search of Junior Stokes.

"Talk about perfect," mumbled Eunice under her breath as she and Jette stood shoulder to shoulder watching Marc jog across the street.

"*Ganohalidohi*," Jette said.

"Hunter," translated Eunice.

Jette looked up at her, impressed.

"He shared a few things during the long dark hours you were missing. Something new for him, actually. You've changed him, Jette."

They continued to watch as Marc swerved and went off on a classic rant at a passing motorist who had the audacity to be minding his own business and driving on his side of the street. Just not quite fast enough to get out of Marc's way.

"He's a work in progress," laughed Jette.

"Aren't they all?"

Marc did make headlines that evening. His arrest of the diamond thief earned only a tiny blip, but the passionate embrace of the Phoenix and the Shield in bold color and flattering light captured every front page in the city. His city. Now their city. The City of Might.

Printed in the United States
141896LV00002B/19/P